"Water, skies and novels should be clear. Roadways and poems should be without obstacles. Hearts and minds should be adventuresome. Love should be forgiving. We find all the right things in Mars Hill's *The Moaner's Bench*."
—Nikki Giovanni, poet

"What an appropriate metaphor—*The Moaner's Bench*—for growing up under the rigors of religion in the South. you don't have to be either Baptist or Southern to enjoy this book. You just have to be, or have been, young at some point. Mars Hill has the South down pat."
—Janice Daugharty, author of *Whistle, Paw Paw Patch, Necessary Lies* and *Dark of the Moon*

"Warm, funny and wonderfully observed."
—*Publishers Weekly*

"*The Moaner's Bench* is as intriguing and ruggedly beautiful as the Arkansas people and places it chronicles."
—*Schenectady Daily Gazette*

"A rich, enthralling saga. [*The Moaner's Bench*] chronicles the joys, pains, successes and failures of a boy who wants badly to be a man and doesn't understand why time seems to be the measure of one. Hill paints vivid, poetic descriptions and has a knack for well-timed humor."
—*Emerge*

The Moaner's Bench

The Moaner's Bench

Mars Hill

HarperPerennial
A Division of HarperCollinsPublishers

A hardcover edition of this book was published in 1998 by HarperFlamingo, an imprint of HarperCollins Publishers.

HarperCollins books may be purchased for educational, business, or sales promotional use. For information please write: Special Markets Department, HarperCollins Publishers, Inc., 10 East 53rd Street, New York, NY 10022.

First HarperPerennial edition published 1999.

Designed by Kyoko Watanabe

The Library of Congress has catalogued the hardcover edition as follows:

    The moaner's bench / by Mars Hill. — 1st ed.
      p.   cm.
    ISBN 0-06-019102-3
    1. Afro-Americans—Arkansas—Fiction. I. Title.
   PS3558.I399M63   1998
   813'.54—dc21   97-53078

ISBN 0-06-093058-6 (pbk.)

99 00 01 02 03 ❖/RRD 10 9 8 7 6 5 4 3 2 1

Acknowledgments

The years spent writing this book cause me to remember and to thank many people who provided resource information and invaluable critiques during the writing. First I remember and thank William Kennedy for starting the work shop at Skidmore in 1987, where I went to do playwriting and instead was directed to the fiction writer's course.

Dr. Mark Nepo, Dr. Eugene Meribelli, and Dr. Eugene Garber offered much needed structural help at SUNYA. Also at SUNYA, Dr. Allan Ballard's encouraging words after reading the first chapter added greatly to my confidence.

The Black Writer's Collective, directed by Henry Evans and Brian Ansara, gave me an opportunity to read and I was critiqued by other writers of different genres.

In 1988, I joined The Hudson Valley Writers Group—fiction only. Joachim Frank directed the group that followed Dr. Garber's format. The critics who read my many long chapters were: Frank Gould, Moses Cash, Carol Shriver, Penina Spinka, Frank Copa, Mary Ellen Barrett, Kelly Lopez, and Joachim Frank.

Near the end of the first draft in 1990, I met Peter Buchard. Peter wrote *One Galant Rush,* the book on which the movie *Glory* is based. Peter repeated much of the criticism I had already received. Peter, however, moved me into adding many of the finishing touches I needed for consideration of publication.

My family and friends who provided me with resourceful information are many: much of the information in Chapter Four came from Mr. Romey Jerman (deceased), Mr. Ed Martin, Mrs. Nan Roaf, my cousins Carry Noble and Thomas Hill Jr., my sisters Geneva Pope and Deloris Harris, Mr. Louis Tidwell (over 100 years old), and my nephew Austin Hill (a history buff). Also, Harvey Bradley (my boyhood friend who has done much independent research) and Ben Dorrough (another boyhood friend who has an excellent memory).

1

Now I see what the hawk's eyes must have seen, soaring high above the purple forest, the powerful wandering Arkansas River, branching out through its many creeks and bayous snaking their way through the hills, the alluvial soils of the plains, the lowlands, seeking the scattered fields of corn, cotton, sleeping farms of rice and hay while the trunk kept steady on its way to the mighty Mississippi. This trapezoid, this patch of earth quilted in between the confederates, is part of the heartland. Texased and Oklahomaed on the west, Louisianaed on the south, Missouried on the north, Tennesseed and Mississippied on the east, Arkansas, land of my mother and father, land of my birth, on which I rest my memory of a time long passed.

After my father died, I went to live with Uncle Pet, who owned a general store. The store was next to his big white rambling five-bedroom house with three porches. It was architecturally overdone, with dormers and gables that served no useful purpose since the attic was only a crawl space. Unlike the house, the store was a long simple shotgun structure with a steep pitched roof and a low colonnaded front porch.

Not only did Uncle Pet sell flour, lard, sugar, salt, cheese, and ham, to name a few of the items in his stock, he reigned over the affairs of the community and dictated to people under his control. Uncle Pet had religion, and he believed in conversion and submersion. He wanted everybody to follow God exactly as he did. Those who didn't have his kind of religion he ostracized as misfits. No matter how much money a person or his family had, how intelligent, good-looking, or talented, if the person didn't profess Christ, submit to baptism, and keep a membership in the Baptist Church, that person was lesser in Uncle Pet's eyes.

Uncle Pet, like most other people in our community, believed that true religion demanded sanction, confirmation, certification, and a miracle as a sign of proof from God himself. Without that proof, acquired through much praying and suffering until all sins were purged and washed away, God would not allow conversion, prerequisite for admission into the great company of *the Faithful*—the chosen of God.

Uncle Pet noted his leadership among The Faithful each Sunday when he knelt to pray. Bowing on one knee from a six-foot frame, head held high, one hand on the back of a chair, well-dressed in a pinstriped seersucker suit, highly shined black round-toe loafers, a starched white shirt with a black tie and stick pin, gold watch fob dangling from a protruding, Buddha-like belly, a rather long, shaved head with a large frontal lobe, beautiful big white teeth accentuated with several gold crowns on the sides, a stern, noble, naturally hairless face, slanted, penetrating dark-brown eyes, balanced features, he looked as if he was fixing to give God orders rather than ask him for something.

Uncle Pet and his wife, Aint Babe, never had any children of their own. He filled that void in his life by taking in boys and girls who, as in the case of my cousin Saravania and myself, had lost one of their parents. He even moved a distant handicapped cousin, Happy Bill, and his mother from the bottom country and took them under his wing until they could build their own house.

When I was growing up in Arkansas, Baptists didn't christen babies. If you were born in a Baptist family, you remained a sinner, outside the church, until you found religion, repented your sins, and joined the church. Baptists would never ask, "What is your denomination?" because for them, you had none without "religion." The importance of *what kind?* was driven home to me at thirteen, when I witnessed Uncle Pet's interrogation of Geeche Tommie Beard one summer Saturday evening in the store.

"Is that all, Mr. . . . er . . . er . . . ?" Uncle Pet stammered as he looked intently at the stranger.

"Beard, Tommie Beard," Beard replied in a thick Geeche accent seldom heard by us because we weren't used to Geeches in Arkansas. They are also known as Gullahs and come from the sea islands and coastal districts of South Carolina, Georgia, and northeastern Florida. Their accent, language pattern, and close-knit lifestyle set them apart as strange to most of us. If we complained about being cheated, we would say, "He took our money." A Geeche would say, "He took *we* money." We would ask, "What is it?" A Geeche would ask, "What it *is*?" For "There he is," a Geeche would say, "*There* he." For "Where is he?" a Geeche would ask, "Where he *is*?" Though the children went to school and church with us, their speech patterns remained the same.

"I'll git it straight next time," Uncle Pet replied.

"Tha-that all right, Mitter Pet. That all right," Beard allowed.

"All right, sir," Uncle Pet said, tapping on the bag that held Beard's groceries. "You new eround heah, Mr. Beard." Asking and answering his own question.

"New. Yes sir, I new."

"You . . . er . . . church man, Mr. Beard?"

"Yes sir, I iah."

"Whut religion?—schuuh." Uncle Pet paused and discharged his characteristic gush of air, due to a chronic shortness of breath. Swimmers and brakes on Greyhound buses made the same noise. "If I'm not being too nosy?"

"Baptiss. Mittinary Baptiss."

A big smile came over Uncle Pet's face. "That right?"

Beard's mouth was full of snuff juice. I noticed him looking around for a spittoon.

Uncle Pet noticed also. "Sun,er . . . er, boy, git that spittoon for Mr. . . . er-r-r, Beard."

Sun was my nickname. Papa named me Mark Andrew, after himself and my grandfather. I moved quickly.

Beard squirted into the spittoon. A long string of okrafied spit hung stubbornly from his lip. He wiped it off with his shirtsleeve. "Been a Baptiss all my life. Me 'n my family."

"Praise the Lord, Brother Beard! I'm a Baptist too. You know, lots er folks say they Baptist, but they ain't really been *born ergin*—schuuh. Tell me, Brother Beard—schuuh—how do you know you been converted 'n you truly got religion?—schuuh—not that I doubt you or anything, but you know how it is wid us Baptist—schuuh—when we truly been born ergin of the Holy Spirit—schuuh— we like to talk erbout it, 'n we like to heah other Baptist talk erbout it."

Brother Beard reached for the spittoon. He took his time, spat, and wiped again. That same long brown slimy string hung from his mouth as before, for which he repeated his shirtsleeve habit. "I talk erbout it."

"You know, when I was lookin' for religion, I had to have er sign from God Himself—schuuh—as proof I had been saved." Uncle Pet paused to see if Brother Beard was listening.

Brother Beard lifted up a hundred-pound sack of feed, hoisted it to his shoulder, and carried it out to his wagon. He came back for his other things. "I talk erbout it."

Uncle Pet handed Brother Beard the rest of his items. "I prayed 'n asked God to cleanse my soul so I would be fit to receive His sign."

"I prayed too—prayed hard. Don't mind talkin' erbout it." He half muttered something to himself as he walked to his wagon. Straightened his groceries. Stepped up on the wheel, and sat on his tall seat.

Uncle Pet stood on the porch of his store, poised and waiting for Brother Beard to "talk erbout it."

Brother Beard picked up his reins and drove away. He didn't even look back once.

Uncle Pet's right hand went to his slick, shining head. He rubbed it in a puzzled fashion. "Huh, strange-talkin', strange-actin' fellah—schuuh. Wonder wheah he come from." He hobbled back inside the store without so much as acknowledging my presence. He reappeared. "Sun . . . er . . . er, boy, git er broom and sweep this store out.—schuuh—Clean up eround heah."

Young as I was, I had a feeling Uncle Pet was overreaching. Expecting Brother Beard to testify to *him*, not to God.

As I was sweeping the store out, Saravania, who had recently come to live with us, entered. She was developed far beyond her thirteen years. Saravania was something to behold! She was slightly above five feet tall. Working in the garden under the hot Arkansas sun had deepened her earthy rich ginger-brown skin in spite of the wide floppy straw hat she wore. The piercing swell that pressed against her dress revealed impressions of her firm nipples, which stood out like two exclamation marks. Her breasts were already the size of two nice cantaloupes. The independent quivering movements of her round plump buttocks beneath her loosely fitting long cotton dress, gathered and tied at the waist—revealing part of her perfect legs—suggested good times to my imagination. Her gray "cat's eyes"—as we called them—took some getting used to. She, of course, was not conscious of any difference. I loved the way she swayed back and forth when she carried cooked food and groceries to and from the house, then returned to help me clean the store. Her help took the form of a number of questions about how to clerk in the store.

Saravania talked with a lisp. She couldn't pronounce her *s*'s. *Sun* came out *Thun*.

"Thun," she said. "Do you know how to work theth thcalth?"

"Nothing to it," I bragged.

"Thuppoth I wanted five poundth er thugar. How would you wait on me?"

"Well, I'd put yo' sack on the scale 'n scoop the stuff in till it showed five pounds heah." I pointed to the spot on the scale. "Then I'd move this little dial over to five cents er pound 'n read twenty-five cents right underneath."

"That thavth time figurin' it out with er penthil, eh, Thun?"

"Yeah, but you don't need er pencil for that," I said.

We tolerated Methodists, though certainly they didn't have a chance in hell of going to heaven like us Baptists. My older sister Jessie married the son of a sanctified family—that is, the Church of God and Christ. They were Holy Rollers compared to the more sedate Baptists; with their massive following, the Baptists thought the Saints were beneath them. Sometimes the two intermarried and went to school together, but on Sundays they stayed away from each other. Still, Jessie's husband was OK because he had been up north and attained some stature in the world. Though he hadn't professed any religion, it wasn't polite to come straight out and call him a common sinner like everybody else outside the church, because he was in the family. They dressed it up and simply said, "He's unconnected to any church at this time." Translated, that meant, "We're goin' to work on 'im—make er Baptist out of 'im." When my sister converted to a Saint instead, I thought my father would start a religious war.

I watched him frantically raking the wall for his hat and cane and taking off like he was going to put out a fire when he first found out Jessie had converted. I hopped and skipped along beside him—on our way to Jessie's house, Over In The Hills—every bit as puffed up and angry as he was. He kept mumbling about what a shame it was and how he was going to talk some sense into that girl's head if he had to kill her to do it.

I think it's er shame too, Papa, I thought. "We Baptists, ain't we, Papa?"

"We Baptists 'n we gon' stay Baptists as long as I got breath in this body."

It did my heart good to be in harmony with Papa. I was more than sure that he couldn't possibly be wrong about anything. Whenever he would let me, I was his shadow.

I thought, *That Jessie's gonna git it.* I had no idea what *it* was, since she had long passed the age of being whipped. I satisfied myself that Papa would take care of it good and proper. I skipped up a little ahead of him as we neared Jessie's house.

"Y'all come on in," Jessie said. "Papa, you wringin' wet. Gimme yo' hat 'n set down. You know y' shouldn't be walkin' way over heah in this hot weather like this. Let me git y' some cool water."

Junior came to the door. Even though I was his uncle, there wasn't much difference in our ages.

"I wanna talk to you, Jessie," Papa said.

"Sho, Papa," Jessie said, moving toward the door. "Junior, y'all go on out 'n play. We'll call y' when we through."

Junior and I went outside. I was eager to listen to what they were going to say, but they closed the door. That stupid Junior was more interested in some irrelevant mud houses and June bugs rolling up cow dung into nasty little balls than in rich, juicy, informative gossip.

When Papa finally came out of the house, he was in a bigger hurry than when he left home. Jessie was running behind him with his hat. "Papa, wait!"

"Come on, boy, let's go! Been er Baptist all yo' life. Yo' grandfather wuz er Baptist. Yo' grandmother, yo' uncles, everybody in yo' family. How kin y' do this to us? How kin y' do it to yo'self?"

Jessie managed to get his hat partly on his head. He squashed it on and kept strutting. I jogged to keep up with him. I looked back; Jessie was standing with her arms folded looking lost and sad until we moved out of sight. As far as Papa and I were concerned, Sister Jessie became a forgotten member of our family. At least that's how angry we were at that moment.

Catholics were foreigners. A few of our people who didn't have farms of their own hired out to the Catholic farm consortium during cotton-chopping and cotton-picking time. Quite a few also attended the Catholic school, but for one of us to join their church—and a few did—was to become an outcast. The Faithful simply didn't know how to deal with such a person.

I used to marvel at how those Sisters could do all that hard farm work wrapped like mummies in those long black dresses in that hot weather. Every time I met or talked to one of them, she was caring and respectful. They mystified me.

Uncle Pet believed that to have a man in a white backwards collar go between you and your God was unthinkable, un-Christian, and definitely un-Baptist. "Worst of all—schuuh—none of um got religion. All y' gotta do to join they church is show up, raise yo' han', 'n they'll let y' in.—schuuh—Then they got that little birdbath where the priest dips his fingers—schuuh—throws er few drops er water at y', calling his-self baptizing y', like the Methodist.—schuuh—Everbody knows John the Baptist baptized Jesus in the River Jordan—schuuh—'n I'm quite sho he didn't lead 'Im out theah in all that water just to sprinkle er little of it in His face.—schuuh—Bible says you must be baptized!—schuuh—That means submerged—put under!"

Uncle Pet was the boss in the little church that I attended. His dominance stemmed from the fact that the church was named after Uncle Pet's father (my grandfather, M. A. Hughes), the founder. In addition, Papa, Uncle Pet's brother, was superintendent of the Sunday school and a head deacon. That constituted a strong family tradition in the organization that few were willing to openly contest.

The front of Hughes Chapel was a simple attempt at a pointed arch, flanked by stained glass windows over the main entrance. The ornate architectural motif on and around the double doors at the entrance wove comfortably with the marble cornerstone, DEDICATED TO THE LOVING MEMORY OF M. A. HUGHES 1874. A whitewashed covered well stood at the northeast corner. The little country edifice, representing the state of the art for its day, stood in the midst of five acres of forested red Arkansas clay. The graveyard took a good portion of the land.

Stately oaks, whose mighty roots sought water deep beneath the surface stratum, provided ever-present and ever-pleasant shade, as they had done for generations past. Beneath their giant umbrellas, we would spread our goodies for Easter, Mother's Day, Children's Day, box suppers, and Saturday night barbecues. Beneath their umbrellas we parked our cars, held our wedding receptions, argued religion and church politics. Beneath their umbrellas, men and boys dug the graves of departed Brothers and Sisters, hunted Easter eggs, and—to avoid that disgusting outhouse—pissed against the moldy bark. Young lovers found each other in the nighttime shadows of oak foliage.

Inside the simple frame structure, finished with dark brown stained wood, punctuated along the sides with stained glass windows, the first thing that struck one's eye upon entering was country folks' attempt at decorating and dressing up the pulpit with an ornately embroidered cloth that draped like curtains. Long tasseled ropes hung to the floor at the center and the sides. Two tall colored candles flanked the big open Bible on top. The communion table also served for collecting money. It always sported a handsome vase of flowers, wild when they were in season, placed directly in the center.

Consistent with traditional conformist patterns, symmetry, inside and out, was as natural as planting the same furrows of cotton or corn each spring, generation after generation. If possible, The Faithful would have placed the bell tower directly in the center where the double doors were. They manifested their conservatism even in the wearing of pants: they didn't trust suspenders alone, so they added a belt to hold things up.

Behind the choir seats on the right was the Brothers' amen corner. Symmetrically opposite was the Sisters' amen corner. Uncle Pet's special seat was directly in front of the Brothers' corner. They lined the sanctuary walls with flattering pictures of the dead pastors, whom Papa called "the Cadre Rigor Mortis," and the boasting tall maroon-upholstered pastor's chair they placed directly in the center. Four feet directly in front of the communion table was the menacing, dreaded moaner's bench. That relic of the dark ages was simply constructed of dark wood and even harder than the church seats. It wasn't built, however, for sitting, leaning back, or reclining in any direction that approached comfort. It was built for one thing and one thing only—to torture a confession of faith out of sinners. Like an electric chair, they pulled it out when needed once a year. Otherwise they stored it away until the victims were readied for the next July.

One Sunday morning, a week or so before revival started, Uncle Pet rose to put the finger on Brother Wiley, who was in the process of kneeling to receive sacrament. "Brother Pastor, with all due brotherly love and in keeping with good conduct *and* Christian spirit—schuuh"—pruning his words—"understand me now—schuuh—I don't like to do this, but I feel it is my Christian duty, 'n yo' Christian duty also—schuuh—if you see somebody doin' wrong—sinnin' 'n breakin' the rules er the church—schuuh—it is yo' *duty* to bring um before the pastor and members of this church." Brother Wiley stood there with a hangdog look on his face as if he had wet his pants. His big sweaty hands clutched tightly to a little thimble of grape juice as if his very life depended on it.

Uncle Pet continued. "Now, passin' the other night, I saw Brother Wiley at that all-night hoedown they had up the Pike."

"Brother Wiley?" someone in the congregation gasped.

"You know that thing where that ol' Boditley sings all them ol' low-down songs and picks the devil's guitar."

Reverend Jarrett looked over his wire-framed glasses. "Is that true, Brother Wiley?"

Looking like a turkey the day before Thanksgiving, Brother Wiley croaked, "Well . . . er . . . er . . . Brother Pet . . . I . . . I can splain."

"Please do, Brother Wiley. I'm sho everbody wants to heah erbout it."

People in the congregation snickered.

"Well . . . er . . . er . . . Brother Pet . . . er . . . er . . . er . . . I wuz up there lookin' fer my sister. She . . . she . . . er sinner done *gone* erstray!"

That familiar lopsided smile crept into the corner of Uncle Pet's mouth. He knew he had caught his prey in a bald-faced lie. "You jist added to yo' sins, Brother Wiley.—schuuh—Wuz that yo' sister you wuz dancin' wid?" Snickering turned to laughter, and when it subsided, Uncle Pet got back down to business. "Now, I still love you, Brother Wiley. Not only because that *also* is my Christian duty, but—schuuh—because of the forgiving spirit in my heart and my goodwill toward my neighbor.—schuuh—Now, I'm goin' to recommend to the church that you repent to our pastor, to the Deacon Board, and to the members of this church befo' you be allowed to commune with us—"

A sense of relief crept over Brother Wiley's face too soon. He thought he would be allowed to take communion after he repented.

"Schuuh—in six months."

Brother Wiley lowered his head again and set the thimble back on the table.

Reverend Jarrett, an educated man with no power, succumbed to Uncle Pet's demands after an empty speech about forgiveness and a quote from the Bible about Jesus and the woman at the well.

"Now I feel it's only fair to warn you, Brother Wiley—schuuh—if you're caught ergin, I will personally recommend that you be put out of this church. With all due respect 'n love, I jist want to make that cleah."

Reverend Jarrett raised his hands, palms facing The Faithful. "We're going to pray for you, Brother Wiley, that God will give you strength to do His will."

The church replied, "Ehhhh-men."

That was no idle threat. Uncle Pet had his spies. If Brother Wiley was caught again, he would indeed be put out. I had seen Uncle Pet ride herd on many sinners, hypocrites, and backsliders. Some would stammer like Brother Wiley. Others scratched where they didn't itch, looked down at their feet, or babbled incoherent or nonsensical responses, but none dared tell him to go to hell, which was what I thought they should have done.

With that kind of background, it was imperative—*mandatory*—even at the ripe old age of thirteen, that I seek and find Christ. Get religion! There were many fascinating stories on how to get religion. All of The Faithful had their own version. I had heard most of them by the time I was twelve. They all involved much self-imposed fasting, praying, solitude, pain, and suffering. All involved miracles.

Sister Grey testified that she had prayed in the bell tower of the church and found her miracle. I knew they locked the building when it was empty. I wondered if that almost three-hundred-pound woman had scaled that thirty-foot tower and climbed in through the louvers near the top.

She said she asked the Lord to let her know if she had religion by causing the bell in the tower to ring three times. When it did, she came roaring down from that tower praising the Lord and testifying! For a long time, my young mind was trying to find room for Sister Grey's enormous body in the upper portion of that tiny tower.

Brother Butler, who was afraid to walk past the cemetery even in broad daylight, claimed he found the miracle while praying in his barn. He asked the Lord to let him know if he had religion by lifting up the wagon tongue three times and rolling the wagon out of the barn, without the help of a horse or a man. If that wagon tongue had moved even an inch, Brother Butler would have been so terrified he would have forgotten who, what, and what for.

Every year after we laid by crops, usually the Fourth of July, the church held a big revival. Those revivals lasted two weeks. The pastor sidestepped them. They called in a fire and brimstone evangelist, paid him cash or whatever he could barter, and the ordeal began.

The church called sinners to the moaners' bench from miles around. Most were young country girls and boys. Some were older men and women—veterans—who had not found the miracle during previous revivals. Those repeaters were honest fools, driven by aberrations, ambition, or the fear of ostracism from their clan.

First night of the revival, we moaners were all in the anteroom. Through the walls we could hear:

> *IIIIII love the Lord,*
> *He heard my cryyy-yyy . . .*

Meanwhile, in the anteroom, two mothers of the church were teaching us the art of humility, submission, lamentation, and how to stand frustration. Crying, looking sad, getting down on our knees, clasping our hands in front of our faces with our heads bowed and our eyes closed, and rocking back and forth were parts of the ritual as we learned to become serious moaners.

There was much laying on of hands by Mother this and Mother that. Long slender bony fingers. Fat puffy ones. Short stubby ones. Sweat, mixed with cheap cologne, produced a rather confused, sweet-smelling funk—a noxious odor.

> *Every time I*
> *Feel the spirit*
> *Moving in my heart*
> *I will pray.*
> *Every time I . . .*

"That's yo' Unka Pet singin', Sun," said Mother Fat-Fingers. As if I couldn't hear. I was sure people in Pine Ridge six miles away could hear him.

Deacon Tiggins stuck his head in the door. "Y'all got um ready yet?"

I felt like a steer going to the dipping vat. Mother Bony-Hands took over. "Ready as they ga' git. Sun, you jes' don't look like no moaner t' me." She rubbed her bony fingers over my face again, maybe thinking that was going to make me look the part. I was happy when she shifted attention from me to Saravania and rubbed her face for a change. "You neither, Saravania," Mother Bony-Hands told my cousin. "Y'all two look like you fixin' t' go to er picture show er som'um. This is ser'ous business, y'all."

"How ith a moaner thuppothed to—?" Saravania started to ask, but Mother Bony-Hands stifled her words.

"Shhhhhh, chile! Don't y' know y' ain't s'posed t' talk when y' on the bench?" I guessed we were supposed to look like we were on our way to the electric chair. We heard more singing coming through the walls of the ante-room.

> *Up on the mountain,*
> *Where my Lord spoke,*
> *Out of his mouth came*
> *Fire and smoke.*
> *Every time I . . .*

Deacon Tiggins stuck his head in the door again. "Brother Pet said t' line um up 'n bring um on out."

Deacon Tiggins, followed by Mothers Bony-Hands and Fat-Fingers, led us into the meeting. They positioned us as if we were fixing to be sold.

> *Ain't but the one train*
> *Runs on this track,*
> *It runs to heaven,*
> *Runs right back.*
> *Every time I*
> *Feel the spirit—*

Uncle Pet, who was leading the song, was in rare form. I had a feeling of hopeless insufficiency, being thrust into the middle of that high court of religious fever, completely controlled by my Uncle Pet and his nest of zealots. The sound was loud even in the anteroom. In the middle of it, I was almost overcome. All of those voices seemed to be coming directly at me. I didn't dare look anybody in the face. I glimpsed Uncle Pet out of the corner of my eye as he watched my every move. Mama and my sisters Geneva and Verleen were watching me from the audience. My brother, Elbert, was sitting in a different seat with his buddies.

Reverend Jarrett rose slowly and moved ceremoniously to the pulpit. The congregation kept humming quietly:

> *Every time I*
> *Feel the spirit—*

Reverend Jarrett spoke. "Praise the Lord, children! Praise the Lord! Some of you young folks are looking mighty scared tonight. There's nothing to be afraid of if you'll repent your sins and come on to Christ while you're young. Say eh-man, church."

"Eh-man."

"I told you I'd get him here, didn't I? The Lord has blessed us to have this outstanding man of the gospel come to pour out his soul to us for the next *two* weeks. If he can't help you find your way to Jesus, I don't know who can. Say eh-man!"

"Eh-man!"

"Say 'Praise the Lord!'"

"Praise the Lord!" The voice of Sister Bony-Hands rose above the others.

"Say 'Thank you, Jesus!'"

"Thank you, Jesus!"

"I don't wanna git loose here now. So, without going any further, I'll turn you over into the capable hands of the Reverend Bradford E. Taylor!"

Bony-Hands, Fat-Fingers, and Deacon Tiggins went down the line, forcing all of us moaners to our knees.

The Sisters in their amen corner started vocalizing prematurely:

> *Sinner, pleeeease don't let this harvest pass,*
> *Sinner, pleeeease don't let this harvest pass*
> *And the deeeevil git yo' soul at last.*

The harvest was just beginning, and they sounded as if we were on our way to hell already.

The whole church rose as the Reverend Taylor strode to the pulpit. He grabbed Reverend Jarrett's hand in passing. Reverend Taylor was a tall, smooth-skinned, dark honey-colored specimen, very much in the mold of the Cadre Rigor Mortis that preceded him. He looked to be about forty. He was well dressed in a pearl gray suit, long-collared white shirt, and black and white shoes, complemented with a black and white tie with thin red stripes and a handkerchief to match. "Ha-ha-ha-ha! You just go ahead and git loose if you want to, Reverend. This is the house of the Lord. You're the pastor. You can git loose anytime you feel like it." At the pulpit, he asked, "Can I get er eh-man, church?"

"Eh-h-h-man!"

"Praise God on high!"

"Hallelujah!" Brothers' corner.

"I'm just so happy you invited me here to git loose with you. And believe me, Brother Pastor, that's precisely what I intend to do! Ha-ha-ha-ha—praise the Lord."

"Praise His holy name!" Sisters' corner.

"Moaners, take heed. You have a choice. You can git loose too—*tonight*! All you have to do is stay on your knees after you have prayed till you can't pray no more, but you keep on praying anyhow, and-and you have cried till your tears have run dry, but you keep on crying, you-you have moaned till you're weary, but you keep on moaning anyhow. Yes, you do. Repent your sins! Resolve to live a clean Christian life, and when you're ready, when-when God is satisfied that you are indeed serious, when you have been molded and tested in the fire of God's mighty foundry and found worthy—He *will* show you a sign! Yes He will!"

CHURCH: "Yes He will!"
TAYLOR: "Yes He will!"
CHURCH: "Yes He will!"
TAYLOR: "Ooooh, yes He will!"

We moaners were all on our knees. The different shapes and sizes of our behinds were sticking high up in the air. Reverend Taylor was preaching to our rear ends. I was kneeling next to a juicy-mouthed repeater whom I called Abba-Lord, who kept grunting and wailing some incomprehensible duosyllabic introduction to every fragmented sentence he attempted.

"Abba-Lord, I know—I know why-why-why—"

I was thinking, *How can the Lord answer a prayer He can't begin to understand?*

Funeral parlor fans were flapping like the wings of butterflies. Our arms and elbows rested on whatever space we could find. Our bodies took different positions, sprawled over the bench. Sometimes we maintained those positions for two hours. It was nonstop praying. Uncle Pet had ordered me not to eat too much, so I wouldn't have to go to that stinking outhouse behind the church. If I did have to go, he told me to keep moaning and praying while sitting on the throne.

The Reverend Taylor's voice rose as he said, "You have all heard the story of the prodigal son. How the younger son said, 'Father, give me all I've got coming to me, now!' You know, so many of us are like that. We can't wait to find out from a wise and almighty God what's best for us. We-we get itchy, and-and impatient, and we *leap* before we look. Yes we do. Some of us get a little money, don't have to be much, and-and we throw it away on the first frivolous thing we see. You may as well say eh-man!"

"Ehhhh-man, Reverend!"

"And so it was with that young man. He took everything he had and made a clean break from a good home and a loving father. And he went far away into another country."

"Abba-Lord, forgive this poor sinner for leaving home! I . . . err . . . I . . . errr . . . "

Sisters' corner:

> *If it wutten for Jesus,*
> *I wouldn' ha-a-ve er-r-r frien-n-d.*
> *If it wutten for Jesus,*
> *I wouldn' ha-a-ave er friend.*

"Yes, Lord!"

TAYLOR: "Pray with me a little while now."
BROTHERS' CORNER: "Wel-l-l."
ANOTHER BROTHER: "Talk to us now!"
TAYLOR: "He went into a far country where nobody even knew his name, where he was among a group of strangers."

"Abba-Abba Lord, forgive me for goin' among them strangers! I won't do that ergin. I . . . errr. . . I . . . errr . . . "

TAYLOR: "You know, it don't pay to get too far away from God."
SISTERS' CORNER: "You better b'lieve it." Moaning:

> *Oh I'm on my journey,*
> *And I can-n-n-n't turn 'round—*

And so it went, into the third hour. The pain we were supposed to feel was concentrated in my knees.

SISTERS' CORNER: "Come on spirit! Move him!"
TAYLOR: "You know, sometimes you can get so far away from God you can't get back. Don't let that happen to you sinners. You get too far out there in sin, and one day *death* comes creeping in your room. Too late then! Too late. Help me now."

BROTHERS' CORNER: "Preach! like we know you can!"

TAYLOR: "And in that far country, he wasted all his money on riotous and
wicked living! And my Bible tells me there was a famine in the land,
and he found himself at the mercy of one of those strangers, and-and
the stranger sent him into the field to feed the swine!"

As Taylor took the prodigal through all his trials and conversions, and back
home to his father, his voice rose higher. At last it began to tremble.

BROTHERS' CORNER: "Git it right now! Talk t' us like we know you can!"

Abba-Lord became rambunctious and more motivated. That called for help
from The Faithful: "Move him, Lord! Shake the devil erway from him!"
Church moaning:

> *Every chile of Gooooo-dd*
> *Got t' cry sometimes—*

TAYLOR: "And while he was out there feeding the swine, he sunk so low
he started to eat their leftovers. Stay with me now. But when he was
down to his last contact with sanity . . . and-and his last contact with
humanity, a wonderful thing happened. Yes it did. Somehow he
found the strength, and he lifted his head to the heavens. And he
cried, 'My father!—Myyyyy father!—My father has many hired
servants. And even though I'm no longer worthy to be called his son,
as wretched as I am, as sinful as I am, I will arise!'—Hallelujah!—
Praise God!—'I will ariiiiise! and go to my father! And I will say to
him, "I have sinned against heaven and before thee!"' Honest
confession is good for the soul. Come on home, sinners! Come on
hommmme!"

ABBA-LORD BEGAN TO SHAKE AND TREMBLE: "Abba-Lord, I'm goin' home!
I'm goin' home!"

BOTH CORNERS GOT INTO THE ACT: "Come on home, sinner! Come on
home!"

TAYLOR MOVED IN WITH AUTHORITY: "I can see him now, ragged, dirty,
bearded, scared, stumbling and falling along the way, but coming on
home! And I can see his father, old and bent, with a cane, peeping
and straining to see who it is. Finally, I can see his wrinkled face come
to life. Then, I can see him with his arms outstretched and tears
running down his cheeks. Glory hallelujah! 'My son. Myyyyyyy son
has come hommmmme at last!'"

BOTH CORNERS: "Preach! Preach!"

"He had done foolish things, but he was no fool. Even though he knew his father had forgiven him and received him back into the fold, my Bible tells me, he got down on his knees." Taylor got down on his knees, intoning, "And he said, 'Father! Father!'"

The congregation echoed him: "Father-r-r-r!"

TAYLOR: "'Father-r-r-rrrr! Why are you so good to me?' The father turned to his servants, who seemed a little slow. The head servant, knowing how the older brother felt, even dared to complain. The old man said, 'Don't mess with me now! Bring the best robe and put it on him. Put a *rinnnng* on his finger and sandals on his feeeeet!' Oh glory, praise God! And not only that, he said, 'I want you to kill the fatted calf! We're going to have a party! For this, my son was *dea-a-a-a-a-ad* and is alive again! Was *los-s-s-s-st!* but now he's found! Was *bli-i-i-i-i-nd!* but now he sees!'"

As Reverend Taylor clothed the son and killed the fatted calf, the church was in an uproar. Sisters shouted and rejoiced. Brothers stumbled over each other's feet as they rushed to comfort those shouting Sisters. I dodged in an effort to avoid being trampled, while Saravania quietly moved to an empty seat and kept on praying. Abba-Lord was in a state of hysteria, shaking and jerking.

Taylor, seeing that he had a big fish on his hook, reached out his hands to Abba-Lord and preached directly to him. Abba-Lord twisted, turned, and with his juicy mouth and sweaty body gave us a great show until, breathless, he gave up his hand in fellowship.

I was puzzled, but impressed. Most of all I was happy. I no longer had to sit beside him or listen to his incoherent babbling or suffer his unsolicited showers. Now I could make a beeline for the outhouse.

Once you fessed up and were baptized and taken into the Missionary Baptist Church, it was for better or for worse. They tolerated no talk. It depended on your performance. We were required to attend, pay dues, sing and pray, testify, and help dig graves, not necessarily in that order. Attendance was easy for me because I was a minor and was forced. I had no money, but 25 cents per week was no problem for Uncle Pet. If I was lucky enough to get my hands on a coin, I wasn't about to give it to some old bald-headed, bad-singing deacon. I liked to sing, and I was given high marks as a singer. I took after Uncle Pet, whose good voice rose above other members of our congregation.

Praying aloud was considered an art. Very big in the church. The biggest devil in the congregation could redeem himself if he could express himself while on his knees fulfilling a church ritual.

I sang better than I prayed, while Uncle Pet shone as a singer and a prayer. He had the spirit, and he was articulate. He had a flair for the dramatic.

On any given night of the two-week revival, after a soul-stirring hymn to set the mood and before the sermon, someone always called on Uncle Pet to pray. "Dear God, I ask you to look down from yo' mighty throne and touch the heart of every one of these sinners.—schuuh—Show them that you're God and besides you there is no other.—schuuh—Turn them eround and help them to see the light befo' it is too late.—schuuh—Help them t' realize that you're er most powerful God—schuuh—who can move mountains simply by willing it be done!"

BROTHERS' CORNER: "Talk t' Im, Brother Pet!"
A VOICE FROM THE CONGREGATION: "Take yo' time! Take yo' time!"

"I'm talkin' erbout the God that delivered Daniel from the lion's den,—schuuh—the Hebrew children from the fiery furnace. The same God that heard my prayer one day and set my soul on fire!"

BROTHERS' CORNER: "Talk to the man! Like we know you can!"

"The saaaaame God that holds the lightning 'n thunder in one hand and holds back the mighty storms with the other!"

BROTHERS' CORNER: "Git it right now!"

"Just glance down at these po' moaners one time."

BOTH CORNERS: "One time!"
A SINGLE VOICE FROM THE BROTHERS' CORNER: "That's all it takes!"
UNCLE PET kept a drumbeat in his prayers: "Yes, one tiiiiiime."
VOICE FROM THE BROTHERS' CORNER: "Good God a-mighty! One time!"

Uncle Pet knew to end his prayers on a high note, and when the preacher rose to speak, the spirit was already in the congregation.

The handicapped were welcome in the church and encouraged in the services. My cousin Happy Bill was physically and mentally impaired. We called him Happy Bill because he was so spirited and active during services.

I seldom understood anything Happy Bill said, but he *could* put on a great show. When he was happy—which was all the time—he would keep moaners and everybody else in church long past the accustomed hour. The people liked and sympathized with him. His lead in singing always brought the best support from the people with high spirits and good voices, and his praying did the same.

Happy Bill was not the only one who took encouragement from others. In the case of loud bad singers, the Sisters shouted, "Hep him, Lord. Hep her, Lord." When the singing was unbearable, the Sisters called, "Lord, *pleeeease* hep the chile!"

Testifying was a big test. If a person couldn't testify loud, long, and with fire, their religion was considered weak and suspect. If one could testify well, it went a long way toward proving that one was not among the fakers.

As the days of the revival followed one another, new moaners came through the woods from miles around, often in the heat of day, sometimes at night, to cry and testify and preach like John the Baptist.

Most moaners asked the Lord to perform small miracles, but even those were hard to do in response to weeks and sometimes years of praying and repenting. Some moaners came back year after year trying to find the magic sign.

At first, I tried the tough miracles: "Lord, let me know if I have religion by making that big boulder move six inches." And I was prepared to measure. When the boulder didn't move after thirty minutes, I guessed that unless the Lord was hard of hearing, my request was out of line, and I was ready to negotiate. If the boulder was too heavy, what about a little stone? And I was willing to forget the measuring. After nothing happened, I changed my request from rocks to living things. "Lord, let me know if I have religion by causing that plant to wither and die before my very eyes." Despite the hot sun, there was no change in the plant. It was so hot I was tempted to ask for a burning bush, but if the plant had only grown healthier, what luck would I have with a bush?

A change of bait sometimes works for a fisherman, so I asked for a different demonstration. "Lord, if I have religion, make water spring up behind that big gum tree." Not only did water not spring up anyplace near that tree, but that year the water table was so low that most creeks and ponds had all but dried up.

I thought of asking the Lord to let me know if I had religion by lifting a tree out of the ground by its roots. My mind told me, *Don't be a fool. Lifting a tree out of the ground by its roots would surely involve a twister, a tornado.*

Since I had struck out on moving the boulder and the small stone, the withering plant, and the upspringing water—I chickened out on the burning bush and the tornado—I toned down my request to simpler miracles. "Lord, let me know if I have religion by causing the barn to move. Not a lot. And I don't care in which direction. Please!"

I was prepared to come out of the wilderness like many of my fellow moaners, testifying about my newfound religion. After all, I had less to repent than many young devils I knew on that bench. In fact, Ben Barrow had stolen my girl not more than two weeks before the revival started.

It was customary, sporting, and a sure sign of growing up to treat a girl—or someone you were trying to make your girl—to a cold drink and a barbecue sandwich. Even though I was too young to make my intentions known and receive permission to come courting, I had engaged in some reckless eye-balling with Cora, and she had responded with a smile or two. It was enough to indicate to me that she was my girl. Besides, she lived up the Pike near me. Her brother Usef was one of my buddies. Her father traded in Uncle Pet's store. I had put on some of my best wrestling matches for her benefit. And her brother had told me, "She likes you." With all those circumstantial circum-scriptions, I figured I had everything sewed up.

That night, about two weeks before the revival started, I was prepared to make my move. Naturally, my first weapons were none other than a cold drink and a barbecue sandwich. An act like that had led many a country girl behind a tree to some serious kissing. And if you got her in the mood and if your rabbit foot was working, she might even go further.

Wooden stands were assembled underneath the oaks. Kerosene lamps burned as brightly as they could. A slow-burning fire kept the meat hot. Smoking rags sent up signals to the swarms of mosquitoes. I eased my way up beside where she stood in the night shadows. I smiled.

She smiled back.

"Cora?"

"Whut?" she said.

"Could I buy you a barbecue sammich and a cold drink?"

"If you wanna," she replied.

"Aw right. I be right back."

I couldn't have been gone more than three minutes. When I returned, Ben Barrow had appeared from nowhere. He had Cora pinned against the other side of that same tree, kissing her for all he was worth. Hurt me to my heart. He, of all people—one of the first to come off that bench, preaching, like Abba-Lord, about what the Lord had done for him and what miracles he had seen.

After the revival started, I dismissed my jealousy. Cora and Ben were just demonstrations of the devil to distract me from finding religion. I soon became a sincere, honest moaner.

As a moaner, I was so sad and miserable, I wouldn't eat, sleep, or talk much to anybody. Around the house or in the store, when they explained that I was a moaner, most people understood and left me alone. Not so with the hard-core Chosen of God. They were real troublemakers. They *pushed* me. Some went so far as to kneel on the spot and pray for the hard-hearted thirteen-year-old sinner. They interfered with my concentration and took time away from my search for a miracle.

By now, most of the moaners had left the bench and were enjoying the fel-lowship of the righteous, as much as was permitted until they were baptized and accepted into the full fellowship of the church.

Inside Hughes Chapel the temperature was 95 to 100 degrees every night. They made us feel that we deserved to suffer because it was taking us so long, though they paid the preacher by the week, whether he saved many souls or not. He realized that the fewer he brought in the less likely he would be called back the next year. On the other hand, when a truly great evangelist like Taylor brought in a large number, there was always the possibility that he represented a threat to the existing pastor. Reverend Jarrett, our pastor, couldn't begin to preach like Taylor, which caused some of the deacons to seek another pastor. They had to reckon with Uncle Pet, however, who explained that Reverend Jarrett wasn't much of a preacher, but he was a good pastor. Papa agreed with Uncle Pet, and everyone dropped the matter.

As an evangelist who wasn't attached to a specific church, Taylor depended on being called by the Baptist churches far and wide.

My cousin Saravania and I were the last young people on the bench. I think she was waiting for me to go first. The hard-core veterans had much more to repent, but Saravania and I were under terrible pressure. I visited my father's grave looking for salvation. In spite of the fact that my grandfather founded Hughes Chapel, our family plot was on a knoll up the Pike, right behind Uncle Pet's house. The tombstones nestled among small oak trees accompanied by ash and hickory, all growing in the shadows of imposing pines. The neat little hill was fenced in, but over the years the fence had rotted away until only a small portion of it was still standing. There was a plot within a plot where the headstones were separated from the others by a stone wall and a relatively new whitewashed picket fence. My father and my two older sisters Florence and Vercie lay there along with a few relatives from generations past. Dead flowers lay on my father's sunken grave. Sunlight and rain had bleached and faded the paper, covered with plastic, inside the metal cross that served as its temporary head-marker.

In spite of all the ghost and hant stories that I had heard, I was not afraid of seeing my father's ghost. I loved my father, and I knew he loved me. I knew his ghost would never show itself to me in any of the awful images that made me afraid of other people's ghosts.

Uncle Pet's hired hand, Crazy Charlie Tiggins, spooked me by telling me about the ghosts of people we knew who had died. He told me that right after Vernessa Murray died in an automobile accident near us, he met her ghost coming down the Pike one moon-shiny night, holding her bloody head in her hands. Crazy Charlie claimed he saw another man, Mr. Garland Dawson, who had died a few years earlier, walking toward him. Dawson changed into a white dog as he approached Crazy Charlie.

I hoped to see my father's ghost. I was standing at the north end of his grave, facing his head-marker. I hoped to ask him how to find the miracle. Kneeling, I called on him quietly, as I had often done before he died. "Papa, how did you get religion? Please tell me. I have tried everything. How did y' do it?" I waited for an answer because I knew my father wouldn't lie to me.

Papa didn't give me any sign that he had heard me. He just lay there in his sunken grave with its dead flowers on top and its faded head-marker. Papa didn't say a word.

During the last days and hours of the revival, the Reverend Taylor agonized over Saravania and he brooded over me, maybe because we were related to Uncle Pet. As he preached, sweat saturated his suit and dripped from his face and nose. I decided to settle for even a cheap miracle.

In the hour of my desperation, the devil decided to tempt me with that which he knew I wanted. My fellow moaner, Saravania, was seeking the miracle, I thought, as hard as I was. I had been interested in girls as long as I could remember, but I lacked the nerve to press my courting further than holding hands, some heavy smiling, and reckless eyeballing. I had the sexual interest of a bull and the nerve of a rabbit. Ben Barrow, on the other hand, had the sexual interest of two bulls and a nerve to match.

The back porch of Uncle Pet's white frame house was too small for the rambling structure. From the backyard on the west, one could see two big windows, a screen door, and four white posts that held up a wood shingled roof. Beyond the porch, through the windows, a big rubble-stone fireplace projected through the center of the house. A covered well stood on another small porch located on the south side of the house, facing the store. On my far right, to the north, glowing in the bright moonlight, stood the little false-friendly whitewashed outhouse, with a crescent cut into the door. No amount of paint, plants, perfume, powder, purifiers, potash, pails of lime, or prayers could keep that putrid, profane purgatory from stinking—stinking—stinking!

One night, near the end of the revival, I was praying on the back porch when I heard someone coming around the house from the north end. I looked up and directly into Saravania's face. She kneeled beside me and started praying also. I moved over to the other side of the porch. She followed me. I moved to the edge of the porch. She followed me there as well. Not daring to break my silence, I thought to myself, *What the hell is this, a praying contest?* Finally she said, "Thun, did the Lord thow you anything yet?" I didn't respond. "Did he give you a thine?" I looked at her but didn't respond. "Thun, why don't you talk to me?" Pause. "I can't thtand it when you won't talk to me."

I turned my head away. I had been warned of temptations the devil would put in your way, especially when you were about to find the miracle. I'd been warned by Uncle Pet, Reverend Taylor, and many of The Faithful not to *let this harvest pass.*

A panoramic moon hung fixed in space out there somewhere beyond the branches of the trees. The stars were like grains of sugar sprinkled over a blackberry cobbler. The hot night sounds were broken by the chirping of the crickets and the chickadees, and intermittently the general cacophony was punctuated by the hooting of an owl, the call of a mourning dove, or the insistent message of a whippoorwill.

Saravania moved closer. I felt her soft breast against my shoulder. I smelled her hot sweet breath against my neck. Her breath came fast and she quivered and shook. "Thun. Thun. Thun."

I clenched my fist and repeated to myself the words of my favorite Psalm.

> The Lord is my shepherd; I shall not want.
> He maketh me to lie down in green pastures: he
>   leadeth me beside the still waters.
> He restoreth my soul: he leadeth me in the paths of
>   righteousness for his name's sake.
> Yea, though I walk through the valley and the shadow
>   of death, I will fear no evil: for thou art with me; thy
>   rod and thy staff they comfort me . . .

The words *rod* and *staff* brought my rod close to bursting the buttons on my pants. But a near miracle was taking place. My frantic need to get off the bench was stronger than my need for Saravania. I defied the devil! I left Saravania panting and sobbing in the moonlight. Crazed by my love for Saravania, shaken to my very soul, I kept praying!

Within the next two days—on a Friday before the final weekend; revival ended on Sunday—I was camped at my favorite praying spot. It was back in the woods about 150 yards from our house, near my father's grave. There a clump of tall pines surrounding an oak stump. The fallen needles of the pines mixed with oak leaves to form a soft natural pallet. Lying still, I looked upward at a stretch of sky. It might rain and it might not. A country boy, I was good at reading clouds. A white cloud carried no rain. I watched several white clouds pass. Finally a black cloud drifted in my direction. I said to myself, "That's *my* cloud. That cloud is my *miracle!*"

THE DEVIL SPOKE: "That cloud is no miracle. Pray for a big miracle, the kind that Ezekiel and Moses saw."

I ANSWERED HIM: "Those miracles are out of style. God don't make such miracles anymore."

THE DEVIL ANSWERED: "Don't give in and join the fakers. Wait for a *real* miracle, like your Uncle Pet and your papa did."

When he mentioned my father, I became suspicious. *How did the devil know what kind of miracle my papa had seen? The devil would have to do better than that.* Saravania's cantaloupes flashed in my head. I kept having visions of her pretty ass rolling like loose ball bearings in her cinched-in cotton dress. I could see her shapely legs, her stockings rolled down to a place above her knees. "Thun-Thun-Thun" echoed in my memory. The worst part was that she said that she had found her miracle the day after our encounter in the moonlight. She had already testified, leaving me with the rest of the repeaters.

If *she* had found the miracle, there might not *be* a miracle. If Papa and Uncle Pet had found it there must be a miracle! Then I thought, *Suppose I am the miracle? Perhaps the miracle is in me? Or—*

The dark cloud came closer and closer. Suddenly I sat up, clasped my hands, and spoke to God. "Lord, if I have religion, if I am saved, let the dark cloud block the sun. Let it rain *here* . . . and then . . ." I hesitated. I wondered if I ought to ask Him to throw in a little thunder and a flash or two of lightning, but not wanting to be too greedy, I told God, "Cancel the thunder and lightning. Let it rain a little, then let the cloud drift by. Let the sun reappear." I lay back with my hands cupped behind my head. The cloud took away the sunlight. Then I waited three, five, seven minutes. *It came to pass*, after seven minutes, a light sprinkle wet my skin. Then the dark cloud rolled away and the hot Arkansas sunlight began to bake the soil again.

I kept my miracle a secret until that evening when I saw the church doors open.

I knew I wasn't following the beaten path, because I didn't come roaring out of the woods testifying and preaching like some of the other moaners had done. Saravania had been unemotional when she confessed. She sounded as if she was reading from a grocery list. Her testimony had brought whispers from The Faithful Sisters: "That gal ain't got nothin'." Because I wouldn't moan and shout, I would be compared to Saravania, but I discovered that I didn't give a damn what The Faithful thought. I was so happy and relieved, I didn't even care what Uncle Pet thought. I had worked and I had suffered, and I had found my miracle.

At that time, the Ink Spots had made a record, "If That Isn't Love, It Will Have to Do Until the Real Thing Comes Along." That night I adopted the same attitude as the song: "If This Ain't Religion, It Will Have to Do Until the Real Thing Comes Along."

Riding to church that night in the 1934 gray Plymouth, which only had a few miles on it though it was over a year old, I could still smell new paint. With only a few hours on my religion, I felt new as well. Crazy Charlie Tiggins drove slowly, almost crawled. Uncle Pet sat beside him. Saravania and I sat in back. Uncle Pet broke a long silence.

"Well, boy,—schuuh—you got one mo' night after tonight. I can't, for the life of me, understand why you ain't seen or heard som'um—schuuh—after all that praying you been doin'."

The tires made a grinding noise on the gravel.

I said nothing.

Uncle Pet spoke again. "I could see it if you wuz a hard-hearted sinner—schuuh—like our friend Charlie heah."

Charlie glanced at Uncle Pet and started to laugh. He plainly didn't give a damn. "Hard-hearted, huh?"

"Yes, y' hard-hearted, Charlie Tiggins.—schuuh—How long y' been wid me? More'n three yeahs?"

"Over fo', ol' man," Charlie said.

"Over fo' yeahs and you won't even set down on the moaners' bench."

"Tell me som'um, ol' man?"

"Whut?"

"Did you hire me to do yo' work or to git me on that moaners' bench?"

"You er good hand, Charlie.—schuuh—I got no complaints erbout yo' work. But it's my Christian duty to bring sinners to Christ."

"Ol' man, you can't force nobody. Why try so hard? Take Sun back theah. We wuz buddies, but for two weeks I ain't heard a word from that kid. It just ain't natural. What y'all doin' to this boy?"

Uncle Pet looked at Crazy Charlie as if he couldn't believe what he had just heard. "You know som'um, Charlie Tiggins?"

"Whut's that, ol' man?"

"You goin' t' hell wid yo' eyes open."

Crazy Charlie roared with laughter.

It was the same laughter I had witnessed when Uncle Pet attempted to whip him. He had whipped other hired hands who lived and worked for him. It was common knowledge that Uncle Pet had held a gun on Gene Cannon, the hired hand who preceded Crazy Charlie, and lashed him with a bullwhip until he was tired. I never knew what it was about, but knowing Uncle Pet, it probably had something to do with Gene's heavy drinking, or he may have "bigged" a girl. Either one could draw Uncle Pet's wrath.

When I saw them on their way to the store, I knew something was wrong. I had felt the sting of his switches before. I could see that look in his eyes and that special limp he had when he was mad. After they went inside, I stationed myself on a barrel and peeped through the window. I didn't hear the first part of the conversation. It took me some time to get my barrel in place without making too much noise. When I was finally stationed, Uncle Pet was fixing to draw the whip back. Crazy Charlie was standing there with his hands deep in his overalls and a big smile on his face as if Uncle Pet was fixing to give him a citation. "Hold it, ol' man! If you hit me with that whip, both er yo' arms go' rot off."

Uncle Pet paused. Reached down in his coveralls for his little long-barreled derringer that shot special shotgun shells. We called it the foot gun because

Uncle Pet had accidentally shot himself in the foot with it, trying to kill a barn rat. "Sooo, you baaad, huh?"

Crazy Charlie pulled his owl-headed pistol halfway out of his pocket. "Bad as I need to be, ol' man." It was a standoff. Charlie broke the silence. "How it go' look, ol' man? Headlines in er *Gazette,* 'Pet Hughes, Well-Known Merchant 'n Farmer, Kills Hired Hand in Squabble. Deacon Faces Jail for Murder.' Or worse yet. 'Hired Hand Kills Pet Hughes in Squabble.' You can whip Sun wid them switches. He's still a kid, but you can't whip me, ol' man. I'm twenty-two yeahs ol'. Now if y' wanna shoot it out, I don't mind dyin'." He let out a crazy roar of laughter and looked straight at Uncle Pet. He knew Uncle Pet was one of the best shots in the county.

Uncle Pet figured he must have been crazy. He had already stated that he didn't mind dying. "You er crazy nigger, Charlie Tiggins."

My heart leaped for joy when he laid the whip on the counter and let the gun slide back into his pocket.

Crazy Charlie was happy to relax also. "Some people call me crazy, ol' man." More laughter. Actually the two men liked each other. Anyone could see that.

"You know you bigged that Nelson girl. You go' have to support that child. I'm go' see to that . . ."

I heard my Aint Babe calling. Not wanting to be discovered, I eased myself down off the barrel and went back over to the house.

All the time Uncle Pet and Charlie talked, Saravania tried to catch my eye. Since that night on the porch, I had tried to ignore her, but she kept on teasing me. I glanced at her. She smiled and puffed out her lower lip. I caught my breath. God help me she was beautiful! Why did something always hold me back? Maybe it was knowing Saravania was a distant cousin. An inner voice kept telling me, *You don't go with your blood kin.* There were people known or rumored to have taken up with their own daughters. I only had to think of Uncle Pet about to whip Crazy Charlie to know what he would do to me if he caught me messing with my cousin. I could almost hear him talking. "Boy, you crazy? I'll skin you erlive if I ketch you smellin' eround Saravania. She's yo' cousin!"

Saravania caught my eye again and slipped her little soft and sweaty hand over mine and squeezed. That time I squeezed also and held on tight. Her eyes widened and her mouth flew open. I guess she thought that at last I had found the miracle! I put my finger to my lips asking her to be quiet, and she got the drift. We looked into each other's eyes. We were as happy and as close as any two young lovers could be. We held on to each other, dreading the end of the short ride.

As the revival swept toward its conclusion, I could hear a familiar, moving hymn resonate from inside the church.

Must Jesus bear-the cross alonnnne
Annnnd all the world go freeeeee?
Noooo, there's er cross fer everyooooone,
And there's er cross fer meeee—

Crazy Charlie parked the car. Uncle Pet stepped down and started limping toward the church when he noticed that Saravania and I were still sitting in the car. He shouted, "Whut you two waitin' fer?"

We froze. Charlie, still behind the wheel, planned to pick up my Aint Babe. He knew what was happening in the backseat. In a harsh whisper, he warned us, "Sun! Saravania! Y'all break it up now! You two cousins, you know that. Ol' man find out erbout this, it'll be hell to pay."

We pulled at our clothes and rearranged our expressions.

Saravania gave a quick wave and smiled shyly. "Bye, Charlie."

"Bye, Saravania, baby." He looked at me and waited to see if I would break my silence.

I raised my hand slowly. "Bye, Charlie."

"All right! That's my buddy ergin!" He was laughing wildly as he drove away.

When Uncle Pet got out of the car, he went into the door on the southwest for the deacons. Saravania and I went around to the moaners' entrance. We squeezed hands again. We took one more long and mournful look at each other and slipped quietly inside.

2

Aint Babe, whose real name was Janie, was a one-woman war department. She was only five feet two inches tall, but she was built solid with sturdy, shapely legs. Though in her fifties, she had no fat on her body and moved with almost lightning speed. Pictures of her youth showed a good-looking woman. Little as she was, she could and would shoot, cut, and hit with any instrument of injury and death she could find. I never knew her to hurt anyone, but she had everybody for miles around buffaloed into thinking she might. That included Uncle Pet. I should say, especially Uncle Pet.

When cooking on her big wood-burning stove, she kept a kettle of boiling-hot water ready. I've seen Uncle Pet do some Olympic-style hopping getting out of the house with her in hot pursuit. Then he would straighten up and start whistling as though nothing had happened. She, of course, was "a crazy woman." She was known, however, to have let off a double-barreled shotgun blast after hearing strange noises around the store. If thieves wanted to take something—and they always did—they had best take it during the day because, being a light sleeper, Aint Babe owned the night. As a consequence of her vigilance, no one that I knew of ever broke into the store.

My Aint Babe was one of the best cooks in the county. I'll go further and say she was one of the best cooks in the world! The complimentary expression "This food will make you slap yo' Aint Emma" was apt in her case.

The Sunday afternoon after Saravania and I had been baptized in the little pond one-half mile down the Pike, Aint Babe prepared one of her special feasts. They killed a goose for the occasion. We put all scavenger animals in a pen and fed them pure corn, bran, or oats for two weeks before they were ready for the table. She stuffed the goose with cornbread dressing. She also baked a big country ham that came straight from our own smokehouse. The night before, she had prepared her rolls with undiluted, caked, pure yeast, and they had risen at least six inches before they were ready for the oven. Talk about good! Her candied yams were better than county fair. There was fried corn, okra, lima beans, turnip greens, crowder peas, squash, tomatoes, string beans, and Irish potatoes. All kinds of raw vegetables—not known as salad to us—came directly from our garden. Added to that basic cuisine was rust-brown gravy, liberally engaged with chunks of giblets and liver. Surrounding that were a number of side dishes consisting of pear preserves, blackberry preserves, preserves of muscadines, and watermelon rinds. There was also a big pan of hot buttermilk cornbread. For dessert—served after the big dining room table had been cleared—she had baked two cakes, a chocolate and a coconut, plus a big blackberry cobbler. You could always count on one or two egg custards, and my favorite, the most delicious, well-filled, ever-loving sweet potato pies this side of heaven. To wash all that down, there were tall glasses of ice tea, lemonade, and my favorite, ice-cold buttermilk with droplets of pure butter laced throughout. Aint Babe spread all that out in the middle of our long, sturdy oak dining room table. The table sat in the middle of the long dining room at the rear of the house. A large open-hearth fireplace separated the dining room from the front of the house—the living room area.

Standing in the garden, one could see the dining room sprawled across the entire house except for the kitchen, which flanked it on the right. I had cut and neatly stacked plenty of wood for the cooking stove on the back porch the Saturday evening before the main cooking began Sunday morning. I had also drawn three buckets of water and set them on the shelves of the small porch on the south side of the house where the covered well stood facing the store. I had raked and cleaned beneath the house, as well as tidied up the back and front yards—all "man's work." Milking cows, churning, making beds, washing clothes, cooking, and taking care of the house were decidedly "women's work." Having finished all of my work on Saturday—men's chores being forbidden on Sundays, except for feeding animals—I was left with nothing to do except stand around and watch my cousin Saravania, Aint Babe, and her quiet, buxom widowed sister, Mrs. Minerva, get everything ready.

"See these linens down heah?" Aint Babe asked, as she bent and opened the bottom drawer of the big chest, which sat to the right of the fireplace.

"Y' never thowed them to me before, Aint Babe," Saravania responded.

"Don't show 'em t' nobody 'cept fer special times like today."

"Yeth ma'am," Saravania said, and waited for orders.

"Now, I want y' t' pick out the right size 'n cover the tables, the china closet, 'n all this stuff that needs it."

"Babe! Babe!" Mrs. Minerva's voice came from the kitchen.

"Whut's the matter?" Aint Babe dropped the linens on the chair.

"Y' better git in heah 'n look at this bird!"

Aint Babe turned and dashed toward the kitchen.

Saravania waved at me through the dining room window. I waved back and sat there watching her neatly unfold the linens and place them on the tables. When she finished, she placed big bowls of roses mixed with wildflowers next to the napkins. There were decorated bottles, used for vases, carefully displayed on most of the furniture.

As Aint Babe entered the dining room again, Saravania was busy wiping and positioning the painted bottles. "Aint Babe."

"Yes, chile?"

"Who painted all of theth pretty bottleth?"

"Different girls of mine who lived heah over the yeahs. They did um at that school they went to." She helped Saravania wipe and position the bottles.

"Y' muthta had er lot of them. Thom er theth are tho pretty."

"This one right heah wuz done many yeahs ergo by my Sarah."

"Y' had er Tharah before me?"

"Sho God did, chile. She wuz Pet's sister's chile. She wuz yo' age too—thirteen. Yes she wuz."

"Whut happened to her, Aint Babe?"

"Oh, she growed up 'n got marr'ed."

"Whut wuz she—," Saravania began.

"Now this one right heah wuz done by a very bright girl."

It was obvious that Aint Babe wanted to change the subject.

"She wuz the smartest one er my girls—bookwise. Pet got her into Baptist College up there at Little Rock." She shook the vase. "We need some mo' water t' fill these up." She walked to the screened door near where I stood. "Sun boy, bring Aint Babe er bucket er water. Standin' out there lookin' like you lost."

"Fer drinkin' or fer flowers, Aint Babe?" I asked.

"Fer flowers." Aint Babe went back into the kitchen.

Saravania waved and smiled at me again. I could see she was in a playful mood. She pointed at the stuffed deer head over the mantelpiece. She mimed placing it over her head and coming after me with her head down in a goring position.

I, in turn, mimed taking one of the shotguns that hung directly beneath the deer's head, aiming, and shooting her.

She responded by grabbing her chest and falling to the floor laughing.

As Aint Babe entered the dining room, I laughingly called out to her, "Aint Babe, did y' ever know er deer to grab his chest and fall to the ground laughing after he'd been shot?"

"Naw, I didn't. Now scat! 'N *you* git busy settin' this table, Miss Funny-Bones. Time's flyin' 'n you two fartin' eround. Y' gonna make me mad now, doggone it! Yes y' is. Folks hungry." Aint Babe opened the door to the big china closet as she continued fussing. Saravania got the message and began taking the dishes out of the china closet and setting the table. I watched as she sashayed around the big ornately carved oak table that sat heavily on a handsome Persian rug. The rest of the wood floor was scrubbed and polished.

Reverend Taylor, Uncle Pet, and Deacon Tiggins were sitting on the front porch talking. Everyone had something to do except me. I was bored. It was

Sunday, and there was little to do except "Remember the Sabbath day and keep it holy," which was strictly adhered to in that house and in that community. Nobody could cut wood, cut hair, work in the fields or the garden, pitch horseshoes, shoot marbles, wrestle, play ball, skip rope, foot race, swim, or even play mama-peg (a game played by flipping a pocket knife on wood or the ground so that one of the two blades stuck in certain positions for so many points). Cards or games of chance were forbidden at all times. I couldn't even play a tune on my harp or the homemade guitar that I had rigged up on the side of the blacksmith shop. I had nailed several strings of haywire to the pine boards and stretched the wire by wedging two bottles or two bricks at each end.

As I sat watching Saravania marching back and forth to the store—after she had finished in the dining room—my mind wandered back to those carefree days of my early boyhood, which were filled with so many different things to do. I did have a brand-new religion with no more than a few hours on it, but though I had endured two weeks of solitude to find the miracle, I was still a boy and needed action.

On one of her trips to the icebox, Saravania smiled and asked me to come help her. I took some of the things and walked with her to the store. She was wearing a long colorful apron over her Sunday clothes. I was still in my suit and tie waiting for dinner. We were barely inside the door and out of sight when we locked onto each other like two magnets. Blood rushed to my head. We were quivering and shaking. Brought on by the sweltering heat, accentuated by our passion, sweat poured down our faces.

All those feelings came back that I had experienced that moonlit night on the back porch, only this time I wasn't holding back, afraid of missing the miracle. Every fiber of my body told me that the sweet girl in my arms looking longingly up at me was the miracle.

Never having kissed a girl before except on the neck or cheek, I didn't know how to go about it. Saravania ran her tiny right hand up the middle of my back until it reached the back of my head. As short as she was beneath me, she stretched her arm and with her fingers started to stroke the back of my head. It went through my body like the Holy Ghost. I was sure she hadn't had any experience either, but how did she know so much? The best was yet to come.

With her left hand she squeezed and dug into my back. It began to hurt. I never knew that hurting could feel so good. We held each other so tight we felt welded together. Our clothes were wet and sticking to our bodies and to each other. Slowly she tiptoed, breathed her hot breath around my neck, behind my ear, and finally in my ear. Then she kissed me ever so lightly on my forehead, eyes, and nose. She worked her way up to my mouth. She proceeded to kiss me a little on the lips. I began to feel a sensation such as I never had known or imagined existed. Before I knew it, she had slipped the tip of her tongue between my tightly closed lips and started massaging my tightly closed teeth.

Completely naive to what she was searching for, I began to wonder if she was trying to brush my teeth on the sly. She continued massaging and prying with the tip of her tongue—knocking at the door—until my instincts finally screamed, *Open your stupid mouth!* The loud noise must have waked up my brain, and I did as the voice commanded. When I did, her slippery probing tongue, which seemingly had a mind of its own, quickly found its way inside my mouth and within seconds began swift wobbling revolutions that gave me to know it was not a brush job. It was the first time I had tasted a tongue. In fact, other than seeing my buddy Ben kissing Cora, who I had thought was my girl, and Pete DiGasspri, the white construction boss, kissing his Jezebel wife, I had made no close-up observations in the kissing department. I had absolutely no idea they were sticking their tongues in each other's mouths. My first taste was that of cinnamon. Then it changed to lemon, then vanilla-apple-maple-grape-strawberry-molasses. I became completely confused, and the taste no longer mattered. That was when it happened.

That swelling, that tight pressure building up in my groin, felt as if it was about to explode. I thought I was going to pee in my pants. I discovered it was far more serious than that. For the first time I experienced a tickling, hurting feeling—far more sensational than I had felt during any of my wet dreams. Finally, when I could no longer hold it, a powerful gush rushed forth. In my mind, I levitated from the floor! The sensation traveled to the top of my head, into my hair, down through my arms and fingers, through the rest of my body down through my toes and, it seemed, to my toenails. I felt like screaming, "Deliverance! Deliverance!" I tried to scream but made only muffled choking sounds. Fortunately, her tongue was blocking my throat, and I couldn't get any sound out.

Saravania was as engrossed as I was, if that was possible. As the sweat poured down, I could also taste the salt as it overflowed into my mouth. I could smell a little sweet musk coming through her powder that called up ancient instincts I never knew were there. There was a natural fragrance in her hair that came from her scalp. As her nimble body swayed in rhythm with mine, I felt another buildup in my groin that manifested itself in stiff body parts. In truth, every linear part of my body was stiff and hard: my arms, my fingers, my toes. My family-making sack felt swollen and balloonlike as if someone was pumping air into it.

The pressure built again. I felt a wet slimy sensation exactly where the pressure was building and started mumbling and straining for words to express my deeper feelings. A second big gush came forth more powerful than the first. The choked screams came again as the slimy liquid began to ooze down my legs into my shoes.

Saravania had gone completely out of control with ecstasy and passion. Coming to my senses a little, I could hear Aint Babe calling, "Saravania! Saravania!" There was no response. Saravania was so out of it she couldn't hear. "Saravania! You Saravania! Whut the devil is that chile doing?"

"Answer Aint Babe." I tried to get her together.

She went to the door and answered in a strained, broken voice. "Yeth ma'am! Whut y' want, Aint Babe?"

"While y' out there, bring me back a couple er lemons, and hurry up, chile!"

"Yeth ma'am!" She walked back from the door straight into my arms.

I embraced her briefly. "Come on now. If we start that ergain we gon' git caught. Wait till tonight, OK?"

"OK. I'll thlip out to the back porch."

"What time?" I asked.

"Thundown."

"Nooo. Not thundown. Wait till they go t' thleep."

She playfully punched me in the chest for teasing her about her lisp.

"OK, thoon as they go to thleep."

"OK, OK. Let me hep y' wid some er this stuff so they won't think nothin'."

"I jutht hope that ol' bald-headed man don't find out erbout thith, 'cauth I'll be long gone to Flint for thure." Flint, Michigan, was where her grandfather lived.

"I hate to think whut would happen to me," I said.

"Me too. He'd try t' kill y'." She fell into my arms again and backed me against some sacks of bran stacked on the floor. Kissing me softly, she whispered, "Thun. Thun . . . "

"Yes, Saravania?"

"I don't ever want t' leave you."

"I don't want y' t' leave either . . . not ever," I said.

"'N I don't ever want you t' leave me."

"I won't leave y'," I promised.

She slipped her tongue in my mouth again.

I tore her loose. "Saravania, Saravania, we gon' git caught. Come on now; wait till tonight. Straighten yo' dress out and fix yo' hair," I said.

She started to laugh. "If y' could thee yo'thelf now."

"Whut's the matter wid m'thelf?"

She playfully hit me in the chest again for teasing her. "Yo' tie ith all crooked, 'n yo' thirt ith all wet 'n wrinkled." She started to fix it.

"I'll straighten it out. You jist hurry up."

"OK, OK."

She loaded me with bags and pans. She took bottles, lemons, and small bags, and we walked slowly toward the house. When we entered, Aint Babe grabbed the stuff from her arms. "Doggone it. Whah you two been? I been waitin' fer this stuff."

"We been gittin' the stuff together, Aint Babe," Saravania lied.

"You wuz out there playin' eround; that's whut y' wuz doin'. Look at y'—y' wring'n wet. Done sweated right through y' pretty dress. You too, Sun. Jist look at yo' new suit. Now go change y' clothes 'n hurry back so y' can hep me set the table. Now scat! Both er y'! Doggone kids mess eround 'n make me mad now. Yes y' will."

I listened quietly to the conversation taking place on the porch while I was changing my shirt. My room was just to the right of the front porch.

Uncle Pet called from the porch. "Janie!"

"Whut y' want, Pet?"

"Whut's holdin' things up in there? The Reverend is hungry."

"Now don't go puttin' it on the Reverend. Jist hold yo' water. It'll be ready when it's ready. It's gotta be right, Reverend. You understand, don't y'?"

Chuckling, "Yes, Sister Hughes. Now don't you worry about me. I'll just be more dangerous when I get there." To Uncle Pet, "I'm afraid she's got your number, Brother Deacon."

Deacon Tiggins, always looking for a free meal, had a problem keeping his nose out of other people's business. To make matters worse, he was an older brother to Crazy Charlie, but one would never know it. He wasn't exactly what I considered an ugly man, even though he was skinny; he just had ugly ways that made him look much worse than he might have. "How y' coming wid that boy, Brother Pet?"

"Y' mean Sun?"

"Y' got some mo' boys eround heah I don't know erbout?"

"He still got er wild streak in im."

"How long y' think it'll take t' git that wild streak outa im?"

"Well, Brother Tiggins, that'll depend on how long he can weather the leather."

Tiggins let go with a big laugh. "Long as he can weather the leather—that's er good one. I swear it is. Y' ain't got hold of im wid that bullwhip yet, is y'?"

"He ain't graduated to that league yet, but if he passes the first test, I'll do the rest."

Tiggins bent over laughing.

Reverend Taylor, who had not found it funny, rose to my defense. "I don't know, Brother Deacon, he made a big step today by coming to know the Lord. Boys his age go through a phase, you know. At least that's what I've found with mine."

"Well, I know that, Reverend," Uncle Pet allowed.

"Anyway, let us pray that he'll be a fine young man like I'm sure you were at thirteen."

Uncle Pet chuckled defensively. "Don't git m' wrong, Reverend; he's my own flesh and blood. I took him when my brother died. My brother wuz sick fer years.—schuuh—His mother and older brother had t' take care of the rest of the family. That boy, bein' next t' the baby, simply got outta hand. That's why my brother wanted me t' have im—schuuh—'cause he needs a man t' straighten him out."

"God bless you, Brother Hughes. The Lord will help you."

Deacon Tiggins hit his corncob pipe in his hand and looked ominously out of the corner of his eyes. "'N you gon' hep the Lord hep you, eh, Brother Pet?"

Uncle Pet looked in another direction.

Tiggins wouldn't let it go. He took a long drag from his pipe. "Reminds me of a joke I heard once. You'll excuse me, Reverend, if I tell er little preacher joke—nothin' bad."

"Go right ahead, Deacon. I tell a few deacon jokes once in a while myself—nothing bad. This *is* going to be good, though, isn't it?"

"Let us pray that it will," Tiggins chuckled. "Well, Brother Jones took er garden wheah the grass had gone wild and crowded out all the plants 'n flowers. Weeds had grown up all over the place. Well sir, he got t' work. He cut down all the weeds, chopped out all the tall grass, cultivated all the plants 'n flowers, 'n lo 'n behold they all came out pretty as y' please. The preacher came walkin' by 'n said, 'Brother Jones, you 'n the Lord have certainly done a wonderful job wid this garden.' Brother Jones stopped for a minute 'n said, 'Thank y', Reverend, but y' shoulda seen it when the Lord had it by His-self.'"

Aint Babe interrupted their laughter with the dinner bell. "Y'all come on 'n let's eat. Jist go right in, Reverend. Make yo'self at home, Brother Tiggins," Aint Babe said as she ushered them into the dining room.

"Now you know I'm gonna make myself at home."

"Y' know y' welcome, welcome. Jist go right on in." Aint Babe stood proudly, fanning herself—her big colorful apron starched and ruffled to perfection.

I walked into the dining room behind them. The smell of fly spray in the room couldn't dull my appetite once I got a whiff of that food.

"Now, y'all be seated, be seated. Reverend, you set at this end."

"Thank you, Sister Hughes."

"Brother Tiggins, you set right heah on the side next t' yo' brother. Wheah is Charlie?" Aint Babe asked.

Uncle Pet picked up his napkin. "Probably 'sleep somewhere, if I know him. Sun . . . er . . . boy, go in there 'n wake im up. Tell im t' come t' dinner."

I exited to Charlie's room, which was next to mine. It was empty. From there I yelled, "He's not in heah!"

Aint Babe's voice came back from the dining room, "Try the store!"

I trotted over to the store and found Charlie sitting behind the sacks of bran putting on his shoes. His reddish-brown woolly hair was full of bran dust. His upper body, rippling with bulging tan muscles, had splotches of the white dust as well. Charlie's eyes were red, not only from sleeping but from nipping, which he did on weekends. He had hidden his bottle in the store, which explained why he was napping in there. My heart pumped and radiated fear at what he must have seen and heard. "Charlie! You—you been there all the time?" I stammered.

"Erbout er hour," Charlie said casually, putting on his shirt.

"That—that means you saw us."

"Course I saw y'. Heard y' too." Mimicking Saravania, "Thun, don't ever leave me. If you could thee yo'thelf now." Mimicking me, "Whut's the matter wid m'thelf?" and Saravania's response, "Yo' tie'th all crooked, and yo' thirt'th all wet." Charlie belched out his hearty laugh. "Do that sound like I heard y'? When she backed you up against these sacks er bran, yo' butt wuz right in my face."

"Sorry erbout that, Charlie. Whut y' gon' do?"

"Ain't made up m' mind yet."

"Well, when y' gon' make it up?"

"Ooooh, I don't know . . . Maybe soon . . . maybe never. Depends."

"On whut?" I asked.

"Ooooh, I'll think er som'um. Might want y' t' run some errands t' one er m' marr'ed women." Charlie continued buttoning up his clothes while he was bandying words with me. He was obviously enjoying himself.

"Ah, Charlie, come on. Stop jokin' eround. Y' gon' tell Uncle Pet? That's all I wanna know."

"Naw, I ain't gon' tell Uncle Pet. I'm gon' tell Aint Babe." A big laugh.

"Y' may as well tell Uncle Pet. I git it worse when he gits it from her."

"I know whut," Charlie said.

"Whut?"

"I think I'll tell Jesus. Y' know that song y'all always singin'? How's it go?" He attempted to sing the first few words.

> *I must tell Jesus,*
> *I must tell Jesus—*

It was so bad, I took it away from him.

> *IIIIIII must tell Jeeeesus,*
> *I must tell Jeeeee-ees-us.*
> *I cannot beaaaar this burden aloooone—*

Charlie applauded. "Boy sho' can sang."

"Tell y' whut, Big Charlie, if y' gon' tell somebody, I'd much rather it wuz Jesus 'cause you bein' er sinner, he ain't gon' listen to you no-how."

A big laugh, then he shut it off abruptly. "All right, li'l bro, I ain't nobody t' be givin' advice no way, specially erbout gittin' some pussy. I'm jist thinkin' erbout how much it'll cost y' if the ol' man finds out. Y' gon' need at least fifty asses, minimum, t' take whut he gon' put on yo' one po' li'l ass. Sho, I had me some pussy fo' I wuz yo' age, but my situation wuz much different from yours."

"How wuz it different, Charlie?"

"I didn't have t' deal wid Uncle Pet. That ol' man tried t' whip me once." He put his hand on my shoulder as we started out of the store. "Now come on, let's go eat."

They had already started when we quietly tiptoed into the dining room.

Uncle Pet looked up from his plate. "We wuz waitin' fer y'."

Deacon Tiggins asked in an annoyed manner, "Y' didn't heah that bell?"

Crazy Charlie ignored him and sat down.

"He wouldn't heah my shotgun," Uncle Pet said.

"Gooood night, it wuz loud ernough t' wake up Lazarus," Deacon Tiggins fussed.

I sat quietly.

"Pass me the rolls, please," Charlie asked his brother.

"You'd been heah, you'da got your'n pipin' hot like the rest of us. You listenin' t' me?" Deacon Tiggins mouthed on.

Charlie looked at Uncle Pet. "You say som'um, ol' man?"

Uncle Pet chuckled and kept eating.

Tiggins looked annoyed at being ignored—even sulked.

The table was quiet.

Reverend Taylor broke the silence. "Where's yours and your sister's plate, Sister Hughes?"

"I wouldn't worry erbout them if I wuz you, Reverend. I bet they the least hungry people in this room," Uncle Pet said.

Aint Babe and Mrs. Minerva looked at each other, chuckled, and kept fanning. "We have t' keep our hands free for servin', Reverend," Aint Babe said.

Quiet Mrs. Minerva chimed in, "That's right, Reverend. Don't worry erbout us; jist go erhead 'n enjoy y'self." She turned and went back into the kitchen.

Aint Babe watched the table like a mother hen. "Now, y'all go right erhead 'n enjoy yo'selves. Yes indeed. I'll feel bad if y' don't."

Reverend Taylor looked up and wiped his mouth. "I'm going to make sure that your spirits are uplifted before I leave this table, Sister Hughes."

She guffawed. Everybody else laughed.

"And, Sister Hughes, it looks as though I'm getting a-plenty help in my efforts. I haven't seen this young man's face since he sat down. Mean business, don't you, Sun?"

Everyone had a laugh at my expense. Reverend Taylor had displayed his sense of humor many times during the revival. Even if he had not been funny, everyone would have laughed anyway out of respect. It was amazing how much weight a good minister carried everywhere he went. Even jackleg preachers were respected, to their faces. I'm sure that's why so many ignorant, unprepared, insecure hams went into the business even if they couldn't pastor a church or become an evangelist. I often wondered how long it would be before Deacon Tiggins hung out his shingle. It was indeed a pleasure to sit at the table with such a man as Reverend Taylor. He helped himself to more of the candied yams and passed them to Deacon Tiggins, who had the nerve to say, "Now, you sho y' got enough, Reverend? 'Cause I'm sho there's plenty mo' wheah this come from."

"I'm sure there is, Deacon Tiggins. If the spirit so moves me, I'll be back." He looked puzzled at Deacon Tiggins's generous offer of Uncle Pet's food.

Uncle Pet registered concern but kept quiet. Finally he spoke up. "Jist help yo'self t' whatever y' see, Reverend. If y' don't see it, speak up 'n we'll see if we can git it fer y'."

With his mouth full, the Reverend said, "I will, Brother Deacon, I certainly will."

While the food was passed around a second time, Aint Babe came out of the kitchen with another big bowl of piping hot gravy for the goose and dressing. As she started back to the kitchen she noticed the crooked ribbon in Saravania's hair. She stopped and straightened it and pulled Saravania's ear playfully.

Saravania smiled and turned her head to the side in girlish fashion without looking up at Aint Babe.

Aint Babe continued to the kitchen. She almost bumped into her wide-rumped sister, Mrs. Minerva, carrying a platter full of hot rolls.

"Oh my goodness! Smells good. Smells reeeal good. Yes indeed!" Those words went up from the table.

Saravania was not excited about the rolls. She was too busy watching me from under her raised fork—the few times she did take a bite. I noticed she had barely touched her food. *This girl's going to let the whole thing out. Can't she see all these people watching?* I thought. As for me, the food was so good it was all I could do to keep from cramming my mouth and holding my knife and fork as if I was ready to stab somebody rather than how Uncle Pet had taught me. He had already thrown me a warning glimpse when the Reverend made the comment about not taking my face out of my plate.

Having traveled all over the country and Canada to the National Baptist Conventions, Uncle Pet had picked up some of the formal manners and styles of more sophisticated, educated Negro people he admired. He especially wanted to display this in the presence of one who was paying him the honor of dining at his table. He often lamented the fact that he had only a third- or fourth-grade education, but his handwriting was fluid, and it had the flair of a trained person, especially his signature. Few people could rival him in arithmetic—a great deal of which he did in his head. As for etiquette, he delighted in passing on what he regarded as proper manners—which he had copied from others in bits and pieces over the years—to those over whom he had absolute control.

"Always hold yo' fork in yo' left hand—"

"Whut if y' left-handed?" I interrupted.

He continued, "—between yo' first and index fingers, controllin' wid yo' thumb." He demonstrated as he continued. "Y' hold y' knife the same way in yo' right hand—schuuh—'n cut erway from yo' left hand wid the knife."

He went on with other important rules. "Never put yo' elbows on the table. Place yo' napkin eround yo' shirt collar—schuuh—on the inside and let it hang neatly over yo' tie and jacket. Some people put um in they lap. And whatever y' do—schuuh—don't put too much food in yo' mouth at one time, and never, ever make loud smacking noises while y' eatin'. Always ask t' be excused before leavin' the table. Cattle, squirrels, rabbits, even mules and horses know how to eat—schuuh—naturally. Dogs, hogs, 'n people don't. But most people can be taught."

Even Deacon Tiggins, who had copied Uncle Pet as best he could, had picked up his habits. Crazy Charlie did it in Uncle Pet's presence to keep down a fuss. Aint Babe and her sister, Mrs. Minerva, on the other hand, ate in the kitchen with their hands and really greased it up in old-fashioned style. For that reason the lady of the house always opted to do the serving, especially when guests came. Uncle Pet knew that if he dared invade her space with his high-and-mighty manners, he would get a good cussing out and some boiling-hot water on his behind if he stayed in her kitchen too long. Uncle Pet didn't like it, but "There ain't er doggone thing he can do erbout it. There now, I said my piece—yes I did," was Aint Babe's response.

Aint Babe never violated the order of things, but she always reserved a corner for herself. She was a good wife, by her own admission, but she could be hell on wheels if she had to—also by her own admission. She could read and write, but she refused to learn how to type. She could plan and pack for trips as well as anyone alive, but she never tried to drive, and she didn't like going on trips. "Runnin' all over the country, puttin' on airs—not fer me."

"Sister Hughes, you and Brother Deacon here are to be congratulated for raising such fine, mannerly children. They are so well behaved and orderly. It is indeed a credit to you and them. I mean that sincerely."

Uncle Pet and Aint Babe spoke at the same time, "Thank you, Reverend."

Reverend Taylor continued, "Of course the carpenter can't build a house nor the sculptor create the masterpiece without the proper materials to work with."

"Eh-man," mumbled Deacon Tiggins—his mouth crammed with food.

Aint Babe said, "The Lord's been good t' us, Reverend—mighty good," affectionately placing her hand on Saravania's head.

"The way I look at it, Reverend—schuuh—it's like cultivatin' a crop . . . not too much, but jiiist ernough at the right time, and if the good Lord blesses y' wid rain, chances is y' gon' have er good crop. Now if any of them things is missin', it could mess up the whole season."

"Meaning, Brother Deacon?"

"Meanin', Reverend, all we can do is whut the good Lord gives us the strength and wisdom to do based on our experience.—schuuh—'Course I'm sho you know that."

"What's your point, Brother Deacon?"

"Whut I'm drivin' at is—schuuh—I will do whutever it takes t' raise this boy—schuuh—and Saravania heah. 'Course you know whut the Bible says erbout sparin' the rod and spoilin' the chile."

Aint Babe cast a disapproving eye at Uncle Pet for even suggesting that he would whip a girl, knowing full well that he only meant me. He was never known to lay a hand on any of the three or four girls who preceded Saravania.

"Sister Hughes." Reverend Taylor wiped his mouth. "Everything is sooo delicious. If I ate your cooking all the time I shudder to think what I'd weigh." With a quick glance at Uncle Pet sitting there with his belly hanging over into his lap, the Reverend quickly changed his tune. "I mean, I doubt if I could be an evangelist because I'd never want to leave home." He cleaned it up quite well, only it was too late. Uncle Pet had that aware expression on his face. He was far too cunning, however, to say anything.

"I'm glad y' enjoyin' it, Reverend. Jist help yo'self—yes indeed," Aint Babe said, and exited to the kitchen.

"I shall. I certainly shall. Saravania dear, would you pass me some more of those crowder peas, please? It's a weakness of mine—especially with okra."

Saravania handed the bowl across the table. "You want thom more cornbread, Reverend?"

"No thanks, Saravania, the peas will be fine. Now, back to what you were saying, Brother Deacon. Didn't mean to cut you off. Now, on this business of discipline, Mrs. Taylor and I have five at home. Traveling a lot in the ministry keeps me from disciplining the way I might. But the Lord has been good to us, and it is seldom necessary for us to get out the belt. Most of the time we punish by taking something away, especially at this age."

Uncle Pet coughed up a dry laugh. "Would you pass me the peas, Reverend, please?"

"Sooo, young lady, you go to Eighth Street," the Reverend said as he passed Uncle Pet the peas.

"Yeth thir," Saravania responded.

"Two of ours go there. I'll tell them about you. What grade are you in?" the Reverend asked.

"Ninth."

"Our Cathrine's in the ninth."

"Well, I'm going into the ninth," Saravania clarified.

"Same with Cathrine. I know you must find it a little different out here in the country, having been brought up in the city."

"Yeth thir, but I like it." She glanced at me beneath her raised fork. I wanted to stop her from looking at me. Was she trying to alert everybody at the table to what was going on between us?

"I can see you do. Well, it's good to have relatives like Brother Deacon Hughes and Sister Hughes, and let's not forget Sister Minerva, not to mention your cousin—who's your own age. He's somebody you can have fun with and maybe study with."

I almost choked on my buttermilk. Saravania slapped me on the back.

"Whut's the matter wid you, boy, went down the wrong pipe?" Uncle Pet inquired. He poured a glass of water and passed it to me.

"God bless you, Sun. Brother Deacon tells me you've got a fine voice. I'm sure with your background, you'll use that voice in the service of the Lord."

"Yes sir, Reverend," I managed, hoping to avoid a question-and-answer session.

Deacon Tiggins saved me, for the time being, by treating us to his annoying voice. "Think you'll ever be as good er Christian as yo' Uncle Pet heah, boy?"

"I don't know, sir, Deacon Tiggins."

"Whut y' say?"

"I said I don't know, sir."

"Whut y' mean y' don't know? Yo' papa wuz er good Christian, superintendent er the Sunday school, one er the head deacons in the church, 'n you settin' there tellin' me you don't know 'n y' jist been baptized?"

Crazy Charlie was obviously annoyed by his brother's troublemaking. "He tol' y' he didn't know, didn't he?"

"I heard that, but that ain't whut I'm after."

"Whut y' after then, brother?"

Deacon Tiggins gave a sinister chuckle. "Brother Pet knows whut I'm after. You bein' whut you is, how would you know?"

Crazy Charlie looked at his older brother hard and long but wisely kept his mouth shut. I wondered if he disliked him as much as I did.

Uncle Pet took a deep breath. "My name is Hess, 'n I ain't in that mess," meaning No comment.

Deacon Tiggins pressed the issue. "We blessed t' have er man er God at the table, Brother Pet. Don't y' think we should heah mo' from er member who has newly confessed 'n been baptized?"

"We got time, Deacon Tiggins—we got time," Uncle Pet said.

Tiggins hung on. "I would like t' heah som'um right now! We can praise God anytime, day or night! Ain't that right, Reverend?"

Reverend Taylor interceded diplomatically by calmly shifting the focus away from me. "You haven't said much, Brother Charlie."

"Erbout whut?" Charlie looked at the Reverend.

"About anything."

"Som'um in particular y' want me t' speak on, Reverend?" Charlie beckoned for another roll.

Uncle Pet made sure he offered the guest first. "More rolls, Reverend?"

"Please, Brother Deacon. My goodness, Sister Hughes, these are good. The whole feast is simply delicious."

Aint Babe spoke from the kitchen: "Jist help yo'self, Reverend! Help yo'-self!"

Piling up his plate again, "Now I know you're a Christian, aren't you, Brother Charlie?"

Uncle Pet spoke up: "Y' know mo 'n the rest of us heah, Reverend."

The Reverend started to take a bite but stopped the fork in midair. "But I thought—" He pointed from Uncle Pet to Charlie, then to Deacon Tiggins.

Uncle Pet began, "You thought because—"

Crazy Charlie picked it up: "I can speak fer m'self, ol' man. You thought because I live heah 'n work fer the ol' man I have t' belong t' church."

"That's precisely what I thought."

"I s'pose it's natural fer y' t' think that, knowin' the ol' man heah."

"I did m' best, Reverend," Uncle Pet said disgustedly.

"God knows I have," Deacon Tiggins added.

Reverend Taylor boasted, "We had a fine bunch of candidates this year. You should not have let this harvest pass, Charlie."

"Eh-man," Uncle Pet responded.

"Just what is your outlook on life, Charlie? What about your soul? Do you think you can make it without the Lord?"

"You got er lot er questions there, Reverend. I'll jist take the first one. I ain't much on big words." Chewing his food. "It's pretty simple t' me—life, that is. I figure I give er man er good day's work fer er day's pay. I treat his livestock, his property, and his family like my papa raised me t' do. I treat him the way I wanna be treated. After that, I like t' have me some good times. Fer as the church is concerned, I respect y'all, and if I happen t' come ercross one er them signs, or miracles, y'all always talkin' erbout—who knows? I might be settin' up heah talkin' jist like y'all." He wiped his hands and mouth, rose from the table. "Now, if y'all will excuse m', I got some 'portant business t' take care of."

"I bet," Uncle Pet said.

Crazy Charlie gave me a quick wink and left the table, chuckling.

As Charlie was leaving, Aint Babe and Mrs. Minerva entered with the two big layer cakes and two sweet potato pies.

"Ain't y' gon' stay fer yo' dessert, Charlie?"

Crazy Charlie's voice came from the living room. "I'll git it later tonight, Aint Babe!"

"Charlie don't care nothin' erbout no sweets no-how," Mrs. Minerva mumbled in a low voice, and chuckled.

Aint Babe confirmed the statement. "Ol' Crazy Charlie never did—once in er while maybe."

As I sat eating my sweet potato pie, with each melting mellow bite I could taste sweet blessings—good things coming my way. And so sudden. With colors too—all those beautiful colors of spring and summer circling and dancing across the screen of my mind. Like red and white morning glories covering our pastures, rich yellow sunflowers in bloom, tall above my head, purple and green honeysuckles on a dewy morning, from which I would often suck wild sweet nectar. Dark blue rich muscadines hanging high in the gum. The red heart of a big watermelon, laced with oblong black seeds lined up in military formation—nature's order of things. But this is hot July, and all the crops are laid by. Soon the browns, hazels, crimsons, yellows, and oranges will own the fields. The pines will accentuate the golds and yellows with their perennial greens. And the hickories and scaly barks will give up their harvest to squirrels and us kids.

Crowning that dream, Saravania was sitting beside me, craving and waiting for thundown, the swell of her ripening breast pressing piercingly against a white cotton dress, her little hands gripping her fork delicately, her gray cat's eyes sneaking a glance at me so often I was troubled that it wouldn't go unnoticed. Aint Babe sensed it, I felt sure. But knowing the taboo of any messing around with kin, I think she chose to treat it as young teens—cousins playing around. Deacon Tiggins, on the other hand, harbored no such notion. He saw what he saw, and I felt sure he would draw his own conclusions, which, since he was eager to make a case against me, would naturally be against my interests.

My probing thoughts flashed to an image of my new role in life. I was a new member of the church. I was attending city school. I was wearing a new belt-back brown suit, white and tan shoes. I was not too happy with Crazy Charlie's homeboy-style haircut, but hair would grow back. True, I missed a lot of the fun I had down the Pike when Papa was alive, but I couldn't go back to that. Some things I could do very well without. The relief flour and molasses, the aid boxes from Chicago—even though I was very glad to see them come. I could do very well without the worn-out shoes with cardboard placed inside to keep my feet off the cold ground, which it never did. The insults heaped on my sick father because he had fallen on hard times after the 1929 crash. The degradation and hardships borne by my mother, who was reduced to working as a peddler to keep the family alive, pained me, though I kept quiet. The fact that my brother had to sacrifice his boyhood and education and take the role of a man at thirteen to help feed the family never set well with me. Worst of all, my family had scattered in all directions after Papa died.

For the first time, the fact came home to me that I was at a crossroads in my life. Except for my worry about being discovered and skinned alive—worse still, having Saravania sent to Flint, Michigan—I felt good inside. I felt so good that I dared not let anybody in authority know about it, for they would surely take steps to wipe that grin off my hidden inside face. After all, what right did an overgrown thirteen-year-old boy have to be happy? "There's grown folks out there who ain't happy. In love? Whut y' talkin' erbout, boy? Y' ain't dry behind the ears yet—little mannish rascal." Happiness at that age wasn't even an issue. It was duty, obedience, dedication to work and study. The very idea of plotting to get my first piece that very night—from my cousin, at that, was incomprehensible and quite against the order of things. If Deacon Tiggins knew about that or even suspected it, he would tear down fences and walls to tell Uncle Pet so he could get more Uncle Tom medals to go along with his ass-kissing citations. I knew that neither he nor Uncle Pet thought much of my new religion and would constantly seek ways to put it to the test.

Reverend Taylor was stuffed and ready to retire to the front porch. "Sister Hughes, Sister Minerva, Brother Deacon, I have never in my life had such a feast. Your reputation precedes you, however. Now I can bear witness to all Pine Ridge that what they say about your cooking is more than true. Thank you so much. Saravania, Sun, you two remind me of mine who are about your ages. God speed. I know you will do good work in school and in the Lord's vineyard. I have no fear about it, and don't you. So work hard while it is day, for when night comes no man can work." He started to get up from the table.

Deacon Tiggins held up his hand. "Jist er minute, Reverend—jist er minute. Ain't we gon' pray?"

Uncle Pet had a question on his face. "Reverend prayed befo' dinner." He chuckled lightly.

"I know that, but this was such a fine dinner and the Lord's been so good t' me—t' all of us—well, I'll be honest wid y'all, I'm jist so filled up wid the Holy Ghost ergin I can't git it outta my system."

According to all of my indicators, I wanted badly to tell him, it wasn't the

Holy Ghost that he was full of, especially after all the food he had consumed.

Uncle Pet and Reverend Taylor looked at each other and sat back down to humor that sanctimonious hypocrite. "Very well then, Deacon Tiggins, why don't you lead us in prayer."

Instead of praying, Tiggins began singing a hymn.

"Beeee-fo' this time ernother yeaaaah—"

All assembled repeated the words.

Tiggins continued to lead the singing.

"IIIIIII may be dead and gonnnne—"

I thought to myself, *I certainly hope so, for my sake.* I didn't like Deacon Tiggins, but I knew it was sinful to harbor such thoughts about another Brother. Tall and gaunt, veins protruding from his long neck, he looked like a turkey with TB. His Adam's apple kept bobbing up and down out of control. He looked nothing like Crazy Charlie—who was well built—except around the eyes and nose. I couldn't abide his obvious Uncle Toming and obnoxious manners. It was all the more offensive because, as a child, I had no rights that grown-ups had to respect. It was the order of things. If a Baptist felt like calling a prayer meeting, he could do so on the spot. They seldom exercised that option except during revival when one of The Faithful came in contact with a moaner. But revival was over, and I was no longer on the moaners' bench.

As the hymn continued, Aint Babe and Mrs. Minerva, who were greasing it up in the kitchen, came to the door and joined the others. Saravania and I looked at each other and dryly joined in, knowing it was expected of us.

Finally, Deacon Tiggins ended the hymn and announced what he had been leading up to all along. "Ask Brother Sun Hughes t' lead us in er word of prayer."

Of course I knew that as a new member I would be tested, but not around the dinner table. I also knew that Uncle Pet couldn't wait to get me in church so he could call on me to lead a hymn, testify, or go down on my knees and pray like him and every other God-fearing Baptist. Deacon Tiggins, wanting to impress Uncle Pet and the Reverend, had jumped the gun and decided to test me immediately.

It was customary to call on another Sister or Brother if the spirit so moved you to do so. I felt so moved and exercised my prerogative with lightning speed. "I call on Sister Saravania."

She felt just as "so moved" as I did and immediately called on Uncle Pet.

Uncle Pet spoke with a mean commanding voice that gave me to know that I had better cough up some kind of prayer. "Brother Sun Hughes, will you *please* lead us in prayer?" He may as well have said, "That's an order."

No longer able to escape, I got on my knees and mumbled the Lord's Prayer in nothing flat. The only thing even I heard was "Forever and ever, eh-man." Technically, I was more than right, since Deacon Tiggins only asked for a word and I gave him four.

Reverend Taylor was about to explode with laughter. He looked at me with tears in his eyes and said, "Brother Sun, that is, without doubt, the fastest delivery of the Lord's Prayer I have ever *not* heard." He started to chuckle.

Saravania couldn't contain herself, begged to be excused and hurried into the kitchen. Aint Babe and Mrs. Minerva followed her. We could hear them in the kitchen getting it all out. Deacon Tiggins sat stone-faced. Uncle Pet sat shaking his head and grunting in utter disgust.

Chuckling, Reverend Taylor said, "Well, Deacon, it *was* the Lord's Prayer."

Tiggins was clearly outdone and outmaneuvered, but, as a boy, I couldn't gloat or give any signs of having bested him. Finally he noticed Uncle Pet shaking his head, and he started to imitate him.

I begged to be excused and went to my room to await "thundown" and the wonderful treat that I had coming with my cousin Saravania.

3

Loud, bearded snoring trumpeted from Uncle Pet's and Aint Babe's room. I waited with a patient Arkansas moon grown old in a midnight summer sky. A tomcat on the prowl scurried, hissed, and fussed after being frightened when he accidentally came upon me sitting on the back porch. I listened to night sounds that squeaked and guzzled and moaned from creatures unmuted by time. Night sounds that had peaked earlier on with exclamations full and round-toned, then dulled and dwindled with the hours to an elliptical, apostrophized stillness accentuated only by stirrings that broke the deeper quiet.

Footsteps made crushing sounds on the rocks coming up the Pike. I listened. Unable to see the figure clearly, I guessed it was Crazy Charlie, who'd been on the prowl himself. When I heard him clear his throat, I was sure.

When he turned off the Pike and started toward the back of the house I stood up so he could see me. "Charlie," I whispered.

"Sssss." Charlie caught me by the arm and led me to his room, which was in the front of the house near the Pike. "Don't y' know y' can git shot like that? Jumpin' out on a man in the dark?" He pulled his owl-head pistol out and laid it on his dresser.

"Y' wouldn' shoot me, would y', Charlie?"

"Not if I knowed it wuz you. Coulda been er prowler. How could I tell in the dark like that?"

"Prowlers sleep this time er night," I said, and sat in a chair.

"If I wuz er prowler that's exactly whut I'd want y' t' think so I could rob y' blind." He started taking off his clothes. "Well, how'd y' make out?" Before I could answer, "Not too good, I see, else y' wouldn' be settin' out there on that back porch in the dark by yo'self."

"How did you make out, Charlie?"

"Me? Made out fine. Tore it up." He chuckled quietly. "You'll see the evidence in er few months from now if she comes in on time."

"You make her sound like er milk cow, Charlie."

"Tell y' the truth, li'l bro, I've seen much better-looking milk cows. But I ain't complainin', she been good t' me." Charlie muffled a laugh. "But whut happened that yours didn't show up?"

"I don't know. I can't figure it out. Somethin' musta scared her off."

"Did y' knock on her window? 'Course y' can't do too much knockin' eround heah at night 'cause Aint Babe would heah it 'n come at y' wid that shotgun."

"I know that. Saravania didn't sleep in her room, Charlie."

"How y' know?"

"'Cause I peeped through the window when the light wuz on 'n saw Mrs. Minerva wuz in that room fixin' t' go t' bed."

"Hmmm, som'um's up, li'l bro, 'n I think I know whut it is."

"Whut?"

"Y'all been found out, that's whut. Did y' see Saravania at all?"

"Never saw her since before sundown."

"Who helped take the stuff back over t' the store 'n put it in the icebox?"

"I tried t' help, but Aint Babe wouldn' let me. She wouldn' leave us alone fer er minute."

"She knows, li'l bro."

"How y' think she found out?"

"Somebody tol' her."

"Who? You wuz the only one who saw us, 'n you left before we finished eatin'. So who do y' think it wuz?"

"Who wuz payin' y' all that attention? Who kept pickin' at y', tryin' t' make y' testify 'n pray?"

"But he didn't see nothin', Charlie—"

"Didn't have t' see nothin', from the way Saravania wuz acting at the table. You don't know im like I do; he's got lots er hell in im. He's m' brother, but he's er mean son of er bitch, 'specially when he's jealous er somebody."

"Jealous er who, me?"

"Y' be surprised. It ain't jist you; it's who you is. The ol' man got mor'n anybody eround heah. Lots er folks jealous er that. You bein' his nephew makes you er part er all that."

"But the Deacon 'n Uncle Pet—they good friends," I said.

"Sure, but that's 'cause the ol' man's got som'um, 'n lot er folks kiss up t' im 'cause they respect im 'cause he got som'um or they scared of im. Why y' think he carry that foot gun wid im all the time? I heah whut they say behind his back. Yo' papa they liked. Y' Uncle Pet, they scared of—all except me."

"Y' mean t' say the Deacon don't like Uncle Pet?"

"The Deacon likes whut Uncle Pet got, 'n who he is."

"Y' think Uncle Pet knows that?"

"Sho he knows it. He also knows that he can find out erbout anything he want t' know from the Deacon."

I sat and looked into space, not knowing what to do or what the next day would bring. My exalted state that looked so bright only a few hours before had suddenly turned to sundown.

*　　　*　　　*

We finished breakfast that Monday morning as early as we had before we laid by crops. The table was quiet. Saravania kept her head down and was about to cry. Uncle Pet—the perfect farmer—paid no attention to stopping work until harvest time, kept everyone busy and on the same schedule. He wasn't about to pay a hired hand $25 per month plus room and board to sit around and wait for harvest like most farmers.

Charlie finished, excused himself, and started for his team. I grabbed my hat and started behind him as I had done all summer. Uncle Pet hadn't said anything so I figured he would pass it up this time and wait to see what would develop between Saravania and me. Wrong. I hadn't taken more than a few steps when—

"Wait er minute, boy.—schuuh—Go over to the sto' 'n wait fer m'."

I knew what that meant, having had the experience too many times before. This, however, was the first time I had faced a whipping for smelling around a girl.

I didn't have to wait long before Uncle Pet hobbled in. He didn't have anything in his hand; I thought perhaps I had graduated to the bullwhip league.

He walked past the bullwhip and came back with a long leather strap. "So y' think y' er man now?"

"Whut y' gon' whip m' fer?"

"Y' mean y' don't know?"

"Whut did I do?"

"It's not whut y' did; it's erbout whut y' wuz erbout t' do. Y' been smellin' eround that girl, that's whut.—schuuh—'N she yo' blood cousin.—schuuh— Now take yo' clothes off."

"Take my clothes off?"

"Take um off. I'm gon' teach y' er lesson."

I simply stood there without responding. I figured that whatever lesson he had to teach me I could learn it much faster clothed. I thought about my sister Geneva's solution: when in doubt, run. I couldn't run. Uncle Pet had locked the door behind him when he came into the store.

Before I could respond, he started beating. "I bought y' er new suit— schuuh"—then a blow—"sendin' y' t' city school—schuuh"—a blow—"feedin' 'n clothin' y'—schuuh"—a blow—"tryin' t' make er man outta y'"—a blow— "'n this is the thanks I git fer it."

At first I wouldn't cry, but the beating became so severe I cried out, "Y' beatin' me on whut that ol' Deacon tol' y', 'n he ain't seen no more 'n you!"

"Don't you sass me, boy!" He beat and beat until I had welts all over my body, but he kept blowing and beating.

Finally I heard Aint Babe's voice. Then I heard a key turning in the lock and she entered. "All right, Pet! That's ernough now!"

He ignored her and kept beating.

She yelled again and ran between us. "Doggone it! I said that's ernough! Now I know y' ain't gonna hit me. Git on outta heah, Sun. Charlie's waitin' fer y'. Y' oughtner whip that boy when y' mad—"

She was dressing him down when I left and joined Charlie. Saravania was standing at the gate crying bitterly. I had stopped crying and was more angry than hurt. When I stepped up on the wagon, Charlie took off. He looked glad to take me away from that sad scene. We were quiet all the way to the fields, since what we feared had already happened.

Near sundown we stopped work and headed back home. I would rather have gone anywhere except there. I dreaded having to face Saravania. I was almost fourteen, tall and growing fast into young manhood. My pride had been snatched away from me on suspicion alone. My status as the only boy my age from my community attending city school, my new religion, my mastery as a plowboy, my ability to do any other work in the fields, to weigh, count, and even mark things in the book and wait on customers in the store, to drive the new Plymouth to church and the little pond near our house, wash it and drive it back, all of those things earned me the same kind of beatings Uncle Pet had inflicted on Gene Cannon, our cousin Jeff Todd, and others before my time. How quickly he found that secret smile on my inside face and wiped it away before I had time to really enjoy it.

The big question on my mind was Saravania. What would happen to her? I knew he wouldn't dare whip her. Aint Babe wouldn't let him. Would they keep a sharp eye on us in the future? Would they take away what few privileges she had—like visiting a young girl her age who lived up the Pike or taking a bath alone? They had already moved her into the bedroom next to theirs. What did Deacon Tiggins tell Uncle Pet that caused him to take such drastic measures? Would he do what I feared most? Would he send Saravania to her grandfather in faraway Flint, Michigan?

Our wagon had barely turned right onto the Pike when I saw the gray Plymouth parked in front of the house. It was always in the garage unless Uncle Pet was going someplace. Shortly, I saw him hobbling out to the car. As we came a little closer, I saw Saravania on the porch. Dressed in her Sunday clothes, she was hugging Aint Babe and Mrs. Minerva. Two bags sat beside her.

Uncle Pet honked the horn. "All right, y'all, we can't miss that train."

When I heard the word *train*, my mind leaped in panic over whatever else followed. Then I saw Saravania crying. She crawled into the backseat of the Plymouth. I lost all control. The car headed toward Pine Ridge. When Saravania saw me, she screamed and clawed at the back window of the car. I leaped off the wagon like a panther and took off after them. Being one of the fastest runners around, even in brogans, I was gaining on the car until Uncle Pet put it in third, then high gear, and pulled away, leaving me in a cloud of dust. I kept running and would have run the five miles to Pine Ridge if I hadn't heard Charlie's voice behind me.

"Sun! Sun boy! Let her go! Let her go!"

I slowed down, finally stopped, and sat on the side of the road crying uncontrollably.

Poor Charlie finally arrived. He was puffing and blowing—out of breath. "I be damned if you ain't the fastest sucker I ever saw. You need to be . . . up there . . . in Hot Springs . . . on one er them . . . racetracks . . . wid them . . . hosses." He sat beside me and grabbed me by the head playfully. "Come on now, li'l bro. Y' git er chance t' see her ergin. Hell, the way you move, you can run from Arkansas t' Flint, Michigan."

I stopped crying and looked up at him.

Crazy Charlie started laughing.

"Whut y' laughin' erbout?"

"If you could *thee yo'thelf* in the mirror. . . . Y' look er hundred yeahs ol' wid all that white-lookin' shit in yo' hair, y' eyebrows, y' eyelashes—all over y'." He helped me to my feet. "Come on, I gotta go take care o' m' team, then we'll see if we can scare up some supper."

"I ain't hungry."

"I know y' ain't."

Charlie put his hands on my raw sore shoulder, and we started back to the house. The sun had gone all the way down, and night shadows were bouncing across the Pike and among the trees. Night sounds began their mystical music again. The moon was peeping over the horizon in the east. Rocks and gravel churned beneath our clodhoppers.

I was used to discipline from Mama and Papa; however, it was discipline with love. "This is hurting me worse than it is you" sounded ridiculous at the time, but now it began to make sense. Uncle Pet made no such statement. He clearly enjoyed what he was doing in the name of his Christian duty.

With the abrupt change in my affairs, I envisioned a bleak future, and I began to question the possibility of a better future in the past. It was an assessment of the naked truth remembered. It was about my earliest memory of Papa and Mama, who would wrestle demons for me. Of Ben, my playmate, who was always helping me "git sum'um done." Of Black Nelson and Elbert, my heroes. Of Mr. Durbey, who was always ready with a nickel. Of Professor L. Carrington Woodside, who showed me about as much warmth as a woolly mammoth but taught me arithmetic and English.

My mind got busy reflecting on my past. I was too young to have lost so much. First there was Spot, my puppy, Mr. Durbey, then Papa, and now Saravania, my first love. When would I ever see her happy face again? When would I hold her again? When would I hear her sweet lisp? "Thundown . . . thundown, Thun, that's when we'll meet . . . thundown."

I began to realize that I could have borne this loss better if Papa was alive. I began to experience more fully the inescapable impact and awesome loneliness of a fatherless boy.

I needed relief. I needed to start all over. My mind went back home, back to memories, back to my earlier days, to recount exactly what had taken place in my life up to that point.

4

Mama was rushing and fussing at everybody in the house. Only one among seven siblings, it was difficult to focus on who everybody was. They were my older sisters, Jessie, Hazel, Deloris, and Geneva, and my older brother, Elbert. The baby was my sister Verleen, who turned out to be Mama's last child. Mama wore her bushy hair in two thick balls gathered in the back. Her long dress and swift movements made her seem taller than her five feet six inches. She had an easy smile that revealed a gold crown on each side among her beautiful white teeth and accentuated her handsome face. After nine children—two died—she was still a young woman in her thirties.

"Y'all pick up eround heah 'n git this place in order. Yo' papa be heah befo' y' know it."

"Whut's Papa gon' eat?" Jessie asked.

"Well, he can't have nothin' sweet. Well, he can have sweet milk, whole wheat bread, chicken 'n fish, fruit—things like that. Wheah's that letter they sent from the hospital?" Mama dashed into another room to look.

Nearing my third birthday, I naturally trailed behind her trying to get as much information as I could about this stranger my sisters and Elbert were calling Papa.

"Deloris—Geneva—Hazel—" Mama stammered.

"Which one er us y' want, Mama?" Deloris asked.

"You'll do. Take care er yo' brother 'n the baby fer er while. I'm too busy now."

It was dark outside. The whole house was in an uproar. Everybody was excited and seemed to know what was happening except me. I wasn't about to let my confusion stand in the way of all the commotion, so I joined the bigger people around me.

Mama was turning and moving swiftly from room to room. She placed a vase here and fluffed a pillow there. The big dining room table was laid out with candles, silverware, napkins, plates, and water glasses placed just so. The aroma of delicious food filled the house. Coal oil lamps were burning brightly in every room. Chairs were covered with white slips. A tall chair sat at the head of the table. As time drew nigh, I learned that the many questions I was eager to ask would simply have to wait.

Finally, I heard horses snorting outside, then voices. Everyone inside froze. Suddenly there was a mad surge toward the front door. Everyone went outside and gathered on the front porch. I squeezed through and held on to Mama's dress. She was already holding the baby in her arms, and I had to settle for second best.

The bright moonlight allowed me to see a tall lean figure get down from a big buggy that had two sleek-looking horses hitched to it.

"Want me t' hep y', Mr. Andra?" the driver asked.

The tall man chuckled. "Y' want me t' git back in?"

"Naw sir." The driver realized the foolishness of his question and said no more.

"Jist put the surrey up, unharness um, 'n bring that trunk inside." The tall man took a briefcase and a walking cane from the big buggy. He squinted at the gathering on the front porch, then pulled his floppy hat down over his eyes, draped his long blue overcoat around his shoulders, slowly opened the gate of the white picket fence, and started to make his way up the narrow path. Suddenly the gathering surged toward him. They surrounded him and began asking him all kinds of questions except the ones I wanted to ask. Principally, who was he? Where was Hot Springs, and why had he been there?

In time, I learned that he was Papa. Hot Springs is a resort area where he had gone for treatments after he became a diabetic. There he saw doctors and bathed in the hot waters that spring up from the earth. The black Baptists owned a house there where members who could afford it went when they were sick. There was also talk of Papa's thirty-third-degree Masonry aiding in his going there and staying a few months.

It was fall. The nights were chilly, and we all gathered around the red-hot potbellied stove in the living room. Since my brother and my older sisters called the tall gaunt stranger Papa, I joined the group, and it soon became easy for me to do the same.

As time passed I discovered that Papa could do things with his hands that amazed me. He astonished my older sisters and my brother, Elbert, also. He did many string tricks. He made crows' feet, Jacob's ladder, Jacob's coffin, and a cup and saucer.

He told my sister Deloris, who was nine, "If you go into the closet, close your eyes, look up at the sky, 'n rub yo' stomach, I bet I can tell y' whut y' doin'." Deloris, being eager to test the trick, went immediately into the closet and closed her eyes. Shortly, her voice came from the closet, "OK, Papa, whut am I doin'?" Papa said, "You're in there actin' er fool." He roared with laughter. Seeing him so overjoyed, everybody joined him.

The trick I considered daring and dangerous was his greatest. He only played that one once, on seven-year-old Elbert. Papa must have learned the trick during his railroad days. He gave Elbert a pocket knife and poured a puddle of water on the floor. He told Elbert, "I bet I can wipe that puddle er water up without touching it." "Impossible," everyone said. He had Elbert sit on the floor and straddle the puddle. Then he placed his long powerful hand in front of Elbert and told him to stab it. Elbert was reluctant. Everybody was concerned. Papa insisted. Finally Elbert took a stab. Before anybody knew what was happening, Papa grabbed Elbert's legs, snatched him over the puddle, and wiped it up as pretty as you please with the seat of Elbert's pants. He lay on the floor and laughed until he cried. Everybody was laughing along with him except Elbert. Elbert did not laugh to accommodate anyone, not even Papa. When the joke was on him, that's precisely how he took it.

Those were some of my first memories of life with Papa—my introduction to life itself. As the years passed, the tall gaunt man, Papa, unfolded many discoveries to me.

In 1906 Papa bought and built on 1.63 acres on Highway 15 (the Pike). One could go all the way from Pine Ridge, Arkansas, to Louisiana on the Pike. Nine children were born in the first house before it burned. Papa built a larger new house on a bluff, on the west side of the highway, farther back from the road. The new house was surrounded by tall gums, big oaks, and a few pines. It was built by carpenters who knew their trade, rather than by the family with help from neighbors and relatives (as had been, and still was, the custom). By facing east, the front porch, with its soothing swing, was cool and pleasant in the evening, while the trees provided good shade in the morning and during the day. My pains, my rejoicings, my sorrows, my home, my world took shape and sculpted my being on those acres.

Behind the store across Wagon Road West from our house, I often met my buddy Ben, and we planned what we would git done. The blacksmith shop, only a few feet from the store, was where I watched Mr. Durbey work. I also drew a crowd, mostly on Saturdays, when wrestling white and colored boys who dared to challenge me.

Directly behind the store was the woodpile, then the barn. I watched a sow give birth to a litter of beautiful piglets in one of the stalls of that barn, and she ate them as they came out. I told Papa what was happening, but we were able to save only three of the little creatures. We fed them from a bottle with a nipple on it rather than let them near their crazy mother. The piglets, of course, soon became pets.

On the other side of the house, I gathered vegetables from our garden, ripped my pants, and scarred my knee trying to reach a pear high on a top branch.

Immediately behind our house, I entered our little smokehouse and watched the slow, twirling hickory smoke from the eternal hot bed of coals weave its white, curling clouds up among the lazily dripping hams, shoulders, and ribs of hog meat.

I often wandered to the chicken house directly behind the smokehouse and gathered brown and white eggs from cackling hens.

The infamous little outhouse at the far end of our garden sat on a knoll near the fence. I dreaded that little house, not only for its smell but for its attractiveness to long black snakes.

Securely placed in the far corner of the garden was Spot's grave. Verleen and I had placed a crude wire fence around it. Weeds had grown up along the fence, but we kept the grave site itself clean and the wooden cross hammered into the ground.

Papa spoke of the early black settlers like the Leddens, who had sold him the land for our homestead, the Tilsons, who had provided land for the first Hughes Chapel and Tilson School, the Beardens and the Martins—all close neighbors and cofounders of community institutions down the Pike. Papa's mother and father had come along since the Civil War. Farther up the Pike, where Uncle Pet had settled, were the Nashes (Aint Babe's family), the Germans, the Walkers, and the Bradleys. All of those families owned considerable acres of land.

Over In The Hills, west of us, the Plumbers, the Roafs, the Simses, the McCraneys, the Cashes, and the Templetons (Mama's family) lived on their own land. Most of those families were free and independent long before the Civil War. Even their mothers and fathers had been free, which meant that they had settled in that community when Arkansas was still a territory. Part of the Louisiana Purchase, it didn't become a state until 1837.

Bottomland along the Arkansas and Mississippi Rivers was expensive and hard to come by. Most of the slaves who were brought into Arkansas after it became a territory were used to cultivate cotton for the big plantation owners of river bottomland. Hilly and forest lands were taken by black farmers and poorer whites.

Grandpa Templeton, who was born in 1853, sixteen years after Arkansas became a state, was believed to have owned over 1000 acres of that forest land. His penchant for doing things in a big way extended to his family-making, since he was the father of twenty-two children. Raising those children must have agreed with both him and Grandma Fannie because they lived to see their seventies.

A picture of Grandpa Templeton reveals a long black beard, a collarless shirt, and thick bushy black hair that framed his strong black face. His most distinguishing features, however, were his big round dark eyes with long eyelashes, above which were very heavy black eyebrows. His image was stoic, solid—no trace of a smile in his face. Papa said that he was a strict disciplinarian, a frontier settler who "kept no truck with nonsense." When he laughed, which was seldom, everybody laughed. He had a delayed-action preparatory drawl that lasted what seemed like three minutes. It was not unlike an irritated baby who would frighten you by holding its breath a long time before finally squalling.

Even after most farmers started using mules and horses, Grandpa Templeton created quite a sight by driving a pair of oxen to town—his wagon loaded with charcoal. No one would dare tell him, "Git some mules!"

I was very young, but I remember Grandma Fannie Templeton's visits. I even have a dim vision of visiting her. It was a large house Over In The Hills, and I ran up and down the rambling halls. Off the hallway were many bedrooms. There was a big rubble-stone fireplace and a charcoal kiln outside.

When Grandma Fannie came visiting, she sounded like Santa. We could hear her high voice in the distance before her wagon, driven by some relative, descended Blueberry Hill—"Merry Christmas! Merry Christmas!" Like Santa, her wagon was loaded with good things to eat. Cheerful and laughing, she was fanning herself, and sweat was pouring down her round, naturally red-tinted face. She was the color of Arkansas clay. "Kitty, ya'll chillen, help Grandma wid these things."

Slowly, someone helped her out of the wagon and up the stairs to the back porch. Inside, someone pulled out a big rocking chair for her. She slowly parked her rather short plump body and continued fanning and talking. She took off her shawl and gave it to Mama. Then she removed her bonnet and revealed a bushel basket of long gray hair. Then Grandma Fannie doled out the socks, gloves, and shawls she had knitted for our family.

I remember on one occasion she reared back in her rocker and a blood-curdling scream came from our cat. "Whut's the matter wid that cat?" Grandma Fannie asked innocently.

"Your rocker's on his tail," my sister Geneva said.

She quickly rocked forward, releasing the cat's tail. "Oh, my goodness. I guess I'd scream too if somebody rocked on my feet like that," she said with a concerned look on her face.

"Or my tail, Grandma," Geneva rejoined with the wit that she displayed even at the age of six.

Grandma Fannie laughed good-naturedly. "Go on erway from heah, chile. You can't grow no tail."

Papa said that his father, Grandpa Hughes, was born a slave in Georgia. After the Civil War, he followed the trend of other freedmen and headed north walking. Arkansas can be cold in winter and chilly in spring. After traveling over 800 miles and finding the temperature 50 degrees at night, such a change in the climate in early spring indicated to him that he had reached the North. If he had traveled 170 miles farther, he would have reached Memphis, Tennessee—which, to him, would have been a real northern city.

His slave name was Holmes. When he awoke one morning and found himself among huge pine trees, he looked around at the beautiful surroundings, had an instant bright idea, and changed his name on the spot to Huge. When asked why, he replied, "I never wanted a slave name in my life. I certainly wuddn't gonna start out in a pretty new place like this wid some ol' slave name." When white functionaries wrote his name on deeds and birth certificates, however, they decided that the ignorant "nigra" must have been trying to say Hughes. Since it was official according to "white folks," no one cared about Grandpa Huge's real intention or knew that the name he had chosen had ever been changed. The important thing is that Grandpa Huge knew, and he passed it on to his wife, sons, and daughters.

I never even saw a picture of Grandpa Huge. The name Huge was a contradiction, physically speaking, according to Papa, because he was short, not that big but strongly built. My uncle Thomas, Grandpa's youngest son, was said to be almost a true reproduction of his father. He had blocked, sculptured features with a strong, prominent chin and a long well-shaped head that rose straight up from his long neck without any overhang in the rear. He boasted of his pure African stock.

Resistance to slavery was a family trait. Grandpa Huge told stories of one of his older brothers who ran away every chance he got. One time he made it as far northward as the Tennessee border before they caught him. When they brought him back in shackles, he went on a hunger strike. Jails, beatings, Bible lessons, preaching—nothing worked for that strapping young man, short of freedom. Finally, the slave-master crippled him by chopping off part of his foot. Better to have a crippled commodity than none at all, the slave-master reasoned. Grandpa Huge swelled with pride when speaking of his renegade brother. Grandpa instilled in his children the idea "You're as good as anybody. Jist because somebody tells y' you ain't don't make it so." It was easy to see where Uncle Pet got his boasting about being "er proud ol' black man."

Papa said Grandpa Huge could do arithmetic better than anyone in the community—mostly in his head. Somehow he had learned to read and write in some fashion and stressed the importance of those skills to his children. Grandpa Huge was a leader. We remembered him as one of the principal founders, as well as the first pastor, of Hughes Chapel, the church that bears his name.

The first Hughes Chapel was a lean-to, or brush arbor, organized and constructed on an acre of land bought from one of the founders in the late 1860s. It was located back in the woods, joining Grandpa's land about a mile west of the Pike. Because the first church had no bell, Grandpa Huge blew a bugle to alert members to services, funerals, weddings, and community meetings. The seats were crude benches rough hewn from logs by the men of the congregation.

In the early 1900s, the founders bought three more acres of land on the

Pike and built a log cabin for the second Hughes Chapel. They soon tore the log cabin down and built a new church with a bell tower. The sons of the founders controlled that church until the congregation outgrew it. Then they constructed another brush arbor until they could build a larger church and add two more acres for a graveyard. That was the church of my boyhood.

In 1890 Grandpa Mark Andrew and Grandma Caroline "Hughes"—having no choice but to answer to the changed spelling and pronunciation of their last name—bought 240 acres of forest and farm land.

A swelling grassy bluff rose from among handsome timbers to greet us as our wagon slowly clucked into the clearing. Ferns and flowers fixed in their wildness fussed with weeds and bushes for a dominion they were bound to lose. Gleaming rays, filtered through trees, entered dancing through a gossamer haze before a sleepy sun retired the day. A few stray cattle grazing nearby accepted our presence with a mere glance that barely interrupted their feeding. Birds, squirrels, lizards, rabbits, early evening sounds of night creatures registered as lowly corporals to the quiet tranquillity of that plot. Just beyond a clump of bushes to the west, Alligator Creek snaked its way lazily from the hills, through the site and our farms, on its way to Bayou Bartholomew.

Mr. Sam stopped the team. Papa and Mama got down slowly and walked ceremoniously over to a growth of trees and weeds. With his cane, Papa fumbled with the remains of an old metal pot half buried in the ground. There was a scattered pile of old bricks nearby that bore witness to years past. There was another growth of tall weeds and bushes to his right that was greener than the rest.

"That's where the ol' well usta be," I said.

"How'd you know that?" Papa asked.

"You took Elbert 'n me by heah befo', Papa."

"So I did, so I did."

When we turned around, Mama had deployed Hazel, Deloris, Geneva, and Verleen to the orchard, on the far end of the site, with buckets. The remaining unattended trees in the orchard bore limbs that drooped and sagged from their sweet ripened riders like weather-beaten, broken-down scarecrows. First plums had already riveted the ground with their black and purple, beneath and around the trees. Birds and ants must have had enough plums because there were many unpecked specimens. Withered limbs lay close to where they fell, still boastfully bearing the delicious weight that caused them to fall.

"This is er shame, all this fruit goin' t' waste like this," said Mama.

Mr. Sam had his mouth full. I followed his example. "Not all of um, Kitty. I'm gon' take care of er mess of um right heah 'n now."

"You gon' be dangerous t' be near in er hour or so, Sam Riley," Papa remarked.

"Y' better worry erbout y' son heah, he gon' be near y' all night," Mr. Sam countered.

Grandpa Hughes had met and married Caroline in the late 1860s. She had come to Arkansas from the Carolinas, also as a freedwoman. She was above average height, had a round, regular, well-proportioned face, with large round intelligent eyes. Her skin was a smooth velvet blackness like an African mahogany finish that complemented well her natural good looks. She carried herself with mindful authority that befitted the pioneer temper of her time and passed that legacy on to her four sons and two daughters.

Grandma and Grandpa Hughes had done well in the new "land of opportunity." In some thirty years, the couple, who were ex-slaves, had accumulated more than a sufficient amount of land, built a house, raised a family, and contributed substantially to the religious and social life of their community.

Late one evening, while driving a spirited team of horses down the road, Grandpa Hughes met a man who he and everyone knew was mentally deranged. The man was carrying a pitchfork. After a brief conversation, during which Grandpa Hughes tried to humor him, knowing his condition, the man stuck one of the horses with the pitchfork. The horses took off, and Grandpa Hughes lost control. He fell out of the wagon, his foot was caught in the reins, and he was dragged, helpless, a considerable distance. The horses headed home. It was dark when someone heard them snorting and the wagon rumbling outside. They found Grandpa Hughes lying bloodied and broken behind his wagon. They took him inside and tried to nurse him back to health, but he would blow his bugle no more. He died in his healthy, strong middle age. They buried him in the old cemetery near the original site of Hughes Chapel, among the huge pines from which he took his name.

Grandma Hughes rose to the occasion and took charge of the farm and her family of six. She carried on in the tradition of Grandpa Hughes as best she could. The oldest child, Uncle E.J., was a young man. Uncle Pet and Papa were old enough to go away to work on the railroad. Aint Sarah was old enough to get married. Uncle Thomas and his sister Cary were the only two who were still too young to "root for themselves." Uncle Thomas was still a teenager, and Cary was a very young woman.

Uncle E.J., the Lazy—he was called lazy because he didn't like drudgery—was studying at Branch College in Pine Ridge when Grandpa Hughes died. He was one of the first teachers sent down the Pike to work in the country. Papa never said how extensive Uncle E.J.'s college training was at that time, but it must have been enough for him to qualify for the elementary school level.

Uncle E.J. carved out a reputation for himself as a man who knew exactly how to get out of hard work. Papa said, "E.J. wutten afraid of hard work. He could set down right beside it, 'n if it didn't bother him, he wutten erbout t' bother it."

Uncle E.J. learned early in life that teachers and preachers were especially exempt from manual labor, better known as hard work. His distaste for drudgery, or his love for those professions, drove him to become both. He was tall and quiet. His manners were warm and impeccable. One of his techniques for preventing the curse of hard labor from touching him was to dress in a suit and tie with a starched white collar every day. As a teacher, he was good, but as a minister, he stood little chance among the squalling firebrands that came to our community. Preaching was only a sideline for Uncle E.J. anyway, since most of the time he was trying to invent something, to get rich and escape the plague of hard work forever.

In his quest to solve the problem of perpetual motion or at least harness the wasted energy that trains produced as they rumbled over the tracks, Uncle E.J. toyed with a method of transforming that wasted energy, through electro-mechanical devices, into pure electrical energy that could be utilized in the many machines of his day. To learn more about electricity and mechanics, he bought many books on the subjects and signed a promissory note that he was unable to meet when it came due. His creditors were impatient and unwilling to wait until his big ideas paid off. His creditors began to froth at the mouth, paw in the earth, gnash and champ at the bit in their efforts to get their money. Because he had sold all of his interest in the land to his brothers, the creditors couldn't place a lien on his property. They tried to bluff Papa and Uncle Pet into paying Uncle E.J.'s debt—even threatened them—but the creditors didn't have a leg to stand on, even in Arkansas at that time. Papa and Uncle Pet reminded them that neither of them had cosigned anything, neither had Grandma Hughes. Unable to make Papa, Uncle Pet, or Grandma Hughes pay, unable to place a lien on any of their lands or properties, that left only Uncle E.J.'s bare behind.

Acutely aware of white folks' passion for getting even, especially against a black man, Papa and Uncle Pet wasted no time in packing Uncle E.J., without his badly used books, and putting his fortune-seeking petuddy on the first thing smoking. They didn't send him to St. Louis, Chicago, New York, or Detroit, where most black people went at that time. They sent him as far as they could within the boundaries of the United States. That place was southern California.

Uncle E.J., the dreamer, the proud would-be inventor, wanted to hang around and pay his debt like a man. Uncle Pet and Papa, the realists, didn't want him hanging around for fear they would have to cut him down and bury him.

Uncle E.J., with all of his hang-ups, failures, and inclinations for getting into trouble, provided the leadership that all his brothers and others followed. He came along at a time of great inventions and inventors, both black and white. In those books, he must have read about the black inventors: Grandville T. Woods' invention of the railroad sensor and the air brake, Louis Latimer's fine carbon wire, which went into Edison's lightbulb, and, of course, the wonderful things George Washington Carver was doing at Tuskegee in chemistry.

Uncle E.J. encouraged his youngest brother, Thomas, to attend Tuskegee. E.J. also started one of the first country stores on the Pike, if not the first, black or white. He was the first teacher sent down the Pike to work with black children. Though he sold or traded all he had, he never failed to advise and encourage his brothers and sisters to start businesses and buy and own as much land as possible. It was his idea, adopted by Uncle Pet, to buy land that whites were likely to want so that when the city expanded, he could make them pay dearly for it simply because they didn't want a black man to own it.

I grew up hearing about the letters that Uncle E.J. wrote two or three times each year from faraway California. It was like hearing from a foreign country. He wanted to pay his debt. He had patented his ideas with the U.S. patent office, but he could never raise enough money from the poor salary his church paid him to afford working models of his inventions. He also wanted to visit, but Papa and Uncle Pet told him that his debtors hadn't given up trying to track him down. They were sure that Papa and Uncle Pet knew where he was. They also knew that the brothers met each year for over twenty years at the National Baptist Convention, but they were never able to do more than harass Papa and Uncle Pet and try to trick them into telling where Uncle E.J. was.

Uncle E.J. was married for a short while only once before he left Pine Ridge. There were no children. Though I never saw him while I was growing up, his image as a prodigious scholar following his dream of trying to get his inventions off the ground never faded.

After graduating from Tuskegee in 1913, two years before Booker T. Washington died, Uncle Thomas returned home to Pine Ridge. The new graduate had recently left a college where he was expected to find a young woman to marry. It was ironic that Washington's philosophy of "Let down your buckets where you are" proved to be fulfilling in Uncle Thomas' selection of a wife.

Aint Grace's family had moved to our community from Baton Rouge, Louisiana, and bought land adjoining that of the Hugheses. Some of her brothers and sisters looked so white that many people, especially white people, could not tell that the Gilmoores had African blood. Reverend Gilmoore, however, was a minister in the African-American tradition and identified with that culture. Aint Grace being young and pretty and Uncle Thomas being handsome and educated, Thomas got permission and "came er courtin'." It wasn't long before they were married. Uncle Thomas obtained a position as professor of agriculture at Branch College in Pine Ridge. Following in the footsteps of Uncle E.J., Uncle Pet, and Papa, he also opened a country store less than a quarter of a mile from Uncle Pet's business.

Unlike Uncle E.J., Uncle Thomas never avoided hard work or shirked his duties. On the contrary, he had a reputation for doing the work of two men. Short, muscular, and exceptionally strong, he was known for his physical as well as his mental abilities. Papa and Uncle Pet told many stories of how he would cut twice as much wood as the average man, load and take it to Pine Ridge by himself. That meant that he made twice as much for his efforts. No one in the community, including the McCraneys, known to be the toughest characters around except for Black Nelson, could match Uncle Thomas wrestling or boxing. Being short and muscular, he would undermine his often taller opponents. In bulldog fashion, once he gained a hold there was no shaking him loose, and a pin was inevitable.

Of the many stories told by Uncle Thomas's two brothers, who coddled him because he was educated and the baby, none topped the one told by his wife, Aint Grace, who was an excellent storyteller in her own right: Cows, being the stupidest animals on the farm next to horses, threw their weight around, often lying down in the middle of the road and refusing to move. One day, boldness caused one to walk up on the porch of Uncle Thomas's store while he was away and park her half-ton carcass in front of the doorway. Aint Grace took a broom to her, with no success. She then tried a stick, but there was no movement. Not wanting to scald the stupid creature, she poured cold water on her. The cow merely shook it off and maintained her position. Finally, Aint Grace tried coaxing the stubborn homesteader off the porch with a bucket of oats, but evidently her gourmet taste buds called for something more exotic that day. When Uncle Thomas arrived, the complacent lounger was still lying there calmly chewing her cud and enjoying the evening breeze. Customers had to walk around to the side door to get into the store. Several of them had tried to get the cow to move but met with the same result as Aint Grace.

"What's this cow doing lying on the porch?" Uncle Thomas asked when he arrived.

"Can't get her to move," Aint Grace replied.

Aint Grace went on with the story. "Thomas said, 'Take my briefcase.' He took off his suit coat. Then he got down on the floor and put his shoulder to the side of that cow. He braced his feet against the wall, grunted a couple of times, and slid that half-ton animal off the porch onto the ground. The cow was so outdone that she dropped her cud and took off into the woods where she belonged."

Aint Grace's complexion and hair permitted her to pass for white, if she had desired. Her bearing, culture, and loyalty to her Thomas, however, prevented her from even considering such a thing. She told another story about her and

Uncle Thomas's brush with the mores and vicious habits of the white man's South. While Uncle Thomas was away during the day, a certain "ol' white man" whom she called "Mr. So-'n-so white man," tried to revert back to the practices of slavery by taking a black man's wife at will. Each time Thomas returned home, there sat Mr. So-'n-so. Instead of buying what he wanted and moving on, as most people did, he set up camp.

Uncle Thomas, who had a reputation for being straightforward, as well as for having lifted a half-ton cow off his porch single-handed, listened quietly to Aint Grace's complaint about that Mr. So-'n-so white man. The next day when Uncle Thomas came home, there sat Mr. So-'n-so in his favorite spot. Mr. So-'n-so started out, as usual, trying to pass the time of day by discussing the weather, Uncle Thomas's job, how well he thought the young couple were getting along, and a litany of "white folks' bull." Uncle Thomas coolly waited until Mr. So-'n-so had finished. Then he set his briefcase down, looked Mr. So-'n-so straight in the eye, and said, "Mr. So-'n-so."

"Yes, Tom."

"Don't come back anymore."

"Whut y' mean, Tom?"

"I mean, don't come back anymore."

"Well, don't y' want m' business, boy? I can take it elsewhere, y' know."

Uncle Thomas moved closer to Mr. So-'n-so and whispered in a deadly, menacing manner, "Don't-come-back-any-more."

Mr. So-'n-so turned red and stormed out of the store.

Aint Grace, Uncle Thomas, and everyone else knew what could happen to a black man who dared go up against a white one, even when the white one was a no-good lout and the black man was a businessman and a college professor. Uncle Thomas and Aint Grace packed up, closed the store, and quietly moved only 35 miles away to Little Rock, hoping to find a haven. In Little Rock, they opened another business, and their second son was born, but after a while, the venomous mouth of the reptilian South dripped poison in the little pool of their new haven.

Papa said that Uncle Thomas didn't want to leave the South. His roots were there. He owned land there, had launched his business there, had a good profession, and had started his family there. After all, he had studied under Booker T. Washington, who counseled graduates to go back home, start a business, teach, and help those less fortunate than you. He tried hard to make it work, but it was not to be.

A simple matter of weights and measures threatened his very life. Uncle Thomas was doing business with another white man. The man got the idea that Uncle Thomas was being "a smart nigger." Few things infuriate white folks, especially insecure white folks, more than smartness and education in a black man. The white man said it was one number. Uncle Thomas used figures to prove to him that it was another. Instead of going over the figures, assuming he was able, or calling in a third person to check them, the white man became unraveled and started calling names. The argument finally escalated into threats, and the white man left in a huff, as Mr. So-'n-so had done. "You wait'll I git back, nigger." That time there was no time to pack the family and leave town quietly. He had to throw something together and leave in a hurry.

That time Uncle Thomas put over 700 miles between him and his beloved homeland and landed in the big city of Chicago. As soon as he could, he sent for his family. Like Uncle E.J. before him, he never set foot in Arkansas again except for an overnight visit he paid us on his way back home to Chicago from the National Baptist Convention one year. As the years passed, I discovered for myself the truth of many stories told to me by Papa about members of my family and why, as men, they were forced to "catch the first thing smoking."

5

It was late fall. Small farmers had picked their full bales of cotton and had only small amounts left over, called remedies. A remedy was not enough to make a four- or five-hundred-pound bale (a bale required twelve to fifteen hundred pounds of raw cotton), and nobody wanted to take a chance on storing it until the next season. They put those leftovers in their barns or cotton pens temporarily and called Papa. He was always happy to take it off their hands.

It was after school, so Papa allowed me to go along with him and Elbert to pick up Mr. Grey's remedy. They lived close by, down the Pike on the left, a short distance up into the gentle hills. I had gone with them to Mr. Thigpen's place, which was the long ride I enjoyed most. On our way, Elbert remarked, "I heard that ol' Mr. Grey can't read and write."

"Who tol' you that?"

"Oh, I heard it. I heard that neither he nor she can read or write."

"Well, I don't know erbout his readin', but Brother Grey can figure like the devil."

"You sho erbout that, Papa?"

"Sho as I'm settin' heah."

"I sho would like t' see it." Elbert turned the mules left on their wagon road. The wagon rocked on up the little incline.

I saw that mischievous expression come into Papa's face. I hadn't seen that look much since the time we had so much fun sitting around our potbellied stove playing games.

"So, you'd like t' see it, huh, Elbert?"

"I'd pay money, if I had it."

"I'll prove it t' you."

Papa was no angel. He liked to have fun. That gave him charm and endeared him to people, rather than rendering him a suspicious, untrustworthy person—as it often did others. His family and friends found ways to reconcile and find humor in his behavior. They often said, "Well, that's M.A. fer you." A big laugh usually followed.

Uncle Pet, to the contrary, seldom found him amusing and often told him so. Mama never said much. She simply watched him with the eye of a hawk, especially when helpless women came seeking his aid. Old Mr. Grey was another one who was onto Papa's little antics. Like most of Papa's friends, he thoroughly enjoyed and expected them.

The Greys lived in a quaint little house surrounded by a beautiful flower garden. There was a vegetable garden on the far side. An orchard, which included a cultivated vineyard with blue-black grapes straining the heavily laden vines, was in the rear. Handsome tall oaks and a few pines graced the spacious front. The vine-covered front porch featured a swing and two inviting rockers. The little road that led to the barn in the rear continued around the house, making it unnecessary to turn around in order to leave. They were indeed gentle people who loved children, though they had none of their own.

They had everything in order. I don't remember visiting their house without them feeding me more than I could eat, then loading me down with tea cakes, pecans, grapes, and peanuts to take home. We, of course, had most of those foods, but somehow they tasted better coming from little old Mr. and Mrs. Grey.

When we arrived, Mr. Grey was waiting for us. Before we reached the house, his voice sounded out, "Hey there, M.A.! Y'all jist pull right up heah— git down 'n come on in."

Mrs. Grey was waving from the porch. "Yes, indeed. Y'all git down 'n come on in—make y'selves at home."

Papa got off the wagon, extending his hand. "How you, Brother Grey? Sister Grey?" He tipped his hat.

"We puddy good fer ol' folks, M.A. How you feelin' these days?" They spoke at the same time as if they had practiced.

"I'm pretty good fer er sick man."

Mrs. Grey spoke up. "How is Sister Hughes 'n the rest er them chillens er your'n?"

"They all fine," Papa said.

Mr. Grey chimed in. "I see y' got two young men wid y' heah. Elbert, you 'n Sun—" I hopped down off the wagon before he finished. "See? Don't have t' say nothin' t' that boy Sun. He's at home, ha-ha-ha."

Mrs. Grey, leaving to get seats and refreshments, called, "He sho God is. How you Elbert? Sun?"

"Fine, how you, Miz Grey?" We both spoke at the same time.

"Brother Grey, we don't mean to rush, but I wanna take er look at that cotton y' got back there. It gits dark early now, y' know."

"I understand, M.A. Y'all wait 'n at least git y'self er cool drink fo' we git down t' business."

Papa looked around the grounds. "This sho' is a fine place y' got heah, Brother Grey, certainly is. I always did like this place. Sorta put me in mind er our old home-place."

Mr. Grey spat a big brown squirt of tobacco juice, part of which ran down his chin like a string of spaghetti finding a clinging home. He slowly took out a big red and white handkerchief and captured the slimy stray mucus, relieving the nauseating feeling in my stomach not a minute too soon.

"Now that y' mention it, I guess it is sorta like yo' pa's ol' place, M.A. House settin' on a bluff, flat land runnin' off in the back. 'Course, t'ain't nothin' like as big as yo' pa's place, but it's ernough fer the ol' lady 'n me."

"How many acres y' got back theah, Brother Grey?"

"Forty. That includes the acre 'n er half this house settin' on."

Papa waved his hands in the direction of the back. "You got the rest er this in cotton?"

Mr. Grey looked up at Papa. "My God no, M.A. Where would I git the hands t' handle that much cotton? I don't have er gang er chillens like you, 'member?"

Trying to get the old man going. "You got plenty er money, Brother Grey. You could hire it out."

"Yeah, 'n go broke."

Papa laughed. "Brother Grey, you got 'bout as much chance goin' broke as Simmons National."

Mrs. Grey came out with lemonade and chocolate cake. "Now y'all jist hep yo'selves." She motioned to Elbert and me, then she went back into the house. "Now you jist hold tight, M.A. I got some good cold buttermilk 'n biscuits fer you—seeing as how you cain't have nothin' sweet wid yo' diii—whatever y' call that thing you got."

"Diabetes, Sister Grey." Papa was lustfully eyeing the cake and lemonade.

"I knowed t'was som'um wid er di . . ."

Papa looked as if he was going to cry if he didn't get some of that lemonade and cake. He graciously took biscuits and buttermilk but was unable to keep his eyes off our plates.

"How many acres you said you got in cotton back there, Brother Grey?"

"I didn't say, M.A., but it's only erbout thirteen. Got erbout eight in corn, two, two 'n er half in peanuts 'n potatoes, erbout one 'n er half in peas 'n melons. Then my wife keeps this big garden eround heah. She do er lotta cannin' from that. The other twenty acres I leave in timber for firewood 'n post. Whut I need t' grow er lotta cotton fer?"

"Cash, Brother Grey, cash."

"Don't need it. Wouldn' know whut t' do wid it if I had it. Y' see, I ain't atta goin' up North t' conventions 'n things like you 'n yo' brother Pet. I don't have no big family or nothin'. Whut I go do wid er lotta cash?"

"That sounds mighty convincin', Brother Grey, to er man who don't know you, but y' see, I ain't that man. I bet you got money in every posthole eround heah."

"Not every posthole, M.A. Think I'm er fool?"

They laughed and slapped each other on the back.

Papa kept eyeing the door to see if Mrs. Grey was coming back. Finally he couldn't restrain himself any longer. "Brother Grey, do you suppose I could impose on your wife t' bring me out a piece er that cake 'n some lemonade? I don't think er little of it'll hurt me."

"Well, M.A., I don't wanna make y' sick." Mr. Grey looked around at us as if seeking our approval. Fat chance. We weren't approving any such thing. Keeping Papa away from sweets had become a full-time family occupation.

"Whut's makin' me sick is seein' y'all eat it 'n me not havin' any. Now I like biscuits 'n buttermilk, don't git me wrong, but compared to chocolate cake 'n lemonade?"

Mr. Grey squirted another mouthful of brown tobacco juice. Papa, who found such habits as smoking, chewing, and especially snuff-dipping objectionable, looked at us with a funny expression on his face.

"Well, M.A., y' know y' 'tirely welcome if y' certain t'wont hurt y'. Lucinda! Lucinda!"

From inside, "Yes, George?"

"Bring M.A. er small piece er cake 'n er small glass er lemonade fo' he bite somebody!"

"Whut erbout his di thing?" Mrs. Grey asked.

"He said er little won't hurt im!"

We heard Mrs. Grey singing a hymn inside. Elbert and I were ready for another piece of cake and more lemonade.

Mr. Grey looked at our empty plates. "Lucinda!"

"Yes, George?"

"These boys don't have no di-whut-y'-call-it. Bring some mo' out fer them!"

"All right!" Mrs. Grey's voice responded.

"M.A., whut sort er med'cine do y' take fer this di thing? Jist how do y' remedy whatever t'is y' got?"

"Well, Brother Grey, every mornin' 'n night, I have t' give m'self er shot er something called insulin."

"Insulin, y' say?"

"Tha's right, insulin. It comes in er little bottle erbout sooo big." Papa held his index finger and thumb apart to indicate the size.

"I see. Whut else do y' have t' do, M.A.? Whut erbout yo' eatin'? Whut kin y' have?"

"Well, Brother Grey, I kin have er lot er things—," Papa attempted to answer.

"That right?" Mr. Grey interrupted.

"—that I don't like but not ernough er anything, ercordin' t' that silly diet."

"But y' still have t' follow it if y' wanna stay eround, don't y'?"

"Well, Brother Grey, I'll tell y', if I had t' eat only whut they got on that diet, I don't know if it would be worth it," Papa said in a serious mood, and looked into space.

"Y' don't mean that, M.A."

Papa snapped out of it by changing the subject. "How many bales did y' have this fall, Brother Grey?"

"Well, M.A., first pickin' we got three 'n er half. That's why I got in touch wid y'; can't do nothin' wid no half-bale—which I don't have t' tell you."

"Well, as always, I'm gon' t' give y' er fair price fer it, Brother Grey."

Mr. Grey spat again. Good thing we weren't eating. I don't think I could have taken it. "I know you is, M.A." He looked at Papa in a knowing fashion as if to say, "You bet yo' ever-lovin' sweet petuddy you are."

Mr. Grey continued, "Now on the second pickin', I figure I oughta git eround two 'n half, two 'n three-quarters bales, in which case I'll be callin' y' ergin—if we can do business on this'un. Erbout half-bale er acre all y' gon' git on hill land, y' know. 'Course, who is I talkin' t'; y' got plenty er yo' own, even if y' don't farm it."

Papa chuckled until he saw the small portion Mrs. Grey brought him.

They finished the weighing beside the barn in back of Mr. Grey's house. Papa completed his calculations.

"Twelve hund'ed thirty pounds . . . at nine cents er pound . . . ercordin' t' my figures . . . that comes t' . . . exactly . . . ninety-six dollars 'n twenty-six cents." Papa winked his eye at Elbert, then stood back and waited for Mr. Grey to respond.

Mr. Grey simply looked up at Papa without saying a word. Then he did a very strange thing for a man only sixty-odd years out of slavery, according to Papa. He took a stick, got down on his knees, and started making crude figures in the dirt. Not knowing how to multiply and carry figures, he simply added 1230 nine times.

By the time he had finished, the sun was going down, but Mr. Grey didn't "give a damned." He literally had figures all around the wagon. Then he went back and double-checked. Finally, he looked up at Papa and asked, "Whut did you say you got?"

Papa hesitated. "Unless I made er mistake, I got ninety-six dollars . . . 'n change."

"That's funny. That sho is funny, but somehow I ain't laughin'."

"Er, maybe it ain't quite funny ernuff fer y', Brother Grey."

"Maybe so."

Finally, Papa popped the big question. "Er, I saw y' down there on y' knees like er good Methodist. I thought maybe we wuz in fer a little prayer meetin'."

Mr. Grey simply shook his head.

This is where Papa's charisma paid off. "Well now, it's jist possible I coulda made er mistake, not havin' m' glasses 'n all. Tell me, Brother Grey, whut did you git?"

"Never knowed y' t' use glasses befo'. Well, way I figured it . . . I don't know nothin' erbout no multiplyin' 'n all, but I kin add like the devil. My addition tells me nine twelves is er hunded 'n eight. Now turnin' eround ergin and addin' thirty that same way nine times, I git two sebny. So, I figure it gotta be two dollar, sebny cents. Now I figure if'n I add that two dollar sebny cents t' that one hunded 'n eight dollars I already got over heah, I come up wid one hunded ten dollar 'n sebny cents y' owe me."

Papa looked at Mr. Grey, then looked back at his figures, then he looked at Elbert, who was standing there with his mouth open in disbelief. "As I said, Brother Grey, I don't have my glasses, but I take yo' word for it."

"Don't take my word; take my figures."

Papa took out his money sack and paid Mr. Grey. Mrs. Grey had prepared a sack full of goodies for us, which included the rest of the chocolate cake. She informed us that the cake was for Mama and the other children. Papa heaped praises on Mrs. Grey for her cooking. Mr. Grey took Papa over to the hog pen and showed him the stock that he would soon butcher. They finally shook hands, and we were on our way.

"Told y' that old man could figure, didn't I?"

"Y' sho did, Papa, 'n good too."

"You'd think after all these years he would learn how to multiply," Papa said, and glanced back at me buried in the cotton.

"Sho would save some wear 'n tear on his knees if he'd learn how t' multiply . . . multiply . . . multiply . . . multiply . . ." That's what I heard Elbert repeating as I dozed.

As the wagon rocked on toward the house, all was quiet, and darkness descended upon us. Suddenly I heard ruffling of the paper bag. Greedy munching followed.

"Mama gon' be mad," Elbert said.

"Not if you don't tell her," Papa responded.

The soft, warm, snug comfort of the cushioning cotton enveloped my small six-year-old frame, but I couldn't go to sleep.

Back home, Mama had supper ready. Papa, Elbert, and I ate again like three hungry field hands.

To remedy his diabetes, Papa took his regular shot of insulin, and we all went to bed.

6

Growing up, my brother Elbert and I made our own toys. We bent a piece of stiff, thick wire, took a metal rim from the hub of a wagon, and steered that rim for miles along country paths, over tree limbs, through mud holes, up hills—often without it falling over once.

We made beam shooters and hunted birds and rabbits. Our favorite way of making a beam shooter was from the Y-shaped fork of a tree limb. We cut two pieces of rubber from a tire tube, stretched them over each prong of the notched forks, and tied them tightly with a string. We cut a piece of leather from an old shoe and tied it to the other ends of the rubber strips to hold the rock. I broke bottles, knocked over cans, and certainly tormented cows and horses with this ancient weapon, but I never hit a bird or a rabbit.

A slingshot, however, is a different matter. I can see why Goliath was in trouble. They outlawed slingshots in our community, and for a very good reason, I discovered. Somehow I came into possession of a mighty sling. I kept it hidden for fear someone would take it away from me. One day I was watching Mr. Parsons' beef cattle grazing in the pasture across the Pike from our house. They were all bunched up together—as cattle always are. *How could I miss?* I thought, as I carefully fished the neatly folded sling out of my loose-fitting overall pocket. At a distance of some fifty feet, I placed a good-size rock into the leather pouch. I wound the sling over my head a few times and let go of one end. The rock hit the steer's head with a muffled thud! He fell to the ground instantly, kicking and groaning. I moved closer to the fence to get a better look. The creature's tongue hung out of his mouth! His eyes were rolled back in their sockets like ball bearings. I was only a skinny boy, but the power of that sling taught me a lesson.

When I saw how much damage I had done, I became frightened and confused. I had nothing against animals, certainly not that steer. I wanted to help him. But how could I undo the damage I had caused? *Such a big animal to be so sensitive. Can't even take a little rock to the head . . . dumb beast. Lyin' theah with yo' tongue hangin' out yo' mouth 'n yo' eyes rolled back in yo' head. Come on. Git up from there.* The cow only groaned and kicked. *I'll have to do something before this thing dies on me. Maybe a cold towel on his head. Yea, that's it, a cold towel. But where could I get a cold towel without being discovered? Sloan's liniment! That will either cure him or kill him. But I don't want to kill him. Almost did that already. Whiskey! Whiskey is used for everything. Why not for this steer? Where am I gonna get whiskey?* My idea department was exhausted. Besides, if I hung around any longer somebody might see me. *I'll never be able to lie my way out of this one. Papa will have to pay for this cow, sho as shootin'. My butt won't heal for a year after he's finished with me.* With all those thoughts running through my mind, I felt my skinny legs moving away from the scene as if they had a brain of their own.

I was sitting in the barn wondering what to do when Elbert showed up with a pocketful of marbles. "Want a chance t' win some er yo' marbles back?"

"Let me borrow yo' aggie?" I asked.

"Whut happened t' yo'ren?" Elbert inquired.

"You know whut happened to mine. You won it in that last game we played," I reminded him.

"Oh yeah. Forgot erbout that, won so much er yo' stuff." He drew a circle and placed his marbles in the ring, the same ones that had belonged to me only the day before. "Lag up," Elbert said.

Certain skills I grasped readily. Others I labored over for a while until something clicked that personalized it for me. Learning how to hold a marble correctly took me some time. Meanwhile, I paid a heavy price by losing sack after sack of them, including my most precious aggies, the shooting marble.

On that particular occasion I did even worse than usual. "Gittin' so it ain't no fun no mo'. I didn't know y' could git worse at this game," Elbert remarked as he took what was left of my marbles. "I got no business doin' this, but y' so bad, I'm gonna give y' some pointers. Y' gotta keep that aggie on that index finger, 'n hold it wid the finger next to it 'n yo' thumb. Got that? Then y' kick it out wid yo' thumb, like this."

"Like this?" My shot went far wide of the marbles.

"Well, that's sorta the idea, only y' gotta aim the marble. Y' gotta aim it!"

I tried again with disastrous results. Finally Elbert tired of me, picked up his marbles, and walked away. "Y' jist practice on how to hold yo' aggie 'n yo' aimin', maybe one day y'll git it."

I was happy when he left. I couldn't keep my mind on marbles and think about that poor steer at the same time. Elbert was only a few feet away when my legs started moving as if I was going into our house. Instead I kept right on past the house and across the Pike to where the steer had met with his accident. On the way, I kept having visions of a dead steer stretched out waiting for the dogs and buzzards. Someone would certainly have to drag it into the woods; otherwise we wouldn't be able to stand the stink. Even from the woods, the winds carried, and that stink was "walkin' 'n talkin' to y'."

As I approached, I couldn't see clearly. Other cattle had moved into the spot where the steer had lain and were blocking my view. I moved cautiously.

Wondering what had happened to my charge, I stooped down to see if I could see his feet among the other cattle. No feet. Maybe he had crawled off someplace else to die. I moved slowly south to the other side of the herd. There, I spotted him. He wasn't grazing like the other cattle. He was weaving and bobbing like a drunk man. Loose wet shit was dripping down his hind legs. He wobbled a few feet and stopped. His tongue had gone back inside his mouth, and his eyes were no longer dancing around in his head like spinning aggies. I stood for a long time watching him struggle to regain his legs.

Mr. Durbey noticed me standing over on the other side of the Pike by myself, watching the steer with my hands deep in my pockets. "Hey, young fella! Sun!"

"You call me, Mr. Durbey?" I asked.

"Yo' name's still Sun, ain't it?" From the front of his shop he walked over to the edge of the road. His greasy blacksmith's garb got more ragged as the days passed. His long muscular arms were streaked with sweat. He was wiping his powerful grimy hands on his equally grimy apron. His sturdy six-foot frame slumped from years of hard work and age. "Whut y' doin' standin' over there by yo'self? Y' see them cattle every day. Whut y' doin', watchin' um grow er som'um? Come on over heah. Want y' t' fetch me a bucket er cool wauter. I got y' nickel waitin' fer y'. He-he-he," he chuckled good-naturedly.

I appreciated the reprieve. I smiled deep down inside, knowing my steer was going to live. I moved swiftly to get the water for a reason far more important than the nickel.

Mr. Durbey enjoyed the cool water, straight from our well, which boasted the best in the community. While he chuckled and drank, allowing the water to trickle down his dirty, greasy overalls—to cool him off in the process—I carefully took the sling out of my pocket and dropped it into the hot fireplace of the bellows. It burned quickly.

Before Mr. Durbey returned to his work, he fished a nickel out of his dirty pockets. "Here y' go, Sun. Aaaaah, that did an ol' man good. Goooood wauter. Mighty good wauter."

"Thank y', Mr. Durbey," I said.

"Thank you, Sun." He grabbed the handle of his bellows and pumped in more air. He took his long iron and poked in the coals to increase the heat. I stood and watched him put a straight piece of steel in the fire and pump the bellows a few more times until the piece was white with heat. He used long metal tongs to handle the hot metal. Placing it on the big anvil, he hammered away until he had shaped a perfect horseshoe.

As he hammered, he hummed "I'm on the Battlefield for My Lord," "Just a Little Talk with Jesus," "Just to Behold His Face," or "Just a Closer Walk with Thee." I found that just a little hard to understand, since Mr. Durbey never set foot inside any church.

*   *   *

It's strange how I felt about that steer. It was my boyish curiosity that prompted me to find out what the sling could do. Boys get into trouble because they can't distinguish between an abstract idea and a real-life happening until it is too late. Yet my playmates and I thought nothing of tying a can to a strange dog's tail and watching him struggle to get it off. We put a cat that had shit in the house in a croker sack, tied it up, and dropped it in the bayou. I participated in that cruelty only once. I knew it was wrong and lamented over it, to myself, for a long time.

Some boys tied rags and paper to a cat's tail and set fire to it. Others chopped off a cat's head. I never witnessed or participated in any of those acts, but I knew those who did. I'm not forgetting that croker sack that we threw in the bayou.

We lived close to the earth. Controlling the soil and animals was in the order of things. Our food and our lives depended upon it. Every creature had to stay within bounds.

Generally mild and pleasant, Arkansas weather could become cruelly cold in winter. Papa and our neighbors built barns, henhouses, birdhouses, and doghouses. We went wild with excitement every spring when the martins came! Swift, strong wings—gray and elegant, throbbing, guttural sounds—they greeted us. They swarmed all over the little house Papa had built. He had bored holes in one end and elevated it on a pole.

Convention time! In their workshop, they laid eggs, protected their young, and battled hawks. I watched a hawk soaring and gliding, looking for prey. Most of the time he was looking for our young chickens instead of the rather well-protected baby martins inside the birdhouse. No matter. Three or four martins would form squadrons the minute the hawk appeared. They attacked from the top, from the sides, and from beneath. The big hawk was helpless in the fight except for his ugly struggle to get out of harm's way. They chased him as far as I could see. Then they returned throbbing—victorious!

Martins were our constant companions all summer. I never saw a dead one. We fed them but never interfered with their little house, their eggs, or their young. It was a mutually dependent, caring relationship.

As they had told us it was spring, they just as timely introduced us to fall. One chilly morning, we woke up and there was no fluttering of their strong wings. No feathery sleek coats of gray. No familiar throbbing. Workshop closed, the little house empty.

Nothing thrilled me as much as, or was more beautiful than, baby chicks, pigs, kittens, pups, calves, colts, birds, rabbits, ducklings, goslings, guineas, and mules. I loved them all but had to learn that those babies grew up.

As a country boy, I saw older family members chop off a chicken's head and watch it flutter and bleed to death. They threw it into a pot of boiling water while it was still alive, and picked the feathers. Then they gutted it and cut it up for supper, Sunday dinner, or breakfast. As I grew older, I learned to take a chicken by its head, get a good tight grip using its head as a knob, and wring its head from its body.

Dogs, cows, mules, and horses had names. We never used the pronoun *it* when referring to those animals. Chickens, hogs, geese, any animal raised for slaughter, we referred to as *it*, regardless of its gender, when we spoke of it in a general sense. As a boy, I wondered about that. We had chickens and pigs as pets. We also gave them names. As children, we could never eat a piece of barbecued George, or the fried drumstick of Miss Lula.

Since Papa wasn't a hunter, we loved dogs only as pets. In our community, we valued most dogs according to their worth as hunters or herders. Regardless of their status, sucking eggs, killing chickens, and, of course, going mad were automatic death sentences. Any member of the community could carry out the execution. A stranger or anyone could kill a mad dog. Poisoning dogs or killing them because they hung up with your bitch was a no-no, especially if he was a good hunting dog.

The saddest day of my young life happened when I was six. My father caught our beautiful pup, Spot, with a half-eaten young chicken in his mouth. We named him Spot because he sported a pretty brown, black, and white coat. With slick short hair, he had big lionlike paws solidly supporting powerful legs and a sleek, well-shaped body. He had a big round head, out of which stared shiny brown eyes, almost covered by long cabbagelike flapping ears. I'm sure he must have been part bloodhound. In a word, he was beautiful. Why did he have to be a criminal? Against the order of things?

I suppose part of it was our fault. We had indulged the puppy in all our games. This included playing with young pigs, goslings, and chickens. As a baby he played with other babies on equal terms, including young chickens. As he grew older, he kept playing, but somehow he developed a sense of his own power and the chickens' vulnerability. Whatever the case, Spot developed a taste.

We stood close together that hot summer morning. My younger sister, Verleen, and I held each other's sweaty little hands tight. All of the family was there. My older sisters, Geneva, Deloris, Hazel, and Jessie, stood in a circle. Elbert, my older brother, stood over to the side. Mama stood on the far south end of the front porch. Sadness shrouded every face. No one uttered a word.

Papa walked out on the porch with his Winchester. A pair of wide white suspenders, with gold buckles, supported his loose-fitting gray pants. His black-gray short-cropped hair accentuated his prominent forehead and strong chiseled face. A white collarless shirt, opened at the neck, revealed a few gray hairs. His rather average-sized shoes turned slightly outward at the heels. They didn't look big enough to carry his tall frame.

Spot stopped gnawing on his chicken and looked up at Papa. He was licking his chops and wagging his tail like a windshield wiper. Though Papa hadn't whipped him or scowled at him, Spot instinctively knew he was breaking the law. He sensed he was in trouble. Ordinarily he would have run up to Papa and leaped all over him for a pat or a rub. Spot stood his ground while Papa slowly raised his Winchester, cocked it in the process, and took aim for what seemed an eternity. Verleen and I shook with fear. Finally, the hand-wringing, teeth-gritting, flesh-crawling, breath-stopping tenseness was shattered. TAA-YAW-W-W-W-W-W! Echoes resounded through the tall gums and oaks that stood guard in front of our acreage. Beautiful Spot's brains and blood lay scattered beneath the red rose bush in the hot morning sun beside his half-eaten chicken.

It silenced all my fun. Ended. Drained. Wasted. I had my first experience with hopeless despair. A bitter taste crept into my mouth. Ugly images of Spot's bloody scattered brains and mangled head pushed back all good feelings—crowded my every thought. Colors faded into ragged shades—tangled messes.

Nothing came together for me for a long time. It would not pass, or let me pass. The swelling in my chest wouldn't let me breathe. A choking sensation lay heavy there.

Papa slowly took the Winchester from his shoulder. Verleen and I kept holding each other's hand—trembling at the horror. Why couldn't Papa forgive Spot this one time? Give him another chance? Why? Why? Why couldn't there be a reform school for dogs?

Still standing on the porch, Papa spoke in a matter-of-fact tone of voice—unemotional. "I hated to kill that dog, but once they git the taste er chicken, you'll never be able t' break um." It was the order of things.

He turned to Elbert. "Take im erway, 'n that chicken too—whut's left of it," Papa ordered.

Verleen and I protested simultaneously. "We take care of im."

"He was our dog, Papa, 'n we take care of im." The words simply flowed from my mouth. The thought of Spot being dragged out into the woods and left for buzzards to pick his bones was more than we could stand. We would give him a proper funeral and burial. Papa chuckled and walked slowly back into the house.

I disagreed with Papa strongly, to myself, of course, but hating him for shooting our Spot never entered my mind. After all, how could Papa be wrong? I loved Spot with all my being, but I loved Papa in a different way. Somehow, without having to be told, I sensed for the first time in my young life that this was how things were. As bitter as it was, this was how things would continue to be. This was the order of things.

Verleen and I took Spot's limp bloody body and his half-eaten chicken to the corner of our orchard. We dug a hole two feet deep with a hoe and laid Spot to rest with his chicken beside him. We covered him with red loamy Arkansas clay. We hammered a crude wooden cross at the head of his grave—made from a crate and a stick. Standing with our hands folded, we bid him a final good-bye. Verleen said, "Don't worry, Spot. There'll be lots of puppies like you in heaven, and you won't have t' worry erbout dyin' no mo'."

7

I felt a quick nibble—a tickling sensation at my bare toes. The first time, I paid it no attention—dismissed it as a twig. Another strike! More forceful this time. Hello! I looked down and saw the little demon coiled to repeat. His powder-brown tail was vertical in the air, mysteriously buzzing his constant electric warning like a desperate escapee trying to gain access by lying on the bell. He must have activated his system before I stepped too close. The snake being small and hidden, I didn't hear or see him.

Verleen and I lost interest in the sweet dark ripe blueberries we were picking in the little patch back of our house. I quickly backed off before he could strike again. At the same time, I pushed the unsuspecting Verleen back with a trembling hand and announced quietly, "I been bit." Verleen looked down at the angry little rattler—still buzzing like crazy—ready to strike again.

"Sun—Sun—come on!" We dropped our pails, berries and all, and took off down the little Blueberry Hill. Heads back, sucking wind, our skinny long legs moved our thin frames along with the speed of young sprinters at the height of competition.

"Sun been bit! Sun been bit!" Verleen screamed.

Deloris, who was in charge of us, ran out to the Pike to get help. She returned quickly to the back porch wringing her hands. "Lord, I don't know whut t' do erbout no snakebite." She turned and ran back to the Pike. That time she returned with old Bob Sikes. He was sweating and puffing from trying to keep up with her. Bob Sikes was our closest white neighbor. Fortunately, he was passing at a critical time. He wore a floppy felt hat with holes in it, overalls, and brogans. He was shy, in his fifties, average size, and a pipe-smoker.

"How long ergo d't happen?" he asked, taking a big handkerchief from his pocket. He twisted the handkerchief into a rope with his big red rough hands.

"Erbout three, fo' minutes ergo," Deloris said.

"Git me er stick. Hurry up!" Bob Sikes demanded. First he tied the handkerchief high around my thigh. Then he tied the stick to the handkerchief and began to twist. "Git me some mo' rags 'n er big pan er coal oil. Make it snappy!"

Deloris came back quickly with all the items. Always thinking, she also brought two more short sticks. "Heah's yo' stuff, Mr. Sikes."

"How erbout er couple mo'—" He saw the sticks before he could get the words out of his mouth. "That's good, 'Lois. That's fine." He tied another tourniquet lower down on my leg to prevent the poison from traveling farther up—hoping it hadn't already done so. That done, he flipped out a big pocket knife, struck a match, and held the blade over the flame briefly. He cooled it in a small pail of water, which Deloris had furnished. Then he took my swelling foot in his hand and quickly made a slit where the rattler's teeth had penetrated. The blood squirted out into the pan. The clear coal oil turned green immediately. Deloris poured that out and put in more oil. Bob Sikes submerged my bleeding foot in the clean oil, and it also turned green. He motioned for her to empty that also—knowing that she could get more from our store when he needed it. He was trying to block and draw off as much poison as possible before it traveled to the vital organs of my body. Coal oil drew out the poison.

I thought to myself, *Maybe he didn't like those first two shades of green. Perhaps he's goin' to keep changing till he finds one that suits him.* It was foolish to think of something funny at a time like that. It gave me a little fright. I recoiled with the satisfaction that I had kept my foolish thoughts to myself.

It was indeed foolish. I had only felt the tightness of my swollen foot and leg up to the lower tourniquet, plus the tickling sensation of Bob Sikes' blade. Other than the original shock of the bite, I really felt little discomfort.

Bob Sikes and Deloris were changing the oil again when Papa drove up with his sidekick, Mr. Sam Riley. "Whut wuz y' doin' up there on that hill in the first place?" Papa asked, a worried look on his face.

"We wuz pickin' blueberries, Papa," Verleen blurted out.

"Wid no shoes on? 'Lois, you know better'n t' let these chirren outta yo' sight when they left wid you." Deloris kept working, without a word. Unlike Geneva and Verleen, she knew when to keep her mouth shut.

"Y'all know erbout wheah it wuz?" Papa asked.

"Follow me, Papa. I show y'." Verleen started walking in the direction of the hill.

"You stay right heah, young lady. Want the same thing t' happen t' you?" Papa asked.

"Think y' be able t' find im, M.A.?" Bob Sikes asked.

"He ain't gone no wheah, Bob Sikes. Mean devil," Papa said as he walked away. Mr. Sam Riley followed.

"Sam Riley, you ain't got on no shoes either. You think maybe you too ugly fer a rattlesnake t' bite y'?"

Mr. Sam Riley brushed his shortly cropped hair back, simulated tidying up his tattered overalls. "In that case, y' can take yo' shoes off 'n give um t' me, 'cause I'm twice as putty as you." He let go with a gut-ripping laugh.

"That co'n liquor gone t' y' head, Sam Riley," Papa answered. They were soon out of hearing distance.

Deloris was still bothered by what Papa had said. "He ain't gone no wheah? How come he ain't gone no wheah? He can still crawl, can't he?"

"He's sick'n this heah boy erbout now. Our blood ain't no good fer them either," Bob Sikes said.

Deloris, Verleen, and I looked stunned.

I thought, *I've been living around snakes all my six years and don't know anything about them. Except to kill one, whenever and wherever I find him.* There was only one exception. They taught us, "Never kill a king snake." An immediate explanation usually followed from whoever gave the advice. "King snakes is friend to man. They ain't pisen. They don't eat chickens or suck eggs. And they kill all other snakes they find. 'N they so putty."

There were as many snake stories as there were bear, panther, and hant stories. Also, they were different for each snake. At six, I had seen many of those snakes in action. I had seen the long black snake in our chicken house swallowing eggs. I ran to the house and reported it to the grown-ups. I had also seen the little green garden snakes in the early spring crawling among the flowers. They were the first to awaken from a winter's sleep somewhere in a rotten log. They were harmless. "Nobody scared er them," they said. Snakes gave me the willies, harmless or not.

I had seen the infamous water moccasin at Bartholomew Bridge swallowing frogs and fish. His venom was quite poisonous. Not as powerful as the rattler's, but he had never been known to help anyone he had bitten. If treated in time, the average person could survive the moccasin's bite.

I had watched the dreaded coach whip speeding down a freshly plowed row behind Elbert. I had watched Olie Riley catch up with it and chop it in half with a sharp hoe. The coach whip was a six- to ten-foot speed demon, which was supposed to catch you and wrap its long black body around your arms and legs, thereby disabling you, then stick its tail up your nose and smother you to death.

They circulated another story that the coach whip would wrap its body around your neck and choke you to death. Others' stories had the snake hanging the victim from a tree and whistling for another coach whip, while standing on its tail. My young mind went astray trying to figure out how a long black snake could do all those things to a strong healthy man carrying a cane cutter, a hoe, a sharp ax, or a switchblade.

The pilot snake—a first cousin to the dreaded rattler—also made his home in our area. He was covered with bright brown colors; he had no rattlers and was shorter and smaller than the rattler. The rattlesnake is known for his rattlers, the water moccasin for hanging around water and possessing a skin that looks like the leather of a moccasin. The stinging snake is known for his stinger, the coach whip for his long black slender body that resembles a whip, and the mighty king snake for his nobility, beauty, and strength. But what qualities, good or bad, could one attribute to the pilot snake on the basis of his name? Every time I saw one of the suckers, which was seldom, it was lying around as if it was lost. The pilot snake was too lazy to get out of the way of my hoe or stick and was the easiest for me to see and kill.

The spread-natter flattened out on the ground to camouflage himself. He must have been kin to the cobra. His hissing was fearsome, and his venom was very poisonous.

The fat, slick-skinned, scaleless lamp-eel lived in and around water. They were specially plentiful during the yearly high rise. I suppose they are related to edible eels—also found in water. The lamp-eel, however, is very poisonous. In addition, he was said to electrocute his victim with his bite. I always thought that was fantastic. A triple threat—he bites, poisons, and electrocutes you at the same time.

The snake that provoked the most controversial stories was the shining black, red-bellied, snub-tailed stinging snake. According to rumors, he was more dangerous than even the rattler, since he struck without warning. He was very mysterious and unpredictable. We never saw one crawling around. He was always near water and among the rocks but never seen in the water. We never heard one hissing or making any sound whatsoever. We never saw one eating or mating like other snakes.

The stories abounded. A cow drinking from a creek accidentally stepped too close to the dreaded stinger. One pop of the mighty tail, she went down immediately and was dead within a minute. A young child wandered down the rocky slopes of a bayou bridge, disrupted the hidden menace, and the lightning tail hit her. She was no more.

The most fantastic story was that of the deadly tail missing a man and striking a tree instead. Within minutes, the leaves on the tree withered. Within a week or so, the tree died.

When I heard that, I began to question the validity of all stinging snake stories. The only place I had seen the fat round red-bellied black menace was on the rocky banks of Bayou Bartholomew. Someone pointed out the deadly silent killer to me. It lay there among the boulders, its shiny black scales glistening in the hot sun. Its head was hidden. Indeed its whole body lay tangled among the rocks that made up the sloped wings of the old steel bridge across Bartholomew.

In spite of Bob Sikes and Deloris soaking and changing oil, my foot was hardly recognizable. Even so, I still hadn't felt the full effect of the poison in my body.

"Well, heah he is," Papa said, holding up the dead snake.

"Li'l ol' devil, ain't cha?" Bob Sikes said.

"You er lucky boy. Rattlers known t' git fifteen, twenty yeahs ol'. One er them had bit cha . . . ," Mr. Sam Riley said. He shook his head morbidly and squirted a mouthful of Brown Mule tobacco juice on the ground from a wad wallowing around in his left jaw.

"Did y' count his rattlers, Andy?" Bob Sikes asked.

"Same age as Sun. Six yeahs ol'," Papa replied.

"Lucky boy. Sam's right. Good thing he wutten one er them ol' uns," Bob Sikes remarked as he tightened the tourniquet on the lower part of my leg and prepared to leave.

"They tell me if y' wear them rattlers in yo' hat, you'll never have ernother headache," Mr. Sam Riley said, taking a bite from his plug.

"Well, I don't know erbout all that, but I do know y' better keep er close eye on this boy fer er few days till that poison's outta his system. Probably gon' have er fever. Be er li'l sick." Bob Sikes was cleaning up his knife and washing his hands with some soap and water Deloris had brought. She also brought a cool bucket of water, along with some tea cakes on a plate.

Drinking from one of the gourds hanging on the porch, Bob Sikes said, "Jist som'um erbout water from a gourd makes it taste so much better," as he let the cool water run down his chest. "Thank y', 'Lois. Y' know, you make er mighty fine nurse."

"Yes sir," Deloris acknowledged, taking the gourd.

"You the one who made er mighty fine doctor, Bob Sikes. I jist don't know how t' thank y'. Sho is er good thing you come along when y' did," Papa said.

"Man upstairs musta been in it. It don't take but five or six minutes, y' know, fo' that pisen done travel t' yo' heart, 'n that's it. End er the war," Mr. Sam Riley said as he spat out his wad, washed out his mouth with some of the water from the bucket, and waded into the tea cakes.

I thought, *I'd rather take a whipping than drink from that gourd or that bucket, for that matter*. To me, drinking behind dippers and chewers was nasty.

"Y' don't mind, 'Lois, I'm gon' take my tea cakes wid me. Don't wanna spoil my supper," Bob Sikes said.

"Take as many as y' want," Papa said. "'Lois, git some mo'.'"

"Two, three er these'll be fine, Andy."

"'Lois, run out t' the sto' 'n git one er them paper sacks t' put these tea cakes in," Papa directed.

Bob Sikes owned a small spread about a quarter of a mile down the Pike. Papa called him Bob Sikes, his full name, rather than Mr. Sikes—as he did other white *and* black men of stature in the community.

The Sikes boys often tied ropes across the Pike when we were on our way down to Barnard's or Newman's store. They never really did anything to us. Nevertheless, the threat was sufficient to strike fear into a young boy walking along a lonely country road.

Papa said, "You got as much right t' travel that Pike as anybody else. I'm gonna tell Bob Sikes to control them devilish boys er his. They older'n y'all."

When I was eight, the younger boy came up to Mr. Durbey's blacksmith shop one Saturday, and we got into a wrestling match. Even though he was two years older and bigger, I threw his butt all over the place. It was my first real encounter with a white boy. It amazed me how delicate and easy he was. I had found many black boys easy as well. In fairness, I was the best wrestler around for my age. With long stringy brown hair falling in his face, the Sikes boy bled at the least little scratch. Like Spot with the chickens, I instinctively developed a sense of physical superiority over white boys.

I had played with Junior Barnard whenever we went down to their store, but we never wrestled. It didn't mean anything to me, but the Barnards considered themselves better than the poor Sikes boys.

Sam Riley carefully picked the rattlers from the dead little snake's tail and emptied them into Papa's hands. Papa took his gray felt Stetson off and carefully placed the rattlers behind the black sweatband, rattle by precious rattle, as if he really thought they would ward off headaches.

The swelling in my foot and lower leg increased. I began to feel a throbbing pain as night approached.

Finally, Mama, Elbert, Hazel, and Geneva came home from the fields. Mama didn't bother about supper and assigned the task to Hazel. "Lord, y'all, lettin' my chile set out heah like this on this hard bench. Er—Jessie—Hazel—Deloris—Geneva—Elbert—"

"Which one er us y' want, Mama?" Elbert asked.

"I want you. Git some firewood fer yo' sister so she kin start supper. I want . . . Andra, go git Miz Melinda."

"Whut you want wid her? Ain't nobody havin' no baby eround heah. Better not be," Papa affirmed.

"Do *you* know how t' take care of er sick chile who's been snake-bit?" Mama inquired.

"Well, er . . . er, well—" Papa stammered.

"I didn't think so. Hurry up!"

Papa donned his flapped Stetson hat with the rattlers behind the black band, grabbed his cane, and left.

"Deloris, I want you t' git the bed ready. Git a lotta pillows so my chile won't be layin' flat," Mama said.

"I already fixed the bed. Mama," Deloris smiled.

"If everybody wuz—" Mama thought better of it. No time to spend on compliments now. "Y' got plenty pillows?" Mama asked as she picked me up and headed for the bedroom. "How you feel, Sun?"

"I don't feel good, Mama," I said.

"Ol' rattlesnake bit my baby like that," Mama lamented.

"Papa 'n Mr. Sam Riley killed him," I said.

"Yes, I know. I'm glad they found him. I hope they find his mama and kill her too," Mama declared.

"He tried t' warn me, Mama, but I didn't heah im," I said in the snake's defense.

"Ol' rattlesnake ain't good fer nothin' 'cept t' crawl eround bitin' people," Mama complained.

"He wutten ol', Mama. He wuz six yeahs ol' jist like me," I said, defending the young snake again.

"I'm gon' have that patch burned back there. Been wantin' t' expand my garden anyhow," Mama said.

"Noooo! Mama, no! You'll burn up they house and all the blueberries," I protested.

"I don't care nothin' erbout they house! Them silly blueberries either! Whut y' doin' takin' up fer them devilish snakes? He almost killed y'. If he'd been a little bigger, he would have. Don't talk foolishness, chile," Mama said. She fixed my pillow, making sure my head was up and my foot down.

"Y' feel like eatin' som'um?" Mama asked.

"I want y' t' feed the snake. Make—sssssure he git my supper. I . . . I . . ." I mumbled something incoherently.

The sun had set. Dark shadows were dancing on familiar walls. Dull thumping permeated my brain. Round balls of red-purple cotton clouds rolled across the screen of my subconscious vision. Pictures of bearded white men I had seen in our family Bible began to float in and out of focus.

Pitchforks and devils mixing pots of people crying and begging for deliverance seized my mind.

Toad frogs and devil horses, grand-dads, grasshoppers, and dragonflies gathered in convention. Bugs. Millions and millions of black bugs began to fall and form like locusts in the valley of my unbelievings. Bugs turned into maggots, boiling over. Working their maggoty mess in putrid, foul-smelling carrion. Lizards leaping through sinews of copious cobblestone.

Maggots turned into snakes. Screaming, steaming, their hallo wills are hollow. Fog spewing from gaping, growling mouths of sawtooth monsters. Teeth turned into stalagmites. I was consumed in an underground cavern—too narrow to escape. Choking . . . choking . . . choking . . . I pass into the gates of death. I can see the blue death crowding my space, heir to my weakness. Forcing . . . forcing . . . forcing. Horrid lamp-eels, stinging butterflies, kissing bats, vituperous hoot owls, poison rabbits, grotesque chickens pecking holes in my coffin. Singing mules dressed in choir robes chanting a sad song for my funeral. Cows as midwives tending baby squirrels. Spot is there grinning, his shapeless head out of focus.

Rolling, cottony revolving gray-white clouds, roaming in planetary movements.

I see a round, chiseled skull of ice. A crater within, with craggy crevices. Smooth, oniony oval, with ragged inside edges—reaching, growing, freezing toward covering a Jell-O-like filling. Deep inside the crater, I touch its edges with my fingers. My fingers stroke at the surface to smooth, shape, and form a complete, perfect round—something? Glowing in the shine. One with the revolving clouds.

A faded, ragged figure began to take shape. Long, slender bony . . . really cantilever extensions from thin stooped shoulders. A solemn face, high cheekbones, somewhat broad hooked nose. The round form, draped with long white braids. More in focus now. Reddish-brown wrinkled covering accentuated by a white dress. A glowing oil lamp, a white handkerchief tied around the upper portion of thick gray braids.

The cool white rag touched my forehead softly, gently.

"Sun . . . Sun boy . . . Sun. You heah me?" Miz Melinda asked.

"Ye-e-e—Ye-s-s-um," I squeaked.

She continued mopping my forehead. "We thought fer sho we guy lose you. Y' been er mighty sick boy. Kitty, Kitty," Miz Melinda called quietly.

Mama entered quickly, dressed in her long nightgown. "How y' feel, Sun? Thank God y' come out of it." She dipped a rag into a washpan, wrung it out, and started rubbing my swollen foot and leg. "Miz Melinda, why don't you git some sleep? You been settin' up wid my boy fer two days and nights now. He must be better now he come to."

"Kitty, you don't know nothin' erbout no snakebite, do y'?" Miz Melinda asked.

"No ma'am, I can't say that I do, but I know you gotta be tired," Mama said.

"Ain't no such er thing. This chile ain't outta danger yet. Y'all think 'cause it wuz such a young snake, he ain't as pisen. No matter erbout his age. He jist is pisen is he guy git. Jist wutten able t' 'ject as much venom, that's all. If he had been, this chile would'na made it. He so young. Grown person mo' able t' fight it off." She checked the poultice on my foot.

"I git some mo' poke salad," Mama said.

"Bring me some mo' er that clay too 'n some vinegar," Miz Melinda said. She took off the poultice. "It drawin' pretty good. But we got er long way t' go," she said, and felt my head. "This chile still got er hot fever. Gotta break this fever. Gotta break it, or we ain't done nothin'."

Mama returned with the poke salad, clay, and vinegar. Miz Melinda worked the mud with bony fingers. She laid it flat on a white cloth. She chopped up the poke salad leaves and laid them over the mud, then saturated it with vinegar and other medicines. She took my swollen foot in her long white apron. Placed the poultice over the wound and tied it on.

As Miz Melinda worked, Mama stood there with a pan of cold water. She felt my swollen foot and leg. "Do y' think it went down some?"

"Not yet, Kitty," Miz Melinda said, and held up the discarded poultice. She pointed to the area. "See how yellow-green 'tis eround the wound?"

"Yes'um, I see it," Mama said.

"Well, that mean it still mo' pisen t' come out. Come on now, Sun, drink yo' tea. Dis heah catnip tea hep break dat fever. It runnin' too long t' suit me," Miz Melinda said, lifting my throbbing head with one hand and holding the teaspoon with the other. I felt pain I couldn't explain. It telegraphed to the back of my tight drum head with every twitch.

Outside me, I was an observer—peeping in. I was neither asleep nor awake. I couldn't sleep. Every drop of catnip I sipped was a giant boulder, hurtling down, down deep, craggy caverns.

When my head was once again teetering on that precipice of biblical images—throbbing regular again—there, focused from a white forest of tangled braids, the tired, wrinkled smile of Miz Melinda.

How could this quiet, patient wader of deep waters, this tender caretaker, possibly be the mother of that stinking Ligah and that bullying, overbearing, too tall Vera Nellie?

Even more strange was Mr. Joe, the father of those two. During the high rise of Bartholomew, a crowd of us were standing on the banks at the bridge watching young men dive into the bayou. Most were good swimmers. Others should have stayed on the banks with us beginners and waited for the deep waters to subside. Reedy, knowing he was a beginner, dived into the water and started to go under. Mr. Osben, who could swim, dived in after him. Reedy grabbed Mr. Osben through fear, and they both went under. I watched Mr. Joe swim out on his back and finally surface with both men in his grasp. Mr. Joe was definitely a hero. Like most heroes, he was not a braggart. Considered it "all in a day's work." I remembered him straightening the shoulder straps on his tattered overalls and squirting snuff juice to the side of the road. "Y'all boys oughta learn how t' swim 'fo y' start jumpin' in deep wauter," Mr. Joe chuckled good-naturedly, then slinked away up the Pike, his dripping curly hair glued to his head, his tall, stooped frame in perfect cadence, his leathery bare feet paying no attention to the gravel and rocks beneath.

Days and nights passed. So did my extended state of agony. I grew weary of the biblical images of strange-looking white men in long robes, flowing wind-blown hair, long hooked noses, and carved walking sticks with snakes twirled around them. I longed to see Mama and Papa, Mr. Sam Riley—as ragged as he was, Mr. Durbey with his greasy cap and blacksmith garb, Bob Sikes—with cool water running down his hairy chest. And where on earth are Uncle Pet, Aint Babe, Jessie, Hazel, Deloris, Elbert, Geneva, and Verleen? Where are my sisters and brother?

Often the snake's head was in striking distance of the man's hand. When the man held the stick high, the snake came alive. Licked out his tongue. Ready to strike at the man's head. "Look out!" I screamed, and jerked myself out of the nightmare to the miserable veil of consciousness I had endured so long.

A cool rag mopped my brow. "Der now, you havin' ernother one er them nightmares."

Mama entered dressed in her nightgown, with crushed peaches in a bowl. "Y' gotta git som'um in yo' stomach, Sun. Y' jist cain't go on like this." She tried to feed me while Miz Melinda went for more sassafras tea. It was to no avail. The peaches came right up, as the rest of the food had done for days.

"Lord, don't do this to me. Y' took my first two chirren. Please don't take my boy. Please, Lord. Please . . . please . . ." It was only a whisper, but I thought I heard a prayer. I looked in Mama's face as best I could, and I could have sworn I saw tears streaming down her cheeks.

Tired, weak, and worn, I soon fell back into biblical images of white men and young white girls—my age and younger—with long white gowns, long silver hair streaming over their shoulders. Their chubby hands and white wings were projecting from beneath the gowns. Some of the children were in flight. *Why can't I do that?* I thought. Then lo and behold, I was flying!

Gliding, diving, and sailing, I thought, *At last a dream!* When suddenly, a man with a long fork stood guard outside my room. I had to get inside and prop my head up and put my foot on the floor. The man looked at me with red shining eyes. He wore a crown on his head and was dressed like the clown I had seen at the minstrel show at Tilson School. I gave him my ticket and entered.

The whole Bearden family were conducting a country fair. They were selling babies. Wrapping them up in newspapers and passing them in assembly-line fashion to—who else but Vera Nellie. She, in turn, was smiling and roasting those babies over a barbecue pit dug in the ground. Smoke and fire were everywhere. Somehow Spot was mixed with these babies. Spot was grinning as stinky Ligah was wrapping him up.

It was more than I could bear. "Stop! Stop! You stinking, pee-smelling Ligah!"

Through the veil, I felt the same cool rag mopping my forehead again. Through a small spectrum of my vision I discerned bony copper-colored fingers. Looking beyond that, I saw Mama standing talking to Uncle Pet. I thought I heard something about a doctor, "if he don't git better soon." Papa entered and joined the conversation. I thought I saw a sad face and Papa moving very slowly.

"I already sent fer Dr. Brian. Never forgive myself fer not takin' him in the first place," I thought I heard Papa say. I heard Elbert outside chopping wood. I peeped outside and for the first time realized it was day.

Papa walked over to Miz Melinda. "Well, Sister Melinda, whut you think? Is he too weak t' move?"

"Thought y'all wuz sich powerful Christens. This boy's er Hughes 'n I's er Bearden. Ain't naire one of um been known t' give up no fight 'cause the goin' git rough," Miz Melinda said without so much as looking up at Papa. She checked the poultice again and shook her head as a good sign.

Mama tried feeding me some chicken soup. I didn't remember throwing it up or swallowing it. "He didn't eat in a week," I thought I heard somebody say. I was tired. I was weak. I was worn.

> *Precious Lord,*
> *Take my hand.*
> *Lead me on,*
> *Let me stand.*
> *I am tired,*
> *I am weak,*
> *I am worn . . .*

I had heard "Precious Lord" butchered by many people at Hughes Chapel. I had also heard the song done right by none other than the great Jeremiah Robinson from Pine Ridge, with Uncle Pet doing the bass. There wasn't an empty seat or a dry eye in the house.

Why would that song come into my slumber? I was only six, the same age as my rattlesnake. If anybody really needed proof, Papa had six rattlers behind the black band of his Stetson to prove it. They also served to keep headaches away. Papa was a lucky man. *I'm goin' to be lucky too. I'm goin' to see Spot and we . . . we're goin' to be together again for always. I'm goin' to see Spot, goin' to see Spot. . . . I'm goin' to see . . .*

A window opened. A cool breeze swept across my face. A click in my head. I sat straight up in bed. Fever broken!

Miz Melinda stood up and leaned over me. A broad smile spread all over her wrinkled face. For the first time I could see she was truly Vera Nellie's mother. She was without doubt a naturally pretty woman. At that moment, I began to understand why Elbert disagreed with me when I described Vera Nellie as long, tall, and ugly.

"Kitty, Kitty," Miz Melinda called gently.

Mama rushed in with a frightened look on her face. "Sun . . . Sun . . ." Mama stopped in her tracks when she saw me sitting up in bed. She approached slowly. She felt my forehead. Took a rag and started wiping my face. "Thank you, Lord. Thank you, Lord. Thank you."

"Mama, I'm hungry," I said, and moved the rag from my face.

Mama turned to Miz Melinda and they embraced each other crying.

"Mama, could I have something to eat?" I said.

Mama looked at me, smiling. "Where is yo' manners, young man?"

"Pleeeeease," I said.

8

It was too far for us to see what it was, that spring of 1928. Then a team of reddish-brown, bony, hungry-looking mules descended the hill immediately south of Mr. Durbey's shop. They were pulling a rickety overloaded wagon. As the caravan came into focus, we could see the leader. He was a tall, bent, bony old man with a long gray bushy handlebar mustache. He wore a loose-fitting brown khaki shirt and pants, a pair of leather sandals laced over his pants and up his legs like a gladiator, and a wide floppy straw hat. He carried a long handmade wooden staff. Sweat poured down his face, and his clothes were saturated. He looked like a hillbilly Moses.

Two women were sitting in the driver's seat with two small children. One of them was ginger-colored with big thick braids. The other one was black with a red and white bandanna tied around her head. Both were good-looking women; however, the ginger-colored one marred her looks by filling her bottom lip with snuff. A bony-faced old woman in a white cotton dress, furled collar buttoned up to her neck, pleated and ruffled in front, with big ruffled sleeves, sat in a chair behind the front seat. She topped her outfit off with a white ruffled bonnet with long hanging strings. She was completely surrounded by old furniture. Without looking to either side, she sat stoic, stiff, and dignified. I guessed that she must be the wife of Old Moses.

Walking opposite Old Mose on the other side of the wagon was a thin man, a little above average height, bony-faced, who looked to be in his forties. He wore brown khaki pants, a white T-shirt, a holey gray felt hat turned up in the front, and a pair of overrun, worn-out tan slippers. He and Old Mose were chewers.

The wagon was overflowing with household junk. I could see the ends of slats, brooms, washtubs stuffed full of sundry things, old sheets and quilts covering and hanging in a haphazard fashion. At the tail end of the wagon beneath the pile was a coop full of clucking chickens and a pen with two grunting pigs inside.

Following the wagon was the rest of the caravan: a cow, led by an older boy, a goat, led by a girl, and a calf, led by another girl. There were fourteen boys and girls, all sizes and ages. Bringing up the rear was a little boy busy throwing rocks, who behaved as if he was about my age. As I watched from the porch of our store with Papa and Mr. Durbey, one of his rocks barely missed me.

The skinny man with the felt hat yelled back at the boy. "Thought I tol' y' t' stop throwin' them damned rocks. Now if I have t' come back there, y' gon' be glad t' stop." The man quickly changed his attitude and greeted us as the wagon pulled up. "Good evenin', y'all."

"Woah!" the ginger-colored woman said, and reared back on the reins.

"Good evenin'." Papa and Mr. Durbey spoke.

My eyes were glued on the boy who threw the rock. Close up, I noticed his disfigurement immediately. A nipple the size of my thumb hung from his chin. In addition, he had scars on his face, legs, and rusty feet. He wore a single garment: a ragged pair of short pants cut from a man's trousers. They were two sizes too big and were held up by a rope. His woolly hair was reddish-brown from going bareheaded in the sun plus a residue of red Arkansas clay. A layer of dirt as old as he was protected him. The summer heat bore down, and sweat had burrowed little rivers and canals over the exposed parts of his body. He smelled worse than the goat his sister led.

"This it, Udell?" the ginger-colored woman asked.

"This it, ain't it, Pa?" the thin man asked Old Mose.

"Yeah, purty sho."

"Whut y' lookin' fer?" Mr. Durbey asked.

"We lookin' fer Wagon Road West jist on the other side er Hughes grocery store," Old Mose replied.

"This is it right heah," Papa said, squinting to make out whom he was talking to.

"You Mr. Hughes?" Udell asked.

"I'm Andrew Hughes."

"My name's Barrow. Udell Barrow."

Papa tipped his hat but said nothing.

"We been on the road since early this mornin' all the way from Cleveland County. Wonder if we could trouble y' fer some wauter?" Udell asked.

"Hep yo'self. Theah's er trough out theah fer yo' animals too."

"Much obliged," Udell said, and motioned the shabby-looking caravan to pull into Wagon Road West.

While they walked toward the well, the dirty little boy came up to me and asked, "Whut's yo' name, boy?"

"My name's Sun. Whut's yo's?"

"That short fer son of er bitch?" he quipped, and laughed and laughed.

I didn't respond. I rather busied myself looking at his disfigured face. I had never seen anything like it.

"Whut the hell y' lookin' at? Ain't y' nevah seen er man befo'?"

"You ain't no man," I responded.

"Man ernuff t' stomp er mud hole in yo' skinny little ass, I bet."

"Y' never did tell m' y' name."

"I'm the baddest man evah come down the Pike. I'll snatch out yo' blood vessels, jump down yo' thoat, paralyze yo' livah, salivate yo' kidney, plug up yo' lungs, 'n stop yo' heart from beatin'," the boy rattled off. It was obviously something he had memorized from his older brothers.

"Som'um like that could kill er person. Why don't y' take er bath befo' y' start all that?"

"Uh-uh. That did it. I'm gon' whup yo' ass till yo' nose bleed. Then I'm gon' whup it till it stops." The boy mimed rolling up his sleeves on his shirtless arms. Then he picked up two small sticks and placed one on each of our shoulders. He positioned himself like a wrestler and placed his hands on his hips. "Dare y' t' knock that off."

I started laughing because I thought he was getting ready to fight. When instead he poised for a wrestling match, I knew he was in trouble.

"Whut the hell y' laughin' erbout? Go on. Knock it off. I dare y'—double-dog dare y'," the boy said.

I still said nothing and continued laughing at the foolish boy—whatever his name was.

"Aw right then, since you skeerd t' knock mine off, dare me t' knock yo's off. Go 'head! Dare m'!"

Still I said nothing and made no move.

"I dare y' t' dare me!" He became frustrated. "Double-dog dare y' t' dare me, goddammit!"

The more he talked, the more I laughed. If only he could have seen himself standing there, the very picture of an orphan, a funny-looking disfigured face, much smaller than I, smelling like a goat, talking about "I double-dog dare y' t' dare me!"

Finally he became so angry at me laughing at him, he forgot about his silly chip ritual and tackled me. I simply wrenched my hands clear of him, stepped aside, and stood there.

"Whut's yo' name, boy?" I asked again.

"Whut y' wanna know m' name fer? That ain't gon' hep y' er bit now."

He grabbed me again. I broke the hold again. "I don't like t' throw people without knowin' they name."

He became more angry at the remark and pressed the attack. I kept breaking his holds and circling him. I could have thrown him fifteen times by then if I had wanted to, but I really didn't want to get that close to him.

Finally a voice came from the direction of the well. "Ben! Whut y' doin', startin' trouble ergin? Leave that boy erlone 'n come over heah 'n git some er this wauter. Come on, now!" Mr. Udell ordered.

"Y' got lucky that time. Jist remember, we got er score t' settle atter I git m' wauter," Ben said as he moved toward the well.

I stood there and watched him climb the little incline to our well in the backyard.

Ben looked around and saw me standing there. "Well, Sunnnn, ain't y' comin'?"

The nerve of this boy, I thought. *I've known him all of five minutes, and already he's inviting me into my own backyard to drink some of my own water with his ugly self.*

When I walked up the incline, I got a clear view of what was going on among the assembly of the Barrow family. One of the oldest boys had drawn a bucket of the cool fresh water from our fifty-foot-deep well. I had never seen so many chewers and dippers rinsing and spitting. The only ones who didn't chew or dip were the young children and the black-skinned lady. I discovered later that Old Mose was a triple threat who smoked, chewed, and dipped consecutively and continually.

Mr. Udell had camped on our bench and was fanning himself with his ragged felt hat. The two women were competing with each other to serve him water, mop his brow, and rub his back and shoulders. Old Mose stashed himself on our back porch stairs and gripped his staff. Tall slender Grandma Mose was attending him.

Before anyone took a drink, Old Mose rose and stretched out his long bony hand. All quieted down, even Ben. "Dear God, we wanna pause heah 'n giah y' thanks fer seein' us safely all the way heah from Cleveland County t' this County Jefferson. If it be pleasin' t' y', if it's alright in yo' sight, we will call this place New Barrowtown. Wanna thank y' for givin' us the strength t' travel such er long distance. We wanna thank y' fer givin' the mules strength t' travel so fer. We wanna thank y' fer giving the chirren the strength t' travel so fer."

Mr. Udell looked over at Old Mose disgustedly.

I thought he had pretty much covered everyone and everything except the goat, pigs, and chickens.

Not good enough; pious Mose kept praying. "Dear God, want y' t' look down from yo' mighty throne on high and bless this family. Continue t' bless this family. Bless this wauter we're erbout t' drink, 'n bless this yo' humble servant. These 'n other blessings we ax in the name of yo' son Jesus. Eh-man 'n eh-man 'n eh-man."

"Pa, y' pray too long. Specially fer blessin' er damned drink er wauter," Mr. Udell said as he took the first drink.

"Have t' use every opportunity I can t' bring sinners like you t' Christ."

"By the time you git though prayin', Christ be done gone."

They passed the bucket and dipper to Pious Mose next, then to the women and older children. Ben and the baby were last. After everybody drank, Ben offered me a drink of my own water. Again I was stopped in my tracks. I must have spent most of the first forty minutes of our meeting laughing at him or scratching my head trying to figure out where he got so much brass. I would not have drunk behind those chewers and dippers unless I was stranded and dying in a desert.

Evidently, water revived Pious Mose's vocal cords. Not only was he blessed with a tall wiry powerful frame—though stooped from age, he also possessed one of the clearest, most distinct musical voices I had ever heard. He had a hoarse quality and a wide range, between baritone and tenor. Also plenty of volume, emitted from the pit of his stomach, that produced a pleasing spiritual resonance that captured the listener. In a word, the old man could sing:

> *Amazing grace, how sweet the sound*
> *That saves a wretch like meeee.*
> *I once was lost, but now I'm found,*
> *Was blind, but now I seeeee.*

Most of the others joined him. The singing became louder. Soon Papa came out of the store. Some customers followed him. Mr. Durbey joined the crowd, and a couple of his white customers came with him. They stood far in the back, half laughing, a curious look on their faces.

Mr. Durbey, who had never seen Pious Mose before, acted as if he was his long lost brother. He went over and stood beside him, put his greasy smutty blacksmith's hands on the singer's shoulders, and took up the bass. He displayed more nerve than ability.

Udell was unimpressed. He was too wrapped up in his own well-being. His two women were all over him, attending his every need.

"These darn shoes hurtin' m' feet. I ain't never walked this fer in all m' life," Udell complained.

"Maybe y' got some er them rocks in y' shoes," the dark woman said as she squatted down and removed them.

"See? Whut'd I tell y'?" She emptied some gravel on the ground from Udell's worn-out shoes.

"By God, Ella, y' right. No wonder m' feet wuz killin' m'."

"Y' shoulda been ridin' the wagon like I tol' y'," the ginger-colored woman said.

"'N jist wheah wuz I gon' set, in Ma's lap?"

"Y' done set in Ma's lap fer the last time. Y' ma's gittin' too ol'. Cain't do it no mo'."

"Did I ax y', Ma?"

"No, y'—"

"Then whut the hell is y' talkin' erbout?" Udell snapped back.

"Y' ought'n talk t' y' ma like that," she said, and started to cry. "Brought y' into this world. I ain't gon' be heah too much longer. Saw it in er dream t'other night." She became preachy. "Good Lord's gon' call m' home! Yes, He is!" Grandma Mose lamented.

"Aw, Ma, dry up. Y' healthier'n any of us, 'n y' know it. So jist dry up." Udell rubbed his hands over his feet and grimaced. "I jist ain't use t' all this walkin' 'n carrin' on."

"Come t' Christ. Jist come on t' Christ, that's whut y' need t' do. Jist stop sinnin' 'n come on t' Christ," Grandma Mose preached.

"Dry up, I said! 'N I mean it!" Udell ordered.

"Y' ought'n talk t' yo' ol' ma like that, Udell. She brought y' into this world. Ain't gon' be heah too much longer t'—" The ginger-colored woman attempted to chastise Udell.

"Shut up, Orathia!" Udell ordered firmly.

"Well, I—"

"Raht now!" Udell gave her a look.

Orathia stopped like a cut-off faucet. She reached into the pouch she carried around her waist and pulled out a small box of snuff. She pulled her bottom lip down and stuffed it until it was protruding and disfiguring her otherwise pretty face. Then she quietly and obediently proceeded to pamper her Udell.

In spite of Udell's rebuke of Orathia, Ella dared to try her hand at chastising him. "Y' ought'n talk t' y' ma like that, Udell. She brought y' into this—"

"Is I gon' heah yo' mouth too? Whut the hell *you* got t' do wid it, Ella!" Udell scolded.

Udell's voice had that hoarse quality like his father's, only Udell never tried to sing. His voice was high-pitched, and he whined when he talked. He also had his father's stooped shoulders, pigeon toes, and swift gate. His thin bony face, thin lips, sunken eyes, and protruding forehead were like his mother's.

Pious Mose was busy receiving compliments for his singing.

"That sho wuz some powerful singin', Mr. . . . er . . . er . . . ," Mr. Durbey stammered.

"Barrow. Charlie Barrow."

"Powerful. Yes sir, powerful!" Mr. Durbey repeated.

Papa and the others agreed. "It sho wuz."

"You ain't bad yo'self, Mr. . . . ," Pious Mose lied.

"Durbey. Gene Durbey."

"Y' don't mind if I call y' Gene, do y'?"

"'Course not. 'Course not. Jist don't call me late fer dinner." Mr. Durbey quickly tried to laugh off the worn-out joke when he found no expected response. "Errr . . . go on, Charlie, wid whut y' wuz sayin'."

"Errr . . . whut . . . I wuz sayin', Gene?" Pious Mose had forgotten.

"Yeah. Y' know. The part erbout how good m' bassin' is 'side yo' leadin'," Mr. Durbey wished.

"Oh yeah, that part. You wuz right on time, Gene. Knowed every word."

"He-he-he-he. Y' really think so, Charlie?"

"Yes sir, Gene, I do; otherwise I wouldn' say it. Lord don't like no liar, y' know."

"Say, listen heah, Charlie, you 'n me erbout the same age—"

"I'm sixty-eight," Pious Mose said quickly.

"Errr . . . errr . . . sho you is. Errr, whut I wuz fixin' t' say is, since you 'n me sound so good together—you leadin' 'n me bringin' up the bass, why don't we go on the road together? I bet we could do all right in the church circles eround heah. Whut y' say, Charlie?" Mr. Durbey looked Pious Mose in the eye like an excited boy proposing a marble tournament.

"Well, Gene, y' look like er blacksmith. Whut y' gon' do wid yer shop?"

Papa was standing in the background shaking his head and laughing at such a wild idea.

"Whut y' laughin' erbout, M.A.? Y' don't think we good 'nuff t' make it on the road? The Deep River Boys started jist like this, I heah. So did the Shilohs Er Joy." Mr. Durbey dared to dream.

"That word *boy*, don't that start y' t' thinkin' erbout som'um?" Papa asked.

"Soooo, y' think we too ol'," Mr. Durbey objected.

"Did I say that?" Papa walked over to Pious Mose. "Mr. Barrow, that wuz, without er doubt, some of the best singin' I heard in a long time. I'm er deacon at Hughes Chapel. We would be happy t' have y' come and sing t' us any time—jist any time."

"Thank y' fer axin' m', Brother Deacon. 'N don't be surprised when y' see m' walkin' in wid the light er the Holy Spirit glowin' eround m' body," Pious Mose replied.

"Well, however y' come, y' welcome anytime—anytime," Papa said as he turned and walked toward the store.

Mr. Durbey and the customers followed.

"How y' gon' invite him 'dout me if we suppose t' be er duet? How he gon' sound 'dout me singin' bass?"

Papa must have refrained from telling Mr. Durbey, "Much better." Mr. Durbey was behaving like a kid who had been put out of a ball game. Papa only laughed and shook his head. When he started into the store, Mr. Durbey blocked his entrance.

"Brother Durbey, ain't I been tryin' t' git y' t' come t' church wid m' fer yeahs? Ain't y' broke promise after promise t' me 'n even yo' own daughter?"

"Well . . . errr . . . M.A., I had things t' do them times."

"Like whut, sleepin', milkin' yo' goat?"

"Don't talk lightly erbout m' goat. Her milk twice as rich as any cow y' got—butter too. 'N she easy t' milk."

"I wouldn' care if she milked herself, churned 'n made her own butter 'n cheese, plus serve it t' m', I wouldn' have no stinkin' goat eround chewing up everything in sight." Papa went inside the store to his customers.

Mr. Durbey stood outside and fussed. "Y' jist don't like m' goat, M.A. Never did. That's all right; I like her. 'N ernother thing. I'm beginnin' t' think y' don't like m' bassin' neither. That's all right too, M.A. Plenty folks who do—plenty."

"Then go sing t' them!" Papa's voice came from inside the store.

Mr. Durbey shook his head disgustedly and moseyed over to his shop, fussing to himself.

The fussing from Udell and his mother became louder.

Pious Mose rushed over to Udell and shook his staff in his face. "I heard y' over heah talkin' t' yo' ma like that! Think y' er bad scamp, don't y'? Well y' ain't too bad fer me. I'm still y' pa, 'n I'll lay into y' wid this stick if the good Lord gimma strength."

"Aw, Pa, don't go gittin' y'self all worked up now. Save yo' strength fer the unloadin' 'n settin' up," Udell said in an attempt to settle the old man down.

"Don't tell m' erbout savin' no strength. I kin lay into y' 'n still have plenty o' strength t' do my part." Pious Mose pushed the long stick against Udell.

Udell grabbed it. "Pa, go on fo' y' hurt y'self now!"

"Give it to im, Charlie! Give it to im fer talkin' t' m' like that," Grandma Mose exhorted her husband.

It quickly became obvious the two men were playing. Udell was only trying to keep his father from getting too excited while they tussled.

"Pa, why don't y' go on now while the goin's good?" The old man kept tussling. "Y' goin' mess eround 'n make m' mad, dammit." But Udell held his father at bay.

The Barrow family functioned on the pecking order. Only Udell could peck up *and* down. It was clear that Pious Mose was under his son. They simply kept up the front of the old man having control out of respect for tradition—the order of things.

A.D. was the oldest boy. Though his sister Joline was older, he was over her by virtue of being a boy. This order was true in most families. My papa was liberal in that respect. He gave trust and authority to Deloris because she was smart.

A.D. was almost a carbon copy of his father. He had Udell's bony features, his sunken eyes, as well as his loud hoarse voice, only A.D. was quite a bit shorter. Already fifteen or sixteen, he had no chance of reaching the height of some of his sisters, or some of his younger brothers, for that matter.

"Udell! Udell! Y' better git ovah heah fo' I lay one of um out!" A.D. yelled.

"Y' better take care er whut evah it is fo' I come ovah theah 'n lay *you* out!" Udell yelled back.

"Udell, we wanna git t' the sto'. Y'all takin' too long," a tall skinny young lady said.

"Don't let yo' mouth overload yo' ass, young lady. You know better'n t' be rushin' me like that," Udell said as he took his sweet time.

Three of the kids had already called him Udell. It was the first time I had ever heard children, no matter what age, call their papa by his first name. The very thought of it gave me a funny fearful feeling, akin to what I could only imagine blasphemy to feel like or using filthy language laced with curse words in Papa's presence. Udell's allowing his children to call him by his first name was a contradiction, in view of the fact that he called his parents Ma and Pa, though there was where his respect ended.

Ben was never idle. That is, his body wasn't. He'd left me alone since I stood him down and Udell yelled at him. He began picking on his sister Corine. When he tired of her, he foolishly switched to his older brothers and sisters, all of whom could outrun and beat him as if he was a stray. Everybody in the family yelled at him for one devilish act or another. His antics included putting grass in his sister's hair, kicking dirt on her legs, and throwing rocks. His favorite was sticking Corine in the rear with a pin and watching her rocket three times her height.

The store was full of Barrows. Papa called for Deloris to come over and give him a hand. Though she was only twelve or thirteen, she had shown leadership ability, plus she had an eye like a hawk. Nobody was likely to slip anything into their pockets while she was around—not even Ben. As a consequence, she was more respected than liked, which was fine with her.

Pious Mose, Grandma Mose, Udell, Orathia, and A.D.—all smokers, chewers, and dippers of one sort or another—crowded around the tobacco counter and ordered Bull Durham, Ideal snuff, and Brown Mule. Ella was the only one of the grown-ups who didn't use tobacco.

Ella and three of the smaller children were bunched around the candy counter.

"Mama, I want er nickel worth er kisses," the oldest girl said.

"Now Joline, y' know I ain't got no money," Ella emphasized.

"Whut happened t' the money we made choppin'?" Joline inquired.

"Y' know yo' Pa took that money. Y' jist gon' have t' wait."

"Udell! Udell!" Joline called.

"Whut y' callin' me fer, Joline? Cain't y' see I'm busy?"

I did a double take. There was no doubt that Joline was Udell's child also. I had been under the impression that Orathia was the mother of all the children.

Ben went behind the counter and picked up a big butcher knife.

Orathia saw him, rushed behind the counter, and took it away from him. "Ben, keep yo' behind away from behind Mr. Hughes's counter!" She popped him on his head a couple of times. "Ketch y' back heah ergin I'm gon' git er switch t' y'."

"Oh, Mama, I wutten doin' nothin'."

"When you ain't doin' nothin', that's when I git fo' mo' gray hairs t' go erlong wid these y' already gi' m'."

"Mama, we want some candy," Corine, the pretty, skinny, ginger-colored girl said. She was obviously a product of Udell and Orathia.

"Y' gon' have t' wait like everbody else, Corine," Orathia counseled.

"But that's all we been doin', Mama," Corine whined to her mother.

"Well, y' jist gon' have t' wait some mo'. Yo' papa be through in er minute."

Udell was busy paying for his nasty Brown Mule and Orathia's equally nasty snuff. After he finished, he went over to Orathia and all the kids gathered around her. He fussed and wrangled with them, then he went over to Ella and the kids surrounding her and repeated the ritual. There were two older kids, a young girl around fifteen or sixteen and a boy who looked seventeen or eighteen. They were obviously sister and brother. They stayed to themselves and didn't say anything, unlike the other kids. They seemed rather lost and last in the shuffle.

Though I was not quite seven, I had already summed up the relationships among the Barrows. I knew, from what I had seen, that there were two mothers and one father. I knew that three of the thirteen belonged to Ella because of the way they gathered around her. Eight belonged to Orathia. From the resemblance of the older brother and sister to Udell, there was possibly another mother someplace who was part of Udell's harem.

"Kin I git anything else fer y'all?" Papa asked.

"Well, there is one little thing, Mr. Hughes. Since you er businessman eround heah, I wonder if y' know anybody who can use some hep? Or maybe you can use some?" Udell used his best manners.

"Whut kinda work? First of all, who y' talkin' erbout, yo'self or—?"

"*Me?*" Udell reacted as if Papa had asked him to give up chewing. Then he attempted to smooth it over. "Well, yeah, me too, but I wuz mostly talkin' erbout all this crew heah. I got some mighty fine choppers, pickers, cutters, shuckers—"

"Shuckers 'n drivers?"—which meant "shuckers and jivers."

Udell didn't appreciate the way Papa finished his litany. He paused for a minute, which made it obvious that he got Papa's snide remark. Not only did he get it, but his deeply sunken eyes snapped around so quickly I could almost hear them click like an empty gun. An angry little grin crept into the corner of his tobacco-juiced mouth. "Yes . . . sir, we got drivers. My boy Halley, the big tall one over there, A.D., and my boy Howard," referring to the boy who had said nothing. "All them can drive."

Papa wrote a note on a piece of paper and gave it to him. "Whut little farmin' I do, m' family takes care of, but this man needs some field hands. He's got a big farm down the Pike, payin' seventy-five cents er day fer grown-ups 'n thirty-five fer yo' young'uns."

While Udell was gazing at the note, Mrs. Margurett Stowald, our closest neighbor and daughter of Mr. Durbey, walked in. She was a nice-looking woman with big brown eyes. She was pleasingly plump, full-breasted, about forty, with a quick, ready smile. She wore a loose-fitting flower-patterned cotton dress, a wide floppy straw hat, and a pair of immaculate white shoes. "Oh, 'cuse m', Mr. Andra. I'll come back," she said in a high voice, then started to leave.

Papa rushed from behind the counter and stopped her. "Hold on, Miz Marge. We kin git whut y' want."

"Oh, thank y', Mr. Andra. All I want is a ten-cent can er Calumet 'n er pound er lard."

"Need some flour, Miz Marge?"

"Sho do. How'd y' know that, Mr. Andra?" Miz Marge laughed—too much in my opinion.

"Been sellin' t' y' er long time, Miz Marge—long time," Papa waved for Deloris to bring the order.

"Want m' t' put this on y' bill, Miz Marge?"

"If y' would be so kind, Mr. Andra."

"Be glad to," Papa said. "How's Jim?"

"Jim's fine. Ha-ha-ha. Jist fine, thank y'. How's Kitty 'n the chirren?"

"Everbody's gittin' erlong fine, Miz Marge."

"That's good. Ha-ha-ha. Whut erbout yo'self, Mr. Andra?" She was referring to Papa's diabetes.

"I have m' bad 'n m' good days, but I'm holdin' on."

Miz Marge looked around at the crowd in the store inquisitively. Udell looked up from the note and got an eyeful of the nice-looking woman. When she glanced in his direction, he tipped his ragged hat.

Half embarrassed, Miz Marge half bowed at the stranger, picked up her brown paper sack, and strolled out of the store. "Bye, Mr. Andra."

"Bye, Miz Marge." Papa looked at Deloris. "'Lois, mark sixty cents next t' Stowald."

"I already did, Papa."

"Good girl." Papa smiled. "Well, Mr. Barrow, sorry we wuz innerupted there."

"That's all right, Mr. Andra. Y' gotta take care er yo' regular customers." He was still fussing with the note. "'Cuse m', Mr. Andra, but I cain't quite make out this name y' write heah." Udell held up the paper higher.

"Parsons. Parsons. Lives down the Pike erbout er mile 'n er half on the left-hand side. Got er big cotton farm erbout eight miles ferther down near Cleveland County."

From a distance, I could see that Udell was holding the paper the wide way instead of the long way. It bothered me like a crooked picture on the wall, though I had no idea why he was holding the note that way. Papa wasn't fooled by Udell's pretense of not being able to read his writing. The truth was, Udell couldn't read *any* writing.

Though Papa never had more than a third- or fourth-grade education, he wrote beautifully and had taught himself to read and figure well.

Most people who couldn't read were too embarrassed to admit it. The common excuses were "Forgot my glasses," "The light's too dim [or too bright]," or Udell's excuse, "I can't read yo' writin'." Papa was used to those excuses; however, I never saw him slight anyone because of their handicap. He accepted their excuses without question.

Outside the store, we could hear hammering again. Ben was still hammering on a cast-iron harrow parked in the barnyard. It was used to break up, refine, and smooth the soil for spring planting. Udell had warned Ben about it before, but he continued. The families had gathered what they had bought and were preparing to leave. Deloris was watching their every move. Udell went first. I followed him when I saw him speed up in Ben's direction. Shortly before we reached the unsuspecting hammerer, the harrow's cast-iron handle gave up as if to say, "I can't take this no mo'," and fell to the ground. Ben stood there looking at it in dismay.

Udell didn't break his gait. He went straight for Ben's head. Such a whaling-whaling-whaling, as he kept repeating, "You had t' keep on nailin'-nailin'-nailin'!"

Neither Mama nor Papa would hit us about the head. They believed it would affect children's thinking and render them foolish as grown-ups. They simply didn't slap us around. When we did something that called for a whipping, a whipping is what we got, but with a belt or a switch, generally on our butts or around the legs. Mama was a pincher. I often thought I inherited my wrestling skills from her. She would catch you, pin you to the ground, and "pinch er plug outta y'." I'd much rather she used a strap or a switch than undergo one of her pinchings. I always found the expression "This is hurtin' me worse than it is you" to be out of place for a whipping, if not sublimely ridiculous. I was always tempted to ask, but didn't dare, "Why don't we switch places?"

The Barrows were just the opposite of my parents. The head was the first part of the body they attacked. My parents thought blows to the head made children silly; the Barrows thought they settled their children down and wised them up.

Udell seemed to think that nailing on Ben's head was sufficient compensation for the handle he broke. In his anger, he conveniently forgot even to apologize. He was wise enough to know that if he had, he would have prompted the question of payment for damages.

The sun was fast setting at the end of Wagon Road West. Heat waves appeared to dance at the feet of a yellow glow, like a big ball splashed into a bowl of paint and crushed against a red horizon far into the hills that received the round descending. Distant trees were silhouetted black against an illustration board of colors. The caravan slowly wormed its way up Wagon Road West past the little hill where I had met with my little rattler. Ben brought up the rear as usual.

9

About two hundred feet south of our house, perched on a hill, stood the big rambling old abandoned Walker house. It was surrounded by tall oaks, gums, and a few pines. The house and its surroundings had once been an elegant estate with colonnaded porches, long open hallways, gables, dormers, and at least two fireplaces. It sat farther back from the road than our house and had a long circling driveway. It had been white, trimmed in green.

Most of the windows were knocked out. Ragged shutters dangled from their frames. Peeling scales of the green paint that once made the facade look handsome now only accentuated the decay. Rain, wind, and hail had played havoc with the roof and were taking their toll on supporting timbers and floors. A natural curiosity for kids, we had dared to inspect the dwindling dwelling on several occasions but had ceased the practice since underbrush had taken over. Besides, everyone knew an old abandoned house such as that was haunted and dangerous. Bushes, weeds, and tall grass took full advantage of each spring and the fertile soil that had accumulated around the old building. It was also a haven for wasp nests and worse yet, hornet nests and long black snakes.

When we saw the Barrows ascending the little hill in back of our house, we wondered where they were going. Our questions were soon answered. In a few days, we looked up at the old Walker house; they had cleared the weeds and bushes, and smoke was coming out of one of the chimneys. Somehow they must have gotten permission to use the place until they built their own.

The Walkers' well was not usable; therefore they made a pilgrimage to our well at least three times a day. Papa became worried about the water supply. Constant heavy usage could cause its depletion. Fortunately, it was enough for drinking, after Papa directed them to use the bayou to water their animals.

At the same time that the Barrows were doing temporary work on the old Walker house, they were cutting, burning, raking, and clearing for New Barrowtown across the way on their new 4 acres. Much to Papa's chagrin, old Mrs. Laughton had sold to the Barrows the land at the top of the hill, which joined our 1.63 acres on the west. Udell, the women, the girls, and all of the boys except William T., who was too young, were busy. Even Grandma Mose occupied herself shelling peas while sitting in her old rocker, singing "Them Old Songs er Zion" and squirting snuff spit.

The hot sun was bearing down. All of the men were stripped to the waist except Pious Mose. He kept his khakis on even though they were soaking wet. He even had his shirt buttoned up to the top. He claimed he was cooler than those who took off their shirts. "Once yo' clothes is soaked, when the cool air blows over um, it cools y' off." What cool air? All I saw were heat waves dancing off bodies, clothed and unclothed. I thought, *Some of those heat waves must have gotten to Pious Mose's brains.*

I soon learned better; Pious Mose was working like a mule. Not only was he working, but he was singing to the top of his lungs while doing so. He treated the whole neighborhood to an open-air concert. He sang one song after the other: "Leaning on Jesus," "Swing Low, Sweet Chariot," "I Shall Not Be Moved," "Go Down Moses," "Onward Christian Soldiers," "Is the Old Ship er Zion," and "Walk with Me Lord" were among the many.

Mr. Durbey became disenchanted with his new friend, Charlie, and started criticizing him to Papa. "Nevah heard so much singin' in all m' life. Man sings all the time. Cain't git er word in edgewise. Y' stop t' talk to im 'n he starts singin'. Y' say good mornin' 'n he sings good mornin' back t' y'. Singin' in the mornin', singin' in the evenin', singin' at supper time—singin', singin', singin'."

"The man's full er the Holy Ghost, Brother Durbey," Papa said.

"He's full er som'um. Theah simply ain't that much Holy Ghost in the worl', M.A.," Mr. Durbey said. "Worse'n somebody who laugh all the time."

"Or talk?" Papa said.

"'Zactly. Or talk," Mr. Durbey repeated.

Day by day, Barrowtown started to take shape, such as it was. Up from the red earth, raw and dripping with new sap, void of all pretense to style, design, or convention, a potpourri of ideas—all Barrow's, all bad—the little home struggled upward to the bright hot sunlight of day.

The Barrows managed quite efficiently to defile, disfigure, and disgrace a perfectly handsome wooded area and render it a slum before the first person moved in. The foundation blocks were leaning in and out. They looked like a confused, bowlegged, slew-footed centipede. The siding was a mangled unfinished crossword puzzle, apparently worked on by an idiot. The roof looked like Mr. Sam Riley's hat when he was in the happy state of a deranged, disabled drunk. If a board was too long, it was the board's fault. Same thing if it was too short. The roof wasn't built to keep out water; rather, it was meant to channel the water more directly to the bedrooms, kitchen, and living rooms, if one could call them that. Since most shacks were one or two rooms, at most, in decay and disarray, I thought more rooms than that in the same condition deserved a longer name. Thus, "shackamore." The name stuck.

Less than five weeks had passed before the family moved into the little shackamore, lock, stock, and Barrow. Mr. Durbey said, "They must sleep stacked on top er each other." I had no idea where eighteen people slept in such a small place. Papa forbade any of us to go inside; therefore I couldn't count the bedrooms. Judging from other shackamores that size and our house, it couldn't have had more than two bedrooms. There were nine of us, and we had three bedrooms, one of which was dormitory size. There was also an attachment to the smokehouse where old Mr. Pie lived. And the teacher slept in the parlor during school months.

Neighbors west of us coming to the Pike stopped, if no one was looking, and gazed at the little mistake in reverence as if at a grave. Some took off their hats and scratched their heads. When it became obvious that the Barrows had finished except for a few sheds for the goat and other animals, people stood and shook their heads in disbelief.

Before the summer was half over the Barrows had settled in. Pious Mose and Grandma Mose had moved back to Cleveland County and only visited on the weekends. Like it or not, our closest neighbors became people with whom we had little in common. They did no farming, not even truck farming. They weren't merchants. They didn't attend church. I doubt if any of them could read or write. Except for Pious Mose and Grandma Mose, they had absolutely no respect for Sunday. Their women cut and sawed wood alongside their men.

Papa was patient. He commanded respect because he always gave it, even when he knew it wasn't deserved. He simply couldn't sink to a low level even when provoked. In private, he referred to the whole family as "them Udells." However, in person, he called the boys "son" and the girls "daughter" or "young lady." He called Orathia and Ella "Miz." He reserved "Brother Charlie" for Pious Mose and "Sister Barrow" for Grandma Mose. Udell, he paid the least respect of all. He didn't call him anything whenever he could avoid it. When he had to call his name, he called him plain "Udell." Udell, on the other hand, always called Papa "Mr. Andra," even when they disagreed, which was frequently.

Their first little encounter came early. Udell wanted to set up an account, like the Stowalds, the Rileys, and others.

"How come y' let them have it, 'n y' turn me down?" Udell asked.

"I know the people I let open accounts wid me. Sometimes I make er mistake, but that's how this business goes," Papa said.

"Y' let Ma 'n Pa open one, 'n y' don't know them no longer'n y' knowed me," Udell said.

"That's quite true. I'm not in the habit of chastisin' grown people, but since y' asked, if I had met you separate, I never woulda thought y' wuz they son," Papa said.

"Whut y' mean?" Udell asked.

"Oh, y' look like yo' ma in the face. Y' walk jist like yo' pa, 'n y' talk jist like im, but y' ain't like um in no other way I seen," Papa said.

"I still don't know whut you mean, Mr. Andra."

"Well, let's take the water situation. You should know by now that I ain't the kind er man who would deny y' water. I got all kinds er people come by heah 'n use my well." Papa paused. "All kinds—whites, blacks, Gypsies, drunks, tramps, rednecks, 'n peckerwoods"—Udell chuckled at those descriptions—"even my cousin the mailman, preachers, 'n travelin' salesmen, folks fer miles eround, they all know erbout this well. It's er good deep well 'n it can take er lot, but constant heavy use, it won't take."

"Whut's the matter? Y' want m' t' pay y' fer the wauter? Is that it?" Udell asked gruffly.

"No. That's not it at all. Fact is, we've been pullin' up sand in the bucket lately. I didn't say anything t' y' 'cause I could see you wuz busy buildin', but you seem t' be through wid that, and I suggest you dig yo'self er well."

"Dig . . . er well?" Udell exclaimed with a half grin in the corner of his mouth.

"Not half as bad as y' think," Papa said.

"I hope not," Udell responded.

"Y' most likely t' be on the same slope as Jim Stowald n' me. Y' probably won't have t' dig more'n twenty, twenty-five feet to the first layer of water." Papa's traveling to the annual National Baptist Convention for twenty years had improved his speech pattern. I never heard him say "wauter" like many people in the community. "I had my well bored and tiles sunk; that's why mine is fifty feet deep, and it's fed from two layers."

"I ain't got no money t' have no well bored," Udell said.

"That's whut I'm drivin' at. You got plenty boys. I had all girls then. You can dig yo' own well, man."

"How come them girls couldn't hep y'? Mine can," Udell affirmed.

"Well, that's up t' you." Papa paused. "Anyway . . ."

"How I'm gon' keep the dirt from fallin' back in if I dig er hole big ernuff fer er man t' work?" Udell asked.

"When yo' hole git that deep, drive er couple er posts on the sides 'n pull the dirt up wid er pully 'n bucket. Then build yo' sides as you go down. Keep knockin' the sides down 'n addin' to um from the top. Some people add from the bottom," Papa explained.

Udell didn't act enthused. Instead of thanking Papa, he seemed annoyed that Papa had laid out more work for him to do. His face seemed to express, "I jist spent most er the summer buildin' that goddamned house. Gittin' kinda tired er people findin' things fer me t' do—'specially you."

"Y' don't have t' worry, Mr. Andra. I won't be troublin' y' erbout yo' wauter no mo'." Udell snatched his ten-cent plug of Brown Mule off the counter and stalked out in a huff.

"Triflin' devil," Papa said out loud to himself.

Udell seemed to have the idea that what was his was his and what was ours was his as well. He seemed to have trouble seeing the difference. He was obviously spoiled. The pampering by Orathia and Ella had intensified since they had moved into the little shackamore. They were preening and grooming morning, noon, and night. Most of the family wore rags and were dirty, but not Udell. He knew nothing about dressing like Papa, Uncle Pet, or other men in our community, but his pants and shirts—though tattered—were always clean, starched, and ironed. They kept his hair clipped close and shaped with an English front style, and he was always clean shaven. He made a fetish of keeping his hands clean and oiled. He even smelled better than the women, except Ella. Too bad he didn't pass some of that personal hygienic pride on to his son Benjamin.

While the family were away all day working in some white man's cotton or corn field, Udell was reclining on the homemade hammock they had rigged up for him. It was made from old cotton sacks and strung by rope between two posts. There was always a skeleton crew. One of the women and a younger child handled his every need and did the cooking for hungry mouths after a hard day's work. In the evenings, however, and on weekends, they waited on him hand and foot as if he was a pharaoh. All that attention by his women and children had gone to his head, and it made him "damned mad" when people like Papa couldn't see just how precious he was.

Not only was he a king where he came from in Cleveland County, but he had only been among the highfalutin Main Pike people for a few weeks and one of our women had already succumbed to his magic charms. Instead of taking Papa's advice and digging his own well, Udell started taking water from Mr. Jim Stowald. He was also having his way with another of Mr. Jim's prized possessions, namely, his precious wife, sweet 'Tata Pie, Miz Marge.

As summer rocked on, Ben and I had become playmates, much against Papa's and Mama's wishes. Even though we were being raised differently, we still had much in common. My parents thought we children—especially me—were bound to pick up "them Udells'" bad habits. They never took into consideration that the Udells were moving into our community, not we into theirs. People with a tradition of doing things a certain way weren't going to suddenly change and start living life according to Udell. Udell was a prince at Barrowtown, but he and his family were simply outcasts and looked down upon by most families in our community.

About June of that summer, some three months after they had moved to the community, Ben and I were on our way from the main garden, a quarter of a mile from our house on the right side of Wagon Road West, to the store to pick up some seeds Mama needed to finish what she was planting. We were rolling our wheel rims, taken from abandoned wagon hubs and paddled by a stiff wire bent to form a guide.

Suddenly a ruling wind crowded our space, wrapping chilly arms about our thinly clad frames. Raw sap, filtered and strained from persimmon bark and holly berries, agitated my nostrils, oozed through mucous membranes, contaminating saliva in my mouth. I tasted an alien danger. Hot, salty sweat, cooled, dried, then drafted on my face, arms, shoulders, and legs like spit gone awry. A savage foreboding gripped my deepest feelings when surging currents rendered me weightless and helpless against them.

We looked toward the sky; the heavens were angry. Giant manatees configurated into galloping camels leaping in and out of a daunting sun. Birds silhouetted against a revolving, turbulent background. Clouds and smoke became gray, white, black, red. Thunder repeated its ancient ritual; lightning unleashed its secret fingers. The devil was beating his wife.

Then the rains came. We were prepared to be drenched, but the hard crystal drops were dry. They stung our heads, shoulders, arms, and the tops of our bare feet, but strangely, we weren't getting wet. We gathered up our rims and paddles. Ben dashed for the shelter of a big oak tree.

"No! No!" I screamed. "Papa said nevah stand under a tree when it's lightnin'!"

"How come?" Ben asked.

"'Cause lightnin' strike the tree 'n you too! You be dead!" I screamed.

"Ooh, shit!" Ben said as he came from beneath the tree. "I'm s'posed t' stand out heah so the lightnin' can git er clean shot at m' 'stead er the tree, huh?"

The crystal drops increased to almost the size of goose eggs. The maddening hard rain intensified. We covered our heads as best we could with our rims and paddles, but the unrelenting dry rain drew blood from our little hands and feet as well as our other uncovered parts. The winds ripped leaves and limbs from the trees. Grass, weeds, and white lilies lay prostrated together on both sides of Wagon Road West.

The brightest day, within minutes, slipped from sight. It rudely cast us into darkest night.

"Come on! Let's run!" I yelled, then took off. Ben followed, coughing and barking in the dark.

We were racing. Lightning was flashing, lighting up the path and trees deep into the surrounding woods. The hail beat us unmercifully. Running as fast as we could, another big flash revealed the Stowalds' house on the left. I finally dashed up on the porch, out of breath and bleeding. Ben followed.

"Miz Marge! Miz Marge!" I called, but there was no answer.

I had stopped on plenty of occasions when she was in the garden or someplace in the back of the house. On those occasions, I had gone around to the back. I didn't dare go tramping through her house without her inviting me inside, and it wasn't practical in that situation to go around to the back, so I waited on the porch, happy to be protected from the brunt of the storm.

Strong winds carried the big dry crystal drops, battered shingles from the roof, and attacked us on the porch. I still would not barge inside.

"Miz Marge! Miz Marge!" I called again, but there was no answer.

"How in the hell y' 'spect anybody t' heah y' in this stohm?" With that, Ben opened the door and went inside. I followed at a respectable distance behind.

The rapid beating on the shingled roof sounded like a thousand hooves thundering over barren tundra. Still we could hear the sound of voices coming from the bedroom to our left. We froze. The voices became more distinctive. One was that of a man. We put our fingers to our lips and said nothing. I knew it wasn't Mr. Jim, because I had seen him headed for town earlier that morning with his regular load of winter wood.

"Miz Marge!" I called again.

"That you, Sun?" Miz Marge's voice came from the bedroom.

"Yes ma'am," I answered.

"Hold on. Miz Marge'll be there in er minute. Jist set down and make yo'-self at home."

After a brief wait, Miz Marge cracked the door and peeped out. When she did the funk flowed. It overtook her and filled the parlor. It was so strong and forceful I'm quite sure it went on out the front door to Wagon Road West, then on out to the Pike. I doubt if the storm could have had any effect on a bad smell like that.

"Some hailstorm, ain't it! Jist terrible—terrible! You all right, Sun?" She noticed Ben standing in back of me. "Ha-ha-ha-ha. I thought y' wuz by yo'self. I see y' got Ben wid y'. Look like y'all jist made it inside in time." Miz Marge obviously couldn't see how bruised and bloodied we were. "Y'all jist make yo'selves at home." She headed for the kitchen. "Miz Marge'll see if she can find y'all some nice fresh tea cakes. Jist baked yestedy. Ha-ha-ha-ha." She entered the kitchen.

She had tried to fix her hair, but it wasn't good enough. Her clothes were dry, but sweat was pouring off her face and neck. I decided there and then, I didn't want any more of Miz Marge's tea cakes.

The minute she left, Ben started pointing toward the bedroom. He whispered something, but I couldn't make out what it was. He tiptoed over to me and whispered in my ear, "I know who that is in theah."

"Who?" I asked.

"Udell," Ben whispered.

"Yo' papa?"

"You know anybody else named Udell eround heah?" Ben kept shaking his head.

"Ooooooohh!" I could hardly contain myself. Curiosity was taking its toll on my imagination. *Whut on earth wuz Mr. Udell doin' in Mr. Jim's bedroom wid his wife while Mr. Jim wuz away? As gentle as Mr. Jim was, would he put up wid som'um like that once he found out? Whut uh scandal!* I thought.

Not only did Mr. Udell have no respect, he was lacking in the commonsense department as well. I already knew Miz Marge thought snake hips were on a snake rather than a switching woman, and black-eyed peas forgot to duck, but I thought Udell—though trifling and selfish—at least had better sense than to leave the door open while he was with another man's wife. Not only that, Mr. Udell had left his old ragged hat on a chair in the parlor as if he was at home. Ben had pointed it out to me before he whispered in my ear.

Shortly, Miz Marge came into the parlor with the tea cakes. Not wanting to arouse suspicion, I tucked two of them in my nasty pockets. *It can't make them any nastier than they already are after being handled by Miz Marge,* I thought. I had no intention of eating them anyway.

Miz Marge saw Ben looking at his papa's hat. The cat was out of the bag. Little did she know that it was out when I first heard a man's voice. When she opened the door and that funk came marching out, the cat had already turned the corner and was in the home stretch. In her simple mind, we were much too young to know about the F word. Even though I had never heard it used at home, I certainly had heard Ben use it aplenty in the few months I had known him. I had also seen a mean, fearless bull hunching cow after cow in the pasture directly across the Pike in front of our store. I certainly didn't think that was a new form of milking. Ben and I had watched bloody battles between male dogs over a female. Finally the winner was hung up with the female and the bloody battle would escalate between the winner and the losers. The winner would escape by running under the house, dragging the female behind him. We had also watched what was considered the Romeo of animal lovers, the slow-grinding, "taking his timing" bow hog. A rooster mounting a hen and pecking her brains out we didn't find exciting. We saw no instrument, which led us to ask, "What's the point?"

Miz Marge decided to try her silly hand at covering up. "Ha-ha-ha-ha. I see y' lookin' at yo' papa's hat. Ha-ha-ha-ha-ha. He come down er few minutes ergo t' git some cool wauter 'n I thought I'd have him fix the slats in our old bed while he wuz heah. Ha-ha-ha-ha," Miz Marge lied.

"Yas'um," Ben replied.

"He's so handy at that kind er thing, y' know. Ha-ha."

"Yas'um," Ben replied.

"Y' want m' t' call him?"

At that moment Udell cracked the door. He was wallowing a big wad of Brown Mule tobacco around in his jaws. "Whut y'all boys doin' out heah in er hailstorm like this? Don't y' know it's dangerous?"

Neither Ben nor I responded. Udell tried to back Miz Marge up with her stupid story. "If I had knowed it t'was gonna hail like this, I'd er jist put these pails out 'n caught some er this good clean wauter from the sky. T'would er been nice 'n cool when it melted."

We still didn't respond.

"T'would er been nice 'n melted . . . 'n nice . . . 'n cool . . . 'n nice fo' night-time. Ain't that right, Mr. Udell? Ha-ha-ha," Miz Marge tried. "Y' git the slats in, Mr. Udell?"

"Yeah, I finally got um in. You 'n Mr. Jim gon' have t' take it easy wid that ol' bed. Ain't whut it used t' be."

It was getting too deep in there for me. Besides, the funk was stifling and the storm was over. I rose to leave. Ben followed.

"Thank you fer the tea cakes, Miz Marge," I said.

"Y' welcome, Sun. Inny time. Y'all boys fixin' t' leave?"

"Yes ma'am," we said at the same time.

On our way home we steered our wheels the best we could over the scattered ice nuggets. It was a challenge. We watched a mother bird try to revive her blood-spattered dying young. Ordinarily we would have been shooting at her with our beam shooters. On that occasion, however, I picked up the nest, gave it to Ben, and hoisted him up high enough to lay it in the fork of a tree. Tree branches and green leaves covered Wagon Road West as far as we could see. Shingles had been beaten off Mr. Jim's house and Mr. Durbey's shack. Sparrows and black crows were pecking at the chunks of ice, thinking it was food. Part of a log had fallen across the road. A rednecked woodpecker was drilling a hole in the tall part of a tree that was left standing.

Most life returned to normal with the return of the hot sun. Leave it to the stupid mocking bird to start singing after something untoward had happened. Ben and I did take our beam shooters out and shoot at him. We missed him by a mile. He simply flew to another nearby tree and struck up another tune, only louder. Earthworms had mistaken the temporary darkness for permanent night and crawled out of their holes. They were lying stretched all over the ground. We stopped and gathered as many as we could and put them in our pockets until we could find a can.

In the far distance, we could hear the blues borne on the air from the moanful cry of a freight, mixed with the competing braying of a barnyard jackass.

"Udell wuz pumpin' it to that woman. All that shit erbout fixin' the slats. 'Did y' git it in, Mr. Udell?'" Mimicking. Ben did it so well, I had to laugh. "'Yeah, I finally got it in.' I bet he did. He wuz pumpin' it to that woman like that ol' bull wuz to them cows we saw yestiddy." We laughed some more.

"I'm gon' ax her fer some very nex time I go by there 'n she theah by herself. I might ax her while he theah, he so damned dumb," Ben said.

"You gon' ax her fer some whut?" I asked. "Some mo' tea cakes?"

I remembered the two I had in my pocket and tossed them away. Ben did the same.

"I'm gon' ax her fer some er that ol' pussy, that's whut," Ben replied. "I think she give it t' innybody if y' ax her nice."

"Ben, I keep tellin' y', y' ain't no man, but you don't believe m' do y'? She's ol' ernuff t' be yo' grandmama."

"But she give it t' Udell, 'n I believe my brother A.D. done got some of it too," Ben announced.

"But both er them men. Mr. Udell done proved his many times. How'd y' think you got heah, fool?" I continued. "If y' ax her fer anything y' better make it tea cakes. That is, if y' want some more er them funky tea cakes. I don't want no mo' of um m'self. I wouldn't ax her fer nothin' else if I wuz you."

"You skeered t' say pussy, ain't y'?" Ben waited. "Well, say it," Ben insisted.

I looked at him. He had me in a corner. I didn't want to appear less experienced about sex than he. After all, we had seen the same animals in action. In addition, we had just seen Mr. Udell and Miz Marge together. I still couldn't bring myself to use language I had never heard at home or from most people in our community. Even Mr. Sam Riley covered up the nasty word by using *trim* and *nookie*.

"I ain't skeered neither," I said rather unconvincingly.

"Let me heah y' say it then," Ben continued.

"Say whut?" I pretended to have forgotten. Before he could respond, I attempted to change the subject. "Let me ax you som'um."

"Whut?" Ben asked.

"I know Mr. Udell is Consuella's and Halley's papa, but who is they mama?"

"They mama dead," Ben responded.

"They mama dead?" I asked rhetorically.

"Yeah, long time ergo," Ben said.

"Did you know her?"

"Sho I knowed her. Usta live wid us," Ben said.

"Whut y' call er long time ergo. Y' ain't but almost seven like me," I explained.

"Last yeah. Whut you axin' me so many questions erbout her fer? Whut's it t' y'?" Ben realized he had said more than he intended. "Come on, let's go git them seeds so we can come back 'n git som'um done."

As we neared the store, we heard a loaded wagon coming down the Pike. We heard a familiar voice coaxing old Juber along. We ran out to the Pike and looked up toward the bridge. We could see a fragile, tattered figure walking along beside the wagon tapping a nag of a mule. As the wagon rounded the trees south of our pasture, we could see that it was loaded with winter wood. There was no doubt, it was Mr. Jim Stowald coming home to the woman he loved, his sweet, precious 'Tata Pie.

10

"Stkh-h-h. Stkh-h-h. Stkh-h-h."
Mr. Jim made a sound like he was trying to pick his teeth with his tongue. Something between a smack and a sucking kiss. "Come on, Juber. Come on, mule. Come on now." Encouraging remarks were heard to the rhythmic march of Mr. Jim's feet, backed up by the clucking and squeaking of the loaded little single-horse wagon crunching the melting nuggets of ice from the hail earlier that morning. Cane poles, on top of the load, projected to the rear. "Move erlong now, Juber. Stkh-h-h. Stkh-h-h. Move erlong. Y' doin' fine. Won' be long now. We be home soon." He lightly tapped Juber with the end of his line. A spirited, lively mule would have reacted and broken into a trot. Poor old bony Juber simply took it as a friendly gesture and never even flinched. Ben and I were standing beside the Pike in front of the store watching. Mr. Jim coming home, it was. The old red mule moped along with his head down, foaming at the mouth, resigned to eternal drudgery to the end of his few remaining days.

Mr. Jim was too tall to be short and too short to be tall. He wore an old brown felt hat with holes cut in the top and a jagged pattern cut from the brim. He folded back and pinned the front part of the brim. He kept a full supply of fishhooks, lead, corks, tackle, and a feather behind the black greasy band. Although he wasn't a big man, he was trim, with a small waist, hunched broad shoulders, long arms, and big rippling muscles. His big hands were carved, machinelike claws with oversized nubbed thumbs and fingers that bespoke hard work. His every motion expressed the power and consummate spirit of the woodchopper. His voice, his laughter, his quiet center and resignation to drudgery were highlighted by a few simple pleasures, very much like Juber, the beast whose burden he didn't hesitate to share.

"Stkh-h-h. Stkh-h-h. Won' be long now, Juber. We be home drexly. Git y' some oats, some good hay 'n plenty wauter, y' be fine. Come on now. Come on." Juber let go with a big loud lingering wind-pressured fart. "Now is that the thanks I git fer talkin' nice t' y'? Shame on y', Juber—shame."

Juber started walking with his hind legs wide apart. Another explosion was followed by a big dribbling pile of an A number one, highly nitrofied mulched mixture of oats and hay. Juber strewed a rich natural grade of fertilizer behind him as he turned toward the setting sun on Wagon Road West.

"My Lord, Juber, do y' think y' can afford that? We still got another hill to climb, y' know."

Ben and I fell out on the ground laughing. Mr. Jim pulled Juber to a halt in front of our store.

"Whut y'all boys laughing erbout? Didn't y' ever see er mule move his bowels befo'?" Mr. Jim asked.

"Hi, Mr. Jim," we both said.

"Hi, Sun, Li'l Udell."

Ben took such pleasure in making fun of Mr. Jim that he didn't object to the name Li'l Udell. Besides, if Mr. Jim only knew what we knew.

"Y' gon' enter that mule in the county fair derby this fall, Mr. Jim?" Ben quipped.

A funny little grin crept into the corner of Mr. Jim's mouth as he looked over at Ben. He thought about the snide remark while tying the reins to the hitching post and didn't answer immediately. "Juber?"

"Whut's the matter, Mr. Jim, y' don't think Juber be eround till fall?"

"He-he. Sho . . . Juber be eround long time." He patted Juber on his bones. "Won't y', Juber?"

Juber was busy panting and slobbering, probably thinking about having to climb that hill before he could earn that little hay and oats Mr. Jim was going to ration out to him.

"Whut y' tyin' him up fer, Mr. Jim? Y' think he gon' run off 'n turn yo' load over or som'um?" Ben asked.

"Don' git too big fer yo' britches now, Li'l Udell."

I had too much respect for Mr. Jim, and grown people in general, to join with Ben in making fun of him. I simply stepped aside and pretended to be busy fixing my beam shooter. However, I could hardly keep my frame from shaking with laughter—to myself—as Ben jabbed him with one ridiculous question after the other.

"Wheah wuz y'all boys when the big hail come up?"

"We wuz—" Ben began.

"We wuz playin', Mr. Jim," I interrupted quickly.

"Hope y' wuz close ernuff t' someplace y' could git in outta that stohm," Mr. Jim said.

Ben and I looked at each other. I could see Ben was in a quandary as to how to answer.

"Yes sir," I responded, which was no answer at all, but it served the purpose for the moment.

Papa came out on the porch. He was dressed in a seersucker single-breasted suit, slightly too big for him. Diabetes had taken off the pounds. He complemented his suit with a starched and ironed shirt with attached stiff white collar and a black bow tie, neatly tied into a small knot. Gold studs glittered from his neck down to his waist. His cuffs projected about an inch from his coat sleeve, and he neatly adorned them with gold cuff links that matched his studs. His graying black hair and mustache were neatly trimmed. He looked as elegant as I had ever seen him. "How you, Jim?"

"Oh, putty good. How you, M.A.?"

"Gittin' ready t' git outta heah." Papa flipped his big Bulova into his ruling hand and glanced at the time. Then he held it at a distance and got a better look. I noticed he had changed his gold fob for a more dressy one than he wore every day. On this one, a gold piece dangled from the chain.

"Whut y' all dolled up fer? Convention time ergin?"

"Yeah. Pet supposed t' pick me up in er few minutes. Don't wanna miss that train tonight," Papa said.

"Tonight?" Mr. Jim asked.

"Yeah. I got dressed early 'cause we got er meetin' up at the church first. When I come back home, Kitty'll have my bags ready, all I have t' do is grab my bags, then me 'n Pet kin take off," Papa explained.

"Wheah y'all goin' this yeah?" Mr. Jim asked.

"Niagara Falls over on the Canadian side," Papa said.

"All the way up t' Canada, eh? I declare, M.A., I don't know how y'all do it. You 'n Pet gon' meet up wid yo' brothers E.J. 'n Thomas up theah?"

"Yep. Same as always, Jim."

"Y'all been meetin' this way pud nigh twenty yeahs, ain't y'?"

"Yep. This yeah is twenty. Jim, y' got er good memory," Papa said. "Wheah wuz you when the big stohm hit, Jim?"

"I wuz still in town at Fuller's Feed Sto', lucky fer us. Me 'n Juber jist pulled under the shed. I went inside 'n waited it out. I see y'all got it puddy good down heah too," Mr. Jim said.

"How's the roads?" Papa asked, and checked his watch again.

"Full'er ice, but it's meltin' fast. Trees and limbs wuz all over. Me 'n Juber had t' stop three or fo' times fer me t' chop 'n move stuff outta the way. In town 'n er lotta places along the Pike, them big limbs done fell ercross them hot wires 'n left um danglin' 'n on the ground. Somebody's bulldog grabbed one er them wires 'n he wound up er hot dog. He-heeee. Cooked im right there on the spot. One er them big limbs fell on a store roof, mashed it flatter'n er pancake. Don't look like y'all had that kind er 'citement eround heah," Mr. Jim said.

Ben punched me in the side. I tried to ignore him. I thought, *If Mr. Jim only knew.*

"Whut y' got there on top er yo' load, Jim?" Papa asked.

"Oh, jist er little som'um fer my 'Tata Pie. I wuz kinda worried. If there wuz anythin' wrong down theah, I knowed y' woulda tol' me by now. So I take it she wuz well taken care of," Mr. Jim said.

"I saw Brother Durbey on his way down theah afterward. I'm sure he looked in on her," Papa said.

"Oh, good. Anythin' happen t' her . . ." Mr. Jim lifted a croker sack from the wagon and carefully took out and displayed some rare, beautiful flowers. "These right heah is holly-hawks. These is cattails. These is eagle feathers. 'N these right heah is pepper berries. I didn't sell no wood, so I caught er couple." Mr. Jim reached deeper into his sack and pulled out three nice big fish.

"Wheah'd y' catch um?" Papa asked.

"Caught um outta the river," Mr. Jim said proudly, and took a long drag on his "roll-yo'-own." The fat nubby butt was soaked and stained by then and barely hung from the side of his mouth. "We gon' have um fer supper."

"Y' went all the way to the river?" Papa asked.

"Yep. Where y' think I got them flowers?"

"Y' went all the way to the river wid that load?"

"No. I left Juber at the yard 'n walked to the river."

"But that's three 'n er half, fo' miles." Papa was puzzled and so was I. Ben was on the ground laughing again. To him, Mr. Jim was a circus of one—a minstrel show.

"Well, I didn't sell no wood, 'n I couldn' come home 'dout bringin' the li'l woman som'um." Mr. Jim's butt declared itself a nub and dropped out of his mouth, but not before the saliva had put the pitiful thing out.

Mr. Jim didn't break his stride. He simply reached inside his khakis, pulled out a small can of snuff, pulled down on his bottom lip, and emptied half the can of nasty brown powder inside.

"Y' know, M.A., me 'n 'Tata Pie been marr'ed longer'n you 'n Kitty. Good Lord didn't bless us wid no chirren like He did y'all, but we got ourselves. 'N y' know as well as I do—'Tata Pie like yo' Kitty—there ain't er better woman on earth than my wife. That's why I do anythin' fer her—anythin'," Mr. Jim said proudly.

Papa looked off into the distance. Rather than agreeing with Mr. Jim, Papa tried to change the subject. "Errrr . . . yes. Jim, these flowers sho pretty, all right. 'N—'n them fish look mighty good too—mighty good."

"Well, M.A., I been knowin' y' long ernough t' know whut y' fishin' fer. Send Sun down t' the house wid me 'n I'll have my 'Tata Pie fry um up 'n send y' back er mess."

"That would be nice, Jim. I sho ain't turnin' down no offer like that—no sirree," Papa said.

If Papa had seen Miz Marge go directly from her bedroom into the kitchen after being with Mr. Udell, he wouldn't eat any of that fish, or anything else she touched, I thought.

Papa looked at his watch again. He thought Mr. Jim was leaving; instead, he started up another long conversation.

"Y' know, M.A., everbody ain't as lucky as you 'n me. Some fellas marr'ed long as me 'n you done had all kinds er bad luck wid they wives. If they ain't drinkin' or stealin' from im, they sneakin' eround wid ernother man behind his back. Thank God we don't have t' worry erbout nothin' like that." Mr. Jim discharged a sigh of relief.

Ben laughed so hard, he started coughing.

"Er bug musta crawled up that boy's funny box. He ain't stopped laughin' since we been talkin'. I know Juber ain't the best-lookin' mule in the world, but puddy soon his feelings is gon' git hurt."

Ben was so overcome with laughter, he got up and stumbled over to the fence that ran along the side of our house. Papa and I used Ben and Juber as our opportunity to laugh at Mr. Jim as well. "Y' know better'n t' pay any attention t' that fool boy, Jim. Juber's still pullin' that load, ain't he?" Papa said.

"Oh, I know that, M.A. M' Juber heah's got er good long life ahead er him." Papa took out his watch.

"Well, now, M.A., I wuz thinkin' yeahs instead er minets, he-he." Mr. Jim chuckled at his own attempt at making a joke. He must also have gotten the hint that Papa was in a hurry. "I know y' pressed fer time, M.A. Y'all have er good trip 'n say hello t' ol' Thomas 'n E.J. fer me." He untied Juber and moved slowly toward the little hill in back of our house, heading home on Wagon Road West, directly into the fast-setting sun.

"I will, Jim." Papa had been laughing. He stopped laughing as soon as we started to follow Mr. Jim, and a very serious look came over his face. He seemed to be thinking, *You poor fool. How can I help you?*

The two men had been boys together. Through the years they had gotten along like brothers—indeed, better than Papa and Uncle Pet. They had both gone to Broomsey together, a little one-room school Over In The Hills on Warren Road. Neither had gone beyond the third or fourth grade. As young men, they had worked on the railroad together. They had built their houses and had gotten married during the same period.

Mr. Jim's mother was a Bearden, and he had maintained most of their habits and lifestyle—different from ours. His father owned no land—though his mother's family, who lived east of us, owned plenty. Mr. Jim owned only a home-site with a house and a little land left for a garden. Miz Marge canned and stored plenty of fruits and vegetables during summer and fall—more than enough for two people. He also hunted, trapped, and fished.

Bearden men didn't go to church often except for funerals, and that was only to join the good times men had during grave-digging rituals. Their lifestyle was influenced by Indians and Africans. Mr. Jim, living close to Papa, had adopted some of his more progressive ways. Miz Marge had always been privy to a better style of living than she was exhibiting during her Udell days.

Marrying her was a step up into more respectable society for Mr. Jim. I often saw him dressed up in his fifteen- or twenty-year-old blue serge suit, complemented with a black string tie, highly shined high-top buttoned shoes, and a black hard-top Stetson hat, march up the Pike toward Hughes Chapel with Miz Marge locked to his left arm.

Ben and I lagged behind the slow-moving wagon. When we got to the blueberry patch on the right side of the road, we couldn't resist stepping off to the side and filling our mouths with the sweet succulent blue-black delicacies. Meanwhile the wagon had reached the steepest part of the hill. Poor old Juber was catching hell. He was stumbling, falling to his knees, slobbering, moaning, and grunting something awful. Sounded almost human. My heart hurt for him. Mr. Jim must have felt the same as I did. Never once did he yell at Juber or even tap him with the lines. He simply wrapped the reins around the front post, bent down, put his shoulder to the right rear wheel, and helped power the loaded wagon up the hill. The melted hail made it muddy and slippery. The steep ruts didn't help matters either.

"Stkh-h-h. Stkh-h-h. Come on, Juber. We can do it. We got t' do it. Don't stop, Juber. Stay on yo' feet, boy." Mr. Jim and Juber were struggling.

We stopped picking berries and joined them, pushing from the rear. Our little hands and featherweight bodies couldn't offer much, but Juber needed all the help he could get. Ben slipped and fell on his face. When he got up he was covered with red Arkansas mud.

Finally we made it to the top of the hill. Mr. Jim stopped the wagon. He looked back and saw Ben digging the mud out of his nose and eyes. Mr. Jim rushed back.

"You all right, son?" Mr. Jim said, and took out his big red handkerchief. He wiped and wiped until Ben looked much better.

"I'm all right, Mr. Jim," Ben said, embarrassed.

"Y' sho?"

"Yes sir," Ben said.

"Sho do thank you boys fer hepin'. Juber thanks y' too."

Juber was standing there with his head almost to the ground, sweating, slobbering, and panting. I could count every rib in his bony frame, which was going in and out like a pregnant frog. The way Juber looked at that moment, Papa might indeed have timed his demise with his Bulova.

"Yes sir, you boys is all right. If the good Lord had seen fit t' bless me 'n 'Tata Pie wid some boys, I'd want um t' be jist like you two," Mr. Jim said.

"Yes sir," Ben and I said.

"Only thing, I'd have t' take my belt off t' this un fer laughin' at my mule so much." He showed he was only joking by playfully shaking Ben's head and brushing more of the drying mud off his face. Ben looked awkward and annoyed. He wasn't used to being treated like a boy his age, not to mention like a human being.

Mr. Jim walked over to Juber and patted him on his bony back. "Juber, ol' boy, tried t' tell y' t' save that pile y' left down at the Pike. You'd er had mo' gas t' git up that hill." Juber didn't respond one way or the other. It was all he could do to stand on his own feet—dignity be damned at that point.

"Well, Juber, let's take it on in 'n see if we can scare up some supper," Mr. Jim said as he unraveled the lines.

The wagon clucked on a few more feet to Ben's house. Ensconced in his hammock was Udell, with Miz Ella and Miz Orathia attending to his every need.

"How y'all this evenin'?" Mr. Jim tipped his ragged hat.

"We all right. How you, Mr. Jim?" Miz Ella and Miz Orathia spoke.

"Puddy good fer er ol' man. That Udell theah in that hammock?" Mr. Jim asked.

"Yeah. Thas him," Miz Ella and Miz Orathia said.

Udell rose up slowly. "How y' doin', Mr. Jim?"

"Ah, not bad fer er ol' man," Mr. Jim repeated.

"You ain't hardly ol', Mr. Jim. Bet y' kin do anything I kin do—probably mo'," Udell said.

"Well, I don't know erbout that. All I kin do is take care er 'Tata Pie 'n ol' Juber heah. Anybody can see you doin' better'n that. He-he-he-e-e." Mr. Jim thought he had made another funny.

Ben and I stood there looking at each other. It was so ridiculous, it had ceased being funny. Ben simply walked over to the fence shaking his head.

Miz Orathia almost busted a girdle laughing, but Miz Ella kept a stone face. I surmised she must have known or suspected the same thing we knew. I spotted Mr. Durbey looking in that direction. He was sitting quietly rocking back and forth in his old rocker, reading his Bible—his wire-framed spectacles hanging over his nose—and enjoying the hot summer sunset. The top to his long underwear, which he wore in all seasons, was as smutty and begrimed as his greasy blacksmith's hands.

"Well, guess I'd better mosey on home. One mo' li'l quick stop t' make." Mr. Jim had started to move when Udell got up off his hammock and came to the fence.

"Jist er minute, Mr. Jim. Wanna ax y' som'um," Udell said.

"Whut's that, Udell?"

"Y' know, I wuz down at yo' house today drawing some wauter when that hail come up. I really don't like t' 'pose on nobody, 'specially when they been as good t' me as you 'n Miz Marge . . . "

"Well, did she 'vite y' in? Did she treat y' right?" Mr. Jim inquired.

"Yes sir . . . errr . . . she did. She 'vited me in 'n gimme some tea cakes."

"That's my 'Tata Pie, awright. If y' happen t' drop by while she's bakin' y' can git um while they hot. That's when they real good," Mr. Jim said.

"Well, them wuz good ernough, I'll tell y' that," Udell said.

"Well, that's good. I'm glad t' heah it. Er, whut wuz it y' wuz fixin' t' ax me?" Mr. Jim inquired.

"Mr. Andra wuz tellin' m' I could dig my own well, wid all these boys I got eround heah."

I wondered, *Where in the world was he taking that story? Is he crazy?*

"That's right, y' could," Mr. Jim acknowledged.

"Well, now, that's easier said than done. Truth is, I got the manpower, but I need somebody who knows whut they doin'. He tol' me he had his well dug, but you dug yo' own."

"Ever' foot of it. Dug it over twenty yeahs ergo," Mr. Jim said proudly.

"Who helped y'?" Udell asked.

"Me, myself, 'n me," Mr. Jim answered.

"I bet you know yo' stuff, Mr. Jim," Udell poured it on.

"Y' bet yo' bottom dollar I do. Whut I don't know erbout well diggin' ain't wurth knowin'," Mr. Jim boasted.

"Well, me 'n m' boys don't know nothin'. I sho would be much obliged if you'd jist sho us how t' git started." Udell finally got around to his question. I wondered if he had briefed Miz Marge so their stories would match.

"Why, I'd be happy t' hep y', Udell. Y' jist let me know when y' wanna git started."

"How erbout tomorrow?" Udell said.

"I be down fust thing inner mornin'. 'N I'll bring m' stuff wid me," Mr. Jim said as he prepared to leave.

"We be ready fer y'. 'N I sho do wanna thank y', Mr. Jim." Udell strolled slowly back to his hammock and stretched out so he could continue being beautified and pampered by his women.

All Udell needed to do was put a horse collar over Mr. Jim's shoulders and a bit in his mouth, and he would have had a much better mule than Juber.

Mr. Jim tapped Juber and pulled off. I followed. Ben had started to follow me, though he was filthy as a pig, when Udell called. "Ben! Where y' think y' goin'?"

"Down t' Mr. Jim's wid Sun. We gotta bring som'um back fer Mr. Andra."

"Whut's he bringin' back, er hog or som'um? Sun don' need you t' hep him bring nothin' back. Git on in heah 'n git yo'self cleaned up. Nobody want you trampin' in they house lookin' like y' been wallowin' wid the pigs."

Ben stomped and kicked dirt in disgust, but he knew better than to have Udell interrupt his beauty hour in order to whip him. In Udell's words, he would have beat his ass to a final farewell. It was hardly necessary for me to analyze those words to fear them. Ben stubbornly moseyed on back to his shackamore.

Mr. Jim stopped next door and walked over to Mr. Durbey—who pretended to be deeply involved in his Bible. "How y' feelin', Papa?"

"Oh, I'm feelin' puddy good, son. How you feelin'? Hello there, Sun boy."

"Hi, Mr. Durbey," I responded.

Mr. Jim went back to his croker sack, pulled out a brown paper bag, and reached it to Mr. Durbey.

"Whut's this?"

"Li'l som'um I picked up at the drug sto', Papa. Man said it'll hep y'."

"Hep me whut?"

"Hep y' pass yo' wauter, hep y' stay 'wake, giah y' mo' pep, evahthing."

"How he know all er that 'n I ain't nevah seed im? Is he er doctah?" Mr. Durbey inquired.

"Naw sir, Papa, he ain't no doctah."

"Y' 'spect me t' put som'um in m' stomach when I don' know whut 'tis that somebody, who ain't no doctah, who nevah even seed me, sol' y'? Good God, son, whut ails y'?"

"Jist tryin' t' hep y', Papa." Mr. Jim hung his head like a little boy.

"Y' hep m', all right—hep m' on way f'om heah faster'n I'm goin' already."

Mr. Jim had abiding respect for Mr. Durbey. There was a long silence in which Mr. Durbey looked bleary-eyed into the distance, simply thinking. There was much more on his mind than the pills his son-in-law was trying to get him to take. Most grown-ups would have walked off and left the old man to cogitate, but Mr. Jim waited patiently to be dismissed by his father-in-law.

Finally, Mr. Durbey spoke. "Y' take winter wood t' town in the middle er the summer. Y' buy animals that sometimes don't live overnight. Y' waste all that wood by choppin' it ha'f t' death instead er sawin' it like everbody else, 'n now y' volunteerin' y' services t' dig somebody else's well who—"

I thought sure the old man was going to spill the tea cakes. I started coughing uncontrollably. Mr. Jim slapped me on the back. I was chewing on a piece of sugarcane I had in my pocket.

"Y' all right, Sun boy?" Mr. Durbey got up and came over to me. "Whut's the matter? Some er that juice went down the wrong pipe? Let me git y' er drink er wauter," Mr. Durbey started to go inside.

My throat cleared up in a hurry. "Er, thank y', Mr. Durbey, but I don't want no water. Errrr, I be all right—thank you."

"Y' sho, Sun?" Mr. Durbey asked.

"Yes sir, I'm sho." I was very sure I didn't want to drink out of Mr. Durbey's nasty bucket.

"Y' want anything, Papa? 'Tata Pie's gon' fry some fish."

Mr. Durbey was a fearlessly proud man. "Y' didn't listen t' er thing I said t' y', did y'?"

"Yes sir. I listen."

"But y' ain't gon' do er damned thing erbout it, is y'? You mean well, son. 'N I hate t' talk t' y' like this 'cause y' good. That's the problem, y' too damn good. Folks run all over y', take 'vantage er y'. Y' er *stuff-taker* 'n I hate t' see y' take all that stuff."

There was another period of silence. Mr. Durbey's old mangy dog came and stood by his side. He reached down and patted him on the head. The dog lay down beside him and panted. At the side of the house, Mr. Durbey's goat was chewing on a bush. The nanny goat gave out with an *eek-eek-eek*.

Mr. Durbey looked over at the little milk-giver. "Y' wanna be milked? Don't worry. Papa git eround t' y' soon."

"Why don't y' git rid er these animals, Papa? Y' know y' cain't take care of um no mo'."

Mr. Durbey didn't bother to respond. He reached in his pocket, took out a folded piece of paper, and gave it to Mr. Jim. "Giah that t' Marge."

"Whut is it?"

"Jist some Bible passages I found fer her Sunday school class. We had ernother fight . . . 'n . . . well, jist give it t' her."

Mr. Durbey didn't smoke, dip, chew, or drink. Nevertheless, we all could see he had aged and his pace had slowed. He simply leaned back in his rocker and engaged it in motion. His old tattered Bible seemed to shoot up automatically in front of his face.

I had never been inside Mr. Durbey's shack. I had only seen smoke swirling from his stovepipe chimney as if it was giving off an Indian signal. I had glimpsed dim rays from kerosene lamps escaping from two narrow, dingy windows on the sides. The best evidence of vibrant home life was his little patch on the side and behind his shack. He always managed to keep a robust garden with some green in evidence, even after father frost had spread his brown quilt.

Mr. Jim was good to him, especially when he was failing. Mr. Durbey's daughter, Miz Marge, identified only with whatever gave her pleasure. Sweet potatoes and hot biscuits rich with butter. Fried chicken, fresh pork, buffalo, and drum fish from the Arkansas River. Calico, fine-spun cotton, and silk dresses worn with pumps, wide hats, and white gloves, too delicate to be soiled by entering the likes of a greasy shack. She tried to force her standards, especially about order and cleanliness, on her father, but he would have none of it. It was a source of contention between them, and she would often walk out fussing, while he stood in the door fussing back.

It was said that in better days she had been fast-paced by a beau, up and down the Pike in a handsome shiny black buggy drawn by a swift, sleek brown mare with a beautiful white blaze streaked down her forehead and white that came only to socks length on her legs. That young man had long since moved up the country to Dearborn, Michigan, to work in Mr. Henry Ford's plant. Mr. Jim had been a substitute. When the sun shined, she shined. When it rained, there was still happiness in her voice. Where she walked was always clean. She chose only what tasted good—what felt good; if one man couldn't, maybe two men could.

Juber moped slowly up Wagon Road West. Only a few more feet to go. As any teamster knows, an animal, especially a mule, doesn't need driving once he heads for home and the feed trough. Mr. Jim wrapped the lines around the post of the wagon and walked behind. I walked after him. Juber pulled alongside the woodpile and stopped. Home at last. Mr. Jim had me take the croker sack inside while he unharnessed and fed Juber.

I stepped up on the porch and knocked on the screen door. I heard Miz Marge singing inside.

> *I'm gonna live sooo*
> *God can use me*
> *Anywhere, Lord,*
> *Anytime.*
> *I'm gonna live sooo*
> *God can use me*
> *Anywhere, Lord—*

I knocked again—harder.

"That you, Kid?" Kid was her nickname for Mr. Jim.

"It's me, Miz Marge!"

She came to the door humming,

> *I'm gonna live so*
> *God can use me*

When? I wanted to ask her.

"Oh, it's you, Sun."

"Yes ma'am. Mr. Jim had me bring this stuff inside while he takes care er Juber."

"Jist come on in, Sun. Do's unlocked. Now I wonder whut on earth's in that croker sack?"

I simply said, "Yes ma'am," and held on to the sack.

"Well, do y' know, Sun?"

"Yes ma'am," I responded, but made no effort to open the sack, because Mr. Jim hadn't given me permission.

"Well, ain't y' gon' let Miz Marge see?" She held out her hand.

"Yes ma'am," but I kept my hands on the sack and made no move.

After waiting with her hand outstretched, Miz Marge blinked her big brown eyes and said, "When?"

"When Mr. Jim come in, he can show y'," I said.

"Mr. Jim sho got you young-uns trained. I declare. He-he-he-he-e-e." Miz Marge laughed and laughed.

Miz Marge had put on a nice bright-colored dress. She had fixed her hair in a bushy fashion and tied a white band around the sides leaving the top exposed. She had rouged and powdered her round, plush face. She never used lipstick. She didn't need it. I don't know what happened to Mr. Funk, but the house was smelling like a perfume parlor. My mind flashed back to that morning when Ben and I had come in out of the storm and the smell had raced through the parlor when she opened the bedroom door. Everything now was in order. The dining room table was set. A vase of flowers was in the middle, and colored candles were burning brightly. Everything was ready for Mr. Jim, home from town.

We could hear Mr. Jim on the back porch shedding his old work clothes before he came inside.

"That you, Kid?" Miz Marge inquired.

"Better be me," Mr. Jim's voice came back.

"There's er pan er hot wauter, some clean towels, 'n clean clothes in the room fer y'," Miz Marge announced sweetly.

"Thanks, 'Tata Pie," the voice came back equally as pleasant.

Miz Marge returned to laughing at my refusing to let her look in the bag. I wasn't laughing. What I had seen earlier that morning wouldn't let me laugh.

"Kid, whut in the world's in this sack Sun's holdin' on to like his very life depends on it?"

"Why don't y' take er look 'n see?"

Miz Marge walked over to me and held out her hand. "Is it all right now, Sun?"

"Yes ma'am." I reached her the sack.

She oohed and aahhed with joy as she unwrapped and took out each flower. Finally she came to the bottom of the sack. She picked the sack up and tested the weight. "Hmmm, mighty heavy." She stuck her hand back inside and pulled out one of the fish. She screamed, jumped, and dropped the fish on the floor. "Kid! Why in the devil didn't y' tell me these fish wuz in heah?"

"Y' didn't ax me, 'Tata Pie," Mr. Jim said as he walked into the dining room laughing. Miz Marge was still trembling. In big he-man fashion, Mr. Jim, stripped to the waist, walked over to the delicate frightened damsel and cradled her in his shining muscular arms. He kissed her on the forehead and on her big brown eyes. "How's my 'Tata Pie? Did that mean ol' stohm scare my baby?" He made baby talk, to which she gladly responded in kind.

"I wuz scared half outta my wits. Sho do wish you had been heah. Me heah in this big ol' house by—" She glanced over at me standing there.

"Well, t'was er good thing Udell wuz down heah gittin' wauter or y' might er been heah by yo'self, since Papa didn't make it." Mr. Jim cut her off just in time. "Oh, I almost forgot. Heah's er Bible verse he sent y'."

So, Udell hadn't briefed her. Or if he did, she had forgotten. Knowing Miz Marge, I chose to believe the latter.

"We had ernother big fight yestiddy. He put m' out ergin. He's jist tryin' t' make up. You know how Pa is."

Time was passing. Miz Marge and Mr. Jim were making me sick. I wanted him to get on with cleaning the fish so I could get back before Papa came from church. Ordinarily I would never break in while grown-ups were talking. If break in I must, I'd think of a way to do it skillfully. "I hep y' clean the fish, Mr. Jim."

"Awright, Sun. That reminds me. I gotta hop to it so y' can fry some er these up fer M.A. He 'n Pet leavin' fer the convention tonight. Would y' do that fer me, 'Tata Pie?"

"I be happy to. Git er move on, Kid, I already got er fire in the stove."

With that move, I was able to shut Miz Marge's mouth before the question came up as to where we were during the storm. It had been avoided once when Mr. Jim had asked Ben and me directly and Papa walked up. I wasn't worried so much about Miz Marge, and I would have delighted in telling on Udell. I simply didn't want to see anything happen to my good friend Mr. Jim. The way he loved Miz Marge, something like that would shatter his world.

Everything Mr. Durbey had said was true and more, but Mr. Jim chose to walk around ugly facts and retreat back into what was—to him—the happy world of denial, drudgery, and doing things the hard way. I often wondered if he was as dumb as he appeared. Did he believe Udell was a good neighbor instead of the evil, selfish rascal he was? Did he cut Miz Marge off intentionally when she was about to say she was by herself during the storm?

Night had fallen. Night creatures pumped up their sounds. It would be another hour or so before the moon appeared. I was proud that Papa had trusted me to bring him back his fried fish. I could feel the heat from the pan she had put the succulent brown pieces in, even though she had wrapped them for me carefully in a thick towel. Mr. Jim laughed and joked good-naturedly as we marched along toward our house. He danced the light from his flashlight off Mr. Durbey's shack as we passed. The Barrows had gone inside for the night, and only a dim glimmer was seen from the kerosene lamp. As we descended little Blueberry Hill in back of our house, we heard horse hooves and the cry of fast-moving buggy wheels, grinding and splashing the gravel about. As we got closer we saw the buggy light flashing and heard the lively mare snorting. Through the window, I could see Mama holding a kerosene lamp, peeping out, looking for me.

"That's Pet 'n yo' Papa now. We jist in time. Fish still good 'n hot. He kin eat it on the train. You run on inside, y' heah?" Mr. Jim said. "See y' tomorrah."

"Thank you, Mr. Jim," I said.

"You welcome, Sun. Good night now."

11

Harvest was upon us. Sorghum was the first ready crop. Having healed completely after my ordeal with the little rattler, I was ready also. Nearly seven in 1928, I didn't do much, but I thoroughly enjoyed riding on the wagon with Elbert, Hazel, Deloris, and Geneva. Papa hired Reedy Riley to drive the team and help with the sorghum. Mama stayed home, took care of Verleen, her last-born, and helped Papa with the store.

The best way to test the ripeness of sorghum was to cut or break it at the joint, peel and eat it. Everybody engaged in the ritual with delight. Even the dippers and chewers spat their wads and joined the others. Sorghum was like most fruits, vegetables, and nuts: each stalk had a different taste. I peeled joint after joint of the sweet-smelling tall ripe stalks and gorged myself on their pink-red juices, allowing the mellow moisture to trickle down my bare chest and drip on the new brogans Papa had bought me. (Papa made everybody wear shoes after my snakebite.) After the juice was gone, I pretended I was a tobacco chewer and littered the ground around me spitting out the pulp.

Everybody engaged in an assembly-line operation. First Hazel, Deloris, and Geneva—when she could be found—stripped the tall stalks. Reedy and Elbert followed with cane knifes. One swift whisk severed the tassel at the top. They grabbed the stalk at the top, then one more whisk at the bottom and the stalk was ready to pile. A good cutter like Reedy could hold five stalks at a time before cutting and piling across the rows. After the piling, we picked up the stalks, stacked them neatly on the wagon, and hauled them directly to Mr. Walker's mill. We bundled the fodder and saved it to feed the stock.

Smoke was rising in a twirl from the little mill, much like that from a freight engine parked in the roundhouse. As we approached, we could see that the rising twirls were more steam than smoke. A shabby tin roof deflected the escaping white fog like a lid over a boiling pot. Beneath the roof was a long series of big shiny pans resting on a rectangular brick foundation approximately the length and width of a big wagon. Mr. Walker poured the bubbling red raw juice into one end of the grand pan and cooked it slowly with a wood fire built on a grate below.

He stirred the juice with a long-handled metal spatula—bent at one end like a hoe—shoveling it from one pan to the next. The pans were opened at alternate ends. The farmer who was having his sorghum juice cooked was busy feeding the grinding machine with his stalks. Two brown mules powered the machine, trudging endlessly around the hungry grinder, pulling a long wooden tongue that projected from the top of the giant juice maker. The farmer also piled up the pulpy remains of the stalks at the mouth of the grinder and removed them from time to time.

The captain of this total operation was a giant of a man, Mr. Lieb Walker, who obviously enjoyed every minute of his work. He was another one who wore long underwear in all seasons. The September heat plus the steam from the hot pan combined to baptize him in sweat. He wore a clean white apron, hanging almost to the ground, and a tall white cap. His big brogans were splattered with sticky black goo. A towel hung from his waist that was almost in constant motion as he wiped and worked. His singing, however, reminded me of the braying jackass down the Pike, which I had heard often but never seen. I wished the opposite had been true with Mr. Lieb. Mr. Charlie Barrow he was not. Nevertheless, I did enjoy his funny laugh. It sounded as if he was crying. It was weak and hoarse—came from deep inside his diaphragm. It was a direct contradiction to his strong, rugged frame. He started with a long wheeze—then nothing. His face wrinkled, and his eyes closed. Ropelike blood vessels popped out in bold relief on his neck and forehead. Every one of his big white teeth could be seen, and they were indeed all present and accounted for. At long last, he let go with a rather hushed, disappointing squall that started everybody laughing at him. The old man truly gave validity to the joyful season of harvest.

When Mr. Lieb saw us he sounded off, "Genevaaaaaa! There's my putty gal! There's my putty yellow gal right there! Yas sir, there she is right there! Ha-ha-ha-ha-a-a!" He rammed his hand in his sagging pocket and came up with a nasty greasy little leather purse. "Heah's er nickel fer y', Geneva—yas sir. Whut you lookin' at, 'Lois? You git putty like Geneva you git mo'n that. Ha-ha-haa." Mr. Lieb reached Deloris a nickel also. She politely turned it down and told him to give it to me. I had a feeling that she wanted to tell him to put that nickel elsewhere. Mr. Lieb was the only person I ever heard mention color. Actually, Geneva was a ginger color like Mama, not yellow.

"Aw right, 'Lois. Aw right. Heah's my boy Sun! Lookin' jist like his papa—man after my own heart—man I truly love! Ha-ha-ha-haaaaa!" Mr. Lieb walked over to Elbert and Reedy. "Whut y' got heah, Elbert boy? Looks like some good stawks, y'all."

"We hope so, Mr. Lieb," Elbert said.

"You next. Unload right heah. Yo' papa best man I ever knowed. We been friends long is I kin 'member—yas sir. Ha-ha-ha."

Mr. Lieb would start working the middle pans of the cooking juice first.

When the pans near the end were cooking too fast, he quieted them down by adding some of the partly cooked juice from the middle pans. After dipping it with his big ladle for a while, he threw a few orange peels into the middle pans to give the final product flavor. Then he picked up his long-handled spatula, pushed and pulled the cooking juice, and guided it down to the last few pans. The good time came when he ran off four or five gallons of the newly finished molasses into waiting buckets at the end of the vat that projected from the platform. What would sweet-smelling, tasty, hot Walker molasses be without hot buttered bread to go along with it? After all, Lieb Walker's molasses was the best in the county. This was by his own admission. Mr. Lieb reached below to his big grill and pulled out a large fried hoecake. He gave all of us plates with a big piece of bread, and the sopping contest commenced. When we finished, we washed it all down with cool spring water Reedy had gotten from our spring near the sorghum patch. There was absolutely no better place on earth to be at that moment.

Harvest was one happy adventure after the other. It was graduation day, with a handshake for all those who had challenged the soil and won. It was the surprise, and the mixture of fear and joy, when a bevy of quail fluttered into the air with one great swoop after I came too close with my brogans. It was the late watermelon that served as a bonus to any harvester while gathering corn or picking cotton. How it lay there quietly camouflaged between the furrows with foggy dew blistered on its green. I busted it immediately! And ripped out its heart! And devoured it quickly! Before anybody could get there.

The sweet potato patch was next after the molasses had been sopped, sung over, and bucketed for the winter. Reedy cheerfully responded once more. It was obvious to me that he was far more interested in being near Deloris than he was in cutting cane and digging sweet potatoes. He hung around long after the work was finished, abusing the language and stifling his natural inclination to say what he really wanted.

I loved riding on top of a load of potatoes. What on earth would Papa do with load after load of sweet potatoes? Little did I realize that I would spend the rest of the winter—indeed, many years to come, finding out. Papa selected a space in our huge barn, and we cleared it well. We hauled in dirt, leaves, and pine needles, added straw, and prepared a large round bed. Then we spread the first layer of potatoes on top. Another layer of straw, pine needles, and leaves with a layer of dirt mixed in. As the process continued, the pile began to take on the shape of a cone. Papa, directing the project, installed a square wooden vent in the middle before the stack was too high. After we finished the cone, we spread a final layer of dirt—mostly red Arkansas clay—on top and patted it to a nice smooth finish. Often we added turnips and Irish potatoes for safekeeping.

We baked sweet potatoes in the oven, on the open hearth of our wood-burning stove, in the open fire while standing around warming our hands or cutting wood, in barbecue pits dug in the ground, in the cotton fields, and around wood piles. We also baked them in the fire beneath big steel pots during hog-killing time, in fires around sawmills, on Mr. Lieb's grate at his molasses-making plant, in the smokehouse where we cured meat, and in the fire of the bellows of Mr. Durbey's blacksmith shop.

Not only did we bake, we boiled, fried, stewed, mashed, grated, marinated, cobblerized, candied, and piefied every sweet potato in sight before the next season arrived.

Nearing my seventh birthday, I had only heard of Dr. George Washington Carver. Nevertheless, I guessed that he must have been the only person in the world who knew more about the sweet potato than our family.

It took skill and practice to prepare many of those dishes, but anybody could bake—and often did. When Papa took me along with him and Elbert, we passed over the railroad tracks. Camped along the side were hobos tending their sweet potatoes among the hot coals. Passing over Bartholomew Bridge, we spied a tramp beneath raking his baked sweet potato out of red sparkling embers. When we finally drove up to our house, I knew we would have sweet potatoes for supper in one form or another. Fortunately for me, I was born with a high sweet potato tolerance. I never tired of the yummy yams, no matter how often or in what form they were served.

Peanuts, hickory nuts, walnuts, and hazelnuts rounded out our harvest for the season. We often plowed up peanuts and threw them on top of a load of sweet potatoes. The tops of our barn and chicken house, made green with their cover, were transformed to a rusty brown within two days. It gave me great pleasure to climb up on either building, rake down two or three bunches, gorge myself on the tasty brown peas, and still have room left for supper.

Hickory nuts, walnuts, and scaly bobs (another variety of hickory nut) fatted the harvest with their offerings from the trees, as did the roots, stalks, and plants that preceded them. Grown-ups seldom bothered with hickory nuts or walnuts. Gathering them was considered "the chirren's" domain. And gather them we did. Older children would use croker sacks. We younger ones used buckets. I was amazed at the different sizes and kinds of hickory nuts and scaly bobs. Those gathered from the flat land, like Uncle Pet's, were big and round. Others were big and long. Those gathered from hilly country were smaller but just as sweet—ofttimes sweeter—with a different taste.

Ben gathered nuts with me in the evenings and on Saturdays. Mr. Udell had everybody in the fields during the day. It was the first few weeks of the cotton-picking season and school. Papa allowed that some children started late. However, when Papa heard Udell's comment, "We gotta make as much money as we can befo' Chrismas," he contacted Mr. Joe Bearden, the care-taker, and he brought Miz Forester, the county agent, out of Pine Ridge to investigate.

Miz Forester was a strikingly pretty little black woman. She was firm. Some thought she possessed a mean streak. She totally disarmed opponents and forced would-be suitors to settle for a conversation of respect rather than dalliance.

"What county did you say you came from, Mr. Barrow?" Miz Forester was busy writing, standing beside her shiny black Chevy.

"Cleveland. Erbout fifteen miles down the Pike." Udell was talking to Miz Forester over the fence in front of his Barrowtown shackamore. It was a Sunday afternoon, so all the Barrows were present and listening to every word that came from that educated city woman's mouth.

"All these your children, Mr. Barrow?"

"These is all I claim. You got any, Miz Foster?"

"The name is Forester. And whether I have any or not is quite beside the point." She didn't bother to raise her head. She kept writing. "Did they attend school in Cleveland County, Mr. Barrow?"

"Well . . . no, er, I mean yes."

"Well, which is it, Mr. Barrow?" She looked up quizzically from her paper.

"Well, I put it like this. They don't go doin' cotton-pickin' 'n cotton-chop-pin' time. We gotta live, miz city woman, we gotta live."

"We all have to live, Mr. Barrow." Miz Forester looked Udell in the eye. "It's a matter of how well."

"You sayin' I don't live good?"

"I'm not here to—"

"Oh, I know this heah house ain't like them you folks got up town, wid yo' 'lectik lights 'n all." Udell held out his manicured hands. "You don't see no scars 'n scratches on my hands, do y'?"

"Nice hands, Mr. Barrow. Especially for someone living out here."

"Thank y'." A big smile crept over Udell's face, too soon.

"Can you write with them?" Her big brown eyes flashed directly into Udell's with a touch of scorn and condemnation.

"Whut's writin' got t' do wid it?" Peeved and upset, Udell countered as best he could. "Tha's the trouble wid you edecated folks, y' thank y' got mo' sense 'n everbody else. Y'all got er heep er book learnin' 'n all, but I bet I beat y' when it come t' mother wit. Tha's right, plain ol' evahday motherwit. Tha's whut it take t' git erlong in this worl', mother wit. Y' heah me? Plain ol' mother wit."

"I'm inclined to agree with you, Mr. Barrow—to a point—"

"'N that is—" Udell wasn't about to get taken in as he had before. He waited this time to see what that educated woman had to say.

"If you mean common sense when you speak of mother wit, I agree that there's no substitute for it. I wholeheartedly disagree if you're suggesting that education is not needed to go along with your common sense." Miz Forester put her pencil back into her bag and put one hand on her hip. "Take yourself, for example, Mr. Barrow. I bet you've got a lot of that plain old everyday mother wit that you don't even use."

"Whut y' talkin' erbout, woman?"

"I'm talking about you using some of that mother wit to think about your children's schooling a little more and less about yourself."

"Jist er minit, lady. Jist er minit. Who in the hell do you think you is coming out heah tryin' t' tell me whut t' do wid my chillens?"

Miz Forester took out her pad again, wrote a quick note, and gave it to Udell. "Take this, Mr. Barrow. I realize you can't read it, but Mr. Hughes can. I am the Home Coordinator for Jefferson County. I will expect all of your children to register and be vaccinated at Tilson School tomorrow morning. If you don't know what to do, just follow the Hugheses." She picked up her long skirt and carefully positioned herself behind the steering wheel of her Chevy.

Mr. Udell walked to the side of her car. "Y' know, you er mighty puddy woman t' be so mean. Let me see y' smile—jist once. I bet t'would really be som'um."

Mr. Udell thought of himself as a tamer and lover of women—all women. Even after a heated confrontation with Miz Forester, he had the temerity to try sweet-talking her the minute he was out of hearing distance of Miz Orathia and Miz Ella.

"Come on now, gimme that smile—jist one li'l ol'—"

"Get one of your wives to smile at you, Mr. Barrow. Frankly, I feel very sad when I look at you, and especially when I hear you talk. Please have your children there tomorrow morning. I will personally be there to check." Miz Forester started her Chevy up and drove down the hill on Wagon Road West. Ben and I trailed along behind her to the Pike. She turned left and headed slowly toward Pine Ridge as we waved her good-bye.

Cotton-picking time stirred the blood like nothing else except revival and Christmas. Prices were good. The year 1928 was bountiful, and planters competed with each other for pickers—any pickers. Strapping champion five-hundred-pound-per-day pickers could take home $5 or $6 a day. At $1 per one hundred pounds, even six- and seven-year-olds could make 75 cents to $1 per day. Nobody wanted to see their white gold rot in the field.

Pickers were mothers with babes in arms, city folks who didn't want to be seen riding in a crowded truck full of country folks, both high school and college students, levee workers out of a job, even an occasional jackleg preacher who didn't have a church to take care of him. All became pickers to make money for Christmas. Generally speaking, everybody went when the truck came.

The truly big planters were down on the delta near the Arkansas River. They were almost all white and owned 1000 or more acres. The smaller white farmers with 100 to 200 acres were south of us down in Cleveland County. Many of those farms were poorer than ours. They were farther away from the river—Up In The Hills.

People and animals took on the character of the land. The land was red clay, void of the soil and soul needed for good crops. In late summer, the creeks trickled and minnows died in the ponds. On the few patches near the creeks, the cotton grew high but bore few bolls. Wandering over the long red winding rows, the pickers, with their long stained white sacks dragging, flanked like wild geese, marched steadily. The people and the animals grew out of the soil. The people, like the bony red mules, were formed from the dead soil that God must have cursed, with its scroungy pines and occasional oak that had died and gone to oak heaven, leaving only a rotted gray monument pointing its finger upward like a drowning man. The rednecked woodpecker passed hot summer days boring a hole to a sordid future.

Yes, the people and the animals sprang up from the land—the red clay with rocks on top. They owned the land, but more important, the land owned them. The white people grew lean and long, with stringy, silky yellow manes like tasseling corn. Dark brown snuff and tobacco juice trickled from the corners of their thin lips, contrasting with their dirty pale skins, and made them look as if they had suffered internal injuries that caused blood to ooze from their mouths. Their smell was downright nauseating and dangerous—a sweet-nasty funk—that sneaked up and surprised you. I noticed it especially when wrestling with one of the young boys. It was quite different from our bold, abrasive fumigating knockout variety. It was the difference between being slowly gassed to death or being killed instantly by a bomb. Neither one was meant to bless.

Those hill people were not exactly white trash; they were only trashed by dint of their wedlock to a crust of unforgiving turf that provided them with no opportunity to advance or escape but only to decay like the dead oak and be buried deep in red, rocky Arkansas clay. It seemed to make little difference to them that they were living on the very edge of El Dorado, one of the richest oil fields in the Southwest.

Their voices squeaked. Their drawl measured in tempo and tone was high-sounding over the barren hills. They were the hillbillies, the rednecks, the peckerwoods, the watermelon growers, the dregs of the cotton growers who couldn't afford plantations and river bottomland. They were some of Papa's customers. They were a large part of Mr. Durbey's livelihood, for they had many lean brown and red mules to shoe, plowblades to sharpen, singletrees to fit, and wagon wheels to keep rolling. Generally, I never saw them display arrogance or willful disrespect. Their behavior was modest. Indeed, they had much to be modest about.

Those farmers were no strangers to the Barrows who grew up in their midst. Ma and Pa Barrow still lived among them. The farmers who were able to hire the Barrows picked them up while the early morning dew was weeping on the grass and the cotton bolls. Pickers welcomed the extra weight gained from the moisture. Chevy trucks roared up and down the Pike from early morning until night, packed with cotton or people. It was almost like the big flood the year before when the levee broke and all able-bodied men and boys, Elbert included, were called into action. Even Udell went with the trucks to conduct the family Barrow's picking during this most critical time. After all, they had to depend almost exclusively on wages to survive.

They packed their lunches in buckets and baskets. The sordid fare consisted of cold gravy, soggy biscuits, soggy cornbread, and black-eyed peas. If they were lucky, baked sweet potatoes and warm buttermilk were brought along for Udell. Stewed tomato dumplings were frequently the dessert. It puzzled me why most people who packed those lunches were never able to keep ants out of their food—especially their stewed tomato dumplings—which in my opinion weren't fit for humans or insects to eat.

We picked our few acres of cotton in a few days. I never knew why Papa even bothered. I think it was more out of respect for tradition, being near the cotton belt, than it was for a cash crop. At his best, Papa was a merchant and a broker, especially with cotton. To me it was all fun. Cotton was warm, soft, quiet, and friendly. Cotton was especially made for lovers. What country boy didn't dream of wrestling a young girl onto the top of his sack between cotton rows, the big sky smiling above, but hidden by tall stalks and hopefully from her father. The next best wish was to corner the lass in a covered wagon full of the soft white stuff, rocking and clucking its way to someplace far away—the farther, the better. The absolute coziest hideaway, the farmer's hotel, was the little cotton pen. That is a small building located at strategic points on the farm for storing and weighing the valuable crop.

Harvest was quilting time. It was caning time. It was a time when all living creatures ate well and lived at the top of life's great offerings. It was a time for buying new clothes and new shoes. Some bought new cars—discarded their old Model Ts for self-starting Fords and Chevys. It was a time when the wild, longing cry and winged beauty of geese flying south filled my frame with mysterious, joyful wondering. It was reading, spelling, and arithmetic time. It was teaching and learning time. It was white chalk and blackboard time. It was schoolbell-ringing time. It was "Arkansas, Arkansas, Is the Name Dear," then "Lift Every Voice and Sing" time. It was hide-and-go-seek, baseball, and puzzle time. It was the clean fresh fragrance of newly picked cotton, and Papa's big money time. It was hickory nut, walnut, peanut, and hazelnut time. It was a time when grays and browns and greens and reds and yellows and azures came together in one big celebration of nature's great gifts. It was hog-killing time and time for crackling bread. It was the sweet smell of winter hay, honey gathering, and cornshuckin' time.

12

They had removed the big potbellied stove that normally sat in the middle of the long room, to make space for the temporary stage now awash with glaring lights. They draped the blackboard, the side windows, and two windows at the north end with a black backdrop. They replaced the classroom desks and seats with long hard benches.

A group of men were behind the stage on the left. They dressed in loud banana-yellow suits, which they complemented with black shirts and ties, white shoes, and black socks. One man had a double-tubed horn that was looped and U-shaped at both ends, but one tube, which was larger, terminated with a big round flared mouth, and the other, which was inserted into the larger, terminated with a very small flare. With the long, ring-adorned fingers of his right hand, the man was sliding the smaller shining tube in and out of the other and dipping all the way to the floor, then up to the ceiling, up and down like the long-necked crane I had seen drinking from the bayou. A loud, blaring sound came from the big flared mouth. It sounded and looked exactly like a horn I had seen in Pine Ridge where Papa had taken us to watch a parade. Other men were blowing horns of different shapes and sizes. It seemed that they were trying to see who could blow the loudest. They took turns squeezing in between each other and showing what they could do.

The piano player was dressed in a white suit, with matching accessories. He topped it all off with a black derby tipped to one side. He also sported a long black handkerchief that hung carelessly from his upper coat pocket beside a big red rose pinned to his lapel. The biggest, longest black-brown cigar I had ever seen stuck straight out from the corner of his mouth like a stovepipe from the side of a gabled house. He was all reared back, grinning and banging that piano like a girl fighting.

The one beating the drums was the man I liked most, but he was doing it all wrong. In the first place, he should have been marching like the man I saw on Main Street in Pine Ridge. In addition to his big drum, he had two small drums on the sides and two large-size biscuit pans on a spindle banging against each other. He even had a cowbell among all that junk. He *was* busy. He didn't have time to wipe the sweat from his eyes and face. When it trickled down the side of his mouth, he simply licked it off with his long pink tongue and never missed a beat.

Five pretty, long-legged girls with cropped slicked hair and short tight-fitting dresses filed onstage from behind the curtains. The crowd went wild. Papa twitched his mouth—a habit when he was about to smile or laugh. From the expression on his face when he looked at me, however, I could tell he was concerned and not too happy about bringing me.

The girls did a little dance to the music. One of them walked out in front of the others and started to sing:

> Just Molly 'n me,
> 'N baby makes three,
> We're happy in my blue heaven . . .

Papa started to squirm and twist in his seat. I thought it was chilly, but he took out his big handkerchief and mopped his sweating face.

After she finished the song, the men struck up a lively tune and the girls started to do some kind of dance that required them to turn around and stick their bottoms out at the audience. I heard someone in the audience yell, "Black Bottom!"

That proved to be too much for Papa. After all, he was a deacon in the church and superintendent of the Sunday school. Sitting up front next to the stage with his family watching a bunch of sinful city girls doing the Black Bottom, and God knows what else was coming, would surely get him in trouble with The Faithful: "As a member of the school board, he shoulda been closin' that mess down." He grabbed his hat and cane and was proceeding to rush us out of that sin den when a ragged, face-painted figure blocked us by running up the aisle toward us on his way to the stage. He was chased by an equally ragged, round-faced fat woman with a rolling pin in her hand. Her hair was braided, and she wore an apron wrapped around her tubby waist.

We all tugged at Papa's sleeves to let us see their act before he took us home. After all, Deloris, Hazel, and Elbert had seen minstrel acts at the circus in Pine Ridge. I had heard them talking about it. In Papa's eyes, the clowns must have been different from the show we had been watching. Since it was impossible to squeeze through the crowd, and we were all begging to stay, he gave in and took us back to our seats.

Rushing up the aisle, the clown was yelling, "Help! Helllllp! Don't let that woman take my life! Pleeeeeeeeease! Don't let that woman take my life!" Onstage, he pulled out a *Life* magazine and opened it. "I wouldn' mind it so much, but I ain't read it m'self yet."

The crowd roared. Papa only chuckled.

"All right, y' kin have yo' stupid *Life*, it ain't wurth nothin' no-how." The fat woman twirled the rolling pin in her hands. "How come, atter all the time we been together, y' ain't nevah tol' me how come they call y' How Come, How Come?"

"How come, atter all the time we been together, y' ain't nevah axed me, Sum Flower?"

"That's *Sunflower*, How Come."

"Sunflower? I wuz right the first time 'cause, honey, you is Summmmmm Flower!" The clown gestured at Sunflower's size with his arms and laughed at his own attempt at wit. He flipped the ashes from his big long brown cigar on the stage floor. "But you wanna know how come they call me How Come?"

"Yes, how come, How Come?" Sunflower put her hands on her hips.

"Well, if y' must know, when I wuz born, my mama axed my papa whut t' name me. She tol' me my papa stood there, frozen, lookin' down at me. She said he jist started shaking his head and saying, 'How come? How come? How commmmme?'"

"And yo' mama said?" Sunflower laughingly coaxed him.

"'How come you wanna name the baby How Come?' 'N my papa said, 'Lorrrrd, whut fuah?'"

"And yo' mama said?"

"My mama said, 'Whut Fuah? Is that a middle name?'"

Sunflower bent over laughing. "Whut Fuah? Whut did yo' papa say then? 'N whut fuah?"

"My papa said, 'Lawd, how come 'n whut fuah you do this to me?'"

"Lawd hah mercy. I guess yo' mama wuz wonderin' when them names would end."

"She wuz. My mama said my name wuz turnin' out to be longer than her labor pains. Atter all that, my papa wanted to know whether I wuz er girl or er boy, so he bent over me to find out 'n I peed in his face. That took care er that question."

Sunflower and How Come put on quite a show. They told jokes, Sunflower hit How Come over the head with her fake rolling pin, they did their own version of the Black Bottom, the Charleston, and tap dancing. Finally, How Come ended the show by singing "Unka Bud":

> Unka Bud got this, Unka Bud got that,
> Unka Bud got er . . . arm like er baseball bat,
> Unka Bud—Unka Bud—Unka Bud, doggone it, Unka Bud.
> Unka Bud got cattle ain't never been sick,
> Unka Bud got cotton ain't never been picked,
> Unka Bud—Unka Bud—Unka Bud, doggone't, Unka Bud.
> Unka Bud got corn ain't nevah been shucked,
> Unka Bud got women ain't nevah been . . . hugged,
> Unka Bud—Unka Bud—Unka Bud, doggone it, Unka Bud.

Papa was laughing right along with us as we filed out of the building. In the crowd, I saw the Beardens, the Beards, the Scotts, the Bradleys, the Thomases, the Hickses, the Harrises, the Stewards, the Martins, the Rileys, the Coopers, the Averys, the Olivers, the Davises, the Leddings, the Youngs, the Tilsons (the family that donated the land for the school many years ago), the Tigginses, and the Barrows. Except for the Barrows, all of those people were from the major families who were also members of Hughes Chapel. I thought, *They are all here watching the same show. This hardly puts them in a position to inform on Papa.* Outside, the crowd was overflowing. They were complaining and asking questions about what went on inside.

Tilson, like all country schools in that area, was a long whitewashed one-room building surrounded by tall oaks, pines, and gums. It was within whistling distance of Hughes Chapel, and the most prominent of the five schools within walking distance.

A few new 1928 Fords, a year old, and Chevys and some older T-models were scattered among the horses and buggies, surreys, and wagon teams. There were a few hardy souls who rode saddle horses from far Over In The Hills, down in Cleveland County, and Mr. Thigpen drove his family in a wagon all the way from the bayou country south of us. There were also a small group of Indian and Harley-Davidson motorcycle riders, who made more noise than that quiet community had ever heard except for the Barnards' jackass down the Pike.

In spite of the gas and smoke from the machines, the night air smelled of clean cut hay in the fields nearby, of gum sap and ripe persimmons high up dangling from the limbs, of hazelnut and oak smoke twirling from the neighbors' chimneys nearby, of Chinaberries and hollyhock. Of holly berries and mistletoe. Of new leather and brown cigars. Of Bull Durham and roll-your-owns. Of cheap powder and homemade wine. Of Garret snuff and moonshine. The night air was fresh and chilly but inviting. Lightning bugs jostled for positions to display their radiance among the bushes and trees. A big glowing cotton moon—made just for us—shed its bright light on our merry acre at Tilson. It was a night of magic.

Miz Harmond was a kind, gentle, soft-spoken, good-looking teacher from Pine Ridge, who lived at our house during the week and went home every Friday evening. She returned to us on Monday evenings directly from a day at Tilson.

My lessons were always in order—as were my sisters' and Elbert's—mainly because Miz Harmond was always available. Students would complain, "Shucks, if I had the teacher stayin' at my house, I'd do good too." I thoroughly enjoyed marching to the head of the class after some big dumb country boy or girl had misspelled some simple word that was easy for me.

Not only were students embarrassed by not knowing their lessons, they had to suffer the humiliation of being whipped for not knowing on top of it. With Miz Harmond, it was usually three light taps in the palm of the hand for girls and a little heavier on the behind for boys. Most boys wised up and wore the thickest padding they could find in their pants.

I was never whipped for not knowing my lesson. I just couldn't resist the temptation of tying girls to their seats or pinning notes to their backs. When I couldn't get to their backs, I'd use their braids. If a girl had little enough sense to go to sleep in class, she was a prime candidate to wind up falling out in the aisle when she tried to walk after I had tied her shoestrings together. The old trick of pulling the seat from under a classmate when he was fixing to sit down—I never tried it on girls—was one of my favorites, but it was sure to get me ten licks from Miz Harmond if she caught me. For the girls, I had a different menu, which included some of the tricks I mentioned, plus my army of frogs, beetles, crawdads, worms, locusts, horseflies, thousand-legs, devil-horses, granddads (devil-horses and granddads are insects), and green rubber snakes. Though they lived with these creatures as I did, I never failed to get a scream simply by presenting one of my friends to any girl.

Mama always rose early every morning and baked hot biscuits. She added gravy, rice, ham, eggs, and standards like molasses, milk, and butter to make breakfast complete. Mama baked sweet potatoes along with the biscuits.

She packed our lunch in tin buckets. Buttered biscuits, ham, sweet potatoes, and buttermilk were sure to go with us to Tilson. Many times she added pear preserves, cake, pie, late apples, or big delicious pears. Miz Harmond ate with us at breakfast and supper, but Mama packed her lunch separately. She was a very light eater but enjoyed coffee in the morning. Children were forbidden to drink coffee or tea. Mama and Papa drank coffee only occasionally to settle their stomachs.

Hazel or Deloris served lunch to all of us Hughes children before the sporting games started. We gobbled it down in a hurry, to save time. My favorite sport was wrestling. I discovered my abilities soon after turning seven. The trick was speed and getting the jump on my opponent, the same as in racing and fistfighting. I was not as rugged and strongly built as many of my opponents. I longed for their big powerful wrists and hambone fists. What I had was a wiry frame, skinny legs and wrists, and a big wish. Nevertheless, many of my opponents hit the dirt behind my swift footwork and shifty movements. I threw them over my head, over my shoulder, and from my side. I had a leg movement that tripped them up and flattened them on the ground while I remained standing.

Foot racing was another sport in which I excelled. The big game was baseball, but younger boys seldom had a chance to use the main field.

Sometimes the fistfights were more fun to watch than the games. Some of the Barrows started trouble with many kids who had never fought before. We had plenty of arguments but few bloody fights at Tilson.

A. D. Barrow, about fifteen and the oldest son, had a battling mind. He even fought girls, who were the only people he could beat in a fair fight. He seldom smiled. He had a swagger in his walk that said "I'm bad." He definitely "went for bad." He was short and slightly built. The Barrows had a gang mentality. If one person got in a scrap with a Barrow brother or sister, the whole Barrow family would jump that one. A.D.'s younger brother Carl also went for bad. He was big and strong and stupid. People in our community had a different code. We knew it as "one on one." The Bearden family outnumbered the Barrows by two to one at Tilson. The Barrows tried the gang activity they were used to only once. When A.D. started a fight with Larry Scott and called for big Carl to help him, Carl was immediately surrounded by Beardens, even though Larry wasn't kin.

Larry was a handsome fourteen-year-old boy. His sisters were also pretty. They had just moved to the community from the bayou country. Larry had an awful speech problem—the worst I had ever heard. In trying to get out a word, he would contort his whole body and almost struggle to the ground. His stuttering made it impossible for him to keep up in class. We all felt sorry for him—all except A.D., Carl, and some of the Barrows.

A.D. made fun of Larry during one of the noontime ball games. When Larry was getting the best of the fight, A.D. grabbed a bat and started swinging it at Larry's head. A glancing blow struck Larry's head. He brushed it off and kept coming. Blood was coming from Larry's nose. He had already busted A.D.'s lip with his fists and closed one of his eyes, which was puffed out like a fresh-baked doughnut. Some of the boys tried to hold Larry. I thought that was crazy, since A.D. was the one swinging the bat. Larry was strong; he threw the boys off and kept coming. He couldn't talk and was bleeding but kept advancing toward his man. A.D. kept swinging the bat and backing up. He was clearly afraid of Larry. Finally, someone came back with Miz Harmond.

"Larry!" she yelled. Larry kept coming; A.D. kept swinging and backing up. "A.D.! Put that bat down!"

"Don't ya'll heah Miz Harmond talkin' to y'!" Elbert yelled, and walked over to Larry.

Larry was in a trance and kept coming. A.D. kept swinging and backing up.

Miz Harmond did a dangerous thing. She stepped between them. Elbert stepped beside her. Other kids did the same. Finally, Larry started to smile. He couldn't go through the crowd, so he stopped charging. Elbert went over and took the bat from A.D. and gave it to one of the players. The bloodiest fight at Tilson was over.

The next day, pretty Miz Forester rolled up in her Chevy. Papa and Mr. Joe

Bearden, the caretaker, had got their heads together and summoned her from Pine Ridge again. They were there to meet her when she arrived. Miz Harmond soon joined them. They stood around the car and talked for a few minutes. Miz Forester took out her little book, wrote something on a piece of paper, and gave it to Miz Harmond. Mr. Joe, Papa, and Miz Harmond signed it. Miz Forester shook hands, got in her car, and drove away. That same day, A.D. and Larry were expelled until after Christmas.

Coming home from Tilson was great fun for my buddy Ben and me. We climbed trees to shake limbs for ripe sweet persimmons. On our way through the break near Bayou Bartholomew, we gathered hickory nuts among the dry brown leaves. We shook vines, and the last of the sweet blue-black muscadines tumbled off our heads to the ground. Along the side fences we gathered hazelnuts that had dried and were waiting for our little hands. When we reached Bartholomew, we hunted for smooth, flat rocks, washed to the surface after untold years of being lodged somewhere in the red Arkansas crust. We stooped low and skated those rocks on top of the clear-running shining creek waters as far as we could see.

Expelling A.D. was like throwing Brer Rabbit into the briar patch. He didn't like school anyway. Now he was completely free to roam the countryside, terrorize the neighbors, drink moonshine, sing the blues at all hours of the night, and "git some pussy." Christmas came early for him. He never knew the words to the songs, which meant nothing to him. He made up his own words as he swaggered along with his shirttail out, shoes untied, ragged pants and coat, and that ever-present bottle in his hand. He yelled at the top of his voice:

> *I have had my fun!*
> *If I don't git well noooo mo'!*
> *I said, I had my fun!*
> *If I don't git well noooo mo'!*
> *Don't give er dammed if I don't git nothin' fer Christmus*
> *'N if I don't git well noooo mo'!*

I could hear Papa complaining in the next room. "I'd like to put er muzzle on that fool boy. He's got no respect fer other people—none what-so-ever."

Christmas was indeed in the air. Miz Harmond formed groups and cleaned up the school inside and out. The sexton, old Mr. Tilson, did the general cleaning and supplied the wood for both the church and the school. I loved those details. It was all fun to me. We went into the woods, cut branches from the brush, tied them together, and made brooms to sweep the yard. The building was on blocks; the older boys went underneath and did a thorough cleaning job. We decorated the inside from top to bottom and capped it off with a big tall tree that the older boys had cut and dragged out of the woods in back of the school.

Everything was ready for the Christmas play. Ben, of all people, was dressed as an angel. I told him he still looked like a devil to me. He put up his dukes and was ready to fight right there at the manger. Stupid Carl was one of the wise men from the East, alongside Elbert who was another one. Hazel was one of the attendants at the end. Deloris was the mother Mary. Vera Nellie Bearden, the Scott sisters, and I were shepherds. Miz Harmond had parts for everybody. We exchanged gifts with her and sang "Silent Night," "Holy Child of Bethlehem," "O Christmas Tree," "Jingle Bells," and "The Twelve Days of Christmas."

13

Christmas of 1928 conjured up all the imagination and questions a young boy's mind could conceive. The preparation, the anticipation, the anxiety filled my chest almost to the bursting point. I never went to town and sat on any white man's knee. That simply wasn't plausible in Arkansas in 1928. But I had seen pictures of reindeer pulling a sleigh loaded with wrapped boxes and toys of every description. They were driven by a potbellied, long-haired, bearded, red-faced white man. I wondered how on earth could that big fat man squeeze his way down our small chimney—especially at his age. The man I saw in the picture could barely get through our barn doors. In fact, I didn't think he could get up on top of our roof, especially with all those reindeer and their long horns, plus all that junk he had on that little sleigh, but that's what I was told.

I was also told that after he had completed his appointment at one house, he gave a couple of "Ho-Ho"s, climbed back out the chimney, and flew to the next home. I thought, *Why climb back out the chimney?* It made more sense to me for him to go out the door while he was already down there, especially since he was lugging all that stuff. And how could he deliver all those presents according to each person's request? Mama said that Santa didn't bring anything to boys and girls who doubted him, so I kept quiet, but I had a real problem with the many things the person we called Santa Claus was supposed to be able to do.

"Do Santa Claus go to every house of all the chirren in the whole wide world?"

"Every house," Mama said. "That is, if the chirren been good."

"Do Santa Claus go to everbody's house on Christmus Eve night?"

"Every house" was Mama's standard response.

"Do Santa Claus know all the boys and girls whose house he goes to?"

"All the ones who've been good."

"Do Santa Claus know the ones who been bad too?"

"Every one. He don't leave them nothin'. Not a thing," Mama responded. "Nothin' but er empty stockin'."

"Have I been good, Mama?"

"Well, pretty good. You'd be er lot better if y' stayed away from Ben 'n them Udells."

"Yes ma'am."

We washed our stockings and hung them on the walls in our dormitory room. I put my name on my stocking to make sure Santa wouldn't make a mistake.

The hushed darkness, the creeping silence, the long wait before we were ordered to bed, the long cotton gown that snugly wrapped me about, the chill in the room away from the fire, the toes of bare feet gripping the floor, the itching ears and running nose, the feel of Mama's warm hand tucking me in were my tinglings the night the mysterious man was to steal into my room with toys of joy.

Unable to fall asleep, I tossed and turned and peeped, hoping to get a glimpse of the satisfier, the strange giver who looked so different from Papa. I closed my eyes and imagined I saw him. I hovered between asleep and awake. In that state, I glimpsed a tall lean figure, dressed in a Santa Claus suit and wearing a red stocking cap on his head. His unbuttoned suit was hanging off his shoulders as if he threw it on temporarily. His shoes were run over and unlaced. When he looked over his shoulder I saw his glasses hanging over his nose. He checked every note carefully. There was no big wide black belt, no long flowing white beard, or big high black boots. When the figure turned his back, I could see the tailgate in the rear of his union suit flapped open and hanging loose.

Seeing that, I awoke. The tall figure was stuffing our stockings with all manner of good things. I watched very carefully but dared not disturb him. I was especially partial to that giver because, in my heart, I had suspected and wanted him to be the tall slender figure I first saw getting out of a surrey four years before. The same giver who wiped up a puddle of water on the floor with the seat of Elbert's pants. The same giver who took me to the circus in Pine Ridge. The same giver who took me to old Mr. Grey's to buy his cotton remedy. The giver who walked fast with a cane, wrote clearly with either hand, sold sugar and flour, Nehi drinks, and molasses Stage Planks. Who talked plain and was warm with the gift of laughter. Who with his ruling fingers wrote the script for my life. Yes, I wanted to see the giver who took care of me and gave me half my life. I dozed again, but before I could gain clarity, the thick sticky salve of sleep weighed heavy on my eyelids, and I could no longer struggle and squint to keep them open.

Soon roosters were crowing. Ducks, chickens, guineas, geese, mules and horses, cows and hogs, sounding the alarm, woke up the sun for feeding time. I peeped out the window. Blackbirds darkened the sky as they flew from one barren tree to another. Frosty freckles glistened on dead grass, winter wood, and ax handles. I hopped up like a rabbit and headed straight for my stocking hanging on the wall.

Sure enough, the tall slender Santa had filled it to overflowing with a long striped peppermint stick, all kinds of assorted hard candies, big delicious Washington apples and California navel oranges—both a winter treat in Arkansas, mixed nuts including what were called niggertoes, or Brazil nuts. There was a red wagon on the floor, loaded with painted logs, a sack of beautiful marbles, all sizes and colors, a cap pistol with a big roll of caps and a star-studded holster, and a beautiful brown and black cowboy suit, including a brown hat.

I hardly knew where to start. However, it didn't take me long to decide. After a bite into one of my big apples, I put it aside and started to slip into my new cowboy suit when I heard Mama's voice.

"Did you wash yo'self befo' you put yo' new suit on, Sun?"

"Yes ma'am—" *Wait er minute,* I thought, *how did she know Santa brought me a new suit? She's still in bed.* From what I had seen I was already certain that Santa must be Papa, but I didn't want to spoil it for next Christmas by opening my big mouth. Mama's question confirmed my suspicion. I rushed to the back porch, poured the pan half full of cold water, and took the world's quickest bath.

After putting on my suit, I grabbed my cap pistol, went outside, and proceeded to shoot up everything in sight. When I came back inside, Elbert, Hazel, Deloris, Geneva, and Verleen were out of bed looking at their gifts. I turned my gun on them until Ben came. I let him borrow my cap pistol on every other shot, and we kept the shooting going.

Ben hadn't gotten the toys or new clothes that I had. Santa had brought him only apples, oranges, and candy. His only toys were some firecrackers and torpedoes—if those could be called toys. We lit some of the firecrackers and put them under a can. They made a terrible noise and blew the can high in the sky.

After annoying everyone we could around our house, we were off to the neighbors west of us. Our first stop was Mr. Durbey's shack. He gave us more firecrackers, sparklers, and torpedoes. We didn't dare take any of his fruit or cake. Though it was baked by Miz Marge, once it entered Mr. Durbey's grimy little shack, it was no longer fit for anything except hogs, dogs, and Mr. Durbey—especially if he had to serve it to you.

Our next stop was Mr. Jim and Miz Marge Stowald. Miz Marge loaded us down with a piece of each of the five cakes she had baked: chocolate, coconut, jelly, fruit, and pound cake. I had changed my mind about eating her cooking. She also gave us a bag stuffed with nuts, fruit, and candy. Mr. Jim gave us each more firecrackers, torpedoes, and a green rubber snake.

We headed for the Rileys', shooting and blasting all the way. When we came to the fence, we stuck some firecrackers in a posthole and witnessed a muffled sound when it exploded. It blasted dirt high in the air and made the hole twice as large near the surface. It gave me an idea of how powerful a big firecracker is. Papa said they were small sticks of dynamite. We knew boys who had lost fingers when firecrackers exploded in their hands.

We continued over the fence, through the field, across Alligator Creek, and up the hill, past the spring, through the pines and hickories, and followed the rutted road on to Mr. Sam Riley's house with a fireplace nestled behind vines, bushes, and a flower garden on an acre of land.

Mr. Sam had bought the acre from Uncle Pet years ago. It was on the west side of the road that divided the 40 acres, but in the absence of a survey, one couldn't be sure where the dividing line was. Mr. Sam, with his easygoing, free-living style, couldn't care less. He was truly a child of the soil. He was unsuited for the facade that the elite, more sophisticated Faithful crowd at Hughes Chapel, or any other chapel, for that matter, often exhibited. He concentrated on moonshine—he called it "juice"—loafing, and "trim," which most men called pussy.

He didn't own farmland, a mule, or a horse; therefore he didn't have to worry about them. Having neither mule nor horse, he didn't need a wagon or a buggy. He had no car, truck, or bicycle but walked and hitchhiked everywhere he went, and he went constantly.

Clothes? His entire wardrobe could have fit in a good-sized briefcase, with room to spare. I'm sure he never owned more than two pairs of overalls, two homemade shirts (usually made from flour sacks), one pair of old worn-out shoes, which he wore only in winter, two pair of long drawers, which he wore in all seasons, and an old ragged hat, which he wore in a multitude of ridiculous fashions. I have seen tramps and scarecrows dressed better than Mr. Sam. He truly had plenty of nothing.

Thanks to a hardworking little wife, Miz Maggie (Miz Mag), Mr. Sam was always relatively clean—"ragged as a jaybird in whistling time" but clean. "You always gotta be suspectable," he often said.

Winters could be severe, although cold snaps never lasted more than a few days; 18- and 20-degree temperatures, sometimes snow, were not uncommon. No matter how cold or hot, Mr. Sam's costume remained the same. He would put on an old ragged overcoat if Papa or Uncle Pet gave it to him during cold spells, but his rusty feet were always peeping out of unlaced, run-over, worn-out leather flappers he called shoes. He was blessed to be in a place, and living at a time, where family and friends treated him like an endangered species.

Miz Mag was a plain little woman whose center must have been in her high behind. She wore long dresses, and when she walked, her rumble seat kept bouncing up and down like a saddlebag on the rear of a horse. Her long neck stuck out in front of her, rather like a turkey's. She even moved her head in a back-and-forth motion like a turkey—almost mechanically. We nicknamed her Miz Turkey Neck. Miz Mag was a prudent, snuff-dipping woman who grew many crops in their rather large garden three seasons of the year. She canned fruits and vegetables for winter and hired out to Papa and Uncle Pet during chopping and picking time. She was the mother of Reedy (the oldest), Leala, and Olie. Leala and Olie were quite plain, like their mother, but Reedy was handsome, with smooth dark skin and a tall muscular body. People said Mr. Sam looked like that in his younger days. If that was true, all that remained was his height. Reedy's slightly turkeylike movements reminded me of his mother's. Since he had long strides, however, it wasn't as pronounced.

Leala was pigeon-toed and took short quick steps more like her father. It was sort of a trot-shuffle. She wore a constant grin, and her hair had never been introduced to a comb. She wore the same braids her mother must have given her when she was two. She had large "titties," a small waist, and her mother's behind. If one could get by her face and head, there was some decent-looking woman there. Crazy Charlie said, "Keep the body 'n throw the rest of her erway." I thought that was a pretty raw statement—as if Leala was a fish. I liked Leala. Her head and face notwithstanding, she attracted quite a few young men, one of whom was Crazy Charlie himself.

Olie was a badly coordinated, juicy-mouthed character with his pa's gift for clowning and making friends.

The grand matriarch of the family, however, was Miz Rose, Mr. Sam's mother, a bony little high-spirited woman. I had no idea where Miz Rose came from or why she was considered such an outcast by Papa and others, given her high standing in her family. She was in her eighties but walked spry and straight with the aid of a cane—which I discovered was more style than necessity after seeing her working in the garden and carrying vegetables without any aid. Her braided hair was all white and contrasted well with her dark skin and deep-set, penetrating eyes. She always wore a long dress, a shawl draped over her shoulders, high-buttoned shoes, and a bandanna, the style of her girlhood during the Civil War. She wielded controlling power in the Riley family.

I understood it all better one day when I overheard Papa telling Miss Rose's story. The story was reinforced when I saw what looked like two white men wearing big black hats hugging her. She was born in slavery. Still a young girl, she ran away and ended up in Arkansas, thinking she had made it to the North. She married and raised a family—two families, in fact, simultaneously. Mr. Sam's father, who was black, had some help that he didn't ask for, fathering children, from a white man named Hunt. This help was rendered not once, not twice or thrice, but four times. Mr. Sam wound up with three half-white brothers and one half-white sister. The disgrace was so heinous that the children, who displayed strong white genes, couldn't live in that community in peace. They had all moved—far north to Canada.

All of us were used to light-skinned people in our community and in our families, but no matter how light, they all fiercely proclaimed their African descent. Any person who didn't identify with this concept was severely limited in our midst—unwanted. No one could point to a known white man and say, "That's my father." Papa became angry simply talking about it. "It's always them, coming after our women. We try going after theirs, we wind up gittin' hung and butchered. I got nothin' erginst them boys, but it's a shame when they come all the way down heah from Canada and cain't even talk to they own papa 'n he livin' right over there in hollerin' distance."

Papa took a drink of water and continued. "Sam's papa got t' take the blame fer't, though. After that first child come heah lookin' white, his choice wuz clear: git rid er that woman or git rid er Charlie Hunt. If he wuz too scared t' git rid er Charlie Hunt, he sho coulda got rid er that no-good woman."

Mr. Sam was waiting outside when he heard us shooting.

"Y'all boys come on in. Merry Christmus, Sun, Li'l Udell. Whut did ol' Santa bring y'all boys?"

We took turns rattling it all off to him. Mr. Sam laughed. He went into the back room and came back with more firecrackers and sparklers. His breath reeked with a mixture of tobacco and moonshine as he reached them to us.

Reedy and Olie were still sleeping in their respective corners of the big room. I wondered, *How on earth could anybody sleep on this morning? Why weren't they up checking to see what Santa brought them?*

Leala, Mr. Sam's daughter, slipped up behind me, as she had done before, and put her long fingers over my eyes. When I turned around, my face was buried in her big soft titties. She said, "Whut did y' do, Sun, to make Santa bring y' all that stuff? I know it wutten fer bein' good."

"I wuz good too."

Leala laughed.

Ben motioned for me to bite down on her breast, but I didn't dare. I wrestled myself free instead.

Miz Mag, Mr. Sam's wife, called from the back room, "Merry Christmus, Sun! I wuz jist wonderin' when y' wuz comin'. How is everbody this blessed Christmus mornin'?"

"Merry Christmus, Miz Mag. Everybody is good."

Miz Mag came out of the room with only one plate, heaped full of all kinds of cakes and pies. She stopped quickly in the door when she saw Ben. "See y' got Li'l Udell wid y'—"

"Y' don't have t' say nothin', I'm gittin' outta y' ol' house." Ben started to leave.

I hung my head.

Miz Mag looked at me and reconsidered. "Wait er minute, Li'l Udell."

"Name's Ben." He stopped.

"It's Christmus mornin', Mag," Mr. Sam reminded her.

"Jesus, forgive me. And so 'tis. Come on back, chile, 'n set down, I fix you er plate too." She reached me my plate and went back for Ben's. Reedy and Olie kept snoring and snorting.

The holidays lasted two weeks into the New Year. There were a host of people who hadn't had the pleasure of stuffing me. I made those visits on Sundays to relatives Over In The Hills west of us, neighbors east and up the Pike, especially Uncle Pet and Aint Babe.

It was sad to watch the last leaves of fall tumble into frozen ruts, be swept to corners here and there by winter winds, and fielded by fences. I could feel my joys of the season slipping away when discarded trees lay dying in pastures, along the road, and on wood piles, when holly berries, cotton braids, tinsel strings, and mistletoes were burned in an open fire as so much rubbish, when just a few weeks earlier they had reigned supreme as splendorous decorations.

How sad the berry that baked high in its tree only to become the sweet persimmon waiting for a schoolboy on his way home. Winter had, at last, claimed its season.

Back to Tilson, where I got down to business: Miz Harmond moved me up to a higher group. That usually took place in the fall rather than in the middle of the school year. I still didn't find the homework so challenging that I couldn't find time for the bag of tricks I played on the girls. Now that winter frost had killed or sent into hibernation most of my army of insects, especially my worms, devil-horses, and grasshoppers, I had to lean heavily on my green rubber snake, along with feathers for tickling the ears of sleeping beauties, and sometimes sharp safety pins to get the lift and exact tone to their screams that I wanted.

Larry, who looked taller and stronger than his fourteen years, was back in school after being expelled for fighting with A.D. shortly before Christmas. He couldn't possibly keep up, because of his stuttering and stammering. A.D., a year older than Larry, did not return. He was busy getting drunk, singing the blues, and making babies. His big dumb brother Carl, who was thirteen, dropped out of school also and busied himself rabbit hunting. Indeed, he became one of the best rabbit hunters in our community. He made a business of it. He took whole loads of bloody dead rabbits on his shoulders to Pine Ridge and peddled them for 25 cents each. Udell stood with his hand out the minute big stupid Carl hit the door. Between that money and what the rest of the family made cutting winter wood, the Barrows survived the winter, until ground-breaking time in late March and early April.

Though I didn't know what was happening at seven, mixed feelings surged beneath my conscious ability to express how I felt about girls. Stacy Martin was the prettiest girl I had ever seen. She was tall, with snake hips, a perfect round face, pretty white teeth, long delicate fingers, long bushy black hair, and a mellow, smooth ebony complexion. The problem was, she treated me like a kid, which my boyish mind resented, simply because she was six years older.

One day at lunch, while playing ball, something got in my eye. I made the discomfort worse by rubbing it. Suddenly I felt long soft slender fingers turning my head around. I looked up, and there she was, the girl I had admired for so long from afar but didn't dare to tell. With her actually caressing my head, I was so excited my tongue became paralyzed and I couldn't speak. I always knew she was pretty, but close up, she was dangerously so.

"Jist hold still, Sun. Let me see if I can blow this outta yo' eye."

I tried to respond, but nothing came out.

She turned my eyelid inside out and gave two big puffs of breath. "How do that feel?"

Water was running down my cheeks. I couldn't speak, so I shook my head.

She repeated the process. Again the water flowed from my eye. It must have washed out the annoying trash because I felt instant relief.

When she was close and blew in my eye, her breath, her body smelled so inviting—of a sweet fragrance that tumbled my senses and rendered me weak. When I dared to look into her sleepy dark eyes, it aroused a festival of mixed feelings inside me. Indeed I was baptized in them. Of course, I felt unequal to any challenge and frustrated, but somehow I still heard church bells ring.

Raw peanuts and raw sweet potatoes were my favorites. I never tired of them and frequently overate. I stuffed my pants pockets on one side with the real thing and on the other with the shells and peelings. I reserved my coat pockets for the larger raw sweet potatoes. When I felt hungry, and even when I didn't, I would snake out one of those sweetboys, peel it with my teeth like a squirrel, and crunch down on it. No matter how hard I tried to keep it quiet, I always sounded like a horse eating corn. Unless I muffled the sound by putting my handkerchief over my mouth, I would wind up having Miz Harmond take my goodie away from me.

One time, I began eating before I went to school. When lunchtime came, I dived into that also, as if I hadn't had a bite all day. Shortly after the bell rang, my stomach began to ache as if there were forty devils running around inside. I didn't want to ask to be excused, because we had just returned from lunch. I twisted and turned, but the more I did, the busier the devils became. It felt like those forty devils were joined by forty more. Then there were eighty devils, running around inside my stomach, playing baseball. I squirmed and turned some more, but it was no use; I had to go.

"Miz Harmond, may I be excused, please?"

"But Sun boy, we just came back from lunch. Can't you wait until recess?"

"Yes ma'am." I strained and gritted my teeth. I thought, *It would be beyond shame if I went in my pants, especially with Grace Anderson and the girl I love, Stacy Martin, in the room. That's how nicknames are born.*

Though I had played tricks on most of the girls my age, I had studiously avoided playing them on little Grace Anderson. She was quiet, shy, and smart. She was also pretty, but not flashy. I liked her well enough, not as well as she did me, but she was too young—seven, like I was. Even so, I didn't want to disgrace myself in front of Grace, and definitely not before Stacy Martin.

With those thoughts floating around in my head, I grabbed hold of my seat, and with every sphincter muscle I controlled, I squeezed and tensed and grunted and pushed and pinched trying to force the fermenting garbage back and keep the day's churned raw sweet potatoes, baked sweet potatoes, raw peanuts, thick buttermilk, buttered biscuits, and last night's chicken 'n dumplings, blackberry cobbler, corn bread, and black-eyed peas from blowing my seat apart, disgracing me and my family in the process.

The gas pressure built up tighter and tighter. The mixture of junk in my stomach began to growl at me, *Let me out! Let me out of here!* It was so powerful and painful, I stood up! I was trembling and shaking. My legs were wobbling, and I was bent over trying to hold back the increasing tide.

Miz Harmond was in the middle of listening to Larry, straining and stuttering trying to read. "'N-'n-'n-'n-'n-'n th-th-th-th-th-th-th wo-wo-wo-wo-wolf sa-sa-sa-sa-id, 'Di-di-di-di-di-di'l hu-hu-hu-hu-huff 'n-'n-'n-'n-'n di-di-di-di-di'l pu-pu-pu-pu-puff, 'n-'n-'n-'n di-di-di-di'l blo-blo-blo-blo-blow yo'-yo'-yo'-yo' hou-hou-hou-hou-house dow-dow-dow-dow-down.'"

By the time Larry finished, those pigs had time to build another house and move in. Meanwhile the muscles in my butt were weakening. In a few seconds I could have taken care of the blowing job for the wolf without huffing or puffing. Finally, Miz Harmond noticed me standing there shaking. "What's the matter, Sun?"

"I have to go to the outhouse, Miz Harmond."

"Very well, Sun. Go ahead," she sighed.

The students started to giggle.

Bent over, making short quick steps, I moved to the door. Cautiously I struggled down the steps and started toward the white-washed structure stashed on a bluff about seventy-five feet away. It might as well have been seventy-five miles. Bent double by that time, I proceeded step by precious step toward what to me was a beautiful city on a hill. I made it halfway. The movement churned the mulch more and increased the pressure to the inevitable breaking point. Unable to restrain it further, I snatched down my pants, ripped the buttons from the rear flap of my long drawers, and with my naked behind pointed toward Grace Anderson, the pretty Stacy Martin, Miz Harmond, and the rest of my eagerly waiting classmates—with sound and fury, I put on the show of my life! Like lava from a volcanic eruption, the explosion sent that mixture of smelly lava all over Tilson's playground, the flap to my long drawers, my knickers, and the backs of my shoes.

My two older sisters Hazel and Deloris washed me up as best they could. They wiped my sobbing face, buttoned up my stinking clothes, and quietly took me home, ending a sorry day for me at Tilson.

Vera Nellie Bearden was about twelve, Elbert's age. She thought she could do anything most boys could do. She was one of the few girls who would take a boy on in a wrestling match or a footrace. If the boy was a little slow, she'd win. Older boys didn't pay much attention to her long copper-colored legs squirming around on the ground, showing all of her bloomers as she pinned an opponent. Many of the kids, mostly her relatives, were on the sideline egging her on, when Miz Harmond wasn't looking.

"Grab his arms, Vera Nellie!"

"Don't let that sucker git er nelson on y'!"

"Don't worry; I got im," Vera Nellie said as she changed positions. "Y' give up?"

"No!" the skinny struggling boy said.

"Y' give up?" Vera Nellie twisted his arm more.

"Noooo! I ain't giving in t' no girl."

"Y' gon' give in t' som'um." She yanked his arm again.

"Noooo . . . I mean yes!"

"Yes whut?" Tightening more.

"Yes . . . IIIII give up!" The boy limped away rubbing his arm.

Vera Nellie got up and brushed herself off. Out of all the kids watching the match, she picked on me. "Whut you lookin' at, Outhouse?"

"Don't call me no outhouse," I responded sharply.

"I calls um the way I smells um, Sunny boy," laughing.

I was very sensitive to the joshing I had taken since my performance that day in the schoolyard. Most kids had forgotten it. It made me angry that she was reminding everybody.

"Whut you buckin' yo' eyes fer, Elbert? You don't like it?"

"Girl, you better pick on somebody y' can whup."

"I ain't scared er you, Elbert Hughes. I take you on 'n do y' jist like I did that skinny Fred Martin," Vera Nellie boasted.

"You'll do-do 'n fall back in it."

"That's yo' brother's job. He can do that better 'n anybody I ever seed." Vera Nellie was scoring and laughing loud. Other kids were laughing with her when Miz Harmond rang the bell and we all had to file back inside.

I didn't like Vera Nellie in the first place. She certainly helped me by trashing me in front of my classmates. Now I hated her, but she was too big, too old, and too strong for me to do anything about it. At least I could take comfort in the fact that my big brother hated her too—I thought.

For Easter, at Tilson, the older girls engaged in a bottle decorating contest, and the younger girls did an Easter basket. Boys were grouped according to age, and a foot-racing competition was held for the baskets. Easter was wake-up time. It was getting-back-in-touch time. It was young lover's time. It was cleanup time. It was egg coloring and egg hunting time. It was springtime. Most of all, it was planting time.

The best thing that happened to me that spring was that Mama gave me a plot of land in the corner of the garden to grow whatever I wanted. I suppose it was her subtle way of saying how thankful she was that I had survived the snakebite the year before. I was so happy, I dreamed about it at night and took great pride in digging up the soil with a garden fork and preparing it for planting watermelons. Almost everything Mama planted did well, though she had never tried to grow watermelons. She would only plant a few seeds, here and there, among the corn, beans, and cotton, but never a watermelon patch.

I worked my soil up so there were no clods or grass. With a hoe, I designed big round hills. I lined them up in perfect rows and worked fertilizer into the middle of each hill. I planted two or three seeds in the center of each hill. Within a few days, young shoots broke through the crust and peeped at the sun. As the days passed, the little plants began to stretch their arms. I cultivated them at least twice each week and prayed for rain. The rains came, followed by warm nights, and the vines began to spread across the hills. The grass also began to grow, but not for long. I chopped around each precious plant, eliminating grass and weeds. I watched them day by day as they spread, covering the hills, then the furrows. Soon the vines were a rug of green over the whole patch.

Then one bright summer morning, I visited the plot and noticed little green bulbs growing on the vines. Nature was at work—changing things. This time it was just for me. I started the whole thing. I was helping nature to control what was taking place. In a few days, the little green bulbs had burst wide open, and my green rug became freckled with white flowers. I could hardly wait to see what would happen next, and it wasn't long. After the bees had romanced each flower, the petals began falling away, leaving a tiny button. It was hard and firm. I dared not pick it or even disturb the baby, born of my caring hands. Each day, I watched my buttons grow until they became the size of marbles—then plums, apples, pears, goose eggs, cantaloupes. By the time June came around, my little patch was full of big long delicious watermelons. They were the pride of Mama's wonderful garden!

The year 1928 had been a good one for Papa. Cotton prices were high. He bought lots of remedies and combined them to make many bales of cotton.

With everybody making money, business in the store was good as well. In the early summer of 1929, Papa paid almost $1,000 cash for a new four-door light blue Model A Ford sedan. It had a spare tire on the rear and a trunk. It also had a toolbox on the running board. It had a rearview mirror and other accessories like ashtrays and a glove compartment. The radiator cap, the gas cap, the door handles, the bumpers, and all details were chromed and shining. The old crank, used for starting the T-model, B-model, and early A-model, had been replaced by the self-starter. It was indeed the latest thing.

Mr. Ford was supposed to have said, when asked about colors for the old rugged assembly-line-produced T-model—which made it possible for the average man to own a car—"Tell them they can have any color they want, so long as it's black." Light blue, trimmed in white, was something new for a Ford. However, Uncle Pet had bought the later 1928 A-model in chocolate brown the year before. We thought Papa was trying to outdo his older brother.

Papa had never driven a car before. They gave him a quick lesson at the dealer's, after which he got in the car and drove the seven miles home. He was reared way back, with both hands firmly on the steering wheel. He was stripping gears, and the car was bucking and jumping like a wild bronco. When he drove up, we all gathered around to greet him. We put our lives into his hands, piled into the seats, and insisted that he take us for a ride immediately. Papa backed the car out of the driveway, almost running into the fence. Then we took off, stripping gears, hopping and jumping down the Pike. We went all the way to Cleveland County doing a record-breaking, earth-shaking 35 miles per hour.

Within the next few weeks, Papa, Elbert, and I went all over. Mama didn't care too much for Papa's driving and stayed out of the car except for riding the short distance to church on Sundays. His driving improved rapidly, however, and in a few weeks, he was as good as or better than Uncle Pet—who was still stripping gears, bucking, and jumping. When Papa was asked why he bucked and jumped when he drove, his reply was, "Most people still drivin' horse 'n buggies or wagons 'n mules, and you're complainin'?"

Though the Ford was equal to most tasks off as well as on the highway, Papa was careful to keep it on the highway. He kept it washed and shining under a shed that he had a carpenter build. If he needed to go back in the hills or over on the bayou, he used his horse and buggy or his wagon and mule team.

My big trip was when we went to Monticello. Papa drove a good-looking lady there to visit a sick relative. I found out later I was more of an unasked-for chaperon, at Mama's insistence, than company for Papa. *Imagine Mama not trusting Papa,* I thought.

The most memorable part of the trip was the beautiful mountains, the lilies of the fields, the morning glories that blanketed the pastures as we sailed along—the new Ford eating up the road at 45 and 50 miles per hour. We glided over hill after hill, through valleys, through mountain passes, and around curves without my going to sleep once. It was a hot day. Sweat popped from Papa's forehead; his armpits and areas of his shirt were wet. The pretty lady sat quietly beside him and spoke softly of the beautiful scenery and how thankful she was that Papa was driving her.

I remember painting the town our way in Monticello. The family we visited prepared plenty of good food. There were fruit orchards such as I had never seen. To make everything perfect, there were girls and boys my age to play with.

We enjoyed the Ford most of the summer. In those few months, the car had become like a member of the family. Then, early one sunshiny morning, Papa and Mr. Sam Riley took off for Pine Ridge. Shortly before they reached Bayou Bartholomew, the Ford's motor caught on fire. Papa and Mr. Sam hopped out before the fire could spread to the gas tank. There were no buckets in the car for carrying water. Water wasn't the best thing for putting out a gasoline fire anyway. They proceeded to scoop up gravel with their hands and throw it on the enveloping flames. Other people stopped and tried to help, but the fire was out of control. We all ran down to the disaster, only to watch our beautiful new car burn to a charred skeleton.

There was no such thing as customer's car insurance in Pine Ridge in those days. The dealers must have had insurance from the factory, though. They gave Papa a used 1928 Chevy with low mileage that was the same size as the Ford.

At seven, my experience with white people was limited to Bob Sikes, who saved my life when I was bitten by the rattler, and the Parsons, who gave us milk with their long stringy hair in it, along with other foods, which Mama thanked them for, then promptly fed to the hogs. Farther down the Pike were the Barnards and the Newmans, both Papa's competitors in the grocery business. Those were the closest white neighbors in our community except for another old couple few people knew.

They lived in a small vine-covered cottage diagonally across the Pike from the Parsons. They were known as the Smiths. No first names—simply the Smiths. Papa trusted me to run errands to neighbors nearby. On one occasion I was delivering a note to the Smiths. I took off with the piece of paper stuffed in my pocket. With my best wire paddle, a stiff piece of wire bent 90 degrees at the end, I rolled my rim in front of me. I trotted along on the right side of the Pike and watched for passing cars and trucks—up the little hill immediately south of us, down on the other side, across a small stream that ran alongside the Pike to a small creek, up a small incline, and there on the right were the Smiths.

I stood outside the fence and called, "Mr. Smith!"

No one answered.

"Mr. Smith!"

Still no answer.

"Mr. Smith!"

All was quiet. *Maybe he's in the back,* I thought. I cautiously opened the gate and went inside. I stood at the gate. "Mr. Smith!"

There was still no answer.

I saw a screened porch directly in front of me. I proceeded slowly up the little path, overlapped with flowers from both sides, until I was closer to the house. I started to take another step when a big bad dog came out of the hedges straight toward me. I froze in my tracks. I wanted to run, but he was too close. I never would have made it out of the gate before he tore me apart.

"Theaaaah, doggie, niiiice doggie . . ."

He stopped coming toward me but continued to growl and bare his long white teeth.

"Theaaaah now, doggie. Theaaah now." I toned my voice to try to disguise my fear.

To my amazement, the beast stopped growling and started licking the sides of his mouth and wagging his tail.

"Thaaat's er nice doggie. Thaaaat's er ni-i-i-i-ce doggie." I reached out my hand to pet him on the head—my little attempt at animal taming. Apparently it was too little. When he got close enough for me to pat him, a strange thing happened. As I bent over to touch his big round head, he quickly jumped up, bit me on my bottom lip, and slowly slumped away.

While I stood there bleeding, a thick southern woman's whine came from the screened porch.

"Whu-u-u-ut you want, boy?" She raised her shaggy snaggletoothed head so I could get my first look at her. She had been sitting in her rocking chair watching the whole sorry affair between that dog and me.

"I got a note for Mr. Smith."

"Stick it in the do' theah. I'll git it d'retly." She got up and started to water her flowers.

"Why don't y' call yo' dog off?"

"I don't tell that dog whut t' do, 'n he don't tell me whut t' do." She had a big grin on her face. "'Sides, he knows whut y' taste like already. 'Pears he don't like y'. He ain't gon' bother you, boy."

"He already did." I was mopping the blood from my lip as best I could with my shirtsleeve.

"T'was yo' own fault. Do I look like er Mr. Smith t' you?"

I had never seen Mr. Smith up close, but I said to myself, *I can't say exactly, but I sure hope his looks are an improvement on yours.*

I put the note under the door carefully. I could still hear her chuckling as I went swiftly out the gate. I stopped along the Pike, gathered some green leaves from weeds and bushes, and put them over my bloody bottom lip. With my paddle and rim in my hand, I ran home as fast as I could.

My seventh year on earth brought many changes in my long life, I thought, as I hid behind a clump of bushes just behind Mr. Durbey's blacksmith shop. We were playing hide-and-go-seek with the Barrows. I could hear my heart pounding as I focused my eyes on my sister Geneva—two years older than me—with her hands over her eyes, leaning against a tree as the post, going through the ritual.

"Honey-honey-bee-ball, I-can't-see-y'all! Ready? Oooone! Twoooo! Threeeee! Foooooo'! Fiiiiive! Siiiiiix! Seeeeven! Ready-or-not, I'm-lookin'-fersho!" Geneva took her hands from her eyes and began snooping out people.

She was good at the game and frequently sought out all of her hiders and beat them to the post. My sister Verleen, only five, was the first victim. She hid, if one could call it that, near the post beneath a tall wagon almost in clear view.

I kept my eyes glued on Geneva as she cautiously inched away from her post, looking for other easy prey. While waiting for a chance to dash for the post and win the prize of becoming the seeker, my mind wandered to the number seven. First, I thought about the multiplication tables Miz Harmond was teaching us: *7 x 7 = 49. I was the seventh child of nine. Two were dead . . . whoops, back up—Geneva is the seventh. There were seven days in the week. Geneva counted to the number seven. Crapshooters always tried to make seven. Crops were laid by July Fourth, the seventh month. There were seven children in our family. What could it mean?* I thought.

Random thinking filled space and time for me. It enabled me to concentrate on my goal of getting Geneva far enough from her post. I knew I could beat her in a footrace if given a little more space. After all, I had taken on boys much older than me at Tilson and beat them.

What could they mean—all those sevens? My mind kept scanning back to— *Uh-uh. She just got Elbert. She's quite a distance from her post now. Farther than she's ever been.* I sprang to the tip of my toes and fingers like a panther on the prowl, every muscle tensed to the ready. Juices were pumping.

Geneva inched a little farther—her careful eyes rotating back and forth to her post and my possible hideout. I was the last hider. "You may as well come on out, Sun. You'll nevah make it."

She was only a few feet from me, but she was fast and I knew it. Sweat was popping out on my face, my neck, my arms—indeed my whole body. I wasn't likely to get a better chance. She was standing in one spot, peeping and spying—not really ready to run. A real runner has motion in mind and body before the race begins. *I'll surprise her and get the jump. The minute she moves, I'll burst forth with my speed. Even though she's closer, with any luck, I'll overtake her.*

I began my count: *7 x 1 = 7, 7 x 2 = 14, 7 x 3 = 21, 7 x 4 = 28, 7 x 5 = 35, 7 x 6 = 42, 7 x 7 = 49!* Geneva started to move toward her post. I sprang forward. My skinny legs and arms were whisking past each other like sharp scissors cutting through silk. I was "pickin' um up 'n puttin' um down," like Mama's sewing machine at full throttle. My mouth wide open, my eyes fixed on the post, spit and salty sweat dripping from my chin, my shoulders forward, head back, sucking wind. *She had too much of a start on me.*

Keep on rubbing!

Only a few feet from her post, I was suddenly even with her.

Keep on rubbing!

"Come on, Sun!" Verleen screamed.

"Come on, Sun!" Elbert yelled.

"Come on, Sun!" Ben shouted.

Everybody was shouting, "Come on, Sun!"

Suddenly I wanted to sprout wings. The sly Geneva had not been beaten often, least of all by someone my age. She almost won that one too, but it was not to be. With my fast start and surprise and my determination not to be beaten, my powerful charge took over. It became the most important thing to me on earth at that moment. I passed her at the last second! My mind was still clicking like a clock: *7 x 8 = 56, 7 x 9 = 63, 7 x 10 = 70, 7 x 11 = 77 . . .*

14

In August of 1929, Papa and Uncle Pet went to the National Baptist Convention again. The convention was in Florida. There they met Uncle E.J., who traveled from California, and Uncle Thomas, who traveled from Chicago. That year Papa surprised us by bringing his youngest brother, Uncle Thomas, home with him to spend the night en route back to Chicago. When they arrived it was so exciting, Mama allowed me to stay up long past my bedtime.

The car pulled up at about ten. We heard Papa laughing, then we saw him get out of the car. It was a hot moonlit night. We could see them more clearly as they opened the gate and strolled up the little path to our front porch. Papa was wearing a tan summer suit with a starched white shirt, a polka dot tie, tan shoes, and a brown hard straw hat called a "crust." Uncle Thomas was wearing a blue summer suit complemented by a starched white shirt, a striped blue tie, shined black slippers, and a white straw hat turned up all the way around.

Papa was at least a head taller than his brother. Uncle Thomas was rotund. When he got closer, I could see his pot belly protruding in front of him. Two sturdy-looking bow legs carried his round body. He was smoking a pipe—the first Hughes I'd ever seen who smoked. His outstanding physical characteristic was his walk—all reared back, proud, dignified. He looked like Papa driving a car. His erect posture said to the world "I *am* somebody."

"Kitty, open the do'. Whut y'all waitin' fer? Don't y' see who I brought home wid me?"

Mama, overjoyed, unlatched the door. Papa and Uncle Thomas walked into the living room, taking off their hats, and set down their suitcases.

Mama ignored Papa and rushed straight to Uncle Thomas. "Lawd ha' mercy, boy. Thomas, come heah 'n let me git er good look at y'!"

"How are you, Kitty?" They embraced.

"Boyyyy, y' done gone up there in Chicago 'n got stout. Y' sho lookin' fine!"

"I'm in good health, thank the Lord."

"How is Grace 'n the chirren?"

"They were all fine when I phoned Grace this morning, Kitty."

"How long y' gon' stay wid us, Thomas?"

"My train leaves early tomorrow morning, Kitty. This is just an overnight layover."

"I wuz lucky t' git im t' change trains 'n come this way," Papa said proudly.

"Well, I sho am glad y' did—I sho am," Mama said.

"I haven't seen any of you—except Andra—in almost five years. I figured while I was this close to home, it would have been a shame not to look in on you folks." Uncle Thomas looked at all of us children surrounding him.

I was checking every inch of that man—my uncle Thomas. He had perfectly balanced squared shoulders. No sign of a hunch or a sag. His arms were long and powerful looking, properly fitted with a pair of commanding hands, long straight fingers, clean fingernails. No sign of having been bruised by farming or hard work. He had a large head, a prominent forehead, distinguished widow's peak, cowlicks, and a long neck that shot straight up from his shoulders in the back—no overhang. His chiseled face was like most of the Hugheses', only his was longer. He was clean-shaven with smooth black skin. His eyes were smaller than Papa's—more like Uncle Pet's—but not as slanted and slitted when closed. They were bright, quick, alert, sure, and almost constantly smiling. His self-assured smile exuded confidence, especially when the dimples appeared in his cheeks. It made me glad to be near him. His lips were V-shaped and barely moved when he spoke, quietly, effortlessly enunciating every word. It was one of my first encounters with a polished, educated man of my own flesh and blood, besides Uncle Ruben.

"So-o-o, this is the crew, is it?"

"All 'cept Jessie. She's married 'n lives Over In The Hills," Papa said.

"I don't think any—no, take that back. I think everybody was here except the baby when I left."

"We lost Florence 'n Vercie to that flu when you wuz at Tuskegee. Remember?" Papa asked.

"I remember that. It was a bad epidemic. Lots of people died. Well, I may as well start all over again. Now who exactly is this young lady?" Uncle Thomas went to each of the older children, shook hands, and gave each of them a coin.

Finally he came to me. "So you're Junior. Right, boy?"

"Yes sir."

"There's something wrong with that. Your Papa is Junior. That would make you . . . the third."

Papa and Mama looked at each other as if they were discovering that fact for the first time.

"Y' know, Thomas, you're right. We jist got in the habit of thinkin' of him as Junior," Papa said.

Mama spoke as though it was no discovery to her. "I know he's the third, but who's gonna call him that?"

"Well, we don't have t' worry, 'cause everbody call him Sun anyway," Papa said.

"Y'all chirren better go to bed now. It's long past time," Mama said.

We bid everyone good night and left the room.

I was up early the next morning trying to get another look at my fine-looking uncle, but I was too late. Papa had driven him to Pine Ridge to catch his train.

At least I had a few minutes of glory. For days after Uncle Thomas had gone, I provided the family with laughs, strutting around the house all reared back with my stomach stuck out, a stick in my mouth for a pipe. "Well now, who exactly is this young man?" I mimicked.

Papa was very proud of his baby brother. He often talked of his physical strength as a young buck, growing up in our community. There was no man stronger or capable of as much work as Thomas. "The only boy from eround heah to go t' Tuskegee 'n study under Booker T. Washington and George Washington Carver, befo' yo' brother Ruben joined him," Papa would say, referring to Mama's brother Ruben. Mama remained quiet and went on with her work, since she had heard the story many times before.

I wanted to hear more. "Papa, when did Uncle Thomas go to Tusk-wegee?"

"Let's see . . . he left heah in the fall of 1909. And that's Tus-ke-gee." Papa headed for the store.

I followed him. "Papa, how long did Uncle Thomas stay at Tusk?"

"*Ke-gee. Tus-ke-gee.* Well, he was theah fo' yeahs."

"Wo-o-o weee! That's er lonnnng time. Ain't it?" I stretched my hands apart, equating time with distance.

"It's a pretty long time, but that's whut it takes to finish college."

"Did you ever go to Tus-ke-gee, Papa?"

"Oh yes. Went there a couple er times. Once when we had the National Baptist Convention in Mobile and another time when we had it in Atlanta. It's a beautiful place," Papa said as he straightened items on his shelves, holding them at a distance in order to see without using his glasses.

"Papa, can I go to Tus-ke-gee?"

"Well, y' gotta learn how t' say it first. Y' said it better, but y' still strugglin' wid it. If y' wanna study agriculture or somethin', that's the place for it, but first let's see if we kin git y' outta Tilson. Then y' gotta go to Pine Ridge for high school. Then maybe y' be ready for college. Lots er colleges, y' know." Papa was straining to read something on a label. I wondered why he couldn't see it.

"Wheah is theah lots er colleges?"

"Well, there's Branch right up heah in Pine Ridge. Yo' Mama went up theah fer er while, my sister Cary, yo' sister Jessie, yo' uncle Thomas, yo' uncle Ruben, 'n yo' uncle E.J. Yo' uncle Thomas taught theah befo' he left Pine Ridge."

"Mama went to college?" I was surprised.

"Well, let me back up," Papa said. "Whut they had in them days wuz er branch to the college that taught high school. Y' had to pass that befo' they'd let y' in the college. Y' understand that?"

"Yes . . . sir." I hesitated.

"That wuz befo' the regular Pine Ridge High School wuz built."

"Ohhh." It became clear to me at that point. In the back of my mind I kept thinking about Pine Ridge High, but I didn't know how to express it. Why didn't they all go there before college? So, Branch served for high school and college.

"Yo' uncle E.J. went to Branch High School and College. He taught down heah for a while. We Baptists got er college also, right up heah in Little Rock. We kin educate our own. There's where we train our ministers—" Papa stopped and looked at me hard.

He had noticed me imitating the preachers at Hughes Chapel. He was also proud of my singing and reciting for Children's Day, Mother's Day, Easter, and Christmas. I had overheard him say, "That boy's gonna be er preacher, like his grandpa 'n his Unka E.J."

"Did Grandpa 'n Unka E.J. go theah to be preachers?"

"No. They wuz called," Papa said, sensing he might be opening up another subject.

He couldn't have been more exact. I hesitated respectfully for a moment before asking. Then I looked at the phone on the wall. "Who called um?"

Papa never answered my question. He went on to warn me, "If you don't stay 'way from that riffraff up there on the hill—them Udells—y' won't be going anywheah, jist like them."

"Yes sir," I submitted. However, at that very moment I heard *bob-white . . . bobwhite . . . bobwhite.* It was Ben's birdcall being whistled to me in an unmistakable tone. It was a Saturday morning, and he couldn't wait for us to git som'um done.

Fortunately, the phone rang. While Papa was busy talking, I slipped outside to find Ben.

15

We took off north for Bayou Bartholomew and its tributaries. Near the bayou, where our pasture had been flooded during the spring rains, mud mounds—made by crawfish—punctuated the soft, soggy lay. Salamander tunnels blistered the grassy brown blanket of earth with crooked rows that ended suddenly without an obvious reason. The rows weaved neatly and conveniently around Papa's traps as if the salamander's body resisted metal.

On inspection, the door to my rabbit trap remained menacingly poised still and gaped like a crocodile's watchful teeth—as it had all summer. *Perhaps the fall would bring me some action,* I thought. Ben and I checked the turnip I had put inside the day before; it was still as I had left it.

"Y' ain't gon' ketch shit wid that big ol' ugly-ass box settin' out there in the open like that. Y' think Brer Rabbit is blind 'n stupid like you, Sun-n-n?"

"Don't call me blind 'n stupid."

"My brother Carl said y' gotta put them traps where Brer Rabbit least expect um t' be," Ben said.

"Where's that? In my bedroom?"

"Naw, Mr. Smartass—" Ben stopped momentarily. "Carl said y' gotta put um on the edge er the turnip patch 'n cover um up real-like so the rabbit can't tell the difference between wheah the box is 'n the rest er the ground. Them rabbits is edicated. They been t' rabbit college, fool."

"Even them young uns?"

"Specially them young uns. 'N they can smell real good too. They kin tell the difference between human funk 'n ernother rabbit in er minute."

"So kin I. Y' don't have t' be no college-edicated rabbit t' tell that," I said confidently.

"Y' talkin' er lot er shit. I'm tryin' t' tell y' whut t' do, 'n all you kin do is talk er lot er shit."

"Aw right. So they can smell real good. Whut else?" I waited.

"Well, Carl said handle yo' bait wid gloves so y' won't git that human stink on it. Then y' pass the fur of ernother rabbit over it—so's t' give it that rabbit smell."

"How am I gonna git ernother rabbit t' let me use his fur fer that purpose? Ax him nicely?"

"Y' still talkin' er lot er shit. I'm tryin' t' tell y' how t' ketch er rabbit, 'n all y' kin do is keep talkin' shit." Ben was really disgusted.

"Aw right, how many rabbits you caught wid yo' brother Carl's method?"

"How many?" Ben hesitated.

"Yeah. How many?"

"Well . . . er . . . I ain't been doin' it long as you. I—I—"

"The answer is—none! Right? Y' ain't caught er single one, 'cause if y' had they would er heard y' in Little Rock. Y' would er been down heah like you'd never left. I know y', Ben Barrow."

We followed the tributaries to Bartholomew looking for different colored rocks. We were especially interested in clear rocks. We had learned in school that Arkansas was the only state where diamonds are found. We also believed any grease or oily substance on top of the water was a sure sign of an oil well nearby. We knew we would stumble up on a gusher or a real diamond one day.

Finally we came to the charred remains of our new 1929 Ford sedan. The loss of our beautiful car that summer was a setback—mostly to our pride. The 1928 Chevy, however, took Papa where he needed to go. Fall was upon us, and he kept buying and selling remedies as well as running a busy store. A few weeks before, the Ford had stood proud, shining, and excellent in every detail like a champion charger ready for action. Now only the petrified, tortured frame remained pitifully among the tall dusty bitter summer weeds. On stilts, ragged, rickety, lacking its former style, attention, and purpose—unlike its worthless but hardy green companions in that spot—it was ignorant of how to grow.

How sad. Once-handsome wire spoke wheels were bent, crumpled, and rusting away like the days of summer at the twilight of fall. The sketchy door-frames, through which I had climbed happily and sat beside Papa, were now but a haven for spiderwebs, a silhouette against the haze of an evening sunset. It was a shadow box that could barely make the raging winds whistle against it. Its once-proud trunk, which had sat handsomely at the rear, was now but a craggy tin sieve, rusting, rotting, and wasting back to the dirt. At the bottom of the waste were the jumbled remains of unused tools, like bones from an ancient tomb. The charred rim of the once-elegant spare sat bare—still bolted to the passenger's side of the running board—violated and robbed of its proper function forever.

I quietly, respectfully mimed opening the door, stepped inside, and sat in the remains of the driver's seat. Ben sat beside me. Slowly I put my hands to the crooked, malformed, pitiful steering wheel that projected in front of me like a rusty pitchfork out of hell. Knocking off scaly metal and paint from the steering post, I reared back, like Papa, and stretched my bare, skinny left leg as far as I could in an effort to reach the faraway clutch. I went through the motions of pressing it, stripping the gears, even bucking and jumping. Then sailing along the highway, up and down hills, through valleys, around curves, through mountain passes, past pastures, fields, and rivers, over bridges, and under railroad crossings—on our way to Monticello. After a while, we sighed, got out, brushed the red dust of death from our short pants, and without words continued our search for diamonds among the clear running waters of the creeks and streams that emptied into Bartholomew.

We hadn't gone more than a few feet when Brer Cottontail jumped up from thickets beside us and ran lickety-split for a big hollow tree a few feet away. We had been waiting for a chance like this for years. That rabbit was ours. But how were we going to get him?

"I know, git er fishin' pole, 'n fish him out," Ben said.

"Where we gon' git er fishin' pole?"

"My Mama got er fishin' pole," Ben answered.

"Y' think she let us use it?"

"Helllll naw," Ben replied.

"Whut y' bring it up fer, then?"

"I be right back. Y' watch the hole while I'm gone." Ben left to search in the canebrake nearby. There were always old dried-out castaways people had cut and didn't use.

"Hurry up. He might decide t' come outta there." I posted myself by the hole, ready to grab him if he came out.

Ben's voice came back from a distance. "Y' still think Brer Rabbit is a damned fool. Don't y'?"

Soon Ben returned with a long cane pole. We pushed the pole up the hollow.

"Y' think this pole is long ernough?" I asked.

"It's the longest one I could find." Ben stopped pushing and held his head to the hollow tree. "Heah im? He's movin' up higher."

"Yeah, I heah im. Y' think he might come out?"

"I jist got through tellin' y' he's movin' up higher. And you ax me do I think he's comin' out?" Ben took the pole out of the hollow and slammed it on the ground. "No wonder they call you Sun, you er bright sun of er bitch. Y' know that?"

I simply looked at him. I realized that my question was rather stupid, but it was too late to take it back. I had to think of something to make up for such a question.

"Welllll, Sunnn-shine, y' got any mo' bright ideas? Maybe we could play er little rabbit music, do er little rabbit dance—the cottontail shuffle maybe, or read him some Unka Remus stories, ring er cowbell, throw some salt on his tail, better still, plain kiss his rabbit ass." Ben rolled over laughing at me.

I was sick of being trashed by the likes of Ben Barrow. After all, he was a lesser being than me in my book. There was nothing he could do that I couldn't do better, longer, faster, and with greater force, except curse and use foul language. Suddenly an idea hit me. I sprang to my feet! Gears began turning in my mind. "Don't they use smoke to run bees away from their hives?"

"Yeeeeah. So-o-o-o?" Ben said.

"So, if smoke works on bees, why not on er rabbit?"

"Because bees is bees 'n rabbits is rabbits, that's why." Ben kept laughing.

I stopped listening to him and got busy collecting dried leaves and twigs. "Y' got er match?"

"How I'm gon' smoke if I don't got er match? Sho I got er match." Ben dug down in his ragged pants and fished out a match.

"We need er croker sack or some rags."

"Whut y' lookin' at me fer?" Ben asked.

"I want y' t' go git er sack outta the barn."

Ben took off. He stopped and looked back. "Sun-n-n-n, oh bright onnnnne, don't start the smokin' till I git baaaack."

"I ain't as stupid as y' think, Ben Bow. Who thought of it in the first place?"

"It ain't worked yet," Ben answered, and took off again.

He was back in a flash. Soon we had the smoke swirling up the hollow like a chimney. Ben kept piling on the leaves.

"Git some damp leaves, next to the ground. These dry ones burnin' too fast—not makin' enough smoke," I ordered.

Ben was as anxious as I was, so he gave me no argument. "Look! The smoke's comin' outta all the knotholes 'n the top too! Told y' that damned smoke wuttin' gon' git im outta theah."

"Keep bringin' the leaves, will y'?"

"I'm bringin' um. I'm bringin' um." Ben kept busy while I squatted by the hole, holding the sack.

After about five minutes, we heard a scouring and scratching near the top of the tree.

Ben put his head to the hollow. "I heah som'um . . ."

"I heah it too!"

The scratching became louder.

"He's comin' down!" Ben whispered loudly.

"I heah im! I heah im!" I whispered back just as loudly.

We covered the hole with the sack in our hands. The scratching gave way to scuffling. He was on his way out! He rammed the hole with all the force he could muster! Somehow he got his head past the croker sack and was almost loose when I sunk my fingers into his fur! Ben also grabbed a vital portion of his cottony rear, and we both held on tight! We could smell singed fur along with burning leaves and twigs.

His squeaking cries were mournful. He quivered in our hands as if he was about to freeze. I wondered if rabbits had ever been known to die from fright.

I also wondered why he didn't bite or scratch like most animals under similar circumstances. Cry as he did—sounded almost human—it didn't stop the quick execution of Brer Cottontail. Holding him by his hind legs, one quick chop with the side of my hand broke his neck, and he went limp as a dishrag. I was happy that his suffering ended. I don't think I could have taken more of his crying.

The excitement of finally catching a rabbit was such a joyful victory for us two young hunters that Ben never mentioned his brother Carl's method to me again. I, of course, was equally quiet about the whole affair except the successful part. The important thing between Ben and me was, "We got som'um done."

16

Gene Cannon was about nineteen and almost six feet tall. He possessed big muscles, wide shoulders, a small waist, powerful hands, and a handsome face. One Saturday afternoon in the fall of 1929, he drove Uncle Pet's team of handsome, lively dark brown mules into our backyard pulling a wagonload of corn. The few people who had hired hands didn't normally work them on Saturdays. Since they were paid by the month, there was no extra pay for Saturday. I don't think Uncle Pet was unfair, but he had a reputation for being strict. He paid Gene $20 per month plus laundry, room, and board. That was considered good pay. However, it meant that when Uncle Pet wanted his corn harvested from the lower twenty of the old home-place before the birds and squirrels got to it, that's what Gene did.

Reedy Riley was a slightly taller version of Gene. He was muscular with smooth skin. He had helped us harvest during the preceding fall. He was standing in the backyard laughing and talking with my sister Deloris—on whom he had a crush—while she and my sister Hazel were shelling peas. It soon became obvious that he was also waiting for someone.

"There's ol' Gene," Reedy said as he walked toward the gate. "Whut y' say, Gene?"

"Heyyy, Reedy. Whut y' say?" Gene got down from the wagon.

"Hey, Gene." Deloris waved.

"Hey, sugar! Hey, Miz Hazel." Gene's tone changed when he spoke to Hazel.

"Hey, Gene. How you?" Hazel responded in her sweet fashion.

"I'd be er lot better, Miz Hazel, if you'd only let me." Gene hammed it up by doffing his cap.

"'Splain yo'self, Gene Cannon." Hazel smiled prettily.

"Oh, I know y' Bill Wilson's girl, 'n I got no business pourin' out m' heart t' y' like this." Gene gave a little awkward curtsy.

"Is that whut you doing now?" Hazel asked cutely.

"Huh?" Gene needed clarification.

"Pourin' out yo' heart t' me?"

"Well, maybe I don't pour as good as Bill Wilson. I seen y'all together. You *is* his girl, ain't y', Hazel?"

"True, Bill comes t' see me, but the last time I looked, I wuz still Mr. Andrew Hughes' girl, Gene." Hazel smiled sweetly.

"I *heard* that!" Gene gave a quick bow from the waist.

"But don't worry, Gene Cannon, you pour quite nicely," Hazel said, laughing.

"Laaaawd ha' mercy! Say it ergin! Pleaseeee say it ergin!"

"She jist said it t' see you act er fool," Deloris said.

"That's good ernough fer me. Jist say it one mo' time." Gene put his hand up to his ear to listen.

"Aw right, Gene Cannon, you kin pour erlong wid the best of um," Hazel prompted him further.

"Laaaawd ha' mercy! Don't pour no water on m'! Jist let m' burnnnn, y'all!" Gene went into a dancing gyration—put on a real show, which everyone enjoyed.

"Come on, boy. Stop actin' er fool. I wanna talk t' y'." Reedy walked through the gate and stood beside the wagon.

Ben and I were admiring the beautiful mules.

"Think y' kin handle a pair mules like that, Sun?" Gene asked.

"Sho."

"Ha-ha-ha. Ol' Sun thinks he's er man already. Let me sho y' what er real man is." Gene made a big muscle and bent down to let Ben and me feel it. It was hard as a rock. Which is precisely what he told us.

"Hard as er rock. Ain't it?"

"Yeaaaah!" Ben and I spoke at the same time.

Reedy beckoned for Gene to step behind the chicken house.

Ben and I were busy rubbing the mules' heads and shoulders. However, we could hear them clearly—especially when they were supposed to be whispering. That gave me cause to watch them out of the corner of my eye. I saw Reedy pull out a bottle.

"How many did y' git?" Gene asked.

"I got two pints."

Ben and I kept playing with the mules in order to hear what they were saying.

"Heah it is," Gene said. "Whut you gon' drink, ol' buddy?"

"Whut the fuck y' talkin' erbout? I'm gon' drink part er that, y' mule's ass."

Gene had the bottle upside down guzzling. He almost choked and spit out part of the whiskey when Reedy called him a mule's ass. He went to the ground choking and laughing.

"Gimme that bottle." Reedy snatched it out of his hands. "Well, y' been gittin' much lately?" Reedy asked slyly. "Come on now, let m' heah some er them lies."

Tall tales about the conquest of girls were a ritual part of any stag drinking party. If forced to leave out that topic, young men's vocabularies would have been reduced to a number less than their shoe sizes.

Gene took the bottle down, wiped his mouth with the back of his hand, and staggered around a little, laughing. "Have I been gittin' much? Have *IIII . . . meeee . . . IIII* been gittin' much?"

"I think that wuz the question."

"Well, Reedy, ol' buddy, I hate t' break the bad news t' y', but I been gittin' mo 'n Barnards' ol' jackass down the Pike, 'n they lead two or three mares in there to him every day."

"Who is she? 'N be careful," Reedy warned.

"He-he-he-heeee! My ace boon-coon! He done got skeerd now that I might be covering some er *his* territory. I don't blame y', boy, I probably have. Y' wanna tell me who they is so I won't mention they names?"

"I ain't gon' tell you shit," Reedy protested.

"Aw right. It's *yo'* fune'al. Y' know Stacy Martin, don't y'?"

When he mentioned Stacy Martin, a cold chill went through me. Then I started sweating. I couldn't wait to hear the details, yet I didn't want to hear them. The thought of Gene Cannon, or anybody else, being with the woman I loved hurt me to the quick. It mattered little to me that she was about fifteen and I was only almost eight.

"You know I know Stacy, wid her good-lookin' self. Now don't try t' tell m' y' done got som'er that." Reedy gasped and gapped his eyes in surprise.

"Tore it up! He-he-he-heeeee! Toooore it up! Y' heah me?" Gene bragged fiendishly.

"Aw, niggah, y' know y' lyin'. You ain't got none er that." Reedy laughed nervously, fearing it might be true.

"If I'm lyin', I'm flyin'. Y' don't see no wings on me, do y'?" Gene held up his right hand and placed his left over his heart.

"I been *praaaayin'* fer some er that fer er *lonnnng* time."

"Well, Brer Reedy, yo' prayers been answered, good buddy—good 'n proper too. September twenty-first, round eight-thirty in the evenin'. If y' stand still, 'n hold yo' peace, the Lawd *willlll* provide! Ain't that what the good book say? Let the church say eh-man!" Gene was laughing and rejoicing.

My little heart was broken. I felt sick all over.

"Wheah wuz her mama 'n papa—her sister 'n brother?"

"Her sister 'n mama had gone t' town wid her papa t' do some shoppin'. I don't know wheah that no-good Frank wuz. Probably out somewheah tryin' t' do the same thing I wuz doin'. Anyhow, Stacy wuz there all by her lonesome. He-he-heeee," Gene rubbed it in as he took another big swig from the bottle.

"Whut y' tryin' t' do, kill it?" Reedy grabbed the bottle and turned it up. "Aaaaah—tell m' one mo' thing, Gene."

"Whut's that, Reedy?"

"Wuz it good?"

"Wuz it goooood!" Gene bent over slapping his knees and laughing. "Let's put it like this, ol' buddy: if it wuz any better, I wouldn't want it, 'cause m' weak heart wouldn' be able t' stand it! Umh-umh-ummmmh! I'm tellin' y', ol' buddy, it felt good all down in my toes, in my eyebrows. I didn't know where I wuzzz!" They both went almost to the ground slapping each other's hands and laughing.

"You like her 'cause she got that long bushy hair. Right, Gene?"

"I like um wid long bushy, short bushy, long wavy, short wavy, nappin', sleepin', curly . . ."

"Black, red, gray, gone away . . ." Reedy continued.

"I tell y' like that ol' hoah told that young un, jist gittin' started. The young one wuz primpin' 'n carrin' on—worried t' death erbout her hair. The ol' one tol' her, y' worried erbout the wrong thing, honey. I been out heah er long time, 'n I ain't nevah had no man ax me fer no hair yet." They went into a knee-slapping laugh. "'N no eyes either."

"Gene, you er crazy son of er bitch, I sweah t' God!" Reedy took another drink and gave the bottle to Gene.

"Y' heah the one erbout Sister Riley 'n Sister Tilson?"

"No, but I got er feeling I'm erbout to," Reedy responded.

"Sister Tilson walked up to Sister Riley, reared back, put her hands on her hips—they both snuff dippers, y' know—she said, 'Thithter Riley, I heard that you thaid my husman Henry'th dick got er wart on it.' Sister Riley reared back 'n put her hands on her hips and said, 'Y' got thom wrong info'mation, Thithter Tilthon. I nevah thaid fer thertain yo' huthman Henry'th dick got er wart on it. No thir—nevah thaid that er'tal." Gene spat. "Whut I thaid wuz, it *felt* like it.'"

I had always liked Gene until about two minutes before. Once he mentioned having his way with Stacy Martin, his popularity took a swift downturn with me. I listened to his bad jokes because I had no choice. I couldn't let Ben know how I felt about Stacy. He would have stretched out on the ground laughing again. I simply had to keep quiet.

Both men were laughing hysterically when Reedy suddenly stopped. "Uh-uh. Ain't that Mr. Pet's car?"

"Yeah, that's him." A frightened look came over Gene's face.

"Whut y' gon' do, man?" Reedy asked.

"I ain't gon' run."

"That ain't whut I'm talkin' erbout. Reach me the bottle—reach me the bottle." Reedy held his hand out, but Gene was frozen—afraid to move.

Uncle Pet had gotten out of his car and started hobbling in our direction. I could tell he was angry by his gait. He was dressed in khakis, a hunting cap, and brown leather brogans. He carried his foot gun (a long-barreled derringer that shot small pellets like a shotgun) cradled in his arm. "How y'all this after-noon? How you, Sun boy?"

Everyone responded except Gene. He was visibly shaken.

"So, this is whut y' do when I send y' t' do some'um?"

"I jist stopped heah t' git er drink er water 'n rest the team, Mr. Pet," Gene said nervously, and started moving toward the team.

As he started to pass, Uncle Pet reached out his hand and stopped him. "Hold it right theah." He sniffed Gene's breath. "Er drink er water, huh?"

Gene didn't respond—stood stiff and frozen.

Uncle Pet put his gun in his side pocket and started to search Gene. "Hold still." He pulled the almost empty bottle out of Gene's hip pocket and held it up in his face. "So, this is the water y' been drinkin'?—schuuh—Y' not only a liar, y' er bad liar.—schuuh—Y' er liar, y' er drunk, 'n y' got no manhood erbout y' on top of it.—schuuh—Y' walk eround heah wid yo' head up yo' ass—schuuh—in er dreamworld all the time."

Gene stood quietly with his head down, completely destroyed.

To make matters worse, Hazel and Deloris were still sitting in the backyard shelling peas.

It was so embarrassing, Reedy dropped his head, put his hands in his pock-ets, and started kicking dirt. Ben and I stopped playing with the mules and looked on sadly.

Uncle Pet continued, "Now do y' understand why I treat y' like I do?—schuuh—I'm er Christian. I ain't gonna take nothin' erway from y' that ain't mine.—schuuh—When I send y' t' do som'um 'n I can't trust y' outta my sight befo' y' done sunk back t' that low life I took y' out of—schuuh—out of the goodness er my heart—schuuh—whut do y' expect m' t' do? Let y' git erway wid it? Huh?"

Gene was frozen—wouldn't respond.

"Answer me!" Uncle Pet bore down.

"I—I—I don't know, Mr. Pet."

"Well, you may not know, but I do.—schuuh—I'm gonna dock y'. I ain't gonna pay y' good money 'n feed y' fer y' t' go out heah 'n cheat m'." Uncle Pet pushed his hat back on his head.

"Now I took y' in tryin' t' help yo' family—schuuh—'n you, but if this is the thanks I git fer it—schuuh—I can easily git somebody else.—schuuh—Now I want y' t' take that team home 'n unload that corn befo' it rains on it.—schuuh—If it gits wet, every nickel is coming outta yo' salary.—schuuh—Feed 'n water that team, 'n I'll see y' when I git home." There was an ominous sound in Uncle Pet's voice. He had a reputation for whipping young men who lived with and worked for him.

Gene slowly started to leave, but he hesitated like a big kid.

Uncle Pet turned his attention to me. "Who you, boy?"

"My name Sun Hughes, Uncle Pet."

"You ain't no Hughes.—schuuh—I'm er Hughes. Yo' papa is er Hughes, but you don't look like no Hughes t' me.—schuuh— Y' sho y' er Hughes?"

"Yes sir. I'm er Hughes. I'm er Sun Hughes."

"Ha-ha-ha. You er Sun Hughes, huh? Who is this boy y' got wid y'?"

"This my friend Ben."

"How you, Unka Pet?" Ben said.

"Wheah y' git that Unka Pet stuff from, boy?" Uncle Pet chuckled.

"I got it from Sun."

Gene stopped in his tracks and pouted like a kid. It was obvious he wanted to try to save a little face before leaving. His moonshine must have kicked in and given him a little courage.

"Whut you standin' there all puffed up like er bullfrog fer?—schuuh— Thought I tol' y' t' leave?"

"Mr. Pet, y' didn't have t' 'barrash me befo' everybody like that. Y' coulda waited till we got home," Gene said.

"'Barrash you? Y' 'barrash yo'self by yo' own actions. Kin I hep it if you er fool—schuuh—'n er clown? Boy, you ain't seen no 'barrashment.—schuuh— You wait'll I git you home, I'll show y' some real 'barrashment."

Gene backed off from the two mules a few feet. He turned his cap backward on his head, spit in his hands, rubbed them together, ran, jumped over the top of the first mule, and landed on the far one as pretty as you please. He folded his arms like he was a Buddha or an Indian chief and gave a quiet, simple command: "Mules." The mules took off and headed up the Pike toward home. Gene never turned his head or expressed anything but stubborn, stolid dignity. The loaded wagon pulled by the handsome mules harnessed with bradded black leather rocked steadily out of sight.

"Fool's drunk," Uncle Pet remarked as he limped toward the store. I followed him, and Ben followed me. "Sooo, y' call yo'self er Hughes, huh?"

"Yes sir."

"Well, if y' er Hughes—schuuh—how-come y' got all that hair on yo' head—schuuh—growin' all down in yo' eyes?"

"Gotta git er haircut."

"That y' do, Sun boy, that y' do." Uncle Pet stopped. "Sun, run back t' the car—schuuh—'n bring Unka Pet that briefcase layin' on the backseat?"

Ben followed me. I returned quickly with a brown leather briefcase. "Heah's yo' briefcase, Unka Pet."

Uncle Pet pulled out his big dirty old money sack, fished out a nickel, and gave it to me. "Now you've earned that nickel.—schuuh—Unka Pet don't believe in givin' erway money fer nothin'."

Poor Ben, standing there expecting his nickel, had to find that out the hard way.

"It's er bad habit fer anybody t' git in.—schuuh—Leads t' stealin'." Uncle Pet didn't even look at Ben. He simply put his sack back in his pocket and limped on into the store.

"I heard y' pull up, but I simply didn't have time t' git over there yet," Papa said as Uncle Pet entered the store.

"You go 'head 'n take care er yo' business. Don't worry erbout me." Uncle Pet looked around at the shelves in the store.

"Andra, why don't y' cut this boy's hair?—schuuh—He's too old t' be runnin' eround heah wid all that wool on his head."

"I jist cut his hair last week," Papa responded.

"'N it done growed back like that? You must not cut ernuff off."

"Well, I didn't cut it *all* off 'n shave his head like you do. Besides, you one t' talk erbout wool. Yours'd be jist as long 'n thick if you didn't shave it every week," Papa said.

"Do y' know y' got drinkin' goin' on eround heah?"

"No, I didn't know. Who been drinkin' eround heah?"

"That triflin' hired hand er mine 'n that Reedy Riley.—schuuh—I bet he the one sold it t' im—'n these kids lookin' at um."

"Wheah wuz they drinkin'?"

"Right theah behind yo' chicken house.—schuuh—Now you know that ain't right. Y' oughta pay mo' 'tention—schuuh—t' whut's goin' on eround yo' own property.—schuuh—Keep all them boys erway from heah."

"Well, I can't police this place every minute. I'll speak t' Sam erbout Reedy, but I got young girls they age, 'n boys naturally gonna come eround."

"I got er young girl too, but I got certain hours—schuuh—weekends only, they can come courtin'. They cain't close no do's—schuuh—'n they have t' git they courtin' in befo' nine o'clock."

"That's too early, Pet. Y' talkin' t' yo' brother now, remember? We wuz allowed t' stay till ten—sometimes ten-thirty," Papa said.

"Y' got that all wrong, Andra, it wuz nine.—schuuh—Now y' er deacon, 'n y' superintendent er the Sunday school. Now if y' won't do som'um erbout it—schuuh—I'm gonna have t' do m' duty."

"Meanin'?" Papa spoke with anger in his voice.

"Meanin' I'm gonna have t' bring it befo' the church.—schuuh—Y' m' brother, 'n I'd hate t' have t' do that—but I must do my duty as . . ."

"*Doooo* yo' duty! Shake yo' booty! See if I care! Pet, don't you come 'round heah threatin' me! Who er you anyhow, Moses the lawgiver? Jist 'cause y' got y' head shinin' like that, don't git that confused wid no halo. I know you. Been knowin' y' all m' life, 'n y' ain't no angel!" Papa was angry.

"Shake my booty? Ha-ha . . ." Uncle Pet's hand went to his slick head. "That ain't whut I come down heah t' talk t' y' erbout nohow."

"Whut *did* y' come down heah t' talk t' m' erbout?"

"We talked erbout it some on the train comin' from the convention er few weeks ergo."

"Y' mean redistrictin'?" Papa reminded him.

"Exactly. I couldn't tell y' much erbout it then 'cause lot er the details hadn't been worked out." Uncle Pet took some papers out of his briefcase and spread them on the counter. "I been talkin' t' Reverend Dr. Claxton up heah in Pine Ridge.—schuuh—He give me this plan—all mapped out—fer the changes." Uncle Pet put his glasses on and pointed with a pencil. Papa tried to see without his glasses but had to put them on.

"Heah's er map showin' all the churches in Reverend Barker's district— schuuh—and the ones in Dr. Claxton's district.—schuuh—Dr. Claxton has promised m' that if we can get Hughes Chapel t' come in, it will encourage all of the smaller churches eround heah—schuuh—like Mott Chapel, Mt. Calvery, 'n New Dawn—t' follow."

"Pet, do that mean First Baptist would become the biggest church eround heah?"

"It already is, Andra, you know that."

"Yeah, I do know that. But wouldn't that mean Dr. Claxton would automatically push Reverend Barker out 'n Dr. Claxton would become president of the whole district?"

"Well, not necessarily.—schuuh—It would depend on how all the rest of the churches voted in our regional conference." Uncle Pet took his glasses off.

"In that case, why don't we wait till the conference instead er trying t' git people 'n churches on board in advance. That ain't fair t' Reverend Barker, is it?"

"I cain't, fer the life er me, understand—schuuh—why you so loyal 'n partial t' that uneducated, river-bottom, backwoods preacher.—schuuh—He's er good ernough man 'n all, but he's behind—schuuh—'n he'll leave Hughes Chapel 'n us behind wid im.—schuuh—He's ol'-fashioned 'n jist ain't in the same class wid Dr. Claxton.—schuuh—Y' saw how he shaped up at that convention. I wuz kinda 'shamed of im m'self." Uncle Pet started to lose control.

"'N I cain't, fer the life er me, understand why *you* so impressed wid that Dr. Claxton—wid his proper-talkin', peacock-struttin' self. I think he's all fer hisself, 'n he only talks t' you 'cause y' got some money 'n influence, 'n he'll use all er that he can git." Papa pushed the papers aside. "'N as fer bein' backwoods is concerned, ninety percent er them people at that convention got backwoods backgrounds. Some er them people there made us look like city slickers. You right, I'm not impressed wid education when it's used t' cover up honesty. Reverend Barker may not be so fancy 'n popular at the convention, like yo' Dr. Claxton, but at least I understands him when he talks t' me. I feel he's always been honest wid m'. Lest you forget, Reverend Barker displayed that same honesty while he pastored Hughes Chapel, long before you met this

Dr. Claxton. I didn't heah y' complainin' about his country ways then."

"Andra, y' don't know whut y' talkin' erbout.—schuuh—Y' think I don't have sense ernough t' know when somebody's tryin' t' make er fool outta me?—schuuh—I been knowin' Dr. Claxton fer years. Been goin' t' his church up there in Pine Ridge.—schuuh—He always calls on m' t' take part in the service.—schuuh—He's been t' Hughes Chapel many times, as you know, and I have never felt slighted in that man's company. Y' don't have one single thing y' can point to—schuuh—'cept y' don't like the way he talks 'n walks."

"Whut erbout whut he's tryin' t' git y' t' do right now? Do y' call that—"

"Whut's wrong with campaignin'? Everybody who's seekin' er office try t' git as many people on his side as possible, Andra—schuuh—you know that."

"That's different from trying t' git people t' sign up before the votin' even starts, Pet. Between now 'n conference time, this man could murder somebody. Would y' still vote fer im?"

"Andra, y' talkin' er lot er foolishness now. The man is er man er God. He's er man er the people: city people—schuuh—bayou people, river-bottom people, people Over In The Hills, timber people—all the people.—schuuh—He wuz out t' my place the other day t' drop these papers off, 'n he walked right down the bean rows wid me—schuuh—didn't faze im er bit.—schuuh—Now, I understand he's after votes, but don't fergit, Hughes Chapel would stand t' gain in this too.—schuuh—I ain't no fool, Andra."

"'N I ain't no traitor. I been wid Barker 'n I plan t' stay wid Barker till he loses in er fair fight, 'n I don't call this fair, Pet. I'm sorry."

Uncle Pet became angry, picked up his briefcase, and started limping out of the store. "Y' jist pigheaded! Y' won't listen t' reason!—schuuh—I cain't talk t' y' erbout this! Jist cain't talk t' y'.'"

Papa followed him to the door. "Don't go erway mad now."

"I go 'way any way I please.—schuuh—Callin' me er traitor 'n er fool," Uncle Pet fussed as he limped toward his car. "I don't know who y' think y' talkin' to."

Papa caught him before he got in his car. "When I wuz talkin' t' y' this mornin' on the phone, y' said y' wanted t' talk t' m' erbout Cousin Jeff."

"Oh, yeah. Y' made m' fergit all erbout it." Uncle Pet cooled off a bit.

"*I* made y' forgit?"

"Yes. You 'n yo' crazy talk."

"Le's not git into that ergin," Papa advised.

"Jeff Todd—schuuh—boy I raised when his papa died."

"Y' don't have t' explain t' me who he is, Pet."

"Well, I didn't know how close y' kept abreast of whut he's been doin'—schuuh—since I put him out."

"I heard he been goin' t' seminary school up theah at Branch," Papa said.

"He jist finished."

"That's good. I'm glad t' heah it," Papa said.

"Wait'll y' heah the rest of it. He's er young man. He's been trained.—schuuh—I don't know whut kind er preacher he is yet. I heard im the other night, briefly. He sounded pretty good.—schuuh—Anyway, he axed me erbout comin' on at Hughes Chapel as assistant pastor under Reverend Rider."

"Y' talk t' Reverend Rider erbout this, Pet?"

"Not yet.—schuuh—Thought I'd see how the deacons feel erbout it first."

"Good idea, 'cause he *is* our cousin, 'n people might think—"

"I know whut people might think, Andra.—schuuh—Y' forgit, this won't be the first time er member of our family served as a minister of Hughes Chapel, beginnin' with our papa, the founder."

"That was a long time ergo. Times have changed, but if Jeff is crazy enough to try pastorin' a church he grew up in . . . "

"Who said anything erbout pastorin'?—schuuh—I said assistant pastor."

"Pet, you know as well as I do Reverend Rider won't be at Hughes Chapel much longer."

Uncle Pet looked at Papa in a *how-did-you-know-that?* fashion. "So, Cousin Jeff is all right wid you?"

"Yeah. All right wid me. I'll support him all the way. But as I said, it's a big step fer er young preacher jist gittin' started. I'm gon' pray fer im."

Uncle Pet started his car. "One other li'l thing. Y' got much money in the bank?"

"Some. As y' know, most er my money is tied up in merchandise 'n that stock I bought."

"I don't mean t' be meddlin', but I don't like the way this stock market been actin'," Uncle Pet said, and looked at his watch.

"I don't like it either, but it's done some er that befo'. The big boys still in theah. Cotton prices still good. Y' got some new info'mation?"

"No mo 'n whut I read—I jist got er bad feelin', that's all." Uncle Pet shifted to first gear.

"Whut y' gon' do, Pet?"

"I already did it. I went up theah 'n got my money. Jake North did the same," Uncle Pet said, and left in a cloud of dust headed north.

Ben and I went directly into the store behind Papa. I bought a Stage Plank with the nickel I had earned. The Stage Plank was two long six-inch-wide pieces of molasses breadcake. One cake had white icing, the other, pink icing. I took the pink and gave Ben the white, and we went next door to Mr. Durbey's black-smith shop, enjoying it.

From watching Mama make molasses bread, I guessed that most of the same ingredients went into the delicious Stage Plank. But as good as her molasses bread was, especially while hot, somehow the Stage Plank represented something very special. The first thing that caught my eye was the grotesque, colorful wrapper. It showed a caricature with two of the biggest, widest red lips one could imagine. A row of big white horse teeth were biting down on half of that Stage Plank. A long red tongue with saliva dripping from it protruded from the bottom of the Stage Plank. An extremely small head projected above the grotesque lips. The lips took up most of the wrapper. Knotty individual screws, representing hair, stuck from the tiny head. On each side of the red lips, two bulging red eyes expressed ecstasy.

I don't remember anyone ever mentioning that ridiculous caricature. Everyone simply tossed the wrapping away and enjoyed what was inside. I was about to do the same on this occasion, when I happened to look closer than I had ever done before at that grotesque figure.

My mind drifted back to my trip to Monticello, when I had seen big high billboards along the highway with a caricature similar to the one on the Stage Plank, this figure with his head buried in a big slice of watermelon.

Advertising the plentiful watermelon at that level in that part of the country was about as practical as trying to sell raincoats to ducks. There was a question in my young mind. Why?

I was also confused about the *Arkansas Gazette's* daily cartoon of a caricature called Hambone. Hambone was a big-lipped, simple-looking, overfed, global-round-headed figure with a silly-looking little hat that clung to the back of his bald head and a cigar stub stuffed into his mouth. He spoke in dialect the words that represented the commonsense thinking of the *Gazette*. Most black people in our community had a difficult time trying to figure out certain words long out of use—if they ever were in use.

It didn't penetrate my young consciousness that those ugly, unnatural golliwogs had anything to do with making fun of us. The older people seemed insulated against paying attention to such things. It was never a topic of conversation.

Mr. Durbey was busy hammering away on his anvil. His pace, at near eighty, had slowed considerably, but he was still singing and humming as usual. Many of his customers were poor white farmers who went to town on Saturdays for supplies. While waiting for their horses or mules to be shod, most of them would walk into Papa's store and pick up something or go over to our well and draw a bucket of our cool good-tasting water. Others would sit around the blacksmith shop, tell jokes, and try to talk to Mr. Durbey.

"Well, Unka Eugene—" a white customer began.

"Wait er minute. Hold it right there. Whut wuz that y' called me?" Mr. Durbey stopped working.

"Unka Eugene, why?" The white customer hesitated.

"Wuz my sister 'n yo' mama sisters?"

"Nooo . . . "

"Wuz my brother 'n yo' mama sisters 'n brothers?"

"Whyyy, no . . . "

"Wuz my sister 'n yo' papa brothers 'n sisters?"

"Why, o' coase not."

"Did I marry yo' mama's sister?"

"Whut er y' talkin' erbout?"

"Did my brother marry yo' mama or any er yo' mama's sisters?"

"Y' know better—"

"Well, did *any* er my sisters or brothers marry any er yo' mama's or papa's sisters or brothers?"

"Y' know darn well—"

"Then how in *hell* can I be yo' uncle? My name is Eugene Durbey. Y' can call me Eugene, Mr. Eugene, or Mr. Durbey. Take yo' pick. Born 'n raised in these parts, 'n I wutten no slave. 'N I'll bet my last dollar you and yo' folks wutten no slave-masters either."

The white customer simply looked at the old man as if he was sure Eugene had lost his mind.

Mr. Durbey kept fussing while he worked. "Naw, I wutten no slave, neither wuz m' ma 'n m' pa. Y' in timber country, man. Lots er folks eround heah don't know nothin' erbout no slavery. Born befo' the Civil War too. Born 1852 m'self. That wuz sho befo' the Civil War. Y' in timber country, man. Lots er proud black folks eround heah. Y' lookin' at one of um." Mr. Durbey pumped his bellows. "Yes sirree. Born doin' thunder 'n lightnin'—tossed in wid er sire's litter till I learnt t' twitter. Then I wuz nursed by er ol' mama bear till I wuz two. Then m' ma put m' straddle er wild jackass, gimme er knapsack, 'n er mess er vittles 'n tol' m' t' fend fer m'self. Hell, I lapped wauter till I wuz fourteen. M' ma had so many chillens, she named one Pete 'n the next one Re-Pete. Then she got into the Befo's 'n Afters."

"Befo' 'n After whut?" the customer asked.

"Befo' she decided t' stop 'n After she decided t' stop. Yes sir, I owe that ol' mama bear er lot. When she seed me strugglin' tryin t' make it, she jist rolled over 'n reached me er tittie. She the one got m' started in the blacksmith business. All this wuz Injion country then. That wuz befo' the white man come 'n messed things up fer everbody 'cept the rich. When ol' mama bear saw me packed 'n ready t' leave, she said, 'Son, I want y' t' look out fer Injions. They the best friends y' gon' have in these parts. 'N ernother thing, I want y' t' be er blacksmith, on account er y' got er birthmark on yo' behind shaped like er horseshoe. 'N ernother thing—'"

The customer reached for his money sack. "By God, Eugene, y' gittin' ol'."

"Gittin' ol'? Whut y' talkin' erbout?" Mr. Durbey exclaimed. "I'm still makin' the anvil ring, ain't I?"

He was indeed. He threw on more coal, pumped the old bellows up again, and stuck the partly bent piece of metal in the fire. Quickly it was heated to a sparkling, malleable white. With long tongs, he took the metal out, placed it on the anvil, and hammered out a tune with his big hammer. He never missed a beat.

"Y' still makin' it ring, Eugene, but y' talkin' crazy too. How much I owe y'?" the customer asked.

"Dollar 'n er half."

The customer paid Mr. Durbey and climbed on his wagon, chuckling. "Raised by er ol' mama bear," he said to himself as he drove off down the Pike.

The window shades to the outside world began to rise. I would soon be eight. Some memories were still fresh as the morning dew, but I spent little time dwelling on them, for that was a time of exploration, inspection, and discovery. I searched the heavens on starlit nights for the Dippers—Little and Big. I searched for the North Star and found it. Papa knew exactly where it was. I climbed the vine-wrapped trees and shook their branches and vines for fruits and nuts. I waded in creeks and streams and fished Bartholomew Bayou. Yes, with only a few horrifying exceptions, my world had been a cocoon of warmth and happy happenings. If I had had to think about it at all, I'm sure I would have thought it would remain that way. I knew no other way but at home with Mama and Papa. I had seen Uncle Pet's ruling hand and iron will, the watermelon- and Stage Plank–eating images that had been projected of us—summed up by the supposedly funny Hambone. More important, I had heard Uncle Pet say that he had taken his money out of the banks. I hadn't lived long enough to recognize the real meaning of those warnings.

17

Papa was right about Reverend Rider: he *had* planned to leave Hughes Chapel, but no one expected it to be so soon. Reverend Rider was a "send um to hell and bring um back alive" preacher—straight out of the mode of the Cadre Rigor Mortis. If a church member didn't do what the Reverend wanted, he'd preach that person into hell's burning fires. If one repented and submitted to the pastor's wishes, he would just as readily preach that person back into the good graces of The Faithful. If you died, Reverend Rider would even preach you into heaven. No matter what, you should never make the mistake of dying outside the good graces of Rider. He possessed a powerful voice, had beautiful control, some education, and was regarded as one of the best Baptist preachers in the state. Hughes Chapel paid him $25 or $30 every other Sunday. That wasn't bad pay; however, there were churches around that paid more for a preacher like Rider. It was easy to see why he left when a better offer came along.

The shepherd gone to a greener pasture, the flock wandered, but not for long. When Cousin Jeff Todd didn't get the assistantship immediately after graduation, he went to Memphis to pursue his ministry. Soon, Uncle Pet informed the deacons that he was sending for the young Reverend Todd to become the sixth pastor of Hughes Chapel since Grandpa Hughes.

His first Sunday as pastor was exciting, full of adulation, hugs, and kisses. Sister Fat Fingers spoke. "Our son done come back home. Let us pray that he can take the helm and guide this gospel ship safely through deep muddy waters, through storms and dashing waves on a troubled and dangerous sea to calm and peaceful shores."

"Eeeh-man!" The church echoed.

Cousin Jeff Todd was only about five feet eight inches, but he was muscular and well built. His youthful, athletic appearance made him quite a contrast to the Cadre Rigor Mortis that preceded him. Even a mustache, a closely clipped English front haircut, and dark suits couldn't disguise his boyish good looks. He had a large round head, big penetrating brown eyes, smooth dark skin, regular Hughes features, and a constant winning smile. He was in his mid-twenties. When he tried to look more mature, he always ended up looking younger than he was.

Exactly how Cousin Jeff was related to us was never explained to me, nor did I care. No amount of Todd or other mixture could extinguish his dominant family resemblance.

The young, good-looking Reverend Todd was unmarried, so of course he was prime picking for every young lady at Hughes Chapel and beyond who wasn't related to him or already married. When word spread that he was also a good preacher, the congregation expanded to overflowing—mostly with young females. "I Need Thee Every Hour" became a theme song among them. But all of their singing, praying, shouting, and throwing of empty pocketbooks came to no avail. Within a short time, the good Reverend Cousin Jeff introduced Li'l Bit to the entire church as the new first lady.

Li'l Bit was simply lovely in every way. Besides her beauty, she was warm and caring. She gave of herself to everyone, no matter how little or important. She could also sing. Papa said, "Never wuz there a more perfect match of man and wife, nor of a pastor's wife to his congregation. Never had such a Li'l Bit meant so much to so many at Hughes Chapel."

I would soon turn eight in the fall of 1929. Every function of the church was in full swing. The young Reverend Todd had broken with tradition and conducted his own revival in July. Many of the new members were busy getting involved with the Young People's Choir, the Senior Choir, the Young People's Sunday School, the Senior Sunday School, the Pastor's Aide Society, the Missionary Society, the Benevolent Society, and the BYPU (Baptist Young People's Union).

Young people were coming from Over In The Hills—passing New Dawn, their own church—to hear the soul-stirring sermons of the gifted Reverend Todd. They came from the bayou country east of us—passing Mott Chapel and the Catholics. They came from the bayou country south of us—passing Derrisaw. They came from up the Pike, passing Mt. Zion. Many older people changed their membership to the progressive, spiritual Hughes Chapel and its young firebrand minister.

Good singing always followed good preaching. Hughes Chapel's Senior Choir sang completely a cappella, as did all other country churches in our area. My sister Hazel, Li'l Bit, and Miz Marge Stowald sang soprano. My sister Deloris and Rosie Lee Martin sang alto. Li'l Jimmy Molton and Osbin Bradford sang tenor. Uncle Pet and Ferd Thomas sang bass. Bill Wilson sang lead and conducted. The rest of the choir, especially those with bad voices, were relegated to the rear and encouraged to sing as quietly as possible. In their cases, less was more. Uncle Pet said, "Y' jist cain't kick um out, which is whut I'd like t' do, but that wouldn' be Christian; simply move um so close t' the edge of the cliff so that the slightest whiff of air would do the job fer y'."

Choir festivals were frequent at Hughes Chapel, usually on Sunday afternoons. Choirs came from as far as seventy-five miles away—mostly Baptist, but there may have been a few Methodists, if they were good enough. The Saints didn't have choirs. Even if they did, they wouldn't have been allowed to participate in a Baptist affair.

The outstanding director and singer of all the choirs was a small copper-colored man with curly black hair and a big mustache called Jeremiah Robinson. Jeremiah was a trained musician from Pine Ridge. To people in his choir, as well as those in the congregation, he was known as Professor Robinson. Papa and Uncle Pet, who had known him for years, called him by his first name. He in turn did the same. Though Jeremiah was a city man, he was quite at home with country folks. He had a deep bass voice that belied his rather bantam size. I had never heard anybody with the resonant modulations and pitch of his voice. He intoned each song without effort. He had a robust, hearty laugh that was contagious and a cheerful smile that revealed all of his big white enamels. Highly intelligent, Jeremiah always commanded respect while exuding warmth and friendliness—a rare but noble combination in man or woman.

Jeremiah would try different innovations. One Sunday evening, during a festival, he picked an all-star group of singers from each choir. My sister Hazel and Li'l Bit for soprano, Li'l Jimmy Molton for tenor, my sister Deloris for alto, Bill Wilson for adjunct lead, and Uncle Pet for bass were selected. He chose other good singers as backups. He even called me and some of the other young singers to blend in. He always took the lead and knew precisely where to bring in the other voices. Jeremiah was divinely inspired, rhythmic, dramatic, and masterful. His mouth was wide, but he seldom opened it wide while singing. His Adam's apple oscillated up and down like a crane swallowing a frog. The vibrato from his mellow bass voice came from his gut and resounded throughout the church. Wherever Jeremiah was, beauty and spirit accompanied him.

> *I woke up this morning*
> *With my minnnnd staaaayed on Jesus.*
> *I woke up this morning*
> *With my minnnnd staaaayed on Jesus.*
> *I woke up this morning*
> *With my minnnnd staaayed on Jesus.*
> *Hala-lu, hala-lu, hala-lu,*
> *Hala-lu, hala-luuuu-yah.*

After Jeremiah's lead, he brought in Bill Wilson, Hazel and Li'l Bit, Li'l Jimmy Molton, and Deloris—after which he and Uncle Pet competed to see who could sing the lowest notes. Finally all of us were singing the chorus together. When it was over, Jeremiah and Uncle Pet were slapping each other on the back and laughing. Everybody was in a good mood. Young lovers carried the mood directly into their Sunday night's heavy courting.

As night shadows gathered, Papa piled us into the Chevy and drove us home. My sister Hazel and Bill Wilson walked the three quarters of a mile down the Pike to our house. The parlor was off limits for everybody when young beaux came courting. The teacher, Miz Harmond, slept in the parlor four nights during the week. She went home Friday evenings and returned Monday nights. That left the parlor clear for one of the most important rituals of all, the prenuptial courting of my next to oldest sister, the quiet, sweet, good-looking Hazel.

On those occasions, Mama and Papa stayed in their bedroom, Geneva and Deloris spent time in the kitchen, Elbert was in the bedroom, and my little sister, Verleen, and I spent our time eavesdropping on Hazel and the well-liked, most eligible, soon-to-become brother-in-law, Bill Wilson.

Papa liked Bill because he was the kind of young man he wanted Hazel to marry. Bill was from a fairly well-to-do, respectable, church-going family. He had never been rowdy, loud, or boisterous. I thought just one of those traits would have kept him from being so wooden. He was from up the Pike. Nevertheless, he came all the way down the Pike to Hughes Chapel instead of going to the nearby church his family attended. Bill was muscular, with broad shoulders, a small waist, and a narrow but protruding butt. He dressed neatly but saturated and slicked his hair down with Dixie Peach hair grease. He didn't even smoke. He did, however, have one bad habit—if it could be called bad— he cut patches, that is, whenever he sat down and got back up, his pants stuck between the cheeks of his butt. This meant that things other than his pants could get lodged in between. My sister Geneva said, "No wonder Papa can't find his flashlight." My beam shooter must have fallen prey to his tight cheeks also. There was no telling what he had stuffed between those tight cheeks. I wondered how big an object would have to be before he noticed.

I didn't know what it was, but I knew Bill Wilson needed something to lift him out of dullsville. Reedy Riley was a bootlegger, cursed admirably, and chased women. Gene Cannon drank too much moonshine, told dirty jokes, and chased women. A. D. Barrow sang the blues, drank too much moonshine, cursed with a vengeance, and chased women. Grinning Silvester (Sly) Jefferson dressed like a sporting man, avoided hard work as if it was a poisonous snake, and chased women. Big stupid Carl Barrow was limited to grunting and muttering when trying to talk, appeared to be about as charming as the Barnards' jackass with girls, always picked a fight, and chased rabbits. Most young men in Bill's group possessed some distinguishing negative characteristic. Bill Wilson merely directed the choir—for which he was ill equipped—and tried to pattern his life after Papa and Uncle Pet who, I wager, were more like the former characters I described when they were Bill's age.

A large sofa that let out into a bed was stashed against a wall of our large nice but cluttered parlor. A tall, formidable chifforobe sat on the Persian-rug-covered floor. Its top was full of doilies, candles, decorated bottles, and a coal-oil lamp. A hutch, two large easy chairs placed by windows, and a huge desk competed for space as the choice furniture. A potbellied, bow-legged, wood-burning stove projected into the center of the room. All of this stuff combined, either by height or size, to make life difficult for us eavesdroppers. At the entrance, one of the double doors had a keyhole through which I peeped away a good portion of my growing up.

That Sunday night, after Bill and Hazel arrived and went directly into the parlor, I waited until they settled in, then took up my station by the keyhole. Verleen and I took turns for a while, but she soon became bored and left. When I took up the watch alone, it was easy to see why she left. Bill Wilson was sitting as stiff and erect as a soldier at attention. He couldn't even relax enough to cross his legs. No wonder he picked up everything he sat on. Next thing you knew, he'd pick up the sofa with those tight cheeks. My sister Hazel was sitting erect also, but I could see she was uncomfortable. For two people who had courted as long as they had, I thought they would at least have gotten to know each other. Is that what they call courting—sitting like two mannequins, looking at the walls and picking up everything that wasn't bolted down with those tight cheeks?

Finally, Hazel asked, "Would y' care for some cake?"

"That would be nice. Thank y'."

I scurried down the hall and hid in the dining room when Hazel went to get the cake. After she went back, I took up my post again. Bill even ate his cake like a mechanical mannequin. Slowly and carefully, without conversation, he nibbled away at each small bite. My eyes started to get heavy, but I kept waiting for something exciting to happen. It was like watching water drip or a potato bake.

"Ain't you gon' have some?" Bill asked after a half hour had passed.

"I couldn't eat ernother bite," Hazel said. While waiting for Bill to finish, she got up to put some more wood in the stove.

Bill jumped up as if he'd been stung by a bee or stuck by my hat pin. "Y' oughtin' do that wid me settin' right heah." He gently took the wood and the poker out of her pretty little hands and masterfully put the wood in the stove. Hazel reluctantly released the wood and poker.

I almost applauded. At least I knew he wasn't dead.

"Thank y', but I kin do it," Hazel said.

"Whut would Deacon Andra say if he seed me bein' lax in my manly duties like that?"

Hazel, wisely, didn't bother to respond but sat back down on the sofa.

"Did I ever tell y' who my favorite deacons is in all er Hughes Chapel?" Bill asked.

"Deacon Redford?" Hazel responded.

"Deacon Redford? Why, he can't sing, he can't pray, 'n he sho can't testify. Why would he be my favorite?"

"Well, I jist thought—" Hazel began.

"You er smart girl, Hazel. Y' seed me in action at Hughes Chapel long ernough to know who I model myself after, 'n it sho ain't no Deacon Redford."

"Whut's wrong wid Deacon Redford, besides whut you jist named?"

"Ohhh, nothin' if y' like dull people. Ak-ak-ak-ak," Bill cackled his version of laughing.

Hazel looked at him and put her hand over her mouth to restrain a guffaw. "So you think Deacon Redford is dull, do y'?"

"May the good Lord forgive me fer sayin' so." Bill reached Hazel the plate. He had left a very small piece of cake.

"Why don't y' finish it?"

"Would Deacon Andra Hughes or Deacon Pet Hughes eat everything on the plate? I'll answer that. Definite no. Only er hungry man wid no class would lick his plate clean."

"Who said anythin' erbout lickin'?"

"It ain't polite. Deacon Pet taught me that, 'n I learn fast, y' know. I'm sure Deacon Andra musta passed that on t' you too. Y' know whut, Hazel?"

"Whut?"

"Deacon Pet 'n Deacon Andra is the two deacons I wuz talkin' erbout. I want to pattern my life after them. Y' know whut else, Hazel?"

"Whut?"

"After we git married, I hope t' go t' that National Baptist Convention wid Deacon Pet 'n Deacon Andra. When the rest er them deacons see me gittin' on that train wid Deacon Pet 'n Deacon Andra, they be sho t' offer me that deaconship in Hughes Chapel." Puffed up with pride, Bill sat more stiff and erect than ever.

Hazel looked at him a while, set the saucer on top of the chifforobe, and sat down beside him slowly.

I grew tired of watching nothing. After changing to the other side, I started to get up, and accidentally bumped my head against the phone on the wall. I had forgotten it was there.

Hazel knew immediately who it was. "Sun," she called softly. "Sunnnn." Hazel had a tone in her voice that said *it's-all-right-because-nothin's-goin'-on-in-heah-no-way.* "Sun, will y' please take this plate back t' the kitchen? I'll give y' er nickel."

The word *nickel* got my attention. I still tried to throw my voice to make it sound as if I was down the hall instead of on the verge of falling through the keyhole. "You call me, Hazel?"

"Come heah," she said pleasantly.

I entered slowly. "Whut y' want, Hazel?"

"Ain't y' gon' speak t' Bill?"

"Hi, Bill." I still stood at the door instead of coming over to the sofa—hallowed ground, I figured.

"Hello, Master M. A. Hughes Junior," Bill said in a completely artificial manner. He stood up and started to search for a nickel. "Let me see if I can find er nickel heah." Bill had a big grin on his face. His giving me a nickel for Hazel seemed to make him feel important. "They tell me you gon' be er preacher one er these days. Then it'll be Reverend Master M. A. Hughes Junior, ak-ak-ak-ak."

"Who tol' y' that?" I asked. I wondered where he got that Master bit from. The only place I had heard it was in church on Children's Day, Mother's Day, or some of those special occasions, when the master of ceremonies would call upon one of us boys to recite. Miz Harmond called us by our first names at school.

Bill was still searching for that elusive nickel. I wanted to tell him to turn around, loosen up his cheeks, and I bet plenty of change would fall out. "They tell m' y' preaching eround heah all the time." He finally found the nickel. However, he withheld it. "Befo' I gia y' this nickel, let me heah er li'l sample er yo' preachin'."

I wanted to tell him I really wasn't that hard up for his stinking nickel, but training, and fear of sassing grown-ups, made me hold my tongue. I had a piggy bank with quite a few nickels inside not more than ten feet from his watermelon head. I simply took the plate and left Bill standing there grinning, pinching the nickel, and cutting patches. I desperately wanted to tell him what he could do with that nickel, if he could find the room. I started humming a church song, instead.

There is no room in the inn . . .

"After we git married?" I thought. *What is Bill Wilson talkin' about? My sister Hazel's not marryin' him. He may as well start makin' tracks now because he has a long way to go to get to his house and a much longer distance to go before he can marry my sister—like eternity.*

In the end, I was right; they never married.

Silvester (Sly) Jefferson, far from Papa's favorite, moved into Hazel's life that same fall, after Bill Wilson's lackluster performance. The keyhole was stuffed with cotton, and the door was latched. Except for an occasional throat-clearing, neither Verleen nor I could see or hear a thing. There was no going in and out of the room. No food, drink, or cake was served. If Sly cut any patches, we had to see it before he went into the parlor or when he came out. Security was so tight that Papa became concerned and insisted on a ten o'clock curfew. Mama backed him up.

Sporty Sly, tall, wide shouldered, muscular, and handsome, wore open-collar shirts, neatly creased bell-bottom pants, and highly shined shoes. He wore a constant grin on his high-cheekboned, chiseled dark face and kept his naturally wavy black hair in place with Dixie Peach hair grease like the rest of his country pals. In conversation, Sly revealed far more by his mischievous boyish face, shifty eyes, and chuckling laugh than he did by what he said.

I never saw Sly kiss up to Mama nor Papa in order to court their daughter the way I had seen Jessie's William and Bill do. He went directly for Hazel. It was harder for me to get a nickel from him than to find oil or diamonds. He laughed so hard, I had to join him. I never saw him idly hanging around. By the time I knew anything, Sly was going into the parlor with Hazel and closing the door. Papa's biggest objection to Sly was that he didn't go to church, except to pick up Hazel. His parents were not big landowners, and he had a reputation for being a sport and not being a hard worker. Nevertheless, within a few weeks Hazel was hopelessly, irretrievably in love with him and couldn't wait to get married. It was just before the cotton-picking season, so Mama and Papa tried to get her to wait until they had time to plan the kind of wedding for her that they had for Jessie. Hazel didn't care about that, declared her intentions, and set an early date. I only saw Sly grin, chuckle, and laugh.

I remembered Jessie's wedding. It was the summer of 1926, the year before the big flood. I was almost five. Mama dressed me in a crisply starched and ironed white suit. The extra-large long collars of my white shirt reminded me of two elephant ears flopping about on my chest. My black patent-leather slippers had a black bow near the toe. A pair of ribbed white socks came almost up to my knees. Around my neck, she painstakingly tied a big sissy-looking black and white polka-dot bow tie, and around my waist, a black and white polka-dot belt. I was truly a study in black and white polka dots.

Joy and a feeling of well-being mingled with fields of flowers—tulips, roses, lilies, violets, and morning glories—on that festive occasion. All was honed and whetted to tasteful civility around that place. Cattle grazed in the pasture and licked salt from white blocks at the fence. Mules and horses wallowed in the barnyard, and chickens cackled at the henhouse—another egg had been laid. And on that day, I heard the jackass bray again in the distance, and the mournful cry of the cotton belt far away in the west.

Everybody was there. They came from the bayou country, driving wagons and horse and buggies, riding sidesaddle and straddle. They came from up the Pike, riding their bikes, driving their Model Ts, dressed in their summer best—blue serge suits, spats, suspenders, and wide-brim hats, in gingham, silks, lace, and bonnets. They came with prescient knowledge of what was expected of them; they bore gifts. Yes, they came from Camden, Little Rock, Brinkley, Star City, and Holly Grove. Cousin Mcglotha came all the way from Kansas City. Reverend Barker, Cousin Susie, Reverend Rider, and Miz Harmond came from Pine Ridge. Most of all, they came from Over In The Hills. Mama was the twentieth of twenty-two siblings. Most of them had children, who had children, who also came. William's family, the Simmonses, and their many offspring came. All the Saints and all the New Dawn Baptists came marching in to the wedding on that day.

We spread tables among the tall oaks and gums on our front lawn. People congregated in back of our house, behind and in front of the store, even around Mr. Durbey's blacksmith shop. Mr. Durbey was duked up in a double-breasted blue serge suit that appeared two sizes too large for him. He also wore a hard derby hat that made him look like a retired undertaker who suffered from nostalgia for the business. Mr. Sam Riley wore a white collarless shirt, without a tie, plus shoes—a big concession for him. He looked very uncomfortable. Uncle Pet and Aint Babe came from up the Pike with Gene Cannon and Diane, a young girl who was one of the many orphans Uncle Pet had taken in.

The grand moment finally arrived—the procession. My sister Verleen and I were summoned from the parlor to carry flowers. Verleen was almost four. She looked frightened, but when she learned that I would walk beside her, she calmed down, and we walked out on the front porch and over to the side, as we had been instructed. Next the maids of honor marched out and took their positions. William and his best man came out looking as though they had been drafted. It was the first time I had seen William with a serious look on his face. But what was the best man looking so serious about? He wasn't getting married. Then Mama, Hazel, Deloris, and Geneva came out. My ten-year-old brother, Elbert, and his buddies Rufus Plummer and my cousin Joe Roath came out together, grinning. My sister Jessie marched out with her right arm locked in Papa's left. Jessie, dressed in white, leaned heavily on Papa. She looked very pretty, smiling constantly behind her veil. Papa looked splendid in his blue suit and white gloves. His trimmed gray hair and mustache made him look very distinguished. He was lending—not giving away—his beloved first-born. For she was the gifted one, the one he had sent to Branch, good in her books, sweet, and obedient.

Two of Mama's many sisters, Aint Fannie and Aint Mary, were standing against the wall crying. Uncle Tim and Uncle Ruben—two of Mama's many brothers—were comforting them. I couldn't understand why they were crying. After all, this was supposed to be a happy occasion.

When everyone was ready, Reverend Rider raised his hand. The crowd quieted down. Deep in the forest a dove intoned his sad, lonely coooo-coo-coo.

And the sun shouted through the treetops. A quiet belch, and the taste of squash and sweet potato crept up and lingered in my mouth. They all had come. They all were there. They all were ready. It was, at last, time. And Reverend Rider began.

For Hazel's wedding, I was almost eight, too old to be tossing flowers along the path for the bride to walk on and certainly too old to wear those sissy-looking polka-dot clothes I had been made to wear for Jessie's wedding. Instead of joy, well-being, and fields of flowers, there was a feeling of loss. The prettiest girl in the family was leaving us. That feeling prevailed, not entirely because Hazel didn't choose Bill Wilson, as Papa wanted, but because it was the busiest time of year and the preparations were rushed. Mama said nothing negative about Sly. She simply wanted more time to prepare the same kind of wedding for Hazel as she had for Jessie.

Because of family, and Hazel's relationship to the church, most of the Faithful were there, but it wasn't the crowd that attended Jessie's wedding. Papa performed his duties in a perfunctory manner, with none of the beaming pride there had been for Jessie and William.

When the grand moment arrived, Verleen and I went through the same motions as we had for Jessie, but the cute part was missing. There wasn't enough time for a big host of bridesmaids, but a respectable few appeared. There was no crying among Mama's sisters as there had been for Jessie. The tall, athletic Sly looked handsome in his blue suit. If only he would wipe that boyish grin off his face. In spite of the lack of that celebration that had prevailed at Jessie and William's wedding, when the pretty Hazel appeared and marched down the aisle, I was marching with her because her wonderful smile said "I'm so happy. Don't worry."

Sly behaved so boyishly, I thought of him as an older brother rather than a grown-up whom I was supposed to respect. He seemed to find it equally hard to be treated as an authority figure. During the ceremony, he had his head bent, his mischievous, boyish eyes looking up at Reverend Todd. I could hardly contain my laughter.

As the days rolled by, Papa was busier than ever, running the store, buying cotton remedies, combining them to make a bale, and selling them for a good price—19 or 20 cents per pound. Then, one Saturday morning I saw Elbert returning home, his wagon loaded with the same cotton I had seen him leave with earlier.

Shortly, Papa pulled up behind him driving the Chevy. "The idea, ten cents er pound? I paid twelve cents fer it m'self. Jist unload it in the bin in there. I'll keep it heah till it rots fo' I lose money on it."

"Did y' go to Crossings and Watleys?" Elbert asked.

"Went t' both of um. Crossings offered m' nine 'n a half 'n Watleys offered m' eight. Week ergo, I got nineteen. Same cotton. Whut in the devil's goin' on? Hep unload it, Sun."

"Yes sir," I answered.

It was all fun to me. While we were unloading, my buddy Ben came. He pitched in and helped us—hoping to earn a nickel, of course. We were doing more playing than unloading.

"Now if y'all gon' hep, cut out all that playin'. If y' gon' play, go somewhere else," Elbert directed.

"Papa told me to hep," I said.

"You heard whut I said."

At twelve, Elbert was carrying on as if he thought he was the boss.

"Y' think y' Papa or som'um?" I asked.

"Y' don't have t' do it. Jist go on wid yo' playin'," Elbert warned.

I got back down to some serious work after that warning. I didn't want Papa to be angry with me for something I enjoyed doing. Besides, I was eager to work myself into a position where I could be trusted to drive a team, as well as the Chevy, like Elbert.

We hadn't worked long before Mr. Ed Nettelford, the postman, came with the mail. Mr. Nettelford had a daily route that took him south on the Pike all the way to the Cleveland County line—about twenty miles, then west to the old Warren Road, then northeast along the Warren Road—through Grandpa Templeton's acreage—back to Pine Ridge.

Mr. Nettelford married our cousin, which made him part of our family. He was a tall, well-built man with a friendly laugh and a sophisticated air, accentuated by his wire-frame glasses. Sweat accumulated on his shirt, along the edges of his wide suspenders, and under his arms. I could also see the saturation around the rim of his wide floppy hat when he lifted it to mop his face with his big white handkerchief. His high-top shoes, with thick leather soles, were always laced up to the top and shined to perfection. He seldom left his car— stuck strictly to business. It was a very good, respectable job for a black man to have at that time, even though he had gone to college. He lived in Pine Ridge and was a member of St. Paul, the Reverend Doctor Claxton's church, where the black elite attended. Indeed, he was highly respected in the black and white communities. Papa said he delivered the mail with horse and buggy before cars became available in the early twenties.

Sometimes he worked a half day on Saturday. The mail was light, so he took his time. After he gave Papa his mail and had a drink of water, he and Papa wandered over to the wagon where we were unloading.

Papa was looking at the headlines of the *Arkansas Gazette,* holding it farther away from his eyes than before. "Not er word er warnin' in any er these papers. Banks jist closed overnight 'n nothin' in heah erbout when they gon' open back up. Friend er mine said when he went t' git his money out the other day, they took him in the back and showed him stacks er cash. Didn't look 'tall like they wuz closin'. . . ."

"'N the next day they closed," Mr. Nettelford said, and waved at us. We waved back and kept working. "Lot of banks been pulling that same trick to prevent a run on the funds. So, the highest offer you got was ten cents for this cotton?"

"Not even that, 'n I went all over," Papa said.

Mr. Nettelford propped his foot on a block of wood, mopped his face, and paused for a minute. "I don't know, Andra. Maybe you should've taken it. It could git worse. That crash the other day is behind it."

"Y' don't think they gon' git this crash thing straightened out in er few days, Ed?"

"It don't look good, Andra. Old Hoover's talking about prosperity is just around the corner, but he's not saying what corner. Anyway, the big stock boys are shootin' themselves and jumping out of windows. It don't look good, Andra. Don't look good at all."

"What er y' think will happen, Ed?"

"Well, Andra, if they can't turn things around in a few days, there'll be a depression." Mr. Nettelford started back toward his car.

"That ain't too good fer the Republicans, is it, Ed?"

"Not good at all, Andra. Not good at all. If it keeps up, Democrats'll get in for sure."

"Well, they won't git my vote—southern devils." Papa sounded resigned.

"Won't get mine either, Andra. Hardly any other colored person's, but don't forget, there's a lot of Democrats up north too."

"I don't care who they put up to run. As long as he's connected to these southern crackers like Bilbo, Talmadge, and Culpepper, they'll never git my vote."

"You won't get no argument out of me on that, Andra. Too bad this had to happen now because it looks like bumper crops this year."

"Yeah. There's plenty cotton eround, corn too. I see that over in Europe they raisin' big crops, but wheah we gon' sell it?"

"I don't know, Andra. I'd hate to advise you to sell and things turn around. On the other hand, I'd hate to advise you to keep it and prices go lower. But if I was going to advise you—which I'm not—it would be to sell it as soon as possible and avoid further loss." Mr. Nettelford chuckled good-naturedly, walked over, climbed into his Ford, and waved good-bye.

Papa walked back to the wagon and ordered us to reload, park the wagon under the loft, cover the cotton good so it wouldn't get wet, unharness, feed and water the team, and get ready to take the cotton back early Monday morning.

I wondered why Papa was so bothered about that one load. After all, he would only lose 1 or 2 cents on four or five hundred pounds, or whatever that bale weighed.

Elbert took pleasure in telling me that I didn't know as much as he did about his and Papa's business. "Shows how much you know. We got cotton all over this county that Papa bought already. We jist ain't got eround t' pickin' it up yet."

I kept my mouth shut after that and worked as hard as I could reloading the wagon. Then it dawned on me that our bin could only hold two thousand pounds of raw cotton, which would yield a little over one bale. It was only a "ready-to-haul" station. That's how Papa stayed ahead of other traders in the business: Buy the cotton ahead of time. Keep it in the seller's bin until you were ready for it—usually when the price increased. Collect it with the Chevy—much faster than a wagon. Put the small remedies in the ready-to-haul bin, load the wagon with one bale, and keep Elbert rolling. That way, Papa did three bales per day. His competition was lucky to do one. Sometimes he would hire his competitor's wagon and driver when it made a profit.

Papa never talked much about the stock he lost or the money he lost when the banks closed. One day when he and Mama were looking for some papers in the hutch, they ran across the stock certificates. When Mama asked him what he intended to do with them, he chuckled and remarked, "These stocks can only be used for toilet paper." Quietly, Mama squeezed the stocks into a wad and gave it to him. Papa chuckled at the gesture.

Papa and Elbert kept the old 1928 Chevy humming day and night. Instead of serving as the family car, for highway use only, it became a truckette, something between a car and a truck. Throughout November and December of 1929, after "the shrinking gourd"—as we referred to supply exceeding demand and prices dwindling—became a reality in our lives, I would often hear a car, look out of our dormitory windows, and see bright headlights and the old Chevy loaded to the last grunt with cotton. The bottom had fallen out of the market. After taking a terrible loss on cotton he had bought before the crash, Papa concentrated on trying to climb back up by paying as little as 5 and 6 cents for cotton that he could only get 7 and 8 cents for. There was so much cotton on the market that when the price was destroyed, so was the margin of profit.

At the store, regular good customers who had kept abreast of their bills weren't able to pay. They came in and asked for more credit, and Papa didn't have the heart to turn them down. They paid what they could, but the bills kept getting larger. Finally Papa was forced to cut down on his inventory. Nevertheless, he struggled along. My brother, Elbert, was his good right arm. A big boy at twelve, he had even started to do more driving, which almost drove me mad with envy. He went with Papa everywhere, while I had to settle for small jaunts.

People didn't take the crash seriously during the first few weeks. They regarded it as a slow period. Things were bound to pick up soon. Instead of picking up, they declined farther.

We had plenty to eat, plenty of winter wood. The store was still operating—though at a much reduced rate. Papa wasn't making the kind of money he had been accustomed to during the boom, from 1920 to 1929. Raw cotton that had been as high as 24 cents per pound was selling for 7 and 8 cents per pound. A bushel of corn had dropped from 80 cents to 50 cents. A bushel of wheat dropped from $1.54 to 67 cents in a few weeks and was steadily declining. Papa complained about having to sell items he had bought before the crash for half of what he paid for them.

I was still having fun at Tilson, refurbishing the bag of tricks that I played on the girls. Miz Harmond had us diagramming sentences, doing short division, learning geography, drawing, and writing. So far, I hadn't found any challenge in my schoolwork.

Poor Larry was as far behind as ever—further. I had moved on to a higher grade while helping him with old stuff. Many times I wanted to draw him a diagram, then thought better of it. If he couldn't understand words and writing, he wouldn't be able to read a diagram either. He had courage. He was sixteen or seventeen years old and still stuttering and stammering his way through life. I felt so sorry for Larry. The Maker had provided him with exceptionally good looks and a pleasing disposition but had taken away his power to speak.

Work was fun to me. I loved making fires beneath the big steel kettle and boiling clothes, quilts, and towels, then helping Mama hang them on the line. I enjoyed helping load and unload cotton, cutting and stacking wood. I had even learned to herd the cows and their calves. The lead cow wore a bell that helped us locate the herd. They never wandered too far from the barn. I wanted them to go far into the woods so I would have the adventure of hunting them down and bringing them back. Cows were a lazy bunch, much less intelligent than even horses. They would lie down in the middle of the road and chew their cuds. People had to get out of their vehicles and whip the creatures out of the road.

December presented itself for the first time since the crash. I did not yet know about the shrinking gourd; I was still too involved in my fun world. Winter's whip once again laid bare the acorns, the remaining harvest of nut-bearing scaly bark and hickory nuts. We dug deep into the potato kiln and covered it back up to prevent the frost from seeping in and making the potatoes rot. Mama and all her daughters added their special patches to the multicolored quilt stretched on a frame in the dining room. Mama kept the pedal to her Singer pumping while she guided material around the shoelike stitcher—material that was soon to become a skirt, a pair of pants, a dress, or a shirt. She made more fuss about the loss of a bobbin pin than she did about the burning of our new Ford. I happened to like smooth, shining silver bobbins. They made nice toys, like marbles.

Mr. Durbey dragged himself down to his shop every day, rekindled the hot coal embers with his old bellows, heated some metal to a white glow, and beat out a tune on his trusty anvil.

Mr. Jim had become a cuckold to his wife—a vassal to Mr. Udell. Even he must have known there was something going on between Miz Marge and Udell other than sharing a cool drink of water. They had started openly picking berries and fishing together. Though Mr. Durbey had aged, he was still strong. I think seeing his daughter mistreating Mr. Jim—whom he dearly loved, far more than Miz Marge—broke his lion's heart and started him down a path of no return.

A.D. was still walking the Pike, singing the blues, and making babies, just like he had promised he would do.

The shrinking gourd began to manifest itself. Greasy, dirty, scratching, long-haired, bearded, smelly white men, usually with different foreign accents and knapsacks tied to sticks, started stopping at the store begging for food. Papa would send me over to the house where Mama would pack some cold biscuits and a couple of baked sweet potatoes in a brown sack. They would fall all over themselves thanking Papa, then tramp on down the Pike toward Cleveland County.

"Po' tramp. Things must really be gittin' tough. Never saw so many of um befo'."

"Whut's er tramp, Papa?" I asked.

"Somebody who don't have er home. They jist tramp from one place to ernother lookin' fer somethin' t' eat."

Yes, the warnings were coming true. Even though it hadn't touched me, I could see its markings. The owls must have known—how they hooted at night. The doves cooed. The jackass brayed. The lonesome moan of the freight train cried in the distant west. "Lord, I want to be like Jesus in my heart" was sung more than enough at Hughes Chapel. Hawks hovered near our henhouse. Papa peppered them with TAAAA-YAAW! from his Winchester to keep them at bay.

What did the great Blacksmith in the sky have in mind for us? What would the Maker of all remedies do about the price of cotton—our lives? What would the Merchant of all merchants bring to replenish Papa's store? What would happen to revive us in the land of the shrinking gourd?

18

Christmas of 1929 was subdued. During the fall of that year after the crash, Papa's losses sent us peddling winter wood, trying to make up for money he had been getting from cotton and the store. Fortunately, the harvest was bountiful. With stored foods that we had grown and items from the store that we hadn't, we met most of our needs.

The early months of 1930 before planting season were those of getting by and wondering whether things would turn around. Meanwhile, conditions continued to get worse.

Mr. Nettelford, the mail carrier, was faithful about sharing information with Papa. Bundled up for January weather, big leather gloves gripping the mail, steam spewing from his mouth, fogging his wire-framed glasses, he leaned toward the passenger's door and gave Papa his mail. "Got a bit of good news for you, Andra."

Papa leaned on the side of the car. "I sho could use some, Ed. Whut is it?"

"That new highway they've been talking about all these years—"

"*Talkin'.* Whut erbout it?"

"Looks like they're starting on it this spring. Some outfit from Louisiana got the job."

"Think business'll pick up, Ed? That's the only way it can help me. Oh, I got plenty customers, but wid no jobs, they ain't got no money," Papa lamented.

"It'll help, Andra. They're going all the way to Louisiana with this Pike. They'll need to hire a lot of men. It'll pay over twice as much as you can make in the fields."

"I was thinkin' in terms er business rather than hirin' out, Ed. I've only got one boy big enough, 'n he's jist twelve. Sho cain't send him out there."

Elbert was splitting and stacking winter wood nearby but listening carefully to the conversation.

As for me, I took exception to Papa saying, "I've only got one boy . . ."

"I was just thinking every little bit would help until things get better. I know Elbert is quite young, but how old were you, Andra, when you first went to work on the railroad?"

"I wuz er young man, seventeen yeahs old, 'n m' mama still had er fit."

"Ha-ha-ha-ha. She was right to worry. Those railroad gangs are rough—full of low-lifers. But that's not your situation. It's not like the boy would have to leave home and go with that gang. He'd be coming home every night."

"Ed, you tryin' t' suggest I should let that boy work wid that road buildin' gang?" A look of disapproval grew on Papa's face.

"No! No! Indeed not. Ha-ha-ha." Mr. Nettelford gave a little nervous cover-up laugh. "Forget I mentioned it, Andra. Gotta go. Ha-ha-ha-ha." Mr. Nettelford laughed in his hearty, friendly way and drove slowly down the Pike to his next stop.

Papa lifted his hat and had started slowly back to the store when he heard Elbert's voice.

"I kin make it."

"You kin make whut?" Papa asked.

"I kin make it on that road gang, that's whut." Elbert never stopped splitting wood.

"Whut the devil y' talkin' erbout, boy?"

"Papa, I been doin' almost er man's job fer over er yeah. By the time spring comes, I'll be thirteen. We cain't sell no mo' winter wood. I kin make twice as much as I kin choppin' cotton or plowin'. Hire Mr. Sam or Reedy to break ground on whut I make till Mama kin hep out wid her peddlin'—"

"Tha-tha-that's ernough outta you, young man! Y' ain't goin' out theah on that road wid that rough gang. That's final! 'Hire Reedy'? Reedy be the first one t' git er job on that road. He's almost er man. Might even be er muleskinner. He sho is big ernough. But you barely dry behind the ears. Talkin' erbout 'I kin make it.' Now I don't wanna heah no mo' er yo' fool talk. Y' heah m'?"

"Yes sir." Elbert submitted with his voice, but his body language told me something different.

The old Pike made a dogleg that ran northeasterly from our house for approximately one quarter of a mile down a slope to Bartholomew Bridge. From the bridge it ran northwesterly up another slope. Our pasture ran along the west side of the Pike almost to the bridge. It was a two-lane road. The bridge was only one lane. The through truss—the steel structure on the sides—projected up above the roadway. It spanned about forty feet and rested solidly on concrete abutments. The high concrete wing-walls retained steep embankments of dirt, rocks, and boulders and kept them from crashing into Bayou Bartholomew.

The Pike was hewed, hauled, heaved, and shaped from the lay of the land. From the sleeping, matted earth that bore curses and blessings, over and over, for untold generations. Won't you wake, call out, and tell what you felt when your red children combed and groomed your black-brown loamy topsoil, then sowed their seeds in the warmth of your womb for still another harvest of maize? Were you sleeping when rebel soldiers brought up artillery along the

Pike—only a crude road then—through rain and mud to fortify their positions in the battle for Pine Ridge? Were you sleeping when Bartholomew's stream ran crimson with the blood of Clayton's and Marmaduke's men? Were you sleeping, old Pike, when treasures were buried by your shores, deep in the bosom of your sticky red clay? Were you sleeping when your face was rearranged, rerouted, and a country-cousin county pike—along the old road—was carved out all the way to the Louisiana line? How could you sleep when all creatures that walked, flew, crept, or crawled left their calling cards—in the form of their broken, crushed, splashed, and matted carcasses—as pavings for your long, winding trail?

How can you still smile, mighty Pike, when over your dusty face runaway horses dragged, mutilated, disfigured, and destroyed my grandfather? How can you lie there so quiet, peaceful, and beautiful—an alluring whore, winking and blinking—your two-legged path open to all through the centuries, while a professor's bloody brains spattered your face one moonlight night because of a debt a white man owed and wanted to avoid paying? How can you be so indifferent and allow burning flames from our new Ford to mar and char, swell and defile your lovely face? In days gone by, twisters have traveled your route, panther and bear have crossed your path.

Riding, gliding along your shadowy reaches, graded and groomed up and down your billowing bluffs, you, Pike, guarded by columns of oaks, gums, hickories, and pines—tree soldiers canopying their branches over your veiled face—still letting in radiant daylight sun and the diamond flickering of the moon at night, you are an enigma. On you, Pike, are bright nights—an irresistible lure, a love trap, a mysterious ghost, an ire healer-destroyer, full of fireflies, bats, fears, and tears, worms, kittle-dees, whippoorwill, barking dogs, and hopping frogs. Ferns grow on your shoulders.

From high vantage points, I can see a winding, twisting trail, cutting through green as if through deep freshly fallen snow, a trail made by brown salt and gravel that bored and snaked its way over hills and dips and streams, around curves, past farms and fruits and forests, families and pheasants, I can see *foreverness* to that disappearing—that dark trail of infinity.

Mighty Pike, paradoxical, with your lean, swollen face—oxymoron, defying description—you are a master of cruel kindness. I have gathered blackberries, huckleberries, and muscadines along your banks and stained my hands, my teeth, my face with the sweet juice of their ripeness. I have picked your wildflowers and your poke salad in seasons allowed. I have guided my wheel with precision up and down your banks without it tumbling over once. I have seen lovers, young and old, deep in the grip of your spell on spring and summer nights. I have smelled your sweet fragrance—your natural perfume—after your dust was settled by cleansing rains. I love you. I hate you. I live with you. I am bemused by your vanity.

*   *   *

The end of our 1930 winter greeted us with rainstorms and overflows as usual. Between the two slopes in the Pike from close to our house to Bartholomew Bridge, three feet of water flooded the road. The Arkansas River, seven miles to the north, backed up into the creeks and bayous each year.

It was necessary to pull cars across the deep to prevent water from splashing on the sparkplugs and distributors. I have no idea who started the toll business, but this was the first time I saw Papa become involved. He supervised Elbert, who handled the team. It was 50 cents per haul—75 for drying plugs and distributors. Papa used to make much more but was glad to get what he could. It was just what he needed—after the crash and a hard winter—to buy seeds and feed for spring planting. Roy Barnard, seeing there was money to be made, quickly sent a horse and mule team to muscle in on the little enterprise.

My legs had grown longer and thinner at eight-and-a-half, and my steps had widened. As I grew taller, my buddy Ben seemed to be growing in the opposite direction. He had always been shorter, but the difference became more obvious as we got older. He had not grown milder in his manners, however. Quite the contrary, he had gotten louder. From his brother A.D., he had also picked up the habit of singing the blues at the top of his powerful lungs. The runtier he became, the more aggressive. It was evident that he was ground-bound, like A.D., and would never grow tall and strong like his stupid brother Carl.

Along with reaching the age of wearing long pants came frequent haircuts. A better description: hair butchering. Elbert and I, being the only boys, were subjected to the untrained, unrestrained hands of our older sister Deloris. After Deloris finished cutting my hair, Papa said, "Looks like somebody set y' in er chair and throwed er ax at y'." The second time she tried her hand, he remarked, "Looks like er plucked chicken wid TB." It got so bad, Papa took up the challenge. He placed a bowl on my head and cut around the bowl. He called it "lowering the ears." Deloris remarked, "Looks mo' like y' raisin' corn." She laughed heartily at her opportunity to get back at Papa. Papa, who seldom burst into laughter, started twitching his mouth. A smile appeared in the corner. A chuckle followed. Finally, when he could no longer contain it, he began laughing.

It was cleansing and healthy to hear him laugh during those days. Heaven knows there was little to laugh about. I had watched spring go out of his big heart and turn into gray, cold, trying winter. Papa was known for having good hands and a sharp eye. When he messed my hair up, it was for another reason—even though he hadn't been trained. His eyesight was getting worse. Pride kept him from using his glasses when he should.

Other symptoms began to appear. Papa's pace had slowed, and he began to sit around Mr. Durbey's shop more than I had ever seen him. He used his cane now for real, not just as a prop or for style. In earlier years, I had watched him throw his cane out in front of him, even swing it over his head, as he walked along at a fast clip. That had all changed. He still dressed well on Sundays and special occasions, though his suits were fitting looser. Through the week, however, his pants and coat began to sag. Patches began to appear, and his sweaty floppy hat had looked better.

Papa hadn't gone back to Hot Springs in over five years. Mama and Uncle Pet tried to get him to go for more treatments.

Mama's brother Uncle Ruben drove over from Wabbaseka and offered to help. He was almost six feet tall, husky, but moved fast, like Mama. He had a pronounced forehead, a ready laugh and smile, and a big heart. He was a little older than she, and they were very close. He would make threats in front of Mama and Papa that he would whip us if we needed it, but he never laid a hand on us when we went to work on his farm. "You gotta take care of your health, Andra, that's all there is to it. I got two hundred acres of bottomland down there, and I'll take every one of those children until you come back."

"You'll take all my chirren?" Papa rolled his eyes at Uncle Ruben.

"Oh, I'll give them back to you, Andra. Don't go getting that crazy look on your face. All you have to do is close the store."

"Close my sto', Ruben?"

"How we gon' run it wid you in Hot Springs?" Mama asked.

"You ran it when I wuz there befo'."

"Yeah, but we need all hands in the fields now t' try 'n make some money. There ain't that much in the sto' t' run no mo', is there, Andra?" Mama seemed sorry she had said anything.

"Things gon' change. Y' heah me? Things gon' turn eround—got to. Wait'll this fall when them big crops start comin' in, 'n cotton prices go back up. Them workers on that Pike start spendin' them long paychecks. M. A. Hughes'll be right theah to cash them checks—'n git m' merchandise back, biggah than evah. You'll see. Jist gotta have er little patience, that's all. Business is like that. Up-'n-down. Up-'n-down. All the time. I see er bright future wheah y'all don't see no hope."

"I never said there's no hope, Andra. All I'm saying is for you to get yourself to Hot Springs for the summer. There you'll be around good doctors who'll give good treatment. You'll be living there at the Woodmans'—where you're a member, like before," Uncle Ruben said.

"I had money then. Who's gon' pay for all this?" Papa asked.

"Who's gon' pay if y' don't git well?" Mama asked.

"That's right, Andra. Your health comes first. Sometimes you have to bend with the wind or you'll break," Uncle Ruben said.

"Tell y' whut, let m' see how this new Pike works out. Plus, I gotta plant m' own crops in er few days. I'll need all hands fer that. Kitty's gotta git her garden in. By then it'll be cotton-choppin' time. Then we'll see how many kin go, all 'cept Elbert. How do that sound?"

"It sounds all right except for one thing," Uncle Ruben said, looking at Mama.

"Y' still ain't said nothin' erbout yo'self, Andra," Mama responded.

"That's right. The whole thing is about your health. You need those treatments, Andra," Uncle Ruben said gravely.

"I jist cain't leave now. Maybe in the fall when pickin' season's ovah."

"If it's the money you're worried about, Andrew, don't. I'm sure we'll be able to get it together. What are we for?" Uncle Ruben got in his car and headed toward Pine Ridge.

Early in April, one chilly morning around two o'clock, the earth shook and thunderous rumbling violated our deep slumber. Thinking it was an earthquake or a twister, we rushed out in our nightgowns. Once outside, we heard men's voices, squeaking saddle leather, and horses' hooves. Moving slowly from the north, invading our space like a mighty, dark tide, was a herd of snorting, tramping animals.

It was a bright night, and we could make out images clearly as they approached. A herd of mules covered the entire road and was spilling over into the woods as they moved. A rider on horseback came galloping straight toward our fence. He cracked his bullwhip to direct the herd away from it. His spirited horse, saddled with brown bradded gear, was snorting, slobbering, and prancing. The rider was wearing a rugged cowboy suit with a wide hat, wide chaps on his legs, and boots. He carried only a Winchester in his gear and a canvas pack behind his saddle that bounced up and down as his mount galloped. The horse was a magnificent calico, the likes of which I had never seen. The rider looked like a young lad not much older than Elbert.

My boy's heart pounded in my chest, and I was overcome with envy. I knew immediately, without question, that when I became older, that was what I wanted to do. In fact, I wanted to do it as soon as possible. With all my heart I wanted to be a cowboy. I was born to be a cowboy. It was in my blood. I had to be a cowboy. There was nothing else on God's green earth worth being but a cowboy. I couldn't wait for daybreak.

Papa made us go back to bed, but I couldn't sleep. The rumbling of the herd, the lightning sound of cracking whips, and the vision of that rider on his calico steed crowded my mind. At long last day came. I popped out of bed as if it was Christmas, got dressed, and headed straight for the porch of our store. Ben and some of his brothers soon joined me.

Mr. Durbey came dragging down the hill to his shop. "Whut in tarnation's goin' on down heah? Y' mean somebody want m' to shoe all them mules? He-he-he-he."

"You'd be workin' well into the next century, Brother Durbey," Papa remarked as he joined us.

The herd kept coming. They were gray, red, brown, and calico. They were all shapes and sizes. They were young and mature, with long pretty tails and equally long leafy ears. They were well behaved and easily controlled. I didn't see a poor or limping mule among them. I never saw a horse among them, only beautiful round fat mules. Hundreds and thousands of them, marching, marching, steadily marching. There wasn't a car, buggy, or wagon to be seen on the Pike, not even Mr. Nettelford delivering the mail. There was absolutely no room.

Mama called us for breakfast. After we ate, we all took off for the fields and Mama's garden. Papa stayed and watched what was left of his store.

When we returned that evening, the herds were still marching. A few cowboys were riding along beside them with their bullwhips, which they hardly needed.

Mr. Durbey had closed his shop and was straightening up around the place and talking to Papa. "Heah come Kitty, M.A. He-he-he. Guess she wonderin' whut's goin' on."

"Whut on earth's goin' on? Y' mean t' tell me them mules still comin'?" Mama asked.

"They didn't let up once since they started last night," Papa said.

"Hard t' figure, ain't it, Kitty?" Mr. Durbey said.

"They takin' over the whole Pike. You'd think they'd put som'um in the papers—give folks some kind er warnin'. Whut did y'all find out?"

"Not much. I talked t' one er the foremen, 'n all he could tell m' is these mules is owned by some big trader outta Pine Ridge. They brought um into town on freight cars from Missouri, 'n they corrallin' um further down the Pike heah in Risen," Papa said.

Mr. Durbey joined him. "'N that fool wuz 'poligizin' fer not knowin' mo'."

"Everbody knows G. L. Hewett is the biggest trader in this part of the country. He been buyin' 'n selling Missouri mules for many yeahs. Bought some from im m'self. Question is, whut happened that he's movin' all these mules at one time. I lived heah since I wuz a boy, never saw anything like it befo'. You, Brother Durbey?"

"Never," Mr. Durbey said.

Mama shook her head and went over to the house to supervise getting supper on the table. Hazel and Deloris had come home earlier to start cooking.

The herds kept coming. After supper I went out and watched some more with Ben. The hooves of the animals had dug little holes in the gravel. All grass, bushes, and vegetation was trampled along the shoulders of the Pike. The ground was littered with droppings they had left in their wake. Finally the sun set, and evening shadows gave way to night; still mules kept coming. Ben and I watched the browns, reds, grays, blacks, and calicos turn into silhouettes, marching—constantly marching—south up the hill as far as we could see. We looked north, up the Pike, and the same silhouettes were steadily coming, one endless line, thick as ants marching, steadily marching. Now and then we saw a cowboy pass, his saddle leather crying, his mount snorting and blowing, his whip cracking. Finally we heard Ben's mother, Miz Orathia, calling. Immediately after, I heard Mama calling me also. We watched what little we could before the moon rose, then reluctantly stole inside.

I had become used to the constant rumbling and the earth shaking. Tired from a long day's work in the garden and keeping a constant watch on the herds, I fell fast asleep.

Time seemed only too short before Mama was shaking me. "Rise-'n-shine," she said.

"I'm risin', Mama. But it's too early t' shine," I mumbled, stumbling to the back porch and starting to wash up. "Sun ain't even up 'n shinin' yet."

Mama laughed and shook my shabby haircut. "Boy, you're er mess. I declare."

We headed back to the fields and garden the second day, leaving the herds still constantly marching. The clouds had gathered, and it looked like rain.

Papa took out his watch and looked up at the sky. "Kitty, y' think y' oughtta wait er while? Looks like rain."

"They look like movin' clouds t' me. Might be er few showers, but I doubt if they'll last. I gotta git these collards 'n t'matah plants in today. Rain'll do um good." Mama paused and looked at Papa for a serious moment. "Y' take yo' shot this mornin'? Y' don't look too good t' me, Andra."

"I'm all right, Kitty. Cain't stop."

"I jist hate it so bad y' won't go see Dr. Brian, see whut he say erbout gittin' y' back in Hot Springs fer some mo' treatments."

"I'll go up there soon as the Pike's cleah," Papa said.

"Y' promise?"

"I promise, Kitty." Papa stood like a little boy and let Mama wipe sweat from his face with her apron and fuss over his appearance much as she did mine and my sister Verleen's.

"I sho hope it'll be cleah this evenin' when we come home." Mama turned and followed the wagon up the little hill toward her garden. Behind us, the leather saddles kept crying, the whips kept making their lightning sounds, and the herds kept marching, their rumbling gradually growing weaker.

Mama was right about the showers. They came as she had said. When they were heavy, we went under the wagon—never a tree. When they were light, we simply enjoyed them and kept working. As the day wore on, however, it became evident that the bladder of heaven was too full to be satisfied with a mere squirt here and there. Thunder and lightning became more quarrelsome. Birds became quiet and sought refuge among the limbs of heavily endowed shade trees. Dark clouds rolled in, and night crawlers began squeezing their way out of their sockets like strings of ground sausage. Verleen, Geneva, and I began gathering them up in cans, for fishing. The air became chilly, and the winds would not quiet themselves.

Mama looked up at the sky and gave the order. "Elbert! Hazel! Deloris! Geneva! Er-er-chirren! Y'all gathah up yo' things, 'n let's git on home. That looks like er real stohm cloud."

Indeed it was a storm cloud. Before we got home, it was pouring. Not too much for me, however. I pulled my straw hat down over my ears, took my shoes in my hand, and had a good time wading through mud holes, splashing through the water—the mud squirting between my toes. My little sister, Verleen, was right behind me, imitating my every move.

We arrived home soaked. Papa was standing in the door puffing and blowing with his hat twisted on his head. He was wet also but had a good hot fire going.

"Andra, you shouldn't be out theah tryin' t' git no wood t' start er fire," Mama complained.

"Whut y' mean, tryin'? The fire's goin', ain't it? Y'all jist git outta them wet things so you won't catch no summer cold."

I hated to come inside, but I had to admit it was cozy sitting around a hot fire, drinking sassafras tea sweetened with honey, and to have on warm, dry clothes after it had turned chilly.

The rain came down steadily for a while but slacked up before dark. I could still hear the rumbling of marching hooves, the resonant cadence of snorting, the crying saddle leather, and the authoritative crack of the whip outside. I threw someone's raincoat over me—it was many sizes too big, dragging on the ground. No matter, I ventured outside and continued the watch alone. It was still drizzling rain. Even my buddy Ben stayed inside. If he had known, however, I'm sure he would have been on the job.

The riders had donned their raincoats. They looked more like tepees sitting on their mounts, their wide hats flopping over their ears, soaking wet, their soggy boots holding steady in the stirrups. I saw a rider put the spurs to his mount, gallop up ahead, and steer a stray back in line by cracking his whip. The wet hemp attached to the end of the leather made the sound of a rifle echoing in the distance.

When, oh, when would it end? What did it all mean? I never thought there were so many mules in the world. That trader, Hewett, must be a mighty rich man. How did he feed all those mules—and when? I hadn't seen any feeding wagons come along.

Mules represented power. Why did they always say "horsepower"? Mules were far more powerful than horses—far more intelligent as well. No one ever heard of a mule burning to death in a barn like a stupid horse or a cow. Cows were too lazy and dull to get out of the way, but horses were plain too stupid. Fire attracted them. Only the lowly mule had sense enough not to cross a bridge that looked unsafe. Mules knew when it was twelve noon or quitting time and sometimes dragged their would-be masters, plow and all, to the house. No panther in his right mind would attack a mule, although it wouldn't hesitate to take on a horse or a cow.

Instead of *horsepower*, if I had to judge, it would have been *mulepower*. Instead of "plain old common horse sense," it would have been "plain old common mule sense." However, "a horse's ass" I would let stand. That phrase had been used so well, with such power and authority, by men like Gene Cannon, Reedy Riley, and Udell Barrow, I dared not tamper with it.

What did the eagle ever do to become our national symbol, except prey on other animals, including the farmer's livestock? The faithful mule provided the power that built the railroads, the highways, packed us across deserts, plowed our farms, hauled our timber and our crops. Yes, the lowly sons and daughters of mares and jackasses, who couldn't even reproduce their own kind, gave their all for a few ears of corn, some oats, and hay in return. Yet some overgrown chicken, first cousin to the buzzard, that has flown itself bald-headed trying to get something to eat, the stupid horse, which hasn't sense enough to come out of a fire, and even the dull-witted cow, which is too lazy to do so, have been elevated to a place of honor above that of the faithful, hard-working, sensible mule. Why can't we see that mules are beautiful in a very special way? There should indeed be a National Mule Day.

After solving most of the country's problems in my mind, I heard Mama's familiar voice and responded, "Coming! I'm coming, Mama!" Dripping and chilly, I strolled slowly back toward the house. Flashes of lightning lit up the multicolored herd as they snorted, slobbered, emptied their bowels, farted, and stepped lively toward a destination of which they knew nothing. What was behind such a big movement? If the mules were to be sold, why bring them all the way from Missouri? Or were they sold before they left Missouri? What change was taking place that was different from anything Papa and Mr. Durbey had ever seen?

Early the next morning, I felt Mama's familiar hand. "Wake up, Sun. Y' stayed out theah too long watchin' them stupid mules last night."

The word *stupid* aroused me. I woke up right away and came to the defense of those mules. "Mules ain't stupid, Mama. I know some people who could use some good ol' common mule sense."

"I know some too, for that matter, but people can change. Become governor, or even president. Name me one mule that can do that."

While washing my face, I suddenly stopped in my tracks. I was struck by the startling absence of the rumbling sound I had heard for the past three days and nights.

"Whut's the matter wid you, boy?"

"Mama, listen . . ."

"Listen t' whut?"

I hurried outside, soapy-faced, towel in hand. "They're gone!"

"Oh, y' mean them mules. They stopped marchin' sometime last night. Erbout time, don't y' think?"

"Yes ma'am. I guess so," I said sadly. In my heart, I had begun to enjoy the excitement. The sad quietness left me without a sense of what to do next. Change was upon us. Everything around us was changing. Papa was doing things to make ends meet that he had never done in my memory. The new Pike was slowly inching its way south toward us. And the biggest movement of mules in the history of our area had come to a close. Uncle E.J. wrote Papa about the bad conditions poor people from the dust bowls were creating by migrating to once-faraway California. What were dust bowls? And where were they found?

Mr. Nettelford was early that morning. He had three days' mail backed up. All three editions of the *Arkansas Gazette* were full of news about the marching mules and the deepening Depression. "Well, I guess you wondering what on earth's happening, eh, Andra?"

"I sho am, Ed. Why didn't them devils tell us they wuz marchin' all them mules down our Pike?"

"I heard they didn't want to alarm people. Ha-ha. I-I can't really tell you, Andra." Mr. Nettelford laughed craftily.

"They didn't want t' alarm us—"

"I'm telling you what I heard, Andra." Mr. Nettelford wiped his forehead and gave Papa the rest of his mail. "It's all in your *Gazette* there."

"I don't need no *Gazette* t' tell me erbout the mules. I saw three days er them with m' own eyes . . ."

Noticing Papa extending the paper in front of him, Mr. Nettelford took time to briefly explain. "You're like lots of folks, Andra. You can't get it through your head that this is a real Depression, probably the worst we've ever had before this thing is over. I didn't read the whole thing in detail, but another big man who couldn't meet his payments went belly-up—bankrupt. The man who he loaned the money foreclosed and took the property. In this case, it was all of those mules you saw. It's a big change of fortune, Andra." Mr. Nettelford straightened back up in his seat and shifted to first. "Gotta run. Take care of yourself, Andra."

"Thank y', Ed."

A few days after the herd ended its march, Udell, Carl, and A.D. came down the Pike and turned up Wagon Road West riding and leading a miniherd of mules. One look and I could see there was something wrong with those mules. There were twenty-two of them. Some were limping. Others had big sores. There was one with an ear missing and another with no tail. The one A.D. was riding looked as if he was blind. There were two things in their favor, however: they were all young, fairly round, and plump.

Ben and I were standing on the side of the road watching.

"Wanna buy er mule, Sun? We got all kinds. Y' jist name what kind er fucked-up mule y' want, 'n I gantee y' we got im." A.D. was about to fall off his mount laughing.

"Y' ain't funny worth er damn, A.D.!" Mr. Udell scolded, and spat a mouthful of tobacco juice.

"If y' want one wid er third eye in the middle of his forehead, we got that som-bitch too." A.D. looked back at a gray mule with a big lump.

"That ain't no third eye, fool, that's er lump," Carl said.

"Jist like the one you gon' have, y' keep it up wid yo' smart mouth," Udell warned.

"Lump, bump, third eye, no tail, no ears—fucked up! Jist plain fucked up, Udell! Whatever made y' buy er bunch er lamed, maimed, fucked-up animals like this? Watch this." A.D. steered his mule toward a tree. The mule bumped head-on into the tree. A.D. laughed and laughed.

Ben and I joined him. Finally, Carl and Udell had to laugh also.

"Udell, I s'pose y' gon' use that ol' one erbout 'This mule ain't blind, he jist don't give er damn,' right?"

"The mule ain't blind. He jist obed'ent, that's all," Udell protested.

"Obed'ent my ass, this mule is blind, y' heah me? *B-L-E-I* . . . well anyhow, he's blind! Next thing y' be tellin' us this som-bitch need glasses."

"Y' steered the mule into er tree. The mule been trained, 'n he did whut he wuz tol'—which is mo'n I kin say fer you."

"This is er Missouri mule, Udell. If they all trained t' be so damned obed'ent, let m' see y' steer that un y' ridin' into er tree." A.D. made his point.

"Blind or not, I'm still gon' sell the som-bitch. Jisssst like I bought im I'm gon' sell im," Udell said.

"Who gon' buy im? Somebody blind, like him?" A.D. asked.

"Naw, somebody stupid, like you," Udell came back.

"Who bought im in the first place?"

The argument between A.D. and his father went on as we watched them herd the afflicted into a corral that Udell had built behind his house. I knew then why I hadn't seen any maimed, crippled animals in the marching herd. They had all been separated from the healthy ones when they got off the freight train in Pine Ridge. Udell had picked them up for little or nothing because the owner didn't want to spend money taking care of useless cargo.

The cruelest act of all was when maimed mules were abandoned in the woods or left in somebody's field to wander and die. The owners wouldn't spend the money for the bullets needed to put the animals out of their misery, which might also have meant the expense of dragging them away and burning them.

A few days after the herds ended their march, I heard explosions up the Pike. The muffled sound went on all through the day as the rumbling of marching mules had done. Once again the earth trembled and shook with a rare sensation I had felt only when angry thunder and lightning occurred. As April came to a close, the sound of explosions became more pronounced. It was no surprise that work on the new Pike had begun. Mr. Quaking Pete DiGasspri, a contractor from Louisiana, needed able-bodied men.

Soon Mama's early garden would be ready. Meanwhile, Papa needed money for seeds, feed, and merchandise. The good business he had enjoyed did not return. Things were getting worse. The *Gazette* was full of stories about failed businesses, unemployment, starvation, and people engaging in sensational life-threatening stunts. Though Papa's credit had been good, the bank was not extending more loans—not even on land. After all, what could the bank do with more hilly forest land?

Another option for raising a little cash was sending his family out to chop cotton. Adults could earn 50 cents per day, and children, 25. Papa resisted that with all his might, which was dwindling daily. Besides, we had corn and cotton of our own that needed chopping. Worst of all, "it would put us in the same class with them Udells."

Elbert could make almost $2 per day as a mule skinner on the new Pike.

"That boy is entirely too young, Kitty, I don't care how much he kin make. That rough crew is nothin' but gamblers 'n drunkards. 'N er lot of um carry knives 'n guns. I know 'cause I worked on the railroad m'self, but I was much older. I could take care of m'self. That boy ain't even thirteen yet," Papa said.

"Y' don't have t' convince me, Andra. I'd much rather he hire out as er plowboy, or chop cotton wid us."

Little did Papa or Mama know; Elbert had already talked with Pete DiGasspri and lied about his age. His strong, sturdy build and mature air enabled him to convince DiGasspri. His only problem was getting Papa's consent.

A few days after Papa had refused Elbert's request and Mama backed up the decision, a strange, humiliating incident occurred. Business was so bad at the store, Papa closed it that morning and followed us to the field to supervise. His pace had slowed, his pants sagged more, his floppy felt hat showed white salt streaks where sweat had dried around the band. His eyes had gotten worse, and he leaned heavily on his cane. Papa seldom smiled those days, and his temper was short. With nine mouths to feed and the crash already six months old, he had gotten $9 worth of merchandise from his nearest competitor, Roy Barnard. It wasn't an old debt, and Papa had planned to take care of it as soon as chopping and Mama's peddling opened up. Unfortunately, Barnard couldn't or wouldn't wait. That morning around ten o'clock, while most of us were working in the garden, I heard horses' hooves and crying saddle leather coming east on Wagon Road West. Three riders rode up to our garden fence leading a heifer with our brand on it. They were dressed in cowboy outfits and carried rifles in their saddle gear.

"Mornin', Andy—y'all. I guess this heifer erbout squares whut y' owe m'."

"Whut's the meanin' er this, Mr. Barnard? You turn my heifer loose this minute! I'll pay y' whut I owe y', 'n you know it."

"Sorry, Andy, cain't wait no longer fer m' money. Things were different maybe I could, but times is tough, 'n I'm takin' this heah heifer fer the nine dollars y' owe m'."

"Y' got no right! Y' didn't give me any notice. Whut kind er business is that? That heifer worth far mo'n any nine dollars, 'n you know it."

"Sorry y' feel that way, Andy. Let's go, boys." Barnard and his fellow cowboys rode away leading our heifer.

"I'll have the law on y', Mr. Barnard! Y' cain't git erway wid this!" Papa was hopelessly stalking after them. "Y' cain't take er man's property like this without givin' him notice! Y' think I'm er fool! Y'... y'... dirty ... bastard!" The last words trailed off to a weak, exhausted whisper, as Papa stood there with his back to us, his hat in his hand, shaking his cane high in the air.

But Barnard did get away with it, and very handily. It was at that moment, when I saw Papa standing there yelling at the top of his lungs—which I had never heard him do before—helpless, without any hope of relief or recovery, that I began to feel the awesome effect of the changes taking place. Although Papa was sick, he remained master of all the problems he encountered, and his word was law. I had not reckoned that we couldn't take matters of a white man's law to another white man to get help.

I didn't know it at the time, but what Papa did was dangerous, could have been taken as disrespectful to white folks and made grounds for a lynching. I recalled the story about Professor Evans, who loaned a white man $200. To keep from paying the debt, the white man ambushed the professor on the Pike one moonlit night and blew his brains out with a shotgun. The professor taught school in the bayou country. He was an intelligent man with a winning smile. It was rumored that he was a bootlegger on the side.

Whatever was done to Papa was done to me. Saliva dried up in my mouth, and I couldn't swallow. A bitter taste ensued. I stood there watching him from the rear, shaking and trembling in the wake of Barnard and his men. I started shaking and trembling also. Nobody said a word. He dropped his hat. I walked slowly beside him, picked it up, and gave it to him. He took the hat mechanically without acknowledging my presence.

Papa mumbled something to himself, "Devil . . . ermagine that devil takin' my heifer like that . . ."

I was baptized in hate for Roy Barnard. He had passed as Papa's friend. I had played with his son whenever Papa had an occasion to stop there. As far as I was concerned, Roy Barnard wasn't as good as a rattlesnake. The rattler always warned his victim before he struck.

I wondered, *Why hadn't somebody done something about Professor Evans?* I soon found out that if a white person did you wrong, your danger was increased when you dared to complain. The practice was that all of your complaints against a white person had to be taken up by another, more powerful white man or they would surely come to naught or perhaps cost your life. Why did Roy Barnard change from respecting Papa when he was doing well to such violent disrespect when he was down? Did the crash hit Barnard where it hurt so that he had to go out and illegally take his neighbor's property at gunpoint?

That evening as we were rocking along home on the wagon, everyone remained quiet. Elbert spoke up. "Papa, Pete DiGasspri offered me a job the other day. I tol' him I wuz goin' on eighteen . . ."

"You whut? You went behind my back lookin' fer er job? Y' lost yo' mind, boy?"

"Papa, after whut happened today, I think y' oughtta let m' try it. I'll only be workin' er few miles erway. I'll be home every night. We need the money, 'specially till Mama's garden's ready. Carl Barrow, my age, been working er week. 'N there's others no older than I am. They workin' on they second paycheck."

"Whut others yo' age?"

"Some of the Beardens, the Youngs, 'n er lot er boys from Over In The Hills. I'll be all right, Papa."

"I'll talk t' Pete Degasey."

"DiGasspri, Papa."

"Whut-ever. Whut y' think, Kitty?"

"Already tol' y' whut I think. Who gon' do the plowin' 'n hep wid all the man's work needed eround heah?"

"Wid whut I make we can hire somebody fer seventy-five cents er day t' do the plowin'."

The explosions and hammering became louder as spring grew hotter. I only had a chance to see Elbert at night when he came home from work and on Sundays. Working overtime, six days per week, he brought home long checks. He was right. Papa hired Mr. Sam Riley to do the plowing and other work that needed doing. Sometimes he hired another man to help Mr. Sam.

Mama's garden came in early May. My fascination with becoming a cowboy began to take shape. I was allowed to go to the pasture, rope our gentle mare, and ride her to herd our cows home. I had no saddle and used only a halter instead of a bridle. Elbert taught me to tie a halter. I had wetted and bent my straw hat to make it look like a cowboy's. I mounted the mare's bare back, kicked her in the side, as if I was wearing spurs. The mare broke into a trot very much as she did when hitched to a buggy.

After I drove the cows home for my older sisters to milk, Papa took the wheels off the buggy, and we rolled them to Bayou Bartholomew, where we submerged them in water so they would swell up good and tight overnight. After I brought in wood for the cooking stove, Mama had me heat water in the big metal pot, take a good hot bath, and go to bed.

Before daybreak, Mama woke me and started me getting ready to go to Pine Ridge with her. While Deloris was preparing breakfast, Geneva and I ran down to the bayou and rolled the buggy wheels back home. Papa put on plenty of axle grease and mounted the wheels. While all that was going on, Elbert was feeding the livestock and harnessing the horse. Meanwhile, Mama was busy packing her buggy with tender mustard and turnip greens, various early vegetables—peas, radishes, lettuce, peppers, tomatoes, cucumbers, okra, and string beans, and beautiful flowers. Deloris called everybody to breakfast, which always consisted of hot biscuits, gravy, syrup, ham, eggs, and cornflakes with milk. "Hurry up 'n git dressed now, Sun. Yo' clothes all laid out on the bed fer y'."

When I saw the short pants, I immediately started to rebel. "Mama, I don't wanna wear no short pants! Where my long ones?"

Her voice came back from the kitchen, "You'll put on whut I got laid out fer y', young man! Don't let m' have t' come in theah!"

Not only did she have those stupid short pants laid out, but my Sunday slippers and a pair of silly-looking long white socks.

"Mama! Who's supposed to wear all this Sunday junk?"

"Put um on, Mr. Big Man! Now if I have t' tell y' ergin, y' gon' wish I didn't, 'cause I'm in er hurry, 'n I'll ring er plug outta y'!" Mama went on fussing while she was getting dressed in her peddling best. "Y' heah m'? Can't have y' takin' stuff t' people lookin' like er tramp. Y' gotta be clean 'n presentable when y' sellin' stuff t' folks."

On our way to Pine Ridge, we detoured from Main Street by turning west and going to Cherry Street. We turned right on Cherry on our way into town. I wanted to continue up Main Street where the men were working so I could see Elbert. I soon discovered that Mama had customers on south Cherry Street also, where she began her peddling immediately. Cherry was a beautiful long tree-lined street occupied by wealthy whites, many of whom were professionals. Our first stop was a palatial estate sitting cloistered far back from the street. It was mostly hidden by blooming trees and manicured shrubbery. Mama rang her peddling bell, and a black woman came to the fence.

"Whut y' got this mornin', Kitty?"

"I got early . . ." Mama went through her long list of earlies and ended with the flowers.

"I know the doctor's gon' 'preciate them early peas 'cause he loves um. He sho do," the woman said. She was obviously the maid.

"How is Dr. 'n Miz Clark?" Mama inquired.

"They fine, Kitty. I'll tell um y' ax erbout um."

"How erbout some fresh butter t' go erlong wid them peas, Sister Jones?"

"I'm glad y' thought erbout that, Kitty. I cleah done forgot."

Before Mama had finished, she had sold Sister Jones twice as much as she came to buy.

"Heah's yo' butter, yo' greens, yo' radishes, peas, 'n heah's er petunia fer each of y'."

"But Kitty, I didn't order—"

"No charge fer the petunia, Sister Jones. It's m' callin' card."

"Thannnk you, Kitty. Thank you so much. They soooo pretty." The woman went on and on about the flowers rather than the earlies, as she fished out money and paid.

"Bye, now." Mama waved.

"Bye, Kitty." Sister Jones stood waving as the mare trotted up the street to the next customer.

I thought, *Is this all there is to this peddling?* My sister Geneva had always gone with Mama. This was my first trip. Mama was only practicing a tradition that most truck farmers—black and white—had engaged in for generations in that area. She had done it as a means of unloading surplus, since Papa couldn't sell that produce to people who grew their own. Now, however, it became a means of survival.

Our next stop was different. Mama rang her peddling bell, and a white woman came to the door.

"Whut y' got this mornin', Kitty?"

"I got early peas, mustards, turnips—they good 'n tender—early radishes, tomatoes—"

"Y' got anything er little late, Kitty? All this early stuff make m' wanna go back t' bed," the woman drawled.

"Well, whut would y' like, ma'am?"

"Have yo' boy bring me er quart er yo' early peas, er quarter's worth er yo' early mustard, 'n er quart er yo' precious-early-gittin'-up-in-the-mornin' dewberries. Er, heee." The woman was restraining a laugh.

I took the items in my arms, hopped down from the buggy, walked through the gate, and headed for the front door where the woman was standing. She started to get red in the face and became very upset.

"Sun! Sun!" Mama yelled.

"Yes ma'am." I turned around quickly. It was such a desperate call, I thought my pants were open and my wee-wee was hanging out.

"Go to the back! Go to the back, boy!"

I turned around slowly—confused—walked out through the gate back to the street and then opened the gate on the side and went around to the back of the house. Meanwhile I had been standing no more than five feet from the woman and could have reached her the earlies and gone on to our next house.

"Y' ain't trained that boy no better'n that, Kitty?" the woman said angrily.

"I'm sorry, ma'am. It's his first time. He'll git the hang of it. It won't happen ergin." Mama reached the woman a flower over the fence. "It's m' callin' card, ma'am. I sho hope y' like it."

The woman took the flower, and a smile came over her face.

As for me, my mind was stripping gears trying to figure out whether to go forward, backward, sideways, or straight up.

My protected life in a self-sufficient, fairly affluent family had not prepared me for the inequities and racial practices that everyone around me took for granted. What made it more confusing was that Mama, Papa, and the pastor told us, "We're all the same in the sight of God. You jist as good as anybody, 'n don't let nobody tell you different." To me, it was fast beginning to appear that some folks were *samer* and far *gooder* than others.

Mama didn't scold me for going to the front door. She simply reminded me each time, lest I forget.

"I don't like it either, but it's the South," Mama attempted to explain.

I kept my thoughts on the practices of the South to myself. I certainly wasn't going to question Mama or Papa about something neither of us could do much about. However, there was never a conscious moment when I didn't resent with all my heart being treated in such a smutty manner. It made me feel unclean, unholy, unworthy. The troubling part was, I didn't have the slightest notion of why I felt that way. But who cared about what I resented. We had to stay alive. I delivered our earlies to white people's back doors all over the place. Some houses had side doors rather than back doors. I found myself looking for the back door anyway. How was I supposed to know all houses weren't built with us in mind?

I began to understand the message on the Stage Planks. Alas, that grotesque picture on the wrapping was about us! Nobody else but us! Those big billboards I had seen of ugly characters with their big white teeth and small heads buried in a big slice of watermelon were also about us! Those hitching posts outside white people's homes, black figures all dressed up in courtly fashion, hats off, humbly bowing—they were about us too!

Questions crowded my young mind. What on earth was behind all that? What made us important enough to deserve all that negative attention? Why did they spend good money and go out of their way to make us look bad? It was also very confusing because most white people spoke softly and were always trying to give us something, whether or not we wanted or needed it—especially food. I had been trained well not to eat their food. What I didn't know, in the case of wealthy whites, was that the food was cooked by one of us.

Mama had black customers also. Sometimes I forgot and found myself going to their back doors as well. "Where y' goin', boy? I got er bulldog tied up back there. Y' git too close, he tear yo' ass up. We have t' go t' the back ernough without us doin' it t' ourselves."

"He forgot," Mama said, laughing.

"Yeah, I know. These greens look real good, Kitty. See y' next time. 'N boy, you stay erway from my bulldog, y' heah?"

"Yes sir," I said.

"We always front do' wid each other, remember that," the man said.

"Yes sir."

"We sho do thank y', Mr. Lawson. Heah's some flowers fer you 'n yo' wife. It's m' callin' card."

"Thank y', Kitty. As always, she gon' be glad t' git these."

That man made me know I wasn't alone in feeling the way I did about going to the back door.

Almost all our earlies were gone except what Mama had stashed away for our next stop. It was noon, and time for a break anyway. Even before we got to the house, a haggard, shabby little snaggletoothed woman with her stockings hanging down her legs and run-over, worn-out shoes, braids standing all over her head, ran out into the hot noonday sun and flagged us down.

"Where y' goin', Cuttin Kitty?" the woman asked.

"We comin' t' see you, Cuttin Susie."

"Well, don't jist set there, git down 'n come on in, y'all. Who's this boy? I don't 'member seein' im befo'."

"We call im Sun," Mama said.

"Whut's the matter, Sun? Cat got yo' tongue? Cain't you talk?"

"Yes ma'am. My name's M. A. Hughes the Third. They call me Sun."

"That's right, Sun, talk! Don't ever be scared t' talk whut y' know! My name's Susie Rowell, 'n I ain't never been scared to talk! If anythin', they have t' shut me up. People who scared t' talk always puny-lookin' 'n hungry. That's 'cause they scared t' speak up. Them big fat ones take all the grub from um. Talk whut y' know, Susie!"

Though Cuttin Susie looked as if she'd been hit by a tornado, her little house was spotless. When I got a whiff of the food cooking in her kitchen, she started to look better to me.

"I knowed y' wuz comin' by today, Cuttin Kitty. Good Lord tol' m' in er dream t'other night. Yes He did! The Lord talk t' m', y' know, jist like I'm talkin' t' you right now. Tell it, Susie! Talk whut y' know!" She noticed the sack in Mama's hand. "Whut y' got there, Cuttin Kitty?"

"Jist some things I saved fer you, Cuttin Susie. They from m' early garden."

"Bless yo' heart, Cuttin Kitty. Y' sho is good t' me—er po' ol' widow woman—you 'n Cuttin Andra too. He always brings m' som'um when he comes by—always. Wish I could say the same thing fer Cuttin Pet. Ol' bal'-headed fool. He'll drive his car right by heah, 'n 'less I'm standin' on the sidewalk, he won't even stop. My daughter, Fredia, says she sees him all the time goin' down the street to that big market to sell his stuff in big lots. He don't peddle like y'all, y' know. How soon some people forgit when they git up in the worl', but you jist mark my word, Lord's go' bring um back down! Tell the truth, Susie!"

"You mean he don't ever stop?"

"Oh, he'll stop if I happen t' be out there 'n flag him down. I ain't gon' jump in front of his car no mo', though. That fool nearly run m' down las' time I did that. Tell it like 'tisssss, Susie! Tell it like 't-i-s!"

"Well, I declare. . . ," Mama said as she took the vegetables out of the sack.

"Them greens sho do look good, Cuttin Kitty, them radishes too. Whut's these, early peas? Oh, my God! Bless y', Cuttin Kitty! Bless y'!" Cuttin Susie took everything into her little kitchen. "Y'all jist make yo'selves at home. These vittles'll be ready d'reckly. That boy look so hungry, I'm scared t' git close t' him, fear he might bite me."

Mama laughed. Cuttin Susie brought a plate of tea cakes out. "Y'all hep yo'selves till other stuff's ready. Don't ruin yo' appetites, though."

"If I wuz you, I'd worry mo' erbout him ruinin' my cookie jar, Cuttin Susie," Mama said.

I bit down on a cookie, and the banana and vanilla flavors jumped right out and introduced themselves. The tea cakes simply couldn't be beat. I couldn't wait to taste whatever it was she was cooking in that pot.

"I *will* say this fer Cuttin Pet, though, every fall eround hog-killin' time, he'll come by, blow his horn, 'n leave m' er mess er fresh pork 'n two, three bunches er them great big turnip greens he grow in that slew er his'n. Tell the truth, Susie! Don't leave nothin' out! Give the devil his due!"

"Will he stop long, Cuttin Susie?" Mama inquired.

"Erbout long as er dog at er fire hydrant. He pees on it 'n keeps on trottin'. He got t' git back t' his sto', he says. Like crazy Cuttin Babe gon' set there 'n let somebody run erway wid it. I knowed um befo' he had er sto'. *Taaaalk,* Susie! I knowed im befo' his oldest brother, Cuttin E.J., had er sto'. *Taaalk-taaaalk,* Susie Rowell, whut y' know! Now yo' brother, Cuttin Ruben, he er edicated man. He went t' that big universiry where that Booker T. Washington was. *He* spend mo' time wid m' 'n Cuttin Pet do." Cuttin Susie went into the kitchen and started fixing our plates. I could hardly wait.

"When wuz Ruben by heah, Cuttin Susie?"

"Y'all come on 'n eat. This boy's eyes erbout t' pop outta his head. Y' thought Cuttin Susie wutten gon' ever git through talkin', didn't y', Sun? Y' wuz axin' m' erbout Ruben. Ruben wuz by heah las' week. He stayed er good while too. Gimme five dollas. He knows I'm er po' widow woman what done lose her husman in that ol' war, only t' have colored soldiers come back heah t' be lynched by these white devils while the po' soldier is still in uniform. *Taaaalk,* Susie! *Taaaalk* whut y' know!

"After my husman, Henry, lost his life in that white man's war 'n left me 'n m' daughter wid this li'l ol' ten-dollar-er-month pension, they had nerve ernuff t' send some low-down fish-face white man out heah t' try 'n take it erway from us. Come axin' me t' fill out some papers 'n sign some forms 'n stuff. I tol im if I could do all that I'd git er job at the colored bank, the insurance company, or the fun'el parlor—only I don't like dead folks. Don't like t' be eround nobody who don't say nothin'. I tol im I'd git some kind er edicated work, maybe even his job."

"Whut he say?" Mama asked.

"He turned red'n that jar over there 'n claimed I wuz sassin' im. I tol im sassin' wuz som'um chillens do t' they ma 'n pa, 'n none er that 'plied t' me. I tol im it wuz the rich, greedy white man that brought this repression down on our heads in the first place. Now they tryin' t' make us po' folks, who barely livin', pay fer they hoggish ways."

"You tol im all that, Cuttin Susie?"

"Taaaalk, Susie Rowell, whut y' know! I tol im that 'n mo', Cuttin Kitty. When I got done wid that ugly white man, he wuz glad t' git outta heah! He wuz in such er hurry, he forgot his hat. Hu-hu-hu-huuuu!"

While Cuttin Susie was taaaalking what she knew, and a lot she didn't, I was busy devouring a hot bowl of some of the best chicken 'n dumplings ever. She had also baked a big pan of light, scrumptious buttermilk biscuits. I washed all that down with an ice-cold glass of lemonade. By that time, Cuttin Susie was looking *goooood* to me—bleary eyes and all. Somehow her sloppy stockings with runs everywhere became well-fitted and new. Her shabby wrinkled dress became stylish and pressed. Her run-over, worn-out shoes became fashionable pumps. Her tramplike plow-boy walk became primpy and cute. And her briar patch braids became a bouquet of beautiful flowers.

"Cuttin Kitty . . ." Cuttin Susie's voice became serious for the first time. "How's Cuttin Andra's eyes? How's that di?"

"Diabetes."

"Whutever y' call that thing he got."

"His eyes not whut they used t' be, Cuttin Susie, but we trustin' in the Lord. Ruben, Pet, 'n me been tryin' t' git im t' go back t' Hot Springs fer mo' treatments, but . . ."

"How that ol' repression hittin' y'all? How's he takin' it wid all them mouths t' feed?"

"Well, Cuttin Susie, it ain't like he's feelin' the Holy Spirit erbout it. Like everybody else . . . "

"Is that ol' repression erbout t' close y'all's sto'? That mean you'll be peddlin' mo' t' hep feed yo' family rather than jist fer extra house money, huh, Cuttin Kitty?"

"Whut time is it, Cuttin Susie?"

"Goin' on t'wards two-thirty, Cuttin Kitty. Y'all gittin' ready t' go?"

"Yes ma'am. We gotta git on down the Pike. They tearin' up the ol' Pike, y' know, 'n buildin' er new one."

"I heard erbout that. T'would hep y'all if Elbert wuz ol' ernough t' work on the road. 'Course I know y'all ain't gon' let im, 'cause he ain't quite thirteen yet, is he, Cuttin Kitty?"

"Yes ma'am." Mama recognized that Cuttin Susie had heard all about the tough spot we were in, and wasn't about to fall into her trap. Neither did she want to lose the friendship and good family relationship with nosy Cuttin Susie. I was proud of the way Mama handled it because it would have been too bad to lose such a good cook, especially after meeting her only once.

"Folks keep axin' me how y'all doin' since this repression hit, 'n I tell um Cuttin Andra er smart man. He ain't erbout t' lose his money in no white man's bank 'n in no white man's stock neither. Susie tells um t' mind they own business!"

"That's mighty good advice, Cuttin Susie. We must go. We'll be back next week."

"Thought you wuz gonna say day atter tomorrow, Cuttin Kitty."

"Next week fer sho, Cuttin Susie."

"Y'all be careful goin' back home. Awful lot er explosions, trees fallin', 'n—"

"We goin' out Cherry, then east over t' the Pike. Bye, Cuttin Susie."

"Bye, Cuttin Kitty! Bye, Sun boy!"

Mama didn't say anything until the mare was trotting south on Cherry Street. "If Cuttin Susie's brain wuz as big as her mouth, she'd be real smart."

I looked at the solemn expression on her face and started laughing. It felt so good, I continued. Finally a smile brightened her face and she joined me. We quieted down for a few minutes, looked at each other, and started laughing again. We both realized that after all the troubles we were experiencing, we needed to escape into the warmth and security of our kind of laughter, that very special laughter that meant so much, only to us—the kind of laughter that needed no words to explain it. If it had to be explained—unthinkable to begin with—it was outside of our rhythm.

Shortly before we turned off of Cherry, a young white boy, sixteen or seventeen, pulled up behind us. His machine was smoking, popping, and painfully loud. The rig was a scant set of wheels, a chassis that barely held it together, and a makeshift seat that was tied on by haywire and rope. The exposed radiator looked as if it would explode any minute. As for disaster, there was nothing between the young driver and his Maker except his nerves. Mama pulled the frightened mare to the side and stopped. The gentle horse trembled and shook but held fast until the daredevil and his contraption passed. When he was out of sight, she tapped the mare with the reins and we continued on our way home.

Again Mama's comment was slow but all I needed to get me started again. "He jist *had* t' have er car, didn't he?"

"Yes ma'am." We looked at each other again. That time I almost fell out of the buggy laughing. Mama laughed at me until she cried right along with me. She playfully called me a silly fool boy and kept her hands on my arm to keep me from falling out of the buggy.

As the brown mare trotted south on Cherry Street, we heard explosions east of us. We heard trees crashing to the ground, and roaring, moaning trucks. We saw smoke bellowing toward the sky and smelled burning wood and brush.

Quaking Pete DiGasspri's crew were slowly working their way south. *Elbert's in that crew,* I thought. *If only I could be a water boy. My brother is very near me at this very moment, and I can't go a few blocks to see him.* I didn't dare disturb Mama with my thoughts. We were having too much fun laughing our way through changes. Laughing away from back doors, bad dogs, heat waves dancing off paved city streets, and the jealous insinuations of a little nosy noisy gossiping *taaaalk whut y' know Susie Rowell!* And at last, laughing away from Roy Barnard leading our heifer away and the ugly spectacle of Papa being humiliated and violated in front of his family.

Our wide straw hats shielded our sweating heads and faces from the angry afternoon Arkansas sun, now clearly in the west. We turned left at the country club, went a few blocks over to the Pike, and turned right for a direct shot home. Once in a while I remarked, "If er brains wuz as big as er mouth," or "He jist had t' have er car, didn't he?" and we started laughing all over again.

Suddenly a very welcome cool breeze brushed over us. Far in the west we saw dark clouds moving toward us. Shortly before we came to Sandy Creek, the sun disappeared and we were greeted with a heavy shower.

"Mama, don't y' think we oughtta pull up and go under the bridge until this shower passes?"

"No. Whut would y' do if there wuz no bridge t' go under? If y' paid attention t' every little shower come up y'd never git anythin' done 'n y'd never git anywhere." With that said, she popped open a big black umbrella and kept driving. Soon the sun reappeared, laughing at us. The dark clouds rolled on east of us. The explosions continued back of us, and far in the east colors were bleeding into the shape of a rainbow. As the mare trotted along, I could hear sounds from the choir of colors. The reds were singing lead, the browns alto, the greens tenor, the yellows soprano, and the blues bass.

Mama swatted a big bloodsucking horsefly on the mare's back with her wide leather reins—good shot! The mare took it to mean speed up. Mama slowed her down to her normal trot. Rotating buggy wheels moving swiftly through gravel, throwing rocks against the carriage, sounded like cotton seeds hitting the sides of the big metal hose as it ginned, sucked, and separated the seeds from the cotton.

Change. Two white men in khakis were surveying on our left. Soon the new Pike would inch its way deep into our lives, rearranging, romping, rumbling, and marching like thousands of mules, tramping and defecating on everything in its path. Change. The ruling winds don't ask. It is only for those in its path to react as it blows. Change. Papa had let down his bucket where he was, and surely he could speak of changing from a small house to a larger one that accommodated nine before I was conscious of life. Change. Papa had not watched from the sidelines but had hustled his way to covered surreys, horse and buggies, annual National Baptist Conventions, degreed Masonry, and community leadership before I was born. I entered during the change—the change of fortune. How could he be other than depressed? Instead of situations over which he had full control, changes had set in, and each day that passed was only because of some more amazing grace.

19

"Where's my strap? Where's my
strap? I'm gonna teach you chirren that when I send y' t' do somethin', I mean
fer it t' be done." Papa was feeling the nail where he usually kept the strap, but
someone had laid it under the desk. He was searching high and low for the
long slick piece of leather with which he strapped his razor and our behinds.
Geneva and I saw the strap, but he would have searched until all of us kids
were grown up before either of us would have told him where it was.

Mama, who was appropriately humming "Nearer My God to Thee,"
merely glanced at where the strap was supposed to be, went straight back into
the kitchen, and continued fixing supper. She had a quiet center about her that
never revealed what action she might take when a particular situation
demanded it.

He gave up looking for the strap. High blood sugar had taken its toll on his
eyes and his energy. He went out on the front porch and sat in the swing to
cool off and catch his breath.

After ten minutes or so, he issued an order: "No supper fer them who disobeyed. Not a bite." No response. "Kitty. Kitty," he called Mama. It seemed as
if he knew nothing else to do.

First time he ever did that, I almost wished he had found the strap.

Mama stuck her head out of the screen door. "Supper's ready." She went
straight back to the dining room and waited for everybody to seat themselves.

While Papa was washing his hands, Deloris, Verleen, and Elbert seated
themselves at the table. Geneva and I stood reluctantly to the side, hoping
Papa would change his mind. "Cuttin Dillwood told me that all Sun 'n Geneva
did down at Wabbaseka all week wuz bust 'n eat watermelon 'n hunt pecans.
He said you two didn't pick ernuff cotton to stuff in yo' ear."

I could sense him softening. The only reason he had resorted to making us
go without our supper in the first place was because he couldn't find his strap.
He really didn't have any heart for it until stubborn Geneva, with her usual
bad timing, opened her sulking mouth. "Cuttin Dillwood wuz lyin'."

"Hush yo' mouth now. You know better'n t' talk like that erbout grown
folks," Mama said.

There went our supper. I knew it. That was Geneva for you. She had no tact. No sense of how to get by. Too damn many principles. She would pay any price for what she wanted. Generally she was sullen and quiet. Stubborn, but quiet. The one time I would have paid her to keep her mouth shut, she had to go and open it. *Whatever possessed her to do that?* I thought. *Too late now.*

Papa didn't mince words. "Geneva! Go to yo' room this minute—both of y'!"

"Verleen wuz wid um, Papa," Deloris blurted out as we walked slowly away and she prepared to stuff her gut.

"She still er baby," Papa said.

What he really meant was, she was the baby of the family. She could have been thirty-one and he would have found some excuse to let her eat.

We lay there in that big dormitory-like room dreaming of food. I was so hungry, my stomach was growling and croaking like a thousand bullfrogs. I tried to cry, but there wasn't enough fluid left in my body even for that. My mind drifted to Mama. She hadn't said anything, but I knew she wouldn't let us go to bed hungry.

Mama—with her steady hand—kept food on our table. Not only that, I never saw her turn anyone away, no matter what the situation.

Immediately after supper, everyone went to bed except Mama; however, she had her gown on. It was a hot late August night. Geneva and I were too hungry to sleep, so we heard the commotion when a white woman crawled through Mama and Papa's bedroom window from the front porch.

Papa stuttered when he was excited. When I peeked into the room, which was lit by a kerosene lamp, Papa was standing there in his BVDs, completely discombobulated, trying to get a word out. Mama, dressed in her long night-gown, was standing beside the woman trying to get some sense out of her. She was in such bad shape that we couldn't tell whether she was young or old. In the first place, I could barely see her dirty, bloody face for the long stringy yellow hair hanging all over it. Her arms and legs were all scratched and bleed-ing as if she'd been dragged through a briar patch. Her cotton dress was ripped and torn and hanging from her body. She wore only one white pump, and that was scuffed and broken. She was trembling and shaking. I got a better look at her face when she tried to lift a wad of long hair out of her eyes with long red bony fingers. I also saw one tit hanging outside her dress.

"What happened, miss?" Mama asked.

"Wilford! That son of er bitch! Wilford, you goddamn redneck!"

"Y'all chirren go back t' bed now. Yo' mama 'n me take care er this. There ain't nothin' happenin' in heah that interest you," Papa said in an effort to pro-tect us from the foul language. He may as well have been talking to trees. We simply pretended we didn't know who he was talking to. I thought, as hungry as I was, *This white woman—whoever she is—is putting on a good show,* and I wasn't about to miss one bit of it. Especially until I heard what redneck Wilford had done.

"Is she sick?" Papa asked.

Mama smelt her breath. "She's sick, all right. This woman is drunk."

"You seen Wilford? Any er y'all seen Wilford?" the staggering woman inquired.

"Who is this Wilford?" Mama asked.

The drunk woman went into an uncontrollable coughing laugh. "Who is Wilford? Well, you ever see er po'ass houn'dog whut ain't been fed fer two weeks 'n when he finally run across sum'um t' eat, he makes er dog outta his-self?" She didn't wait for an answer. "Then when he's ett it 'n fucked it, he shits all over whut's left 'n trots off? Well . . . that's Wilford. 'N y'all wanna know som'um else, y'all colored folks ain't begin t' be as nasty—"

"Please, miss, don't tell us no mo' erbout Wilford," Mama said.

"Where she gon' sleep, Kitty?" Papa inquired.

"Where do you think, Andra? There ain't but one place fer her to sleep." Mama helped her toward the parlor.

"But the teacher sleeps in that parlor," Papa said.

"She won't be heah till September. 'Lois, git me some sheets 'n er quilt 'n help me make er pallet. Andra, you go back t' bed 'cause you cain't do nothin' till mornin' nohow. You ain't doing nothin' now, for that matter."

"That Wilford 'n his T-model . . . puttin' me out in the country like this 'n me havin' t' 'pose on y'all good folks like this. I'm gonna kill im, very next time I see im . . . shoot im down like the dog he is." As she was being helped into the parlor, I could see where she had peed all over herself. The water had washed streaks over the dirt and blood on her legs. This had to be the only white person who had ever slept in our house and one of the few who had been inside.

Papa and all the children except Elbert went back to bed. Geneva and I were stashed in the smokehouse, where Elbert told us to wait. After a few minutes, Mama entered carrying a big tray. Elbert followed her with two stools.

"Where's Papa?" were the first words out of my mouth.

Geneva said, "I don't care where he is long's that food's heah."

"Mama, you believe us or Cuttin Dillwood?" I asked.

"Ain't er matter of who I believe. I jist know I ain't gonna let m' chirren go hungry fer nobody."

"Cuttin Dillwood lied," Geneva said as she prepared to eat.

"Shut yo' mouth, chile! Y' talkin' erbout grown folks," Mama said.

"Yea? Well, he told a grown lie. And he's a dog on top of it," Geneva persisted.

"Whut on earth is the matter wid you, chile? Y' know better than t' talk like that. I declare. That's why y' had t' leave that table tonight. Yo' papa had no intention of not lettin' y'all eat. But when you kept runnin' off at the mouth like that, he had no other choice," Mama said.

"Mama, please don't let Papa send us t' Cuttin Dillwood no mo'. 'Cause I ain't goin'," Geneva insisted.

I didn't like Cuttin Dillwood either. He and Uncle Ruben were the only ones in the family who were allowed to whip us, but I couldn't figure out why Geneva was so much more bitter than I was.

Anyway, dinner was served. There were two steaming hot bowls of chicken 'n dumplings, baked yams with the skin falling from the meat and loaded with butter, another bowl of turnip greens laced with ham, two big pieces of hot buttermilk corn bread, also full of butter, and a big tall glass of buttermilk to wash it all down. For dessert, Mama had brought each of us a big bowl of peach cobbler. All my favorites. I don't think I would have gotten that much if I had sat at the table.

Soon roosters were crowing, day was breaking, Sunday morning was upon us. What were we to do with this drunken sleeping white woman? Everybody was up early. Papa and Elbert were cranking up the old Chevy to drive down the Pike to the Parsons'—a white family. Jake Parsons—the oldest son—was a mean, nigger-beating captain at the local state prison farm. Fortunately or unfortunately—depending on your view—he was home for the weekend. When we drove up, the old man, who liked and respected Papa, came to the door when he heard the horn beep. Papa got out and walked up to the gate. "Good mornin', Mr. Parsons."

"Mornin', Andy. Whut brings you out this hour on Sunday mornin'?" Mr. Parsons walked to the gate. He sensed something must be wrong.

Papa went through the whole story of what had happened. "In short, we don't know whut t' do wid this woman and I thought—"

"I understand, Andy. Jake! Jake!" Mr. Parsons called to the house. Miss Birdie came to the door.

"Jake's sleepin', Papa. Whut y' want wid im? Good mornin', Andy, boys."

All together, "Mornin', Miz Birdie."

"Jake! Jake!" Miss Birdie called. "Ja—" Before she could get the rest of it out, a sleepy Jake appeared at the door.

"Whut's all this racket erbout out heah this hour er the mornin'?" Jake growled.

"Andy's got er problem wid er drunk white woman up at his house," Mr. Parsons explained.

"Er drunk white woman? Whut y' want me t' do erbout it?" Jake answered. "I cain't do nothin' wid the sober one I got heah." Jake disappeared back into the house to get his hat and gear.

"Ernother hot day, eh, Andy," Mr. Parsons said.

"Erfraid so, Mr. Parsons. Not nearly as hot as last night, though," Papa answered.

Mr. Parsons laughed out loud. "Andy, I bet y' nearly shit when she crawled through that window on top er y'all, didn't y'?"

Papa laughed.

"Damned if I wouldn' er given a cow t' see that." Mr. Parsons shook his head laughing.

"Well, I'll tell y' this much. It wuttin funny at the time."

"Andy, I always liked y' sense er humor." Mr. Parsons was still laughing as Jake walked out.

"Whut's so funny this early in the mornin'?" He was dressed like Buck Jones. Ten-gallon white hat, wide belt, big buckle with steer horns on it, western pants and shirt—topped off with a pearl-handled pistol—the works. The only thing that localized him was his big long pipe, with the good-smelling tobacco.

"Don't y' see Andy 'n the boys there?" Mr. Parsons asked. "Ain't y' gon' speak?"

"Mornin', Andy." Jake walked straight to his pickup truck without so much as looking at any of us.

"Mornin', Mr. Parsons," Papa responded.

The "Mr. Parsons" formality didn't go unnoticed by the old man, since Papa had always called him just plain Jake before he went to work for the farm, reserving "Mr." for the old man.

"Andy's been knowing y' since y' wuz er pup, y' know," Mr. Parsons said.

Jake didn't respond. He simply busied himself trying to start his truck.

I couldn't stop thinking about how this peckerwood was beating and killing mostly black prisoners on that farm every day. I felt sure that's what Papa and Elbert were thinking as well. Jake was known to be mean. But since he had taken that job at the farm, he had a license for it and had become a terror.

Finally Jake got the truck started and pulled off ahead of us. As we were about to follow him, Miz Birdie came storming out of the house with a gallon of milk. "Andy! Y'all take this to Kitty fer me, will y'?"

"Thank y', Miz Birdie." Little did Miz Birdie know that Mama would always feed the hogs with the milk or any other food white people gave us.

When we returned, the white woman, who had served as a diversion from Geneva and me, was all cleaned up, sitting at the table on the back porch having hot buttered biscuits and coffee. She and Mama had gotten acquainted, and Mama was trying to convert her to a Baptist.

"Y'know, the Lord will forgive us our sins 'n take us into the fold if y' only repent and ask Him to."

The woman was still scared and a little swollen, but she wasn't that bad-looking, as hillbilly women go. "Y' know, Kitty, I wuz raised er Baptist, like you."

"You wuz? Well, I declare!" Mama said.

"Uh-huh. In fact, one er my uncles wuz er preacher," the lady said.

"Wuz that in the Ozarks?" Mama asked.

"That wuz in the Ozarks, long before I come heah."

"Whut wuz it that brought y' heah in particular?"

"Oh, like most country girls, I guess, I had a yen fer the big city."

Hearing Pine Ridge referred to as a big city, Mama stopped wrapping the food and looked quizzically at the frail country woman. "Sooo, you come heah t' Pine Ridge?" Sensing that her question didn't arouse any suspicion in the woman's mind, Mama continued her work.

Jake was standing near the back porch waiting for the woman. He didn't strike up a conversation, so nobody said anything to him. He simply pushed his big cowboy hat back on his head, kicked up dirt, and puffed on his pipe.

"Hi do," the woman said as she walked down the steps carrying the food Mama had given her.

"Hi do," Jake said.

"My goodness. I'm being picked up by none other than Mr. Buck Jones himself," she said.

"This is Mr. Jake Parsons. He'll see to it y' git back home safe," Mama said.

"How you, Kitty?" Jake acknowledged.

"I'm fine, Mr. Parsons," Mama said.

"Y' ready?" Jake started to leave.

"Jist er minute, please." The woman walked back to Mama and took her hands. "Kitty, I can't thank y'all ernuff fer whut y' done. 'N I'm gon' think erbout whut y' tol' me. But there's jist one question."

"Whut's that?" Mama asked.

"Do y' think the good Lord will forgive a skunk like Wilford after whut he done to me?"

"You have to forgive him first, honey. And if he repents and asks, I'm sure the Lord will forgive him."

"Well, the way I figure it, I'll kill im first, 'n if the Lord wants to forgive im, that'll be up t' Him."

Mama laughed. "Y' don't really mean that. Y' still upset. Y' be all right once y' git home."

"Good-bye, Kitty. I'll never fergit y'." She looked around at Papa and the rest of the family, assembled here and there in close proximity. "I'll never fergit none er y'all. Too bad ain't mo' people in the world like y'all."

Mother's Day at Hughes Chapel was right up there with Easter and Children's Day. Father's Day hadn't caught on yet.

The funeral parlor fans were swishing. The wide floppy straw hats were blocking views from all lines of sight. Everybody, big and small, young and old, had on a red rose for mothers living and a white rose for mothers dead. Dixie Peach hair grease was melting and running down Sisters' and Brothers' necks. When it mixed with cheap cologne, the odor of black and brown shoe polish, Vaseline, and healthy sweat, it smelled like evening in swamp-water.

Added to that was the sweet smell of mothers' milk that sometimes oozed through the thin cotton dresses the childbearers wore. Everything was just as it should be.

Babies crying couldn't compete with the spirited singing of the Senior Choir, backed up by Uncle Pet's bass. Once again, Hughes Chapel was rocking.

> *If I could heah*
> *My mother pray ergin,*
> *If I could heah*
> *Her tender voice ergin,*
> *How happy I would be,*
> *T'would mean so much t' me,*
> *If I could heah*
> *My mother praaaay ergin.*

After the welcome address by my sister Deloris, who was bold, articulate, and well rehearsed, the master of ceremonies called for recitations from some of the children. Dressed in a new short-pants blue suit, white ankle-length socks, white shoes, and a blue bow tie, I stumbled awkwardly to the platform in front of the pulpit. After clearing my throat four or five times, with giggling and interruptions from the audience, most of whom would much rather hear me sing, I spurted out the first words to the verse that had been selected for me and rehearsed for two weeks. "Of all—" I was interrupted by loud giggling, mostly from my marble-shooting buddies. "Shh"s from grown-ups quieted them down.

"Jist go erhead, Sun. Don't be nervous," a voice from the audience said. "Wait till some er them git up theah."

I started again.

> *Of all the wonders in all the world*
> *God made for land or sea,*
> *There's none so precious*
> *Or could ever mean more*
> *Than my mother means to me.*

20

It was late August of 1930, and Elbert was driving Deloris, Geneva, and me to cut sorghum. Ben, who had nothing else to do before cotton-picking time, easily begged his father into letting him come along with us. I hopped off the wagon and walked along with him.

Ben made fun of each of our neighbors on Wagon Road West as we walked along, including his own family. "Boy, am I glad t' git outta that funky house. We had butter beans fer supper last night 'n such snowin' 'n coughin' 'n fartin' 'n stinking y' never heard befo'."

"Y' cain't heah stinkin'," I said.

"If it's bad enough, y' kin." He grabbed his nose and looked toward Mr. Durbey's shack. "I been hearin' that funky smell from ol' man Do-Do Durbey ever since we been heah."

I laughed, and listened to Ben carry on about Mr. Durbey until we reached the Stowalds.

"'Member that time we run outta that hail 'n surprised Udell 'n Miz Marge while they wuz knocking off er piece?" Ben asked.

"Yeah, I remember that. Whut erbout it?"

"'Member when she opened that do' 'n that overgrown, ragged-lookin' monster Mr. Funk, who had toenails older'n you 'n me put together, come roarin' outta that bedroom? Y' mean y' didn't heah that?"

"Boy, you got er lot er imagination," I said.

We arrived at our farm, one quarter of a mile west of the Pike, and turned right on a road that led to a little log-and-plank bridge across Alligator Creek. We stopped at the sorghum patch on the other side of the creek and began work. Later that afternoon, I talked Elbert into letting Ben and me look for canes for fishing poles and flutes.

When Ben and I arrived at Mr. Sam's house, the afternoon sun was still high in the sky and it was a beautiful warm fall day. It seemed that even the sunflowers were speaking to each other. Birds were chirping and bearing witness as they had done all summer. Two new Fords were parked on the other side of the fence in a wide open space between tall oaks. Two young white men and young Reedy Riley were hanging their feet out the car windows. They were drinking moonshine, yelling, and cursing.

Mr. Sam came out on the porch eating a big plate of turnip greens and hot corn bread. The food was all over his mouth. "Hi, Sun, Li'l Udell."

"Hi, Mr. Sam," I said.

Ben, however, resented it and snapped back, "My name is Ben. Udell is my papa's name."

Mr. Sam laughed and continued eating. "Y'all boys want som'er this heah grub?"

I hated that word *grub*. It always made me think of the grub worm we used for fish bait.

"No sir," I said. "We gotta git on to the canebrake."

"Hey, bro' Sam!" one of the white men yelled.

"Hey, Mr. Johnny!" Mr. Sam yelled back.

"Come on out heah 'n take er li'l ride wid us," Johnny said.

"'N bring Leana wid y'," the second white man said.

"Wait'll I finish these heah greens," Mr. Sam said. Mr. Sam chugged his mouth full, grabbed his old ragged hat, stumbled out to the coupe, and climbed into the rumble seat.

"Thought I tol' y' t' bring Leana wid y'," the second white man said.

"She busy wid her ma, Mr. Fred."

"Busy wid her ma? Look heah, Sam, we been doin' some mighty fine business t'gether, ain't we?" Fred said.

"Sho has, Mr. Fred—sho has." Taking the bottle Johnny was offering him, he gulped down half the pint.

"We been doin' everthin' t'gether on er equal basis right down t' drinkin' t'gether, ain't that right?"

"Yas sir, Mr. Fred, y'all been doin' mighty good by us. I cain't complain."

"Ain't that right, Reedy?" Johnny asked.

"Yas sir, sho is," Reedy turned to Johnny in a drunken fashion.

"Now that we got that straightened out, why don't y' go on in theah 'n bring Leana on out heah like I tol' y'?" Fred said, and took another drink. "I got me er idea. Why don't you go git her, Reedy."

"Who, me?" Reedy jerked around.

"Yeah, you. Why not? She yo' sister, ain't she? My young sister do anythin' I ax her. Now go on in theah 'n tell her y' gon' treat her t' som'um real nice. Now go on."

"She didn't listen t' Pa, she sho' ain't gon' listen t' me, Mr. Fred," Reedy said as he reached for the bottle.

"Don't look like t' me y'all boys wanna play this heah game fair 'n square, ain't that the way it look t' you, Johnny?"

"That's right. We been good t' y'all—better'n most white men, I bet y'," Johnny admonished.

Fred hit the steering wheel. "Y' know som'um? I know whut's wrong." Fred paused and hit the dashboard. "By God, why'nd we think er this befo'?"

"Think er whut, Fred Hunt?"

"It's plain as the nose on yo' face, Johnny Hunt, 'n tha's plenty plain, I gotta tell y'."

"You ain't no puddy thing y'self, y' know—y' dick-head," Johnny replied.

"Well, whut's wrong is . . . many times as Sam 'n Reedy been t' our house—et wid us, drunk wid us, 'n everthing—we ain't never offered nary one of um our Ella Mae," Fred said with tongue in cheek.

Mr. Sam, who had the bottle turned up guzzling, spat whiskey out all over the rumble seat and the back of the coupe, then started coughing.

"By God, Fred, y' know y' right, we never did," Johnny agreed. "'N t'aint right, seein' as how we share 'n share erlike in everthin'. Why ain't we offered um Ella Mae, or one er the other girls?" Johnny agreed.

Reedy looked at them as if they had suddenly turned into dragons.

"Now, Sam, I know how much you like trim, as you call it—both er y'all. Y'all seen Ella Mae. She got long puddy yaller hair. She got titties 'n er ass on her that'll send er man straight t' heaven," Fred said.

"That's whut I'm scared of, I ain't ready t' go t' heaven yet." Reedy sobered up a bit.

Fred and Johnny laughed. While they were laughing, Leala came out of the house with a basket full of clothes. Her big udders were showing through her loose-fitting cotton dress. She was barefooted and had a white bandanna tied around her head. She proceeded to hang clothes on the line.

Fred stopped laughing and hunched Johnny. "Y' see whut I see?"

"Yeah, I see both er them big rascals," Johnny replied.

"Wait heah." Fred got out of the car. He reached for the bottle and took a long drag. He stuck it in his back pocket and stumbled over toward the fence.

"Sam, ain't y' gon' go over theah 'n say som'um?" Johnny asked.

"Uh-uh. Mr. Fred the one gon' need helpin' fo' this is ovah—gaintee y'."

"But Fred is liquored up. Ain't y' jist er little concerned he gon' mess it up fer both of us? Now if one er y'all boys did it . . . "

"Now tha's the difference twix us, Mr. Johnny. You don't truss yo' women outta yo' sight eround us. You always guardin' um like they in jail er som'um—even them ugly ones whut don't need no guardin'."

Johnny fell over the steering wheel laughing. "By God, you crazy as hell, Sam Riley." Then Johnny stopped laughing. "Whut y' talkin' erbout guardin' fer, Sam? Didn't we jist offer y' Ella Mae?"

"Sure y' did. Tha's jist like a cat offerin' a mice some cheese, or me offerin' you the moon."

"Speakin' er moon, pass me that jug, Mr. Johnny," Reedy interjected.

Miz Mag came out of the house with another basket of clothes before Fred reached the fence. He ignored her and continued.

"Whut y' doin' theah, gal?" Fred asked.

"Hangin' out clothes, Mr. Fred, whut do it look like?"

"Look like you hangin' out them clothes t' me," mimicking. Fred took a lit-tle drunken step backward. "Yas-sir, look jisssst like y'all hangin' out them clothes t' me. Look heah, gal—"

"I got er name, 'n it ain't gal, Mr. Fred."

"O-o-o-h. Aw right then, Leana."

"My name is Leala," she said as she continued hanging her clothes.

"Look heah, Leala, how'd y' like t' set that basket down 'n come wid us fer er li'l ride in one er our brand-new cars? You kin take yo' pick."

"Naw sir, I don't think so."

"Maybe y' didn't heah me good. I said put the basket down 'n come on t' town wid me. I'll buy y' anything y' want: pair shoes, new bandanna, new dress, you name it, 'n we go git it right now," Fred promised.

"She said naw. Didn't y' heah her, Mr. Fred? Whut she look like goin' t' town wid you? Better go git yo'self er white gal 'n leave my Leala erlone," Miz Mag said.

"But I don't want no white gal, Mag. I want Leala." Fred put his hand up to his eyes and faked a cry.

"Yo' wants ain't gon' hurt y' none, Mr. Fred," Miz Mag said diffidently.

Fred pulled out a roll of bills. "See them cabbage leaves? Well, theah's plenty mo' wheah these come from. Now why don't y' git y'self on out heah like I tol' y'?"

When Leala wouldn't come, Fred put his roll back in his pocket, pulled the bottle out of his back pocket, and guzzled the rest of the pint down. "Yeeeee-hu-u-u-u-u!! By God, I'd ruther be sloppy drunk than anything I know! Tha's all right, Maggie. Tha's aw-w-w-w-right, you heah me!! I'mo git some er that fo' it's over wid, y' heah me? Fred Hunt ain't use t' bein' turned down by no nigger gal."

He staggered over to the car, mumbling to himself. He kicked the side of the coupe and almost broke his foot. "Goddammit! Oooooh shit! Come on, y'all, let's git erway from heah. I feel like howlin'. Yeeeeeeeee-hu-u-u-u-u!" He hopped into the black coupe with the rumble seat. Mr. Sam was still sitting in the seat drinking. Reedy was sitting in the black sedan drinking with Johnny. They all had their shirts off. The fumes from that moonshine were talking. We could smell it from fifty feet away. Fred started his motor and revved it up as high as it would go. Johnny followed suit.

Fred yelled, "I'm ready t' how-l-l-l-l, goddammit! 'N when I say I'm ready t' howlllllllll, I mean I'm ready t' howlllllll!!"

Johnny pulled his sedan up beside Fred's coupe. "Hey, Sam, reach me er gal-lon er that corn over heah, will y'?"

"Y' gots t' git it 'cause y' caught me wid it. Now let me heah y' how-l-l-l-l-l, Mr. Johnny!"

"Yeeeeeeeeeeee-h-u-u-u-u-u!" Johnny took a drink out of the jug by flipping it over his shoulder and turning his head to the side, then guzzling. He revved up his motor, alternating with Fred. Fred took off in a straight line, burning rubber and throwing mud and grass in every direction. Suddenly he made a sharp turn around a big oak on two wheels, almost tipping the coupe over. Mr. Sam's hat flew off, revealing his messed-up gray hair. Johnny was right behind him. They almost collided, but Johnny careened his sedan and barely got out of Fred's way. They raced around in that reckless fashion three or four times.

Miz Mag and Leala were standing at the fence. "Sam, git outta that car fo' that fool kills y'."

"Pa! Reedy! Y'all lost yo' minds? Git outta theah! Git out!" Leala screamed.

Mr. Sam stood up and started to get out. As he did, Fred put the Ford in first and took off, jerking Mr. Sam back into his seat. Getting up as much speed as he could, he quickly threw it in second, then third, and within seconds he had disappeared over the hill. Mr. Sam's gray head was bobbing up and down like a cork float getting a bite from a perch. He was laughing at the top of his voice.

Johnny and Reedy were in hot pursuit; soon they all were out of sight.

Miz Mag stood mopping her neck and face with her apron. Leala stood there shaking her head in dismay.

"Dirty dogs. Them ol' Hunt boys jist like they ol' pa. He used yo' grandma till he wuz tired; now he comes back from the grave in the form of his ol' sons, thinkin' they kin go on usin' you. Lord be my judge, I'll die 'n go t' hell fo' I'll let it happen. Good thing yo' grandma's in Risen or she'd be eggin' y' on. She thinks it some kind er honor t' be sought after by er stinkin' white man. Y' jist cain't git that slavery out of her.

"Sam oughtta be 'shame er his-self, carrin' on like that right heah in front er Sun. Whut's Brother Andra gon' think? Whut y'all doin' way over heah anyhow 'dout grown-ups wid y'?"

"We lookin' fer some cane fer fishing poles, Miz Mag. You know wheah we kin find the brake?" I asked.

"Well, Sun, you follah that road till y' come t' a li'l bridge. There's a li'l branch off er Bayou Bartholomew on yo' right. You follow that li'l branch er few feet 'n y' find the canebrake. Y' lucky t'aint much wauter in it this time er yeah. Still, I don't like boys yo' age goin' out in that brake by yo'self—too thick back up in theah. Y' kin git lost easy. Now y'all jist come on in heah 'n I'll fix y' some lemonade 'n tea cakes. I'll send Olie wid y' when he come back. Come on now, he won't be long."

"Yes ma'am," I said, and followed her inside. Ben walked in behind me.

As always, the little house was clean and orderly. The furniture was home-made and simple but suitable. Being from a home where no tobacco was used in any form, I found dipping and chewing nasty and distasteful, especially dipping. I loved Mr. Sam and Miz Mag, but I found his chewing and her dipping hard to take. At eight, I didn't have the slightest notion that dipping, chewing, and smoking were all done with the same tobacco. As many did, I regarded smoking as socially elite (especially ready rolls, cigars, and pipes). Rolling your own was at the bottom of the smoking group. The nasties were the chewers and dippers—the dippers being at the bottom of that group. I never saw a woman chew. I could abide a man with a wad of tobacco in his jaw pushing out one side of his mouth—squirting a clear, clean-looking, reddish-brown or brown, well-directed stream of tobacco juice. But a woman or a man with their bottom lip bulging with nasty, caked, gooey, slimy, saturated snuff always gave me an unclean feeling—hard to accept, no matter how much I liked the person.

Miz Mag was a lifetime certified, government-inspected, Arkansas qualified, bona fide incurable, lip-sagging, sharpshooting, nasty snuff dipper. And Mr. Sam was her counterpart in the chewing department. No matter if they cooked greens, baked potatoes, turkey, and ham, fried chicken, or boiled chitterlings, no odor known to man could stand up to the stench caused by snuff and chewing tobacco juice. When it moved in, it settled for at least two lifetimes. The only way to get rid of it was to burn the house down.

When Miz Mag gave me food, I always enjoyed it better outside.

Inside the Rileys' small house, everything revolved around the fireplace, located on the east wall to the left of the entrance. In fact, it appeared that the fireplace must have been built first and that everything else was added on as an afterthought. One room served as kitchen, living room, dining room, and bath. There were only two bedrooms in the house, and one was littered with dead rabbits, coonskins, and Miz Mag's canned fruit and vegetables.

The low ceiling and walls of the main room were covered with garish flower-patterned wallpaper. In an attempt to repair peeled spots, they had pasted up newspapers—headlines and all. Continually seeing the same words probably didn't bother them, since I was sure only Leala and perhaps Reedy could read. I don't think it ever occurred to Mr. Sam that a papering job required repeating at least once during his lifetime. I was fascinated with some of the old stories on the wall. One was about prohibition being lifted if Roosevelt got in. When it read "See Prohibition, page A–12," I immediately went to the next patch looking for the continuation. I probably would have found it too, if I hadn't been interrupted by Ben, who was busy looking at the old funnies of Alley Oop, the Gumps, Dick Tracy, and Little Orphan Annie.

A leaking roof had stained various areas in the ceiling and on the walls. The plank floor, though clean to a fault, had shrunk and left cracks an inch wide. That's how black snakes had crawled through from time to time and found their way into a pile of clothes or some other cozy spot. Sometimes weeds grew right through those cracks. On the left side of the room was an opening that led to the loft. I could see a portion of the hewn wooden rafters at the top of the ladder.

The house faced the east. A homemade wooden table, draped with a nice white cloth, stood in the northwest corner. A neatly made cart was in the southeast corner. A double-barreled shotgun lay on its rack over the mantel of the fireplace—along with pots, pans, buckets, a poker, dried corn, a fox hide, and cans containing flour, sugar, meal, lard, and dried peas and beans. There was a bridle, a ukulele, some rope, an old saddle, and some garden seed on the side. The floor was crowded with saws, posthole diggers, boots, old shoes, a hammer, an ax, and a rake. Even though the room was crammed and hot, everything was neatly placed. A churn was in the southwest corner of the room. Buckets, bowls, jars, dippers for handling milk and butter, parts to the churn itself, and clean white rags were on the shelves of the churning corner.

Leala entered with her constant grin. She came over to me and grabbed me around my neck playfully. "Wheah Mr. Andra?" Leala asked.

"He home." I muffled out a sound.

"Wheah Elbert, 'Lois, or somebody?"

"They down the hill cuttin' sorghum," I said.

Miz Mag walked in with the lemonade. "Leala, turn that boy loose so he can eat his tea cakes and drink his lemonade while it still cold."

Leala let go of my head. Ben and I took the lemonade. Miz Mag went over to the table for the tea cakes. Leala went over to the churning corner. She took the lid off one of the big clay jars and tested the milk with a spoon.

"Is it clabbered yet?" Miss Mag asked.

"Yas-um, it's ready t' churn." Leala slipped the handle of the churner through the hole in the cap of the clay jar, placed the cap over the big clay jar, placed clean rags around it, and began to churn.

Olie entered carrying a big paper sack. He was dressed in the family uniform for males: overalls, a ragged straw hat, a cotton shirt, and of course, no shoes. His whole outfit cost a dollar and a quarter—tops—when it was new. He gave Miz Mag the sack and came directly over to me for a playful wrestling match. "Heah's ol' Sun. Come on, Sun, let's wrassel."

Olie let me throw him down and get on top. I grabbed him around the neck and he faked being choked.

"Why don't y'all cut that out so we kin git som'um done?" Ben said jealously.

"Whut you gotta git done, li'l Titty Chin?" Olie asked.

"Don't call me Titty Chin," Ben said.

"Everbody else call y' Titty Chin, 'cept Sun," Olie said.

"He better not, 'cause he know I whup his ass."

"Why jist him?" Olie asked.

"'Cause."

"'Cause whut?" Olie asked.

"Jist 'cause, goddammit."

"Hey, hey, Li'l Udell, take that cussin' outside. We don't erlow that eround heah—specially from somebody whut ain't dry behind the ears yet," Miz Mag admonished. "Wheah that boy learn t' do all that foul-mouth cussin' anyhow?"

"From his pa, Udell. Where else?" Olie said.

"It's er shame," Miz Mag said.

"Don't talk erbout my pa," Ben said, rising.

"Whut you gon' do erbout it? You li'l . . ." Miz Mag advanced on Ben with a big wooden spoon in her hand.

Olie was on the floor laughing.

"My name's Ben," he said in a rather troubled voice I had never heard before. He backed down.

"I believe in chillens stayin' in chillen's place. I don't understand why Mr. Andra let you run eround wid one er them Udells anyhow. I jist don't understand it," Miz Mag said.

Ben started to say something, but looked at that spoon and changed his mind.

I thought I'd better get Ben out of there. "Olie, kin you take us to the canebrake so we kin cut some fishing poles and some flutes?"

Still laughing, "Sho, I take y'." He looked over at Leala churning. "First let me git er cup er this heah clabber while it still got that cream in it." Olie held his cup for Leala to fill it up.

"Honest t' goodness, Olie. Why don't y' wait till it's buttermilk?" She took the top off the jar.

"'Cause I like that clabber better, tha's why."

The canebrake was thick, dark, and mysterious, even in the daytime. We tramped along in our bare feet, following a tributary of Bayou Bartholomew that must have been spring fed because most of the tributaries were bone dry in August—even Alligator Creek—except for one small stream. I looked up and could barely see rays from the sun peeking in from time to time. Finally we came to a trail on our left that must have led to something. Olie passed the trail, but Ben wanted to see where it led, and so did I. When Olie looked back, we had already entered.

"Hey. Wheah you two goin'?"

"We wanna see where this trail—" Ben stopped, surprised by what we saw.

A crude little plant—an operation of some sort—was cloaked away in a small clearing. Two fifty-gallon steel oil barrels were full of what looked like hog slop. Two more barrels on a platform were separated from the first barrels by a distance of some thirty feet. A long shiny copper coil connected these barrels. The end of the coil led to a hole that had been dug out and covered over with leaves, sticks, and straw. Ashes were evidence of an extinguished fire. We went back to the barrels full of what looked like hog slop; they were bubbling slowly and had a pungent sour smell—not at all like real slop. Vines were so thick overhead I couldn't see a single ray of sunlight. Foliage on the sides completely enveloped the little operation.

"Come on, let's git outta heah. Y'all boys don't wanna look at this no mo'," Olie said, in a hurry to leave.

"S-s-s-shit, I do. Whut the hell is this rig anyhow?" Ben asked.

"It's fer making slop," Olie said.

"You mean it's a slop factory like they got fer making soap or som'um?" Ben asked.

"You got it. Now come on, let's go," Olie said.

"S-s-s-s-hit, you gotta do better'n that, Olie Riley," Ben said.

"You didn't know they had slop factories?" Olie asked.

"Uh-uh. You ever heah of a slop factory, Sun?" Ben asked.

"Naw. Never did," I said.

"You boys young, only eight, nine yeahs ol'. Wait'll y' git fifteen, sixteen like me 'n Elbert. Bet y' Elbert know all erbout slop factories."

"If this is a slop factory, wheah's the hogs?" I asked.

"Tha's right. Wheah is the hogs?" Ben asked.

"You boys ax too many questions. I don't know wheah the hogs is. Hogs wheah they always is—they in the pen."

"We feed our hogs corn when they in the pen—not slop," I said.

"Theah's plenty corn in this. Believe me. Come on now, let's go cut yo' poles." Olie walked to the main trail; we followed him reluctantly.

We could hear water running in the little tributary beside us. Hickory nuts were falling as squirrels fed overhead. Chickadees and crickets made evening sounds, readying for the night. The sultry quietness quickened our steps as we headed back to the Rileys'. Olie had cut us some fine poles and canes to make flutes and whistles. He slogged along in front of us, hitting a mosquito now and then. Every once in a while he laughed to himself.

"Whut you laughin' erbout, Olie?" I asked.

"Oh, nothin', Sun . . . nothin'."

"I always heard, people who go eround laughin' at nothin' belong on a fuckin' funny farm or som'um," Ben said.

"Boy, y' sho got er big nasty mouth t' be young as you is. Let m' tell y' som'um else—y' gon' belong in er hoss-pital, y' keep motor-mouthin' t' me, y' little titty-chin squirrel-face fart-fetcher."

"I done tol' y' erbout that shit. M' pa give m' er name, 'n it ain't no Titty Chin. It's Ben—Ben—Ben—"

"Ben-Ben-Ben, the Titty-Chin-Chin-Chin—"

Ben picked up a stick and started after Olie. Olie faced him. "Whut y' gon' do wid that stick, boy?"

"I'mo brain y' wid it if y' call me Titty Chin one mo' time."

Before Ben could swing the stick, Olie was on him. He twisted the stick out of Ben's hands and shook him. "Boy, y' too young 'n y' too li'l t' go ergin me or anybody near m' size. It's plain t' see y' got that bein' bad from yo' pa, Udell. Now I'mo take yo' butt back to the house 'n that's it. I don't wanna see y' in my house ergin or nowheah eround. Y' don't notice Sun usin' all them cuss words 'n actin' like you. Why don't y' try t' act like him? Now if y' pick up ernother stick at me I'm liable t' fergit you er kid 'n whup yo' ass. Y' got that?" Olie turned Ben loose and slogged on along in front.

Ben puffed up like a toad and stayed a distance behind us. We could hear him mumbling to himself.

"How long that boy had that thing on his chin?" Olie asked.

"He wuz born wid it on theah," I said.

"Why don't they git it cut off?"

"Cost money t' have er doctor cut that thing off," I said.

As we walked along talking about Ben, my mind drifted back to that slop factory. I knew what we had seen. I was sure Olie knew it also, but Ben and I didn't know who it belonged to. We didn't know if Olie did either.

I was always fascinated with the natural things around me. Many questions floated through my mind. Where did snakes go in winter? Why were owls so stupid—easy to catch or shoot—if they were supposed to be so wise? How could people in China see the same moon and sun as we did? How did maggots turn into flies? Why did horsehairs turn into worms when dropped into mud holes? What was the secret behind burning someone a long distance away by casting a concentrated ray of sunlight with a mirror?

My mind drifted to Ben. Though he was a little devil, and Papa did all he could to keep me away from him—or any other Barrow, for that matter—he would seek me out after each fight we had and act as though nothing had happened. Ben wasn't the kind to say he was sorry about anything; I doubt if he was sorry. He would simply come on back, acting bad and cussing, as he had done when he left. I never saw him cry, even when Mr. Udell beat him. He would holler like he was being murdered, but as soon as the beating was over, he'd come right back down the hill, beckoning for me to come on out so we could git som'um done. There wasn't a tear in either eye.

I asked him one day, "Why do y' holler so loud when y' gittin' er beatin'?"

"To git the son of er bitch t' stop," he replied.

Bad as he was, I felt sorry for him when he would foolishly go up against someone bigger and older and get slapped down.

He never admitted or even recognized defeat, no matter how hard or how long I threw him. He would say, "That'll teach y' not t' fuck wid me, boy. Y' want m' t' whup yo' ass some mo'? By God I'll 'commodate y'," I would respond, "No thanks, I think y' whupped m' ass ernuff fer one day. Come back 'n whup it some mo' t'morrow."

I had gotten used to that nipple on his chin. It didn't bother me like it did most people. As gentle and good-natured as Olie was, he would never go out of his way to insult anybody unless provoked, and even then it would have to be a matter of self-defense. It was clear to me that Ben brought many things on himself with his mouth. Even so, it saddened me to think he would have to go through life like that. A big part of his trouble was caused by that nipple on his chin. It disfigured what otherwise would be a nice-looking boy. Why didn't his parents have it removed? I had felt the tit many times when we were wrestling and playing. There was no bone there, just a soft piece of meat. It should be a simple thing to remove, I thought.

After I thanked Olie for cutting the cane—Ben was still angry—we took off down the hill toward the sorghum patch.

Ben was mumbling louder now. "That big ugly slouchy mealy-mouth son of er bitch. Nobody—I mean nobody—go' fuck over me like that. I'mo have his life, y' wait 'n see."

I caught up with him. "Who y' talkin' t', Ben?"

"I'm talkin' t' myself, goddammit," Ben responded.

"I always heard, people who go eround talkin' t' themselves belong on er funny farm or som'um," I reminded him.

"Don't y' git smart wid me or I'll whup yo' ass right heah 'n now." He stopped in the middle of the road.

"If you ever dream y' kin whup me, you'd better wake up wid er smile on yo' face," I said.

He grabbed me. We held each other in a mad grip. Finally I threw him down in a mud hole and pinned him with a nelson.

"Give up?" I asked him.

"Hell no. You give up?" Ben asked me foolishly.

"Whut y' talkin' erbout? I'm the one holdin' the nelson."

"Like hell, you ain't holdin' no nelson on me," Ben said.

"Let me see y' git up, then," I said.

"Hell, I can git up if I wanna. Let me see you git up," Ben said.

"How can I hold you if I git up?" I asked.

"Told y' you ain't got no nelson on me. You ain't got shit," Ben insisted.

A bumblebee started buzzing around our heads. Rather than be stung, I jumped up and started fighting the bee.

Ben stood up, brushed himself off as best he could, and started making a muscle. "Feel that, boy. Hard as steel. How you gon' hold a man down wid muscles like me? I'mo do the same goddamn thing to that ugly-ass Olie very next time I see im. You tell im that. Y' heah? Y' had ernuff, or y' want me t' beat yo' ass some mo'?"

I simply stood and looked at Ben, trying to figure out what drove him. Why was it he could never admit defeat even after the glowing fact? Why did he have to lie to himself and even act on his own lie, thereby getting himself into more trouble?

In the first place, he wasn't tall like I was. He was skinnier than me. Except for his grandpa and his brother Carl, I hadn't seen any big people in his family. Since he was nearly a year older than I and not nearly as big, it was clear he was somewhat of a runt. He would never be more than average size at the very best, yet he would challenge a bull with nothing to back him up but his mouth. Do unto others before they do unto you was deeply rooted in his very bones.

My mind kept coming back to that tit on his chin. Was this causing him to act like he did? I looked down at the mud hole again and saw some horsehairs that hadn't turned into worms yet. I looked at the tit, then at the horsehairs. Finally I picked up one of the horsehairs, walked over to that bloated fool, and told him to stand still for a minute.

"Whut y' gon' do, son of er bitch?"

"I'm gon' git rid of that piece er meat on yo' chin," I said.

"How y' gon' do that?"

"Wid this horsehair," I replied.

"You crazy?"

"I think it'll work, 'n y' won't have nobody callin' y' all them names ergin," I said.

"Naw. You gon' fuck me up worse'n I am," Ben said.

"Look at it this way. After all these years, Mr. Udell ain't took y' to no doctor t' git it taken off. If I git it started and it festers, he'll have t' take y'."

For the first time in the two years or so I had known Ben, he stopped to think.

"Y' think so?" Ben said.

"Let me try it 'n we'll find out," I said.

"Aw right then, but if you fuck me up, I'mo whup yo' ass worse'n I been doin'," Ben boasted.

I took the long sharp horsehair and tied a loose knot in it. I carefully placed the loop over the tit and pushed it up to Ben's chin. I twirled the ends of the hair around each index finger and began to pull. "That hurt?"

"Uh-uh, not yet," Ben said.

I pulled a little tighter. "How erbout that?" I asked.

"Naw. Not yet."

I pulled tighter the third time. A little blood began to ooze from around the sharp black hair. "How do that feel?" I asked.

"I feel it jist er little, but not much. Tighten up on it some mo'."

"No. It's starting t' bleed. I'd better leave it erlone," I said.

"Go erhead, goddammit, tighten up on it some mo'."

Instead of tightening more, I simply tied the knot so it wouldn't slip. I dipped my finger in the blood on his chin and showed it to him. "See, it's already bleedin'. I'mo leave it alone now," I said.

"Why don't y' cut the son of er bitch all the way off like I tell y'?"

"'Cause I ain't no doctor. Jist leave it right theah, 'n I bet y' in a few days it'll fester 'n fall off," I said.

"'N leave er big scar? Boy, I'm tellin' y' if you fuck up my good-lookin' face—"

"Look like somebody already beat me to that."

"Sunnnnnnnn! Sunnnnnnnnn!" We heard Elbert's voice calling in the distance.

"Whuuuuuuut?" I answered.

"Git on down heah! We fixin' t' leeeeeeeeave!"

"Comennnnnnnnnn'!"

We picked up our canes and headed for the sorghum patch. The warm soft mud felt good mushing up between our toes. Ben toyed with his bloody chin as we rushed along.

21

Hughes Chapel's lot was packed that Saturday night with T-models, A-models, and a few B-models (1931—the latest), mixed with a few horse and buggies and even wagon and mules, driven mostly by people from Over In The Hills. Elbert was driving Papa's 1928 Chevy, making his second run to church that night. I sat between him and Papa. Deloris was the important passenger on that trip. She had prepared a box and dolled herself up for the occasion. Verleen had come earlier with Mama and Geneva.

Young men were gathered around a new car. It was the very latest—a black convertible 1931 B-model Ford, with a rumble seat, whitewall tires, "wire-spoked" wheels, chromed radiator, chromed bumpers, chromed door handles, chromed gas cap, and a spare on the rear with a chromed cover. The white top was down, ready to take some good-looking young lady wherever her heart desired.

Deloris's beau, Rufus Pointer, was dressed in a red belt-back, wide-cuffed, bell-bottomed suit. With it he wore a red tie, red handkerchief, red hat (flopped over his right eye), and red spats that almost covered his red shoes. He looked as if he was on fire. The only color he wore other than red was his shirt—which was an absurd purple. I wanted to ask him if the store had ran out of all other colors or if he thought that the color red was the only way we could find him. Even Papa, who could see colors and objects better at a distance, commented, "Whoever that is sho' wants to be seen, don't he?" When I tried to tell him who it was, Deloris put her hand over my mouth.

I wondered what happened to the nice blues, grays, browns, seersuckers, and pinstripes that Papa, Uncle Pet, and other older men wore.

We didn't recognize the young man who was showing off the new car, but he was also fashionably dressed. His getup was much more civilized than the wild red Rufus was sporting. The strange young man wore a light gray belt-back, double-breasted, cuffed bell-bottomed suit. He topped it off with a polka-dot tie with a matching handkerchief, black slippers—no spats—and a wide gray hat tipped to the side, almost covering his right eye. There was one thing wrong: the suit was two sizes too small. With the coat buttoned, his butt stuck out like Miz Mag's.

"Elbert, you know who that is?" Deloris asked.

Elbert squinted. "Butt looks like Miz Mag's." Precisely what I was thinking. "That's Reedy," Elbert said.

"Reedy? Wheah Reedy git er suit like that?" Papa asked.

"Wheah Reedy git er car like that?" Deloris asked.

"Wheah Reedy git money t' buy clothes and a car like that?" Elbert asked.

"How come he didn't git the suit to fit im?" I asked.

"Probably bought it someplace wheah he couldn't try it on. Git close 'n you'll see wheah he cut his shoes too, I bet," Papa said.

I had heard Papa and Uncle Pet talking about stores that wouldn't allow black people to try on clothing before they bought it. Once you bought it, you couldn't exchange it. If a white person came in while a black person was being waited on, the black person had to step aside and wait until the white person was finished. That practice didn't work too well with most black people. Anyone with one tenth of a brain would simply walk out.

Papa and Uncle Pet wouldn't go into many stores in the first place. If they were pushed aside in any manner, they would walk. If they couldn't try on a pair of shoes before they bought them, they would walk. If they couldn't try on a suit, a coat, or a pair of pants, they would walk. If they were addressed as "boy," they would walk. Consequently, they were limited to a few stores where they and their families had become known over the years. Even if one of those few stores practiced unfair tactics on other unsuspecting black people, they would never try them on Papa and Uncle Pet, "the walkers." I suppose that could be called discriminating among the discriminated against.

Black women had an especially hard time. A dress two or three sizes too large or small marred the good looks of the prettiest girls and accentuated the homeliness of others. Therefore, many of them designed and made their own clothes.

We got out of the car. Rufus sidled over to his girlfriend Deloris, leaving Reedy with his new clothes and new car.

Reedy tipped his hat. "Evenin', Mr. Andra. Evenin', 'Lois."

"Evenin', Reedy," they both spoke at once.

"Y' so dressed up, we didn't know who y' wuz," Deloris said. Rufus took her arm and started to go inside.

Usually sullen and solemn-faced, Reedy smiled broadly and laughed. "Thank y', 'Lois."

Papa had already gone inside. I made it my business to get close enough to see Reedy's shoes. Papa was right. Sure enough, they had been cut where the toes pushed against the leather. They were clearly too small for Reedy's big feet. I had noticed him limp when he took a few steps toward Papa.

While I was close enough, I took a closer look at the coupe he was driving. There was something very familiar about it. *"New dress, new hat, new shoes . . . anything y' want,"* flashed in my mind. It dawned on me. *This is Fred's car.* I had seen Fred flashing a roll of bills. Had heard him trying to get Reedy to put him close to Leala and her "big titties." Besides, they were partners in something.

Elbert, who had gone to park the car, walked up. "Whut y' say, Reedy?"

"Whut y' say, Elbert?"

"This you?" he looked at the car.

"Yea-a-ah, this is me," Reedy replied.

"Nice little buggy. Yes sir, *niiiice* little buggy. You choppin' in *high* cotton now, Reedy Riley," Elbert said.

Reedy laughed. "Aw-w-w, I'm doin' all right fer er po' boy. I ain't up there wid you Hugheses yet."

"I don't know erbout that. Look like you done passed us in the automobile department. I ain't never seen you dressed up like this befo'. Whut y'all do, strike oil er som'um?"

Reedy simply laughed—squeezing every inch he could out of the praise Elbert was heaping on him.

"You comin' in wid us?" Elbert asked.

"Yeah. Sho' is."

Reedy limped along beside Elbert. I brought up the rear, as we filed into Hughes Chapel for the box supper.

A long decorated table was in front of the pulpit. Shoe boxes were neatly placed on the table with a girl's name on each one. All the young ladies were hidden behind a long white sheet draped around the platform, with only their bare feet exposed. Young men inspected those feet and selected a partner. The young lady selected would come from behind the curtain, and her box would be bid on. If the young man had selected the wrong feet—not his girl's—he was permitted to wait until the young lady he liked came out, and bid on her box.

When Elbert, Reedy, and I entered, all eyes were on Reedy. Neither he nor his family made a habit of coming to church. Elbert walked up to the front where the action was. I followed him. Reedy, in his tight shoes, which must have been killing him, sat in the back.

Bill, Rufus, and the other young men began touching toes. All manner of young ladies revealed themselves: short ones, tall ones, fat ones. Some were pretty. Some had pretty faces but bad bodies. Some had bad faces but beautiful bodies. Some had pretty faces and fair bodies. Some had fair faces and fair bodies—plain. There were others who should have stayed behind the curtain.

Deloris had not been picked. The bidding was going hot and heavy. The auctioneer picked up a box that belonged to one of the prettiest girls. "I have in my hands heah the box of Miss Stacy Martin. I'm sure that this pretty young lady has her box stacked . . . wid all kinds er goodies fer one er you young men out theah to enjoy. In addition to that, you will also have the pleasure of her company fer the evenin'. Whut am I bid?"

A rather stupid young man started the bidding with 50 cents. That was exactly twice as much as was usual on the first bid. If the young man had wanted to go unchallenged, he would have started the bid with a minimum of $1.

Stacy's box finally went for the big price of $2.25. That was three days' work for the young man who bought it. I would have paid $5. Stacy Martin was just that pretty.

Deloris's box was next. I naturally assumed Rufus would start the bidding high to eliminate the competition. Rufus revealed his uneasiness by looking at Deloris, then looking to the back of the church. I discovered that he was watching her watch somebody else—Reedy, I guessed. Deloris possessed such an outgoing, confident personality that it was difficult to tell whether she liked a particular beau or not. She paid respect to Rufus because he had asked and received permission to come courting. It wasn't polite for a young lady to do less for her beau in public—especially when they were practically betrothed.

I often wondered what Deloris saw in Rufus. He dressed like a clown. He looked like a clown. He acted like the father of clowns and smelled wild like the rest of his family. He also had hunched shoulders and walked funny, as if he was putting on gloves all the time. I never could see why Deloris took up with him in the first place—except that Elbert liked him. But Elbert never met a man, or an animal, he didn't like.

Rufus wasn't unlikable; he simply couldn't command respect. He trivialized everything. He was from Over In The Hills. New Dawn, Grandma Fannie Templeton's church, should have been his church instead of Hughes Chapel. Many hill country boys sought girls over on the Pike, mostly for prestige. That's where the action was.

Thus Rufus had been on the bench with his buddy Elbert at our church. He was asked to pray, as were all new converts. He was so frightened, it took him twenty minutes to get on his knees. Once on his knees, he uttered, "Bow down, b-b-bow down." Elbert asked him to repeat it. He was fool enough to do so. He got up and sat back in his seat—smiling. End of prayer. Elbert simply couldn't contain himself. In his deep, quiet, serious way, he shook and laughed and cried through the balance of the service. Years later, when things would go wrong, Elbert would say, "Bow down, b-b-bow down," and lighten his day.

Rufus tried to eliminate all competition by opening the bid with "Two 'n er quarter."

A voice trumpeted from the rear. "Two fifty!"

All heads turned to the strange voice in the rear. Rufus looked at Deloris, then Elbert. "Er-er-r-r, two 'n six bits—"

"Three!" Reedy responded before Rufus got the bid out of his mouth.

Rufus pulled out his big red handkerchief and started wiping grease and sweat from his face and neck. Wild, funky fumes sprouted legs and walked across noses like they were gangplanks. He called for time, went over to his buddy Elbert, and whispered in his ear. Elbert nodded his head. "Three 'n er quarter," Rufus squeaked out in a choked voice.

"Five dollars!" Reedy said, and started hobbling up to the table with his money in his hand. It was obvious those tight shoes were killing him, but he managed to squeeze out a smile.

Poor Rufus dropped down in his seat, completely disgusted and exhausted. There was no way he could have answered that, even if he had borrowed one more of the dollars Elbert needed for his own bidding.

Bidding over, the successful young men sat down to enjoy their suppers beside their young ladies. I had never seen Reedy so happy. He and Deloris were laughing and carrying on a friendly conversation. After all, they had known each other since childhood. Deloris, who was raised to be compassionate and considerate, got permission from Reedy, took part of the food over to Rufus, and he accepted. Deloris joked with him for a minute, got him to laugh, and returned to her guest for the evening. Like Papa, she instinctively had a way with people.

I wondered, *How can Reedy be so happy while those tight shoes have a nelson on his feet?* When everybody started to file out of church, I noticed Reedy walking normally, still laughing and talking with Deloris. However, he was carrying the shoe box that the food had been in under his arm. I looked down and saw his big breathing bare feet sticking from under his bell-bottoms. I said nothing to anyone. We got in our cars and headed home.

With a deep darkness upon us, the air was thick and heavy. Chickens roosting made only a subdued fuss now and then. Cows and calves lay close together, chewing on ancient cuds. Mules muttered slightly aroused sounds, halfway between neighing and braying—inherited from the gentle neigh of a mother mare and the hoarse, harsh cry of a braying jackass. Hogs and pigs huddled in the nearest mud hole, piled around and on top of each other like sacks of oats thrown at random. Squirrels had long since ceased whittling sculpture for the day and stolen quietly into their retreats, high in the forks of old oaks. Nocturnal foxes, however, were still on the prowl, sniffing and peeping and spying—seeking that one opening to chicks at rest. Gentle Harvey had growled and barked once, then sold out to good-smelling leftovers from a good-looking gal. Those were some of the sounds and images that penetrated the night. It would be four hours before roosters crowed, and there was no moon to guide wandering feet.

Scratching was heard at the back porch screen where Deloris had moved her cot to escape the heat inside and enjoy the occasional breeze that slipped through during the night.

Mama's voice came through the wall that separated their room from our dormitory space. "Andra, Andra. Do you heah scratchin' or somethin' on the back porch?"

Papa was half asleep. "Whut?"

"I thought I heard a scratchin' noise," Mama said. She was interrupted by the sound again.

"Yeah, I heard it that time," Papa said.

The next instant, I heard Papa getting up. A flashlight shone in the hallway. I heard the sound of a rifle being cocked.

"Who is it?"

As the light penetrated the kitchen on the way to the back porch, a scurrying, rushing noise was heard—then bare feet repeating like flapping geese taking off. A leap that tore off a picket from the fence. Then the rapid clapping of feet in motion, headed up Wagon Road West.

"Halt, or I'll shoot!" Papa yelled.

It was to no avail. By that time the feet had made it up the hill. Soon the repeating beats against hard red Arkansas clay were drowned out by distance and dark night. Since a Winchester is dangerous at a distance of over five miles, Papa could have shot in the direction of the sound and perhaps hit him, but he had no desire to take a life he didn't absolutely have to take.

He uncocked his gun and flashed the light around. "Who in the devil wuz that, I wonder?"

"I don't know, Papa," Deloris responded.

"Andra, git on back in heah. There may be somebody wid im," Mama said.

"If theah wuz, he sho gave im er good demonstration of how fast he could run off 'n leave im," Papa said.

We were all up by that time, trying to find out what had happened. Elbert took the light and walked out into the backyard. He flashed it over by the fence, and there lay a shoe box with a pair of new, cut-up black loafers sticking out. "Heah's er box wid some black shoes in it," Elbert said.

"Who do y' think they belong to?" Papa asked.

I knew immediately and blurted out, "Bet they Reedy's."

Elbert checked the box. "Sun's right. Heah's 'Lois's name right heah."

"Bet I know—," I began.

"Shut yo' mouth, boy, 'n go back t' bed," Deloris said.

Papa chuckled. "Fool boy. Why wouldn't he come eround in the daytime, like er young man should, 'n ask t' see 'Lois 'stead er scratching eround heah in the middle er the night, like a cat, takin' a chance on gittin' shot?"

"I guess he figured you wouldn't let him call on me," Deloris said.

"He could er asked me and found out," Papa said.

"He probably figured it wouldn't do no good, Andra," Mama said.

"Well, the boy is kinda wild heah lately. I'm gon' have t' talk t' Sam erbout im first thing inner mornin'," Papa said.

"There's som'um goin' on. Reedy wuz drivin' a new Ford. He had on new clothes 'n these heah new shoes," Elbert reasoned.

"That ain't none er yo' business. Don't go talkin' that stuff eround. Jist mind yo' own business 'n stay away from im," Papa ordered.

I thought about the slop factory. I hadn't said anything about what Ben, Olie, and I had seen in the canebrake. I wasn't even sure it wasn't on our land or Uncle Pet's.

I had seen Deputy Westbrooks and his men headed south on the Pike many times. It was generally late in the evening. I had also seen them return early in the morning with their Ford loaded with steel barrels, tubes, and coils dangling from the holey barrels. Papa would comment, "Well, ol' Westbrooks 'n his boys done busted ernother one. Wonder whose wuz that?" Sometimes Westbrook had two or three rednecks in the backseat of his Ford. Their heads bobbed up and down as he sped north, his tires grinding the gravel and throwing rocks here and yon. Occasionally he stopped and got a drink of our water, well known to be the best. He wasn't a man who talked a lot, and I never saw him smile. He simply talked crops and weather, asked how business was going, and mentioned how good our water tasted.

His name was enough to strike fear into most people. He wore a semiwide gray western hat with a narrow black band, tipped over his right eye. His wide sweat-stained suspenders were attached to his wide black gun belt. His holster and pistol were the fanciest part of his rather conservative dress. His pearl-handled .38 was camped in a black leather holster with a circular nest of shiny silver brads on the side, from which hung several strips of leather. The end of the holster was tied around his leg with more leather strips. His pants and shirt were regulation khaki.

Nobody knew his first name. He was simply Westbrooks. He looked and could indeed be dangerous. He kept his big railroad watch in his right shirt pocket. The fob dangled from a gold chain, projected through a buttonhole.

He put one of his scuffed cowboy boots on a block of wood, pushed his hat back on his head, and enjoyed his cool water as he chatted with Papa. Then he walked slowly to his car, still making small talk, settled back in his seat, cocked his hat over his right eye, waved good-bye, and drove off.

About two weeks after Papa had gone to talk to Mr. Sam about Reedy, Papa came home with Mr. Sam in the Chevy. When Mr. Sam got out of the car, he was dressed as I had never seen him before. He looked almost decent. He had on a pair of gray suit pants and a white shirt with the collar detached, buttoned all the way to the top. His wide red suspenders were accented by a pair of big silver buckles. He also wore a pair of tan shoes he had put the knife to. He had discarded his old ragged, greasy, sweat-stained floppy hat for a black hard-top Stetson. He had pounded the Stetson in on top, however, until it took on that Sam Riley character. In addition, he made doubly sure the hat was sitting on his head with the bow of the band in the middle of his forehead. This meant the label was over his left ear and the front of the hat was over his right ear. He had even been to the barbershop and gotten a shave and a haircut. Bob Ledden, the barber, had sprinkled some of that awful stuff on him (Bob called it cologne) that smelled like toilet disinfectant to me.

Mr. Sam was in a jolly mood, as usual. "Andra, don't y' slam that do' on my hand and hurt me. You *know* how tender I is. No sir, don't hurt *me* whutever you do!"

"You kin take care er yo'self, Sam Riley. I jist don't wanna mess up my do' on yo' rough hands," Papa said.

Mr. Sam almost swallowed his tobacco juice laughing. He then started spitting all over the place. He didn't bother to come to the porch. He and Papa chatted out by the woodpile. Finally, I saw him humping up the hill on Wagon Road West, his shoes in one hand and a big brown paper bag in the other.

A few days later, at dusk, Westbrooks's black Ford was heading south. I noticed it slowing down as it approached our house. Sure enough it turned right on Wagon Road West and headed up the little hill.

Papa and Mr. Durbey were sitting in front of the blacksmith shop. Westbrooks waved but didn't stop. The Ford left a cloud of dust as it tore up the little hill, as if he was on his way to a fire. And I had a good idea where that fire was.

Papa didn't know about the slop factory, but he certainly knew something was wrong when he saw Westbrooks rushing up the hill in the direction of our farm. I could see a worried look on Papa's face as he said good night to Mr. Durbey and we went into the house for supper.

Inside, Papa, Mama, Deloris, and Elbert were buzzing and talking grown-ups' talk, more or less ignoring me as if I was a chair or a mule or something. Little did they know I could have provided them with shocking information at the slightest prompting.

It was another dark, moonless night. We went to bed wondering what the morrow would bring.

> *Hurry down sunshine,*
> *See what tomorrow bring.*
> *It may bring mo' sunshine,*
> *Then ergin, it might bring rain.*

Everybody was up early the next morning. It was late September, almost time for school to start. Mama and Papa started prodding us about cleaning up the yard, chopping plenty of winter wood, cleaning up the living room and the rest of the house—making it nice for the teacher before school started.

We had only worked a short while when we looked up and saw two cars coming down the little hill in back of our house. The Barrows were all outside watching. Ben passed the slow-moving cars and came flying down the hill in front of them. Mr. Durbey, moping along on his way to his shop, moved quickly to the side of the road and let them pass. The cars pulled up beside our house. Westbrooks got out of his Ford, which was loaded with the wrecked and hole-riddled steel barrels of the slop factory. The coupe was the same car Fred and Reedy had driven. Ben punched me and whispered, "Ain't that the slop factory there?"

"That's it," I said.

Papa came out of the backyard and walked toward the cars. "Mornin', Mr. Westbrooks."

"Mornin', Andy. How y' feelin' this mornin'?"

"Pretty good. Pretty good." Papa was busy looking in the backseat trying to see who it was.

"'Fraid I got some bad news fer y', Andy. Caught them two boys cookin' whiskey early this mornin', around three."

"Ain't that Sam 'n Reedy back theah?" Papa asked.

"That's them. Now I been knowin' Sam long as you have. 'N you know I usually take great pleasure in bustin' stills, but I gotta tell y' t'wasn't no pleasure bustin' this'un. T'wasn't easy either." Westbrooks took out his big red and white handkerchief and mopped his brow.

Papa was shaking. "Sam 'n me growed up together—he's like er brother."

"I know that, Andy. That's why I stopped heah. Theah's one other thing, we don't know fer sho, but it might er been on your or Pet's land."

"Wheah y' find that still, Mr. Westbrooks?" Papa asked.

"Little branch off Alligator Creek, jist fo' y' git t' the bridge—thick cane-brake on the right. Know wheah it is?"

"I think I know erbout wheah it is," Papa said.

"Well, don't matter. Jist thought you oughtta know."

"Mr. Westbrooks, Sam heah can't go to no state farm. He's too ol'. It'll kill'im."

"I know, Andy, 'specially wid Jake Parsons the whippin' boss down theah."

"That's exactly whut I mean. Sam ain't use to that hard work either," Papa said.

"I'm gon' level wid y', Andy. We didn't actually ketch Reedy in the act. We picked im up at the house later. But I don't know if the boy'd be willin' to take the blame fer the ol' man . . ."

"Theah's only one way t' find out." Papa walked over to the car and stuck his head in the rear window. Westbrooks followed and stood listening. Ben and I could hear only part of what Mr. Sam said.

"Whut you laughing erbout, you ol' fool?" Papa asked Mr. Sam.

Sam said something we couldn't hear. Then Papa said, "Don't worry erbout the look on my face. Better be worried erbout y'self. Settin' there, tied up like er hog fixin' t' be castrated."

We overheard Mr. Sam say something about being tender, unable to take any beating. But if he had to, he could take beatings better than he could hard work.

"Listen, y' ol' tobacco-chewin' dirt-darber," Westbrooks said. "Andy's tryin' t' help y'. We all tryin'. Least y' kin do is be serious at a time like this. By God, maybe you'd jist as soon we turn y' over t' Jake Parsons?"

We heard Mr. Sam loud and clear that time. "Oooooh no! I knooooow you don't mean that, Mr. Westbrooks! Sam can't take no beatings! 'N Sam is much too tender fer that hard work!"

"Pa, quiet down now!" Reedy said.

"Reedy, Mr. Westbrooks offered us a proposition heah. He's willing t' take you instead er yo' pa. Whut y' say?" We didn't hear it, but Reedy's response must have been an instant yes.

"You will, Reedy?" Papa said. "Well, y' heard im, Mr. Westbrooks."

"Sho did, Andy. Theah's one mo' thing. Theah's gon' be a fine. Can't tell y' how much, but somebody gon' have t' come up wid some money—possibly five hundred dollars—fo' Sam can go free."

"Well, Mr. Westbrooks, that's er lot er money fer these times. That car er Reedy's should take care of that," Papa said.

"Only that ain't Reedy's car. He don't have no papers t' show it's his. That's some'um else we gotta look into," Westbrooks said, getting into his car.

"I'm gon' talk t' Pet. We'll be up theah soon as we git straightened out."

"You do that, Andy. I'll be able t' give y' mo' details when y' git theah. Sorry erbout this, Andy, but I'm sho you understand. It's really up to the judge now. I'll do the best I can t' git it as low as possible."

Westbrooks and his entourage pulled off slowly and headed north toward Pine Ridge. He was surrounded by an audience of fifteen Barrows. Even Mr. Jim and Mrs. Marge had come down the little hill and were standing at a respectable distance. Mr. Durbey was standing over by the store with his greasy apron and dirty black leather cap. He had a pair of tongs in his hand. Hazel, Deloris, Geneva, Verleen, Mama, and Elbert were standing in our backyard. Papa gave a weak wave and walked briskly toward the house.

Many questions were yet to be answered. Would Mr. Sam go to the pen if Papa and Uncle Pet didn't raise the money? Would Jake beat Reedy like he would a stranger?

Ben and I followed the entourage to the Pike and watched them as they approached Bayou Bartholomew Bridge.

"Well, theah goes our slop factory," Ben said.

"Did y' know whut it wuz when we first saw it?" I asked Ben.

"Damn right I knowed. That ugly-ass Olie didn't fool me fer er minute," Ben said.

"You lyin'. You didn't know nothin'.'"

"Say that one mo' time 'n I'll snatch out er blood vessel, rip off er arm, or som'um," Ben said as he rolled up his sloppy shirtsleeve.

"You heard me the first time. I don't chew my tobacco but"—I was struck by what I saw—"once . . . is . . ." I couldn't believe my eyes, but there it was, or was not. Once the small scab healed on his chin, one wouldn't know the infamous tit had ever existed.

"Whut the hell you starin' at, pussy-face?"

"Not much, y' little bogey-wogey. Why didn't y' tell me?"

"You got eyes. You kin see. Whut y' want m' t' do, kiss yo' ass 'cause y' did er little operation? Come on. Let's git som'um done."

I hadn't seen Ben in a few weeks. He had been in Cleveland County with his grandparents. I didn't dare tell him, but he looked absolutely marvelous for the first time in his life. Too bad I couldn't say the same for his errant personality.

There was still plenty of damp sand in the ditch on the east side of the Pike. Ben and I busied ourselves building castles. I placed a small candle in mine, stood back, and looked at it. Ben was green with envy.

Soon Papa was headed up the Pike in his Chevy to look after his old friend.

22

Hot June spat dragon fires showering Baptist business around about our farms, our rolling hills, our lowlands, our creeks and bayous in forest country. Weeping willows that sat quietly on sloughy banks shared the watering rains, drank deep from creeks and unseen substrata, and springs slowed their givens. Joints from growing stalks popped at night, and the smell of fresh earth rose to greet every nostril. Sweet potato vines spread their azure quilt across each row, and pole beans climbed high toward the heavens and drooped their wings laden with ripened lobes. Quiet sprinkles continued earth's ritual plan, and its living and growing exceeded its dying and decaying. Bumblebees buzzed among berries and bushes. Horseflies galloped among the stock, drawing blood, growing big, brave, and ugly. Everything that crept or crawled gathered at the watering holes. Fresh tenders replaced tender "earlies." Earth's evangelism sprang to full pump, and witnesses were everywhere. Fields and gardens were deep green, speckled with white, pink, and blue. The heathen sun was relentless in its savagery. Snakes crawled night and day, and there were rumors of slobbering mad dogs running loose in the roads.

Deloris and Mama called us all to breakfast early. It was the first time Elbert, just turned thirteen, had honored us with his presence at the breakfast table since he became an almighty mule skinner. He took full advantage of his newly found importance. Pass me this and pass me that. "Any mo' er that rice left?"

The hoecake was always saved for Papa. In fact, it was a symbol of his rank in the family. No one, not even Mama, questioned the importance of the hoecake and Papa's rightful claim to it. Though I had no idea how leftover scraps of dough from cutting out biscuits, balled up and baked in the same pan with the biscuits, ranked so high as a symbol of authority, I maintained the same level of respect for the superbiscuit as everybody else.

As soon as Deloris came to the table with a big steaming pan of biscuits, plus a big hot hoecake at one end of the pan, Elbert spoke up. "Papa, could I have half er yo' hoecake?"

"Give that boy half er my hoecake," Papa ordered.

"'N put plenty butter in between," Elbert added.

"Plenty butter, Deloris," Papa backed Elbert up.

"Any mo' er that chicken left in theah?" Elbert inquired.

"Y'all bring some mo' chicken out heah," Papa echoed.

"Why don't y' jist sign the house over t'im while y' at it, Papa?" Deloris blurted out exactly what I was thinking but didn't dare say.

"Quiet, young lady. Bein' er mule skinner is hard work. Man gotta have plenty t' eat under his belt t' handle er team er mules 'n er dirt zip ten hours er day on that Pike."

"Elbert's er man now?" I asked cynically.

"He's doin' er man's job. Law says you er man at twenty-one, but I say y' start becomin' er man when y' put away child's play 'n start doin' things er man have t' do. Some people don't ever grow up."

Stuffing his face like it was a cotton sack, our newly acknowledged man-child prepared to leave. "Sorry I can't stick eround 'n discuss that wid you folks, but there's er Mr. Pete DiGasspri waitin' fer me."

A truck whistle blew outside. Elbert grabbed his dinner bucket, his work gloves, his pith helmet, and rushed out the door. "See y'all good folks t'night."

"Drank plenty water!" Mama warned.

"Don't git too hot out theah!" Papa added.

Elbert forgot his big red and white handkerchief. He rushed back inside to get it. Mama followed him to the door and started straightening his shirt. He pulled away from her. "Mama, don't let nobody see you doin' that." It was too late. Men in the truck were already laughing at him.

"Come on theah, young mule skinner! Y' holdin' things up heah!" one of the men said jokingly.

I ran to the fence to see him off. He put his helmet on as he ran and buckled it under his chin to keep the wind from blowing it away.

Two of the men playfully pushed him off when he tried to get on the truck. Finally they grabbed him by the hand and pulled him onto the flatbed. The truck took off in a cloud of dust, headed up the Pike. The men were laughing and joking, happy to be working on the new Pike.

If only I could go with them. Why couldn't I be a water boy? At least I would get to watch Elbert drive those mules as a real mule skinner and handle that big shovel, the dirt zip. Elbert had already made it abundantly clear that the water boys on that job were really men, much older than he was. It was also clear to me that all the attention he was getting, plus Papa's what-makes-a-man speech at the breakfast table, had gone straight to his thirteen-year-old mule skinner's head.

After Elbert left, the rest of the family headed for the fields. Instead of being a water boy on the Pike, I soon became one on our farm. Mr. Sam Riley, barefooted and ragged as usual, steadied the plow from row to row. Cultivation, which kept the soil loose, and chopping, which kept the grass from choking and starving the plants, was at a premium until the Fourth of July.

At nine, I pulled my own weight with the hoe as well as my other chores. Papa, who was spending progressively less time at the store, camped beneath the shade of a willow on the bank of Alligator Creek, which ran through our farm. When I reached the end of my row, near where he was sitting, he called me. "Sun, come wid me 'n bring yo' hoe 'n this bucket."

"Yes sir." I followed him across the shallow part of the creek and up the side of a steep hill. The ground became softer as we climbed. Finally Papa stopped and poked around with his cane until he found a spot where it pierced through the leaves and debris. "Take yo' hoe 'n dig right heah," he said, and stood aside.

First I removed a layer of leaves and pine needles. As I dug and raked with my hoe, the ground started to bleed a reddish-brown liquefied mud. I was mystified.

"Keep diggin' 'n rakin'. Clean it all out," Papa said.

Sticks, mud, and leaves came out of the big hole as I dug. Soon mud and water the color of blood bubbled around my hoe.

"Keep diggin'. Rake that stuff outta y' way. Still kinda muddy, ain't it?" Papa said, and pointed with his cane.

The faster I dug, the bigger the bubbling flow became. Finally I was pulling out white sand, and the flow began to clear up.

"Li'l bit mo' 'n y' got it, Sun."

The raking became smooth and easy. The bubbling blood-colored mud became cool, fresh, clear water. Papa rinsed out his felt hat, dipped up a full portion, and drank with great swallows. I lay on my stomach at the edge of the bubbling spring and drank until I could feel my stomach swelling.

"How did y' know this spring was heah, Papa?"

"I wuz raised on this land, remember? All y' have t' know is erbout wheah t'is 'n keep walkin' till the ground feels soft 'n damp. Then look fer er li'l dip in the land. Springs don't usually dry up. They jist fill up 'n y' have t' clean um out."

"Did Grandpa show you the first time?"

"Naw. My oldest brother, E.J., showed me. He called hisself lookin' fer er oil well. Fill the bucket up 'n let's take some er this good stuff to the rest of um."

My mind went back to Ben and me, always looking for oil wells.

Before we headed back, Papa marked a spot on a big oak with his pocket knife. "Papa, theah's already a mark heah."

"Wheah?"

"Right below the mark y' just made."

"Oh, yeah." Papa strained to see. "Well, this one'll make it cleah. That one's growin' over, anyway."

*   *   *

As I lugged the bucket back, I thought about Elbert. How I wished I was more grown up so I could do the things Papa let him do. *Pretty soon he'll be asking to wear Papa's watch*, I thought.

It was only the past winter that Elbert had stayed out of school to haul winter wood until spring. I liked school, but I would much rather have worked with Elbert. Whenever spring arrived early, I was happy because the wood business slacked off and Elbert came to school with the rest of us.

During the fall, Elbert went on all those moonlight trips with Papa to pick up remedies. He was getting to be such a man that soon he'd be going out with girls. He had never been skinny like me. I grew fast and straight like a pine. Elbert grew fast and powerful like an oak. I was swift and wiry, with small wrists and long fingers. Elbert was powerful, deliberate, and enduring, with broad shoulders, big wrists, and strong manly hands. Though he possessed that rugged body, I had never seen him exhibit his ability by wrestling or fighting like me and most boys. He was quiet and constantly working. With his friends, however, he always laughed and talked in a fun-filled manner.

It wasn't that I was jealous of Elbert's position in the family. I simply couldn't wait to get where he was.

After work that day in the field, Mr. Sam hopped on the wagon with our family and drove us south a short distance on Wagon Road West to the old Hughes homestead. The pickers filled the tubs and all the buckets with sweet ripe plums, and we headed home.

When we pulled up in our backyard, odd-looking strangers were drawing water from our well. I had seen all manner of travelers take water, but these people were different. There were three women and two men.

The women wore long colorful dresses and skirts. Two long black plaits came to their waists. Their beautiful heads were wrapped with exotic headbands. Their arms and ears were laden with craftily designed jewelry. Beads and leather made up the rest of their costume. Their makeup would do honor to a minstrel artist. Shining painted red lips, exaggerated long curling eyelashes, and thin arched eyebrows that curved up the sides of their temples to infinity snapped out from a thick layer of cakey powder generously applied to a base of other greasy, mysterious ingredients. Their long, painted, dirty fingernails looked more like claws or talons. Long golden earrings dangled from their earlobes, and they wore brass-bradded sandals that flopped loosely from their dirty feet. They were pretty women, the color of dark red Arkansas clay, slender and delicately built.

The men adorned themselves with almost as much overlay as the women, which included earrings and wide brass-bradded leather belts and wristbands that made them look almost biblical. They had covered their arms, legs, chests, and backs with tattoos.

Papa climbed down off the wagon in a hurry and was walking toward them when he heard Mr. Durbey's voice from the rear of the store. "Don't you worry none, M.A., I got my eye on um. I tol um they could git they wauter 'n git goin'."

As we approached, we walked into a funk wall. Close up, they were dirty to the point of having thick layers of grease on their skin and clothes.

One of the ladies spoke first in a thick accent. "Niiiice man, niiiiice mister, please, we want only water—only water we want. Yes?"

"Well, git yo' water 'n go."

She looked pretty from a distance, but close up, when she opened her mouth, most of her teeth were black and rotted. The inside of her mouth looked as if she had been eating blackberries. She appeared young, but under the thick makeup, thin lines could be seen on her forehead and around her neck and eyes.

The women gathered around Papa, grinning in his face and bowing. One of them went over to the fence, picked up a bag, and began taking out articles. "I have niiiiice sweater forrrr you. Niiiiice talllll handsome man."

Papa needed a sweater like he needed a fever; it was about 97 degrees at that moment.

She draped the sweater over his shoulder. "Sweater fit beautiful. I make you gooood prrrice. Yes?"

Papa politely took the sweater off his shoulder and gave it back to the woman. Close up, her breath smelt like a gaping outhouse.

Mr. Durbey had crossed the road and was standing at the fence with his blacksmith hammer in his hand. "Don't talk nice t' them Gypsies, M.A.! Tell um t' take they wauter 'n git on 'way from eround heah! Right now, they sizin' this place up so they kin come back 'n steal som'um!"

Standing there with his wristbands and belts over his arms, the man spoke up. "We no steal! We no steal—noooo steal! Only sell—only sell!"

If someone talked to me like that I'd feel offended. The Gypsy kept showing all his rotten teeth and trying to peddle his stuff. I wanted one of his wristbands in the worst way. For all their faults, I thought they did beautiful work.

"That's whut every Gypsy I ever seed said. Y'all must git together 'n go over this stuff, like choir practice. 'Me noooo steal.' You Gypsies'll steal the gold fillin' outta er man's mouth wid him lookin' dead at y'. Y'all will steal the sweetness outta sugar! You Gypsies wuz bo'n stealin'!"

"Only sell—only sell! No steal—nooo steal!" He walked over to the fence grinning and holding his stuff out to Mr. Durbey as if he had enjoyed being insulted. "Niiiice band forrrrr strrrong man!"

"Git erway from me wid that Gypsy junk fo' I flatten y' like er hoss-shoe!" Mr. Durbey drew back his hammer.

The man stopped in his tracks, but still tried to sell the wristband. "Only two dollar fifty cents forrrr the nice gentell-man. Only two dollar fifty cents, please. Yes sirrr. Please, nice gentell-man."

"Y' ain't doin' nothin' but tryin' t' gyp m'. Wheah y' s'pose that word come from anyhow?" Mr. Durbey lashed out. The women were still trying to sell items to Papa. "M.A., y' want me t' git rid er these stinkin' Gypsies fer y'? 'Cause y' ain't gon' never do it, way y' goin' erbout it! Y' gotta git rough wid these boogers. Y'all jist wait heah till I come back." Mr. Durbey hobbled as fast as he could toward his shop.

Mama, who had watched the whole thing, went to the back of the wagon and got a bucket of plums. "Now y'all hold yo' handkerchiefs out."

They left Papa like a flash and hovered around Mama. She emptied the bucket of plums into their handkerchiefs. "Now y'all go on back t' yo' tents now, 'n behave yo'selves." Mama went inside to get supper started.

They gathered their stuff up and took off like happy children. The men playfully trekked behind the women and stole plums out of their handkerchiefs.

Mr. Durbey hobbled back over to the fence with his shotgun. "Wheah'd they go?"

"Whut y' gon' do wid that shotgun, Brother Durbey?" Papa asked.

"I wuz gonna scare the hell out of um. If I'd er let go er couple er times in the air wid Mr. Gravedigger heah, you'd er seen some stinkin' Gypsies fly, I bet! He-he-he-heee! They try t' make out they don't know whut y' talkin' erbout. I bet ol' Gravedigger heah speaks er language they understand, stinkin' devils."

Elbert walked up, coming home from work. "Evenin' everybody." Everybody responded. "I jist met er bunch er Gypsies, 'n I saw they tents up by the bayou. They musta come this mo'nin' after I left," Elbert said.

"They did. We jist got rid of um," Papa said.

"That ain't good ernough. We gotta git all the stock inside 'n lock up the chicken house 'cause them Gypsies'll git y', give um half er chance." Elbert sat his lunch pail on the back porch and walked down to the barn. "Remember whut happened er couple er yeahs ago."

"Everbody knows them Gypsies'll steal y' blind, Elbert. That is, everbody 'cept yo' Pa 'n Ma. They goin' eround talkin' nice to um 'n givin' um plums 'n stuff. Last time y' did that, they come back 'n stole yo' chicken 'n yo' 'taters, didn't they?" Mr. Durbey looked at Papa for an answer.

"We don't know fer sho it wuz them. All the chicken I lost over the yeahs wuz not stol' by Gypsies," Papa said.

"All I know is, chickens been out theah all that time 'n nobody bothered um. Them stinkin' Gypsies heah er few days, 'n when they left the chickens left wid um," Mr. Durbey responded.

Elbert overheard Mr. Durbey as he walked back from the barn. "They sho did, Papa. I don't see them geese out theah."

"You look behind the barn? Back er the shop?" Papa asked.

"I looked all around. They must be down at the bayou. Come on, Sun." Elbert took off. I picked up a stick and followed behind him.

"Hey, Elbert! Y' wanna take ol' Gravedigger erlong wid y' in case y' wanna make um understand whut y' talkin' erbout?"

"No, thank y', Mr. Durbey, I think I kin get erlong without him."

"Y'all be careful up theah, y' heah?" Papa warned.

"Yes sir," we both responded together.

I rushed to catch up with him. "Elbert, you ain't scared?"

"Scared er whut, them Gypsies?"

"Naw, them geese. O' course them Gypsies," I said.

"'Course not. Gypsies ain't erbout fightin' nobody."

"They erbout stealin', huh?" I said.

"That, 'n singin' 'n dancin' 'n makin' er lot er babies. They make er lot er stuff wid they hands too."

"Lots er pretty stuff. I saw a wristband fer two fifty. I sho do wish I had it."

"Whut you wish ain't gon' hurt y'. Wheah you gon' git two fifty?"

"Workin' on the new Pike as er water boy," I responded.

"Sun, I keep tellin' y', y' ain't ol' ernuff t' be no water boy, now why don't y' forgit it?"

"You ain't ol' ernuff t' be no mule skinner either, but y' pullin' down them long checks every week," I countered.

"I'm worth every nickel they pay me too, buddy—every penny. I'm right theah doin' the same thing them men over twice my age is doin'."

Down an embankment on our right, the land flattened out. Constant shade from ancient oaks prevented the growth of underbrush and grass. Mulched rotted leaves and residue from floodwaters left a soft carpeted floor. The lazy trickle of tributaries flowing into Bartholomew accentuated the shimmering tranquillity that held sway for us and the exotic pilgrims encamped there. The selvage shadows flickered through a rinsing blue haze. There in that evening quietness, that host of colorful strangers strummed guitars, played, and danced around three beautifully decorated tents that rose elegantly among the oaks. A slow-burning open fire cradled a big steel pot, and close by a team of lean brown horses munched on a pitiful ration of hay. A young boy was putting a spotted dog through his tricks.

As we started to pass, a man and a woman spotted us and ran over to greet us. "Hello, hello, hello, niiice young man-boys. Welcome, welcome! You welcome ourrr home. Yes?" the man said.

"We lookin' fer som'um. We ain't got time t' stop," Elbert said, and kept walking.

I wanted to see that wristband again in the worst way, but Elbert almost walked over both of the Gypsies when they got in his way. A short distance past the camp, we spotted the geese and goslings drinking and playing in a water hole near Bartholomew. Elbert found a stick, and we herded the geese toward home. The Gypsies were busy trying to interest us in some of their items, but my big mule skinner brother completely ignored them.

The lady Gypsy was dangling and rattling beads, earrings, rings, and combs in Elbert's face. "Niiiice young man-boy, beautiful rrring forrr beautiful lady, of you. You come my house, I show you morrre. You come. Yes?" Elbert kept walking.

After failing to interest Elbert in pocket knives, wallets, and belts—things we sold in our store—the man pulled out a wristband. It was almost identical to the one I had seen at the well, only more adorned with shiny brass brads. It was irresistible. I saw the immovable Elbert give it a quick glance out of the corner of his eye. That glance didn't go unnoticed by the Gypsy either.

The Gypsy bore down. He grabbed at Elbert's wrist. "I show you, niiiice man-boy. I show you. I put on. I put on. Yes?"

"It ain't gonna hurt y' t' let im put it on. That's the band I wuz tellin' y' erbout," I said.

Elbert stopped and looked at me. "Put it on him."

I shot my arm out before he got the words out.

The Gypsy fastened the band in the last hole, and it still swallowed my tiny wrist.

"Now you thrrry, nice man-boy, you thrrry." The Gypsy grabbed Elbert's big strong wrist, fastened the band in the second of the four holes, and it fit perfectly. "Beautiful! Beautiful! Niiice man-boy." The man was dragging Elbert. "Now come my home, I have forrrr young man-boy also."

"Naw, I gotta git home wid these geese." The geese had found another water hole nearby and were playing in it.

"Whut you talkin' erbout? Them geese ain't goin' no place," I said.

The Gypsy lady grabbed Elbert's arm and pulled him toward her tent. "You come my home. I make you gooood prrrice. You niiiice man-boy! Niiiice man-boy!"

Before we reached the tent, Elbert was swamped by other Gypsies. The boy who was putting the dog through his paces came straight toward me. He was about my age but not as tall. He had black teeth also and was much in need of a soapy scrubbing in Bartholomew.

Somehow, the stench around the tents wasn't as deadly as when it was around our well. I was sure the horses' odor improved theirs measurably, and the horses had piles of manure beneath them.

"You like marbles?" the boy asked. "I have beautiful marbles forrrr you, young boy." He held out a handful of marbles.

"Y' nothin' but er young boy yo'self," I responded quickly.

The boy grinned at me and showed all of his black teeth. "I show you my dog. Verrry smart. Herrro! Herrro!" The dog came to him and waited for his command. He snapped his fingers for the dog to stand up. The dog stood on his hind legs.

"Hat, please?"

"Whut y' want my hat fer?"

"I show you thrrrick. I show you thrrrick."

"Use yo' own hat," I said.

"I use hat—I use hat of me." The boy took off his cap, pointed to it, waved it in front of Hero's nose, took the hat inside the storage tent nearby, came back out, closed the tent, and commanded Hero to go get it. The dog went to the tent door and fussed around with the ropes but couldn't get in. He then went to the sides but saw no entrance. Without further ado, Hero started digging. The top layer of the ground was soft, and within a few seconds he had dug a hole large enough for him to get underneath, retrieve the cap, and return it to his master.

"Smart dog," I said.

"You have nickel, yes?"

"I have nickel, no. 'N if I did have, I'm not fool ernuff t' give it to you, especially for some dog trick I never asked y' for."

The boy looked at me and showed me more black teeth.

I walked next door, where the lady was trying to get Elbert to come inside to get his fortune told. I peeked inside, and at the entrance sat a heavily laden, dark-reddish-brown-pot-liquor-looking fat woman with a big shiny glass ball in front of her. The odor from her tent, while still stifling and nauseating, was better than in the open air. She had tall weeds smoking beside the candles on her table. It gave the inside an eerie look, and me an eerie feeling. The smoking weeds somehow squelched her odor.

"Step inside, please! Madam Taker-Gooski rrrread palms. Tell you many many seee-krrrets you life. You will be rrrich! You will marrrrry beautiful lady. Have many many beautiful shiilddrren!"

The man, with his armful of bands, grabbed my wrist and put a beautiful band on it that fit perfectly. It was like the one the boy was wearing. "Beautiful! Beautiful forrrr young man-boy. Yes? Yes?"

I turned the band over and over, admiring it by my expression.

"You buy for him, yes?"

"How much fer these two bands?" Elbert finally asked.

"Forrr you, I make verrry especial prrrice, two dollar—one dollar half." The man held up two fingers, then held his other finger halfway across to indicate the half dollar. "Yes, please?"

"No, please!" Elbert responded.

They went back and forth until we walked away with the two handsome bands for 75 cents. Elbert was proud of the deal he had made. The other peddlers were tugging at him as he walked boldly over to the water hole, gathered the geese and goslings together, and we headed home.

"How did y' know he was comin' down that low?" I asked.

"Y' gotta know how t' deal wid Gypsies. If y' kin stand t' smell um, y' kin git some good deals from um."

"But them women look so pretty," I said.

"So do er skunk, but y' don't wanna be near im." Elbert kept herding the geese home.

"How come y' know so much erbout Gypsies? 'N why don't y' like um?"

"Well, you ain't ol' ernuff t' remember, but them Gypsies been through heah befo', many times, 'n every time they leave, some er our stuff leave wid um."

"How y' know it wuz them?"

"Don't know fer sho', but the last time they come through heah we missed two of our turkeys 'n other stuff. We ain't the only ones. People all up 'n down this Pike miss stuff whenever them Gypsies come eround."

We herded the geese and goslings into the hen yard and locked the gate.

"We won't have t' worry erbout these geese, they under lock 'n key," I said.

"We gotta keep um locked up till they leave. I still don't trust um. They got lots er tricks up they sleeves."

Early the next morning, Elbert woke me up calling from outside. I jumped into something quickly and ran out to the hen yard.

Elbert was standing there shaking his head. "They gone, every last one of um."

"Whut y' mean, they gone?" I asked.

"The geese, they all gone."

"Did y' look in the back?" I asked.

"Looked everywheah. They gone, I tell y'."

I ran around the hen yard, looked around, and came back to find Elbert looking at a hole under the fence, trying to figure out how it was done. "How in the world did they do it? Dog didn't bark—nothin'."

I looked at the hole, and my mind immediately went back to the boy and his dog. "Hero!" I said.

"Whut y' talkin' erbout?"

"That li'l spotted dog that Gypsy boy had doin' all them tricks." I told Elbert about the dog digging under the tent and retrieving the boy's cap. Elbert looked at the hole again and noticed a grain of corn nearby. A few steps away he found another—and another. Soon he traced the grains across the Pike. I followed him to where we found feathers on the ground.

"I know how they did it," Elbert said.

"How?" I asked. Then I guessed. "Y' mean they tied er sack er corn—"

Elbert continued, "—to the dog, put er hole in the sack, 'n sent im t' the hen yard."

"But how did he git the scent?" I asked.

"From some of them feathers around the water hole." Elbert grabbed a club. "Now maybe I could use Mr. Durbey's Gravedigger."

"Y' don't suppose they still theah, do y'?"

"Not hardly, but I ain't takin' no chances." Elbert took off running up the Pike.

I grabbed another club and followed him. When we arrived, the camp was empty except for the trash and cans they left behind. Only the goslings were left playing around the water hole.

"Whut did I tell y' erbout them stinking Gypsies. They got us fer five geese this time." Elbert dropped his club in disgust. "Well, I gotta go t' work." He turned swiftly and headed back home. I herded the little motherless goslings behind him.

As the new Pike cut, sawed, blasted, and hammered its way south, the boss of the construction crew, Pete DiGasspri, moved his camp a few miles ahead. It was July. He set up his camp in the same location the Gypsies had recently vacated. Crops had been laid by on the Fourth, and we had time to fish, swim, and pick fruit. Who wanted to do that, however, when the biggest project we were likely to see was in progress right under our noses? Besides, my big brother, Elbert, was in the middle of it—as were Ben's older brothers.

I still had to figure out some way to get a job as a water boy. Walking past the camp one hot summer morning on our way to the bayou, we heard a sweet, singing, soft voice. "Wheah y'all boys goin'?" We stopped, looked, and saw a young, pretty white lady. At least, we thought she was a lady, at that point.

"Y' talkin' t' us, ma'am?" I asked.

"Well, I only see the three of us standin' heah. Whut er y' think?"

"Aw, we goin' down t' the bayou," Ben said.

"Whut y'all goin' down theah fer? Come on over heah er minute."

We looked at each other, then walked slowly toward her.

"Whut y'all boys do fer funnnn eround heah?"

We looked at each other again. "Lots er things . . . ," I said.

"Like whuuut?" she asked.

"Like playin' wid our beam shooters, our paddle wheels—," Ben said.

"Fishin', swimmin', our swings, our guitars," I continued.

She changed her stance by shifting her weight from one leg to the other and sticking her hip out. "Anything else y'all can think of?" She started to unbutton her scanty excuse for a dress and reached inside for one of her breasts.

Ben became fixated like a broken record. "Fishin', swimmin', fishin', fishin', fishin'. . . "

"How much fiiishin' y' gon' do? You boys call that havin' funnnn?"

"Yes ma'am," I said quickly as I kept waving with one hand and covering my eyes with the other, trying to get the crazy woman to cover herself before somebody else saw her.

She paid me no attention, pulled her scanty dress off her shoulders, and bared both of her breasts. "How would you boys like t' play wid these?"

"Both of us?" Ben asked.

"Why, shooo. You can take onnnne, 'n yo' friend heah wid the bulging eyes kin take the other."

I shook my head and tried to speak, but nothing came out. I remembered the white woman who had crawled through our window one night, torn, haggard, and bleeding. One of her breasts was hanging out also. I began to wonder if it was a pattern with white women. Most of all, I was concerned about the stories I had heard about black men being lynched for *looking* at a white woman the wrong way. They called it reckless eyeballing. I had never heard Papa, Mr. Durbey, or even Mr. Udell discuss or mention the dangers of involvement with a white woman. However, from the *Gazette,* overhearing other people talk, and the look I had seen on that white woman's face when I attempted to reach her the vegetables, enough fear had been instilled in me to last. Though I was only eight and had lived relatively separated from whites, the "THOU SHALT NOT" wall was well planted in my mind. Why was it that white woman didn't understand the same?

On the contrary, she was thoroughly enjoying teasing us. So much so, she escalated her boldness. She began hissing and licking out her tongue like a snake. "Y'all boys ever had any pussssy?" She slowly took her long slender fingers and inched her dress up to her waist. She had absolutely nothing on underneath. Instead of bloomers, a nest of black curly hairs greeted us head-on.

"Lawd, ha' mercy!" automatically came out of my mouth.

"Awwww, shiiiit!" Ben said. His eyes became as big and bulging as mine.

As long as he was discussing women, how he'd "like t' do it to um," even how he had "done it to um," he was the baddest, the boldest bull in the pasture. Faced with the real thing, his stream dried up and he was as much at a loss as I was—which was completely.

I put my hands over my eyes and started backing up, when I heard a car behind me. I turned and looked at an average-sized white man dressed in khaki, wearing a pith helmet.

He got out of a Ford and walked toward us. "Whut y'all boys doin' up heah foolin' eround wid my wife?"

"She—she called us over heah," Ben stammered.

"That right, sugar?" the man asked.

"Thaaat's riiight, Peeeete, I shooo did." She embraced Pete and gave him a quick kiss.

Pete? That must be the great Pete DiGasspri, Elbert's boss, I thought.

"Did she ax y' t' go git some water fer her?"

"No sir," I said.

"Did she ax y' t' git some firewood?"

"No sir," Ben said.

"Did she ax y' t' bring som'um outta the storage tent?"

I spoke up: "No sir, she didn't. We wuz on our way t' the bayou—"

"Well, whut then? Don't tell me. I bet I know." He looked at each of us. "She tried t' gia' you boys some pussy, didn't she?"

"Ooooooh!" I put my hands over my mouth and started to leave.

"Wait er minute. Don't go. I got er li'l job fer you boys."

I stopped in my tracks when I heard *job. That is Pete DiGasspri. He's the man I've wanted to meet. Maybe this is my chance at that water boy job I've wanted.*

"Now, let m' explain som'um t' y'. My wife heah is like that. Every time she see some fine-lookin' boys like y'all, she jist loses all control. I done took her t' the doctor, the preacher, 'n everything—'course takin' her t' that preacher wuz er bad mistake—but handsome-lookin' boys like y'all, she jist can't resist um. Starts takin' off her clothes minute she sees um. Y'all some goood-lookin' devils, y' know that? I sho do fear the competition, I gotta tell y'. Jist whut did y'all say when she tried t' gia' y' some?"

"Noooo ma'am!" we said at the same time.

"That's whut I figured. Well, seein' as how y'all boys don't like this stuff, I'll jist have t' suffer erlong 'n git it all m'self. Sho could use some hep, though."

"My papa, Udell, could hep y'," Ben blurted out.

"Naw, naw, that's all right. He's probably overloaded already," Pete responded quickly.

Pete's wife went to her knees laughing.

Mr. Udell was indeed overloaded, if there was such a thing. He had recently added Leala Riley to his harem.

"Besides, she's kinda partic'lar. It ain't jist anybody she'll take up wid. They have t' be er special description. I hate t' admit it, but y'all boys seem t' fit the bill. Y'all two fine-lookin' colored gentlemen, I gotta tell y'. 'Specially this un wid that one strap pinned on that goes over his shoulder 'n them natural-lookin' shoes that make it look like he barefooted. Bet you thought you had everybody fooled, didn't y'? 'N that World War One helment wid that bullet hole through it, really sets things off *jiiist* right. Some kinda new style, I bet. I tell y', I'm from Louisiana, 'n I ain't never seen nothin' quite like it—not even in New Orleans—you, honey?"

"These boys in er class all by they-selves." She smiled and started lifting her dress again. I covered my eyes and peeped through my fingers.

Ben looked at me, then down at his bare feet. He developed a strange-looking smile on his face. I thought he was going to "Awww, shucks" any minute in spite of the fact he was standing there looking like Patches.

I had already asked Ben where he got the helmet with the bullet hole through it. It was his version of the pith helmet worn by the men who were working on the Pike. He had told me, "That's fer me t' know 'n you t' find out." I guessed Udell had found it in the junk pile.

"Whut y'all boys' name?" Pete DiGasspri inquired as he took off his helmet and prepared to eat. His wife was setting up a table outside.

"My name's Ben."

"Ben whut?"

"Ben Barrow."

"My name's Sun Hughes."

"Barrow . . . Hughes . . . You kin t' Elbert?" Pete asked.

"He my brother."

Pete looked at me. "He sho is. I shoulda guessed it. Y'all sho look erlike. Elbert's one er the best mule skinners I got. Fer er sebenteen-yeah-ol' boy, he's quite er man."

"Sebenteen?" Ben blurted out.

I tried to cover it up by agreeing with Pete and taking the opportunity to ask him for that water boy job. "Yes sir. I wuz wondering if you needed any water boys, Mr. DiGasspri?"

"I can always use er good water boy, but I bet yo' papa ain't gon' let you do it. Y' see, all er my water boys are really water men. Carrying two five-gallon buckets ten hours er day can't hardly be done by no eight-, nine-yeah-ol' boy."

"Yes sir," I replied.

"Tell y' whut I'm gon' do, though. Honey, can you use er couple er fine-lookin' gentleman t' hep y' out eround heah?"

"Sho can. In fact, they can start right now by gittin' me some er that good drinkin' water from Hughes's well."

Ben and I each took a bucket and hurried to the well.

"We got us er job. I wonder how much she gon' pay us?" Ben said.

"Whutever it is, it's mo'n we got now."

When we returned with the water, Pete DiGasspri and his wife were inside the tent laughing their heads off at our expense. We overheard them and waited outside.

"'N,'n, 'nnnnn, Pete, the tall one, Sun I think he said his name wuz, he said, he-he-he-heeeee, he said, 'Laaawd, ha' mercy!' He-he-heeeee! 'N-n-nnnn the short one said, 'Awwww, shiiiit!' Ha-ha-ha-haaaaa!"

"You shoulda axed um t' scratch yo' back or som'um," Pete said.

"I didn't think of it at the time. They wuz soooo funny. 'Laaaawd, ha' mercy!' I thought that's whut I wuz doin' when I showed him the best part."

"It shooo is the best part, all right. Come heah."

We could hear them kissing.

"Awwwww, shiiit!" Pete yelled, and they started laughing again.

Finally I called out, "Heah's yo' water, ma'am."

She came out still laughing. We pretended we hadn't heard anything.

Pete DiGasspri and his pretty wife, Lucy, were anything but conventional people. The summer for two eight-year-old "fine-lookin' colored gentleman" was exciting with them, from a boy's point of view. She gave us money and food—mostly store-bought goodies—for helping her. I wouldn't have eaten anything she cooked, anyway. Whenever we got unruly, she'd start pulling up her dress. "You boys better do what I tell y' or I'm gonna have t' give y' some pussy." It worked every time. Not even Ben was willing to face the horrors that such a prospect had to offer in reality.

Lucy DiGasspri was a loose, reckless, devil-may-care Jezebel by our Baptist standards. She belonged in the hall of shame. However, she wasn't obliged to live according to our rules, and as a free, overprotected white woman, she laughed at our reaction to her behavior.

Thick smoke reached for the heavens like white streaks twirling through transparent marble. Deafening dynamite booms wrestled stubbornly rooted stumps from earth's mighty grip. Deep dust settled like darkness at the daily death of the horizon on moonless nights. Even so, Arkansas men kept on rolling, happy to prove their mettle. Happy to be known as one of DiGasspri's crew, which was moving on down the line.

Mr. Durbey had more work than he could handle, especially considering his declining years. Papa's store started to come back as well. There was a bigger market than ever for bologna, cheese, potted meat, sardines, vanilla wafers, and Nehi sodas. Bull Durham and other "roll yo' own" gave way to Lucky Strikes and Camels—all ready-rolled. During lunch and after work, the store was crowded with Pike workers.

Elbert started driving the Chevy more as he became recognized as a man among his fellow mule skinners as well as at home. Papa allowed him to buy a new belt-back, bell-bottom suit. He had gone to the moaner's bench the preceding summer. Therefore he enjoyed showing off his new suit while watching others suffer during the revival that was in progress. Another habit Elbert had picked up that Papa didn't know about was going to the picture show on Saturday evenings.

Elbert still took care of the stock when he came home at night and did errands for Papa. Among the few times I got to be with him was when I helped. One evening when we were feeding the mules, we found a bunch of field rats trapped in a barrel where corn was kept. We took a pitchfork and killed all the rats. We turned the barrel over to empty the dead rats on the floor, and two pints of moonshine fell out. They had been hidden in the bottom of the barrel.

"I wonder who these belong to?" I asked.

"Who do y' think?" Elbert responded.

"Y' mean . . . Papa?"

"I don't mean Mama," Elbert responded as he uncorked the bottle.

"Whut y' gon' do wid it?"

"I'm gon' test it." Elbert smelled the bottle.

"Moonshine?" I asked. "Maybe it ain't whut we think it is. Jist because it's in that kind er bottle don't mean it's—"

Elbert smelled the bottle again. "It's moonshine, all right."

"Whut y' gon' do, give it t' Papa?" I asked.

"Whut? 'N worry him erbout it, in his condition? You oughtta have mo' consideration than that." Without further ado, Elbert turned the bottle up and took a sip. "Aaaaah!" He frowned and shook his head, then reached the bottle to me.

My mind went back to when I had seen Gene Cannon and Reedy Riley drinking behind the henhouse. Called up also was the incident Ben and I had witnessed at Mr. Sam Riley's place with the two white men and the Rileys. This situation, however, wasn't like those; this was Papa. Though I had never seen him take a drink, I had seen him use whiskey in a hot toddy when he had a cold or mix it with black draught when he took a purgative. I stood with the bottle in my hand for a long time, afraid to drink.

"Go ahead, it's only some er Papa's medicine," Elbert said.

Trembling, I put the bottle to my mouth and took a small swig. I spat it out as fast as I could. "This stuff is nasty! No wonder they call it medicine!"

Elbert took the bottle and took another swig—then another—and another. "Y' jist have t' git use to it, tha's all."

"I don't wanna git use to it. Whut y' think Papa gon' do if he smell that stuff on yo' breath?"

"I don't think *Papa's* gon' do anything." He said it in a way to indicate that Papa wasn't in a position to do much, lest he expose himself. He raised the bottle and took another drink.

When we went in that night, Elbert was walking like he was trying to step over treetops. I had him wait outside until I checked to see if the coast was clear. When Papa went out on the front porch and sat in the swing, I eased Elbert inside and put him to bed. He wasn't in bed five minutes before he jumped up and headed for the backyard. I went outside and helped guide the Big Man back inside after he had puked up his guts.

Fortunately, the next day was Sunday. Elbert acted strange and sick at breakfast, which he barely touched. Papa looked across the table at him and mentioned something about having to give that boy some er my medicine. Elbert jumped up from the table and ran outside into the backyard. He was allowed to stay home that Sunday to recover for Pete DiGasspri Monday morning.

Sweaty streaks ran fingerlike creeks down his dust-laden young face. A face decorated with frescoed eyebrows and eyelashes. A face shaded by a turtle-back-shaped brown pith helmet strapped beneath his square adolescent chin. Carved shoulders and back, coated with an oily slick sheen that glowed with varying shaded highlights, caused by pulsating youthful muscles rippling and dancing to the rhythm of his every move. His bare torso, his trunk, tapered to a neat, wide-belted waist. Rugged, ready hands ruled by strong, axle-action wrists. One wrist was cuffed by a brass-studded Gypsy wristband. Loose-fitting khaki pants, drenched with dark waters from sweating creeks, draped over bold brogans.

The new Pike had moved close enough for me to visit Elbert at work for the first time. I stood and watched. He held the handle to the dirt zip with his left hand and the long leather lines with his right. "Muuules," he said quietly and confidently. He tilted the big shiny metal shovel to dig into the lower part of the embankment. Two big strong round black sons of jackasses squatted and dug in like sprinters at the break. Their powerful muscles quivered, twirled, and mixed as at the narrow confluence of mighty merging streams. The beautiful giant beasts began their crawl, the shiny blade dug in and filled the shovel, jussst full. Elbert tipped the lever on the handle of the zip, and the blade tilted upward and stopped the digging. Both hands on the lines, he pulled the rugged drudges up the slope and dumped the dirt in a low spot on the Pike. "Yooooo, mules," Elbert said quietly. The panting, sweat-drenched mules obeyed like well-trained children and stopped instantly.

By contrast, many of the mule skinners carried long punishing bullwhips around their wrists. Some of them used their whips frequently, applying the full length of the plaited leather so often that the animals' backs were sore and raw.

The whistle blew for dinner. Elbert finally saw me standing there. "Whut y' say?"

"Whut y' say?" I responded.

"Whut y' got theah?"

"I don't know whut they put in heah."

"You eat yet?" Elbert asked.

"Yeah."

"But y' still want some er mine, I bet."

"I don't want none er yours," I said.

"That's 'cause Miz DiGasspri's been fillin' y' full er that sto'-bought stuff," Elbert said.

"I ate dinner at home," I said. "How come y' don't have er bullwhip like the rest of the skinners?"

"Don't need one. They don't need um either." Elbert pulled his mules under the shade and put on their feedbags. He opened his bucket, and we sat in the shade.

"Why do they use um, then?" I asked.

"'Cause they mean, some of um. Others jist don't know, and they do whut they see somebody else do. Mules got feelings, like you 'n me. If y' talk to um right 'n treat um good, they do anything y' tell um. They ain't dumb by er long shot."

"That skinner wid them brown mules beat er sore on they back," I said.

"Yeah, I know. Pete catch im doin' that, he gone. Don't do nothin' but burn er mule out. After his shovel's full, he keeps strainin' his mules instead er tripping it. Mule's strong, but he cain't keep that up. They done burned out er lot er good mules on this job."

"Whut they do wid um when they burn um out?" I asked.

"They sell um t' Udell, I guess."

We had a good laugh.

"'N Mr. Udell sell um t' Mr. Jim," I added.

"Exactly."

One wrong loop, pulling one string too taut, the other too loose, putting the wrong finger in the triangular loop or the right finger in the right loop when it was too small or too big, flipping the loops too fast or before all the cords were lined up and ready, a wet or damp string that prevented it from sliding easily— all these things could result in a constricted, ill-formed, unacceptable Jacob's ladder, Jacob's coffin, cup and saucer, or crow's foot. All of these were lessons learned from string tricks performed on my fingers.

Slipping the bottom and top bottles up and down on my homemade guitar attached to the side of the smokehouse required patience and know-how when tuning taut stretched strings of haywire. A crack running with the grain of the wood was certain to lead to a two-part split, a useless beam shooter. Old rotted tire tubes were sure to break no matter how tight they were tied to the prongs of the shooter.

I made sure no knot was tied in my yo-yo when I wanted it to lag and return to me when I gave it a little jerk. To increase my points, I learned to play mama-peg with a two-blade knife instead of one. To beat my opponent's time, I sought out hard clay instead of soft when spinning a top. I chose big toy aggies instead of pretty small ones when involved in a serious marble game. Such were my worries at the end of my DiGasspri summer.

Elbert had to be concerned with a broken singletree, a rubbing collar, a shabby harness that left sores on a mule's back or shoulder. Lack of shoes that ruined hooves, thorns that penetrated the soft part of a mule's foot, festered, and left running sores where maggots could gather and multiply. Broken axles that reduced a rolling wagon to a dragging contraption. Rescuing a calf stuck in the mud, or hunting down a pig that decided acorns, nuts, and roots were better fare than slop.

Pete DiGasspri's job was winding down. Cotton-picking season was claiming its own, minus fathers and sons still working on the new Pike. Crowds in the store dwindled, erasing Papa's aberrant business comeback. People talked of factories begging for help in the North. "Henry Ford is payin' five dollars er day. Plus, y' don't have t' fear fer yo' life if y' have er disagreement wid er white man." Few people in our community were willing to leave their land and all they knew for the faraway promises of the harsh, cold North. Aint Fannie and Uncle James were exceptions, however. They packed up, with their host of children, and bid us a tearful farewell.

Elbert put in every day he could on the new Pike. At night he drove the Chevy and helped Papa pick up remedies. When there was no more work on the Pike, he helped gather our own crops. That done, he went directly into winter wood. He was constantly working. Between Mama's peddling, Elbert's work on the Pike, and Papa's store and remedies, we prevailed intact until well into the winter. Then the dependency for cash fell entirely on Elbert and his winter wood.

Elbert moved swiftly, even on Sunday. He never had time to be a boy. It was OK for me, but he had to be a man for all of us. Elbert became Papa's arms, his legs, and most important, his eyes. He never complained or showed any disobedience toward Mama or Papa. Fighting with any of us was out of the question.

School began that fall without Miz Harmond. She was replaced by a professor, L. Carrington Woodside. Elbert was too busy to start school with the rest of us. Papa was heartbroken. Though Elbert was doing a man's job, to Papa he was still a boy and should have been in school. Mama suffered in silence and kept his school clothes always at the ready.

Driving his team out of the flat along Wagon Road West, Elbert walked patiently beside the loaded wagon talking to his mules almost in the same fashion as Mr. Jim. "Muuules, easy now. I'll tell y' when. Yooooo." Patient and caring he was. Always preparing for the next day, he never looked back at a setting sun. For him, the sun was always rising.

23

A straight line extending from the center of his large blocked forehead down to the tip of his bony nose, then down to his protruding, oscillating Adam's apple would clearly reveal a skewed, angular jawbone that would have looked better on a jackass than on a man. Nevertheless, that jawbone did indeed belong to a man, Professor L. Carrington Woodside. His sculptured face did not improve when viewed from the side or in three-quarter profile. When he laughed or smiled, which was often, his thin lips stretched like rubber bands over big gold-crowned horse teeth that poked out of his overcrowded mouth.

His head possessed irregular cowlicks that appeared to have been made by a nervous, nearsighted cow. They started in the front, as usual, and went straight back; however, when the cow came to the middle of his head, she abruptly changed direction and went straight across. For some unknown reason, though, she had stopped in the middle and licked a large round bald spot near the back. Grazing, I suppose. The mosaic patterns of hair growth produced various continents with islands here and peninsulas there that reminded me very much of our globe. The cleavage of his frontal lobe was forested with a thick growth of shaggy eyebrows that covered and protected deep, sunken, penetrating dark eyes between high cheekbones. Though I couldn't see them, I was sure he had the same set of eyes on both sides and in the back of his head. Added to the Professor's super vision were big cabbage-leaf-sized ears that enabled him to pick up sounds as easily as a dolphin, a whale, or a dog.

L. Carrington did nothing to enhance his sad, gaunt appearance. He dressed his small, straight, plumed figure in the darkest, dullest colors he could find and topped them off with a black bow tie, a stiffly starched white shirt, and a weather-beaten, sweaty-brimmed straw hat. No matter how hot it was, he always wore a coat with a vest that served no purpose other than to provide pockets for his big gold watch, chain, and fob and his ever-present toothpicks.

Unfortunately, I had just gotten the teaching end of Papa's belt before the Professor arrived. I fully deserved the whipping because I had foolishly hammered on the cast-iron cap to Papa's gas tank until the poor thing gave up and fell apart. I was always taken inside for the home revival ceremony. If a whipping was inevitable, that arrangement always suited me better because I could cushion the blows with quilts, chairs, pillows, or any other object I could find. If lucky, I could arrange for Papa to hit the mattress, since his eyesight was failing, rather than my body. In those cases I always yelled the loudest and gave the impression of being most used and abused. Strangely, those were the times Papa would say, "This is hurting me more than it is you." On that particular occasion, however, he omitted the expression.

In my own defense, I wasn't considered a bad boy. It simply happened that my curiosity and energy were increasing at the same time that Papa's were declining. Regardless, the prevailing thought was that boys were by nature and all human experience harder to control and needed a man's hand to their behinds. Everybody knew that boys were made of "nails, snails, 'n puppy-dog tails." Though few people would admit it, a quiet, subdued, easily controlled boy was suspect, and people wondered if there was something wrong with him. They naturally warmed up to a spirited, quick-witted, mischievous boy. Girls preferred that kind of boy also. In that sense, they regarded us in the same way that farmers did mules and horses. The only difference was, they didn't have to inspect our teeth to determine our ages.

Papa was sitting in the swing, fanning and still fussing about the gas cap. "I cain't, for the life of me, figure out what possessed you to take er ax 'n hammer on that gas cap."

I still stuck with Papa even after a whipping. I was sitting at a distance on the edge of the porch when I saw a figure approaching carrying a bag in one hand and twirling a black umbrella with the other. As he came closer, I noticed that his stride was brisk, and he walked like he had an ironing board up his back. Completely erect, he was whistling a jolly tune I had never heard before. As he walked into our front yard, the big gold horse teeth shot out and the rubber-band lips stretched shiningly across them. "Is this the M. A. Hughes residence?"

Squinting, Papa answered hesitantly, "Whyyyy yes, it is. Whut kin I do fer y'?"

He set his bag on the porch and extended his hand. "My name's Professor L. Carrington Woodside."

Papa's face lit up as he stood and pumped the little man's hand. "Oooh, yes, Professor Woodside. We wuz expectin' you. Give me yo' bag, 'n come on in. Let me git you settled. Kitty! Kitty!"

"If you don't mind, Mr. Hughes, I'd just as soon stay out here and talk with you and the boy. Far too nice to be inside. Don't you agree, young man?"

"Yes sir."

"I'm sorry, Professor. This is my youngest son, with whom I'm not too pleased at the moment. We call him Sun."

"Howdy, Sun."

"Howdy, Professor Woodside."

"Whyyy, what did he do?" the professor asked, turning back to Papa.

"Oh, I don't wanna bother you wid it," Papa said.

"I really don't mind, Mr. Hughes. Since I'm going to be living here, I want all of you to regard me as one of the family. I want to know as much about the children as possible. Perhaps I can help."

"Well, since you put it that way . . . You know, Professor, we all been boys, and I confess I did my share of breakin' things when I wuz growin' up, but I don't remember ever taking er ax or a hammer and deliberately hammerin' on something till it fell apart. Am I missin' something?"

"What exactly was it, Mr. Hughes, that he broke?"

Papa reluctantly showed him the broken cap that he still had in his hand.

"He did that with a hammer, you say?" The professor turned the pieces over in his hands and laughed.

"If it had been an accident, I could halfway understand it, but he took a single-blade ax and went to the cap and started hammering on it. I can't figure it out."

"I'm sure you've heard the expression 'An idle mind is the devil's workshop.' There's another one that I like even better, 'A hard head makes a soft behind.'"

"But there's aplenty things around heah fer him to play wid. Why pick on the cap to my gas tank? Theah's no tellin' how long it'll take fer the company to git me another one."

"You won't have to close your gas station, will you?"

"Oh no. Just have to be careful that no water or dirt gets in the tank. Sun, go draw the Professor a cool bucket er water."

I moved quickly because I didn't want to miss anything the Professor had to say. When I returned with the water, they were discussing discipline.

"Boys will be boys, Mr. Hughes, and they have to be introduced to Mr. Hickory early on. Mr. Hickory and I are close friends. I hope you won't mind if I call on him whenever it becomes necessary. That way I'm sure we'll learn."

"You call on him whenever y' want to, Professor. Whenever y' need my help, I'll be right heah to back y' up. He's not a dumb boy. If you kin git it out of im, go right ahead."

"Sure thing, sure thing."

Mama's voice from inside: "Supper's ready!"

"Come on, Professor, let's eat," Papa said.

"Sure thing, sure thing."

We filed into the dining room, where Professor Woodside met Mama and the rest of the family. He was given a choice seat at the other end of the table facing Papa.

I didn't like the way the Professor laughed when he was turning those pieces over in his hands. I didn't like his wanting to become a part of our family and his "Perhaps I can help" remark. I found his "hard head makes a soft behind" adage less than helpful if not completely uncalled for. His "Mr. Hickory and I are close friends" revelation worried me.

My suspicions about the pompous, proper little man were not completely unwarranted. I found out the next day that Professor Woodside was as orderly and precise as he looked. His menacing walk was slower in the classroom but just as deliberate and deadly. We had been used to Miz Harmond and her motherly, caring ways. The Professor, on the other hand, was a strict disciplinarian who laid down hard-and-fast rules from the start.

I escaped his "Mr. Hickory" for the first two weeks because I always knew my lessons. Mr. Hickory was in operation, however, from day one, and his usage increased daily, mostly for not having done the assignments.

As time rolled on, I became bored. The bag of tricks that I had played for years at Tilson, especially on girls, had grown stale and rusty for lack of use. I had to do something to give myself a lift. Nothing gave me a lift quicker than when I lifted a young lady out of her chair. So far, I had found nothing more appropriate for that purpose than a long straight hat pin.

Most of the girls who knew me wouldn't stand or sit anywhere near me because of past experience. Fortunately—for me, unfortunately for the girl—a new girl came to Tilson, Mary Rose, who hadn't experienced the excitement of my "rise 'n shine!" Her father, who I learned was our cousin, made coffins and pine boxes for undertakers. He had moved his business to the country to be closer to the forest his supplies came from.

Miss Mary Rose started to take the seat in front of me, which would have been perfect, but moved to the next aisle, diagonally in front. She was a snooty city girl who walked around with her nose in the air like she was sniffing something unpleasant. She made it clear that she thought she was better than us country kids.

Since her change of seat put her farther away, I was forced to grow a longer arm, which I promptly managed. I waited until L. Carrington was at the blackboard doing long division. That to me seemed quite an appropriate moment. Mary Rose was intensely involved in the instructions. She had leaned over in her seat, striking the thinker's pose. That caused her oversized rear end to gush out good and tight from her small seat. It was a dream come true. Slowly the long arm extended notch by notch until it reached the target—Mary Rose's protruding bottom. A quick prick, and Mary *rooooose!!* She let out a Holy Ghost scream that drew the attention of the whole class; however, they suppressed their urge to laugh out too loud. I, of course, sat saintly with a halo around my head.

Cool and calm, L. Carrington didn't bother to turn around. Instead, he finished what he was doing, then turned around slowly and said quietly, "Sun, come here."

"You call me, Professor Woodside?" I responded in my best innocent saintly tone.

"Come here." That time he was beckoning with his finger.

I walked slowly up to his desk. "Yes sir."

He reached down beside his desk and pulled out two long seasoned hickory switches. Those switches would bend, but they wouldn't break. "Now, bend over."

"Whut did I do, Professor?" I asked in my most faraway voice.

"You know what you did. What you didn't know is that I've got eyes in the back of my head. I could have stopped you when I saw you almost fall into the aisle leaning over to stick that girl with that hat pin."

How did he know it was a hat pin? I thought to myself.

"It's gonna cost you five licks this time. Next time it'll be ten. Now bend over and let's get on with it."

That time there were no pillows, chairs, boxes, quilts, or mattresses to block the licks. Worst of all, Woodside was no ailing man who couldn't see what he was hitting. I didn't even have any padding in my pants that day. It was bad enough to be humiliated in front of the entire class—especially those pretty girls—but to be whipped by a man who knew exactly how to hurt you was a new experience for me. Where before I had received three licks over my padded pants with a ruler from a lady who liked me because I was good in my classwork, now I suddenly received five hard-as-he-could-hit licks on my tightly stretched pants with two seasoned hickory sticks.

Hickory switches cut and always left welts the size of the Professor's finger. If the padding was obvious, Professor Woodside removed it in front of the class. Like Miz Harmond, however, he whipped girls in their hands. Most girls said they would rather take it on their behinds like the boys. He became known as "Red Meat Woodside with His Hickory Hot Holy Ghost."

Where preference had been given to students who did well, now the work became much more difficult, and that number decreased in most of the upper grades. I don't believe it was an accident that there were only older girls in that group. Big boys whom he considered unruly were expelled. In the last part of the third grade, we were introduced to long division, decimals, and simple fractions. In the fourth grade, we were doing complex fractions, more difficult decimals, and long division. English compositions started in the third grade and got harder in the fourth. Latin had been required when Professor Woodside went to school. He declared that if he had his way, we would be studying it also.

That same Professor Woodside who had put welts on my butt as big as his finger stretched his thin shiny lips over his big gold horse teeth and practically ordered me to walk home with him. "Wait up, Sun. We're going to the same house." He even had the gall to try striking up a friendly conversation. "Nothing personal in my butt beatings," his tone suggested.

He talked about how he used a rope to aid him in climbing a tree. I thought, *In your case, I could find a much better use for a tree and a rope.* But then I remembered having seen power line workers climbing telephone poles using that exact method, and I decided there was something to it. I could climb trees much faster that way than any boy around, using my belt instead of a rope. Still, I hated walking home with that man instead of with my buddy Ben.

That night at supper he sat there at his choice spot, getting special treatment, and joked about the events of the day. How much fun we'd had with our projects, during which he had whipped butts from one project to the other. "Sure thing, sure thing."

Teachers were regarded even higher than preachers, in a sense. They could do no wrong. No student would go home and complain to his parents about the teacher. That would just get the student another whipping from his parents. A teacher's authority was unquestioned in our community. The teacher slept in the parlor, the best-furnished room in the house.

As the school year progressed, Professor Woodside revealed more strongly his preference for older girls and his dislike for boys. A "young lady," as he referred to each of them, could get away with behavior that he would put welts on a boy for. One day he forgot himself and whipped a boy over his head and shoulder. The tough unforgiving Mr. Hickory drew blood and left the boy in pitiful shape. The Professor was so angry, his voice changed, he turned red, and he began to tremble and shake. Though he was a good teacher as far as subject matter was concerned, and I learned basic arithmetic and English from him that lasted, I found it difficult to respect the little man after seeing him lose control that way. I discovered that most of the boys and many of the girls felt the same. He had never gone off on me like that, but I got my share of whippings, and he made me toe the mark.

Among the young ladies he was just *too* nice to was my fifteen-year-old sister, Deloris. She was cute—short, dimpled, and developing fast into a woman. I never saw anything out of the way between the Professor and Deloris, but I felt that his attitude toward her was a bit more than a teacher's toward his student. I sensed that at home as well as at school. Mama was subtle, but highly protective of her daughters. She made sure Deloris was never left alone and kept close check on her, especially since she was the friendliest and most outgoing of her daughters. Quiet, perceptive Mama, like most people, respected the Professor as a teacher and didn't think he would do any wrong. Nevertheless, she made sure he never got the chance.

Professor Woodside's attitude toward me was the opposite of what it was to Deloris. I soon discovered that I was no more than a snotty-nosed brat who was in the way to him. Though I could do my decimals, long division, and fractions, it really meant nothing to him. There were no rewards or encouragements for good work as there had been with Miz Harmond.

On a chilly fall night, he carried his disgust for me too far. The large wood-burning stove in the parlor had an apron that projected out in front. We raked red-hot coals out on the apron, where we popped corn and roasted peanuts and sweet potatoes. Often, after we finished our homework, everybody gathered around the hot stove for snacks before bedtime. Sometimes the Professor engaged us in riddles, puzzles, and stories. Rather than go to bed before popcorn and peanuts were ready, I attempted to wait but fell asleep on the floor.

Biblical images of a hot burning hell with sinners—women and men—falling and crawling over each other appeared. They were moaning, groaning, crying, being herded and stuck with a pitchfork by a man in a red union suit, with a forked tail, horns on his head, and fiery red eyes. My mind went back to the images I had seen when I was ill with fever from the snakebite. Suddenly the demon in the red union suit threw more wood on the fire. When he turned his face toward me, I recognized the thin lips stretched rubber-tight over big gold horse teeth. The fire became hotter and hotter as he stirred it with his iron poker. I saw the boy Professor Woodside had beaten being pushed into the fire! I began to twist and turn and wiggle as the fire grew hotter—hotter!—hotter!!

I woke myself up screaming and stamping. I looked down, and sure enough my foot was on fire. My sister Geneva rushed to my aid and put the fire out. I looked over at Professor Woodside, and he was stretched out in his big soft chair hysterical with laughter. He had turned red again, and tears were streaming down his ruddy, wrinkled face. I looked down again at my foot and discovered he had packed cotton between my toes and set fire to it.

"Now, Sun, you know how it feels when you give other people a hot foot." He tried to laugh it off, but neither Elbert nor my sisters thought it was funny.

I had stuck people with hat pins, tied their shoestrings together, even tied them to their seats, and chased them with my army of insects and frogs, but I had never set fire to anybody's feet or caused them any serious injury in my entire career as a prankster. Even if I had, I thought, there was a vast difference between my doing that at nine and Professor Woodside pulling such a prank at forty-nine.

Big blisters quickly formed on my foot. My sisters bathed and put baking soda on the burn. When the blisters burst and left big sores, my sisters treated them with coal oil and wrapped them properly until I was well. Elbert advised everybody to tell Mama and Papa that hot coals had fallen on my foot from the apron of the potbellied stove. Elbert knew our financial situation and didn't want Papa to lose the income from the Professor's room and board.

When Professor Woodside returned the following fall of 1932, I settled down to do my schoolwork and saved my pranks for after school and weekends. Apparently that wasn't good enough for the little man. He had firmly established the fact that he had no respect for boys, and I suspected that his preferential treatment of girls—especially my sister Deloris—was for reasons unrelated to his interest in their education. I was not alone in my thinking, but teachers being so highly respected and powerful, there was no one a mere student could go to for help.

One day, probably during lunch, someone put a frog in Vera Nellie's desk. She jumped twice her height when the frog hopped in her lap. It was a known fact that Vera Nellie didn't like me, nor did I have an undying love for her. So though I had been playing ball the entire lunch period with my buddies, Vera Nellie promptly blamed me. She being one of the older, supposedly pretty girls Professor Woodside was partial to, he jumped at the chance to concur with her. My buddies tried to come to my defense by declaring that I'd never left the playing field, but the little man told them to shut up and sit down.

"Don't you dare dispute me! I'll whip the whole lot of you lying rascals! And if you're too big to whip, I'll expel you so fast, you'll wonder if you ever attended Tilson!"

Out came double trouble, Mr. Hickory. He commanded me to bend over again. He gritted his teeth, and with all his might he delivered ten cutting blows to my innocent behind. I was so angry I refused to cry.

It was observed by one of the girls that he liked so much that Professor Woodside himself was the only person who had gone inside the building before lunch period was over. Though we had no proof, everybody believed that Professor Woodside, who had gotten such a big laugh out of setting fire to my foot, was the real culprit.

I decided there and then that the little man was wicked and needed to go to our moaner's bench. I had turned ten and didn't have the patience to wait for his conversion. I got together with some of my buddies, including the boy he had beaten badly, and we decided to get rid of Red Meat Woodside.

We were prompted by none other than John Dillinger, Youngblood, and our own community's Black Nelson. Those three men were our folk heroes at that time. Dillinger had escaped from prison with a soap pistol he had carved and finished with black shoe polish. Youngblood, a young black inmate, had aided Dillinger and escaped with him. That act alone had endeared John Dillinger to our community. "At least he ain't prejudiced" was the thinking. Black Nelson was imprisoned, then escaped, after he nearly beat to death a white man who had cheated him out of his wages and then kicked him.

Encouraged by those acts of bravery against injustice, I conceived a plan—a boyish plan. I would wait until the Professor surrounded himself with young ladies during lunch period, then I would sneak up behind him and hit him in the head with a brick. When the time came to perform that act, I discovered that I was alone while my buddies lingered in the bushes egging me on. I hid the red brick as best I could beneath my shirt. As I approached, thoughts flashed across my brain. *What will Mama and Papa think? Will I be sent to reform school and never see my brother and sisters again? What if I don't knock him out? He will rise and kill me for sure. What if he sees me with those eyes he has in the back of his head before I let him have it?*

Closing in, I heard him laugh. "Sure thing. What time is it?" He took out his watch. I was very close. None of the girls had noticed me.

Without taking his eyes off his watch, Professor Woodside said, "Where're you going, Sun boy?"

He must have seen my reflection in his watch, or did he really have eyes in the back of his head? I stopped in my tracks, took the brick from under my shirt, and tossed it from hand to hand while I thought up a quick lie. "I'm goin' over heah to hide this brick. I figured if I laid it near you they would never think to look theah."

Professor Woodside stood up. "I see. Quick thinking, Sun. Why don't you let me have it."

He didn't know how badly I wanted to let him have it! Perhaps he did. The girls certainly knew, judging from the expressions on their faces.

"Whoops." He looked at his watch. "I'm afraid we'll have to play your little hide the brick game another time, Sun. Time to go inside."

During recess, immediately after the brick incident, Professor Woodside called me up to his desk. "Sun, I've been thinking, since Larry is having such a hard time keeping up with the rest of his class, you might be able to help him."

"Why me, Professor?"

"He seems to respond to you. I already have my hands full, and since you grasp the subject matter rather easily, and—"

"I'll be happy to help Larry, if I can, Professor Woodside."

"Fine! Fine! Then it's settled. One more thing, Sun. Since you're going to be my assistant, I want you to move up to one of these front seats. Oh, and remember, we'll just keep this arrangement our little secret."

Professor Woodside was at Tilson nearly two more years, but he never again pulled Mr. Hickory on me. He was also reluctant to whip any of the older boys. Instead, he beat the slop out of the younger boys who couldn't defend themselves.

My suspicion about his interest in my sister Deloris was confirmed after he had left Tilson. My quiet but observant sister Geneva discovered, or nosed up on, a letter that L. Carrington had the poor judgment or the excess of arrogance to write to Deloris, expressing how he felt about her. My wiser older sisters had a way of keeping such things among themselves until it was safe to talk about them. Considering the trouble it might have caused an already overburdened family, I suppose they were right.

24

From bluffs raped of soil by plow and scour, cotton and wind, unchecked by root-growing piles from tall timbers, the land was forced to surrender the pink-red of its earth, its deeper womb, far beneath its once rich topsoil, made so from rotting logs, leaves, and bark. Now, from droppings of cows, mules, calves, and horses, manure solicitously sifted and shoveled into plow-stirred gaping rows, cane and corn grew like inverted roots, stunted in their height but, from the work required, made much dearer to our economy. Scuffling, we managed orderly rows of stalks waiting for our knives, much like those that plunged deep, bloody, and quick into the hearts of squealing hogs at killing time.

Also surrendered were the mournful groans of beef cattle at Jake Parsons' slaughterhouse, where the shining dark blood of death ran like creeks and bayous at high rise, down vats and troughs on to the hillside where it waited and rotted and stunk, then was consumed by teaming maggots, flies, and dogs.

Jake Parsons' row of death was real to me, when he Winchestered the animal through the head, then sent home his long shining steel blade to the hilt, through the heart of each waiting two-thousand-pound steer. The ritual conjured up images of what he was doing every day to black prisoners on that work farm where he was a whipping boss. To me, the cold, impassive manner in which Jake Parsons went about everything he did had the stench of death. With his long black pipe hanging from the corner of his never-smiling face, he forged ahead with his slaughter as if he was plugging a watermelon to see if it was ripe. At that very moment our own Reedy Riley and Black Nelson were under his harsh control on that chain gang of hell.

There was the surrender of the blues-singing, bad-talking, whiskey-drinking unruly A. D., the Barrows' oldest son, pointing a double-barreled shotgun at a Bearden who had incurred the wrath of the entire Barrow clan. I never knew what it was about, but the whole disturbance had spilled down the hill onto our property. Big dumb crying Carl, with snot running from his nose, was stalking the dressed-up Bearden with a single-barreled shotgun, aiding his crazy brother, A. D. Udell was cursing and swearing at the man. The man had a smile on his face and seemed unconcerned, as if he was being annoyed by a passel of puppies. I heard him say something like "If the woman didn't want to, she didn't have to." He turned and started walking down the hill. Papa came out and told them to take their fight someplace else away from his property or he would call the law. I had no idea how he was going to call them, since his phone had been disconnected long ago.

Bearden left. The Barrows went back up the hill and kept arguing among themselves. Shortly, Ben came running down the hill looking for Papa. A.D. had shot Udell and needed someone to take him to Pine Ridge before he bled to death. Papa's Chevy was on blocks. Fortunately for Udell, Uncle Pet drove up in his Ford. He didn't like or respect "any of them Udells." His Christian principles, however, would not allow him to let even Udell bleed to death. He hustled Udell into the backseat and rushed him to town.

Uncle Pet never stopped complaining after helping the "useless man," especially since Udell had bled all over his car. The Barrows claimed that A.D. shot Udell accidentally. Mr. Durbey said, "It wuz accidently on purpose. That boy never got along wid his papa."

There was the surrender to a new way of life caused by the long winding new Pike snaking its way south through farms, forest, and fallow fields, over creeks, bayous, and up and down hills, leaving wrecked properties crippled and dispossessed in its wake of eminent domain.

Then there was the life-giving healing tree that grew straight and tall like an obelisk pointing through the smoky fog of hate and fear toward the cosmic heavens of understanding and peace, the way that Grandpa Hughes had pointed years before I was born.

Over two years had passed since the heifer incident when Roy Barnard had humiliated Papa before his family. One cool autumn evening, Papa, Mr. Durbey, and I were sitting around the blacksmith shop when an old man, dressed in cowboy garb, rode up on a beautiful palomino saddle horse. When he pushed his hat back from his forehead I received the shock of my nine years. Roy Barnard had aged almost beyond recognition since I had seen him almost three years earlier. His jaws were sagging like a bloodhound's. His triple chin unfolded and fell in sacks over his hairy chest. Long reddish-gray hairs like a hog's stood out on his arms and his big red wrinkled hands and fingers. His deep red complexion was redeemed only by a big toothy smile and quick, flashing gray cat's eyes. When he opened his mouth to speak, sparkling gold glittered from his irregular teeth, and gushes of air exuded from his large diaphragm.

"Howdy, M.A., Gene, young fellah."

Papa squinted a long time to see who it was before he responded. Then a smile came over his face. "Howdy, Mr. Barnard."

Mr. Durbey nodded and kept working.

I wondered, *Why is Papa smiling at Roy Barnard, who has disrespected and abused him?* I remembered that the last time Roy Barnard tried to speak to Papa, he barely grunted.

"Haven't seen y' in er while," Barnard said.

"Well, I don't git eround much no mo'. Business been slow, as y' know. Whut can I do fer y', Mr. Barnard?"

I knew Papa was sick, but why was he talking nice to the likes of that dog? *Now that creep Roy Barnard's lost his health he comes crawling back around for help,* I thought.

"Well, M.A., I'm in er li'l tight spot. I need a couple er good hands to hep me husk 'n haul the last of a crop er field corn."

"I wish I could hep y', Mr. Barnard, but I don't have nobody fer whut you want."

"I may as well level wid y', M.A. I wouldn't blame y' one bit if y' had no mo' t' do wid the Barnards, way you wuz treated by my damned fool son Roy. Y' don't have t' believe me, but I jist found out erbout it t'other day."

Sooo—it's the old man, Roy Barnard's father. It had been a few years since I had seen him, because Papa had forbidden us to go near Roy Barnard's store after the heifer incident. I remembered him being big, round, and red-faced. He reminded me of the pictures I had seen of Santa Claus. He even behaved like Santa. Unlike his tightwad son, he always gave me candy and made fun-filled conversations. He must have been sick because he had lost so much weight that he looked like his son.

"Whut exactly y' referrin' t', Mr. Barnard?"

"Oh come on, M.A., you know precisely whut I'm referrin' t'. He had no right—no right whut-so-ever—to go onto yo' property, rope yo' heifer, 'n lead her erway fer no measly nine-, ten-dollar debt. Not even if it wuz er thousand. As you kin see, I'm gittin' er li'l ol'"—Mr. Durbey looked up at him—"'n don't git eround any mo', but I been use to seein' you 'n Elbert every fall eround remedy time. When I missed y' two yeahs in er row, I knowed there wuz som'um wrong. We got two jackasses down there. One of um we keep locked up in er corral, but the other one rides eround on horseback and eats fried chicken like he wuz fixin' to be executed 'n it wuz his last meal. But the worst thing wuz, he mistreated a fellow businessman, a good lifetime friend, 'n one of the best neighbors a man could have—'n I mean every word of that, M.A."

"Thank you, Mr. Barnard. We *have* known each other er long time."

"Try er lifetime. I'm gonna tell y' somethin' I bet y' didn't know, M.A."

"Whut's that, Mr. Barnard?"

"Yo' papa, Parson Hughes, got me started when I first come to this timberland. There wuz only er few farmers heah then. I didn't know my ass from Wednesday mornin'."

"Y' sho got that right! Po' white boy didn't know shit from shoe polish," Mr. Durbey, who wasn't supposed to be listening, blurted out.

"Who woke you up, ol' man?" Barnard said.

"Woke m'self up workin' so hard. Doggone noisy hammer."

They all had a good laugh.

"Anyway, M.A., yo' papa interrupted his own work when he seen I didn't know whut I wuz doin'. He come over to my forty, which wuz right next to one er his, 'n showed me how to lay out er row, how to plant cotton 'n corn, 'n most important of all how to treat and handle animals. I tried to owe him—damned sho didn't have nothin' to pay him back then—but he tol' me to make sure 'n hep somebody else if they needed it."

"Is that the forty south of us back in the flats?" Papa asked.

"The same forty. Yo' papa kep a good team of horses 'n mules. He knowed farming inside 'n out. Too bad he wound up bein' killed by the same animals he took such good care of. Everbody knowed that Gates boy belonged on er funny farm. Why they let him have er pitchfork I'll never know. If them horses had been nags, he'd probably be alive today."

"I wuz er teenager at the time, so I remember it well," Papa said.

Papa had vowed that he wouldn't have any more dealings with Roy Barnard. He had assumed that that would include the rest of his family, since most families stuck together right or wrong, but old man Barnard made it clear that he didn't uphold his son in his redneck peckerwood behavior. He wanted Elbert because he had seen him handle mules. He also made it clear that we didn't have to even see his stupid son if we chose not to.

When Papa asked him if Roy would object to us being hired, the old man took off his cowboy hat and revealed his balding head. He told Papa, "I never made er lot er money in life, M.A. But y' see my head? I got bald standin' on it, tellin' people like my son Roy to kiss my hairy ass." He also declared that he was trying to mend fences with Papa because he was scared to death of ghosts, especially preacher ghosts, and he didn't want Parson Huge or Hughes scaring the living bejesus out of him while he was eating supper or "knockin' off er piece."

Elbert and I left early that Saturday morning before sunrise. The wild braying of the jackass, which I had heard over the years, became more pronounced as we neared Barnard's place. Though I had heard all the talk about the beast, I had never seen him. The old man was waiting for us when we arrived at the field. We wasted no time getting on with our husking. By noon we had finished the first patch.

Frost had turned most of the leaves a golden yellow. Trees still gave shade, especially those following the banks of the meandering stream. The soil around Sandy Creek was surprisingly rich, having benefited from the residue of the yearly flood along its banks. Corn grew big and full, four and five ears to a stalk. We spread our lunch beneath a big oak, and the old man told us one dirty joke after the other. I'm sure Papa would have had second thoughts about letting me come if he had heard some of those jokes.

"This young man who wuz er rank sinner married into this strict, respectable Christian family. The young lady knew it, but she set out to polish him up—make er gentleman out of im. At the supper table that evenin', the ol' man asked him to ask the blessin'. It was customary. The young man wuz honest 'n tol' im he didn't know how. They didn't wanna accept that, so his young wife insisted. She tol' im he didn't need to be formal or sound like er preacher or her father. The Lord would be listenin' for his honest words from his heart. He said, 'Well, in that case I'll do it.' He saw that big plate er beef settin' in front of im. He bowed his head 'n clasped his hands in front of im 'n said, 'God bless the cow that had this calf and the bull that bore the rod. If it hadn't been fer that noble long prick of his, we'd have no beef, by God.'"

The jackass had been braying all morning; it turned strangely quiet in the afternoon. When we finished unloading, we discovered why. A group of men were looking into a fortresslike corral that was seven feet high, reinforced with strong timbers and portly columns buttressed from the outside. The large area of the corral was the undisputed domain of the uncontrollable beast. He was fed and watered strictly from the outside. The cleaning of his droppings was done while he was installed and engaged at his pleasure. Men had domesticated oxen, wild horses, mules, donkeys, llamas, and the mighty elephant as beasts of burden. According to the men around the corral, no one had succeeded in passing any loads onto the back of the fearless, and feared, jackass.

He was taller than any big stud horse or bull I had ever seen—some six feet or more, and longer. His tan coat stretched tightly around shining, rippling muscles. Even his stingy ass was lined with muscles—no fat anyplace. His long stiff ironlike legs were like stilts—a replica of the Trojan horse. His long slender tail was almost bare, except for a brush at the end used to whale the daylights out of horseflies, and it extended almost to the ground. His mane was shaggy and mangy. His long ears, shaped like airplane propeller blades, pointed toward the infinite heavens. He moved them past each other in a mechanical fashion like devil's scissors. His crude, primitive face was a veiled collage of baked bones—made alive by quaking, piercing, demonic eyes. When he peed, it foamed and stunk, a fog rose from the ground, and bucketfuls ran freely out of the corral. When he shat—which he did often—a monstrous turd, six or more inches in diameter, exuded like a stovepipe from his oversized black canal. When he walked, the earth shook, and his sharp hooves dug deep into the ground. His crowning glory, however, was his big long swaggering tool. His testicles hung like two elongated melons in a sack and gave vivid testimony to his virility. His only purpose on earth was to use those tools to father the animals that provided the greatest power of all in shaping the nation. "Working like a mule" was no idle saying.

I watched closely as they backed the mare into the small stall. He almost tore the fence down getting to her. His long tool grew longer until it almost touched the ground—which was three feet beneath his belly. Mares as well as men feared him. Once in the stall, she was blindfolded. The gate was opened from the rear, and the snorting jack came on to her. On his own, he would never be able to penetrate. Holes were provided on the sides of the stall for two men to grease the long rod with axle grease and guide it to the target. His hind legs were trembling as he drove home his mule-maker. The greedy jack was deliberate and took his time once he was inside. Slobbering and snorting, he began to hunch. The hunches were so powerful the mare went to her knees groaning. It was quite unnatural for the mare, for no such measures were necessary when mating with a stud. Bulls and dogs are fast once inside. The jack went on in that violent manner for what seemed like eternity. When he was near ejaculation, I thought he was going to drive that poor mare through the wall. At last he finished. The mare had to be rushed out discharging blood and water.

"Git her outta there fast or that wicked son of er bitch'll kill her."

I knew then why they called him a jackass. They had been known to kick mares to death after mating. A mean, selfish, violent, evil creature that had feelings for nothing except what gave him pleasure—that's a jackass.

Nine or ten months after that violent organized rape, a long-legged, long-eared, ugly creature would be born. The mother would care for that hybrid as if it was a beautiful colt. As mules grow to maturity, however, they become round and handsome, once their bodies catch up with their spindled legs and extravagant ears. As a hybrid, mules cannot reproduce. To produce a mule, the same unnatural process is required again between a mare and a jackass.

Much work was required on the farm and in the forest land, especially during spring, summer, and fall. I couldn't understand why people took such a dim view of work. To me it was all fun. I thoroughly enjoyed husking corn, picking cotton, plowing, mending fences, digging sweet potatoes, picking berries, and cutting wood. Perhaps it was because I was limited in the amount I could do.

The old man paid us well and tried to get us to stay a spell. We thanked him and told him if he needed us again to give us a holler. A few weeks later we heard that old man Barnard had told his last joke. Elbert and I had often reminded each other of some line he had spoken, and started laughing all over again. On hearing he was dead, we looked at each other with an emptiness that expressed our feelings. For *that* was no laughing matter.

25

The winter of 1932 entered cold and hard. Christmas had passed with scantiness such as I had not witnessed before. I had grown to be quite a tall skinny lad.

The season for remedies and cotton-picking ended before Christmas. It would be at least three months before the spring rains would flood the Pike and allow Papa to make money towing cars. Pete DiGasspri wouldn't start back on the Pike until April. The only way to supplement stored food supplies was by peddling firewood. Though the Depression had forced many people to go on relief, Papa struggled against it.

Gum and pine, both softwoods, were burned when one didn't have access to red oak and ash. Hickory and white oak, the hardwoods, were sold for railroad cross-ties and manufacturing purposes. The old Hughes tract, some of which was ours, had plenty of red oak and some ash.

Tools used to cut firewood were simple. A sharp crosscut saw, two sharp axes (single or double blade), two wedges (one metal and one wooden), and a sledgehammer. A Nehi bottle full of coal oil was always a welcome ally as a lubricant for the saw.

Papa climbed down off the wagon. He was dressed in baggy gray suit pants and vest, a starched white shirt without the attachable collar, run-over loafers that had been cut at the toe to relieve pressure on his diabetic feet. A gold railroad watch fob dangled from his vest. This outfit was topped off with a floppy gray Stetson and a long black overcoat, two sizes too big, draped over his shoulders. He walked up to a forty-foot oak, placed his hands high on the trunk, and looked up at the top. He moved away a few feet, picked up a handful of dry leaves, and threw them up in the air to see which way the wind was blowing. "Wind's blowin' in the wrong direction, but I guess we can fall it right out through theah." He pointed with his cane. "Chip it on the bottom real deep."

Elbert hopped off the wagon and grabbed the saw. "Sun, git the axes 'n wedges."

I hopped down, grabbed the tools from the wagon bed, and followed him.

Elbert motioned for me to go on the right, and he took the left. We placed the five-foot crosscut saw parallel to the ground, against the leeward side of the tree, and pulled back and forth until it started to bind. That didn't take long, since it was rather dull.

"Wait'll I git the coal oil," I said, and ran back to the wagon, grabbed the Nehi bottle full of oil, took the cork out, and stuffed some pine needles in the mouth of the bottle. Elbert used the needles to sprinkle some of the oil on the saw. We only pulled a few more times before it jammed again.

"Let's take it out 'n chip it. It ain't goin' no further," Elbert said.

We both yanked and yanked until the saw finally came out. Elbert took one of the axes and chipped the underside of the shallow cut.

"Papa said deep," I reminded him.

"Y' think y' kin git it deeper?" Elbert asked doubtfully.

Papa looked at it. "Now that y' chipped it, y' kin saw it deeper, then chip it ergin. Make sure."

We repeated the same operation to get it deeper, then went around on the opposite side of the tree. We placed the saw, horizontally again, above the first cut and proceeded to pull. Soon the good-sized tree cracked, cried, twisted, and popped. We pulled the saw out quickly and scurried away a distance—lest the butt kick back or break the saw, hurting one of us. It made a resounding crash when it fell clear in the exact spot Papa had pointed out.

We proceeded to lop off one-and-a-half- to two-foot-long blocks—the first for stoves, the second for fireplaces—one after the other. My hands became numb with cold. My ragged cloth gloves were more of an annoyance than a source of warmth to my hands. "My hands freezin'."

Papa, sitting on a nearby stump, pointed with his cane. "Er—Elbert, git some kindlin' 'n use some er that coal oil t' make er fire."

Soon we heard the twigs and kindling cracking and popping. The smoky red blaze leaped toward the treetops. I eagerly reached for it, but Papa restrained me.

"Don't put yo' hands right over the fire." He cracked some ice in a nearby mud hole with his cane. "Dip yo' hands in that cold water first. Dry um off. Then put um in yo' pockets, close t' yo' skin. Let um warm up slowly befo' y' go near that fire."

I looked at Papa doubtfully.

"Don't look at me in that tone er voice. Do it."

"But Papa, that water is ice-cold. My hands already freezin'. I—I—"

"Aw right, warm um up over the fire first. If that's the only way y' kin learn."

I knew what he meant. My feet and hands had been cold many times before, but I had always put them in water that was room temperature. Even when I did it at home, I had always ended up wringing my hands and stumping my feet from the pain when they started to warm up. My hands began to ache after I refused to dip them in that ice-cold water. Rather, I massaged them and stuck them deep into my pockets. They still pained me. Papa rose from his stump, came over to me, took my skinny little hands in his big paws, and began to massage. "I told y'. A hard head makes a soft behind."

I wanted to tell Papa my behind was fine; it was my hands and feet that were killing me.

"We gotta hurry up and git this wagon loaded so Elbert kin git on t' town. Git up theah too late, other peddlers beat y' out." Papa continued to massage.

"Mr. Wheaton had t' bring back a load yestiddy; got up theah too late," Elbert commented while he was busy quartering blocks.

Papa was still massaging my hands. Finally they began to feel better, and I returned to the saw to finish the tree.

"If it stays cold like this, y' won't have no trouble gittin' rid of it." Papa looked up at the clouds. "'Course if the sun comes out . . . "

"That's whut happened t' Mr. Wheaton. Sun popped out on im in the afternoon 'n nobody bought er stick er wood," Elbert said.

"Yo' hands feel all right now?" Papa asked as he fished another pair of old holey woolen gloves out of his pockets. "Put these on over them y' got on. Make it snappy now; we gotta git goin'." He pulled out his big gold railroad watch. I was always deeply impressed with how it nestled in his big hand, especially how he flipped the cover with his long ruling fingers of the same hand. "Gittin' on t'wards eight now. By the time we git that wood split 'n loaded, it'll be nine. That means Elbert won't git t' town till eround ten-thirty."

Papa was known for being the most coordinated man in our community. He was evenhanded. The few times I ever saw him pick up an ax, he would switch hands with no effort. A right- or left-handed person had to walk around on the other side. Many people accused him of avoiding work, even when he had been able. I always thought of him as a natural-born director.

"Why y' quarterin' the blocks like that, Elbert?"

"We don't have t' split this wood up out heah. I kin save time by quarterin' the blocks first, hauling um t' the brickyard, unloadin' everthing, splittin' 'n reloadin' in batches, which I'ma have t' do anyway. I want t' be gittin' on the streets no later'n ten, ten-fifteen. This is Saddy, so Sun kin come along 'n split while I haul." Papa thought for a minute, but he couldn't venture an argument. It made sense. The brickyard was dry and level. It was much easier to handle quarter blocks than many more pieces of split wood. Plus, some of the peddlers would always have a fire going. To me the big deal was that I would get a chance to go along and split that wood like a real man.

"Y' wanna do it that way?" Papa asked thoughtfully.

"Yes sir, that's the way I wanna do't."

"Who'd y' see do it like that?" Papa inquired.

"Charlie."

"Y' mean Pet's Crazy Charlie?" Papa asked in a somewhat surprised manner.

"The same," Elbert answered.

"Hmmm. I didn't know Pet wuz peddlin' wood ergin."

"He ain't. All Uncle Pet did wuz drive out theah 'n tell Charlie how t' do't, then he got back in his car and left."

"Did y' talk to im?" Papa inquired.

"Sho did. That's how I got the idea. Charlie made twice as much money as I did and wuz leavin' by three. Uncle Pet said it wuz som'um t' keep Charlie busy till plowin' time."

"Whut Pet chargin' fer er batch?" Papa asked.

"Same as me, everybody else, buck 'n er half. When it's cold, y' kin git buck six bits, two bucks fer it. Sun comes out, y' lucky t' git buck 'n er quarter, sometimes er buck. I seen guys sell it fer six bits. I ain't gon' do that. I'll bring it home first," Elbert said.

"Yeah. Cost y' mo'n that t' feed yo' team," Papa added.

"That's ernother thing. Uncle Pet feed his team wid his own feed. When y' gotta buy it from somebody, it eats right into yo' li'l profit." Elbert hit home.

Papa tried to slough off Elbert's last statement, realizing how short we were every year because of not raising enough feed. He said more to himself than to Elbert, "Pet's always got some scheme nobody else ever heard of."

"We git some snow, I kin make ten, fifteen dollars," Elbert said, looking up at the clouds. "Another thing, he don't use no crosscut saw much no mo'."

I thought to myself, *If he's tryin' to make Papa feel good, he's badly in need of some lessons.*

"Whut do he use then, er mill saw?"

"Som'um on that order. He jacks up his pickup truck—"

"Puts a belt on the wheel, 'n powers his circular saw." Papa finished the statement, clearly annoyed. "Trouble wid that is, y' wind up gittin' rid 'er yo' saplings. Takes forty yeahs t' grow a tree like this un we just cut. If y' cut bigger trees, y' need two good men t' split um."

"I kin split," I cheerfully volunteered.

Elbert looked at me and said nothing.

"Gotta figure a way t' git that old car runnin' ergin," Papa said to himself. "Maybe I kin find ernother splitter."

Papa knew what it took, but he had been whipped to his knees and didn't have the money or the physical strength to pull himself back. Elbert was only fourteen and could only see what was successful. He didn't always consider our own situation, which often prevented the execution of a plan.

While Elbert and I were quartering and loading, we heard blues in the distance.

Unka Bud got guts, Unka Bud got heart,
Unka Bud got great big buttermilk farts,
Unka Bud—Unka Bud—Unka Bud, doggone it, Unka Bud.
Unka Bud got razors ain't never been honed,
Unka Bud got babies ain't never been bo'n,
Unka Bud—Unka Bud—Unka Bud, doggone it, Unka Bud.

"Who is that way out heah in these woods this time er mornin', that crazy A.D.?" Papa asked.

"No sir. It's that crazy Black Nelson," Elbert replied.

"They didn't ketch im yet?" Papa asked.

"I don't think they wanna ketch im," Elbert said.

When Black Nelson had beaten a white man nearly to death for cheating him out of his wages, they gave him two years in prison, but he broke out after three months and was still at large.

Presently Black Nelson came tramping through the woods. As usual his greasy black leather bag was loaded with a multitude of rare things that people called "illegal, immoral, or bad fer yo' health." In other words, everything people wanted. The nickname "Black" suited him to a tee. He was well over six feet and had smooth black skin except for a few long, scattered, straggly hairs projecting from the tip of his chin. His bradded Levi's showed off his sleek powerful body. He wore a pair of motorcycle-type leather boots, braided bands on both wrists, and a black leather cap with more brads. His jacket was open, and I could see his mighty, hairless chest. His manliness was awesome, and he had a reputation to match.

Black Nelson was a hustler, a country drummer without the benefit of a car. He had spent time in the penitentiary for helping an Uncle Tom's chariot to swing low and carry him home. Everybody knew he was living on borrowed time.

He could strike fear into any man simply by standing up and smiling. When he smiled, which was often, his rather slanted small eyes closed completely except for two slits. His big white teeth flashed their beauty, and his round boyish face revealed a soul that belied the danger one might be facing. Actually he was rather nice-looking, but his powerful body rendered that secondary. His age could have been anywhere between nineteen and thirty-eight, depending on how he looked at you. The rumor was, if Black Nelson smiled at you in anger, get ready to meet your Maker, especially if he laughed. He loved children, however, which he proved by fathering quite a few of them.

Black didn't have scars and cuts on his face and neck like most bad men who were still alive. Word was, he avoided getting hit or cut by smiling at you until you were put off guard. Then there were only two licks passed: he would hit you, and you would hit the ground. Though I kept quiet about it, Black Nelson was my hero.

In one part of his mighty bag, he carried cards with pictures of Booker T. Washington, Joe Louis, Jack Johnson, Carter Woodson, W. E. B. Dubois, Paul Robeson, and Joe Baker. In another part there were wristbands, rings, hair grease, hairpins, straightening combs, perfumes, cologne, special chewing tobacco, sweet snuff, Sloan's liniment, snake oil, powder, Babe Ruth and Milky Way candy bars, brass knuckles, pocket knives, fishhooks, needles and thread, silk stockings, rubber snakes, wallets, handkerchiefs, small Bibles, Spanish fly, and rubber condoms.

"How y'all, Mr. Andra, Elbert, Sun?"

Papa squinted. "That you, Black Nelson?"

"Yes sir. How y'all doin'?"

"Oh, pretty good, Black. Right now we tryin' t' git this load t' town befo' it gits too late. Whut y' got in that bag, Black Nelson?"

"Got lots er stuff in heah, Mr. Andra." Black spread a leather mat on the ground and started pulling items out. "Heah's som'um y' gon' love, Mr. Andra." Black pulled out a Jew's harp. He put the harp in his mouth and played "I'm on the Battlefield for My Lord."

"How that sound, Mr. Andra?"

"Not bad, Black Nelson. Not bad."

"Only er dollar six bits 'n y' kin set eround the house and 'muse yo' whole family. The whole community fer that matter." He put the harp away.

"If I set eround 'n played that thing, I'm sure all Cleveland County would come. Whut else y' got?" Papa took out his glasses.

"Soooo . . . y' ain't no music-maker. Let me see . . . heah we go. This heah'll git it from a duck. If y' ain't never missed it, that means y' ain't never had it. 'Cause once y' try it, y'll never ergin be without it, gantee y', Mr. Andra." Black Nelson pulled out a shiny little package neatly wrapped in tinfoil.

Papa looked at it. Flipped it from hand to hand. "Whut is this, Black Nelson?"

"Whut y' flippin' it from hand t' hand fer?" Black inquired.

"I'm tryin' t' cool it off," Papa said.

"Tryin' t' cool it off?" Black let go with one of his famous laughs. "I swear, Mr. Andra, you don't think none er this stuff is hot, do y'?"

"No, no. I wouldn't exactly say that. It's just sweatin' a little bit, that's all." Papa was still trying to read what was on the package. "S-p-a-n-i-s-h fly? Black Nelson, you better fly on erway from heah. Don't you realize y' dealin' with er deacon, boy?"

Black laughed harder as he pulled out another shiny package. "Y' right, Mr. Andra. This little package heah made especially fer deacons. It's much stronger 'n acts twice as fast."

"Y' seem t' be in er mighty good mood, Black Nelson. Hope y' takin' all this the way it's meant," Papa said as he examined a shaving brush.

"From you, Mr. Andra? You like my own papa. I'd rather cut my right arm off than go gin you, and I loves my right arm, God knows. My nookie finger's on that arm." He caught himself. "'Cuse me, Mr. Andra. 'Cuse me."

"Well, I don't want y' t' lose yo' arm." Papa looked at the load Elbert and I had piled on the wagon while he and Black were talking. "'Specially now, 'cause I got a feeling we gon' need y' t' hep git that wagon outta theah. Look how them wheels sinkin' in the ground." To Elbert, he said, "Don't put no mo' on, Elbert. Might have t' take some er that off."

Elbert looked at his beautiful quarters. "Take some of it off?"

Papa walked over to the wagon. "Take er look at them wheels."

Elbert looked at the sinking wheels. "We kin make it. Gotta." He quickly took the lines and tapped the animals on the behind with the slack part of the leather. "Mules!" The wagon didn't budge. Rather, the wheels sank deeper.

Elbert pulled them to the right. "Aw right, mules!" The team strained, but the wagon still wouldn't budge. In addition, the team began to bog down in the soft mud.

"Hold it. Don't try no mo'. Y' only makin' bad matters worse. Take some er that load off like I told y' t' do in the first place," Papa ordered.

"Jist er minute, Mr. Andra." Black Nelson set his big bag on a nearby stump. He walked around on the other side of the wagon and checked the rear wheel. "Yo' problem is mostly on this rear wheel right heah. Cut me er short saplin'." Elbert moved quickly. "Now when I lift this wheel up, stick that saplin' in the rut under the wheel."

"Elbert, give im er hand," Papa said.

"I don't need no hand." Black Nelson backed up to the sinking wheel and took a good grip. The big smile on his face wrinkled as he put all his strength to the wheel. Stubbornly, slowly the wheel came up bringing mud, decayed leaves, and sticks with it. Elbert quickly stuck the sapling beneath.

Papa and I stood in awe. We couldn't believe our eyes.

"Aw right, Elbert. Take um on out," Black Nelson ordered.

"Mules!" A light tap again. The animals squatted, moaned, slobbered, bogged in the mud, stumbled to their knees again and again, but finally struggled out to the little road, with Elbert's beautiful quarters still intact.

"You er strong man, Black Nelson. I knowed some 'n heard er others in my day, but you gotta be up there among the best." Papa was still shaking his head in disbelief.

"Among the best? Whut you talkin' erbout, Mr. Andra? I is the best. Name somebody who kin stand up t' me. Go erhead, name um. I got fo', five days t' kill." Black Nelson laughed heartily.

"Aw right, Black. Maybe you the best, but y' don't mind if I name some mo' strong men who jist might come near yo' territory, do y'?" Papa and Black walked behind the loaded wagon. I brought up the rear.

"I permit that 'cause I wanna heah who you gon' name."

"Well, theah's Ferdinan Tonkin—"

"Ferdinan?" Black laughed so hard he could hardly keep his gait.

"Vernan McElroy—," Papa added.

"Vernan McEl—? Ssshit. 'Cuse me, Mr. Andra." Black laughed harder.

"My young brother Thomas. Lives in Chicago—," Papa added with pride.

"Stop it! Stop it! Mr. Andra, y' killin' me!" Black Nelson was so overcome with laughter, he stopped and went to his knees.

Elbert looked back from the wagon and started laughing also. I joined in. Papa joined the rest of us laughing. "Git up off yo' knees, fool. Y' crazy jist like yo' papa."

"I see right now I'mo need mo'n five days fer this." Black Nelson continued laughing.

"Aw right, Black Nelson, since y' laughed so hard at all the rest of my men, I got one mo' fer y'," Papa said, laughing.

"I don't know if I kin take this, but go erhead," Black said.

"Samson," Papa said jokingly.

"Samson who?" Black Nelson asked sincerely.

Papa looked at him and chuckled. He noticed Elbert slowing the team to a halt. "Keep goin'. Whut y' stoppin' fer?"

"Don't y' wanna ride, Papa?"

"Yeah. I reckon so." Almost out of breath, Papa climbed up on the wagon.

Black Nelson and I walked along in back of the wagon. "I swear, Mr. Andra, I sho do have myself some fun when I come eround y'all. Still like t' know who this Samson is, though."

The wagon clucked along. I strolled behind Black Nelson in the gum boots Papa had bought me and stepped in every puddle of water I could find. I kept a sharp eye out for any hickory or scaly bark nuts or persimmons the squirrels and hunters may have missed. Leaves all gone, it was also easy to spot squirrels' nests high in the forks of tall oaks. And who could tell, Mr. Cottontail might be scared from his bed, jump up, and hightail it through the woods any minute.

Multitudes of winter smells were stored in dead grass, dead leaves, dead weeds, dead sorghum stalks, dead cornstalks, dead squash, dead pumpkins, dead peas, dead beets, dead meat, and dead farts that oozed out of long winter drawers down dry ashy legs and somehow found their way to the marketplace of the good-smelling things, ofttimes without being heard or seen, nevertheless dangerous and deadly.

The wagon clucked on to the little wooden bridge across Alligator Creek, with water running swiftly beneath. The mule pulled to a halt—intelligent enough to doubt such a homemade contraption—and had to be coaxed across by Elbert putting the leather to his behind. As we crossed the little log-and-plank bridge, we suddenly came into our open field.

Brown furrows lay dead, wrapped in winter's grip. Backed-up water from Alligator Creek had claimed the floodplain, as it did each year. Persimmons and gums, topped with mistletoe and muscadine vines, rose toward murky clouds long since empty of crying, whining wild geese winging their way further south to parts unknown. The sweet silence was broken only by the clucking wagon loaded with winter wood, Black Nelson's squeaking leather as he trudged along beside the rocking wagon, my gum boots splashing water, and the mournful pleading of a freight train far in the distance. I was indeed happy to be where I was.

It was fun to be old enough to saw and chop wood with my big brother, especially with Papa there to oversee everything. And to make things perfect, the fearless Black Nelson was walking right in front of me. I was always happy to be wherever Papa took me, and he took me many places.

As the wagon rocked on through mud holes, up and down a little hill by our garden, we finally came to the Stowald house. When we drove up, Mr. Jim, who didn't have anybody to pull the other end of his crosscut saw, was doing the job alone. This was no simple task, and painfully slow. He had built a rack by driving two sharp stakes in the ground crossing each other and then another two, about six feet apart. He lay the wood in the rack and, holding it with his left foot, pushed and pulled the saw with both hands.

We were not as efficient as Uncle Pet, but we could cut four or five times as much wood per day as Mr. Jim. It wasn't because he moved slowly but because he simply didn't know how to improve his operation.

The poor man was seldom able to keep an animal. Little wonder. If the average life span of a horse or mule is twenty years, and one buys him at nineteen and three quarters, one doesn't need a veterinarian to tell how many years he has left.

Not able to keep an animal, Mr. Jim had to drag logs out of the woods harnessed up like he was one. When it came to being independent, Mr. Jim had indomitable pride. He wouldn't ask for help if he was drowning. As unimaginative as he was, he managed to keep plenty of winter wood neatly stacked in cords, half cords, quarter cords, even an eighth of a cord (which is a little less than a batch).

"The mule died" was his middle name. Mr. Jim peddled wood winter and summer, spring and fall. Almost nobody bought wood in the spring and summer except for cooking. Bringing it back home no doubt accounted for seventy-five percent of Mr. Jim's fabulous winter woodpile. Most farmers were far too busy to waste precious time driving a wagon six or seven miles to town just to have people look at their neatly stacked load. Mr. Jim, who owned only about 1.5 acres, didn't have that problem. In order to have a problem like everybody else, it seemed that he ingeniously invented the one of loading up his wagon and driving to town for absolutely nothing. Not even for his health,

since all the drudgery he had invested in dragging, cutting, loading, and hauling took care of that. He had his own way of doing things, usually backward,
and didn't want to be confused by troublesome enlightenment.

Black Nelson repositioned his big leather bag on his broad shoulder. "Well,
y'all, I hate t' leave, but I gotta stop heah 'n see Mr. Jim. One er my favorite
customers."

"Jist er minute, Black Nelson." Papa took out his worn leather pouch.
"How much is that shavin' brush I wuz lookin' at?"

"Well, I us'ally git two fifty fer um, but you er good customer er mine. Gon'
let you have it fer . . . one 'n six bits."

Papa looked down at Black Nelson quizzically. "Y' want m' t' stay er good
customer er yo's, don't y'? Remember, Black Nelson, I used t' sell these. I'm in
er big hurry, so I'll give y' one 'n er quarter fer it, take it or leave it."

"Y' sho drive er hard bargain, Mr. Andra. That brush is made outta pure
'Rabin hoss-tail," Black complained.

"Did that hoss eat slop and go onk-onk?"

"Papa, I gotta go," Elbert said.

Black Nelson laughed and reached Papa the brush. "Go erhead, Mr. Andra,
take 'vantage er my good nature. I know yo' conscience gon' whup y', first
clean shave you take."

"I'm erbout t' cry right now, Black Nelson. Mornin', Jim."

Mr. Jim walked slowly toward the wagon. "Mornin', M.A. How y'all feelin'
this mornin'? Nice load er wood y' got heah. Need splittin', though."

"New idea, Jim. Mules got er chance t' ketch they breath. Gotta git on now
so Elbert kin git this load t' town," Papa said as Elbert tapped the mules and
pulled off.

I hopped on the back of the wagon when Black Nelson stopped at Mr. Jim's.
The next house we came to was Mr. Durbey's shack. Mr. Durbey was leaving
for his shop. He had never moved fast, but even that had slowed to a mere
drag. His greetings, however, were just as lively as ever.

"How y'all feelin' this mornin'?" Mr. Durbey's tone belied his slow talking
and his movements. "Y'all makin' putty good time this mornin'," Mr. Durbey
remarked as the wagon inched on in front of him.

"Tryin' t' git er jump on um if we can," Papa said.

The wagon couldn't have gone more than eight feet before we were on the
Barrows' property. Udell, Orathia, three of the older children, and Ben had
dragged some brush and twigs from in back of their overcrowded little shackamore and were busy breaking them into very temporary firewood batches.

"Mornin', Udell, y'all." Papa swallowed his pride and condescended.

"Mornin', Mr. Andra," all the Barrows sang out simultaneously.

As we passed, Ben broke from the group and tagged along behind the
wagon. He, of course, was hoping to get me into a marble game—too cold for

that, though—or go hunting birds and rabbits with our beam shooters, wading and skating flat rocks on top of the water down by Bridge Bartholomew, walking on stilts, playing music on our homemade guitar nailed to the smokehouse, or perhaps swinging on the big rubber tire in back of our store.

"Where y' goin'?"

"Can't play. Gotta go t' town with Elbert," I said.

"Whut's the matter wid Elbert, scared t' go by hisself?" Ben scoffed.

"Whut make y' think I'm scared, y' little titty-chin scamp," Elbert responded, although Ben no longer had the growth on his chin.

Undaunted, Ben asked, "If y' ain't scared, why don't y' go by yo'self like y' been doin', 'n leave Sun heah so we kin git som'um done?"

"Sun's gon' git som'um done. Don't y' worry erbout it," Elbert came back.

"Kin I come?" Ben asked.

"Nooo! I kin answer that. Now git on back up heah 'n leave Sun alone," Udell yelled.

The wagon moved on through the last muddy spot before we descended little Blueberry Hill in back of our house. Ben reluctantly slowed down, put his hands in his pockets, and pulled out a beam shooter. It was torture.

I pretended disinterest and sat quietly as the wagon pulled up and stopped beside our house. I could see Ben still standing there looking lost.

"Git on back up heah like I tol' y' now!" Mr. Udell's voice resounded down the hill.

Papa climbed down off the wagon. "Y' got feed fer that team?"

"I got ernuff left from yestiddy," Elbert replied.

"Don't forgit t' water um at that pond befo' y' git t' the brickyard," Papa added.

"Yes sir," Elbert answered, anxious to get going.

Papa fished his money pouch out again. "Heah, take this dollar 'n er half case y' need som'um."

"I don't need nothin', Papa," Elbert said. I knew he wanted to add "but for you to let us get going," but he didn't dare.

"Take a dollar anyhow. Never kin tell," Papa insisted.

Elbert took the dollar before Papa thought of something else. "Thanks, Papa. We gotta git goin' now."

"Sun boy, you all right?"

"Yes sir, Papa. I'm all right," I hurried to respond.

Papa took out his big Bulova again. I could hear its click-click-click-click. "Now you stay right theah at that brickyard, y' heah?"

"Yes sir," I said.

"Y' cold?" Papa asked.

"No sir," I hurried to assure him. I could have been freezing, but I wasn't about to let him delay us any further if I could possibly help it. *Didn't he realize other peddlers may have been getting ahead of us at that very moment?* I thought to myself.

"Take some er that coal oil 'n make er fire while Elbert's gone," Papa ordered.

"I'll be workin', Papa. I'll keep warm," I responded. I swelled up inside with the anticipation of being trusted to stay and split wood while my big brother peddled it. I loved splitting wood, even more than sawing it. It meant that I was in on the last job before the wood was actually burned. I longed to see some customer actually burning the wood I had helped to saw and split myself. *This is going to be so easy. Maybe I'll be peddling winter wood in a year or so myself. Soon as I'm big enough to handle a team,* I dreamed.

At last we were about to get started, since Papa had run out of questions. Then I heard Mama's voice from the back porch.

"Wheah's Sun goin'?"

"He's goin' t' town wid Elbert t' hep im wid the wood," Papa said.

"Dressed like that? 'N whut is he gon' eat?" Mama asked, then turned and went back into the house.

"Mama, we gotta go!" I yelled.

"Jist hold yo' hosses, young man," her voice demanded from inside the house.

"We gon' be late fer sho," Elbert said disgustedly.

Mama came out of the house with a big overcoat and a brown paper sack full of God knows what. "Put this coat on 'n take som'um t' eat. Elbert, be sure y' make er fire so he kin keep his hands 'n feet warm. Y' heah?"

Mama made me get off the wagon so she could wrap my thin frame in a man-sized belt-back blue overcoat. No one had to tell me that I looked like a scarecrow. I could feel it. Elbert burst out laughing. Papa turned and started walking toward the house, but I could see his frame shaking from laughter as he walked.

"Mama, I don't wanna wear this thing," I protested.

"You wear it. It won't be funny when y' git on the road 'n that cold wind hit y'," Mama said.

"Where did this dog pallet come from?" I asked as I climbed up on the wagon.

"Yo' Aint Fannie sent that coat heah from Chicago in that last box. Y' better be glad y' got relatives thinkin' erbout y'," Mama said.

"She musta been thinkin' erbout er whale 'stead er me," I said.

When Elbert was overcome with laughter, he never yelled out like a lot of people. It came from deep within. He would shake and tremble, then he would pull out his handkerchief and start wiping tears from his eyes. That's precisely how Mama laughed. And that's exactly what he was doing then.

Elbert tapped the team, and we were off at last. Clouds were still hiding the sun as it strove to peek out from time to time. Instead of the weather warming up, it became colder. In the woods, we were protected and didn't feel the full effect of the wind. It was a different story on the open Pike. Also, I had been busy working or walking and so managed to keep warm. Suddenly, the big long double-breasted dog pallet and I became quite good friends. Elbert, on the other hand, seemed quite comfortable with his jacket and old ragged cotton gloves. We sat side by side in complete silence.

The wagon rolled along northward beside our little pasture on the left, which fenced in our few cows, heifers, and a calf or two. They were huddled together like reliefers waiting for rations. Their reddish-brown coats were woolly and fluffed on their backs; their underbellies matted with dead "cuckerburrows." Their jaws were in constant mechanical motion, munching their cuds. I always wondered what a cud was made of and why they never swallowed them like grass, after all that constant chewing. As still as they were, the silence was always broken by the dangling bell around the lead cow's neck, making it impossible for her to hide, even when let out of the pasture. Of course, in winter, what cow would want to stay away from a cozy barn and some dry fodder, rich pea hay, and the comfort of having her big udders relieved of milk?

In the far northern corner of the pasture, there was a mud hole. Our hogs, which were seldom let out, were bunched up also, rooting in the mud, their stiff hair covered with it. Their long ears covered their eyes. They were grunting and nudging like young students playing musical chairs. The boar nudged his big body in between the lesser hogs and mounted a sow. She just as quickly slid from under him, as if to say, "You crazy, cold as it is? You'd better be tryin' to root up on er nut or er acorn or som'um to keep you alive till that slop gits heah." The boar wasn't discouraged; he simply mounted the much smaller pig next to him, probably his son. Mama hog bit him directly in his sitting apparatus and chased him away from the group.

On our right, near the bank of Bridge Bartholomew, where the Gypsies and the DiGasspris had camped, the land sloped off to a swamp. Tall stately oaks, probably two hundred years old, leafless that time of year, were loaded with noisy blackbirds. They were obviously having a convention, but it seemed no one could get a word in edgewise.

I wondered why blackbirds didn't use the same intelligence as wild geese, hawks, quails, blue jays, woodpeckers, martins, and others of their kin. I knew that geese flew south. Their V formation, their sense of direction, their single-minded commitment to purpose, their strict discipline and leadership reminded me of Uncle Pet. Hunters never shot at geese when they flew over our area. They were always so high even a rifle wasn't likely to reach them with any degree of accuracy. I never saw hunters bother.

I have no idea where other birds went, but they were not to be found when cold January and February winds blew. Even mockingbirds had sense enough to shut up when winter arrived. But not blackbirds. They were like bad singers in church, always insisting on being heard.

They were supposed to be good to eat. Occasionally a shotgun blast would bring four or five of them down, but I never knew anyone to take the time to pick the feathers from their skinny bodies, clean them, and celebrate with "four and twenty black birds baked in a pie."

Often Ben and I would let go a rock in their midst with our beam shooters. They would darken the sky momentarily, only to light on another tree nearby, in clear range of our beam shooters again. There was absolutely nothing for them to feed on, especially in the bare trees, but they loved to flock to them.

Steady rocking and gravel grinding beneath steel-rimmed wooden wheels soothed our impatience and the chill of winter winds. Impetuous impulses prompted the idle mind to wander and roam. When we were three quarters of the way across the one-lane Bartholomew Bridge, my immediate thoughts were interrupted by a truck, headed south, that stopped in front of us. A tall white man hopped out and held up his hand for us to stop. Elbert pulled his team to a quick halt. "Wheah y' gon' wid that wagon, boy?"

"Gon' t' town wid this load," Elbert said.

A voice came from the truck. "Tell um t' back up 'n let us cross first. Then he kin go peddle his damned wood!"

A third white man's voice came from the cab of the truck. "Don't argue wid them niggers, Howie. Boy, if I have t' git outta this truck 'n come over theah, y' gon' be glad t' back that team up! Now goddammit, move it like I tol' y'!"

Elbert was fourteen and I was ten. We weren't prepared to go against three grown men. But Elbert simply didn't know how to back a loaded wagon off a narrow bridge. It was hard enough with the wagon empty. In the face of such force, however, we proceeded to try.

Bartholomew Bridge had steep embankments on both sides. The embankment on the southeast was where Roy Barnard's team had gone off and drowned the past spring. The one on the northeast was where old man Joe Bearden had swum out and saved the drowning Reedy Riley and Osben Bradwell.

Elbert and I were sitting high on a seat that had been placed on top of the load. I got down and walked in front of the team, trying to help guide the tongue and hopefully keep the wagon on the road and prevent it from going down that steep embankment.

Elbert braced his feet against the front pole and yanked on the reins as hard as he could. The wagon didn't budge. He tried again with me putting all of my seventy-five pounds on the tongue. The wagon moved only about six inches backward. It was headed straight for the bridge truss. There was not enough room to get off the bridge.

Seeing we would never make it, I approached the tall man. "Please, mister. Why don't y' jist let us pass? We be right out yo' way."

"Y' talkin' t' the wrong man. I ain't the boss," the tall man said as he kicked gravel from the Pike.

A big man with a potbelly, the one who had yelled at us, jumped from the cab of the truck with a crowbar in his hand. He walked to the north end of the bridge. "Whut's the matter, nigger boys? Y'all need some help? If I have t' give y' some help, it ain't gon' be the kind y' like, by God, I gantee y'." He hit the palm of his powerful left hand with the crowbar.

Elbert yanked on the reins again. This time the wagon backed into the truss.

I struggled with the tongue of the wagon to no avail. The tongue reared straight up into the air, taking me with it as if I was a feather. The horse started to get nervous, unruly.

Unable to move back any farther, I turned and looked at our tormentors. The tall man was leaning against the cab of the truck. The big potbellied one was busy taking a leak on the shoulder of the Pike. "Aw right, let's keep crackin' there. Pry that wheel off that truss 'n back that wagon on off there." He shook his dick in our faces. Then he raised his leg and let go with an earth-quaking, ground-breaking fart. "See if y' kin ketch that'n, boy, 'n tie er ribbon eround it." The tall man laughed. The driver grinned broadly, revealing rotten black-brown teeth.

I tried to figure out why he was doing this. Why did he need to do it? What kind of mother gave birth to a son like that? Perhaps he was what they meant by "er son of er bitch." Then it dawned on me. He was doing it because he felt like it. What's more, he was doing it because it felt good to him. Not only that, he was doing it because there was nobody there to stop him. He was doing it because it wasn't going to cost him anything. Where was Black Nelson when we needed him?

Though Elbert was still only a boy, he had never enjoyed that luxury since Papa had been sick. He had long since learned to do things that most men were doing. After all, he had worked on the levy during the flood. He prided himself on being one of the best mule skinners on the Pike. And he was becoming a fearless ladies' man, according to him.

Elbert hopped off the wagon. He found a pole and placed it between the truss and the wheel. He put his shoulder beneath the pole and slid that wheel out as pretty as you please. He hopped back on the wagon and gave one mighty jerk on the reins along with a backup command. The loaded wagon began to roll backward. When the back wheels reached the incline, they really began to roll.

I could see the rear wheels going toward the steep slope from where I was standing. I yelled to Elbert, "Jump! Jump!" No sooner said than done. One mighty leap and Elbert landed in the middle of the Pike. The speeding wagon kept pulling the frightened team down the slope. Spokes from the right rear wheel shelled from the hub like kernels of dry corn from the cob. The tall load tipped over and rolled, scattering to the ditch below. The wagon tipped upside down. The struggling team were dragged to their bellies. Fortunately, the tongue broke from the wagon and the singletrees detached, so the struggling horse and mule were able to keep on the shoulder and struggle down to the ditch below.

Bitter-tasting gall boiled up from my guts and seeped into my mouth. I was consumed with a sick anger I had never known. I felt as if I was unclothed in the middle of the street with hundreds watching. But most of all, I felt the swelling need to get even for the evil done to us by those beastly devils for absolutely no reason.

Elbert had a hurt look on his face. I had never seen him look so helpless. That unnecessary tragedy cost us a lot that we could ill afford, but three "white citizens" were able to cross Bartholomew Bridge without further inconvenience to them.

His big belly heaving up and down laughing, Big Daddy said, "See there, I knowed y' could do't if y' put yo' shoulder t' the wheel." He turned and gave no further outward sign of human emotion—not even more laughter. Neither did his tall companion. Only the rotten-toothed driver grinned broadly. Big Daddy walked slowly back to his truck, climbed in, and they puttered off.

26

Spring of 1932 was fraught with mixed feelings. I was happy to see it come but sorry for what it brought. The new Pike was *moving on down the line*. A steady rhythm of *bam-sss-shoo! bam-sss-shoo!* intermingled—during the day—with barking, bleating, braying, neighing, mooing, chirping, crowing, sawing, clawing, chopping, sledgehammer blows, falling trees, burning brush, dynamite blasts, the cracks of long whips on mules' hides, the crying roars of dump trucks and rattling Caterpillars, the yells of mule skinners and redneck foremen, and the laughter of the road crew at dinnertime. An unforgiving Arkansas sun bore down on man, beast, and machine, sending heat waves dipping and leaping like ripples on shining, rushing Bartholomew at high rise. Mean, angry heat waves, visible as smoke, galloped into the atmosphere, the firmament, the heavens.

I had watched the approach of the new Pike over the past summer and fall. The road crew had reached Bartholomew before Christmas and knocked off for the winter. The big problem arose when they surveyed the new Pike to straighten out the dogleg and bypass the old bridge we knew so well. The new route cut straight through our property. It had been a summer of excitement and fun for Ben and me, but now when the tall trees near the bayou and close to our house began to fall, so did my heart.

While the building crew worked at Bartholomew on the new bridge, the road crew kept moving on down the line. And move they did! Within days they had cut through our little pasture to within a few feet of our beautiful front yard. Already the new Pike had lopped off at least one quarter of our plot while we watched helplessly. Dust, grime, and smoke covered everything in our house, our store, and worst of all, our spirits.

It was spring, however, and the yearly high rise of Bayou Bartholomew had covered the dogleg part of the old Pike that ran northeast from our house almost to the old Bartholomew Bridge. That part of the Pike dipped downhill, and the water was too deep for cars to drive across. While they were building the new Bartholomew Bridge, the old bridge was the only way to get to the new Pike that had been finished north of Bartholomew. As Papa had done every year since the Depression, he had Elbert harness the team and tow cars across the deep water. I was happy to go along and help. The toll in a twenty-four-hour period could add up to a handsome amount of much needed cash, depending on the tippers.

Late one evening, a sleek Airflow Chrysler was waiting on the high spot at the south end of the old bridge eager to continue south. The car carried special Louisiana plates. The two men in the roomy backseat seemed comfortable enough. One was in his shirtsleeves, wore glasses, and was going over some papers spread out on what looked like a desk in his lap. The small light over his head made everything look cozy inside. After Elbert and I had pulled the squatty, wide, odd-shaped Chrysler across the deep water, the driver gave him $5. Elbert started to give him his $4.50 change, but the driver simply pulled off without so much as a word—leaving Elbert standing there with that big $5 bill!

Papa, with a spring in his walk, approached the puzzled Elbert. "Know who that was?"

Elbert gulped and guessed, "John Dillinger?"

"Nawwww, boy! That was the Kingfish himself!"

Elbert gulped again. "You mean Governor Huey Long?"

Papa's eyes were bad, but he sensed that Huey Long must have left a good tip. "How much he give you?"

Elbert reached the bill to Papa.

Papa smiled. "Ain't that er five-dollar bill?"

"Yes sir."

"That's erbout whut I expected from Huey," Papa said.

I had heard Papa and Uncle Pet discuss the Kingfish many times before. He made the headlines so often it was impossible not to discuss him. Even though he was a Southern Democrat, the party they hated, somehow they regarded Huey as some kind of a backhanded friend to black people, as well as to the common man. At least he wasn't guilty of the blatant hatred expressed by Bilbo, Talmage, Eastland, and Thurman. The Kingfish was admired as much for his outspoken courage as for his stand on racial issues.

In the same spirit, people of our community regarded Dillinger as a kind of Robin Hood. Certainly neither Papa, Uncle Pet, nor any of the people of our community favored robbing, killing, or political corruption. Quite the opposite. The system, however, was so antiblack it had poisoned their minds against anything it stood for. Therefore anybody who bucked the antiblack system—the status quo—for whatever reason, they saw as indirectly representing black people and their struggle against racism.

Black people were so eager to escape the negative image of being lazy and cowardly that when the black outlaw Youngblood escaped with John Dillinger and was at large with him for a few days, Dillinger could have run for president and easily carried the black vote as well as that of many poor and out-of-work whites. In our hearts we were pulling for him to avoid recapture. When he was finally gunned down in Chicago by the FBI, many felt they had lost a friend. To me this thinking only revealed how far good honest people will go when pushed by an unjust and uncaring system.

Huey Long became so powerful that many feared his political ascendancy. He ran for and won a Senate seat. They said he was positioning himself for the presidency. Soon after he traveled down our Pike, he was cut down by an assassin's bullet. Papa and Uncle Pet considered Huey's death a great political loss. They believed Huey could have made some difference for black people in this country. They certainly didn't want anybody else from the South representing black people's interests. Even our own Senator Fulbright—supposedly forward-looking and progressive—kept his Senate seat by voting to "keep niggers in their place." In that kind of environment, all Huey had to do was keep his mouth shut on the race question and automatically look good as far as black people were concerned.

Shortly after we saw Huey Long, the bayou began to go down and cars were able to cross without our towing them. We knew that would be the last of our little enterprise. Before the next high rise the new bridge would be completed, and the little old one-lane bridge over Bartholomew, where I had spent so many bittersweet moments early in my young life, would be remembered like the battle between Marmaduke and Clayton during the Civil War.

Bammm-ssssshoooo! Bammm-ssssshoooo! The tall crane hovered like a mighty dinosaur over the tightly bound cap of the treated wooden pile as it stubbornly penetrated red Arkansas clay and gravel. One by one, day and night the tedious process went on. Nimble men scampered and crawled in the scaffolding to cut off the caps at the right height and recap the top. Since this was a wider part of Bartholomew, it required a two-span bridge. Support columns had to be driven near the center of the bayou.

After the concrete abutments had been poured and the crossbeams set in place and bolted down, it was time to mount the long beams. While my buddy Ben and I watched, a crew of men were placing the stringers on the plates. One of the workers, who was laughing at the time, accidentally made a wrong move, and his thumb was sheared off with one clean cut by one of the beams. The cut was so clean and fast that he didn't notice. When Ben and I saw the blood dripping, I yelled out to him, "You're bleeding!" When he held his hand up and saw that his thumb was missing I thought he was going to fall from the scaffolding. "Oh my God, my thumb's gone!" Other workers helped the injured man off the scaffold, scooped up some red clay, made a poultice, wrapped it with some rags, then rushed him to the doctor in Pine Ridge.

The morning the angry crosscut saws and axes stood poised to destroy our front yard, Pete DiGasspri was nowhere to be found. The line had already been stretched right through our front yard, barely missing the front part of our house, and it was right on the edge of our store. Mama stood silently watching the white string stretched tight across her rose bed. Her honeysuckle grove, which stretched some thirty feet down to the old Pike, so beautiful in bloom and almost as old as most of her children, had but a few moments to live. Mama's front yard, during various seasons, was filled with chrysanthemums, yellow and white jasmine, magnificent magnolias, African violets and African marigolds, tall sunflowers, turban-capped tulips, dark petunias, yellow buttercups, goldenrod, praiseful orchids, and black-eyed Susans. All of this tender-handed love and cultivation had been covered with red dust and grit since the early cock's crow of spring.

Though we were forewarned, and Papa had almost got into trouble with a white man over "eminent doah-main," it was still hard to believe the moment of action. That was when all avenues of reprieve had been exhausted.

"Y' evah heah of eminent doah-main, boy? 'Spect not," the redneck clerk sang.

"Whut's it got t' do wid my property?" Papa asked.

"It's got everthing t' do wid yo' property," the country functionary drawled. "Yo' property happens t' be in line wid State Highway 15. The state got the right t' take anything in her path."

"Without payin' fer it?" Papa asked.

"Y' have t' take that up wid somebody else. I done—"

"Who? I wuz tol' t' take it up wid you."

"Well, y' already done took it up wid me, 'n I done tol' y' I don't know." The functionary started to get hot. Papa was also hot.

"If you don't have the answer, there must be somebody else I can—"

The superfunctionary walked out of his office singing bass drawl to the other's tenor. "Whut seems t' be the trouble?"

Before Papa could answer, the tenor jumped in. "This heah boy seems t' think that his property rights takes preference over the state. Wants t' git paid fer Highway 15 comin' through his land—som'um like that."

"Did y' explain to im—," the bass functionary began.

"Erbout eminent doah-main? I did, 'n he nevah heard of it, naturally."

Papa was really steaming by that time, especially about being called a boy. We watched the two functionaries huddle. Papa wasn't unfamiliar with the ways of southern white men. Papa knew they could be like wounded animals when made to feel insecure about something. He knew they could turn the most innocent situation into a major event that could lead to a black man losing his life.

Seeing much better than Papa, I could observe the tension building. I tugged on his sleeve lightly. "Papa, let's go."

He looked down at my ten-year-old frame. "Hold yo' ho'ses. I ain't finished yet." I wanted him to leave before he was finished by those rednecks. He simply ignored me and kept pecking his cane on the floor impatiently.

Finally the superfunctionary came back to the counter. "Tell y' whut y' do, boy—"

"My name is M. A. Hughes. Has been fer nearly fifty yeahs." Papa looked down at me. "Y' wanna see er boy? *This* is er boy right heah."

I really became worried then. For someone born and raised in the South, Papa had more bare nerve than I thought he should, especially in the absence of any defense except his mouth.

To my surprise, a slight smile came over the man's face, as if he was amused at that fool. I don't know what came over that redneck, but his whole attitude changed, and he tried to become some kind of a cracker statesman right there on the spot. "Well, M. A. Hughes, as straight as I possibly can, I'm gonna tell y' whut I'd do if I wuz you. I'd write to Little Rock or git m'self er lawyer t' do it. Maybe er combination of them two things. Anyway, y' ain't gonna git noplace talkin' t me 'n ol' Lester heah. We jist doin' er job, if y' know whut I mean."

Papa didn't smile or show any emotion. He simply tipped his hat in a gentlemanly fashion, said, "Thank y', sir," turned, and walked out. I followed proudly and gladly.

We were left bare to the snarling, gnashing teeth of crosscut saws, the sharp blades of timber axes, the roar of dump trucks, the rattling cold steel of an unrelenting Caterpillar, at the mercy of a tobacco-chewing, nigger-hating, glad-to-be-white redneck.

"Would it make that much difference to your highway if you moved that line a few feet to the east so my store could be saved?" Papa asked.

"You talkin' to the wrong man, boy. Pete DiGasspri's the man y' wanna see."

"I talked to im last week, and he said he was goin' to save m' orchard, m' store, and as much of m' front yard as possible. Wheah is he anyway?"

"He ain't made no exception fer nobody else. Whut makes y' think he gon' make any fer you? He don't make them kind er decisions nohow." The redneck spat a slimy mouthful of tobacco juice on the ground and looked at his watch.

"Can't y' skip ahead and work until I git a chance t' talk t' him?" Papa pleaded.

"Boy, y' got erbout three minutes 'n I'm gon' start these boys t' work."

Papa was plenty angry. I'd seen him that way only once before, when Roy Barnard took his heifer for a $9 debt. "Can't you wait until I talk with Mr. DiGasspri?" Papa knew that he had done favors for DiGasspri by letting him use his well. Besides, Elbert was one of his best men. Papa thought that if he had one more chance to talk with DiGasspri, he might be able to save something.

Mama walked up beside him. "Andra, you know Pete DiGasspri ain't coming heah this mornin'."

Papa stood there like a statue in line with where the trees would fall. A slight breeze started to blow his floppy hat as if it was going to rain. *Maybe a twister will come and blow this old redneck away,* I thought. I had heard plenty of sermons about how the waters parted for the children of Israel, and when old Pharaoh came after them the waters closed in, and Pharaoh and his army were drowned in the Red Sea. There was even a song about it. *Why can't something like that happen right now? Since we don't have no sea, red or otherwise, around here, a tornado will do just fine.* I prayed for a tornado, but it was not to be.

Redneck looked at his watch. "Seben o'clock on the dot. Y'all boys kin start to work now."

Papa just stood there. The winds became more blustery. Mama's long dress was flapping about. She held tight to her straw hat. The workers knew and loved Papa. Most of them were on his books for money they owed him. Two of the head choppers placed the long sharp crosscut across the big oak that had shaded many barbecues, pastors, Baptist convention visitors, young lovers, schoolteachers, customers, deacons, sinners, liars, thieves, Gypsies, truck drivers, barbers, marble shooters, mama-peg players, horseshoe pitchers, strangers, plain loafers, and the weddings of my two older sisters Jessie and Hazel.

During this entire standoff, Mr. Durbey stood to the side holding a pair of tongs with a horseshoe in it and a big anvil hammer. Normally full of fire and sass, he looked ancient, defeated, and ready to die.

The redneck repeated his command. "I said y'all kin git started now."

One of the workers spoke up. "But Mr. Andra is in the way." He must have known Papa all his life to refer to him as Mr. Andra.

"I'm gon' give y' one mo' chance to move out the way, boy."

"I ain't goin' nowheah till I talk t' Pete DiGasspri."

"Now I done tol' y' Pete DiGasspri ain't heah. I ain't got all day. Anybody who don't wanna start workin' kin go git they time, right now!"

The worker who had spoken dropped his tool, walked over to Papa, and spoke softly to him. "Come on now, Mr. Andra. Pete DiGasspri ain't comin' heah this mornin'." He took Papa by one arm, and Mama took the other. They led his lean, dusty frame over to the store, south of where they were standing. Then Mama and Papa stood and watched. Mr. Durbey followed slowly. The worker returned swiftly to his job and proceeded to saw.

By noon all of our beautiful oaks, gums, and pines were cut and hauled away by log trucks. Except for the pots of flowers Mama had us carry to the back, they dismissed most of our front yard as mere rubbish—nigger trash. But the worst was yet to come. Instead of having the workers dig, cut, and burn the stumps close to Papa's house and business, as they did for whites, they set dynamite beneath the stumps. The blast broke the front windows in our house and tore off the front of our store. Nothing—especially the rights of a black man—could stand in the way of the state. The county. Eminent domain. The new Pike was moving on down the line.

Papa's heart was broken. The new Pike had taken most of his front yard, exposing his once cool shaded porch to the hot sun and the ever-present dust. The only time he could enjoy his favorite swing was late at night after traffic had subsided. The new highway would leave the front yard of our house and the store on the edge of a ditch. Even the little birdhouse Papa had built for the martins had been knocked down by the construction crew. Papa had Mr. Sam Riley brace it back up so that the tall pole with the whitewashed little house on top pointed proudly toward the heavens once more. The martins had returned that spring and conducted business as usual.

About two o'clock that morning, when all were asleep, the loud hoarse voice of the drunken, riotous A.D. came down the old Pike, turned on Wagon Road West—by our house, and went up Blueberry Hill singing his fool head off.

> *Packin' up my suitcase,*
> *Movin' on down the line.*
> *Wellllllll, packing up my suitcase,*
> *And I'm movin' on down the line.*
> *Wellllllll, it ain't nobody worried,*
> *And it ain't nobody cryin'. . .*

27

Unfortunately, the front of Mr. Durbey's little blacksmith shop, to the south of our store, projected a few feet on the wrong side of the white line. Gravedigger, his trusty old double-barreled shotgun, was no match for such an awesome array of hardware and a redneck foreman with the force of the state on his side. As Papa had done the day before, he ranted and fussed and coughed to no avail as the rattling, roaring, smoking iron monster with a steam shovel attached to its rig huffed and puffed off the front part of his little shop. The redneck foreman was prepared to tear the whole shop down, but Elbert and Papa persuaded him to allow some workers to save as much as they could. They were able to leave Mr. Durbey's anvil, his bellows, his tools, and an old stove intact.

"Bet y' think I'm gonna cry, don't y'?" Mr. Durbey said vehemently. "I-I-I-I wouldn't give y' the satisfaction! Y' low-down . . . buzzards! Y'-y' filthy, heartless undertakers!"

"Watch yo' mouth, ol' man!" the redneck foreman warned.

"Whut y' gon' do? Shoot me? Lynch me? I know that's whut y'd like to do, but y' ain't got nerve ernuff to try it while y' outnumbered by all these black folks eround heah! Y'-y' dried-up . . . peckerwood!"

The white man turned purple. Big veins popped out on his forehead. He didn't know how to answer the old man. He simply looked at Mr. Durbey for a long time. "Y'all knowed this road wuz comin' through heah fer over er yeah now. Y' shoulda had all this junk out the way."

"Whut the hell y' talkin' erbout? If the county wants our land, the county oughtta pay fer it erlong wid whutever they move! Y' think we're stupid because we're black?"

The redneck didn't answer Mr. Durbey. He stepped back and gave the workers the nod to begin.

The old man had boasted that he was "raised by an old mama bear till I was two." The same old man had just said, "Bet you think I'm gon' cry, don't y'?" After the foreman and the workers had gone, he looked sadly at his ransacked, serrated shop that was completely exposed, and did indeed break down and cry aloud.

Papa, who had been devastated the day before, limped over to the old man, who was sitting on the side of the embankment looking at the mess, and put a hand on his shoulder. "Don't worry, Brother Durbey, we'll git yo' shop boarded back up tomorrow."

Mr. Durbey stopped crying abruptly. "You'll do no such thing, M.A. I been standin' on m' own two feet all these yeahs, 'n I ain't erbout t' start 'pendin' on you or nobody else. I kin take care er m'self. Besides, you got er whole mess er trouble er yo' own. Cotton-pickin' time's almost heah. Y' oughtta be startin' yo' remedy business." The old man struggled to his feet and grabbed an old greasy croker sack that had some potatoes in it among other things. He staggered. Then, with great effort, he carefully put one foot in front of the other and inched his way up Wagon Road West. Papa told Ben and me to follow him and see that he got home safely. That spoiled our plan to visit the new bridge before nightfall.

The new bridge over Bartholomew had opened early in the fall of 1932. The old bridge, as well as that dogleg section of the old Pike, was closed forever. When Mama and I loaded our buggy and headed north for one of our last peddling trips of the season, I was amazed at how quickly we arrived at the new bridge.

How different the two bridges were. Trees that drank deep from the ancient waters that rushed angrily down the Bartholomew surrounded the old bridge. Waters that overflowed along her banks into her ditches and tributaries during spring slowed to lazy sandy draggy dregs at the end of summer and fall. How different they were. The old bridge was loud and boisterous. Her high rusty steel trusses cried out as if in pain—or perhaps in victorious joy—when she let your wheels trundle day and night over her worn ruffled wooden back. Perhaps it was joy that she never lost a customer who dared to straddle her planked spine. The restful banks, berms, and shoulders of the old bridge and its surroundings, steeped in a gossamer haze, were a mingled cornucopia of boyhood happenings.

My first awakening to the sting of a switch on my spindly legs at the age of four was at the bridge. Papa, as the driving force, propelled my little sister, Verleen, and me all the way home from Bayou Bartholomew screaming at the top of our lungs. The bridge was above the graves of Roy Barnard's horse-and-mule team. There Papa's new 1929 Ford burned to a rusty frame. It was where three evil white men made Elbert and me back up our loaded wagon, sending it crashing down the embankment, almost killing Elbert. It was where I had watched Mr. Joe Bearden swim out on his back and pull two drowning men to safety. It was near the bridge that Ben and I had smoked brer rabbit from one of the hollow trees. I loafed lazily on her banks, skated flat rocks on her shining waters, and dog-paddled across her deeps to the other shore. I found a whole case of snuff that had dropped from a truck near her south end.

Snagged fat perches from among her rocks and landed what was for me the world's biggest catfish in one of her boggy ditches. The banks and tabletop flatlands surrounding Bartholomew after the waters subsided were a haven for many wayfarers, Gypsies, truck drivers, and tent-sheltered evangelists.

At the end of July, however, Bartholomew's banks became holy grounds for The Faithful. New converts, just off the moaner's bench, came to be baptized. Draped in white, they were led barefoot into the bayou crying "Holy Unto the Lord!" After baptism they sang "Lord, I Ain't No Stranger Now!" and one of the all-time favorites, "I'm a Witness for My Lord!"

The new bridge was wide, strong, efficient, rigid, void of all trees, made no sound, and had no soul. Except for the railings, there was no consciousness of crossing a bridge.

The advance road crew had moved on down the line. The business that Papa was getting from the workers moved to Barnard's store, which was closer. Our land, our orchard, our front yard, and our store had been savaged by the shark's teeth of eminent domain. We were left with nothing to show for it but our deeply sickened hearts and the job of salvaging and repairing as much as we could.

Reds, azures, blues, and crimsons had blinked their final disappearance on the panoramic proscenium of the west. The cool kiss of autumn air stole in. Moving from the forest in back of us, up the little hill, and looking back, we saw fireflies explode magically into a painting of flickering comets. Leaping, escaping shadows danced and dotted against the deep dark woods. Night sounds observed their clock, and touch-me-nots closed their petals.

Halfway up Blueberry Hill in back of our house, Mr. Durbey gave out and sat down to catch his breath. Ben and I were ready to help him when we heard a woman and a man walking behind us talking. It was Miz Marge and Udell. They were carrying fishing poles and buckets.

"That you, Pa?" Miz Marge squinted at the old man sitting on the ground.

"Who'd y' think it wuz? Brer Rabbit?"

"Almost dark, so I couldn't see y' good."

"There's none so blind as them who will not see."

"Come on, Pa. Git up 'n let's go home." She tried to pull him up.

"Y' cain't lift me. Y' think y' er man all of er sudden?"

"Mr. Udell . . ." Miz Marge beckoned for Udell to help.

Udell hesitated. He slowly put his pole down, then reached down to help.

"Don't you touch me!" the old man growled. Udell recoiled quickly. "I'd sooner stay out heah all night and catch m' death than fer you to put yo' hands on me."

"*She* axed me t' help y'. Wutten *my* idea."

"I don't need yo' kind er help! 'N don't you ever forgit it!"

"Come on now, Pa. Y' jist bein' fussy now."

"Been fussy all m' life. Too bad y' didn't take after me."

"Who'd I take after, then?"

"Y' sho didn't take after me. That's all I'm gon' say erbout it."

"Meanin' that I musta took after Mama. Is that whut y' tryin' t' say?"

"Keep yo' dead mama outta this. When is y' know'd me t' try t' say anything? I got som'um t' say, I say it. I don't give er damn who heahs it."

"Don't you start ergin, Pa. Don't y' see them boys standin' there?"

"This ain't the first time them boys heard me cuss, 'n I hope it won't be the last."

"Least y' could show er little respect fer yo' daughter."

"Huah! You ain't no daughter er mine. You ain't been no daughter er mine in er long time! 'N as fer as respect is concerned, y' gotta earn it! 'N y' don't do that by sleepin' eround on yo' husband, pretendin' t'—"

"Y' lying, Pa! I'm er Christian woman, 'n my feet is on holy ground."

"Yo' feet ain't been on the ground—holy or otherwise—in yeahs. Layin' flat on yo' back wid yo' legs stickin' up in the air ain't whut I call havin' yo' feet on the ground."

"Y' er wicked old man! That's whut y' is!" She started crying. "I'm gon' tell Kid! I sho is! Soon as I git home! Talkin' t' me like that right in front er these boys 'n Mr. Udell."

"Tell him! Hell, I'll help y'. If he ain't done nothin' in all these yeahs to somebody who needs it"—Mr. Durbey looked at Udell—"he damned sho ain't gon' do nothin' t' me."

"Y' jist don't have no respect fer yo'self or nobody else, Pa. Y' won't clean yo'self up 'n go t' church—"

"I don't go t' church 'cause theah's too many hypocrites theah like you. 'N—"

"Y' live in grease 'n filth—"

"Hell, I'm er blacksmith, woman! How do y' expect m' t' look? Like M.A.? 'N as fer as grease and filth is concerned, I'd rather have dirty hands makin' er honest dollar, a clean heart, and a clear conscience than clean hands and a dirty, smutty heart like you two."

Udell was quieter than I had ever known him to be. He was in an awkward position. He walked off a piece toward his house and turned his head occasionally when Mr. Durbey scored another big point.

"Tryin' t' tell me som'um erbout respect. Y' gotta respect yo'self first. Yo' mama wutten too smart, but she wuz faithful. Least as fer as I know. She damned sho had better sense than t' spread her business all over the county. Not that I think she wuz doin' anything. Y're scorned, woman! Y'-y' er Jezebel! Y'-y' famous fer whut you do! No amount er church-goin'—"

"Shut up, Pa!"

"Who y' tellin' t' shut up!"

"I'm tellin' you! Y'-y' old 'n-'n . . . y' sick . . . 'n-'n y' cranky, y' bullheaded 'n talkin' outta y' head! 'N y' make it impossible fer us t' git erlong." She moved to pick him up again, but he was too heavy. "Y'all help me git im home. He cain't set out heah all night."

Ben and I rushed to his side and tried to help, but he was too heavy for us.

"Mr. Udell, give us a hand," Miz Marge said.

"But the man said he didn't want me t' put my hands on him."

"That's right! I don't. I'd rather rot out heah, 'n really give y' som'um t' smell!"

"Don't pay no ertention t' whut he says! Jist take er hold of im."

Udell reluctantly hobbled back, limping from the gunshot wound he'd gotten from A.D., and reached down to help the old man. Mr. Durbey took a swing at him but missed and started coughing.

"Y' see, he's lost all control. Jist don't pay him no mind."

Udell finally got Mr. Durbey to his feet and tried to put the old man's arm around his shoulder so he could carry him better, but Mr. Durbey jerked his arm down, leaned toward Ben and me, then started ranting and raving again.

"Y' no better than er cur dog! Way y' been carryin' on! Talkin' erbout these boys gon' heah me. These boys ain't no fools, they ten yeahs old. I'd fathered six kids when I wuz that age 'n been divorced twice."

"Tol' y' he's crazy," Miz Marge said, and started inching him along.

"Way y' been carryin' on wid this no-good whoremonger been the talk er the county fer yeahs! Everbody knows it! Even Jim! He jist ain't got up ernough nerve t' do anything erbout it yet."

"Pa, be quiet! Wait'll I git you home."

"Whut y' gon' do, whup me? I wish y'd try it! I still got ernuff left t' send y' erway from heah. 'N if I cain't do it, I'll sick m' goat on y'."

Ben couldn't control himself—he started laughing. I joined him. Soon everybody was laughing except Mr. Durbey.

"That goat turns into a dog wid horns when somebody messes wid me. He'll butt yo' ass clear outta the county!"

The old man was amazing. Once he was on his feet, he was able to walk alone and didn't hesitate to tell us.

"Y'all let go er me 'n give me m' bag! I never asked fer y' help in the first place. Think I'm er baby or som'um?"

"Y' sho, Pa?" Miz Marge asked.

"'Course I'm sho." He slapped her hand down when she wouldn't release him.

"Y' my pa, 'n I love y', but y' one evil ol' cuss, y' know that? Y' won't make friends, 'n y' won't even let me help y'."

"If Jim had listened t' me, he woulda settled the score wid y' long time ergo. Tell y' that much." Mr. Durbey pointed his finger at Udell.

Udell walked along in front, spat tobacco juice, and never bothered to respond.

Miz Marge wasn't a mean person. I still liked her in spite of her obvious faults. She'd give you anything she had. Geneva thought Miz Marge had "missed a few helpings at the brain counter." Maybe that's why Mr. Jim put up with her, I thought. She never neglected Mr. Jim during all those years she was unfaithful to him. She always had his food ready. Kept the house spotless.

She tried to do the same things for Mr. Durbey, but he wouldn't have any part of it. He objected to her straightening up and cleaning his jumbled, messy shack. "I know wheah my stuff is in this junk. Let you in heah wid yo' nice-nasty neatness, 'n I wouldn' be able t' find er thing. Best thing fer y' t' do is stay outta heah. If I need y' I'll call y'."

Miz Marge bragged on Mr. Jim every chance she had as if he was the best thing that ever happened since leather shoes. On Sundays she was seen all dressed up, with a wide floppy hat, white gloves, and often white shoes and pocketbook to match, just to please him. Every other Sunday, when the pastor came, you might see her strolling up the Pike arm in arm with her husband. Mr. Jim walked proudly, chuckling and laughing as if he was glad to get his turn. "Good mornin', Udell, y'all," he would say. Papa said, "If Jim is happy, whut wuz we worried about?"

Mr. Jim and Elbert repaired the front of Mr. Durbey's shop. Once the new Pike was finished and graded, it was far enough away from our store and Mr. Durbey's shop that with care—such as no dynamite—the damage could have been avoided. The old man mustered enough strength to come there every day. Most days he simply sat around, fussed with different little things, but he never got back into his work as he had before. He told a few stories about the old days when Arkansas was young and people came there from all over seeking to better themselves, since Arkansas was the "land of opportunity." He talked about the many ex-slaves who came, bought land, dug wells, planted crops, and started families. Grandpa Hughes was among that number. Mr. Durbey had owned land also, but after his wife died at a young age, he sold his land, opened a blacksmith shop, and made a good living at it—enough for him and his children.

It was finally cotton-picking time. Papa was busy buying remedies, combining them to make bales, and selling them on the market. He had little time to sit around Mr. Durbey's shop listening to tall tales, though his store was practically closed. Mr. Jim was busy cutting winter wood and piling it. Miz Marge and Udell were still carrying on their affair as they had been. After school and on weekends, Ben and I visited the old man to see if he wanted us to bring him some water or run an errand. We were in the best position to know how he was going down daily. He tried to laugh, but his coughing got worse. He started trembling and shaking. Sometimes he could hardly get his breath. He rallied, however, and came back to his shop, claiming that he only had an early winter cold. Mama and Papa, who had gone to see him, thought he would recover and be all right again, but on his way home he could barely make it up the hill in back of our house. He had to stop several times to catch his wind.

Ben and I had gathered hickory nuts for a few days after school and hadn't gone to see him. After four days, we went to his shack. It was chilly, but there was no smoke coming from the chimney. We heard coughing and hacking inside. I knocked and waited.

"Who is it?" a voice finally said.

"It's us, Mr. Durbey," I said.

"Who the devil is *us*?"

"Sun and Ben."

"Do's open. Y'all come on in."

Before Mr. Durbey became ill, I had been inside his one-room shack only a few times. He wasn't sick then, and it was hardly a model for any bachelor to follow. Being sick and unable to do for himself only added to an already bad situation. The wallpaper—old *Arkansas Gazettes*—was peeling badly. The cold air that came from the sides met the air that shot upward through the cracks in the rough wooden plank floor. On a chilly day, one felt warmer outside.

A rickety old stove with a dirty smutty pot and skillet on top, with wired-up pipes sticking out of the tin roof, sat in the middle of the small cramped space. A small table with a kerosene lamp on it and a rickety chair sat near the north wall—facing us as we entered from the south. A small bed propped up on orange crates was in the northeast corner of the room. There was a stinking slop jar near his bed. Many articles hung on the walls: a gourd, a water bucket, a rabbit trap, a coon trap, bags of seeds, a small shelf for Sears catalogs, some magazines, a few books, a grandfather clock, and the Bible. Old Gravedigger, his double-barreled shotgun, sat in the corner near his bed, standing guard over all that junk. Outside, that stupid goat that could turn into a watchdog on a minute's notice was bleating her silly head off, wanting to be milked.

As we entered, Mr. Durbey's ugly rusty feet greeted us as he lay coughing on his filthy little bed. He had long, out-of-control toenails, wore dingy dirty long underwear, and had a ragged gray week-old beard. The room reeked of every unpleasant odor known to man. He had been neglected. It was not customary in our community.

He rose up as best he could. "Whut y'all boys doin' heah this time er day? Why ain't y' out in the cotton fields, like everbody else, or at school?" He spoke in a raspy voice.

"School's out fer today, Mr. Durbey," I said.

"Whut time is it, Sun?"

"It's after six, Mr. Durbey."

"Time sho flies when y'"—he hesitated, gave a weak chuckle—"havin' fun."

"We didn't see y' fer almost er week. We wondered if that barkin' goat er yo's got y' mixed up wid er robber," Ben said in an effort to cheer up the old man.

He looked up and gave a wheezing, uncharacteristic little chuckle. We had grown used to his wholesome loud "Haw-haw-hawwww!"

"That's mighty nice er y'all boys. I erpreciate it. That po' goat ain't been milked in pud niah er week . . ."

"We milk her fer y'," I said.

"That's mighty nice er y' t' offer, Sun. But I'm erfraid she wouldn't take too kindly t' somebody 'sides me. Might go watchdog on y'."

Ben and I spent the rest of the evening with Mr. Durbey. We took out his stinking slop jar, made a fire in his broken-down stove, brought him a bucket of water, and straightened up his filthy place as best we could. Before we left, the old man was sitting up slurping a tin cup of black coffee and trying to tell a funny story.

When Miz Marge or Mr. Jim showed up with his food, she was tired and sweaty from picking cotton all day with Udell and the rest of the Barrow family. Mr. Jim cleaned up, doing what was considered women's work.

The old man was a loner with unyielding pride. Even so, it was customary in that community for people to sit up with the sick or dying, whether you were in the church or not. They also got together, dug your grave, and buried you. Mr. Durbey didn't socialize, make friends, or want anybody to do anything for him, especially if he couldn't repay the favor. His only friends were Papa and Mr. Jim. He refused help from Mama and Papa after he started having coughing attacks. He also refused to have Miz Marge around, claiming she made him feel worse "wid her nit-pickin'." After he had rallied and returned to work, nobody knew how sick he was except Ben and I. He confided in Mr. Jim and told him, "I don't want all them hypocrites and liars makin' er fuss over m'. When the time comes, jist put m' in er pine box, take m' up t' the cemetery at Hughes Chapel, 'n take care er the whole thing."

Knowing his condition, Ben and I looked in on him every day after school. He kept eating less and less. Finally, he was so weak that he didn't recognize us when we tried to talk to him. Then one warm day we walked in and the old man was lying flat on his back with his mouth open, eyes half-closed so that we saw only their whites. His breathing was irregular, and there was a deep throttling sound when he breathed in and a wheezing sound when he breathed out. White foam ran from his mouth and down the sides of his chin. The stink was horrible. Green flies covered his face and were making their way down his throat. We brushed them away but to no avail.

"I think he's dyin'," Ben said.

"Did you ever see a person die befo'?"

"Naw. Did you?"

"Naw. Y' think we oughtta call somebody?" I asked.

"They know he's sick. Look like Miz Marge or Mr. Jim oughtta be heah."

"Mr. Jim come every day, but ain't nothin' he can do. Mr. Jim tried to move him in with them when he first got sick, but he put up such er fuss Mr. Jim forgot it."

We brushed the flies away again. The grandfather clock was ticking slower. It hadn't been wound in a while. The kerosene lamp was almost out of oil and was dimming. We closed the door quietly and left.

I wanted to tell Papa, but he was away buying remedies. Mama was busy preparing supper, but I told her anyway.

"I'll tell Marge when she passes this evenin'. It's her own papa. Seems t' me she oughtta be there wid him. I took him some soup, but he's so weak . . . ," Mama said.

The next day we went straight from school to his place. We expected to find him dead. We opened the door slowly. It was dark inside. All of the oil had long since burned out of the kerosene lamp. Slithers of light were streaking through the small window. We left the door cracked to let in more light. Mr. Durbey was lying still in the same position. His rusty feet with long unruly toenails pointed straight at us as we crept toward his bed. The plank boards squeaked beneath our feet. As we drew nearer his head, we were sure he was dead. We stood over his bearded, gaping, foaming mouth and waited for him to tell us he had breathed his last. We didn't wait long. Another horrible wheezing sound ushered from his volcanic throat, scattering the green flies in the process. After another long wait, another horrible throttling sound quivered deep within his throat. We waited. Finally there was one big gush of air that stopped abruptly when he exhaled.

I whispered quietly to Ben, "He's dead. Mr. Durbey is dead."

"Wait," Ben said.

We waited five minutes or so. The grandfather clock had stopped. Food and foam around his mouth were stinking and rotting.

My thoughts went back to what he loved and how he lived. Mr. Durbey was so tough that it took him three days to draw his last breath. Though he was well into his eighties, I believed he could have easily made it to a hundred if the things that he lived for had not been taken away from him. I found myself asking, when does an old man die? When the old bridge at Bartholomew died. When the daughter that he loved turned into a trollop before his eyes. When his best friend's business was ransacked, and neither he nor anyone else could do anything about it. When his own blacksmith shop was wrecked. When he was no longer able to take care of his goat and had no one he could depend on to do it for him, because Mr. Jim knew nothing about goats. That's when an old man dies.

*   *   *

It was a blustery Saturday. Ben and I were going down the new Pike on our way home with two bags of hickory nuts we had gathered. Mr. Jim met us on his way up the Pike to Hughes Chapel's cemetery. He wore his usual overalls and work shoes. He was leading a nag of a mule that looked as if he should have been left at a mule's cemetery. When we were close enough to notice, we saw what he was hauling in his small one-horse wagon.

"Howdy, Mr. Jim," I said.

"Howdy, Sun, Ben. Wheah y'all boys been?"

"We been gatherin' hickory nuts," we said together, and held up our bags.

I looked at the pine box in the back of the wagon. "Who gon' hep y' dig the grave, Mr. Jim?"

"I dug it yestiddy by myself."

"Why didn't y' ax somebody t' hep y'?" Ben asked.

"Yeah. We woulda helped y'," I said.

"I know that, boys. 'N I wanna thank y'. But y' know how the old man wuz. Never wanted anybody t' do anything fer him when he couldn't return the favor. Come on, Ike." He led the nag and the loaded wagon toward Hughes Chapel's cemetery as we stood on the side of the road and watched sadly. There was no procession. No mourners. Not even Miz Marge. Mr. Durbey did not belong to the church and therefore was outside the grace of The Faithful.

28

Late one Saturday evening, Papa and I were checking what was left of our inventory in the store. A tall smooth dark-skinned young man ambled in.

"Whut y'all doin'?" he asked.

Papa squinted. His eyes had almost failed. "Who's that?"

"Er fella leave heah fer er few days, 'n he's forgotten like er pair er ol' worn-out shoes."

I recognized him immediately. "It's Reedy, Papa!" I blurted out.

"Reedy? Boyyy! When y' git outta that prison?" Papa's face lit up.

"Got out yestiddy," Reedy said as he walked toward Papa and grabbed his hand.

"Stand back, boy! Let m' look at y'!" Papa laughed and put his hands on Reedy's shoulders. "Whut y' talkin' erbout er few days? Y' been gone erway from heah fer two yeahs!" I hadn't seen him that happy in a long time.

Reedy walked over to me and playfully grabbed me in a wrestler's hold. "Soooo! This is ol' Sun! Guess y' smellin' yo' own pee now. Eh, boy?"

"Hi, Reedy," I said.

"This boy's growin' like corn after a good shower on er hot summer night. Bet y' cain't catch im no mo', kin y', Mr. Andra?"

Papa chuckled, but it wasn't funny. Reedy had put his finger on a fact. Papa had never run after me. His command had been enough for me to come when he called. Sensing that he had become so weak and blind that whipping me had become difficult, I followed my sister Geneva's advice, ran and hid until he cooled off, then returned home.

"Well, tell me erbout yo' two yeahs down theah on that farm. How'd ol' Jake treat y'? Must not been too bad. Yo' face look smooth t' me. Not er single scar. 'Course he been knowin' y' since y' wuz er baby."

"My face, huh?" A mean gloomy look came over Reedy's handsome face. He had never been one for smiling. "Jake don't beat y' on yo' face." He began taking off his shirt. Red and white canals crisscrossed his back all over his once smooth black skin. The white streaks were scabs formed from healing. The red streaks were from recent beatings. They were still raw and sore and had pus beneath the scabs that leaked out and caused his shirt to stick to his back.

It all came from Jake Parsons' twenty-foot-long rawhide bullwhip with plaited lash.

Papa shook his head. "Why, that mean devil. He knowed you since y' wuz er baby—right heah from this community. He also knowed you wuz doin' yo' papa's time. How kin he look in our faces? Ol' man Parsons don't approve er this. He—"

"He never spoke t' me or even acted like he knowed who I wuz. T' him, I wuz jist ernother nigger doin' hard time." Reedy started putting his shirt back on. He didn't dare take it all the way off because it would have taken the scabs with it. Papa helped him. Though his back was sore, he never made a face or showed any expression of pain. "You never been t' the farm, did y', Mr. Andra?"

"Naw, son. I never been, thank God. I seen um in balls 'n chains workin' on this very Pike yeahs ergo, but they cut that out after they had so many break-erways. Hold on er minute." Papa took a jar of Vaseline from the shelf. He opened it and rubbed some over Reedy's shirt on the spots where the pus had leaked through and stuck.

"Whut's that fer, Mr. Andra?"

"Whut's it fer? Well, when y' git ready t' go t' bed tonight 'n start t' take this shirt off, I hope it'll be loose enough so it won't take the scabs off 'n leave them sores exposed. Git somebody t' hep y', 'n be sho 'n wrap some clean rags eround yo' back till these sores heal up. Whut do they do on the farm when somebody's cut up like this?"

"They don't do nothin'. We throw some dirt on each other's back t' soak up the blood 'n pus. They don't let us have no rags. Nothin' like that."

"Whut erbout coal oil?" Papa asked.

"If we lucky ernuff t' git er little."

Papa was steadily shaking his head. "I cain't hep thinkin' erbout whut woulda happened t' Sam if they had taken him."

"Jake woulda killed im, that's all. 'N if he didn't, the hard work in that hot sun woulda. Every once in er while y' see er ol' man come in. I never saw er single one of um go back out."

"Whut er y' mean, Reedy? Whut happened to um?"

"They git killed tryin' t' escape." Reedy gave Papa a you-should-know-what-I-mean look.

Papa got the drift and hung his head. "Escape, huh?"

"I saw Jake beat er man t' death once. I wuz on er grave-diggin' detail many times. They don't put no headstone up when y' killed in prison. Jist bury y' like er dog."

"We put er head mark up fer Spot," I said, uncharacteristically interrupting grown-ups.

"Well, Sun, that's mo'n er dead convict gits out theah on that state farm.

Anyway, we couldn't dig mo'n three feet befo' we started digging up some-body's bones. Theah ain't no tellin' how many convicts they jist plain killed out theah fer little er nothin'."

"Whut would Jake beat y' fer?"

"Talkin' while y' workin' or standin' in line. Shoes tied wrong. Stretchin'. . . ."

"Stretchin'?" Papa asked.

"Thinkin'. . . ."

"Whut y' talkin' erbout, Reedy?"

"That's right. Jake claimed he could read minds. That's whut he use t' take *me* down fer. Thinkin'."

"I never heard er such foolishness." Papa sat on the counter.

Reedy pulled up a keg of nails, placed a board over it, and sat on top. "That's right, he didn't like me 'cause I didn't laugh 'n grin. He said I musta been thinkin'."

"Well, wuz y'?" Papa asked slyly.

"Wuz I whut?"

"Wuz y' thinkin'?"

"Every minute!" Reedy laughed.

Papa joined him. "Whut wuz y' thinkin', Reedy?"

"I'll give y' three guesses, Mr. Andra."

"How t' git out! How t' git out! 'N how t' git out!"

"Y' got um *all* right, Mr. Andra. I know I ain't nobody's smiler, grinner, or laugher, but that Jake make me look like er circus clown by comparison. You been knowin 'im all his life, y' ever see im smile?"

"Well, I thought I did once, but it turned out he'd accidently slammed his truck door on his hand," Papa said.

We all laughed.

"The ol' man, Jake's papa, is always smilin'. But the mama looks like she's suckin' on som'um all the time," Papa said, laughing.

"It's that mama that Jake takes after," Reedy said. "He looks like he's in pain all the time."

"Seems like whut you tellin' me is y' don't have t' do nothin' fer Jake t' beat y'. In that case, whut do y' do t' keep im *from* beatin' y'? 'Cause whutever it wuz, you sho didn't do it."

"I didn't know how. Most er them ol' boys come from them plantations down on the river bottom. 'N they use t' them white folks kickin' um eround. I ain't never worked fer nobody 'cept you, Mr. Pet, 'n Papa."

"If I wuz you, I'd forgit erbout that work y' did fer yo' papa. Makin' moon-shine ain't exactly the kind er work experience most bosses wanna heah erbout."

I stretched out on the floor.

Reedy laughed. "Anyway, Mr. Andra, the only way t' keep Jake off y' is t' snitch fer im on them other boys. 'Course if them boys ever caught y', yo' life wutten worth er nickel."

"Y' mean them boys would beat y' up er som'um?"

"No, they wouldn't lay er hand on y'." Reedy slid his finger across his throat. "They'd cut yo' thoat from ear t' ear. I seen that happen. Sucker looked like he had two mouths."

"You saw that happen?"

"We call it 'happy hour.'"

"Happy hour?" Papa asked.

"Ol' crazy Black Nelson named it that."

"Wuz you in that same gang wid Black Nelson?"

"Same gang. But Jake didn't know we knowed each other or he woulda separated us."

"Jake didn't know you 'n Black Nelson knowed each other? But y' both from right heah like he is."

"I tol' y', he acted like he didn't know me. All niggers wuz the same t' him."

"I read in the papers that Black Nelson broke jail, but they didn't give no details. Said som'um erbout one er the whippin' bosses' horse draggin' im while he wuz tryin' t' stop the prisoner, 'n—"

Impatiently, Reedy snapped, "Paper's lyin'."

"Whut?"

"I said the paper's lyin'. I wuz there 'n saw the whole thing."

"Well, whut happened? Whut did Black do that caused Jake t' whip im?"

"Jake *tried* t' whip im. Black Nelson's always sellin' som'um. You know that."

"He's er drummer without er car. I know," Papa said.

"Is Sun 'sleep?" Reedy asked.

I made a snoring sound and snorted.

"Yeah, he's gone. Go on," Papa said.

I was coiled up on the floor with my eyes closed, but my ears were open.

"Well, Black Nelson had been sellin' them dirty books. Jake found out erbout it 'n ordered one of his snitchers t' find out who it wuz. Ordinarily he wouldn't er said nothin' 'cause he knows that Black Nelson is er *bad nigger*. In fact, we used t' call Black 'Mr. Bad Nigger.' But Jake's reputation wuz on the line, so he approached Black while we wuz on a field detail."

Papa laughed and shook his head. "Mr. Bad Nigger."

Sneaking a peep, I saw Reedy lean back against some sacks of feed, when Papa gave him a strawberry Nehi. He swigged on the tall bottle as he told the story.

"Black Nelson let Jake whip im er few lashes. Then he stuck his powerful arm out to ward off the blows from that bloody bullwhip. Finally Black wrapped the long tail of the whip around his left arm. Jake wuz settin' on his horse. He tried t' unravel the whip so he could keep whippin'. When Jake couldn't git the whip unraveled, he made the mistake of wrappin' the other end of the whip around his saddlehorn. Then he put the spurs t' his horse 'n tried t' drag Black Nelson. He did it fer er while till Black wrapped the whip eround er saplin'. The uneven pull caused the belly buckle t' slip. Black Nelson gave one mighty yank 'n the whole saddle came off, takin' Jake wid it.

"Jake had such er mean reputation as er capt'um that sometimes he wouldn't let other guards back im up. He thinks of us black folks like animal trainers think of lions 'n tigers. He knows we got strength 'n muscles, but he don't give us any credit fer havin' any sense at all. He bragged that he could control any nigger he ever saw wid the crack of his whip 'n er pistol t' back im up. He wuz doggone neah right most er the time. Whenever he took er man down, he sel-dom left the comfort of his saddle. All he had t' do wuz order them other nig-gers t' strip er man 'n take im down. It wuz usually er "Yasssuh, Capt'um," 'n they'd overpower the man.

"After Black Nelson pulled Jake off his horse, he unwrapped the whip from the sapling. Then he took up the slack in the whip till he wuz close ernough t' smell Jake's tobacco-smokin', whiskey-stinkin' breath. Jake went fer his gun. Too late! Black Nelson overpowered him, twisted the gun out of his hand 'n kicked it outta reach. Jake hollered fer some of the other prisoners t' grab er hold of im. Two of the prisoners dared t' try t' hold Black Nelson's arms. Black gave one of um a backhand lick that sent im reelin' over some bushes. He stumbled t' his feet bleedin' 'n spittin' blood. The other prisoner took off. 'Grab im, I tell y'!' Jake yelled."

"Did you try t' hep?" Papa asked.

"Meee?" Reedy asked, surprised. "I thought Black wuz doin' er pretty good job widout my hep."

"I meant did y' try t' hep Jake?"

"Jake's horse had gone off 'n started eatin' grass. I figured if his own horse wutten helpin' im, I wutten erbout t'. 'Grab im, I tol' y'!' Jake hollered ergin. None er the prisoners liked Jake, not even the snitchers, but they wuz so scared of im that ernother one tried. Black Nelson sent him bleedin' 'n mop-pin' his mouth with his ragged shirtsleeve same as he'd done the other one.

"Finally, Jake looked dead at me 'n said, 'I'm givin' y' er order, boy. Take this nigger off me 'n take im down!' I stood there 'n looked at im. Whut I saw wuz not the white god settin' high astride a spirited white horse wearin' a white cowboy hat, some strings er yeller hair fallin' in his face, er fierce long bull-whip draggin' the furrows, er pearl-handled pistol hangin' from his side, er long black pipe stickin' outta his mouth 'neath his long red nose 'n over his steam-shovel chin. Whut I saw wuz not the devil-god who drew blood, ripped 'n cut through my back with every lash of his black-snake rawhide. It wuz not the quiet voice of the devil-god whose very sweat that oozed from the armpits of his white cowboy shirt drew fear from young strong black men that he lorded over. That was not whut I saw. Jake wuz dirty 'n bleedin'. His long stringy hair hung in his ugly red face. His gun had been wrestled from his hand 'n kicked out of reach! His bullwhip had been taken from im 'n wuz now in the powerful hands of Capt'um Black.

"Two prisoners had already felt the force of Capt'um Black's backhand blows 'n wanted no mo'. 'N that helpless Jake wuz ordering me t' take Black Nelson down. I'd rather try t' shave er lion. As crazy as that white man wuz, he couldn't begin t' be as crazy as er grinnin' worked-up Black Nelson.

"Black cracked that bullwhip at ernother crazy fool who tried t' rush im. Cut his shirt right off! Left his arms 'n back bleedin'. The rest of um backed off.

"Capt'um Black started givin' Capt'um Jake some of his own medicine. 'N believe you me, Mr. Andra, it wuz some baaaaad stuff! He whipped big bad Jake till the angels in heaven got the message. He whipped im fer ol' 'n new. He whipped im all on his back, his arms, his legs, his face, his fingers, his neck, in the palm of his hands, under the pit of his arms, all underneath his feet—"

Papa fell off the counter laughing. "Reedy! Boy! You go on erway from heah wid yo' crazy self!"

"I ain't lyin', Mr. Andra. I felt like I wuz in er revival meetin' on the moaner's bench. I wuz so full er the Holy Spirit that I wanted t' shout!" Reedy said.

"Reedy, that wutten no Holy Spirit you wuz full of," Papa informed him.

"It sho felt like it." Reedy raised his clasped hands in the air. "Our Father who art in heaven must've made er note er that beatin'. He whipped Jake's white ass—'cuse me, Mr. Andra—till his soul wuz satisfied! Then he jumped on Jake's white horse 'n rode off. Never befo' had black men witnessed such er righteous whippin' fer such er righteous cause so well taken care of under Arkansas' hot sun!"

A few days after Reedy told Papa—us—his story, who came hobbling into our closing store but Jake Parsons! He looked like something left by a tornado. His right arm was in a sling. He had bandages all over his head and half of his face. His fancy cowboy shoes had been replaced by ugly house slippers. His khaki pants had been cut almost up to his behind, and white bandages were showing on his legs. He was moving like Mr. Durbey shortly before he died. Nevertheless, he still puffed on his long black pipe that stuck out over his steam-shovel chin. Reedy was right, Black Nelson almost killed Jake. Anybody else would have been in bed, precisely where he belonged.

"How you, M.A.?"

"P-p-pretty good, Mr. . . . Parsons. How you?" Papa finally got it out.

"I been better, as y' can see."

Papa moved fast to get Jake a seat before he fell. "Why-why don't y' set down heah, Mr. Parsons?"

"This is still er place er business, ain't it? Not some place t' hang out."

"It's been known fer both. Pretty soon it won't be either one," Papa said.

"Whut y' mean, M.A.?"

"We closin' out, Mr. Parsons. Business ain't whut it useta be. Cain't keep goin' when times is hard like this 'n don't seem like it gon' change soon."

"Thought that new Pike brought y' lots er business."

"Did fer er while, but they done moved on down the line. Whut kin I git fer y', Mr. Parsons?"

"Couple er packages er Old Granger, box er matches, 'n er ten-inch file."

"Erfraid I can't hep y' on the file, Mr. Parsons."

"You are closin' out. Never knowed y' t' be outta files."

"Sold the last one yestiddy. Anything else?"

"Naw. I guess that'll wrap it up, M.A."

The horn blew outside.

"Keep yo' shirt on, woman! Byyy God."

"That Miz Birdie out there?"

"Yeaaaah. She didn't want me t' come up heah. You know how that is."

"Sho do. But she's got er point, till y' git well."

"Now don't you start, M.A."

"No sir. I read som'um erbout yo' accident, 'n I wanted t' git down theah t' see y', but I cain't git eround any mo'. Them spirited horses kin be dangerous. I reckon y' kin never be too careful wid um."

"Got m' foot caught in the stirrup. Damned horse drug m'. . . musta been er mile or mo'. I'm lucky t' be erlive, M.A."

I wanted badly to say, "It looks more as if he drug you fifty miles."

Papa, probably thinking the same thing, covered it up. "That bad, wuz it?"

"Pretty bad, M.A. Pretty bad."

"Well, one good thing, y' still wid us. Thank God," Papa lied.

"Yep, M.A. Guess the Ol' Man wutten ready fer m' yet."

I could hardly contain myself. I wanted to say, "The Ol' Man may not have been ready, but I'm quite sure Black Nelson, Reedy, and those convicts were." I was glad my buddy Ben wasn't there. Nothing could have kept him from laughing at those two grown men standing there lying to each other. He would have been stretched out in the middle of the floor, as he usually was, kicking like a fool, completely out of control.

"The Lord's blessed y', Mr. Parsons. I guess y'll be goin' back on yo' job in er few weeks."

"Naaaaw, M.A. Ten yeahs is ernough."

"It's been ten yeahs?"

"It woulda been ten yeahs this fall. I had ernuff. I neglected m' farm, m' cattle . . . My wife, Birdie, claims I neglected her . . . "

The truck horn blew again.

"Thought I tol' y' t' lay off that horn, woman! See whut I mean? How much do I owe y', M.A.?" Jake picked up his bag.

"Oooooh, that'll beeee ten, ten 'n five, twenty-five cents, Mr. Parsons."

Jake tried to reach for his money sack with his right hand but couldn't reach it. "Kin y' git that fer m', M.A.?"

"Sure thing, Mr. Parsons." Papa reached in Jake's back pocket and gave him his money bag.

Jake sat the bag on the counter and fished out a quarter. "There y' are, M.A."

"Thank y', Mr. Parsons. Sorry I cain't say hurry back, but as y' kin see, I don't have much left."

"Wish it wuz otherwise, M.A. Y' run er good business heah fer many yeahs."

The horn blew again.

"Byyy God! That woman's gonna drive m' t' drink, some mo'. You take it easy, M.A." Jake hobbled out the door swearing at Miz Birdie, and she was swearing right back.

"You too, Mr. Parsons. Give m' best t' yo' papa."

Jake yelled back, "That ol' dog won't hunt no mo'. I ain't givin' him nothin'."

Papa stood and watched Jake go out the door and struggle to get into his truck. He chuckled. "Well, I declare. Ain't nothin' like fear t' make er white man stop actin' like he thinks he's God. After he's done all that sinnin' 'n killin' of black folks, he finally met his match in that crazy Black Nelson. Now he's tryin' t' crawl back 'n be er human being. But he misses the point entirely. He ain't er bit sorry fer whut he did, but he's plenty sorry 'n 'shamed he got caught. 'Course most sinners is like that. They wait till they at death's do' befo' they start worryin' erbout they soul's salvation."

"Yes sir," I said.

29

"Aw right, boy. Cut out all that noise. Rise 'n shine."

"Oh, man! Y' jist saved m' life." I shook my head, relieved.

"Whut y' mean? Somebody after y'?"

"Barkin' lions," I said.

"We goin' t' the Flats this morning. Got t' cut er load 'n git on t' town befo' it gits too late."

Happy to be alive, still happier to be called upon to be my older brother's helper, I bounced out of bed, jumped into my clothes, then joined Elbert and Papa at the breakfast table for some hot buttered biscuits, molasses, and buttermilk. We loaded the wagon and were off to the Flats.

The Flats were part of the land Grandpa Hughes had left. During early spring when Bartholomew overflowed, water backed up in Alligator Creek, ran through his land, and flooded most of the Flats. When the water drained, residue was left that gave the Flats very rich soil. When I asked why they chose the hilly land for crops instead of the Flats, Papa explained that we could get more crops during the year where the land didn't flood.

Over the years, Uncle Pet had bought his brothers out, and now he owned the Flats. Being a merchant, Papa didn't need or want a lot of land. He did maintain certain timber rights, however, when he sold to Uncle Pet. Those rights did not stop Uncle Pet from complaining when he thought Papa was cutting too much—especially when it was the expensive white oak.

As the wagon trundled past Grandpa Hughes's old homestead on Wagon Road West, we came to a fork. Elbert took the road to the left. It was a narrower road that hadn't been traveled much. Weeds and bushes covered its path, and it was necessary to cut and remove fallen trees and limbs before we could continue. Suddenly the road ran out and we came into an expansive, panoramic clearing.

The fat flat land lay sleeping beneath a blanket of brown dead leaves, dead logs, and dead branches. It was one of the few times I had been in the Flats in my entire ten years. How soft and forgiving the brown blanket was beneath my boots. How ancient and quaint. How glad the tall, slender, stately oaks stood guard against any intrusion into their Alligator Creek heaven. Even in winter their bushy heads gathered moplike at the top of a long handsome trunk and mingled with evergreens, leafless vines, squirrel's nests, and owl's nests high above the quiet landscape, blocking out the seeping sun. How dark and deep with mysteries spawned before my time. Before Papa's time. Even before Grandpa Hughes's time. This land—this *before* land. This *now* and *after* land. This land of my father's father. This all but forgotten land. Our own lumber land, deposited, and now being called upon to yield some of its red oaks to help us through this ugly year—this ugly time.

That forgotten land of Papa's boyhood was an unquestionable echo chamber. When Elbert walked off a distance, looking for dead oaks first, he yelled, "Over here!" The sound of his voice vibrated through the trees for miles around.

Papa told us stories of deer, bobcat, timber wolves, black bear, and panther that made their home in the Flats. I immediately asked, "Whut are we doin' heah?" Papa assured me that people had long since forced those wonderful creatures to move. Their voices were no longer heard in those parts. Only the ghostly legacy of their past lingered in old men like Mr. Joe Bearden and Mr. Durbey, as long as he was alive.

We returned to the Flats many times that winter. Papa had shown us what trees to cut when thinning a forest and which ones to leave standing. As spring approached, Papa's feet became so bad that he could no longer go to the Flats with us. He was forced to trust Elbert and me to go into the deep dark woods without him.

Soon the bottom dropped out of the wood business, but we kept peddling. Elbert was forced to break his own rule and take 75 cents for a load he normally got twice that much for.

We had heard the *tramp-tramp-tramp* before as our loaded wagon clucked out of the woods. I had asked Elbert to stop, but he was always in a hurry to get his load to town. I had other ideas and didn't hesitate to tell him. "Y' think that's er ghost of some of them wild animals hantin' these woods, don't y'?"

"Whut y' mean?" Elbert cut his eyes at me.

"Y' know. All them stories Mr. Durbey tol' erbout bein' raised by an ol' mama bear. 'N the one erbout Papa's cousin outrunnin' a panther."

"Y' think them stories scare me?"

"Yeah. I do."

"Shoooot! I'm er man. You ain't nothin' but er snotty-nosed boy. 'N you think I'm scared like you."

"Tell y' whut. Since you think I'm so snotty-nosed 'n scared, if y' stop the wagon, I'll go see whut's makin' that trampin' noise."

"Woooah!" Elbert stopped the wagon and hopped down. "You so big, bad, 'n brave, let's see whut y' gon' do."

I hopped off the wagon, grabbed an ax, and headed back to the thicket where I heard the tramping. I was shaking in my bowels, but I couldn't let Elbert know that.

"Hey! Wait er minute!" Elbert yelled when he saw I meant business. He took the other ax off the wagon and joined me. "Y' crazy, y' know that? One er these times y' gon' git mor'n y' asked fer."

We chopped away the underbrush as we crept slowly and carefully toward the increasing sound of the *tramp-tramp-tramp*.

"Whut do y' think—"

"Ssssssh!" Elbert shut me up. As we hacked away and got closer, the tramping noise became louder and more rhythmic. It sounded like the very heartbeat of the earth. As if it knew no time. No beginning. No ending.

We kept hacking away. Finally we broke through on a trampled circular path. The splintered remains of a big oak had died in a fight with the powerful god of lightning. In its death struggle, instead of strong limbs that bore acorns for sows and boars and rested the nests of owls and squirrels, its craggy twisted fingers pointed in all directions, some straight toward the heavens. The rest of its mangled body lay dying and bleeding as it seasoned for our crosscut saw. If not cut for wood, it would decay into the rich soil as so many of its ancestors had done. For now, however, the dead snag was the eternal circular track, a sight that moved me to tremble, around which a dying billy goat was destined to trundle day and night until it wasted away. As in my dream, death must surely be the unrealized, the unrehearsed, the ultimate of all nothingness, the firmament and author of all *unneccessarylessness*.

Split, snaggled, narrow hooves tooling and retooling the same mulch of leaves, twigs, grass, dirt, and droppings, *tramp-tramp-tramp* to the dull rhythm of a throbbing pain, exerting the same energy as feet mashing grapes, only it is not for "what the wine sellers buy." Above the haggard hooves, bony legs connected to bulging ball-shaped knees that lazily bent mechanically to execute each step. Shaggy, mud-knotted hair hung from its belly like old wallpaper from a leaking ceiling. On his back and down his protruding ribbed side, splashes of white skin showed where the hanging hair had peeled off. When he rotated so I could see his rear, two lean balls hung down like zucchini squash. From his waste canal, defecated excretion mixed with debris to form beads that dragged the ground dangling as he tramped. Below the puffed, displaced, rancid nose and jaw, an ugly grin revealed bare bone and teeth. Above the jaw was a wound that had pierced the right eye and caused such a transformation. An insipid imitation of life in limbo. A latter-day zombie.

As we stood and watched, the goat never broke his pace. He never looked or acknowledged our presence. *Tramp-tramp-tramp*. His head was turned toward the dead trunk of the big oak. I threw a stick in his path, trying to get his attention. The stick broke his gait only momentarily. When it was pushed aside by the constant tramping, the death rhythm resumed. Elbert and I looked at each other. We couldn't believe our eyes.

"Wonder how long he's been like that?" Elbert said.

"I heard this trampin' a week ago, remember?"

"Yeah. I remember. You did mention it."

"I wonder why is he holdin' his head like that?" I asked.

"Y' mean all twisted t' one side?"

"Yeah."

"He musta been in er fight. Besides his eye, one er his horns is messed up, 'n the thing got infected."

"That musta been it. Either that or lightning struck him, like that tree. Look at them green flies swarming all over his head." I thought about Mr. Durbey, how the green flies were swarming all over his mouth and down his throat.

Suddenly we smelled the full stink of rotting flesh.

"That's a drop-dead stink if I ever smelt one," Elbert said.

"I've never known a goat t' smell good at his very best. How do y' expect one t' smell that's rottin' on his feet?"

I noticed maggots dropping from the side of his head and wiggling on the ground.

"The maggots is eatin' his brains," I said.

"Wonder how much longer will he last like that?"

"He's already been goin' for er week. He's the walkin' dead. No tellin' how much longer he can last. Don't y' think we oughtta put im out of his misery?"

"We don't know whose goat it is. Let's go," Elbert said.

We climbed back on the wagon and continued toward the Pike. We could hear the *tramp-tramp-tramp* in the distance.

We always stopped and tried to feed the dying goat some hay on each trip we made to the Flats, only to have it trampled into the ground. His tramping had slowed considerably. Finally he was barely moving. Winding down like an old clock. His spunky *tramp-tramp* rhythm had died down to a drag. His stink had sent a message to the big chicks, and they were perched in the nearby trees. Dressed in their black funeral suits, the undertakers waited.

"Why don't they attack 'n git it over with? Theah's enuff of um."

"Big chicks don't attack nothin' till they sure it's dead," Elbert responded.

"They won't have much when they git him. He's almost wasted away," I reasoned.

"Buzzards'll take whut they kin git."

We had cut our load that day so Elbert could get an early start the next morning. After we clucked and rocked a short distance, we came to a limb that had fallen across the rough rutted road. Elbert drove around it. That took us into the brush. Suddenly the horse and mule reared up, tucked their tails, and tried to run. They had stumbled into an awakening hornet's nest. I was thrown from the spring-cushioned seat we were sitting on, directly in front of the wheels of the loaded wagon. Fortunately the seat fell on top of me. The front and rear wheels of the loaded wagon ran over the seat with me underneath. Elbert leaped off the wagon and ran back to where I was lying.

"Y' hurt? Sun, y' hurt?" He pulled the seat off me.

I got up slowly. "I—I don't . . . think so . . ."

I didn't feel that anything was crushed or broken. Other than being speechless, I was okay. My mind flashed back to being smothered by that seat as those wheels rolled over my head and body. *Suppose that seat hadn't cushioned the heavy wheels. I might have been killed or hurt so badly I would never be the same.*

As spring approached and the rains came, Elbert and I made our last trip to the Flats. Customers were no longer buying winter wood. The small amount they bought for cooking wasn't worth the effort. Besides, the rains were flooding the Flats as they did each year.

We had long since given up on feeding the goat and had even stopped watching his death march. That being our last trip, we stopped to pay what was left of him one last visit. We knew he must be dead and that the hovering black-suited undertakers had taken their toll. When we approached the treaded circle, it was quiet and gloomy. No more tramping. No more rhythm of the march. The goat's skeleton lay at the south end of the snag. Small pieces of soggy brown hair were scattered over the path. Black greasy spots remained as a dreary reminder.

Papa's eyes were worse. Home remedies came from many people. The insulin wasn't doing the job. Papa wouldn't stay on his diet, even though the sores on his feet had spread to his legs and other parts of his body. He would eat his diet food while Mama was watching. At night he would sneak into the kitchen and gobble down a whole pie or half of a layer cake.

One of the home remedies suggested was the mother's milk of a young woman who had a suckling baby. A brown buxom young woman laid her baby on a pallet next to the window in the parlor. When she squatted and placed the pillow just so, I could see her cleavage. She rose and took off her shawl. Her bulging breast was full of milk that leaked from her protruding nipples. She was jolly—laughed a lot. I had never seen her before. Why was she here? She removed her colorful bandanna and revealed bushy black hair. With her dimpled cheeks and perfect white teeth, she was a joy to look at. They closed the door, but I peeped through what I had come to regard as my keyhole and saw Papa sitting on the couch with his head leaning back. The young woman took out one of her large breasts and squirted milk into Papa's eyes. Mama and other women were wiping splattered milk from his face and clothes.

*   *   *

It was an early spring that nineteen-hundred-and-thirty-third year. It was only mid-March. Mama said she wanted an early garden to help feed the family, especially since Papa's remedy business had been so bad the fall of 1932, and the store had closed. Plowing of the garden preceded all farming. We turned every inch of soil, created new rows, and put fertilizer in each trench before we planted.

I had turned eleven in the fall of 1932. I had begged Papa since I was nine to let me plow. I pointed out to him that I was keeping pace with Elbert on the other end of a crosscut saw. I was splitting and stacking winter wood. On several occasions, Elbert had let me drive the team out of the Flats (of course we never told Papa about the wagon running over me). I could also keep pace with my older sisters when it came to hoeing, husking, and gathering crops.

"I'd better git Reedy. Er man kin git mo' respect out of er mule." Papa pondered. "I don't believe in er boy plowin' befo' he's twelve."

"Elbert plowed when he was ten," I countered. "'N he wuz workin' on the new highway as er mule skinner befo' he wuz thirteen."

Papa was quiet for a moment. "Think we oughtta let him try it, Elbert?"

"Won't hurt t' let im try it."

"Hook that mule up 'n see whut he kin do wid that turn plow." Papa relented.

Elbert did the first three turns to give me the idea. Then he gave it to me. The sharp shining blade of the earth tool cut with ice-cream-dipper precision into the caked, loamy loaf with dead grass on top and peeled off eight-inch swirls, lap after gleaming lap.

To me it was wizardry. A transforming constancy in action. I was controlling nature with a shining tool. A swift-moving mule. My voice and the tilt of my fingers on the plow handles steadied the peeling. To get the mule to go right, not a shrill, sharp "Geeeeeeee!" but a quiet, self-assured, deep-voiced manly "Geeeeee-e-e-e." If the command was not obeyed, up the volume but maintain the deep manly voice.

"Never let the mule get the idea that you're only ten years old, you don't know whut you're doin', and you're scared of im. Even though all of that's true," Elbert advised me.

"I already know that 'Geeee' means right, 'Hawwwww' means left, 'n 'Whuaah' means stop. Why y' tellin' me that?"

"Yeah, y' do. The mule knows that too, but if he gits the idea that you're weak or shaky erbout it by the way y' say it, he ain't gon' pay y' no mind."

I showed that Elbert. I lowered my voice to a miserable trembling pitch that scratched my throat. I barely whispered "Muuullle" when I wanted him to go, "Whuuuaaaah" for stop. For "Geeeee" and "Haaaaaw," I literally growled in my best man's voice. Papa and Elbert laughed all day. My growling and straining, however, had turned a big beautiful swatch of land by three in the afternoon, and I was ready for the next patch.

When I looked at the dark shining swirls glistening in the sun, I was beside myself with a feeling of accomplishment, since I knew that earlier that morning that same dead brown field lay decimated by winter. Perhaps this was an introduction, at last, into my brother Elbert's class of manhood. Who knows? The next step could be wearing Papa's watch fob or even sharing part of his treasured hoecake!

Before taking on another patch, Papa and Elbert showed me how to prepare fresh new rows for planting. Elbert hitched the team to the harrow. Then he pulled it over my beautiful swirls until the clods were broken into a billion pieces and the plot leveled smooth and granular. Elbert hitched one animal to a plow that had a ten-inch blade. Papa hobbled to the far end of the patch and stood still. Elbert pointed his mule directly at Papa, using the space between the mule's ears for his sight. After that he laid off each row three feet from the one before. Then he hitched two animals up to pull the mighty middle-buster. That plow was big and bad with a sharp blade. The shining wings of the middle-buster threw the rows into a pile and left a big clean ditch for water between each row. Then he passed the harrow over the new rows and leveled each one very much as he had leveled the swirled patch. He used a six-inch blade to open a small ditch in each row. We placed fertilizer in the ditches, and the rows were ready for planting. Mama and the girls came in for that precious task. Quite often all other work ceased and everyone took a bucket full of seeds.

"Make sure you put them pole beans three feet apart," Mama ordered. "Put the corn two feet apart. Trail the radishes and the beets. I'll do the squash m'self. Be careful wid them tomato plants. We don't have too many this yeah."

"Whut erbout the sweet potatoes, Kitty?" Papa asked.

"We'll git t' them tomorrow."

After the seeds were planted, everybody, except Papa, grabbed a rake or a hoe and covered the seeds. This had to be done quickly before the birds unplanted the seeds we had just put down.

Within a week, we had planted most of Mama's big early garden. We then started breaking ground in the fields for corn, sorghum, peanuts, potatoes, and a few acres of the almighty cash crop, king cotton. I developed into a real plowboy. I was even currying and harnessing my own mule. I took up the slack in the chains when the plow blade was running too deep. I put on the feed bag at dinnertime. I unhitched and took my mule to Alligator Creek before we started work for the afternoon.

We had cut most of the red oak on our farmland over past winters. This year Papa took the opportunity to clear off a good-sized patch near Alligator Creek. It was not a matter of thinning out some of the trees so others could grow, but cutting everything and burning the underbrush. Only stumps were left. Stumps were a nuisance. Hard to plow around because of the roots, they were one of the drawbacks to rich new ground. Cultivating plants in new ground was also more difficult because of the looseness of the soil and the tenderness of the fast-growing plants. In spite of the troubles, the abundance of the crops made it all worthwhile.

In early May the garden had been picked for its first givens, and the fields bristled with growth and promise of a good crop. Blessed rains and warm nights were mother's milk for happy plants that wafted in nocturnal breezes, and the hand of God calmed the troubled waters.

"Exodus chapter ten, fourth verse. 'Else, if thou refuse to let my people go, behold, tomorrow will bring the locusts into thy coast: And they shall cover the face of the earth, that one cannot be able to see the earth: and they shall eat the residue of that which is escaped, which remaineth unto you from the hail, and shall eat every tree which groweth for you out of the field.'"

"That wuz er good readin', Sun, but whut do y' think it means?" the fat Sister Grey inquired, peeping over her funny-looking wire-framed glasses.

I didn't have the foggiest idea what Sister Grey might want it to mean. I had heard sermons about how God sent locusts into Egypt and they had destroyed the crops—even the trees—plenty of times. The preachers had dwelled on the subject longer and more often than I thought I needed. Besides, I thought the Bible reading explained things in detail quite beyond my feeble powers to improve them.

I didn't dare say it, but I harbored the same thoughts about big dumb Fat-Fingers, Sister Grey, as I did about myself. Having had her for my Sunday school teacher for over a year, I realized that whatever explanation I might give wouldn't satisfy her hungry ignorance. She would only go into some long drawn-out rope-jumping verbiage and leave the whole class in a state of epileptic seizures showing how little she knew. I also knew that if I complained, a little boy's thoughts about one of The Faithful carried so little weight that a grunt could have changed the balance. Therefore I didn't need to think long about my answer to her question.

"I don't know, Miz Grey."

"Aawww, don't gimma that, Sun. You smart. Y' read that better'n me."

That was not a compliment, considering the fact that Sister Fat-Fingers Grey stumbled over her own lips when she attempted to read.

My regular Sunday school teacher had left, and Sister Grey was substituting until Papa could find someone more qualified. Since Papa was superintendent of the Sunday school, I asked him how long it would take to find somebody better qualified. I wanted to say that I felt better qualified, if that was all he was waiting for, but that, of course, would have been disrespecting a grown-up—one of The Faithful at that.

I approached it another way. "Papa, do you suppose God would be mad at me if I changed to Deacon Thomas's Sunday school class?"

"Whut fer? That's fer older kids."

"Miz Grey reads too good. Sometimes I don't understand her."

"Boy, whut you talkin' erbout?" Papa looked at me out of the corner of his eyes.

"Well, when she comes to a big word in the Bible, instead er backin' up, gittin' er good fresh start, 'n jumpin' right over that word, she'll stand right there 'n fight wid it. She's so smart that the next thing y' know she's changed it t' er brand-new word."

Papa twisted the corner of his mouth. It was a familiar habit when he was about to laugh. "Sister Grey is only fillin' in."

"Fer two yeahs?"

"Askin' her t' move now would hurt her feelings. Besides, who would I git t' take her place?"

Any other English-speaking person, I wanted to say.

We left the fields early because of a hailstorm. After the storm, the afternoon sun reappeared full-blown and spat at us in anger. As we descended Blueberry Hill, a persistent humming sound invaded our space. Mysteriously, low-flying dark clouds descended upon our heads. The team neighed nervously and broke into a trot. Our cur whined and ran beneath the moving wagon. Birds dotted through trees looking for shelter. Young cottontails scurried into the woods. Rusty toads hopped hurriedly across Wagon Road West. The humming volume and dark clouds intensified. We were cast into darkness, roosters crowed, owls hooted, and dogs howled in the distance. Before we could get out of the wagon, missiles flew into our faces. The strange insects covered our straw hats, our arms, our hands, our legs, our entire bodies. Then we heard them filling the wagon bed and the buckets like falling hail. They crawled all over the horse and mule. The animals were almost out of control as we worked desperately to unharness them and get them inside the barn.

"Oh my God! Oh my God!" Papa uttered desperately.

"They heah! They heah, Andra!" Mama said as she hurried to get us inside.

"All that hard work, seeds, everything, wasted—lost."

"Whut is these things, Papa? Grasshoppers?" Deloris inquired.

"They grasshoppers, all right! The worst kind. I ain't seen these things eround heah since befo' you wuz born."

"They locust, ain't they, Papa?"

"How'd you know that, Sun?"

"I read erbout um in Sunday school."

We fought the busy pest as best we could, crushing and smashing them with boards, buckets, shovels, our bare hands—anything we could find. After they had settled in the trees, on the roofs, on the windows, on the sides of our house, the store, the barn, the chicken house, the flowers, the grass, all over the road, we were able to see a bleary, blinking sun's mighty red eye disappearing behind a speckled locust horizon.

Elbert, Papa, and I rushed into the house as soon as we had closed the animals inside their stalls and fed them. Inside, Mama and the girls had closed all windows and sealed all cracks by stuffing them with rags. As we prepared to eat supper inside, supper was being eaten outside as well. Our night began with the sound of an eternal gnawing and sawing.

When I tried to look out the window, it was covered with the menacing creatures. In the evening shadows I could see them darting through the sickened air. We were completely surrounded!

With all the windows closed, it was baking inside. I felt stifled and smothered. As the gnawing and sawing went on, tiny chips like pebbles were sprinkling the roof, the ground, and everything that lay bare.

The next morning when we went outside, the ground was covered with green leaves they had stripped from the trees. Trees stood naked and stark before a merciless sun. Fortunately, the brown horsefly-sized grasshopper menace was short-lived. The millions that lived and gnawed away did so over the dead bodies of their own kind. As they died on the ground, they were in the process of eating the residue of the leaves that had fallen.

Chickens, geese, gunnies, ducks, birds, and hogs feasted on the insect carcasses. Dogs didn't know exactly what to do with the ancient pest. After a few attempts at eating the wingy, fidgety things, they gave up and looked for something more appetizing and filling.

Mama dreaded coming outside. When she did, she moved slowly and sadly through the few flower beds we had been able to salvage when the new Pike went through. Only short stems were left. She went to the garden we had planted by the house. It was devastated. She looked up at the fruit trees, whose limbs had been sagging with young fruit. The limbs were stripped bare. Those that were not, soon would be because the devil's grasshoppers were busy finishing their total destruction.

Elbert and I had harnessed the team and were waiting for the family to load so we could visit the fields. The wagon clucked slowly up Wagon Road West. It was indeed an eerie feeling riding through that barren desertlike community of trees. Stark, stripped, helpless stalagmites where only yesterday there was a heavenly grove arched overhead, thick with sounds of life and nature's greens. As we expected, the garden was ravaged. Stripped of every bean. Every pea. Every leaf on the young sweet potato vine. Every bloom and leaf on okra stalks. Every young squash and blooming promise of squashes to come. Every waving leaf on every cornstalk. All vegetation.

Elbert and I walked through the slushy green residue of leaves and plants of all descriptions mixed with the nasty bodies of those ancient soldiers of death. Before we reached the fields, we could smell the strange odor of the dead and dying marauders mixed with that of freshly destroyed plants.

The fields were full of birds, frogs, lizards, tortoises, and ants claiming their share of the dead and dying locusts. As we neared Alligator Creek, we had to be careful. Snakes had crawled up from the creek to gobble down the free meal. In the creek, fish rose to the top and snapped the floating brown bodies. We crossed the creek. Cotton and corn had been growing on that side. Nothing but stripped stalks. The new ground, which had been thick with tall tasseling blue-green corn—five and six ears to the stalk—looked as if they ate it for dessert. The stalks were pitifully naked.

Hughes Chapel's farmers and truck patchers were standing around on the littered grounds beneath the barren shadeless oaks discussing the nature of the devils, and their losses.

"They come every seven yeahs."

"Every four hundred, I heard."

"Bible says they come in heah from Egypt."

"Wheah you see that in the Bible?"

"It's in theah . . ."

"Wheah?"

"They already cleaned me out. Wonder how much longer they gon' stay?"

"They erbout died out now. 'Magine doin' all that damage in fo' days . . ."

Then all The Faithful there assembled filed inside and began praising the Lord. Once again Pastor Jarrett called on Uncle Pet to lead us in prayer. Once again the moaning began and continued through the prayer and the service.

> *I-I-I-I love the Lord,*
> *He heard my cry-y-y-y* (repeat in moaning fashion)
> *An-n-n-nd pitied every groan-n-n-n* (repeat in moaning
>   fashion)
> *Lo-o-n-n-n-g-g-g as I live*
> *When trouble riiiis-s-s-s-e* (repeat in moaning fashion)
> *I-I-I'l-l-l-l hasten to His throne-e-e-e.*

Many of the songs were uplifting, spiritual, sad, but beautiful. Moaning made me feel none of those emotions. I always felt devastated, powerless, under siege. Moaning was not even considered singing. It was meant to cause humility, submission, a complete sense of inadequacy. As if there weren't too many of those feelings among The Faithful already.

Soon they would pull out the bench, and revival would begin. This year we could start a month early. The devil's grasshoppers had ushered in an ancient hell and laid by our crops for us.

30

Hazel and her husband, Silvester—
who had moved next door, into the store—started to rumble. We heard blows
and screams. We hurried over to see Hazel's lips and eyes puffed up and her
face a bloody mess.

"Whut's wrong over heah? Silvester, whut's wrong wid you? Y' lost yo'
mind?" Papa asked.

"Whut you do wid your'n when she git outta line, Father?" Silvester always
paid Papa great respect, even when beating up his daughter.

"I never hit Kitty er day in her life! Y' carrin' on like that trash up theah on
the hill. I declare!" Papa looked closely at what had been a smooth, pretty face.
"Look at yo' face! I want y' to git yo' things 'n come home wid me right now."

Hazel dabbed at her swollen lips with a wet towel in an effort to stop the
bleeding and get the swelling down. At her best, she was considered the prettiest of all the girls. She had very soft, smooth black skin. She had a well-shaped
nose, just right. Her forehead and the general shape of her face were a perfect
oval; the pointed part formed her chin. Her lovely face was set off by a bushy
haze of thick black hair. Her constant ready smile revealed perfect white teeth.
Her eyes were big round brown moons that sparkled under natural long eyelashes and eyebrows, which she was constantly shaping. Added to the blessings
nature had provided her was a pleasing disposition and a soft voice, which one
had to listen to very carefully in order to hear. She had inherited our mother's
temperament, including her shyness. I had never seen my sister Hazel lose her
temper—until the moment Papa told her to get her things and come home.

That formerly angelic, beat-up model of a young woman stood up and hobbled over to Papa, put her hands on her hips, and conjured up a voice I had
never heard before. With fervor and vibrato she announced, "Papa, I'm not a
li'l girl anymore. And I'll thank y' to stop treatin' me like one. I'm a full-grown
woman, and I married who I wanted to marry. I didn't marry Bill Wilson,
'cause I don't love Bill Wilson. You *love* Bill Wilson so much, marry him yo'-
self!" Papa was startled. He stopped in his tracks.

"Maybe y' wouldn't look like y' been kicked in the face by er mule if y'd
married Bill Wilson. This is no man! This is somethin' in britches! Y' oughtta
be ershamed er yo'self!"

Tall, handsome, athletic-looking Silvester sat on the edge of the table, pulled at the sleeves of his T-shirt, and looked out the window as if he was expecting someone to come in and help him.

"Sooo, Silvester 'n me had er li'l fight, that's our business! And I will thank you t' stay out of—"

"Y' call that er fight? 'N-'n y' call yo'self er Hughes? I got calves 'n chickens wid mo' sense 'n you, chile. Who do y' take after anyhow?"

"I'll jist thank y' t' leave Silvester 'n me be."

Papa stopped talking to Hazel and turned to Silvester. "I jist got one mo' thing t' say. If y' gonna stay over heah in this sto', don't ever hit her ergin. I may not be much good anymo', but she my flesh 'n blood, 'n I won't stand t' see her treated like this right in front er my eyes."

Silvester dropped his head like a little boy and spoke in a low hoarse voice. "I understand y', Father."

"Y' jist mind yo' own business, Papa. Silvester 'n me will give y' yo' ol' sto'."

Papa shook his head in disgust and walked out. My heart fell with his. It was my first lesson in the victim's denial in my family. I knew Hazel loved Papa, even while she was sassing him. Udell was the only other man I'd ever seen beat his wife—wives. I couldn't understand why they didn't leave any better than I could understand Hazel. On the contrary, they clung to Udell more than ever. Papa mumbled something like "Never thought I'd see the day er chile er mine'd sass me like that." He sat in the swing on his front porch and fanned himself with his hat. I went to the well, drew him a bucket of cool water, and brought it to him.

Papa was desperate for money. The locusts had left us hard-pressed. He had already exhausted his money for supplies and animal feed. Food for us was plentiful, however.

Papa, being a gentleman farmer and a merchant, hadn't mastered the art of raising enough feed for our farm animals to last from one harvest to the next, as Uncle Pet had done. While he had the store, and money was coming in from his trading during the cotton season, the feed problem didn't exist. Having to depend solely on farming, which he never cared for, clearly took him out of his element. Consequently, during the period before crops were laid by on July Fourth until harvest, we had to buy oats, corn, bran, and sometimes even hay. It wasn't that we didn't have the land; it was the unwise use of the land and the failure to protect crops with good fences. No one could control droughts or locusts—which came about every seven years. However, with pesticides, the worms, beetles, and birds could be reasonably controlled. And allowing cattle, mules, horses, and hogs to simply break through a weak fence was unforgivable. Those animals could do more damage in one night than all the insects and pests of the entire summer.

When one of Papa's mules would stuff his stomach with green plants, it bloated him. We would find him lying near the house moaning and groaning with a bellyache. Mr. Sam Riley, who prided himself on being an animal doctor, would run his arm up to his shoulder into the rear of the animal and pull out the undigested stinking horseshit, often to no avail. Once a mule or horse went down with a bloated belly, it seldom arose. With whatever team we had left, we would tie a rope around the animal's hind legs and drag the inflated carcass bouncing and dripping deep into the woods. The place and time of the funeral service was soon noted by the black-suited buzzards we called big chicks, ceremoniously circling the hot summer skies over the spot where the body lay. Papa would have to buy another nag at a time when he could least afford it.

The year 1933 brought overloads to our troubles. Papa was forced to close the store. For the first time, the entire family had been hired out to chop cotton earlier that spring. I knew Papa was sinking when he spent most of the hot summer days finding odd jobs for Mr. Sam Riley and his son, Reedy. He also managed to get the old Chevy off blocks and running again.

When we pulled up in the driveway, Papa almost ran over a sawhorse that had been left too close. That was another warning that diabetes was taking its toll on his eyes. I covered my ears as he put the old Chevy in reverse. It sounded as if he had been taking gear-stripping lessons. He finally got it in reverse, and the car jumped and bucked backward. It barely missed a tall stranger, who hopped up on an embankment out of danger. When Papa put it in first to go forward, the stranger playfully jumped all the way up on the embankment and stood there grinning.

Mr. Sam Riley, who had been talking to the stranger, walked up to the car laughing. "Hold it there, cowboy. If Brer Durbey wuz alive, he'd wanna shoe that filly fer y'."

"I could sho use some new tires, Sam Riley," Papa said as he crawled out of the car.

"'Fraid y' gon' have t' take that wild bronco elsewhere, Andra," Mr. Sam said, and laughed.

The tall stranger came down off the embankment and joined in the laughter as if he was an old friend. Papa looked at him and waited for an introduction.

Mr. Sam stopped laughing. "Andra, want y' t' meet er young fella heah calls hisself . . . Dor . . . Dor—"

"Dobrite Gangarist from Texas. Glad t' meet y', Mr. Hughes. Mr. Riley heah wuz tellin' me erbout y'." He vigorously extended his hand.

Papa was caught off guard, half smiling but more curious than anything. "Mr. . . . . Gangright?" Dobrite's dress was conspicuous. It looked like a costume.

"Dobrite Gangarist," Dobrite corrected him.

His physical appearance was his calling card. He was well over six feet tall and well built. His hair was closely clipped and edged just so. He had a rich, smooth, dark brown complexion that bespoke city life—not exposed to hard work and the hot sun. His big well-manicured hands looked the same way. He sported a light tan pair of riding pants, something we only saw white people wear—wealthy ones at that. He had on a beautiful pair of highly shined tan riding boots. Though the weather was too hot—sweat was pouring down his face—he wore a well-tailored western leather vest loaded with shiny silver brads and strips of leather hanging from everywhere. Beneath the vest he had the stamina to wear an open-collar, string-tied, embroidered western shirt. He topped all that off with a wide-brim ten-gallon hat with an ornate black band. His hat was tipped elegantly to the side of his rather long head.

Nothing was spared that might accentuate Dobrite's western appearance. That included a well-shaped thin mustache, two big rings, and a big railroad watch. Indeed he was the picture of success. Considering the heat, he even smelled good.

"Texas, y' say?" Papa eyed the young man.

"Yes sir. Li'l ol' state joinin' your'n west er heah."

I thought Dobrite was a bit too flippant.

"Ever been t' Texas, Mr. Hughes?"

"Oh yes, many times. But Texas is er big state. Which part y' from?"

"Me? I'm from all over, but m' main base is Houston. Whut brought you t' Texas, Mr. Hughes—good weather, oil, timber, or wuz it our prutty women?" Dobrite finished with a big laugh and grabbed Papa by the shoulder in a much too familiar fashion for a complete stranger.

Not amused, Papa focused on Dobrite's hand grasping his shoulder. Dobrite quickly got the message and released his grip.

"When I wuz er young man—maybe younger'n you—I did er stint on the railroad. It took me through all er the major towns: Texarkana, Fort Worth, Dallas, Houston, San Antonio, all the way t' Brownsville."

"Go any ferther 'n y'd be in the Gulf," Dobrite said.

"That's right." Papa half-smiled for the first time. "Fer over twenty-some yeahs now, me 'n m' brothers been goin' t' the National Baptist Convention that's held all over the country 'n er couple er times in Canada. Texas, bein' so big, naturally gits picked quite er few times."

"Y' er man after my own heart, Mr. Hughes. I love t' travel. Ain't met nobody like you since I been heah." Dobrite flipped out a package of ready-rolled cigarettes, revealing a slight bulge beneath his western leather vest. The bulge had to be a pistol. He also wore a leather wristband, more adorned than King Nebuchadnezzar's. "Ready-rolled, Mr. Hughes?" Sticking them in Papa's face.

"No, thanks."

"Mr. Riley?"

"No, thanks. Don't smoke cigarettes," Mr. Sam responded.

"I ermagine most er y'all eround heah roll y' own, right?" Dobrite boasted.

Mr. Sam looked at him hard and long before answering. "Well, you ermagine wrong, young fella. Andra heah had plenty er them Camels 'n Lucky Strikes too right heah in this sto' we standin' next t'. Ain't that right, Andra?"

"We may not be as up-t'-date as Houston in our li'l town, but we have managed t' git ernough supplies t' carry on most er the bad habits y'all use t'."

"Y' think smokin's er bad habit, Mr. Hughes?"

"Do y' think it's er good habit, Mr. Gangarist? Oh, I got no right t' talk erbout it like that. Sold too much er all kinds er tobacco in my day. I jist never used it m'self. Neither did m' mama 'n papa. All in the way y' raised, I guess. Besides, it's erginst my religion."

"I know, y'all good Baptists eround heah. I'm er good Baptist m'self, most er the time. However, I do have this one li'l habit . . ."

"Smokin'?" Mr. Sam asked.

"Much worse'n that. Makin' money," Dobrite said, and laughed heartily.

We all laughed, including me, who didn't ordinarily become involved in grown-up conversations.

Dobrite pointed his thumb at me. "Look at that boy laughin'."

Dobrite had a sinister look on his rather handsome face. It was the kind of face whose hypnotic charm one could neither completely trust nor resist. He definitely had a way of communicating with gullibles and doubters alike, and with patience won them all over—almost all.

"This is the plan, gentlemen." Dobrite spread out a big map on the table. "Now heah's yo' land right heah. Right, Mr. Hughes?" Dobrite pointed with a pencil.

Papa took his time putting on his glasses. "This forty heah's in crops. This is my timber land over heah."

"*And*, this is Mr. Pet's timber land right heah. He's yo' brother."

"That's part of it," Papa affirmed.

"First we have t' cruise this land t' make sure we cut the right trees. Don't wanna go over the line 'n cut somebody else's timber." Dobrite made too much of a point of his own honesty to suit me.

"No, we don't wanna do that. 'Course I know wheah mine is."

"Good, good. Now, I assume that since you er merchant who do er li'l farmin' on the side, y' not hardly equipped t' do any loggin' 'n truckin'. Am I correct?" Dobrite looked Papa in the eye and waited for what he knew would be the answer.

"You correct t' assume that."

"Thought so. Now, heah's whah *I* come in. *Enter Dobrite Gangarist!* with mules, loggers, chains, wagons, saws, axes, log hooks, coal oil—right down to snakebite medicine." Dobrite laughed loud and pulled out a half-pint of whiskey.

"How do we git paid, Mr. Gangarist, and when?"

"Fair ernuff question, fair ernuff." He playfully beat out a jingle with his pencil:

> This is the way we pay our bills,
> Pay our bills,
> Pay our bills,
> This is the way we pay our bills,
> Early Saddy mornin'.

He gave a big laugh, then snapped into serious composure.

Papa looked at Dobrite with a curious expression. But whatever ailed Dobrite, Papa couldn't let it interfere with his chance to get his hands on some badly needed cash.

"Remember that li'l jingle, Mr. Hughes?" Getting too familiar again, slapping Papa on the shoulder. Papa responded with a dry chuckle. "Cheer up, Mr. Hughes. I'm the one takin' all the chances heah. S'pose er tree falls on one er the wagons or the truck, one er the mules, or—heaven forbid—one er my men? I'd be messed up! Even er mule—er good mule—cost four, five hunded dollars. God knows whut one er them trucks would cost. All you gotta do is set back 'n draw yo' check on Saddy. Now—I'm tellin' y' now—I might wanna borrow er animal or two. Y'll be paid fer um. Maybe er wagon or som'um." Dobrite took out his book. "Now I got nine people in heah, includin' you."

Papa put his glasses on again. "Who all y' got heah?"

"Look at it. I'm sure y' know all of um."

"I see y' got Parsons heah," Papa said.

"Yep, Barnard too. Yo' two white neighbors down the Pike heah."

"Ledden, Walker, Steward . . . I don't see Pet heah." Papa waited for a response but received none. "Wheah is Pet?"

"Er . . . er . . . Mr. Pet's comin' in later. He already promised. We'll git im," Dobrite assured Papa.

Papa gave him back his book. Dobrite mounted his pretty black stallion, tipped his hat, and galloped up the Pike.

Hughes Chapel was packed. It was a first Sunday. I had just finished singing "Just to Behold His Face" when Pastor Jarrett rose to give his collection plate sermon. "You see, He's a mind reader—yes He is. He's a mind regulator and a heart fixer! He's a mighty warrior in the time of battle—yes He is! He's a soul stirrer, a healer, and a doctor! He's a loving and forgiving God. He's my all and all!"

"*We heah y'!*" the church responded.

"Don't let me get loose here now!"

About as likely as a mule picking cotton, I thought, considering what a spiritless preacher Pastor Jarrett was. He wiped the sweat from his face with a huge handkerchief that looked more like a tablecloth. Every time he had "gotten loose" in the past, I had felt like walking out.

Pastor Jarrett's preaching reminded me of Papa's gear-shifting: we put up with it because we couldn't do any better. The only reason we tolerated Pastor Jarrett was that he was educated, an excellent politician, and had Uncle Pet's ear.

"Go erhead 'n git loose if you feel like it, Reverend!" the church commanded.

"Jist let the Holy Spirit lead y'!" From the Brothers' amen corner.

"Praise God from on high!" From the Sisters' amen corner.

"Something tells me to stop and take up collection while the spirit is still roaming around in here. Let the church say eh-man!"

"Ehhh-man!" the church responded.

"Today being Young People's Day, we are fortunate to have with us some young men who will carry on in the tradition of their fathers and their grandfathers. We have already heard that beautiful rendition from young Brother Sun Hughes. Mark my word, with a voice like that, this boy could become another Roland Hayes! The other one I'm sure will become a deacon in this church—"

Elbert looked around to see whom the pastor was talking about.

"Don't be looking around, Brother Elbert. I'm talking about you. Everybody knows this young man. He's only a teenager, but he has already courageously taken on the responsibilities of a man. And I understand he's doing quite well at it. He has helped build our new highway, working right along beside men twice his age and drawing the same pay. I take my hat off to this young man, who stepped to the front when his father, Brother Deacon Hughes, was no longer able to carry on. God bless you, Brother Elbert. It's good to see you all dressed up in your belt-back suit with those bell-bottoms and your spats and so forth. Think I'll talk to Sister Jarrett about getting me one of those—"

Uncle Pet interjected, "That one he's wearin' is ernuff fer all of us, Reverend."

The church laughed, including Mama and Papa. Elbert didn't share in the laughter at his expense.

"Anyway, I'm choosing you to take up the main collection this morning. I want you to take this end of the table."

Papa had a big proud smile on his face.

Elbert stood and marched to the table. The pleated pants to his brown suit were at least two inches too long, causing the wide bell-bottomed cuffs to drag the floor. The belt-backed jacket, with the big wide lapels, looked as if it was cut for a chef. Elbert had a big flower pinned to the left lapel. An equally large handkerchief hung from his chest pocket that looked as if he was waving down a train. In the three-pocket double-breasted pearl gray vest, he sported one of Papa's gold chains with a fob dangling from it. Accompanying that garb was a pair of what he called tan and white shoes that looked red to me. They must have cost all of $2.50. Good shoes cost $5. A flaring pair of light beige spats, buckled halfway up to his knees, completely covered the white part of those wing-toed monstrosities. It was just as well. Only he, the family, and God ever knew about the white part of those shoes. His shirt was white, and his tie was every color in the spectrum. His hair was plastered so close to his scalp with Dixie Peach, it looked as if it had been painted on.

He had bought that outfit for Easter but did not want to change because it was September. Stubbornly ignoring all advice to the contrary, having taken his cue from a Sears catalog, Elbert held on to his newly acquired notions of fashion. He didn't want to hear anything I had to say while he was getting dressed.

"That suit, with that big wide hat 'n them spats, y' look like y' jist escaped from Ringlin' Brothers."

"You er pickle-headed knucklehead—still peein' in the bed. Whut would you know erbout dressin' in the latest style?" Elbert said as he walked all over my feet primping in front of the mirror. "If I listened t' you, I'd be dressed like Papa 'n Uncle Pet."

"Y' know whut would improve that outfit?" I asked.

"Whut?"

"No clothes at all. Jist go out there naked."

"You crazy!" Elbert playfully bopped me on the side of my head and strolled out. He yelled back, "Women gon' like it, bet'cha."

"Blind women!" I yelled back.

"Now our second young man, who due to his age will take the lead in the collection. He is a visitor to our community from the great state of Texas, I understand. Did I get that right, Brother Dobrite?" Pastor Jarrett asked.

"That's right, Reverend." Dobrite stood up and straightened his suit.

"I've only known this young man a short time. He appears to me to be a person who's going a long way in a short time. Praise the Lord."

"Ehhh-man," the church responded.

I noticed Papa and Uncle Pet quietly casting glances at each other.

Pastor Jarrett continued, "Without further ado, I'm going to have this young man come up here and help take up this collection with Brother Hughes."

Considering our standards, Dobrite was far more tastefully dressed than Elbert. His bearing as a well-dressed man of affairs, which he was, contrasted with the strivings of a young country boy trying to be stylish. His pinstriped suit fitted properly and flowed from his tall frame. He wore no spats over his black wingtip Nunbush slippers. His light blue tie and handkerchief matched. His thin gold chain and watch fob hung gracefully from his pearl gray vest. Unlike Papa's chain on Elbert, Dobrite's chain had a watch attached to it.

Sweat began to pop out on Elbert's forehead. That was the first evidence that he was at least aware of his inferior position. He eyeballed Dobrite slyly, not knowing what else to do.

Dobrite glanced at Elbert with curious detachment. He seemed to be choking back an urge to burst out laughing. His eyes seemed to be saying, "Who let that boy out of the house dressed like that?"

I'm sure Pastor Jarrett didn't intend it, but anytime one was called to take collection, a privilege reserved for males, a power struggle was automatically created. It mattered little that it was a green country boy against an adversary who reminded me of a riverboat gambler. It was clearly no contest.

This became evident very quickly when Dobrite pulled out his beautiful gold watch, checked the time, and placed the timepiece on the table. "Good mornin', church!"

"Mornin'," the church responded.

"I don't think y'all heard m' 'cause I sho didn't heah y'all. Let's try it ergin. Good mornin', church!!"

"*Good mornin', Brother Do-Right!!*"

"Y' got my name wrong, but at least I got some noise outta y'. Now say eh-man!"

"Ehhhh-man!"

"My name's Dobrite Gangrist, 'n I'm er Baptist. A Texas Baptist, that is."

I wanted desperately to add, "One with a very big mouth, as well."

"Been er Baptist all m' life. My mother 'n father wuz Baptist 'n they mother 'n father befo' them . . ." Dobrite preached on.

"Ehhh-man!! Ehhh-man!!" The church liked him.

"Now Pastor Jarrett already tol' y'all I'm from Texas. I tol' y' too. As y' know, Texas is er big state 'n we do things in er big way out there. Now I have tried t' tone m'self down 'n not let that show. But it seems the mo' I try t' hide it, the mo' it pops out. Y'all know whut I'm talkin' erbout? Sorta like er rabbit tryin' t' hide the fact he's got big ears. That's whut makes him er rabbit. No self-respectin' rabbit wants t' be mistaken fer er skunk or som'um. Know whut I mean? Y'all know whut I'm talkin' erbout, don't y'?"

The church laughed. He got them in a good mood.

"Now, y'all know I'm er businessman, 'n I believe in doin' things in er business way. Why don't y'all say eh-man!" Dobrite exhorted them.

"Ehhhhh-man!!"

"That's whut I'm talkin' erbout! Now, I know y'all got er buildin' fund heah. Am I right, Reverend?"

"We sure do," Reverend Jarrett responded.

"Never saw er Baptist church that didn't have one." Dobrite looked up in the ceiling. "From whut I see, if y' don't have er buildin' fund, y' need one. Come on now, y'all, praise the Lord!"

"Praise the Lord, Brother Do-Right!!" Some of the Brothers were amused by Dobrite's antics and were urging him on—as if he needed it.

Dobrite took out his wallet. That's the moment the entire church was waiting for. "Now I'm gonna start this collection off wid er ten-dollar bill. Now I didn't mean t' take up all that time. But you know how it is when the spirit moves y'."

"Ehhh-man, Brother Do-Right! Jist hep yo'self!"

"Now I know Brother Elbert heah wants t' say som'um 'n answer me."

Elbert looked faint. His mouth flew open, and he rolled his eyes at Dobrite. More sweat began pouring off his face and down the front of his brown belt-back, all the way to his light beige spats. He wiped again and again with his big handkerchief but to little avail. I began to feel sorry for my big brother, as I'm sure others did. Finally, Elbert gained what could pass for control of himself.

"Well, Sisters 'n Brothers, I ain't from Texas, 'n I sho ain't no businessman—not yet. But I am er Baptist. I am er member er this church, same as the rest er my family. My granddaddy started this church. Anyway, Brother Dobrite, I'm gonna match yo' ten dollars. I don't have all of it on me right now, 'cause I didn't come prepared fer such er big sum. I'm gonna put in two dollars right now 'n pledge eight mo' till I kin git t' the bank."

Papa fanned furiously. Mama looked straight ahead—fixated. My sisters and I froze in disbelief. Ten dollars was over one week's work on the new Pike.

Uncle Pet managed a face-saving laugh on Elbert's behalf and pulled out his dirty money sack.

Dobrite continued, "Now I'm gonna see how many er you good deacons gon' follow me. Now I don't wanna see no silver, lest they silver dollars. Small silver somehow hurts my eyes. Them ushers will pass the baskets fer yo' silver. I want y'all t'be quiet erbout it 'cause the noise also hurts my ears, unless it's paper. Now, all y'all wid ten dollars jist line up, march by this table, 'n lay yo' money down so everybody can see y'."

Pastor Jarrett stepped down out of the pulpit with his $10 in his hand. "I may have to go on a diet next week, but I won't be outdone in my own church."

"Eh-man," Uncle Pet said as he followed the pastor.

Deacon's wives, Mama and Aint Babe included, were turning their heads, digging in their bosoms, and rolling down their stockings pulling out bills to make up the $10. They were humming "Nearer My God to Thee" as they marched sadly by putting down their hard-to-get cash and having to look at all that money on the table. It was more like looking at someone lying in a coffin.

"God bless the cheerful giver," Pastor Jarrett kept repeating in an effort to lift their spirits. "God bless the cheerful giver . . ."

After a week of cutting and logging, Papa was up early that Saturday morning. It was a very special day. He had sold Dobrite Gangarist over $300 worth of timber. That didn't include the use of his wagon and team. He had hired Reedy to cut and load the logs, and his father, Mr. Sam Riley, to haul them out to the Pike so the trucks could pick them up and take them to Pine Ridge. Papa had also wound up using his own tools when Dobrite complained of the late delivery of men and equipment from his last job. Roy Barnard, Parsons, and other sellers had gone overboard helping the young prosperous-looking timber man. Dobrite rode out to the different sites every day on a beautiful black stallion—the best in the stable. He had won the hearts of all he came in touch with. My sisters thought he was the cutest thing who ever put on a pair of britches.

I had heard Papa and Uncle Pet discussing Dobrite that Sunday after church.

"How much timber did you sell this Dobrite, Pet?" Papa inquired.

"I didn't sell im any."

"He tol' me you wuz comin' in."

"Well, I thought erbout it. Then I thought I'd wait er while," Uncle Pet said.

"He must have money. Y' see how he spends."

"That's whut bothers me. I don't really need t' sell right now, but don't you be guided by me, because you need it now. I could be wrong erbout the young man."

Papa looked very strange. I could see he was worried. He and Uncle Pet quarreled and didn't get along at times, but they never forgot they were brothers. Papa had absolute respect for Uncle Pet's judgment in business matters.

When we arrived in the old Chevy, Roy Barnard was standing talking to one of the owners of the mill where Dobrite sold the logs. When Barnard saw Papa, he rushed over to him with a big grin on his face, acting friendly. That was the same Roy Barnard who had roped our heifer.

"Hello, Andy, Sun," Barnard said.

"Good mornin'. . . Mr. Barnard," Papa said dryly.

I said nothing.

"Can't you speak, Sun?" Barnard asked.

"Hi," I managed to force out.

"Hi, whut?" Barnard waited.

"Hi . . . Mr. . . . Barnard." I almost gagged on that one.

"Guess y' got im up too early, Andy." Barnard tried to excuse my behavior.

What did that white man think? That we were dumb animals and had no memory? I had watched him humiliate my father before my family, and he expected us to forget it and act as if nothing ever happened? He must want something.

"Wheah's yo' friend, the young colored boy who bought all our timber?"

So I was right; he does want something.

"I wuz jist gittin' ready t' ask you the same thing," Papa said.

"Why, he tol' me he wuz stayin' at yo' place. He said he would soon be er member er yo' family 'cause he's gittin ready t' marry one er yo' daughters," Barnard said.

"He tol' you that?"

"Sho did."

"Whut time did he tell y' he's payin'?" Papa asked.

"Six-thirty. Whut time did he tell you?"

"He tol' me seven-thirty," Papa said.

Barnard and Papa looked at each other. Other sellers started to arrive. Each had been given a different time to be paid. Each had heard a different story about the other.

At ten o'clock, it became obvious that all those men had been had. One by one they started to leave. Papa and I were the last to go. We kept looking back over our shoulders hoping, hoping, hoping . . .

31

I was eleven in the fall of 1933. Time to take on more responsibility. The old Chevy was on blocks again. Even if it hadn't been, Papa's eyes had become too bad for him to drive, and Elbert couldn't be spared. I was driving us to town in the wagon to pick up relief rations for the family. Mama had headed for the fields an hour earlier with Elbert, Geneva, Deloris, and Verleen to see what they could salvage from what the locusts had left and gather vegetables from the late garden we had planted. The only other hand that might have been spared from the field was Verleen, but she was too young, and a girl simply wasn't allowed to handle a team. Driving a horse and buggy was permissible, but never a team—especially a mismatched team.

I was ashamed of our mismatched team, but one of the mules had died, and the horse, which normally pulled the buggy, had to help the remaining mule pull the wagon. It wouldn't have been so bad if they had been round, fat, and good-looking, but those two critters were just this side of nagdom, fugitives from the glue factory. My pain was aggravated when we passed Uncle Pet's place and saw his hired hand, Crazy Charlie, preparing to leave with two round beautiful mules. We saw Uncle Pet get into his Ford and head for town just in front of us.

Uncle Pet and Papa simply nodded at each other. They were feuding, as usual, over religious politics.

Papa sat there stoically as the rickety old wagon rocked along up Olive Street all the way to Barraque. Right on Barraque to Main—left again on Main and on to the relief station. His gray felt Stetson flopped over his eyes. The sweat stains on the black band had crept all the way up to the crest in front and beyond. As hot as it was at that early hour, Papa had shaved, wore a clean white shirt, wide suspenders, a gray suit coat, and a baggy pair of faded pants that had been worn more than the coat. The coat and pants would have fit a man twice his size, but somehow he managed to look respectable.

He never said a word to me in the form of a conversation. After all, our mission was not one to celebrate, and it was not in the order of things to discuss anything other than fun with "young-uns." There was nothing funny to discuss, especially after the Dobrite and Hazel incidents, so we kept quiet. When we came to Barraque, however, Papa instinctively said, "Turn right heah." Again at Main, he said, "Turn left heah." Finally we arrived at the station. I'm sure it was instinct that enabled him to call the turns, because of an incident I had witnessed earlier on our way.

After Silvester and Hazel moved, Papa rented the store to the school district. Papa was on the board, but nobody worried about conflict of interest in that community at that time.

Papa still bought cotton remedies that fall. In better days, I had seen him and Elbert leave in the dark and come back at twelve or one o'clock at night. The old Chevy would be loaded down with cotton. It was immediately stored in our barn and locked up along with other remedies. Papa had a moral and religious conviction against stealing and pounded that into our heads. However, I'm not too sure he bothered to police every vendor he bought remedies from.

During those months of plenty, Papa would return with new shoes, materials for making clothes, big cakes of cheese, whole rolls of bologna, giant peppermint sticks, assorted candies, and jellied doughnuts. Mama brought portions of these goodies over from our store. The penetrating aroma that seeped through the house bespoke well-being and good times. We still had plenty after harvest was over, going into the Christmas season. After the holidays, the months of January through early May were lean and cold. We never went hungry, but the diet was monotonous.

The winter of 1932–33 was especially hard because Papa had tried his hand at what he was least qualified to do—cotton farming—during the summer of 1932. We lived in a forested, hilly area more suitable for timber, truck farming, and livestock. Most cotton was raised on flat river bottomland.

Cuttin Dillwood, a mean short fat jackleg preacher with a bulging bag around his testicles, told Papa about some rich river bottom farmland he could lease. It turned out it wasn't exactly river bottomland, but it was close to a bayou. "Bale er acre if it grows er pound. Cotton grows taller'n er man. You'll thank me once fall gits heah," Cuttin Dillwood assured him. "Y' got all these chillen heah—put um t' work. Grow some cotton. Make some *real* money fer er change!"

"But how will I be able t' work all this land I got 'n that too?" Papa asked.

"Fergit erbout this hill country. Come on down t' Wabbaseka 'n make some money fer you 'n yo' family while y' got the chance."

"I don't know, Cuz, this may not be much, but it's mine."

"It's you'rn all right, includin' the red clay, the rocks, the po' crops 'n hard knocks. Ain't nothin' gon' grow on land like this, certainly not cotton. Man cain't even raise er hard-on on this po'-ass land."

I thought that was foul talk for a preacher—even a jackleg preacher like Cuttin Dillwood.

"Oh, I don't know erbout that, Cuz. I got nine on it, 'n they didn't git heah by me jist laughin' loud. Two of um died, but they wuz heah."

"See, if they'd been down theah on good rich river bottomland, they'd still be heah."

"I'm no good at this farmin', Cuz. Pet's the one who knows whut he's doin' when it comes t' farmin'. Besides, wid my health bein' whut it is . . ."

"I'm thinkin' erbout that. Y' make some money, y' be able t' go back t' Hot Springs, git yo' health back."

"It'd be different if I wuz able t' work 'n—"

"Hold it. Hold it. Y' talkin' t' *me*, remember? I didn't notice y' doin' er lot er work when y' weighed two hundred 'n forty pounds. Y' sho didn't have no diabetes then. All I ever saw you and Pet do wuz stand eround 'n supervise. Well, since y' had so much practice at it, y' be right at home."

"You ain't nothin' but the devil, Cuz." Papa worked his lips at Cuttin Dillwood and held back the urge to laugh.

"Yeah, I know, but I got him covered too." Dillwood shook his small Bible. "I'll put this heah Bible on im. Where wuz I? Oh yeah. Y' kin put Elbert t' doin' the plowin'. Let Kitty 'n the rest er these chillen do the choppin', jist like y' been doin'. This boy heah 'n Verleen kin bring the wauter, when they ain't choppin'—"

"She's the baby," Papa blurted out.

"I know she's the baby, but everybody go when the wagon come if y' wanna make some money."

Papa took out his big tablecloth-sized handkerchief, mopped his forehead, then looked far off into the distance as if he was summoning some magical powers to aid him in resolving that puzzling dilemma. Actually all he was doing was ignoring Cuttin Dillwood's advice about putting Verleen to work.

"I'll come by every night 'n read y'all some Scriptures."

"Where y' go be t' do that?" Papa asked.

"Right next do' on the joinin' forty. Where'd y' think I wuz gonna be?"

"Somewhere preachin'," Papa said.

"Well, I'm gon' do that mostly on Sundays. Lord done called me t' preach, so I gotta do that. Remember whut happened to Jonah when he disobeyed? He was swallowed up by er *big* ol' fish!"

"I feel som'um like that right now," Papa said.

"Heee-heee-he-he-heeee. You always good fer er big laugh, Andra, I declare. Well, whut should I tell the man?"

"Gimme er little mo' time t' think erbout it."

"Don't take too long now. Deals like this ain't gon' hang eround forever."

Apparently, Cuttin Dillwood got Johnson grass confused with cotton because that was the only plant that grew "taller'n er a man" on that land. The cotton, if one could find it, didn't grow at all. It had no room even to try. I swear those acres had to be the place where Noah's ark landed. Every kind of killer grass known to man thrived there in abundance. Besides Johnson, there was crabgrass, moody grass, bluegrass, grazing grass, and devil grass, all choking the life out of the few doomed cotton plants that dared to show their heads. Johnson grass was so pervasive, I asked Papa if there was a market for that instead of cotton. We told many jokes about that grass and that horrible summer, but alas, it was no joke. The locusts and Dobrite forced Papa to take the steps that we had so long avoided, through pride and struggle, in spite of the Depression.

Papa made his way to the line. Many people shook his hand and even offered him their places. This was not without cause, considering that many of them owed him money, but the main reason they offered was because of his health and their long-standing respect for him. He, of course, declined and had me stand in line until his turn.

As I stood in that dingy room marked "Colored" that smelled of pine tar disinfectant and listened to those southern voices—all white—affirming their rights over ours by using the word *boy* in every other sentence, I had to do something to transform my mind out of that reality. I was much too young for such morbidity. What could I do? I didn't want to sing, because I thought they might think me completely loco, although some of the older people were singing.

It always depressed me no end when I heard old people singing those old songs of Zion. Usually it was a signal that they had some kind of problem they couldn't do anything about. What they were singing was always in direct contradiction to what was happening—completely unsuitable for the occasion. If there was a drought and the crops were burning up, they would sing "Didn't It Rain, Children." During a flood, it was "Them Bones, Them Bones, Them Dry Bones." For someone sick, "Whut You Gon' Do When Death Comes Er Creeping in Yo' Room" is not exactly a selection to cheer them up. During a tornado, no one wants to hear "I'll Fly Erway," and "I Once Was Lost, but Now I'm Found" doesn't help a person who is still lost.

When I saw those disrespectful rednecks behind the desk—and even those on the line, many of whom were no better off than we were—throwing their weight around, I felt "What a Friend We Have in Jesus" was more appropriate in church. I felt more like singing one of the Barrows' old blues songs, "I'd Rather Be Sloppy Drunk Than Anything I Know," "Blow the Man Down," or "Joshua Fit the Battle 'Round Jericho."

In any case, I needed something to lift me out of the doldrums, the mundane, the ordinary, onto a heavenly plane. I looked at my diabetic, waning, almost blind father, and I thought of something he had done quite handsomely as we were rocking along in that old wagon on our way to town that morning. Shortly before we reached Uncle Pet's place, the Nelson family had laid some white pillows in a swing on the porch. Papa, always a gentleman, graciously tipped his hat to the pillows and said in a loud clear voice, "Good mornin', y'all."

32

Arkansas' growing season allowed for at least three crops of greens, onions, Irish potatoes, beans, peas, corn, and some melons. Because the sores on Papa's feet were worse and he could barely walk, Mama took over. She had Elbert reopen trenches in the rows in the garden, and we promptly replanted as many vegetables as time permitted. A seasoned plowboy after my experience earlier in March, I kept busy turning over the ground. When those patches were ready, we sowed more mustard and turnip seeds. The late crops came up quickly. By August we were eating greens, beans, and peas from the garden again. Other vegetables, along with melons, came later. Cotton, corn, sweet potatoes, peanuts, and sorghum crops were finished.

When fall arrived, we went to white people's cotton fields trying to make enough money to keep us going. Farmers farther south and some of the growers along the river bottom had escaped the locusts.

In previous years, we had picked cotton only for Uncle Ruben and Uncle Pet. Uncle Ruben's bottomland farm at Wabbaseka had escaped the locust attack, but he didn't plant cotton that year because he was too busy with his duties as a professor of agriculture at Branch College in Pine Ridge and vaccinating animals for the state. Uncle Pet's crops had been wiped out also, and for the first time, he had nothing for us to do.

Papa hobbled out to the wagon and went with Elbert a few times to buy remedies, when they could find them. When he couldn't go to do the bargaining, we ended up losing money. Elbert hadn't learned the fine points that Papa knew instinctively about bargaining. No one in that area had. Elbert worked and behaved like a man because he had to. We often forgot that he was only fifteen. I had become a trusted plowboy nearing my eleventh birthday. I took care of animals, cut wood with most men, and picked two hundred pounds of cotton a day, considered good even for a grown man. I picked as many berries, husked as much corn, milked as many cows (considered women's work), boiled and washed clothes and bedding, and made soap as well. I still didn't receive the same respect or trust as Elbert. Papa still treated me as an immature boy. That meant I had to be disciplined by a man, whether I needed it or not.

I was getting to know more about the outside world. Elbert had sneaked and taken me to see my first cowboy picture show and let me drive the team back home. I had more responsibilities than when I was younger, but I was never kept out of school like Elbert, nor was I depended on to run things as he was.

Ben and I still found time to run our hub rims on errands, swim and fish in Bartholomew, make beam shooters, and improve our musical talents by picking out tunes on the homemade guitars we had hooked up on the side of the smokehouse and the barn. We had also gotten much better at playing the harp. One could even make out the tunes we were trying to play, especially when we were imitating the sound of a freight train. With all of my extra activities, I wasn't always punctual in doing things Papa asked me to do. Sometimes I couldn't be found. When Papa attempted to whip me—we were whipped, never beaten or abused—I'd run away and hide until he cooled off. Not to come when called was being disobedient. No one in our family dared defy such an order except Geneva. Her reasoning was, "If I'm going to be whipped whether I come back or run, I'll run. No whipping is a pleasure. Why let him do it when he's mad. If he gets you after he's cooled off, it's more or less to keep his word. And it's never as bad. It also gives more time for heavy padding."

Our family structure had changed over the years. Though Papa suffered from diabetes all the years I knew him, he was always in full control while everyone was under his roof.

My sister Deloris, next to Hazel, was almost eighteen. Dufus Rufus and Reedy were trying to get her to make up her mind between the two of them. She laughingly told Papa that she wanted them both. It was obvious to me that looks weren't how she measured the two. Neither was intelligence. Though Rufus came from a respectable landowning family Over In The Hills, he impressed me as a silly, badly dressed, knock-kneed, greasy-haired hunchback who shouldn't have been allowed out of the house except on a leash. Deloris loved power. The more, the better. Rufus was born to be controlled by anyone except Rufus. He was especially suited to the whims of a cute, smart little young woman like Deloris. On the other hand, Reedy had outbid Rufus at the box supper for Deloris's box some years before. Not to his credit, however, he had risked his life by sneaking around our house late at night in the dark. He had even run off and left his shoes when Papa went to investigate. On the other hand, he had proven that he was a loyal, trustworthy person when he served two years in prison for his father. He had never wavered in pursuit of Deloris's hand. Besides being sincere, physically Reedy made Rufus look like a bad mistake.

At twelve, Geneva had earned the reputation of being the most independent thinker of the family. She had not won any rewards for that. Quite the opposite. She rivaled only me in whippings. But as a boy, I was supposed to be whipped. She would run away, but that never worked. Her weaknesses: she loved to eat, and she was deathly afraid of the dark. Those habits made her easy to find at dinnertime and at night. Contrary, stubborn, and quiet, she could be funny and quite witty. When she did speak, she hit home runs.

"You gainin' weight," she commented to a boy at church.

"It's these pants I got on," the boy replied.

"You ain't got no pants on yo' face," Geneva answered.

One of the guests was admiring how tall she had grown since the last time he had seen her. "Do you cook?" he asked.

"If I git hot enough, I have been known to burn."

Papa recognized that Geneva inherited her wit directly from him. Once, while giving her one of her many whippings, he used the worn-out statement "This is hurting me worse than it is you."

"How do you knoooooow?" Geneva snapped back.

Papa stopped whipping, mostly *at* her since he couldn't see well, and told her to get out of there. I overheard him telling Mama, "I had to git rid er that gal befo' I laughed in her face."

My sister Verleen was the baby. This meant that all of her transgressions were far less serious than those of the rest of us—especially mine. It wasn't that I didn't deserve my whippings—and I took them like a man, yelling my head off—I simply objected to the injustice of the double standard. If Verleen did the exact same thing that I did, she most likely got away with a scolding at worst. He explained to me that I was older and should know better. What Papa was really telling me was, "She's the baby." Don't mess with his hoecake or his baby. Verleen was never mean about her special place as baby. She treated it as her divine right that needed no touting.

Most of my whippings came as a result of my relationship with Ben. Papa could never get used to the idea that my closest friend was a Barrow. He even worried about Elbert when he became interested in one of the budding Barrow girls. He lectured him on what could happen if he "knocked up" a fourteen-year-old girl. The busy Elbert took his advice and went elsewhere to do his courting.

That fall, shortly after Elbert yielded, I engaged myself in a boyish romance with one of the forbidden Barrow girls. She was a pretty little skinny girl with a high-pitched hoarse voice. I had my eyes on her for some time but never the opportunity to make my move. Coming home on Wagon Road West from gathering hickory nuts late one evening, I struck up a conversation with her. She giggled and laughed at my immature attempts to court her. We walked slowly behind the others, hitting and playing with each other. When we came to the ruddy red clay hill opposite our garden, I mustered up enough nerve to ask her to "gimma some."

"Give you some whut?" she shot back.

"You know." I tried to put my arms around her.

"Naw I don't." She twisted away from me.

I figured that as long as she had lived in that sin den with her father, Udell, she had to know exactly what I was talking about when I said "some." Everybody knew what *some* meant. After all, her brother Ben knew all about "gittin' some," "tearin' it up," and "poppin' it to her." At least, he knew the words.

I decided to press harder. I started to wrestle with her. Ben had told me that when they said no, that was a sure sign they truly liked you. Because with women, no really meant yes. A real man never took no for an answer. The way he put it, women really didn't know their own minds, and a real man had to push ahead until a no-no turned into a yes-yes. According to Doctor Ben, who studied under his father, Udell, a grand master, it was up to the man to get a woman hot.

Armed with all that information on how to handle a woman, I proceeded to try to take me *some!* I was ready too. My little rod was pushing my pants out like a tent pole. Being the best wrestler around, it was no problem to throw Corine down.

"Nooo, Sun! I said noooo! You crazy?"

"I'm gon' make y' hot, then we see who's crazy. Come on. You know y' want it."

"Let me up! I don't know whut y' talkin' erbout!"

I pried, tugged, and pulled, but she still managed to keep her legs closed and her bloomers on. We were both exhausted.

"Sun, please git up. Y' done got some, so why don't y' git up?"

"Whut y' mean? I didn't git nothin' but a wrestlin' match. I ain't givin' up till you git hot," I insisted, and rolled in the dirt with Corine until we bumped against Verleen's long skinny legs.

"Ooooooh! I'm gon' telllll Papa!"

I looked up, and she was standing over us. She didn't wait for a response but took off running toward the house.

We both jumped up, brushed the red dust from our clothes, and took off after her. "If you tell, I'm gon' tell erbout you 'n Ben in the barn!" Corine yelled to Verleen.

"Tell m' y' er young man now. Rollin' eround on the ground wid one er them Barrow gals. Y' ain't dry behind the ears yet. Git my strap 'n come heah," Papa said.

I looked down at the tub in which he was soaking his infected, stinking feet. In the past few weeks, he had rarely been out of the house. Gaping sores on both feet and legs reeked with the foul smell of rotting flesh in spite of Lysol, Pinesol, and other efforts to keep the odor under control. I went over to the wall, took the strap off the hook, and laid it where he could reach it.

"Did y' heah whut I said?"

"Theah's yo' strap layin' right beside y'."

He felt around on the wrong side of where the strap was. I realized then that his eyesight was gone.

"I'm gonna teach y' theah ain't but one man in this house." He finally found the strap. "Now come heah like I tol' y'." He tried to stand up but had to sit back down.

I choked up. Seeing him like that, I couldn't take it anymore. I quietly walked out the door. I passed Mama on her way to take care of him. Papa was still ranting about what he was going to do to me when he got his hands on me. Then I heard him tell Mama that he couldn't whip me anymore.

Outside, night had fallen. I couldn't control myself. The tears flowed like rainwater. The bitter salt taste that washed down my face mixed with the deep-down hurt I felt inside. I looked up at the freckle-faced sky and searched for the Big Dipper. Then the Little Dipper. After that the polestar. I closed my eyes and tried to inhale the stars. I was glad to stand there in that spot, in our backyard by the picket fence, alone with my thoughts of what Papa meant to me. To us all. What would the future hold? Where would we go? How could our family go on without his guidance? His courage? His wit? His strong hands and ruling fingers? His caring and his love? A cold fear welled up inside me. I quivered and shook, and the tears flowed again. When it was all out, I got control. I reasoned, *If I don't cry, Papa won't die.*

In early September, Papa had scraped up enough money to make his yearly trip to the National Baptist Convention. He and Uncle Pet forgot their perennial quarreling, dressed in their summer suits and their straw hats, and took the train to Memphis. There they met Uncle E.J. and Uncle Thomas, as they had done for years.

Mama and Uncle Ruben tried to get Papa to forgo that convention and concentrate on his health. For reasons that we could only guess, he made the questionable journey anyway. Walking, carrying bags, and the extra activity had infected his already sore feet, which led to gangrene.

That evening in early November, after he tried to whip me and couldn't, the house was packed with women and a few old men. Most of them were The Faithful. I came in from the backyard, where I had set up headquarters. Papa was sitting in a chair. Sister Fat-Fingers Grey had her fat hands on his forehead and was praying for him.

"Prayer can move mountains, Brother Hughes! Prayer changes things! Prayer can conquer all!"

Papa got up in the middle of Sister Grey's prayer and stumbled to the window. He fumbled at the curtains. "It's dark in heah."

It was still daylight outside, and the room was lit up with coal oil lamps.

"Why don't y' lay down, Andra, before y' fall?" Mama advised.

He was suffering. He felt behind him for the bed and lay down. Sister Grey and other women were helping him.

Resisting lying flat on his back, he rose up quickly, shivering and shaking. "It's cold in heah."

Everyone else was comfortable. It was hot to me.

"Kitty! Deloris!"

They hovered around him.

"I want . . . I want y' t' promise me . . . "

"Whut y' want us t' do, Andra?" Mama asked.

"I know y' cain't keep this family together . . . "

"Yes we can, Andra," Mama said, crying.

"Naw, Kitty, y' can't. Send Deloris t' Chicago . . . wid her Uncle Thomas. . . . I already spoke wid im. . . . Elbert can stay heah 'n hep y' wid Geneva 'n the baby . . . "

"Whut erbout Sun, Papa?" Deloris was crying.

"That's m' main worry. He's gittin' big. . . . Boys need er man t' control um at his age. . . . I wanna git im away from them Barrows. . . . Send im t' Pet. . . . Send im t' Pet . . . "

He became unbalanced and started pulling at the curtains and talking out of his head. He was so sick, I couldn't bear to watch him. I went into the backyard again and the cool night.

Over by the store, a crowd had gathered around a huge bonfire. The death watch was on. Unnoticed, I found my way to the edge of the crowd. Many of the men were people from whom Papa had bought cotton remedies. I had never seen them before. They came from all over. Mr. Jim Stowald, Bob Sikes, Mr. Joe Bearden and his clan, Mr. Sam Riley with Reedy and Olie, and Mr. Gus Thigpen were people I had always known. They were discussing things they remembered about Papa.

"M.A. wuz asked which part of the chicken he liked best. He said he liked all parts best."

Mr. Joe Bearden kept his cool while everyone else was laughing.

"M.A. said he really didn't mind hard work—for other people," Mr. Jim Stowald contributed his little wit.

"Somebody repeated the old saying 'Winnin' is not everything.' M.A. thought for a minute 'n said, 'That's true, Brother, but whut good things can y' say erbout losin'?'"

Another big laugh.

Mr. Joe Bearden spat a mouthful of snuff juice into the blazing fire.

"Well, guess it's my turn. I'm gon' take m' time 'cause M.A. 'n me go wayyyy back. 'N bein' er ol' man, I deserve t' take m' time. Many yeahs ergo when M.A. wuz er young man, the farmers got together t' talk erbout puttin' er cattle gap eround heah. [When a road runs through a fenced-in area for livestock, a grille, or cattle gap, goes where the gate would be.] Meetin' wuz goin' pretty good till Henry Martin showed up, liquored up. Most of us had pretty much agreed we didn't need no gap eround heah like they did down in the bayou country. Who wuz gonna put up the land? Henry Martin said, 'I think we oughtta have one! Cattle gap—whut we need! Theah's mo' ways'n one t' skin er cat, y' know.' M.A. tol' im t' name some of um. Henry Martin kept on talkin': 'Never do today whut, wid any luck, y' may be able t' put off till it's too late.' M.A. tol im t' make up his mind. Did he want the gap or didn't he? Henry Martin wuz so drunk, he started talkin' in riddles. Went back t' nursery rhymes. 'Bah-bah black sheep, have you any black milk?' He wuz so drunk, he started talkin' t' the man in the moon. 'N got mad when the man didn't talk back. 'Hey, up theah! Don't y' heah m' talkin' t' y'?' T' make it worse, it wuz er half-moon. He thought the man had gone t' bed." The men were beside themselves laughing.

"He 'n M.A. growed up together. M.A. would tell im anything he felt like. Finally M.A. got sick of im 'n tol' im he wuz too dumb t' grow er wisdom tooth. Tol' im t' set down 'n shut up, 'n 'If I want yo' advice, I'll give it t' y'.'"

"Yeah. M.A. er good man." Mr. Jim's voice cracked. "Yes sir, er good Christian man. Er family man. Sho gon' miss my best friend."

Mr. Sam Riley spat in the fire and took a swig from his bottle. "Well, bad as I hate it, we all gotta go sometime." Took another swig. "The man upstairs wants M.A. today."

"How do y' know that, Sam Riley? Y' talk to im?" Bob Sikes asked, pushing his hat back on his head.

"That's right, Sam Riley. How do you know? Y' moonshine tol' y' so?" Mr. Thigpen asked.

The whole crowd was laughing except Mr. Gus Thigpen. Mr. Thigpen sported a long handlebar mustache. He was always clean and neatly dressed even in overalls and shined brogans. He lived down in the bayou country with his family and was a successful farmer. I had gone with Papa and Elbert to pick up a remedy from him at one time. His wife was a good-looking woman, so were his daughters. The sons looked too much like him—hunched, round shoulders, rotund with a slouched walk. They were much older than Elbert and me and lived too far away for us to be friends.

Mr. Thigpen squatted down, poked in the fire, and maintained an evil grin in the corner of his mouth. His shifting eyes, wrinkled forehead, and body language told a different story from the painted smile on his square, animated face. His big white teeth were always showing like the chrome-plated grille on our Chevy.

"Y'all doin' whut y' always do. Wait till er man's on his deathbed, then y' start sayin' all these good things erbout im. If I didn't know better I'd er thought y' wuz talkin' erbout somebody I didn't know 'stead er M.A."

There was a silence.

Mr. Thigpen continued, "If y' doin' all this lyin' now, man ain't dead yet, I can 'magine how y' gon' pile um on at the funeral." Mr. Thigpen had a thick, hoarse, hacking, ominous laugh.

The men listened hesitantly. "The M.A. I knowed wuz er real rascal. Oh, he had er lot er flair, which he used t' charm y', but if y' didn't watch im he'd cheat y'. Ha-ha-ha. Jim heah called im er good Christian family man. Oh, he put on er big front, all right. Big deacon in that church up theah his pa started 'n he 'n Pet own—"

"Wait er minute, Gus. M.A. 'n Pet don't own no church. Case y' don't know—'n I see y' don't—my pa wuz one of the founders, along wid Parson Hughes 'n Ed Tilson. Nobody nor nobody's family owns Hughes Chapel. If that wuz true I'd own part of it m'self," Mr. Joe Bearden said.

"They run it. Whut's the difference? All this business erbout M.A. bein' such er Christian family man"—he spat in the fire and gave that accusing laugh again—"all front. The M.A. I know drank mo' corn liquor 'n chase mo' women—"

"Don't y' see that boy standin' theah?" Mr. Sam Riley cut in.

"If that boy don't know erbout it, he don't know who I'm talkin' erbout. If he already knows, then he knows I'm speakin' the truth."

"These men eround heah been mispronouncin' yo' name all evenin', Gus. They been sayin' Mr. Thigpen when they shoulda been sayin' Mr. Pig Pen!" Mr. Sam Riley said with a laugh.

The men laughed along with him.

Mr. Thigpen rammed his hand in his pocket and started after Mr. Sam Riley. That was a mistake considering the fact that Reedy and Olie were standing in the crowd. Mr. Joe Bearden grabbed Mr. Thigpen. Immediately, Mr. Jim Stowald, Bob Sikes, and other men surrounded him. He was so angry, sweat popped out on his forehead. I thought he might have a gun until he spoke.

"Y' call me outta my name! Y' whisky-guzzlin' son of a bitch, I'll cut y' damned thoat!"

"Why don't y'all turn im loose 'n let im come on over heah! Ain't nothin' the matter wid Gus 'cept he's jealous. He wuz always jealous er M.A. Even when we wuz boys. It's all 'cause M.A. took some gals erway from y' when we wuz young. Y' goin' t' y' grave wid it?" Mr. Sam Riley was standing by the woodpile with an ax in his hand.

"Y'all boys cut this out now, both er y'! This ain't no way t' act no matter whut! Y' standin' on ernother man's property—him inside on his deathbed— 'n y'all gon' start er fight. How'd y' like fer im t' treat you like that?" Mr. Joe Bearden's speech calmed them down. "Y' oughtta be 'shamed er y'selves."

Someone in the crowd said, "M.A. wouldn't do nothin' like that!" The crowd responded, "Nawwww, he wouldn't!"

I had heard enough. I slipped away while they were still talking. Mr. Joe Bearden seemed to have things under control.

I had only seen Papa once in a place that raised a question in my mind. He was walking on a path near Tilson School on his way home. He was moving briskly, placing his cane in front and swinging it back and forth in cadence. It was hot, his shirt was wet, his hat was turned down over his eyes, and sweat was pouring down his face. I was with Ben and three other boys. We were on our way to play with Ned Witherspoon—a boy who had lived near the church only a year. When we heard someone coming, we moved to the side of the trail. I was farther away from home than I was supposed to be. At first I didn't hide, but when Ben whispered, "It's y' papa," I ducked down behind one of the taller boys. Papa tipped his hat, said "Howdy, boys," and kept walking. He obviously didn't recognize anyone.

"I bet I know wheah yo' papa been," Ben said suspiciously.

"He been checkin' on that new spread the church jist opened up fer buryin'," I responded.

"Ssssshittt, he been buryin' it in that new widow Witherspoon, who lives on the spread jist behind the graveyard." Ben stopped in the middle of the path and fell out kicking and laughing, which is what he always did when he thought he had scored.

I didn't think it was funny. I turned around and started back home. Ben followed behind.

"Hey, whut's the matter? I don't say nothin' when you talk erbout Udell."

I kept walking and refused to talk with him. *How dare he compare my father to the likes of a low-life lout like that Mr. Udell,* I thought to myself.

The widow Witherspoon had moved to our community after her husband died. She was a good-looking woman who wore her hair in a big roll piled high back on her head. She spoke quietly in a low voice. She became a Sunday school teacher shortly after she joined Hughes Chapel. She had two older daughters and one younger. Her boy, whom we were going to see, was a big-jointed, freckled-faced, loud-mouthed kid, about my age. There was talk about a relationship between Papa and the widow Witherspoon but no proof. The widow finally married one of the prominent deacons in the church, which put an end to the rumor.

The most persistent rumor I had heard was that Papa and Miz Marge Stowald, Mr. Jim's wife, had a thing going on for years, before Mama broke it up. To me, these were all rumors. I never saw or heard anybody say they saw Papa with any woman except Mama. I never saw Papa take a drink, except in a hot toddy when he had a cold. I never saw him cheat anybody, unless one would consider the time when he jokingly maneuvered old Brother Grey into some crude figuring in order to win a moneyless bet he had made with Elbert. I never saw Papa or Mama raise their hands in anger against each other. Seldom did I hear them disagree. They never quarreled. I never heard them talk about how much they loved each other. They were already busy living their love.

My love for Papa wasn't based on whether he did everything right, nor did I always have to agree with him. If that had been the case, I would have hated him after he killed Spot. Ben's father, Udell, was just the opposite of Papa, but I'm sure Ben loved him without reservation at the same time he was talking about him as if he wasn't human.

What angry ugly voice could penetrate and spoil my sweet thoughts of Papa who as a human was oh-so-human? What could shake my faith or stain his name? I knew him too well.

Inside, I made my way past the dining room table—laden with food—past the death watchers and the long sad faces of The Faithful who had offered their last bit of devotion, hope, and prayers for Papa's survival. I walked close to where he lay. His chest was rising and falling. Death was rattling deep in his throat. His eyes were set in eternity. The long ruling fingers that projected from his once powerful hands lay motionless by his side. His infected feet lay partly uncovered, and his raw sores leaked gangrene pus that stained a wad of white towels that were changed regularly. His toes pointed toward the fancy steelwork at the foot of his feather-mattressed bed. The stink of Pinesol and Lysol mixed with that of his rotting flesh. A baby cried in the next room. The young mother who had held her breast and squirted milk into Papa's eyes excused herself quietly to attend to it.

I watched Papa for a while and wished it would soon be over. He had been dying all night. I hated to see him suffer. It was useless for me to try to sleep or eat. I wandered back outside. The bonfire had simmered down, and some of the men had left while others had come. Mr. Gus Thigpen was discussing the Bible with one of the local jackleg preachers. Mr. Sam Riley was nodding. Bob Sikes was having a conversation with Mr. Joe Bearden and Mr. Jim Stowald. I heard crowing nearby, which was answered in the distance. Chirping birds awoke, and far in the east a brightness became visible on the horizon.

At daybreak I found myself walking toward the garden and the fields on Wagon Road West. It was a frosty November morning. Browns, reds, yellows, and purples had splattered the woolly green and blue with faster strokes and leafily quilted the ground with their softness. Snakes had slid out of the dwindling warm vibrancy of fall into the rasping cold of ensuing winter—there to sleep unnoticed until the warm suns of spring. A squirrel scurried around a naked oak, stopped to peep, then stole hurriedly into its nest in the fork of the tree. A woodpecker riveted his staccato in the top of a dead snag. *Let the mock-*

ingbird imitate him, I thought. There were no mockingbirds in sight, though. *Where did they go?*

I didn't know what to do with myself. When I came to the garden, I walked between a row of sticks loaded with late dried string-bean vines. Many of the vines were frosted, and yellowing beans that had grown since the plague of locusts were hanging lazily. Black potato vines sprawled across the patch in the wake of killer frosts. Garden cornstalks stood straight and brown and dead. Tops of onions, tomatoes, beets, and carrots were strewn, half-eaten, over the ground. I walked on across the barren fields to Alligator Creek. Then I turned east and followed the creek to our fence. Turned north and followed the fence across the creek, balancing myself as I walked on a big log. Then I climbed a steep hill. I picked up a stick and walked slowly, as Papa had done, until the ground started to feel soft beneath my boots. I poked around the leaves with the stick until I found the soft spot I was looking for. Since the spring had been used late into the fall, I didn't need a hoe or a shovel to clean it out. I stooped and raked leaves and debris out with my hands. Wine-colored liquid spewed for a while, then turned clear. Though I wasn't thirsty, I scooped the water up with both hands and drank. It was as cold and fresh and sweet as ever.

Is he gone? Is he peaceful, at last? I'd better run back and find out. I took off like a frightened deer. Sucking wind, I ran as I did when the rattlesnake bit me, when I was six. As I did when I had beaten my sister Geneva, when we were playing hide-and-go-seek, when I was seven. As I did when I outran a bad dog and climbed over the fence to keep him from tearing me apart, when I was eight. Like the time I raced and beat other boys my age and older at Tilson. As I descended Blueberry Hill, I noticed that more cars, wagons, motorcycles, and buggies had filled the lot behind the store and in back of the house. I slowed my pace to a walk and slipped past people sitting and standing around with their hands in their pockets. The sun was out, and the day was much warmer than the night had been. *Was he gone?*

Squeezing past fat ladies and big tall men, I finally entered Papa's bedroom. He was still lying in the same position. His chest was rising and falling slower than the last time I had seen him. His mouth was half-open. His face was sunken, his eyes glassy and fixed. This had gone on all night and half the next day. That night in the backyard I had thought, *If I don't cry, Papa won't die.* I knew he was strong-hearted and would take his time, but the watching and waiting was heavy and beyond my young imagination.

Ben and I had watched Mr. Durbey die, and I knew it could take time for the breath to leave a strong, determined man's body. What a difference, I thought. Mr. Durbey died alone, with flies and maggots threatening to devour his body before he stopped breathing. Papa, on the other hand, was surrounded by his family, The Faithful, and many friends and acquaintances in a day-and-night vigil, waiting for him to breathe his last.

Mr. Durbey had died neglected except for Ben and me. Though Papa was consumed with sores on his feet and legs, they bathed and cleaned and treated him when he needed it. They even changed his sheets as he lay dying. I watched for a short while, then stole quietly out of the room.

Overcome by sleep, I lay in a corner of the dining room. When I awoke, it was dark. I peeped into the room once more, and Papa was still struggling. I thought, *Papa knows what he's doing—even now.*

I wandered out to the bonfire once more. The crowd was larger than it had been the night before. I went to the barn and crawled into the cotton bin. When I awoke and peeped outside, the lot was empty. The bonfire had dwindled to coals and ashes. I brushed myself off and walked toward the back door of the house. I knew, without being told, that it was over. When I entered the house, I saw no one. *Where is Mama? Where is my family? Most of all, where is Papa?* I didn't look in any of the other rooms. I walked slowly through the kitchen, the dining room, and stopped at the entrance of Papa's bedroom. I could see his profile as he lay on his back near the big front window in his room. The room was spotless. I still smelled the rot coming through the Pinesol and Lysol, but it wasn't as strong as it had been. I walked inside and moved close to Papa's body. He had been washed, shaved, and wrapped in clean white sheets. His ruling hands lay folded across his chest. I placed my small bony hands over his and looked carefully at his closed sunken eyes. Then I looked at that familiar smile beneath his trimmed black and white mustache. Papa was peaceful at last. I did not cry. Rather, I felt a great sense of relief, and victory. Especially at his enduring smile.

> *There is a fountain filled with blood*
> *Drawn from Emmanuel's veins,*
> *And sinners washed beneath the flood*
> *Lose all their guilt and stain . . .*

Hughes Chapel was packed far beyond capacity for Papa's funeral. They couldn't close the front doors, and a seat was out of the question. Few people could sing Papa's favorite hymn—certainly he couldn't, although each Sunday found him fervently trying. But where Papa and many others had failed, the great Jeremiah Robinson from Pine Ridge knew exactly how to approach the dull song and make it ring with the spirit. Jeremiah sang the first verse. He put Uncle Pet on bass. Then he broke the song into parts and had the tenors, sopranos, and altos come in on cue and blend at the end. It was Jeremiah's controlled, melodic bass voice, however, that brought the church to its feet. He closed his eyes. His protruding Adam's apple moved up and down as if it was mechanically controlled. His small frame trembled, and beautiful sounds rolled out of his big mustached mouth. Jeremiah and Papa loved each other like brothers. After Papa's favorite, Jeremiah followed with a litany of songs that The Faithful sang: "He Never Have Left Me Alone," "I Shall Not Be Moved," "Lord, I Want to Be a Christian in My Heart," "The Old Ship of Zion," "Walk with Me, Lord," "Have You Got Good Religion?" "I Woke Up This Morning with My Mind Stayed on Jesus," and the all-time favorite, "Precious Lord."

Reverend Barker was an old friend of Papa's who had been the pastor of Hughes Chapel many years ago. Papa had selected Reverend Barker to preach his funeral long before it had anything to do with church politics. The stocky, round-faced, blue-suited Reverend Barker was the leader of the district that Papa followed when a split came about. Uncle Pet followed the Reverend Doctor Claxton. Papa and Uncle Pet feuded for years over their differences concerning the two opposing organizations. Papa's funeral, however, was not the place or the time to mention anything that could be considered political. Reverend Barker stuck strictly to his personal knowledge of Papa and the importance of his Christian life as an example for others to follow. In spite of Uncle Pet's assessment of Reverend Barker as an uneducated backwoodsman, to me he sounded better than that highfalutin Reverend Doctor Claxton. Reverend Barker eulogized Papa in a way that everybody understood. He often injected Papa's sense of humor, which made it seem more like a celebration than the sad types of funerals I had heard. Only at the end did Reverend Barker's eulogy become emotional—as always when a sermon refers to death himself.

"Early, early Wednesday morning, after M.A. had struggled with old death for more than three nights and two days, after he had *fought* the good fight!— for those of you who don't know, M.A. was a *soldier* in the army of the Lord. Yes, he was!—after he had done his best, almighty God in His righteous wisdom looked down from His blessed throne on high! and-and He said, '*Enough is enough!* My soldier is tiiiired! And he neeeeds his rest! He has traveled a long, hard, and dusty road! Yes, he has! Not only that, he has worked faithfully in my vineyard in the heat of the day! He's one of my favorites, and I don't wanna see him suffer no more!'

"Somebody said, 'But he's not that old of a man. And, and, he's got a loving wife and young chirren.' And, and God said, 'Don't you think I know that? I-I-I-I-I *made* him, his wife, and his chirren! I-I-I-I created the universe! With this mighty hand, I scooped up matter from my immortal storehouse—rolled it up into a small ball, tossed it into space with a flip of my finger, and lo, it became the planet earth! I reached back into my immortal bag as a farmer would a sack of grain, and with one mighty motion, I planted the stars in the heavens! And when I was good and ready, I stepped out of the heavenly clouds of infinity. I planted one foot on eternity and placed the other on my everlasting holy word! With one hand, I held back the dark! With the other, I hung out the sun!

And brought forth light into a dark and dreary world! I clapped my hands, lightning flashed, and thunder rolled! I'm the God of Abraham, Isaac, Jacob, and Moses! The same God who gave Samson back his strength! The same God who delivered the Hebrew children from the fiery furnace, Daniel from the lion's den! The s-a-a-a-me God who don't know how to do wrong! So don't worry about M.A.'s family. I-I-I-I-I-'m God! And I'll make a way out of no way!'"

Reverend Barker knew whom he was preaching to. He knew what The Faithful expected. He acted out the passage on God with hand gestures and props. After a few squalls like that, they were on their feet. The spirit was in the house.

"E-h-h-h-ah-man!! God will make er way out of no way!!"

"Yes He will!!"

Reverend Barker mopped his pudgy face with a big white handkerchief. "God knows how much we can bear. With His golden scepter, He tapped one of His favorite angels on his shoulder. Gabriel, I think He called him."

"Gabriel!!" From the church.

"'Gabriel, I know you're busy, but this is your job.'"

"Tell us erbout it!"

"Gabriel said, 'Yes Master, but whatever You will, I'll obey.' Master said, 'Do you see that white house down on Highway 15—Main Pike they call it?' Gabriel said, 'Yes Master, I see it.' Master said, 'My servant M.A. lives in that house, and, and old death has him tied to his deathbed. Not only that, he's afflicted with sores like another one of my servants named Job! And, and, like Job, M.A. has kept the faith in spite of his affliction!'"

"Yes he did!!"

"'I want you to fly on down there, and tell old death that I said end it! And bring my servant M.A. on home to me!' Gabriel said, 'Master, are his papers in order?' Master said, 'Papers are all in order. M.A. sealed it with me in this church, on the moaner's bench long time ago! Go on, like I told you, Gabriel, and bring my servant home!'"

"Bring him home!!"

"'Before you leave, Gabriel, I want you to take care of his wardrobe! I want you to get out his golden slippers—size eleven. He's a tall man, so pick out an extra long white robe!'"

"That's whut He tol' im!"

"'Get down his golden crown, and I-I-I-I will place it on his head! I'll wipe the sweat from his brow and the teaaars from his eyeeeees! I'll ease his aching pain! Be on your way, Gabriel, and bring my servant M.A. on home to glory!! Gaaaa-briellllll!! Gabriel!!'"

The church was in an uproar. Reverend Barker did what the masters of his craft usually do. Once he had roused the church to a high spiritual pitch, he broke it off and slowly, dramatically returned to his seat beside Reverend Jarrett, who was crying tears of joy.

Uncle Pet was laughing, as he always did when he was happy with a preacher's performance. It mattered not that he and the good Reverend Barker were on opposite sides of the fence politically. He appreciated a master when he heard one. Reverend Barker was only living up to his reputation.

P. U. Muller was the richest black man in Pine Ridge. He handled the majority of the funerals for black people in our area. His black-suited, white-gloved, well-trimmed scavengers always gave me an unpleasant smothering eerie feeling. They reminded me of those buzzards hovering over that goat waiting for him to die. I wondered, even at eleven, why a man like P. U. Muller, who simply picked up, embalmed, and prepared dead bodies, deserved to make so much money, when Papa, who was running a store that kept his community supplied with most of its daily needs, had been forced out of business. Though I had never seen P. U. Muller in person, I had seen his black-suited buzzards in operation since I was four.

The black-suited buzzards were very efficient. On signal, three of them marched like soldiers around Papa's beige coffin. Two of them carefully removed the multitude of flowers while the chief buzzard unscrewed the cover. Carefully he lifted the half-cover up and propped its hinges. He fussed with the white ruffles and tilted Papa's head this way and that far longer than I thought was necessary, as if he wanted to make sure Papa was comfortable. For a minute there I thought he was going to tickle his chin. Finally he beckoned for people to line up. The two buzzard helpers went into action getting people into position, helping children, the old, and the crippled.

The line dragged because many people stood and stared as if it would bring him back.

"He sho looks natural."

"Don't look like he been sick at all."

"P.U. did er wonderful job."

"That's the kind er job I want done on me."

"Sho gon' miss im. Sho is . . . "

Such comments went on for what seemed like hours. I was counting the people I knew. Mr. Jim Stowald wept bitterly. Miz Marge followed suit. Mr. Sam Riley wore his Sunday best. His starched white-collared shirt was buttoned up to his neck. His wide gray suspenders held up a pair of blue pants that flopped over a pair of rough-looking clodhoppers. He was liquored up for the occasion. Reedy said later, "That's the only way we could git him to come." Bob Sikes was the lone white person in the line. He had his hat in his hand. It was the first time I had seen the bald spot on the back of his head. He looked drawn and sad.

As superintendent of the Sunday school and a merchant, Papa knew many young people. He couldn't make out who they were when his eyes became worse. They found it amusing when he called them by the wrong name and had to be corrected. Children loved Papa. Many of them were wiping tears from their eyes when they viewed their friend's body.

The big surprise was when I saw Mr. Gus Thigpen and his family in the line. They were in their Sunday best. That sly little grin was still in the corner of his mouth. I couldn't figure out if it was an "I'm glad you're dead, you rascal you" grin or just his patented painted grin.

Emotions were kept under control until Mr. Lieb Walker came to the coffin. Mr. Lieb rendered many services in the community. He was known best for making molasses. Big, tall, and powerfully built, he looked down at Papa's body and started to cry out loud.

"M.A., M.A.! Why did you leave m'? Why, M.A.!! Whyyyy!!"

One of the black-suited buzzards tried to move him.

"Leave me alone! M.A. wuz the best friend I ever had!! Now you fixin' t' stick im in the ground and throw dirt on im!!" He bent over the coffin and wept like a child.

Mr. Lieb's outburst started Mama and my sisters crying. Uncle Pet was supportive, but he didn't cry. Uncle Ruben was wiping his own tears and trying to comfort us at the same time. At one point, Uncle Pet held me on his knee. I felt uncomfortable sitting on anybody's knee. Elbert looked frightened. It was something he didn't know how to deal with. He was left as man of the house at fifteen.

The black-suited ones finally brought the family up to view the body. They had dressed Papa in his blue serge double-breasted suit, a white shirt, and a blue bow tie. His face was fuller. His eyes were not sunk deep in their sockets as when I first saw him dead. The eternal smile was more pronounced on his friendly face. With tears flowing, Mama bent over and kissed him on the lips. Crying, my older sisters grabbed his hands and didn't want to let go. Hazel had to be pulled away from the coffin. She screamed and cried. Elbert had cried himself out and stood like a statue, staring. My baby sister, Verleen, was trying to do whatever she saw her older sisters do. Geneva was showing her own private grief by covering her head completely and crying buckets. I had cried that way once in the backyard.

When we came outside to follow the hearse to the family cemetery, cars and trucks were lined up all down the Pike. I thought about my good friend Mr. Durbey. For him there were no followers, no pallbearers, no family except Mr. Jim Stowald—not even his own daughter, Miz Marge—and no mourners to follow him to his final resting place. Only Ben and I tried to follow and mourn him, but Mr. Jim wouldn't let us. The Faithful rendered their hearts to Papa. Even Mr. Gus Thigpen, his critic, was there, but there was no one to cry for Mr. Durbey.

*   *   *

Back home after the burial, "Y'all chirren take y' shoes off befo' y' come in the house. Don't track all that mud in heah." Mama tried her best to sound normal, but there were tears in her voice.

Slowly, she started packing my things.

"Mama, why don't you lay down? I'll pack Sun's things," Deloris said.

"Brother Pet will be heah soon, 'n y' know how he is erbout waitin'. I'll hep y'."

Mama would not sit down, though she was visibly tired. She and Deloris had my small bag packed and ready before we heard the Ford's horn outside.

Uncle Pet parked on Wagon Road West and got out of his car. He walked up on the porch. Mama came to the door, and I followed.

"How you, Kitty?" He stood at the door. "Why don't y' git some rest 'n let these chirren help y'?"

"I will, Brother Pet. I jist didn't want you to have to wait. Sun is all ready. Now you be a good boy, 'n obey yo' Uncle Pet, y' heah?"

"Yes ma'am."

"Uncle Pet is good to little boys who obey, but he can be a doctor when they need a little straightening-out medicine," Uncle Pet said.

Uncle Pet took my bag and headed for the car. Mama and my sisters and brother came to the door. We hugged and said our good-byes. They were tearful, but I did not cry. Outside, the sun had set and night sounds filled the air.

Uncle Pet backed up and turned the Ford around, stripping gears in the process, and headed up the Pike. I waved and looked out of the window as long as I could see. I was on my way to my new home and my new life.

That left Elbert, the oldest boy, Deloris, the oldest of the children who were still at home, Geneva, and Verleen, the baby, with Mama.

I would be fourteen in November of 1935. I feel ashamed for having cried after the car outran me yesterday evening when Saravania was being taken away to Flint, Michigan.

Dry spit caked around the corners of my mouth arouses my most recent memory. Yesterday's tears had streaked patterns into the dusty paste beneath my sad, puffed eyes. Creased wrinkles in the homespun quilt sagged toward the floor, squished and hedged their shapes on my buttocks. A blue hand-knitted replica of an owl in relief on a rectangular white piece of cloth lay diamond shaped on a fluffed white pillow. My ashy feet and legs have taken on the appearance of my scuffed, worn brogans sitting nearby. The wick of the coal oil lamp is flickering to stay alive when all the oil is gone. Aunt Babe stares dimly from a big doctored turn-of-the-century photograph hanging tilted from the north wall. A chest of drawers supports a large ornately framed mirror and sits beneath the photograph. Greenish flower-patterned wallpaper begins to distinguish itself as daylight begins to creep through open window shades. Roosters never forget, and their voices echo near and far throughout the countryside. The sultry July night air recedes only to herald the beginning of another wicked day.

I am tired, but I can't rest. Sleepy, but I can't lie down. Crazy Charlie rubbed the welts on my back and the rest of my body with Vaseline before I was *supposed* to go to bed last night after the worst day of my life. Sitting with my hands holding my chin as if it might escape, my body was still and quiet, but my mind romped, leaped, cried, yelled, played, and prayed through the length of my remembered days throughout the night.

I hear Crazy Charlie stirring in the next room. He's putting on his boots, getting ready to feed the mules, hogs, and cows. I will have to join him soon to take care of the chickens, ducks, geese, and the nasty little caged wild foxes in the blacksmith shop. Aunt Babe is making her move as well. Breakfast, however, is the farthest thing from my mind.

The Prodigal Son I am not. Returning home is out of the question. During the time since Papa died and I left to live with Uncle Pet, many changes have occurred. Deloris has moved to Chicago and is living with Uncle Thomas. Elbert is living in the store. Mama, Geneva, and Verleen are still at home, but Mama—still a young woman, in her early forties—is being courted by a crazy Geeche named Tad Bloodso.

Should I catch a freight to Chicago, where Deloris, Aunt Fanny, and many other relatives live? There I would be close to Saravania and could visit. I'm already doing the work of a man at thirteen. Maybe we could get married. What about Missouri Street School, which I attend in Pine Ridge, and all the friends I have made there? I heard Uncle Pet say he's buying me a new balloon tire bicycle to ride back and forth. I want that bicycle so bad, it almost makes the beatings seem worth it.

What kind of confusion is this? Only three days ago I sat at the dinner table, stuffing food away like a magician, and felt so good about my life that I dared not let anyone in authority look deep inside me and see the happy grin on my inside face. I was dressed in a new brown suit, brown and white shoes, and a straw hat to set it off. I had joined the company of The Faithful—a big step, as Reverend Taylor pointed out. I had driven the new Plymouth to the pond, *alone,* and washed it. Had indulged in some heavy breathing, kissing, and rubbing with my cousin Saravania and had every intention of climaxing the job the night we were found out and I was severely overruled by Uncle Pet's brown leather the next morning.

I had reached a degree of manhood that had escaped me at home where we had depended on our older brother, Elbert, for our very existence. At Uncle Pet's place, it's Crazy Charlie who is second in command. A fly buzzes past my face several times and finally lands on my forehead. Being deep in concentration, I don't bother to brush it off.

My mind wanders back to the little knoll where I prayed and agonized while I was on the moaner's bench. I remember the hopeless despair I experienced when my Spot was killed. I remember the snakebite, the wagon incident, and Papa's death—worst of all—which sent me back to that spring on the side of the hill, where I had to think, reflect, regenerate, and re-create myself. I know now that Spot's grave in the corner of the garden, the bridge at Bartholomew where our wagon was forced off the road and Elbert was almost killed, the blueberry patch where the little rattler bit me, and now the little knoll are all like the moaner's bench in my life. And I may return to this wooden frame after a hot day in the fields. I'm ready-rolled, so I step into my brogans and grab my straw hat from the wall, and walk out into the hot air to do my chores.